C.O.P.

CASH OVER PEOPLE

POLICE CORRUPTION. THE ULTIMATE BETRAYAL

Rodney R. Pittman

D1332699

iUniverse, Inc.

New York Lincoln Shanghai

C.O.P.
CASH OVER PEOPLE

Copyright © 2007 by Rodney R. Pittman

iUniverse books may be ordered through booksellers or by contacting:

iUniverse
2021 Pine Lake Road, Suite 100
Lincoln, NE 68512
www.iuniverse.com
1-800-Authors (1-800-288-4677)

This is a work of fiction. All of the characters, names, incidents, organizations, and dialogue in this novel are either the products of the author's imagination or are used fictitiously.

ISBN: 978-0-595-44729-9 (pbk)
ISBN: 978-0-595-89050-7 (ebk)

Printed in the United States of America

THANKS TO:

My parents Robert and Bessie Pittman

My brothers and sister

Robert Jr.

Reginald

Renee

Raphael

my daughter Randi Nicole

and a host of nieces, nephews

Desmon, Devon, Sharra, Shanee, Jasmin, Azaria, Kayla, Anthony

SPECIAL THANKS FOR INSPIRATION TO:

V. Whittington

There are laws, rules and regulations that we the public must adhere to.
Some live the exception.

PROLOGUE

▼

Between the three of us, Stoney, Sleeper and me, when Stoney hustled his marks, he played the game so painstakingly precise that he could creep up on a fifth of loneliness with a padded soul. He had an unwavering passion to be the best cop, ladies man, hustler, whatever. My man Stoney Brooks. The Stoneman! Even to God, he was stone cold to the bone.

I thought he could handle the business that we were involved in because he appeared nonchalant in character, cool, calm and collective when he played blackjack with the devil. They were on first name basis. He wore an ice-cold poker face that could deceive anyone. This might seem difficult to understand, but Stoney knew how to sweet talk like the warmth of summer, and at the same time, twist his words to perform like old man winter. He spilled a platinum rap so tight that he could cut diamonds with his tongue, and induce the grim reaper to tears. Make him surrender his cloak and sickle. And to think, I had more doubts about Sleeper than Stoney.

It was exciting at first, manipulating the public the way we did by exploiting their blind faith in us. I've never had so much fun before in my entire life. We had it all; power, prestige and privilege. The marks had no idea where we were coming from, until we slammed the judge's gavel onto the block. We were so good at what we did that we felt invincible. We believed that no one could touch us. Doing what we did was easier than taking candy from babies and we enjoyed it immensely.

When the majority of the marks heard the dreadful news that we laid on them, they dropped the phone immediately and we heard all kinds of chaotic hell going on in the background; hyperventilated cries of denial, bloodcurdling screams and inarticulate pants of acute shock. From hearing what sounded like a sack of potatoes hit the floor, we could tell that they had fainted. And weirdly, sometimes we heard hysterical laughter, as if we had induced the mark into a psychotic fit.

The whole idea was to cause as much pandemonium as possible, in the least amount of time possible, delivering the maximum shock effect. We first sent the mark soaring to the high heavens by showering them with blissful praises. When they were just about to walk through the pearly gates of heaven, we gave them the bad news that there was some sort of mix-up in the books. Which sent them zooming on a spiral downward, bypassing the formidable abyss, straight to hell.

If after they got over the initial shock, they picked up the phone and pled their cases desperately, as though we were vengeful gods on judgment day. Vigilantes prepared to judge and punish them by giving them a one-way ticket straight to hell in a flaming hand basket mounted on racing slicks.

Every now and then when we hung out together; completed our clique, Stoney, Sleeper and me, for thrills, we set the stage for entertainment and made merciless blackmailing telephone calls right in front of each other, for bragging rights. Lights, no cameras, but a hell of a lot of action. Needless to say, for our own protection, we never taped the conversations. Although, it would've been great for posterity.

After we discovered or came in contact with the only piece of evidence or information that could tie a person to a crime; cold case or otherwise—preferably someone who had a lot of money, or a high paying job—we did a little research to gather as much information about them as we could. Then we'd construct a pitch-line, which was like preparing a manuscript for a short play. Then we'd contact the mark using disposable cell phones, or through public telephones located miles from where we lived. When we spoke to the mark, we initiated the arrangement by leading them with an enigmatic conversation about diddlysquat jack shit, preferably hyping them on their past achievements. When they were feeling at ease, as though everything were hunky dory—we could tell they were by listening to and feeling the level of comfort in their voices—within a few seconds, we transformed their bright and cherry lives into an apocalypse. Make them break down, cry and grovel. And weirdly, in some cases, urinate or defecate on themselves.

Surprisingly, three of the marks had heart attacks right over the phone. Fortunately for us, they recovered. Subsequently, they wished they had died for the dire circumstances in which they were forced to live with.

I had once stopped a court appointed lawyer for driving intoxicated, and asked him to submit to a sobriety test. He stepped unsteadily out of the car and almost fell into oncoming traffic, and I found a gram of cocaine on the floor of his car. To let him off the hook, so that he could keep his license to practice in the Commonwealth of Massachusetts, he agreed to give me free legal services for a year, and a summers use of his beachfront home in Hawaii. Another time, a postal worker who would've done anything to keep his record clean, so that he could hold onto his job, offered me the sexual services of his wife, his ten-year-old daughter and eight-year-old son. All but himself.

It was amazing to learn what some people would do to hold on to their jobs, or to stop their reputations from becoming blemished. Which chances are, would be detrimental to their livelihood. The list of favors that people offered and the kinds of promises that they made were mind-boggling and endless. Things got so crazy at one time that I couldn't tell what was going to happen next.

To pacify his niggling conscious, Stoney called what he did 'making the criminals pay dearly for their grave mistakes.' Which he thought would initiate the beginning of their long and costly road to rehabilitation. To have the opportunity to play God and assume the role of jury, judge and executioner, and to inflict his own brand of vigilante justice, Sleeper called what he did 'bleeding the bastards, medieval style.' Undeniably and straight-up, to get what I wanted out of life, I called it 'pumping the suckers.' A sucker is anyone who messed up, then didn't cover their tracks. Anyone!

Spanky

CHAPTER 1

▼

Ten years after joining the Boston police department, ten years before his retirement, Stoney Brooks paced agitatedly across the living room floor of his luxurious mansion on 24 Hillshire Boulevard, in Dover, Massachusetts. The extravagant manor has a sizable reception area, a grandiose ballroom, a Jacuzzi and fireplace in the master bedroom, a fully stocked wine cellar, and a twelve seat movie theater. The spacious master bedroom has an elegant Russian steam bath off to the side; a place that he frequents at least four times a week to enjoy body massages at the firm hands of a robust Russian woman staying in the states on a temporary work visa. The mansion is blessed with a gourmet kitchen that would make any cook proud to create their delicacies in. To entertain his guests cordially, he has a world-renowned five star chef on retainer who caters the most extravagant affairs.

Stoney relished in the hospitality of these areas every day, but his favorite space is the red and gold schemed Paisley sports room. It boasts of a professional length pool table, a twenty-five thousand dollar technically advanced surround sound stereo system—its fifty speakers implanted stealthily throughout the mansion—a complete wet bar, and a wall sized, high definition, flat screen television connected to the huge satellite dish rooted in the backyard. It pumps in over two thousand channels from around the world, but he mostly watches the discovery channel. Collectively, the mansion delivers warm feelings of permanence, as if he had lived there forever—he resided in eloquent dreams of immaculate grandeur. Understandably, it's a comfortable refuge from the outside world; an escape from all that ails. Until recently, the mansion was everything that he had dreamed it would be.

He lives in an exclusive gated community that's kept so secure that crime and solicitation were completely unheard of. Even visitors weren't allowed to roam freely, unless accompanied by one of the twenty-armed security guards. The locality is so extravagant that there's an early ear picturesque Venetian water fountain placed at the gates entrance, designed by a famous Italian artist on the skids, and a private subcontractor wheeled in fifty foot potted palm trees in the middle of each spring. The area is so strikingly attractive, that a reporter had once described the experience of his visit as entering through the pearly gates of heaven.

To cast suspicion of the mountain of wealth that he has amassed through many illicit ventures, he arranged to have the deed put in a dead uncle's name. He was once a high-priced divorce attorney who practiced his trade in Marin County, California, a prosperous area where the rich and glitzy reside. Bizarrely, the locale is also know for its high divorce and suicide rates.

He keeps a cramped little two room studio apartment in the South End of Boston, mainly to show inquiring minds that that was his primary place of meager residence. He stops by every now and then to collect the mail, give the place a light dusting, talk to the neighbors, keep up appearances.

Glancing at the luxury surrounding him in his lavish domain, he found much conflict. In remembering how each item was paid for, he saw mistrust and betrayal flowing in drapes of crimson. The exquisite priceless art and other costly fixtures lining the living room ridiculed him when he walked by them, or even glance in their direction. Their eyes leered accusingly, they laughed scathingly, and whispered his name hauntingly. They treated him as though he was simply an object for want, made him feel as though he was nothing but another lifeless fixture dressing the mansion. A heartless clump of materialistic glob created to take up space for someone's idealistic whims.

The faceless children have been calling out to him everyday for the past year, in hopes that he'd hear them, then respond receptively. Yet, he didn't, their voices blocked by his ignorance to give atonement to his bleeding soul. He had traveled just past the fine borderline that separated the sane from the insane, never to return. He was still aware of his everyday activities and going-ons, but everyone has their limits. The idea that he could have been hallucinating never once entered his mind He wouldn't allow it to, for his gilded pride. Therefore, he accepted the paranormal occurrences as a reality, and incorporated them into his waking days. He responded defiantly to their warnings, lived in a harrowing madness that only he knew existed. A sinister world separated from everything civilized and composed.

Feeling the mounting stress from the children sneering at him, their diminutive voices taunting him, he had finally reached his limit and exploded, "What're you looking at, you pieces of shit?" He circled the living room, raving like an enraged lunatic. "I said, what the hell are you staring at? Damn you!"

He ran to the priceless Ming vase mounted on a French marble-topped, three-legged stand, just behind the far left end of the Persian couch. Its ancient Chinese design formed a pair of menacing eyes that poked, prodded and pricked him cripplingly with scorns of tell tale. He tried arduously to pierce the vase with a heated stare, but to no avail. He ordered, "Answer me, dammit! I asked you a question. What in the hell are you staring at?" His shaking hands dragged frustratingly over his head, over his bloodshot eyes, cupped his mouth. "Don't act like you don't hear me." He stepped to only inches away and examined the meticulous ancient Chinese freestyle design. "I know there's someone in there. I can see you peeking at me from behind that Bonsai tree. And you, I see you hiding under the bridge. I hear you giggling. I can see ..." he swallowed remorsefully, "... your eyes."

The dark eyes on the vase focused intently on him, aggravated him until he could no longer bear its presence. Their voices rode him mercilessly like a sweltering sun in the Sahara desert. Their syllables stabbed him callously, like shots fired from an AK-47.

Now highly frustrated at its torturous silence, he snatched the twenty-five pound vase from its stand, and hoisted it high over his head until his elbows locked. Idling, his blood pressure shot through the roof, higher than it's ever been before, he blasted, "I know you can talk! Tell me, dammit! Why do you keep staring at me?"

He considered whether there would be some gratification in what he was about to do. Ignoring his denial, he was sure there would be. He laughed hysterically, grunted heavily and flung the vase into the fireplace. After smashing it into a thousand pieces, he jumped up and down excitedly, rejoiced mightily, "Yeah! I killed the little rat bastards!" He danced in a festive circle around the chunks of ancient clay, clapped his hands exuberantly.

Hearing the thunderous crash, his servant stormed from his bedroom and dashed to the living room. He stopped twice along the way to slip on his slippers. Entering the living room, he knotted his robe, thinking worriedly, almost every fricken night, the same damn thing. And it's getting worse. I'm getting tired of this mess. When's he going to get some help?

Standing in the living room doorway, Carlton said coolly, "Sir," with his obviously fake English accent, "are you all right? I heard this awful crashing sound and I came at once." He noticed the devastated priceless Ming lying shattered in and about the fireplace, and his eyes popped out of their sockets. He gushed, "Sir, that was a priceless Ming! It's ... It's irreplaceable!"

Stoney jumped on him, "That was a piece of shit. It kept harassing me, and it wouldn't stop." He stared desperately at Carlton. "It tormented me, so I killed it. I had to destroy it, don't you see? It was trying to drive me crazy, and I ain't crazy. You know I ain't crazy, Carlton." He drew closer. "Don't you understand?" He spanned the room perplexedly, pointed to an authentic Rembrandt hanging on the wall just behind the couch. During an uncontrollable outburst the week before, he had assaulted it with a letter opener. He had stabbed the painting with such a sizzling viciousness, that he had left two golf ball sized holes in the sheetrock behind it. Later that evening, when he had come downstairs through the darkness to retrieve a book that he had left on the couch, he had the most harrowing experience of his life. Carlton had left the lights on in the next room over, which was easily seen glowing through the Rembrandts eyes—it looked like a ghost from Christmas past. The next morning, instead of removing the painting from the wall, he stood on the couch and patched the eyes with duck tape. "They keep staring at me, accusing me of doing these awful things. Things that I know I didn't do. They're trying to imply that I did something horrible. Something horrendous. They keep insinuating that I ... that I ...," he paused, fell short of disclosing what they implied. His fists clenched infuriatingly. "... they keep running it into the ground. They won't leave me alone. They won't stop."

Carlton often downplayed his frequent psychotic behavior in sarcastic ways. His eyes returned a sleepy butlers look, he sighed. "I think you should try to get some rest, sir. Maybe an hour in the Jacuzzi might do you some good. Or perhaps you could have that stoutly woman come by, and massage the tension from out of your ..."

"I don't want to take a bath, and I'm not sleepy," he huffed. "And dammit, don't patronize me, as if I'm a little kid." He highlighted the end of each sentence with stomping his right foot, as a child throwing a tantrum. "I don't want to go to sleep!" **'STOMP!'** "They won't let me sleep!" **'STOMP!'** "Every time I close my eyes, I see them!" **'STOMP!'** He paced nervously in front of Carlton, amid a storm of hysteria. He stopped, faced him and explained, "They get together and hold hands, then dance in a circle around me." He stepped even closer, and Carlton saw the distress in his bloodshot eyes. "And I want to grab them, to twist their little fricken heads off, so they'd shut the hell up." He stammered, "An-An-And they sing these infuriating nursery rhymes that drive me up the damn wall, and I'm tired of it. All day long, hickory dickory dock, the mouse ran up the cock. Jack be nimble. Jack be slick. Jack likes to talk a lot of shit. Mary had a little lamb, whose fleet was white as snow. A pimp caught up to her, slaughtered the lamb, and now the girl's his hoe. It's maddening! I-I-I can't take it anymore."

Carton didn't believe a word of what he said, but gaped blankly. Yet, he did consider the rhymes to be quite amusing. He asked calmly, "What did you say you saw, sir?"

Stoney stared into his doubting eyes, and suddenly remembered not the oath he took when he joined the police force, but what was to him a more important one. The oath that initiated him into the Dixie Club. A pitiless secret society that he and two other police officers had started ten years ago, to make money to supplement their incomes.

Dropping his shoulders, as well as his enthusiasm to proceed with what he's been wanting to get off his chest, he sighed grievingly, turned and walked away. He stated hopelessly, "Never mind, Carlton. It's nothing. You're right, it's absolutely nothing. I'll try to get some rest. I'll pour myself a drink, and try to get some shuteye. Maybe that's all I need."

Although Carlton knew exactly what was bothering him, he played it off, not wanting to get involved. He, like most people, had his own fair share of personal problems to deal with. Helping him deal with his meant adding another job to his full list of daily chores. Another arduous task that he could surely do without.

Stoney approached the portable bar, it slid from underneath the glass topped coffee table. He plopped on the couch, then grabbed a bottle of scotch. He swung his heavy construction boots up to rest on the glass surface and nearly shattered it.

The bang startled Carlton and he snapped in a half circle. "Sir!"

"Now what do you want?"

He replied politely, "Don't you think you should remove your boots before placing your feet up there? If you're not careful, you could do a substantial amount of damage to …"

Stoney twisted his neck strenuously, peered coldly. "So what! It's my gotdamn table. If I break the damn thing, then it's broke! It's just as simple as that." He looked at the glass surface. "And then again, that might not be a bad idea. That way, the little crumb snatcher with the curly blonde hair won't be able to look up at me anymore. If I could, I'd snatch those horned rimmed glasses off his face, and smash'em … break'em into a million pieces. Then I'd shove each piece right up his ass. That'd teach the little punk to mess with me. Coming into my home, disrespecting me like that."

Although he heard every word, he replied, "What did you say, sir?"

"Nothing. I didn't say anything."

"But I heard you as clear as …"

Stoneys facial expression blared, 'How dare you challenge me! I'm your employer. More than your bread and butter.' He shouted, "I said, I didn't say jack, dammit!" He turned around completely and leered at him, hoping his angry eyes would threaten him to go away.

Carlton returned his stare. He had several ways of telling Stoney what was on his mind. He stared discontentedly, his eyebrows rose confoundedly to meet in the center of his forehead. Suddenly, one big wrinkle came into view just under his hairline. "Sir!"

Stoney faced the fireplace, threw in back, "You ain't left yet? Now what do you want?"

"After disposing of the refuse, will you be needing me anymore this evening?"

He waved his hand dismissively. "No!" With an English accent, he said facetiously, "I don't think I'll be needing you anymore this evening." He said inaudibly, "Why don't you go take a dip in the English Channel."

Although he heard some parts of the statement that he had just made, he ignored verbal insults. Knowing that it came with the territory. It was part of the job. Furthermore, he knew it didn't pay to respond to belittling or demeaning gibberish. "Sir! I beg your pardon."

"Nothing. I didn't say anything. Just talking to myself."

Over the last few months, he had slowly developed a nasty habit of lashing out at nearly everyone, for no apparent reason that anyone could see. Although, some of his close friends believe that it was because of how he felt on the inside.

Carlton cleared his throat. "Very well sir."

When responding to Stoneys guests at some diner parties, he was instructed to hold his nose up high, and hold his right hand up in front. A limp wrist, dainty like, as if about to flip a coin, or insert one into a slot. At some of his fancy black-tie affairs, he made him wear a tuxedo, and ordered him to click his heels ever so often, giving the atmosphere the Baron Von field marshal effect. And sometimes, to complete the scene, as he was about to leave the room, he smacked the palm of his hand over his pruned lips, making a popping sound. A few times he even went so far as to don a revolutionary military jacket, complete with a few dozen costume medals. The year before, at a Halloween party, he had dressed as a medieval court jester. The suit fit perfectly, but the humor was nowhere to be found. Didn't even have the same zip code.

Before he left the living room, he remembered a message that he was supposed to deliver. "Sir. Your fiancé called a short while ago. She asked if you could return her call at your earliest connivance." He waited for a reply.

Hearing nothing but a grunt, he left.

He had met Katherine several years before, at a dinner party that a married couple he knew had hosted. They introduced her to him, in hopes that he'd seriously consider the institution of marriage. Ever since that dinner party, he hasn't spoken a word to them for making that arrangement. Instead of thanking them, he told them that if he ever saw them again, he'd arrest them for spite. He'd beat them silly with his nightstick, then create the false charges later, after he figures how much he disliked them for their not staying clear of his personal affairs.

She's a young woman of twenty-five years who's been partying ever since she was twelve. She's the type of daddy's little girl that he despised for her overruling femininity, but loved passionately for her sporadically naughty ways. She broke every rule in the book when it came to lovemaking. It was a lifetime quest. Once, persuaded by her tantalizing sex appeal, they had sex in the bathroom of an airplane, five miles in the air. While the flight attendant banged away on the door, they banged away in the bathroom. Twice, they had sex in the balcony at the cinema 54 movie theater. The first time, 'Batman' was playing. The second time, 'Batman Returns' was playing. For some reason, the Black Knight drove her wild with passion. As wrong as he felt his actions were, he had no self-control over someone so sexually demanding. Someone who was so wrong for him. And yet, so right.

At first, being with her was simply divine. Like a breath of fresh air. He enjoyed the late night diners by the seashore in Cap Cod. The stimulating cozy fireside chats. The long walks in the park just after sunset, and the exhaustive sexual encounters. That first month was what his long sought after fantasies were made of.

During the weeks to follow, the relationship turned into an average association. He had developed a sour ear from her continual whining and nagging. When frequenting her issues, he felt as though someone was dragging fingernails over miniature chalkboards installed in his ears. Other times, her troublesome personality sent electrical shock waves circling the base of his skull, zooming down his back, forcing him to stand straight, stick out his chest and clench his fists. His feelings went from wanting to use his handcuffs on her, to add to their sexual pleasures. To his wanting to use his nightstick, to beat her senseless, to add to his greater pleasure. The sex was great, but the mouth that accompanied her needed to be gagged or sewn shut. He believed unreservedly that she was nothing but the groundskeeper for a great vagina.

In public, standing behind her, he sometimes simulated a strong-arm on a Viking ship in the middle ages, delivering a hearty flogging. He topped it off with making believe that he threw a bucket of salt water into the wounds. Afterwards, he smiled gleefully, feeling great satisfaction.

The first major argument they had was about the way she dressed in public. She wore jeans that snuggled her apple bottom so tight, that it appeared as though Levi Strauss had painted them on. Although, that's one of the attributes that attracted him to her—a sexy round mound—after they began dating, he didn't like her walking around with men drooling at her all the time. He told her that only brainless nitwits try to get what they want by using perverted seduction. And did the shit hit the fan after he made that statement. Since then he's learned to keep his mouth shut, say as little as possible, and never volunteer information.

Katherine, he wondered of drearily, staring into the fireplace. She's daddy's' little innocent saber tooth vamp. Girl can suck all of the I's out of the word Mississippi, and leave a hell of a limp river behind. I must've been out of my mind when I spilled my guts out to her that night I was drunk, babbling about our secret operation; The Dixie Club. Expecting her to keep her mouth shut is like my wishing I'll never be disappointed another day in my life. One day she's going to turn on me. I can feel it deep in my bones. She's getting to be a thorn in my side, her and that 'give me this and give me that' dialogue. She sounds like a broken record. I'll give her a call tomorrow sometime, or maybe the day after. I don't feel like hearing it right now. I don't feel like hearing anything right now. Right now, all I want to do is …

He brought the bottle of scotch to his lips, closed his eyes, then took several hearty swallows. Feeling the alcohol burn his throat, he inhaled deeply, attempting to cool himself. He wheezed, "Damn, that's good stuff."

Minutes later, he picked up the remote control to the C.D. player, then aimed at the stereo system across the room. He pressed a few buttons with some difficulty, for his double vision, and soothing music filled the room. "Kenny G.," he said. "Little boy blue, come blow that horn."

He ran the back of his right hand across his mouth, then brought the bottle to his lips and tipped it again. This time, he didn't stop drinking until the half-full one liter bottle was completely empty.

After he had finished, he looked awkwardly at the bottle, tried to read the label. The words wiggled as heat waves, and the letters jumped from place to place, appeared jumbled, as if he was dyslexic. He gave up trying to give himself a

hard time, and dropped the bottle next to him. He tilted hi_
degrees, stared intently at the ceiling, and his eyes followed _
shell like designs surrounding the crystal chandelier. Most insta_
him, surrendered him to the tranquility of the rolling waves on a.. ocean surface.

Without warning, they shuffled from place to place, like watching a street shark hustle at three-card-monty. He focused on his prized wining gun collection, felt woozy, and the room began spinning wildly out of control. He snapped his head several times to attempt to stop the effect, but only succeeded in becoming dizzier. The room spun faster and faster, his stomach became unsettled, and he felt queasy. To avoid becoming nauseous, he closed his eyes tight and fell back against the couch. At that moment, he experienced the effects of having a wrecked equilibrium, like being in outer space, having no symmetry.

I haven't learned anything yet, he thought. The first time I got plastered was at age fourteen. The second time, a week later. The third time, not to long after. At the Boy Scouts jamboree. When my dog was and killed by that drunken bastard who I use to live next door to. Again, at the family picnic, when my older brother came home from college that summer. Another time when my ...”

He passed out.

Scurrying to a time of innocence for relief of the pressures of what he had become; a hustler in blue, he remembered a time not to long ago. After high school, Stoney, his close friends called him Stone—when he played high school football, a rugged running back, his diehard fans called him ‘The Stoneman’—went to a second rate technical school to break into the world of hi-tech computers. He had heard that a person can make fair living in that particular field of technology. Shortly after his graduation, he hit the work force with a psyched anticipation of having a new and exciting career. However, he quickly discovered that his meager certificate had about as much bang as a wet firecracker floating in a bowl of chicken noodle soup. He wanted a hell of a lot more out of life.

He also had a secret desire to write and publish an international bestselling novel. An idea that's been on the backburner ever since he attended middle school. He believed wholeheartedly that writers were especially talented people. Spellbinders with the God given ability to sweep people away into an exciting adventure, in another place and time. Holding them captivated with brilliantly arranged choice words. Praiseworthy individuals with the capability to make their readers forget all about their worldly problems, if just for a little while. People who can transform other peoples lives for the better, by bestowing hope with written inspirations. Give them words to live by. He would've started working on the idea after he took a few English literature classes in high school, but he thought he never had anything exciting to say. That would soon change.

During this time period, he lived in the two room studio apartment, located on the top floor of a brownstone on Mass. Avenue, near the Tremont Street intersection. Most days, his long sought desires of being rich mushroomed into glamorous dreams of enchanted castles and pie in the sky. He felt as though everyone he went to high school with had accomplished more than he did. He wasn't a jealous man, but he did feel that life was unfair.

He grew up staying out of trouble. He was a decent kid who didn't sidle with the wrong crowds. He ate his spinach, like his mother told him to. He ate his Rice Crispies and drank his Ovaltine every morning, before he went to school. After becoming an adult, he asked himself, where's the reward? Where's the excitement? Where are the gorgeous women, the fine automobiles and the spacious house with the tennis court and Olympic size swimming pool in the backyard? When does life begin?

He was quoted in the high school dyad as saying 'living meager paycheck to paycheck is like hanging by a silk thread over a school of hungry piranhas. Clad in nothing but a Venus Beach g-string, and maybe some underarm deodorant for seasoning.'

Why shouldn't he have been able to enjoy himself? He was a hard working individual entitled to take pleasure in the American dream. At the back of his mind, he knew his fancy dreams would only come to fruition with a hefty price tag. Because he had fed envy and covetousness into his desires, he allowed his desperation to grow until he could no longer hold onto his integrity, to obtain the luxuries of life through honest, hard work. Before long, the numbers on the price tag had changed to the price of his soul.

He became disgusted sometimes, staring drearily from the only window of his apartment. Made him feel pure hell, anguished him to no end. This particular Friday evening was no exception. Most people in the area, yuppies in general, were either enjoying themselves, or were planning to enjoy themselves later on that evening. He couldn't stay out late, because like Cinderfella, his one million dollar stretch limousine turned into a five dollar hooptie precisely at midnight.

Listening to Nelly and Tim McGraw sing one of their hits 'Over And Over' on the radio, he wandered aimlessly around his apartment in a pair of wrinkled boxer shorts and flip-flops, clutching a warm can of Budweiser beer. Passing by the bedroom, he stopped briefly and listened to the excitement pouring through a Radio Shack police scanner. People caught up in the displeasures of life; two neighbors in a heated dispute over a parking spot, shots fired in a nearby housing project, a domestic dispute, a car accident.

Feeling the need for some encouragement, give him hope for a better tomorrow, he glanced over the beds headboard and admired his lifelong inspirations. Three pictures that he's treasured ever since Junior high. On the left, the Reverend Dr. Martin Luther King. On the right, John Fitzpatrick Kennedy. In the middle, the greatest rock sensation of the sixties, Jimi Hendrix.

Abruptly, he heard the familiar awe-inspiring hum of a finely tuned Italian sports car, and rushed to the window to look outside. He damn near broke his neck tripping over the wires to the playstation. A young prominent sales and marketing attorney for a well-established law firm in downtown Boston, who lives in a twelve room luxurious penthouse in the same building, had just arrived in his brand spanking new, candy-apple red, Ferrari 308 GTI. It resembled the type of car that Tom Sellick once drove in the television detective sitcom 'Magnum P.I.' The car was aeronautically designed so perfectly, that at a standstill, it appeared to be going one hundred and fifty miles per hour. As he trafficked in or out of the apartment building, as he sometimes strode by the car, his heart raced out of control with the anticipation of having one just like it some day.

The attorney pulled up to and parked behind a rust bucket, Stoneys' 1973 Ford, Pinto. He rammed the bumper recklessly and jarred it loose, and the muffler fell to the ground. The attorney jumped out of the Ferrari laughing up a storm, and selfishly neglected to examine his hanging bumper and dropped muffler, but hustled to the passenger side door.

Listening to a simmering drum role, Stoney wondered dolefully, now what's this clown going to throw in my face and shove down my throat?

The young attorney opened the door to the Ferrari, and a glamorous Hollywood type sexy female, a bombshell of a woman, whose tanned flesh screamed 'every inch of me is just like this!', stepped daintily out onto the sidewalk, taking her glorious sweet ass time. She held out her hand, hinting to ask for assistance, and her gorgeous legs stretched out for miles. Six-foot legs, on a six-foot tall woman. The seemingly painted-on white spandex mini skirt she wore nudged itself higher with each move she made, revealing that she was not wearing undergarments.

She giggled boisterously, as if to flaunt, 'We have money! We have identities! Let us pass to the front of the line!' Stoney understood it to be the kind of laugh that only people with loads of money were aloud to use. Maybe millions. It's the kind of laugh that proclaims your status quo.

After the young attorney slammed the door shut, two beeps pierced the air, signaling the alarm was on. As the couple walked up the short flight of stairs leading to the apartment building, Stoney followed them until his forehead grated the screen. When he could hear their voices no longer, he looked to the end table, to the right of the sleep sofa, and glanced lustfully at a framed picture of a glamorous Swedish supermodel that he had clipped from a Maxim magazine. He then became angry at himself for the many times he's lied to his guests about her being his fiancé.

He wondered if he'd ever have a woman like her someday, knowing that with no finance, there would probably be no romance in his life. The mere thought of him making love to a woman that gorgeous made him salivate like a dog. Gave him a hard-on the size of the Rock of Gibraltar, and excited him to the point of blacking out.

Reflecting enviously on his neighbor and the luxuries he possessed, he closed his eyes despondently, glanced to the evening sky and grumbled miserably, "Please God, humor me. Tell me why that fat baldheaded jackass is living my dream?"

Suddenly, an unforgettable incident that had occurred eleven years prior flashed inconveniently through his mind. It happened on a scorching mid August afternoon, it was at least eighty degrees. Although the sun had gone down, the torturous humidity was still as chunky as clam chowder. Since he didn't have an air-conditioner, it often became unbearable to stay inside. As pools of sweat ran liberally down the sides of his face, he contemplated taking a stroll, going out for a breath of fresh air. Because he wasn't satisfied with his position in the workplace, hadn't discovered his niche in life, his mind wandered often, and most walks seemed an empty expedition across vast regions of gray sidewalks under blue skies. Like sleepwalking, the finer details of his surroundings often escaped him, unless brought to his attention, charged at him with the full force of its significance.

To fill the void, he picked a popular destination and decided to wander to the Copley Square Library, or to the Stop and Shop Supermarket, for want of a cooler environment. Or he'd have a few ice cold beers with two of his closest friends; Spanky and Sleeper. Maybe shoot a few rounds of pool at the amusement center and arcade on Brookline Avenue. Or better yet, he could go to the Science Christian Monitor and sit on the front lawn, enjoy the cool grass, fifty yards from the bustling Massachusetts Avenue traffic. Perhaps he'd meet a girl there, or mingle with the locals. Many Northeastern University and Berkley Conservatory of Music students found the area to be a reasonably calm place to chill. Some enjoyed a vigorous game of Frisbee or sat on blankets, and some studied their lessons, while others listened to ipods and chatted amongst themselves. Some roller-bladed or dared fate by skateboarding hazardously on a few cement structures.

Sometimes it was more interesting to merely sit at the side of the lengthy wading pool, enjoy a gentle breeze frequenting the still waters. Observe the flow of traffic, a parade of assorted life forms. Some circling the pool wonderingly with profound thoughts etched on their faces, philosophical theories running fluidly through their heads, contemplating this and that. From time to time, he saw expressions on those wanting to shake their heads like an Etch-A-Sketch toy to start their day, year or lives over again. He was familiar with this look. Saw it in the mirror from time to time.

On occasion, and sometimes to his amusement, an often inebriated and grime ridden homeless man named Andrew—he seemed to know by full names most police officers walking their beats in the area, had a hidden rapport with them—would stumble by and preach to anyone who would listen about having ethics, and the life, liberty and pursuit of unhappiness. It seemed an undying quest, his subconscious provoked him twenty-four seven. Somewhere along the way he was blinded by the starry lights. He discovered that life is all about the choices we make, and that even fake gold glittered.

Every day at six thirty sharp, a middle-aged Caucasian man wearing a pair of gold trimmed horned rim glasses—a well-established edible flesh peddler of sorts, the sole proprietor of a nearby butcher shop—strolled vigorously down Massachusetts Avenue. A profitable time, because most people in the area were just getting off work, out of school, hustling to and from where ever.

Weirdly, he thought it wholesome business to advertise his produce by passing out leaflets dressed in a bloodied butchers apron, tee shirt and jeans. He looked like a surgeon just out of the emergency room, or a cold-blooded killer scurrying from a carnage. Perhaps mangled bodies lay splayed across his meat shop, positioned as manikins for sale to some fine young cannibals. Maybe he prided himself on being organized, with having severed appendages with liquorish twizzlers tied around the wrists and ankles arrayed in one section. Decapitated heads with broccoli wreaths circling their necks lined neatly on a shelf in another area. Torsos braised in basil sauce stacked in another room not to far away, maybe in the freezer section. The display case fashioned with an assortment of fried ladyfingers, sautéed man toes, and pickled ass cheeks.

Most people believed his profession implausible, as he was fitted securely with two veteran war era prosthetic arms. Reinforced plastic limbs, the ends fitted with stainless steel split hooks that cracked ajar, operated by wiring surgically attached to the muscles in his shoulders. To open and close the hooks, he only had to raise a shoulder slightly. It was never learned by anyone how he lost his arms, and no one knew if he's had this handicap since birth.

The Friday before, he had stopped to talk to Stoney, just casual conversation. He wondered how he could handle an assortment of blades without causing damage to other parts of his body. Surely he couldn't do any more damage to his hands and arms. The butcher pulled an advertising leaflet from the pocket in his apron, then handed it to him. Stoney eyed him distastefully, but accepted the leaflet. He then inquired as to, 'How can you advertise for your business, dressed like that? No offense, but it looks like you just murdered someone with a meat cleaver.'

The butcher studied his physical make-up absorbedly, and became deeply engrossed. He smiled haughtily, then took a seat beside him, less than a foot away. He wiped the sweat of his labor from his brow, then replied, 'Young man, I make no qualms about my business. That way there's no doubt in anyone's mind as to what I do for a living.'

Stoney studied the leaflet. 'There's no doubt in my mind what you are. You're a butcher.'

'Touché! Give the young man a cigar. You're very perceptive.' He stated jokily, 'I'm going to have to work hard to sell to you.' He flared a pretentious smile. 'So, what's it going to be?'

'Huh?' Stoney asked, slightly confused.

'My meats. I got some delicious cuts just for you back at the shop. I give out sample platters to my new customers. One bite, and you'll never stop … eating.' He sounded as though it was personal. He grew a little eager. 'Are you interested?'

He studied the leaflet again, wondering about the man, wondered about the suspicious pause in between the words 'stop' and 'eating.' 'I suppose it looks okay, prices and all. However, I never agree to things like this, perishables and such, unless I see them first. Had a uncle who ordered a side of beef through the mail one time. From somewhere near Houston, Texas. Clear across the country. He had plans to sell to his family, friends and neighbors and wrack up. Make a lot of cash. Didn't turn out that way though. He got ripped off. The meat was spoiled. His experience taught me a very valuable lesson about agreeing to things that I haven't seen.'

'Then you'll have to stop by my place sometime. It's not too far, only down the street a bit. Left on Sycamore Lane, third shop on the left. It's right next door to a little place called 'Big Daddy Woo Woos Smoke Shop. I'm sure they'll be something there that'll catch your eye, turn your fancy.'

Stoney nodded. 'Maybe. I might pick up a few steaks. Some filet mignons.'

The butcher went on to explain, 'I trim my meats to the bone, young man. Everything I sell is as fresh as the morning dew. I'm an expert in my profession. Been at it for eons. There's no fat in my meats, assuring that you'll get all that you bargain for. I season them with the choicest mouthwatering herbs, delicious temptations from the garden of Eden. I am the essence of times of many times. I've lived in the shadows of many men, as I'm sure I'll make you a permanent customer to the end of your days. I'll make sure that you get the best, so you can tell all your friends about me. My reputation's been built on word of mouth. Literally.'

Stoney nodded again, still slightly confused. 'Yeah. I might do that.' He thought about the butchers last statement, then asked, 'If your reputations been built on word of mouth, then what's with the leaflets?'

The butcher looked toward the afternoon sky in heavy contemplation, nodded assuredly. 'Oh yeah. I'm definitely going to have to work hard to sell to you. You don't let nothing slip by, and that's good. It'll keep me on my toes. There's an old saying that goes, Pick your friends. Don't let them pick you. In my case, having customers come to me is one thing.' He stated repulsively, 'Any worthless hooligan can come traipsing into my shop, making unpardonably requests, making a mockery of my profession. Telling me how to run my business, how to cut and season my meats. There's no challenge in them, because they're an easy sell. They come to me with preconceived notions on their taste buds. Their minds are fixated on what they want, and what they've had. It's no contest. Now, going out to handpick the most elite clientele with virgin tongues is altogether different. They're the cream of the crop. I get much pleasure, gratification and satisfaction in selling to them, because they meet a certain criteria. Their passions are left to be molded, like eager cadets. They're exactly who I'm looking for, because their palates haven't been spoiled with the lust of what they've already had. They grow to be grateful customers who I can rely upon. They appreciate my business, and are much obliged.' He smiled cunningly. 'Now it seems as though they can't live without me.'

The butcher rose to his feet, then extended his blood stained hook. He waited for Stoney to grasp, and then shake; make a deal. He stared at it with a hefty repulse, reluctant to accept. He kept his hands on his lap, and a deplorable feeling bubbled up from his gut, settled at the back of his tongue. He looked up at the man and stated skeptically, 'I might stop by sometime.'

The butchers prosthetic arm dropped and swung by his side. 'That's all right, cause I have a lot of faith in you. You're special, I got special cuts for you. You'll like my meats, I guarantee. Like I said before. One bite, and you'll never stop ... eating. You come by sometime, ya hear?'

Stoney didn't respond, only stared thoroughly as the butcher neared him briefly, then walked past him. At one point, when he was only a few inches away, he felt an arctic chill grasp his soul and shivered uncontrollably. He felt an electric surge, a strange urge entice him to buy as many of his products as he could afford. And if he ran out of money, then he would beg, borrow or steal to finance the rest. A lifetime commitment. A solemn contract made the old fashioned way, a few words and a handshake.

He eyed the butcher through the corners of his eyes, figured him to be quite unconventional. He imagined he gave a filleted orientation when presenting his goods to his choice individuals, dressed in a cherry red tuxedo and tails, complete with fluorescent spats—looked like a pimped out Willy Wonka. He wore a large colorful peacock feather tucked in the band of his purple top hat, and Fifty Cents' hit 'The Candy Shop' played in the background. Tap dancing gaily from display to display, he satisfied a tally of sinful customers in every respect, with meats prepared just as he had described. Just as he had promised. They were so terribly satisfied that they never stopped ... eating.

The words the butcher spoke didn't confuse him in the least, but the way he pronounced them did take him for a loop. It sounded as though he made a genuine declaration. Stoney was spellbound. Captivated. He felt the power of his influence overwhelm him with strong feelings of submission.

Feeling that he had lost nothing in the transaction, when the butcher was nearly out of sight, he washed the episode from his mind entirely. Wrote him off as an eccentric loony. A perverted weirdo.

Then, weirdly, he wasn't sure of what the man had tried to sell him. Realized years later that he was vying to trade for his soul.

C H A P T E R   2

▼

Still unconscious, he traveled back nine years, to a time just after his graduation from the police academy in Pittsfield, Massachusetts. He, Spanky and Sleeper—two of his closest friends that he's known ever since high school—were sitting in a sports bar in North Station, in downtown Boston, celebrating their victorious ascend into the ranks of Boston's finest.

It's five o'clock and most people were just getting off from work. As the bar became filled to its capacity with lawyers, engineers, secretaries, construction workers and a few others, they discussed what promises their futures might hold. What possible fortunes the next day might bring. Who would have to go to the bathroom next? Which woman walking by had the most sizable breasts and curvaceous round mound?

On Stoneys left is Robert Sinclair. When he was younger, he felt his name was too serious for whatever, so he adopted the nickname 'Spanky.' He's a six foot-four, two hundred and sixty pound prankster. To break the seriousness of life's everyday harsh realities, he often tells corny jokes and pulls childish pranks. Most of which are insulting and not amusing. To most people, he's your average smartass who believes that he holds the upper hand. Even when he's dead wrong.

Once, while driving in rush-hour traffic, he rear-ended a man. He jumped out of his car and then punched the guy out, arguing that he had bad breaks. Of course he was wrong for doing so, but he argued that he was right. Right up to when they cancelled his insurance policy. He was also arrested by a state trooper, then charged with road rage. However, the case was dismissed upon completion of six months of anger management.

He's single and lives alone in a five-room apartment in Dorchester, Massachusetts. Near the Savin Hill area. He doesn't believe in marriage at an early age. He believes in sewing his wild oats until they become fully cooked. Until they're burnt. Until his sixty-fifth birthday.

To break the monotony of his quiet and sometimes lonely apartment, he went out and brought a roommate. A pet bulldog he named Spike. He's fifteen inches tall, fifteen inches round, and has little stubby bowlegs. He calls them 'little tree stumps.' After having his tail cut off, he thought that Spike was very upset with him. To alleviate the grudge, he fed him steak and potatoes for nearly four months. By the end of the third month, the dog had gotten so fat that he had to carry him up and down the stairs. Before and after taking him for walks.

That was a few years ago, and he's since then shed a few pounds. Now Spanky considers him to be a lean mean fighting machine. However, he believes that he'll always keep the trauma of having his tail clipped at the back of his mind.

He's very sensitive about his dog, and believes that he's a reincarnated ex-marine soldier who was killed in the line of duty, because he was easy to train and is well disciplined. He only had to train him for five minutes on how to do things like fetch his slippers or bring him the newspaper, and he remembered easily.

When Spike came charging at him after a long days work, he enjoyed it when he jumped onto his lap and licked him all over his face. It made him feel special, adored. Unlike when he was a child, when his mother use to do something similar. Anytime his face appeared dry and ashen, she spat a loogey into her hand and smeared it all over his face, thinking it would improve matters. It only succeeded in making him smell like cigarettes, coffee and polident.

He talks to him often when they're alone, like a close friend, or a psychologist. Sometimes he'd ask questions about what to do about certain real-life matters. If Spike plod down on his belly and covered his ears, then that meant 'Hell no! Don't do it!' However, he also behaved like this when he squeezed the cheese. But if he sat up straight and delivered a look of encouragement, that meant 'Yes! By all means. Do it!' Most of the time, as crazy as it seems, Spanky respected his decisions. To him, Spike made more sense than most people he knew.

One time Spankys' VCR had went on the blitz, and he became highly upset. He unplugged it, then asked Spike if he could throw it out the window. Spike sat up and delivered a cheerful look of encouragement, probably because he felt he hadn't done anything wrong. He was merely happy that his master had addressed him. Sure enough, Spanky threw the VCR out the window. He lives on the third floor.

Sitting on the other side of Spanky is Bruno Knight. Growing up in Boston, with sleeping through most of his high school classes, he's earned the nickname 'Sleeper,' and sports the name well. In talking with someone whom he didn't believe was telling the truth, he often remarks, 'Com'on! Ya putting me ta sleep. Ya gotta come up with something better than that.' He's almost as tall as Spanky, and weighs two hundred and thirty pounds.

Sleeper grew up and still lives in Roslindale, Massachusetts with his wife Elizabeth and their newborn, Junior. As a child, Sleeper was the silent type who hung out with a gang of troublesome misfits. As everyone made suggestions about what they should do for the day, Sleeper seldom offered any advice, thinking his ideas were never good enough. He always left it up to them to plan his pastime. Even if they were going to get into mischief. Hence the saying, 'there are leaders, and there are followers.' Sleeper is certainly a follower.

"Okay," Stoney said, "which one of you cheap bastards is paying for the next round?"

"I got it," Spanky replied. "You guys are so damn cheap, you probably reuse your generic brand condoms."

"What're you talking about? I paid for the last round. Now it's you guys turn to set me up."

"Com'on you guys," Sleeper said. "Ya both sound like a couple of cackling old bitties. Ya act like somebody's trying to bleed ya, medieval style. We're only talking about a few lousy bucks. You guys act like you're on some kind of a tight ass budget or something. Ya putting me ta sleep with all this 'whose turn is it' jazz. Ya gotta come up with something better than this. I know both of you got loads of money."

"Not me," Stoney said. "Just because we're on the force now, doesn't mean that I can start throwing money all over the place." He looked up, closed his eyes and smiled. "I got this beautiful dream car in mind that I've been saving for." He stated exhilaratingly, "A Porsche Carrera! I don't care how long it takes, I'm going to get it. I've wanted one like it ever since we were in high school."

Spanky looked into his lap glumly. "You know guys, I've been thinking. You hear all this pity patty depressing shit we've been talking about for the past few years? We shouldn't have to be concerned with something as trifling as whose turn is it to buy a couple of beers. Now that we're cops, I think we've have the prime opportunity to make some easy big bucks."

"Shhhhh!" Stoney hushed. Appearing especially paranoid, he scanned the vicinity, searching for flies on the wall; unwelcome ears. "Keep your voice down. Your loud jokes aren't going to do anything but get us into some serious trouble."

Spanky sighed. Lowering his voice, he told Stoney, "This ain't a joke, buddy boy. I'm talking about some serious stuff here. I'm talking about the oldest profession in the book."

Sleeper's eyes widened. He excited, "Prostitution!"

"No, ya bonehead! I'm talking about one that's even older than that. In the Garden of Eden, that serpent ran a game down on Adam and Eve so smoothly, that there still talking about it in this day and time. I'm talking about cashing in on the weak. I'm talking about hustling."

"Look, you guys," Stoney said, "we just got on the force. I'm not about to screw up. I'd be a disgrace to everybody I know. Especially my parents."

"Who's talking about screwing up? I'm just talking about making a few extra bucks. You know, the way a few of the veterans do it. A little here, a little there, it all adds up. Besides, who's gonna tell?"

"I don't know about this," Sleeper said skeptically. "Like Stoney said. We just graduated from the academy, and we don't know anything about what it's like out there. As far as having the right connections are concerned. Like some of the vets."

"Look, guys," Spanky said, "if we don't take the money, then someone else will. What do you think this is, a democratic society? The way things work in this country is the person with the most money calls the shots. That's the bottom line. It's just as simple as that and everyone knows it." He whispered secretively, like a secret agent delivering an important message to a fellow agent. "It's been heavily rumored that some secret organizations in our very own government are involved with hustles. Just to stir up revenue." He glanced at a few patrons nearby, then back to Stoney and Sleeper. "Guys, I'm only telling you what I heard, and believe. Only because it makes sense."

Sleeper pretended as though he was smoking a joint, told Stoney, "I think he's been smoking some of that primo shit he took from one of his arrestees."

"Ya better lay off that stuff, Spanks," Stoney chuckled. "You're killing brain cells by the truckload. You'll be a strong candidate for Alzheimers if ya keep that up."

Spanky's serious disposition didn't waver an iota. "I can't believe you two don't know about what's been going on." He looked to the ceiling and mumbled inaudibly, "I'm sitting here with a couple of naive shits."

Sleepers laughter disappeared, after Spanky started to explain. "What I'm saying is that it's only logical that some false terrorist attacks serve their purposes. Some people believe that September eleventh was all about Americas need for oil. Another example of the government hustling is the Tuskegee Experiment? About fifty years ago, they tested for the long term effects of syphilis on a group of African American men in the South. As far as lost lives are concerned, or, expendable casualties of war, Uncle Sam figures the ends justifies the means. For our government, in the case of a terrorist threat, it makes it easier for them to take away civil liberties and turn the country into a police state. You know, marshal law and all that good stuff. Most people, that is, most law abiding citizens, feel it's okay to give up their identities; fingerprints, mug shots, submit to DNA samples or whatever, if they feel it will make them feel safer when they go out to public places, or travel. Especially if they're taking an airplane. Plus, it makes it easier for lawbreakers to get caught. And here's the payoff. Because of the economical state of affairs in America, the more people in prison, the better the economy for some who work in state and government. Get it?" He paused to catch the expressions in their eyes. "It means job security for us and the entire system of justice; workers in the penal system, the various social services departments, straight on down the line. If you remove a spouse from the household, the crippling financial domino effect begins with dysfunctional poor families whose members sometimes give up hope for the sudden hardships placed on them. The results being, they lower their moral standards of living and sometimes resort to crime for survival. Because the country's getting tough on illegal immigrant workers, a lot of people are getting deported. In the future, their menial jobs will be done by inmates in prison for a fraction of the cost."

When Stoney and Sleeper glanced earnestly at each other, Spanky could tell that they considered his every word.. Neither interrupted, as they were all ears and ready to listen to more of his depraved ideas.

Sleeper declared, "We took an oath. What you're talking about doing wouldn't be right."

For a fleeting moment, Spanky leered spitefully at him from the corners of his eyes, felt the sting of his undermining comment. He urged, "Com'on Sleeper. You don't believe in that 'justice for all' bullshit, do you? It's a crock of shit and you know it. That's not a viable reality, so don't even throw that shit in my face. Reality, to me, is not taking the bullet for some poor Joe Shmoe good-for-nothing piece of trash who probably doesn't even like cops. He gets into trouble all the time because he can't control himself. He has a record as long as my arm, uses drugs on a daily basis, and is a drunken disorderly slob. An asshole. A looser. People like that could care less about me or my family. What's more, as the numbers put it, most people don't even like cops until they need one. The only thing that matters to me, is my family and I having what we need to get by on. Just like the next person, I want a beautiful house in a safe neighborhood for my kids to grow up in. If I ever find the right woman to marry. I want brand new cars to transport them safely from 'A' to 'B', and loads of money keep to them comfortable. Lastly, and most importantly, I want to be able to be there for them. Alive and in good physical condition. With all of my body parts functioning properly." He waited for a second, then added, "Especially my Johnson!"

If Spanky were to join the military, he'd definitely be the type of soldier who'd take cover in his foxhole amidst a hail of enemy gunfire, with his helmet strapped securely over his groin area. He's not a sex fanatic, but he's gotten comfortable with the idea of having something in between his legs. Like most men, life without their penis' would be a living nightmare. Since he was ten years old, he considered his penis to be a physical declaration of his manhood.

Just before he graduated from the police academy, he went out and brought a tailor-made bulletproof jockstrap, which he wore for the first six months of service. The hell with what his colleagues thought. He was merely protecting his ass with a heavily padded slingshot. A bulletproof chastity belt. A golden thong. The only person he feared was Lorena Bobbitt. He's a typical American male who believes that if you have no ding-dong, you'll have no music in your life.

After selling his pitch, he sat back in his chair, folded his arms and allowed his devious proposal to marinate in their minds. Breaking the long silence, Stoney said, "I don't know about all of this. I have a feeling that this is some deep shit you're talking about us getting involved in. I'm going to need some time to think it over."

"Me too," Sleeper said. "I'm gonna have to think real hard about this. We're talking about our futures here. Our careers. That's nothing to pass lightly."

"I guess I can't ask for more than that from you guys. We'll talk about it again in a couple of weeks." He smiled comfortably. "For now, let's get something to drink. I'm thirsty as all hell." He turned around. "Where'd that waitress take off to?" He held his right hand high over his head, then whistled. "Over here! Some beers for my friends, when you get a chance." He told Stoney and Sleeper, "It'll be on me this time. I want you guys to think about it real hard, what I've been telling you. There's a lot of moolah out there, and all we have to do is take it. It's easy pickings."

The waitress, a middle-aged blond woman named Paula had just arrived at their table. She parked her tray on her burly hips, then eyed them one by one. "What can I get for you boys?"

Spanky glanced at his buddies with a wacky expression caked on his mug, and they knew it announced the approach of a corny joke. He smiled crazily. "Well, we'd like two pitchers of Budweiser draft delivered every ten minutes, until someone passes out or dies of alcohol poisoning. After that, bring one every fifteen minutes."

Paula giggled. "Two pitchers of Budweiser, coming right up."

After she went to the bar to fill their order, Spanky rubbed his hands together, looked like a mad scientist on the brink of a Nobel prize winning discovery. Eyeing Stoney and Sleeper, he whispered fiendishly, "Money, dammit! Is there anything else in life?"

A few awkward moments cruised by, then Spanky went on to say, "You know, guys. I heard the damndest thing about week ago, from one of the detainees arrested on a class B distribution charge. When his lawyer came to see him, he told his client that he may have to go away for a little while, since he was busted for holding a kilo of cocaine. His client told him that all he had to do was pay the right person, then he could get off with a slap on the wrist. Maybe a suspended sentence and a few hours of community service. The lawyer told him that the case had progressed too far into the system, so he couldn't make it disappear with a few payoffs. He told him that he should've offered the arresting officer a substantial bride, because on the street, the acronym for cop stands for 'cash over people.'" He snickered unenthusiastically. "Ain't that some shit?"

CHAPTER 3

▼

In the same dream, two weeks later, after their shift had ended, the three met at the same bar, sat at the same table; a cubby less than twenty feet from the rear entrance. A favorable spot because the noise emitting from the kitchen smothered their conversation. Also, Spanky had a paranoid thing about sitting with his back facing the entrance. He felt that he needed to see who was coming in, and who was leaving. Not saying a word, he folded his hands neatly, then placed them on the table. He eyed Stoney and Sleeper inquisitively, trying to figure which way their deliberations leaned. He found no expressions that appeased him and grew inpatient. He hurled a question into the air. "What's it going to be, guys? You've had some time to think about it, so ..." he showed empty palms, signaling for a reply. Sleeper was easier to read, so he focused on him. "I know you've seen what I've witnessed on the streets."

Sleeper said, "What's that?"

"Plenty of opportunities to generate some serious cash flow."

Stoney felt hesitant about saying, "In keeping my eyes opened around the station house, and a few other places, I guess I did see a few others in the department doing their thing. Mostly hush hush, on the down low. And now that I've taken the time to put things into their proper perspective, I also saw those drug dealers around town, riding around in their tricked-out luxury cars." He proclaimed enviously, "They make more money from one drug deal than I could in an entire year." Shook his head in detest. "It doesn't take a rocket scientist to figure the math, but I think it stinks."

"I saw the same things too," Sleeper threw in. "It turns my stomach to know that some of them have been getting away with total chaos. I mean, we go through the hell of laying our lives on the line to arrest them, and they're back out on the street practically the same day. Especially the big time dealers. They're making a laughing stock out of our legal system, standing in court with their one million dollar attorneys. I have to agree with you about money being the only and final answer. Since we're getting very little praise out of doing our jobs, we might as well get it out of taking the money that some criminals have accumulated illegitimately."

A smile creased Spankys' lips. "You know, guys? The way I look at it, we'd be doing the public a favor if we did things our way ... since we know the truth about what's *really* going on. Last week alone, Stoney must've brought in over thirty prostitutes. Ten of them with their Johns. Jailing the Johns doesn't do a damn thing. But if you mess with their finances, then they start listening. As for the low-life drug dealers, when they get back on the streets, it's simply business as usual. You set up a few big drug deals on video camera, then sell them the tape, explaining that it's the only copy. Their money can either feed their infested egos, or do us some real good by making our lives comfortable, or by putting our kids through college."

Stoney looked into his lap submissively. "I guess your right." He looked at Spanky. "So, how do we get started?"

Spanky considered the eagerness of how the question was posed. "Well, I've been thinking of how to organize this, and I think we should do something called a swap hustle."

Sleepers eyes widened curiously. "A swap hustle? What'n the hell's that?"

"That means that each of us should hustle who the next guy arrests. This way, it throws off suspicion. Take for example you, Stoney. You work in the domestics unit. You arrest prostitutes, their pimps, sometimes their Johns, et cetera et cetera." He focused on Sleeper. "Every now and then the Johns will turn out to be well esteemed individuals with status quo. You can apply pressure to them any way you see fit, to take them for whatever it's worth; money, stock information, property or inside connections on anything. Even pimps don't want to do time, thinking someone will move in on their women. An example of the payoff is that Sgt. Johnson in traffic pulled over a drunk driver one night, the owner of a well-known steak house in Cambridge. To avoid the arrest and get a DUI on his record, the guy offered Johnson free diners for a year, and he accepted. Most people in professional positions will pay anything to keep silent their arrest for solicitation of a prostitute, or for pumping one of those pretty boys who hang out in those cheesy blue-boy clubs in the downtown Boston area. They'll pay a hell of a lot more if you can get it on video tape. Recently, in the media, there was something about the Evangelical leader Ted Haggard buying a methamphetamine substance from a gay escort. The escort went on television and blabbed it all. Chances are, the escort tried to blackmail him with the information. When Haggard didn't pay up, that's when he was exposed. Things like this happen more often than we'd like to believe." He turned his attention to Sleeper. "Since you're in narcotics, I'll put the squeeze on the drug dealers you arrest. Especially the ones who've fucked up real bad, and need a way out of the mess they've made of themselves. Those guys will pay almost anything so that they don't get sent up. And you, Stoney, you're going to have the most fun."

Stoney asked skeptically, "Oh yeah?" He smiled frailly. "Spanky, enlighten me."

Spanky nodded for sure. "Oh yes indeed, my good friend. You see, since I'm in homicide, you're going to hustle the people who I can connect to a murder. Most anyone in the right mind would do anything on earth, to see that you accidentally lost very crucial pieces of evidence that could implicate them in a murder investigation. Cold case or otherwise. Information that I just happened to chance upon at a crime scene, that only we know exists. Since we're the first ones on the crime scene—even before the crime scene investigators show up and do their thing—we can collect the only piece of evidence that could tie a person to the crime committed. When you attempt to establish contact to initiate the hustle, they may simply hang up on you, because of the weight of their doubt for a conviction. Which maybe in the form of unknown evidence that they're in possession of, which they can produce at any given time to exonerate their self. If that's the case, then it's no big deal. You simple move on to the next sucker. However, if you're right, then you got 'em by the balls. The strange thing about this is that if you got 'em, without a doubt, you'll know it. Several peculiar things will happen when you get a solid hook. You may hear them stop breathing on the other end of the phone line. Or they may gasp for air, like they're having the life sucked right out of them. In case they faint, you may hear their dead weight drop to the floor, like a two hundred pound tuna. On the other hand, and even better yet, they may discharge a comical effect from having been slapped silly with shock. Stoney, when you get one, or even a couple of these absolute signs that you've got them, then you hunker down for the long haul, and pump that fucker dry for as much as you can. You strap yourself in and reel that son-of-a-bitch in like a prize winning trophy marlin." He paused again to allow the excitement to linger, then went on. "The plus side to this hustle is that sometimes you can offer evidence that will exonerate a person. Instead of the defendant paying a lot of money to some tight ass shark lawyer who'll only bargain for a shorter sentence, they'll pay you half of the same amount to ensure their innocence. So they can remain among the free and able. Besides, some people who're sent to prison aren't guilty anyway. Sometimes the mayor or governor incarcerates people on trumped up charges, or even with no evidence, only to show their constituents that they're getting tough on crime. Typically during an election year."

Spanky knew how to lay and sell his eggs. Ever so often, they ended up scrambled, which was seldom his preference. After he presented his get-rich-quick plan; fed his pitch, he sat back in his chair, crossed his arms and smiled haughtily. "Well guys, what do you think? How does it sound so far?" He believed Sleeper was sold, but Stoney was a complete toss-up. He couldn't read his rock-solid poker face if it was to save his life. His eyes shot back and forth in between the two. He added nothing to sweeten the pot.

Finally, Stoney nodded vaguely, an indistinct smiled creased his lips. Yet, his eyes remained skeptical. He finally spoke up, said plainly, "Yeah. I think I can hang with this hustling business for a little while. Sounds like a lot of fun. I'll go along with it, as long as it doesn't get too complicated. Too messy."

"Me too," Sleeper said. "Sounds like a cake walk. I didn't say anything at first because I think you already knew I was sold. I was just waiting to see what Stoney was going to say. It's just like you said before, easy pickings."

"It is," Spanky assured. "Easy as pie. But it'll taste even better once you get a hefty slice. In a couple of months, we should be off to a pretty good start. We'll talk in more detail somewhere else. This place has too many big eared people floating around. For now, let's have a couple of beers to toast our little hush-hush secret organization, arrangement, or whatever the hell it is we have." He looked to the ceiling and a marvelous idea hit him dead cold. "Ya know, guys. I was thinking. We have a group that doesn't have a name. And its just so happens that something came to me a few days ago, as I watched an old black and white civil war movie starring Clark Gable." He held up his hands to form a picture frame, as though holding an elongated paging sign. Like the ones some limo drivers held at airports, when they're looking for someone who they've never seen before. "Tell me how you like this." He whispered, "The Dixie Club!"

After announcing the name he had in mind, it grew so quiet that they appeared to be actors in the nineteen-eighties commercial, 'When E.F. Hutton talks, everybody listens.' Sleeper gave his opinion, "I like it! It has a nice ring to it." He laughed. "It doesn't mean shit, but it sounds good."

Spanky snickered. "You would say some dumb shit like that." He looked at Stoney. "And you, Stoneman? What do you say?"

"It's sounds confederate," he replied contemptuously, "like the old south. Jim Crow. Days of slavery, and all that other sick shit." He peered slyly at Spanky. "This doesn't have anything to do with the good old boys network, does it?"

Spanky shook his head. "Of course not. I just think it sounds neat, like the General Lee, on the old sitcom 'The Dukes of Hazard.'" He blurted, "Com'on, Stone! You know I'm heavily into the early era muscle cars." He paused. "Don't worry. You won't get an email inviting you to a cross burning. Like Sleeper said, it doesn't mean jack shit. You know me, and we've been friends for a long time. You know I don't believe in all that bullshit. In this situation, the only thing that matters is the money we'll be raking in, hand over foot."

"Well, all right. I guess I can deal with it. I just can't wait until the cash starts rolling in." He bitched and griped to the high heavens. "That old beat-up car I'm driving is on its last leg. I'm not even sure if I should give it the respect of calling it a car anymore. On the way to work this morning, twice I had to jump out in the middle of the pouring rain to get a jumpstart because the damn thing kept shutting off. What's worse is that I was standing on the side of the road with my uniform on, and nobody wanted to stop and help me." He scratched his head. "Sometimes I just can't figure people out." He fumed, "Dammit! I'm a police officer!" As if it were a reality, he stated, "People are supposed to respect me and my authority. I'm standing there all soak and wet, holding the damn jumper cables, and no one wanted to give me fifteen shitten ass seconds of their fricken worthless time to help me. And I had to …"

His old 1973 Ford, Pinto was indeed on its way to the cemetery. Before he attempted to start the car each day, when he got inside, he said a quick prayer. Then he had to pump the accelerator thirty times before turning the key. Sadly, he only got one shot before the carburetor over-flooded, and he had to get out again to check up under the hood to see what went wrong. At least twice a day on the way to work or where ever, he has to get out of his car with no matter what he's wearing to perform automotive surgery in the middle of day or nighttime bumper-to-bumper expressway traffic. The car is an outdated no-frills automobile. It has no air conditioning, no heat, no power steering, no power breaks, no power windows or door locks. The v-belt circled only the alternator and the camshaft. He wasn't mechanically inclined, so he considered the basic knowledge of how an engine operates to be rocket science. To his great pleasure, it would surely be a thrill to see the last of that non-starting, bald-tired, shredded interior, push-starting, fume smelling rust bucket. The floors were so rusted that from a distance, his feet were seen dragging the ground, like he was driving the Flintstone Mobile. Since he believed the car was already dead, he wrote a eulogy and taped it to the dashboard.

Hearing him rant and rave about nothing that mattered, Spanky finally cut him off by shouting, "Hey!" He lowered his voice. "Don't worry about it for now." With a serious stare lasting more than three seconds, he stressed, "As long as we get started and keep everything confidential between the three of us, at no matter what the cost, we should be okay. Most importantly, we'll keep no video or audio recordings of anything. Nothing!" He told Stoney, "You'll be driving a new Porsche before the end of the year. One that's paid for."

Spanky was a jokester who hyped people into his schemes by selling exaggerated pipedreams. He once sold Sleeper a supposedly mint condition car that he'd been trying to get rid of for almost a year. After he had finally lifted the rugs in the back seating area two months later, he discovered that he too had a Flintstone Mobile. The holes in the back floorboards were so huge that some mornings he found stray dogs, cats or other small animals sleeping in the back seat. The front seat was used as a rest room.

Stoney sighed with relief. "Yeah, the good life. That's just what I've been dreaming about for some time now. Finally, a comfortable life is within reach." He closed his eyes and imagined what the good life would entail. The good life, because for a long time, when he was much younger, he couldn't understand why there was so much violence, corruption and mayhem going on in poorer communities. Now that he understands finances—money and the importance of its necessity—he understood everything. Simply put, he figured that if people in poor communities fell into a lot of capitol and resources, then discrimination between the cultures would be outdated. You could afford what you needed to make your community a better place to live in. Instead of picketing city hall on deaf ears, waiting for forty acres and a mule. With most people being able to afford what they needed, there wouldn't be as much violence; random or otherwise. When you don't have annoying bill collectors chewing at your ass everyday, you can live an almost stress-free life. You can afford to do anything you want to do, or go anywhere you want to go, on a moments notice. If this were the case, chances are, you'd be a more pleasant person, with not many problems to complain about. You'd have nearly everything you'd need to satisfy your every whim. Everyday frustrating problems would be the farthest thing from your mind. Leaving you to suffer only little everyday inconveniences, almost ensuring that you'd have a very healthy attitude toward life. Most skirmishes like traffic jams are easily chucked off, because you'd have more important and pleasurable things on your mind. Wonderful things that make life worth living. Like being able to sit at the diner table with your family, in a beautiful home, as you enjoy delicious gourmet food over pleasant and intellectually stimulating conversation.

Sleeper was sold on the idea easily because he's a family man, and has fundamental needs on his mind all the time. He wants his family to live comfortably, to be able to raise them in a safe neighborhood, and then send his children off to the college of their choice someday. Coming from a large, lower-middle class family, he remembers often how many intense arguments there were in the household for the scarcity of a dollar. He would've welcomed any ideas to make some extra money, and thought secondly of the risks involved.

CHAPTER 4

▼

Moments later, Stoney was wakened by a gentle hand pushing his shoulder. Carlton attempted to rouse him, saying, "Sir! Wake up! Sir, it's sunrise. What would you like to have for breakfast on this superb morning?" His perky attitude was gentlemanly sublime. Always courteous.

Because Stoney experienced a mind-bending hangover, suffered a tremendous headache, the, his voice came over as a rackety pandemonium. He cracked his eyes open and peered at Carlton with a sinister leer. He yawned and stretched, spewed hoarsely, "Huh? What?" After realizing who it was, he shut his eyes tight for the barrage of sunlight paining his pupils. Forcing a few words past his parched throat, he said hoarsely, "Oh, it's you."

Wondering drearily of his wrinkled clothes, Carlton implied, "Looks like you tied another one on last night, sir." Hoping to get a response this time, he asked, "What would you like for breakfast today?"

Before Stoney cracked his eyes again, he cupped his hand over his brow, cleared his throat and accidentally coughed up a wad of phlegm. Didn't have anywhere to spit, so he swallowed it. Didn't taste good at all. "I think I can go for one of your English omelets this morning. And leave out those damn hot peppers. That stuff comes back on me something awful."

"Splendid sir. Will that be all?"

Stoneys squinted excruciatingly, massaged his temples, making a lax attempt to will the headache to leave. No dice! "Put a couple of aspirins on the side. No, make that three aspirins." He corrected him self again, "Just bring the whole damn bottle of that extra strength stuff." Massaging his scalp, he complained, "Damn, my head is killing me."

Carlton Spotted the empty bottle of scotch lying next to him, smirked, then remarked casually, "Heavens to mergatroid! I wonder why."

"You're not getting paid to get flip," Stoney said smartly. He ran his hands through his muddled hair. "Now go make my breakfast."

"Very well, sir. An omelet, and a bottle of extra strength aspirins. Coming right up." He turned to leave, then all of a sudden stopped in his tracks. "Sir?"

Stoney didn't bother to look at him. "Yeah. What is it?"

"Will you be going to work today?"

He released a heavy sigh. "Yeah, I suppose so. The bills aren't going to pay themselves."

"Very well, sir. As you eat, then bathe, I shall press your clothes."

"Yeah yeah yeah," he huffed. "Hurry up with those aspirins, will ya?"

CHAPTER 5

▼

After Stoney completed a twelve-hour work shift, he jumped into his Porsche and hit the asphalt. After arriving home, as Carlton had predicted, he went straight to the living room, plopped on the couch, then grabbed a fresh bottle of scotch. Hearing the bottle clink, he came out to greet him. Entering the living room, he cleared his throat and announced good-humouredly, "Good evening, sir."

Sitting on the couch, slumped, rubbed the back of his neck, as though he was on his last leg. He replied grouchily, "What'n the hell is so good about it?"

Carlton ignored the attitude that he had become familiar with. "What will you have for dinner tonight, sir?"

Normally, he'd have a full spread prepared when Stoney arrived. But he noticed that he hasn't been eating much lately. He had gradually replaced his meals with liquor. He's been drinking up a storm nearly everyday, because it was the only way that he knew how to distort the days events and recollections of his jaded past, without waiting for time to take its natural course to fog his memory. The immediate effect worked, but the hangover he received on the morning after plagued him doggedly. What he suffered most were the earth shattering head-aches, and blinding streaks of light that stabbed through the slits of the Venetian blinds. Every morning was like waking up from the dead. Before he cracked his eyes ajar, the first thing that he reached for were his dark sunglasses. His aviator shades.

"I'm not hungry right now, Carlton. Why don't you just fix a cold sandwich or something light? Then leave it in the kitchen somewhere. I'll find it if I get hungry."

He realized that even if he did fix the sandwich, the chances were more likely to result in him eating it, or throwing it out the next morning. Nevertheless, he always prepared the sandwich because it made him feel complete about doing his job. "Very well, sir. I'll leave it in the fridge. In the crisper section."

After he left the living room, Stoney raised the one-liter bottle of Jack Daniels to his lips and guzzle down a quarter of its contents. Less than ten minutes later, he felt lightheaded, and a little self-conscious. Many troublesome thoughts of his past illicit dealings swarmed through his mind unreservedly. Observing the many graphic images flashing intermittently, a few left him unnerved and distressed, drove him mad.

After passing out, his subconscious took over, and he could no longer control what entered his mind. Fading in and out of conscious, he fought monotonously to resist the childrens unbearable presence. He swam desperately on the couch amidst a turbulent suffering, moaned in agony, cried aloud, "No! No! No!" He implored, "Please, go away! I … I didn't do it. It wasn't me."

Moments later, the grandfather clock whispered hoarsely, "STONEY! STONEY! Over here, Stoney. It's my turn tonight. Get off your lazy ass and come over here, if you can make it. Com'on Stoney. Don't make us wait too long."

The eyeless Rembrandt jeered, "Hey, ya boozehound. I owe ya one for what ya did to my eyes. Get over here!"

The prize winning gun collection mocked, "You ain't nothing but a sleazy belly whopping, pitch fork carrying imp." It shouted, "Get the fuck over here, boy!"

"Hidey hidey ho ho, Stoney!" the chandelier goaded, sounding like a typical street hustler. "Ya no-good pilfering pig. Word on the street, I hear tell ya been puttin cash ova ya peeps. C'mon over here and get what for."

Two candle holders over the fireplace mantel bobbed and chanted simultaneously, "Cash over people! Cash over people! Stoney's got a bank account as big as a steeple!"

A miniature marble figure of Apollo jumped from its stand on the coffee table. It danced the mamba, snapped his fingers and sang, "Hey, Stoney baby. Break out the champagne. There's a party over here, cause it's my birthday. Can ya get down like this?" It drooled, "Shiiiit! I can shake my ass all night long. Jus dancing to the beat on your nice new stereo set. Didn't cost you a damn thing. A little hustle here, a little hustle there, and presto! Music every where."

The eighty-five inch flat screen plasma television spat forward, "No! Over here, bitch. Come git some." It grew a pair of stumpy muscular midget legs, raising the set two feet from the floor. It danced a waltz, taking composed steps, as though performing Tai Chi. It pestered him by spelling, "I was suppose ta go to the baseball park by myself this Saturday morning. I can't because my mother thinks that there's a child molester out there who's waiting to get me. To do horrible things to me. I keep telling her that there's nobody out there, and that I know who the real maniacs are. But she won't believe me. She doesn't believe that the people who are supposed to be protecting us would do things like that, just to get overtime pay. I keep telling her that it's only you, Larry and Curley; The Three Stooges." It beseeched, "Stoney, please tell her there's nobody out there, so she'll stop worrying and crying all the time. Pleeeeeeease!"

He couldn't stand the punishment any longer and burst from the starting blocks. He ran frantically to the center of the living room, leered at the objects tormenting him and shouted, "What're you looking at?" He faced the television, stared focally at the picture tube. "I see you in there, you big headed son-of-a-bitch. What'n the hell are you looking at?"

Staring at the screen, the dark picture tube hazed into an indistinct image, a fuzzy outline of a human figure. The image became sharper, and he saw the unambiguous outline of a child's upper body. It was definitely a young boy, seemingly frail in stature. He crossed his eyes, stuck out his tongue and his eye brows bounced up and down contemptuously. He urged Stoney to, "Come turn me on, then turn me off. You can even flip through my channels, if you'd like. I know you like stuff like that. Don't you, Stoney? People like you like being able to do anything you want, to whom ever you wish to do it to. Never mind the integrity you swore to preserve. That don't mean shit no more. I know your type. You're a rat-face manipulator." The little boy giggled, "All the channels I have, I see assholes like you all the time."

He became more irate for the insults knocking him into a frenzy. He shook his fist at the television and blasted, "Shut up!" Stomped his right foot. "Shut the fuck up!" He covered his ears for the torturous words scorning him. He pointed to the television and cautioned through gnashed teeth, "I'm warning you for the last time. Shut the fuck up!" Because the occurrences were extraordinarily bizarre in nature, coupled with the notion that he thought he was loosing his mind, he believed that there was nothing that he could do to stop the insanity from swallowing him whole. He *assumed* that he had no control over the matter. Therefore, felt totally helpless.

Stewing at the television, the image faded to nothing, and a blanket of quick relief surrounded him completely. Moments later, to his grave dissatisfaction, the young boys face reappeared, caused him to revisit the many unstable and out of control emotions he believed would never inconvenience him. He teased, "I'm looking at you, Stoney. Do you have a problem with that? If you do, I don't know why. It never seemed to bother you before. I thought you liked it when people paid close attention to you. Especially when you're driving around in that nice new Porsche. Why am I here? you might ask. Well, I wanted to see what a real man looks like. I hardly ever get to see a sight like you, with my having to stay here, all cooped up in this little box. And to think, I wanted to be just like you when I grew up—a supposedly man of honor." He laughed, "You're a cop, and you're supposed to help people. Stoney, please help me get out of this box?" He beseeched, "Pleeeeeease! Oh please oh please oh please oh please! I promise I'll be good." He turned his back to Stoney, pulled down his pants, bent over and flashed the bright side of the moon.

Stoney trembled irately. His jaw locked tight, his eyes squinted to a close. The veins on the sides of his head surfaced so high that they could be seen pulsating from twenty feet away. He pounded his temples frustratingly with clenched fists, grunted, "You fucken miserable ..." Unleashing his fury, he ran toward the television at top speed. He kicked at the picture tube, shattered it into a thousand pieces. He stood in front of the destroyed television set and laughed hysterically. "How'd you like that, mother fucker?" He leaned forward, cupped his right ear. "What's that? You say something?" He stood upright. "You ain't talking so much now, are you? Now that I busted your ass good." He held his right fist over his head in victory and shouted, "Yeah! Ya piece of shit!"

Just when he thought he had defeated the television, the boy laughed, "Ouuu-uuch! Boy, that really smarts." He asked sympathetically, "Stoney, is your foot okay? I hope I didn't hurt you. I would never want to hurt a man of your quality. You're too special. We have to take care of people like you." He laughed aloud, "And who said the age of chivalry was long passed. Man, you're priceless. I love ya, Stoneman. You remind me of that redheaded guy ... um ... what's his name? That's it! His name's Bozo. Bozo the clown."

Feeling defeated, he felt there was no point in responding further. Dropping his shoulders, as well as his enthusiasm to proceed, he stumbled to the couch. About to flop his dead weight onto it, he looked up and found Carlton standing silent in the doorway, wearing a dour mask of disapproval. He asked calmly, "Sir, why did you do that?" He held up his hand to stop Stoney from responding, then answered his own question. "Don't tell me. I already know. It talked too much. Didn't it, sir? It kept staring at you, harassing and pointing its fingers at you. Am I correct, sir?"

Stoney was too despondent to respond, and simply ignored him altogether. He sat on the couch, picked up a bottle of Jack Daniels, raised it to his lips and took a long swig.

Not wanting to get into it, knowing that he would only evade the issues, Carlton turned and walked away, throwing behind, "I shall return shortly to clean up the mess, sir."

Before he returned, because Stoney was dead tired from not getting enough sleep for the past few weeks, and mostly because he was about eighty-five percent inebriated, he had passed out again.

*   *   *   *

Minutes later, Carlton had returned to the living room to clean up the broken glass. Hovering above Stoney's seemingly lifeless body, appearing to mourn the dead. Twisting his lips dolefully, he made a few skeptical faces. My God! he thought. A conscious can be your best friend, or if abused, your worst enemy. Too bad some of us have to learn the hard way. He shrugged his shoulders and remarked, "Oh well. The riches of the world can never be obtained without cost."

He dropped the broom on the floor accidentally, and it made a loud slapping sound, rousing Stoney from his sleep. He mumbled, "Huh? What?" He smacked his lips a few times, cracked his eyes ajar and saw Carlton standing in front of the television. He returned to sleep.

Carlton noticed his eyes open briefly. "It's just me, sir. No need to be alarmed. I only dropped the broom."

Stoney grumbled, "Oh. Yeah. Okay. Okay."

After Carlton had finished cleaning up the mess, he left the room. Stoney opened his eyes once again, then glanced at the newspaper laying beside him. The front page bold print headlines read, 'Child Molester Stalks New England Area.'

He closed his eyes and fell unconscious.

*   *   *   *

With the article in mind, he found himself in Spankys' living room, a few years prior. He, Spanky and Sleeper had gathered to watch the Super Bowl. As Sleeper and Stoney sat on a couch, opening beer cans and large bags of pretzels and potato chips, Spanky stood in front of the television set, fine-tuning the color. "This is going to be a hellova good game," he proclaimed. "I got fifty on the Rams, because I know they're going to kick some ass tonight. Anybody want to cover that action?"

"I'll take some of that," Stoney replied. "The Dolphins are looking pretty decent today. Although their quarterback's on the injured list."

"I've got five dollars," Sleeper said. "Anybody want to work with that?"

Stoney and Spanky looked at each other dryly, then to Sleeper. It appeared as though he had told a bad joke that didn't have a punch line. It left them hanging in anticipation.

Sleeper's the conservative type, thinking continually about the wife and child he had to support. He often slammed the atmosphere with understandings that didn't jive with the rest of the crew. Being a family man, he had different priorities. He was more responsible than his cronies.

"I'll tell you what, you cheap bastard," Spanky responded jokily. "Why don't you take that lil ole measly five spot, and stick it ya ass as far as you can ram it. When it reaches maturity, turns into something I can work with, maybe a twenty ..." Stoney began laughing, and Spanky continued, "... pull it out of your ass, then we'll talk business. Oh, and don't forget to wipe it off. I like my money green. Not brown with corn colored poker dots."

Stoney and Spanky laughed, gave each other a high five. Stoney repeated, "And don't forget to wipe it off. That's funny. I like that."

"I'm sure you did," Spanky chuckled. "Thank you."

"Ha ha ha," Sleeper said wryly, mimicking their laughter. "That's very funny. Hilarious even." He clutched his left side. "That was so funny, I'm in pain. I think I'm dying with laughter over here. Spanky, you're about as funny as a bald-headed Chihuahua with whooping cough."

Stoneys laughter picked up. He pointed at Sleeper. "Now that's even funnier."

After their laughter simmered, Spanky sat on a lazy-boy recliner, then popped opened a cold can of Budweiser beer. "Before the game starts, I want to tell you guys about a little top secret operation that some of the detectives down at the station have been working on. This'll kill ya. You're not going to believe it. This thing's going on clear across New England."

"Wow!" Sleepers eyes widened. "The whole station's in on it? Damn! How far is this hustling shit gonna go?"

Spanky eyed Sleeper resignedly. "I didn't say the whole station was in on it. Why don't you clean the pigeon shit out of your ears?" He repeated clearly, "I said *some* of the detectives." He emphasized, "Some! Some! Did you hear me that time?"

"Yeah yeah yeah," Sleeper said. "So, what's it all about?"

Spanky sat back in his chair, then explained, "Since the country's all up in fears about child molesters, and anything of that nature, some of the guys have hired a mysterious character to drive around on the inner city streets, and act suspicious. The guys name is Thomas Trumbell, and he lives in Reading, Massachusetts. He does his thing mostly in the morning time, when the schoolchildren are waiting for their buses, or are on their way to their pick-up spots. He pulls over to a child routinely and asks if they've seen his lost puppy. Or if they'd like some candy. You know, something harmless. That way if he's pulled over by an officer who's not onto what's going on, he won't get into any serious trouble. And if he's brought in on suspicion, then all he has to do is call one of the officers from our precinct, and they'll go to wherever he's being held. They'll verify his status with the police force—that's he's doing undercover work to catch the suspect—then he'll returns to the streets to continue ..."

"I don't get it," Sleeper interrupted. "So you put somebody out there to ask children a couple of questions. What's the point?"

"Yeah," Stoney said, then repeated, "What's the point?"

Spanky smiled assuredly. He sipped his beer, then stated, "Special detail pay for some of the detectives in the domestics unit, with no dangerous risks involved."

"I see," Sleeper nodded. "Overtime, with no risks."

Stoney asked inquiringly, "How do you get overtime out of doing something like that?"

Spanky peered at Stoney and Sleeper. "Damn! You guys are slow as molasses." He went on to explain. "When the mothers all across New England cry wolf to the top officials, the same officials then push to get funds allocated for detectives to work special details. Then they sit around at some of the children's bus stops, early in the morning, with no fears of a psycho child molester in existence, and make special detail pay."

"That's amazing," Sleeper said. He sipped his beer. "How'd somebody come up with something as horrifying as that?" He laughed, "It's disgusting!"

"It's not an original idea. We merely simulated a real-life situation that's going on right now in Ithaca, New York. As we speak, there's some kind of a psycho child molester up there, running around kidnapping, molesting and killing children. His name's Louis Lent. He's about twenty six years old, has a thick moustache, black hair, about six feet tall, and weighs about one hundred and seventy five pounds. They know all about him, but haven't caught him yet because he's in hiding. He also goes by an alias. I think it's ..." he rubbed his chin, looked to the ceiling for a second, "... I think it's Steve ... something or other. I'm not sure. Anyway, we found a guy who matches the same description, and the detectives sent him to work. It's going on so good right now, that the state wants to bring in the F.B.I. Everybody wants a piece of this action."

Sleeper sat gaping in awe.

Stoney looked into his lap for a moment. "Ya know, hustling perverts who sleep with prostitutes, or putting the squeeze on low-life drug dealers is one thing. I can deal with that. But, with putting fear into the hearts of all those innocent woman and children, don't you think that's going too far? Doesn't that bother you at all?"

Spanky slid to the edge of his recliner, looked at Stoney for a moment, then sighed jadedly. He rose to his feet, stuck his hands into his pockets, walked around to the back of the recliner. He leaned over it, clasped his hands, then brought his elbows to rest on top of the chairs backrest. For a moment longer, he remained in deep thought. He finally replied, "Well, I thought about it. I thought about it long and hard, but that Detective Thompson is a pretty persuasive son-of-a-bitch. He sold some of the guys down at the station on the idea that it's nothing but a little ole harmless hustle, to get some overtime pay. Besides, it's at the tax payers expense. Everybody screws the city, you guys know that. The politicians have been doing it for eons. Now it's time for us little guys to cash in. As for the women and children, well, we've only been doing it mostly to poor towns. You know, people with no voice in what goes on. Towns that nobody really cares much for. Towns that have a lot of people who are doing nothing but sponging from the welfare system. They're getting theirs, and we're getting ours. Shit! Some parts of this city are so messed up, it's a shame. With all of the drug problems and random violence going on, it's crazy! It's pathetic! It's ludicrous! Of course, we can stop a lot of it if we want to. But why don't we? Why don't we get orders from the top to stop the shipment of drugs at no matter what the cost? Aren't we supposed to be laying our lives on the line for something? Why isn't the manufacturing and distribution of firearms monitored closely? Simple! If we get serious with correcting these problems, then there won't be much work to do. They'll have to start laying some of us off. On the force, that means no busy homicide departments, and no busy narcotics unit. From some politicians, straight on down to the workers in the welfare and transitional departments, they won't have much to do. The bottom line is that with no bad guys, you need no good guys. We're only allowed to go on the warpath if one thing occurs." He stared intently at them. "That's if someone kills a cop. I think you both know the truth about that."

He returned to his seat. "It doesn't bother me as much as when I first heard about what they were doing. Other times I think about it, it doesn't bother me at all. Especially when I'm out there doing my job, and a civilian gives me a hard time for nothing. If you try to be nice guy in today's system, you'll be a sure bet to finish last."

When he was much younger, he was conditioned to believe there were mostly minorities on the welfare system. Years ago, when he was younger, anytime the media mentioned welfare in the city of Boston, they flashed a picture of a poor minority woman, surrounded by a couple of filthily dressed children, clinging to her skirt tail.

Now that he's older, and since the times have changed, he prefers to deal with the truth. No matter how ugly it appears to be. He understood that you can play to its advantage, give yourself the edge. He's been made aware of the facts of Americas economic system through the school of hard knocks. He now understands that all of the minorities in America on the welfare system only account for a small percentage of those on the system altogether. He also believes that the U.S. government needs a bad guy to blame for some of its ill-fated woes. Never mind the fact that his grandparents were on welfare when they first settled in America many years ago. That was yesterday, and this is today. It's a whole different ballgame, and the name of the game is called controlling the influence. When talking of someone else as being the bad guy, the spotlight is removed from yourself. Just the same, he considers most people in poor minorities to be hopeless beggars with no will to better themselves. He has no room for empathy in his life, it wouldn't fit in.

After soothing his inflated ego with a long, drawn out, self-serving explanation, he took a breather, sipped his beer, focused on the television. When the national anthem began playing, he sprang to his feet and removed his baseball cap. He held it over his heart and proclaimed, "That's my mother fucken song they're playing. Ya gotta love this country."

After the Anthem finished playing, Sleeper told Spanky, "By the way, congratulations on your promotion. How did you get it anyway? I thought James Goldfield was next in line to advance. You know, that guy in domestics who suddenly quit the force. Saying he had to take care of his sick mother."

"You guys are going to get a kick out of this," Spanky laughed. "I knew I deserved it more than he did. So, I hustled it away from him."

Stoney looked at him sideways. "You did what?"

"You heard me."

Sleeper stared at Spanky for a long moment. "How in the hell did you do that?"

"About a month ago, he asked me to go on a shakedown with him, to cover his back. While there, I set him up for the take down. Since I knew where it was going to go down, I arrived a few hours ahead of time and set up a video camera in a car to catch the transaction. One in which I kept my back to the camera, so that my identity would remain unknown. Then I sent him a copy of the tape, explaining that I was a concerned citizen who taped what he did." He laughed, "Simply put, he panicked and quit the force, before the scandalous shit hit the fan."

Stoney and Sleeper could tell that he believed wholeheartedly in what he did. Without the slightest inclination of what was ethically wrong with it. To Spanky, the ends justified the means. Whatever the means were. For that matter, whatever the ends were.

From hearing of his unscrupulous actions, both felt that at the back of their minds something ominous would arise to shadow them. Stoney, more so than Sleeper, because Sleeper was more of a follower without questions kind of person. Rather than a leader with a constant thirst for answers to lead him from the darkness. He always put his conscious on hold, as if he could afford to wait for a better time to give the thought serious consideration. If the idea sounded good, then he was down with it, no questions asked. He didn't like webby technicalities. Questions.

When Sleeper was eight years old, then called by his first name, Bruno, he use to run with a gang of misfit kids. He was the youngest of the bunch, they called themselves 'The Rat Pack!' They use to get into all sorts of mischief almost everyday; stealing fruit from the neighbors trees or a sidewalk market place, or spray painting a dog. Sometimes they strapped a firecracker to a stray cats tail, or water ballooned cars driving through an underpass on the highway. On some rare occasions, they left a brown paper bag filled with dog feces on a neighbors doorstep. The lit the bag on fire, rang the doorbell, then stood about fifty yards away and watched the action unfold. They had a ball, the time of their lives. No kid could ask for a more fulfilling childhood.

One day, after returning from a frog hunting expedition in the graveyard near Jamaica Plain, the others in the gang decided to play a practical joke on him. They explained to him that since he was the only virgin in the gang, if he wanted to remain a member, he'd have to loose his virginity. They even went so far as to pick out a girl for him to have sex with. An exciting older woman who knew all the ropes. A girl from their future high school, so they told him. After they set everything up, all he had to do was march in there and do his duty for the boys in the gang. Do them proud like. He was happily obliged. He was ecstatic.

It was mid July.

During the summer vacations, his parents allowed him to stay outside until eight thirty in the evening. The place was inside of the old widower Mrs. Grudwigs garage. At sunset, the entire gang stood at the entrance and cheered Bruno exuberantly, as if marching off to battle. Before Bruno entered the garage, they explained to him that the girl was waiting for him in a stall near the back end of the garage. They told him that she was already undressed, and that she'd be lying down, underneath a blanket. Armed with this information, he entered the garage eagerly and felt his way through the darkness, and subsequently found her. With no hesitation, he removed his pants and slipped under the blanket. He mounted the young lady, slid his little tally-wacker inside of her and rode like a champ. He knew his father would've been proud of his take-charge son.

Less than a few seconds into the lustful carnage, the others is the gang crept into the garage and followed the grunting sounds all the way to the back. When they found Bruno, two members in the gang pulled out flashlights and turned them on. There, they discovered Bruno hard at work, attempting to have sex with the young lady. They broke out laughing and begged him to stop, shouting, 'Get up, you fool! That's not a real girl.'

They found it more hilarious when he refused. When they explained to him that he was poking one of their fathers sex toys; a plastic blow-up doll, he dismounted it, rose to his feet, then began laughing just as hard as the others. He swore on a stack of bibles that he knew what was going on.

Besides the minor friction burns he suffered on his penis, knees and hips, from grinding against the plastic, he survived with minimal damage to his pride.

As Stoney gaped peculiarly at Spanky, in the dream, he pushed himself further into the couch, shook his head solemnly. He shut his eyes and faded away, drifted effortlessly to nowhere.

*   *   *   *

Moments later, he heard Carlton calling, "Sir! Sir!" He reached out and tapped his shoulder. "Mr. Brooks!"

It was Monday morning.

Stoney peeped his eyes ajar, and some of the sleep crust fell into his eyes. He blinked a few times, rubbed his eyes with the back of his right hand. He eyed Carlton, hovering over him. "Wha … what time is it?" The words barely made their way past his parched throat. He swallowed dryly, wet his dry lips, and realized that the taste sitting on his tongue was disgustingly horrendous. Moldy, like a pair of old shoes fished from the river basin.

Carlton held his head high, looked down the straight of his nose. "I do believe it's time for you to prepare yourself for work, sir."

Stoney made another effort to speak. Felt like he was twisting his own arm, searching for politically correct words, "Oh, yeah. Sure. Work." He squirmed in place to loosen his stiff clothes, which he had ironed into ruffles while he slept. The hollows of his armpits burned torturously from grinding his shirt into his skin. He flapped his arms like a duck, allowing his irritated armpits to breathe. He stretched thoroughly, yawned exhaustively.

Carlton made it known, "Your clothes are pressed, and your bath water was readied ten minutes ago, sir. Its temperature is exactly as you like …"

"Aw c'mon, Carlton," Stoney huffed. Peered at him through the corners of his eyes, squinting, trying to let in as little light as possible. "Why do you have to start my …" he yawned again, "… day off with all this 'it's exactly as you like' bullshit? Why do you always have to complicate everything? Why can't you simply tell me to get my lazy ass up, and go to work?" He looked into his lap glumly, rubbed the back of his aching neck. Felt like someone had smacked him there with a fifty pound catfish. He mumbled, "Damn! It's like waking up to a tight ass robot. I don't know how people in the future are going to do it, but I ain't ready for that kinda shit yet."

"Sir, this is certainly not you. Are you all right?" He realized it was a senseless question, feeling the response would probably illogical.

Stoney bowed his head and sighed, knew that he was right. This attitude I have, he thought, it's not me at all. Damn! What in the hell am I turning into?

Looking at Carlton, his eyes apologized way before he found the words. "You're right, Carlton. This definitely ain't me at all. I'm … I'm sorry. I didn't mean to offend you."

"That's all right, sir. I understand." He managed to break a faint smile into his unbendable stiff upper lip. "No offense taken." Most of the time when he talked, only his jaw moved ever so slightly, and never his lips. He went to the kitchen.

Feeling like he'd been working incessantly with a pickax in the quarries under a sweltering Texas sun all day, he struggled to bench press his weight from the couch, grunted exhaustively, "Aaaarrrrgggg!" His underwear delivered the all-powerful atomic wedgy, so he waddled like a duck to the bathroom. He held his hand over his brow to shield his eyes from the torturous morning sunlight light prying its way in through the Venetian blinds, over the huge bay window.

He opened the bathroom door, but before he entered, he lifted his left knee to the midsection and snapped it out to the side, hoping to rid himself of this mischievous toil; the dreaded wedgy. He felt relieved for his success, as failure required an early morning gold mining excavation, with his fingers. He chucked a few words past his parched throat, just loud enough so that Carlton could hear. "You want to get me a couple of extra strength aspirins?"

He barely heard Carltons reply coming from the kitchen. "Coming, sir."

While in the bathroom, Stoney stood in front of the sink, gazed attentively into the mirror and noticed the swollen veins surrounding his pupils. He thought his eyes resembled a pair of crimson cue balls. The skin on his face appeared ashen, wrinkled, like a crumpled sheet of sandpaper. He rubbed the bristly hairs of his five o'clock shadow and commented, "Looks like shit. Feels like shit." He paused, then finished, "Must be shit."

He experienced an early morning dizzy spell, and leaned onto the sink and stiffened his body so that he wouldn't collapse. He bowed his head for a moment to collect himself. Feeling the dizzy spell had diminished, he suddenly felt several pairs of inquisitive eyes probing and dissecting him, and realized he wasn't alone. He raised his head at a snail's pace and looked into the mirror, and saw a massive amount of anguish riddled across the children's faces, blemished from the traumatic ramifications of his misguided actions. Though, their naïve hearts remained cheerful and uninhibited.

He suddenly felt an unnatural tingling sensation creeping over his skin. He frowned agonizingly, as if about to cry out in intense pain. Without breaking his eyes from theirs, he took several steps backward, closed his eyes tight in an attempt to erase the visualization. He stepped inside of the shower, turned the hot water on, then removed his clothes. The order in which he did this was of no significance.

Showering in a steam-filled bathroom, he heard soft footsteps traipsing, lurking just on the other side of the shower partition. He became frightened, unsure of what to make of it. He froze in place, listened carefully. Because he had the children in mind, his troubled subconscious challenged his reality. He muttered, "I thought it was only in my mind, reflected from inanimate objects."

Could it be …?

Are they …?

He heard a voice say, "Your breakfast is ready, sir."

Stoney heaved a heavy sigh, thinking, Damn that Carlton! Creeping around here like a fricken cat burglar. The asshole just rammed two years down my throat. Maybe I should tie a cowbell around his ass. That way I'd hear him coming a mile away.

He continued showering. Through the steam covered shower partition, he saw Carlton bending over to collect his wet clothes, to throw into the laundry bin. Carlton became puzzled as to how the clothes had gotten soaked, then asked Stoney, "Sir, are you okay?"

He waited for a response, but there was none.

Moments later, he tried again, and received the same results.

The thought to look inside of the shower entered his mind, but he left the issue alone. He was satisfied knowing that Stoney was awake, showering, amidst the course of his day. He left the bathroom, carrying the wet clothes off to the laundry room.

After Stoney heard the bathroom door close, he blurted, "And stay out! Ya sneaky tiptoeing son-of-a-bitch. What's wrong with you, prowling around here like that? What do you think this is, a fricken mortuary?"

My God, he thought. His heart racing a mile a minute. That kind of stuff gets ya adrenalin pumping something fierce. I almost ran into a brick wall on that one. Sneaky bastard!

*   *   *   *

Getting dressed wasn't too difficult. He managed to find his arms and legs and insert them where they belonged with little trouble. It was the order of putting on those damn socks and shoes that was very confusing. Was it one sock, then one shoe? Or was it two socks, and then two shoes? Or could it be two shoes, and no socks? Or was it the shoes first, and then the socks? No. The first way sounded just fine.

Sometimes the order rambled uncertainly in his head for a while before it sorted itself out. Like when he first learned how to use a computer to write basic letters in high school, he caught on to it eventually. But those first few weeks of exploring the menus were enough to send him scurrying to the emergency ward with a migraine headache, filled with mind-boggling questions and no answers. He had gotten so mad at the damned thing that he had slammed the monitor and keyboard to the floor, then stomped them repeatedly until they broke into a hundred pieces. That day, he couldn't have been more pleased that he put the computer out of its misery. Even after the principal suspended him for two days, and made his parents pay for replacing the computer, he was sure that he came out ahead on that episode. Would swear to it.

After completing his dress; mountain climbing boots, white gym socks, jeans and a red and gray plaid shirt, he marched down the stairs and into the kitchen. He didn't really march, but he likes to think that he always does. Doing so reminds him of the enjoyable police training he endured when he stayed at the police academy for six months. All that hut-hut, one-two and comradeship stuff were what gym locker-room dreams were made of. Like alcoholics anonymous.

He entered the kitchen and saw the nourishing breakfast that Carlton had pre-pared, laid spread like a country buffet. There was a plate of scrambled eggs with American cheese, just the way he liked them. Wheat toast with butter, and a few thick slices of Canadian bacon. To drink, there was a tall glass of orange juice, and a cup of steaming hot coffee. His eyes rejoiced, but his stomach cringed and wrestled itself into a square knot. Taking in the savory aroma, at first, it smelled fantastic. Seconds later, a disgusting taste wormed its way up his throat and set-tled at the back of his tongue, and he nearly vomited. Holding his hand over his mouth, he swallowed twice to keep the disgusting taste from taking over his entire mouth. He cleared his throat for the repulse that lingered, then hollered, "Carlton!"

Seconds later, Carlton entered the kitchen from his bedroom. He stood over the neatly made table and looked at Stoney. "Is there something wrong, sir?"

Stoney asked plainly, "Where's the cereal?"

Carltons eyebrows jumped inquisitively. "Cereal, sir?"

"Yeah. You heard me. You know what I'm talking about, because we go through this shit at least three times a week. I'm talking about that stuff that goes snap-crackle-pop. Where is it?"

"But sir," he looked at the food on the table, "this is more nourishing than that children's cereal. Only people who don't care about themselves eat foods like that. After last night, you'll need something like this to replace some of the nutri-ents that …"

Stoneys patience grew thin. He angered, "I'm through with the games, Carl-ton. Now either you give me my spackle-crap-tap, or I'm gonna pull it outta ya ass!" He pointed to the delicious breakfast simmering on the table. "If you like this shit so much, then you eat it."

Carlton knew that he would never attempt to do such a thing, assault him. He realized that his spewing violent words only meant that he was getting a little upset.

Knowing that Stoney always had the last say, he resigned. "Very well, sir. I shall get it." He turned around and reached into a cupboard and pulled out a box of Rice Crispies, sat it on the table. He went to the sink and removed a bowl from the drying rack. He pulled open the silverware drawer and retrieved a spoon. He dropped the spoon into the ceramic bowl, making a loud clanging sound, then plopped the bowl onto the table. Hearing his attitude from his sloppiness prompted Stoney to ask, "You got a problem?"

Carlton told him directly. "Sir, I do."

"Spill it."

"Sir, you hired me to take care of you. Did you not?"

Stoney shrugged his shoulders insensitively. "Yeah. So?"

"Then how can I do my job, if you won't let me. Part of my job is to see that you get off to a good, healthy start in the morning. But that seems to be an unreasonable request."

Stoney sighed regrettably, knowing that he was telling the truth. He explained calmly, "Look, Carlton," he paused, searching for passive words, "you're doing a fine job. It's ... um ... it's not you. It's me. I haven't been feeling so good lately. I haven't been myself at all. I have a whole bunch of things going on in my mind. Things that I need to sort out."

"Well then, I suggest that you take a sabbatical, sir."

Stoney twisted his head curiously. "A sub. A subbat. A what?"

"A lengthy rest. A break from all that ails you."

At first, Stoney thought that he was talking about the police force. In the back of his mind, he knew that he referred to his involvement with the Dixie Club. Carlton saw on a daily basis how it chipped away small pieces of his soul. Leaving a big black gapping hole large enough so that his morals, ethics and principals could drain through.

Stoney picked up the box of cereal and replied, "I can't right now." He started to say, "I'm in the middle of ..." he thought better of it, changed him mind and said, "There's too much that's got to be done right now." He poured the Rice Crispies into the bowl.

"Sir, you really should think about it. Now that I think about it, I haven't see you relax in years."

"I'll think about it, Carlton," he said to appease him. "For now, I have to hurry up and eat my breakfast. I gotta get outta here."

"Very well, sir," Carlton walked to the kitchen doorway, said along the way, "I'll see you when you return. Have a nice day, sir."

Stoney threw halfheartedly, "Yeah." Before Carton got too far away, he added, "Hey. Um ..." Carlton turned halfway, "... I'm sorry."

Carlton smiled dimly. It wasn't distinctly outlined on his face, but Stoney knew it was definitely there. It meant that he accepted his apology. It meant a lot to him that he did.

*   *   *   *

While eating his breakfast, he closed his eyes for a moment and drifted away. He found himself talking on a public telephone, two miles from his house, to one of the Marks that he arrested earlier that year. Although they agreed to do a swap hustle, him with Spanky, sometimes he couldn't help but to hustle a few of his own marks.

After the phone rang three times, a little girl answered, "Who is it?"

Stoney asked politely, "May I speak to Anthony Dole?"

The little girl pulled the phone away from her ear and yelled, "Daddy! Someone wants to talk to you!"

Immediately, he heard a deep voice bellow, "Thank you, sweetie! I'll be right there."

The little girl placed the phone on something hard, perhaps a table of some sort. Seconds later, he heard the pitter patter of footsteps running away from the phone. He heard a door slam, the little girl shouted, "It's my turn to use the swing. You been on it all day. It's not fair."

Moments later, he heard heavy footsteps approaching the phone. A man said, "Yes. Who's calling?"

Stoney lingered in a hushed silence, before he responded politely, "Anthony … Dole!"

The hesitation in between the way he stated Anthony's first and last name made him wonder. After a few moments, he said, "Um … yes. I … ah … I don't recognize the voice, although you do sound vaguely familiar. Who am I speaking with?"

"I'm one of the teachers at your daughter's school."

"I see. And your name is …"

"My name is … ah … Henry Thompson."

The pause created a suspicion in Anthony's mind. He said inaudibly, "Henry Thompson. Henry Thompson. The names doesn't ring a bell. I'm familiar with most of the teachers at my daughters school. I don't recall ever meeting you."

"I'm new there."

"Um … what did you say your name was?"

"Ah … I said it was Jack. Jack Robinson."

An uncomfortable suspicion grew in Anthony's mind. "I thought you said your name was Henry Thompson?"

"Well, I did. At first."

It all of a sudden hit Anthony that someone was playing childish games with him, and he didn't like it at all. Mostly because he had no idea of who he was speaking with. He was definitely at a disadvantage. Because of the level of confidence and casual tone of the caller, he stayed on the line to attempt to get to the bottom of why this was happening. At the back of his mind, in the pride department, he knew the caller had to be outright arrogant to call his house and put him through this bullshit. Of course, unless he had a good reason to be so bodacious. He proceeded cautiously by asking firmly, "Who is this, and what do you want?"

Feeling his emotions fluctuate, Stoney remained calm and replied, "Well, Anthony, who I am isn't important. Are you alone at the moment?"

Anthony didn't know why, but he felt that he should answer the question. Maybe it would lead to getting some answers. He replied shakily, "Sure." Stoney could tell by his response that he was beginning to feel a little uneasy. Perturbed. He spat anxiously, "I'm not a man who plays games. Either you state your business, or I'm hanging up. Then I'm going to make an attempt to have the call traced. And if I find out who you are, Mr., you're going to be in big trouble."

Hearing how frustrated Anthony was becoming, he felt he should release some slack and throw the dog a bone, give him a taste. Let him hold onto it, then pull it back, as a tease. "Well, I guess you can say that I'm a ... a sort of ... a sort of a friend. A very ..." he emphasized, "... *concerned friend*, who doesn't want to see you get into any more trouble than you're already in."

He heard a weighty silence rumbling on the other end of the line, and knew that Anthony was in deep thought about what the statement might've meant. Had Anthony been a faithful man of unwavering conviction, he would've remained steadfast to his innocence, and been able to refute any alleged challenges without fear of reprisal. He had doubts about his personal standing because of his past illicit actions, so he listened closely. A blanket of insecure warmth engulfed his body, and Stoney could feel the uncertainty in his voice when he asked timidly, "What are you talking about? Is this a practical joke or something? If it is, I've no time for this ..."

Stoney laughed. "Oh, I guarantee you, Mr. Dole. This is no joke." He stopped laughing, then repeated sternly, "This ... is ... no ... joke."

Feeling the callousness in the callers voice, Anthony asked, "Then what do you want?" He rambled on, as if he believed for a moment longer that the caller had to be playing games. "Out with it!" He stuttered, "I-I-I don't have time for games. I'm a very busy man, and I have important obligations to …"

Stoney cut him off by agreeing facetiously, "I'm sure you do, Mr. Dole. Besides a few other important undertakings in your life, you're also in the entertainment industry. Am I right?"

Sounding a tad snobbish, he disagreed sharply. "No! No! I don't dawdle in that sort of nonsense. My business is purely on a professional level of …"

"Mr. Dole, you *are* in the business of entertainment. I should know. I caught your debut during one of your busy evenings, after you left work, about a month ago. You put on a very good show. You know, right before you were supposed to meet some of your friends at the gym to play a few games of squash." Stoney paused to let Anthony absorb the general idea of what he was getting at. "I can agree with you on one thing, Mr. Dole. You *are* a very busy man. I can testify to that." He waited for a few seconds, then decided that he couldn't hold back any longer. He read proficiently from a prepared statement, laying out what he had discovered. "You have a very lucrative position at the bank where you work as an assistant vice president. You have stocks, bonds and blue chips totaling well over one and a half million dollars. You also have a part ownership in a prosperous little bed and breakfast, slash, ski lodge, in Manchester, New Hampshire. You have a glamorous wife who's the chairperson of the local P.T.A. in your district. You have four children; one is in elementary school, two are in middle school, and the oldest attends high school. As for your place of residence, you live in Milton, Massachusetts. In a big white fancy mansion, white picket fence, three car garage, with a swimming pool and tennis court on the grounds." After Stoney had finished reading the statement, he could tell that he had Anthony's' full and undivided attention. Since he was in a hypnotic trance, Stoney went on to say, "Yeap, Mr. Dole, the community looks up to your family with complete respect and admiration. One could even say that you have all the makings of a perfect fantasy life; happily ever after and all that cute shit. Am I correct, Mr. Dole?"

Anthony snapped out of his trance, feeling the caller tread on sacred ground when he mentioned his dearly loved family. He became defensive and fired angrily, "Look, Mr., if you don't tell me what you want this instant, then …" the hesitation was because he still believed that it would be to his advantage to keep a cool head, "… I'm going to … to hang up!"

"I wouldn't do that, Mr. Dole," Stoney calmed. "I wouldn't do that at all. I wouldn't want to see you or your family, well, you know, disgraced, or dragged through some kind of a societal scandal, or anything like that. And about your wife and children, I wouldn't want them to suffer, or loose respect for you." He chuckled, "I wouldn't want your fantasy bubble to *explode*."

Anthony felt his temperature rise at least twenty degrees. He tugged nervously at his collar several times to vent the heat trapped in his shirt. Moments later, large patches of sweat grew on his forehead, beaded together intermittently and trickled lickety-split down the sides of his face. Suddenly, he felt, more like believed, that the mysterious caller had to have something on him to be so bold. Yet, he couldn't figure out what. Now, his tone became docile. He asked submissively, "Mr., what's this all about?"

Stoney felt that now was the right time to disclose a piece of imperative information. Still reading from his notes, he explained, "About a month ago, after you left work, you went to a parking lot located in between Hancock Street and Central Avenue. That's what this is all about, Mr. Dole. It's all about you ..." he chuckled, "... doing the nasty with a young lady of the night. A prostitute! Mr. Dole," he laughed, "asses and elbows were flying high. The young lady who accompanied you goes by the street name of Starlight. Am I correct, Mr. Dole?" Stoney believed that asking rhetorical questions did more tormenting than name-calling. It challenged a person's intellect. "I manage to get my hands on the only copy of the video tape from a parking lot attendant. And ya know, Mr. Dole, surprisingly, you take a pretty good picture. Considering the position you were in. Especially with these advanced high quality surveillance cameras they have out there on the market. The tape clearly shows you paying her some money, both of you getting into your car, and the motion of the car going up and down." He repeated slowly, "Up and down, Mr. Dole. It also shows the whole scene when the police showed up to arrest you and the prostitute. Until now, it was all hush-hush and on the down low because of your high priced lawyer friends. Your case was settled by your agreeing to stay out of trouble for six months. After that, the whole mess would be dismissed. Then you would've had your record sealed, and no one would've been the wiser. Mr. Dole, I have only one thing to say." He laughed, "That's a hellova way to wear out a pair of shock absorbers."

There was no response, and he thought for a moment that Anthony had went into acute shock, or had fainted. As a few others have done in the past. Listening closely, he heard sputters of distressed wheezing, and he realized that Anthony was having trouble breathing. This is why he didn't interrupt him as he spilled a horrible tale of 'a night to remember.'

He lost partial control of his motor skills, but managed to sputter a few angry syllables. "You ... You lo li, scu su bast!" Ten minutes ago, he would've been able to say clearly, 'You low life, scum sucking bastard!' He finally managed to get control of his thought process, then ranted and raved, "What are you going to do with that information? I can't have anyone finding out about that regrettable incident. I'll ... my reputation will be destroyed. My wife, I'm sure she'll leave me, and ..."

Stoney assisted him in setting up the dominoes that would surely topple, one after the other. "... and your job will fire you. Your business partners will distance their selves from you. Your community and church will chastise you and your family. Your children and their friends will have a hard time keeping their respect for you. Your neighbors will distance themselves from you, giving your whole family the silent treatment, pointing their fingers at you as they whisper ugly rumors of bondage and sadomasochistic behavior. You know, adults running around clad scantly in chaps, spanking each other. Tony, old boy. When the ax falls, it'll cut bone deep." He took a deep breath, then continued on a more pleasurable note. "But, let's not get too far ahead of ourselves, Mr. Dole. I'm here to do you a favor, before that doggone tape falls into the wrong hands. We wouldn't want that to happen. Now, would we?"

"Ah ... no. Certainly not. It would destroy my life, and everything that I have worked so hard at ..."

Stoney cut him off. "I mean, I'm not saying that it won't happen, as long as you do the right thing. Then there shouldn't be a problem. Otherwise, a copy of the videotape and your rap sheet will be sent to your boss, your wife's parents, your kids schools, the golf club that you belong to, et cetera et cetera? That could turn into something really ugly, wouldn't it?"

He agreed wholeheartedly. "Yeah. I'm sure it would be very embarrassing."

"In that case, I'll tell ya what I'm gonna do. I could destroy the tape, if you'd like."

Anthony waited for him to say more. He knew there would be, because nothing was as simple as that. Especially something as complicated as the grotesque ugliness that this unknown caller was laying out before him. He half cupped the phones mouthpiece and whispered, in case someone else in the house might be listening. He flattened the door leading to his gilded pride, then begged with nil shame. "Mister, sir, whoever you are, could you please do that for me?"

"Sure I would," Stoney said happily. "No problemo, my friend! And I'm going to do this because I like you."

"You ... you like me?" Anthony sounded skeptical.

"Um ... no," he laughed. "I was just kidding. You know why I don't like you, Mr. Dole? I'm going to tell you why I don't like you. I don't like you because you have everything a man needs to live on, and yet, you're a disgusting, selfish, perverted son-of-a-bitch, who really doesn't care about diddlysquat jack shit. Especially your own family. I say this because you could've fucked up everything you have by bumping uglies with a mange infested street walker. How can I possibly respect somebody like you?" He paused, then continued. "But, I also understand that we're all human, and we all make mistakes. I also believe that everyone deserves a second chance, which is the main reason why I'm going to destroy these documents."

After having been pampered with a false sense of security, Anthony cried happy tears of joy. "I'd really appreciate it if you would. I've worked all my lifer to get where I am, and I just can't see having everything ..."

While hurling a boatload of praises, Stoney felt that it was the perfect time to shoot him down, right while he was flying high. Spanky and Sleeper were good when they rolled their hustles. Simply good. But the Stoneman held a captive audience. He had them tossing roses on stage and applauding for an encore. Had them bum rushing backstage to ask for his autograph. He took his marks on the rollercoaster ride of their lives. Sometimes he began with a slow ascent, then a sudden gravity defying drop. The remaining ride contained many perverted twists and shaky turns. Sometimes the turns and twists came before the drop. He was brilliant at what he did. He sung a praiseworthy song, gave a little soft-shoe, then painted an ugly picture before he mentioned anything about money. "But ... ah ... all for a price, Mr. Dole. This here's American, and ain't a gotdamn thing free. Not even a blam damn ham sandwich. You wanna dance, do the watussi? You gotta pay the pied pop-eyed piper. Now git up offa my tip on that ... Mr. Dole."

Hearing the bottom line, the stipulation hit Anthony like a million volts of electricity. He froze, stuck in limbo, imagined giving his hard-earned life savings to a total stranger. Someone who he had never seen before, and chances are, will never see. Certainly someone who he would've preferred to see dead, hanging by his testicles from a rooster tree on a snowy Christmas morning. Anthony nodded loathingly. "I had a feeling you were heading in that direction." A nauseous taste rose from the pit of his gut and simmered about his tongue. He spat hastily, "Shit! I just knew it! How much is it going to ..."

"Relax," Stoney appeased. "I'm not a greedy person."

"After I pay you, how will I know you won't turn into a blood sucking parasite and try the same fucken thing in the near future? After you spend the money, you'd grow desperate for more?"

"Tsk tsk tsk, Mr. Dole. How mundane. Such foul language for a prominent man of your stature. As I said before, Mr. Dole., I'm not a greedy man. You'll just have to take my word for it. Either that, or risk everything that your wife may take from you in what I'm sure will be a very bitter divorce."

"Okay okay," he hastened. "I understand. Now how much is it going to cost?"

Stoney stated plainly, "Fifty thousand dollars."

After hearing the staggering figure, Anthony screamed, "**WHAT!**"

His wife heard the yell and rushed into the room. After noticing her husbands distraught condition, Stoney heard her ask, "Tony, sweetheart, are you okay?" She wiped the sweat from his brow with a napkin. "My poor baby, did something bad happen?"

Kidding around, Stoney told Anthony, "Here's a better idea. Tell her to give me some head. If it's good, I'll take off two dollars."

Anthony gritted angrily, "You fucken miserable ..." he stopped talking abruptly, covered the mouthpiece.

"What?" His wife said. "Tony, what's going on? Who are you talking to?"

"It's nothing, sweetheart," he replied calmly. "One of my friends and business partners who I play golf with just suffered a massive cardiac arrest. He died a few minutes ago."

"Your friends are dying all right," Stoney chuckled. "That is, your friends at the bank. There's Ben Franklin, Thomas Jefferson and old Honest Abe."

Stoney heard her muffled voice say, "I'm so sorry, sweetheart. Give his wife my condolences, and we'll talk about it after you hang up. I'm going to prepare some snacks for the children."

A few moments later, Anthony spoke angrily into the phone. "What are you? Some kind of a sick twisted moron."

"Relax," Stoney said. "I was only kidding. You sleep with whores, and chances are, you've already slept with your wife. That means that she unknowingly slept with that whore as well, and every John that she's had dealings with. As for me, that just wouldn't do. I wouldn't touch your wife even if I wore a full body condom. No sir. No thank you."

Eager to get the telephone conversation over with, Anthony said, "That's a lot of money. A hell of a lot of money."

"Even with considering what's at risk?" Stoney asked. "The money's nothing. But your family life, just like the MasterCard commercial says, 'that's priceless!' Or so it should be."

There was a long hesitation, then Anthony asked, "Can I think about it?"

"Sure," Stoney laughed. "I'll give you three seconds." He stopped laughing and took on a serious tone. "Then I'll hang up. After that, I'll send copies of everything I have to your job, your family, your neighbors, your children's schools, your business partners ..."

After Stoney arranged an initial payoff, he sat in silence for a few minutes to attempt to justify his actions. Most of the time, he succeeded. Anthony Dole, he wondered. That's another one who won't learn by his mistakes. I can feel it. It's not my fault he can't keep his Johnson in his pants. He needs intervention. Somebody has to help him. Even if it's against his will. Therefore, I'm doing him some good, like giving him an outrageous speeding ticket. He'll be looking over his shoulder the next time he decides to recklessly endanger the lives of those around him. I'm sure he'll appreciate it in the long run. He'll also think second the next time he thinks about cheating on his wife and add fire to the perverse world of prostitution. The man should be ashamed of himself, brining those kinds of issues home to his wife. A nice family like that, and he's willing to throw it all away for a few seconds of immoral and disgusting pleasure. Damn near every guy I know would die for a chance to have a straight set up like he has.

"Okay okay!" Anthony huffed. "Shit! I'll get the money. It'll take a few days, but I'll get it."

"Good. Then it's settled. I'll get back in touch with you in a few days, to tell you where you can drop the money off at."

"Will you be there?"

"Don't be ridiculous. My identity must remain a secret. Like I said before, Mr. Dole, I'm just a friend. A very *distant* friend. I'll talk to you in a couple of days. By the way," he laughed, "give my best to your Mrs., and your little ones."

$$*\qquad*\qquad*\qquad*$$

He placed another local call, and a twenty-five year old rap sensation named Tito Ramirez answered the phone energetically. Hearing the commotion going on in the background, Stoney guessed that he was amidst an entourage of close friends, flunkies, groupies, record producers, managers, personal valets, et cetera et cetera. "Tito here."

"Tito? Tito Ramirez?"

"Yeah. This is Tito. Who's this?"

Stoney grew excited. "Oh wow! I can't believe I actually got you on the horn."

"Yo man!" Tito angered. "Who's this calling me from out of the blue? And how in the hell did you get this unlisted number?"

"Have one of you boys take down your messages," Stoney heard a older man say in the background. "We gotta get on schedule with this track. This is sure money."

"Com'on," Tito told his manager. "Why you always gotta be on my ass?" He spoke into his cell phone. "Yo! Who's this?"

"I'm sorry, Tito. I really didn't mean to disrespect you like this, all unannounced and shit. I'm nobody important, just a diehard fan. One of your greatest. I've been following you for years, from when you were just fifteen, rapping on the streets at Park Street Station in downtown Boston. I heard your new CD you just put out for the first time today, and man, that shit is the bomb diggidy! I must've played it a hundred times already."

Still angry, Tito asked, "Who's this?"

"I'm sorry, Mr. Ramirez. Excuse my manors. My name's DJ-Fuzz. I know you've heard of 2-PAC. My group use to go by the name 3-POC, three people obsessed with cash. I'm with two other guys." He said sadly, "But it didn't catch on. Nobody liked us. I guess they thought we were mocking the brother. God rest his soul. Anyway, we got some new stuff.. We're a future beacon in the industry. Like 2-PAC said in one of his hits, 'All eyes on me' You know what I mean? We're just tryinta get our shit heard all over, then signed to a good label. Like you did."

Tito figured the caller to be an enthusiastic nobody, trying to make it big in the music industry from making connections with somebody important. "Look kid. I feel ya passion and all, cause I was just like you at one time. But I can't talk right now. I'm at a studio in New York City, trying to burn a new CD."

"Aw man! That's great. Congrats to you on that. I give you much props, bro. I know it's gonna be some serious shit!"

"Of course it will." He boasted, "Hey! They don't call me Tito 'Zapata' Ramirez for nothing. But, I guess I can understand where you're coming from. I use to have as much drive as you, when I first got into the business."

"I appreciate that," Stoney said. "I really do. But I have to ask you something important, and then I'll let you go. I know you're a busy man and all."

"I think I can spare a second." He laughed. "Especially for one of my protégés."

At that moment, four young women entered the studio and rushed to Tito, contending for his attention. An especially beautiful young lady caught his eye, and he told Stoney, "Hold on a sec."

He pointed to Natasha Woods, Miss Black District of Columbia for two years running. The remaining three backed off immediately. He told her. "Damn, you's a fine lil mama! What's your name, baby girl?"

The young lady replied shyly, "Natasha."

"Check this out, Natasha. I'm gonna finish this conversation, then we can talk for a quick minute, cause I got a CD to burn. Business first, then we can grab something to eat. Talk for a while. Get them digits."

"Okay."

"You wait right next to me, an I'll be with you in a sec."

Tito told Stoney, "Hey, look here. I got my hands full right now. So I'm gonna haft to let you …"

"Getting all the ladies," Stoney said excitedly. "All that fine tail. I hear that."

Tito laughed. "Hey! It comes with the turf."

"Just one more thing, and I'll be out of you hair."

Tito sighed tiredly. "Listen. I appreciate your being a fan and all but …"

Stoney cut him off, "Tito, in order to make it to where you're at, I know you've had to want it real bad. I read a recent column on you in the Rolling Stones magazine, saying how rough it was for you coming up in the hood. Especially with your coming from a broken home and all. Going through that shit, with having the odds stacked against you, and still come out successful, I know you have great dedication. But what I'd really like to know is … how bad did you want success?"

Tito studied the question for a moment, visualized the hardships he's endured through his ascent to the big time. He replied, "I felt as though I would've done anything to get this far. For me, there's no other life style, only rap. It's like I was born to do it."

"Any major sacrifices?"

"Plenty. Damn near cost me my soul."

"I'm sure of that," Stoney agreed. "Paying with your soul is the devils price. It means you'd do anything to get what you want out of life."

"Say what?"

"Anything, even kill for the money to finance your first demo tape. You killed someone at a bank heist up in queens last January. And I got the only piece of evidence that proves that you were in on the robbery."

Tito glanced at the caller ID screen on his cell phone, saw a blank, then shouted angrily into the receiver. "Yo man! Who the fuck is this, calling me with this dumb shit?"

"You told the authorities that you weren't even in the state, when the shit went down. But I know otherwise, because I have the surveillance tape from Macys Department Store. On it, it clearly shows you purchasing a black ski mask at nine-thirty on the morning of the heist. What were you going to do?" Stoney laughed, "Ski your way through Harlem?"

As Stoney filled him in on the gruesome details of what had happened during the bank heist, Tito said absolutely nothing. "An off duty security guard almost ruined your plans by showing up unexpectedly, didn't he? That's when one of your long time buddies took him out. And he's the only one that's been caught, so far. Luckily for you he's kept his mouth shut. And you're returning the favor by sending him plenty of money to fill his canteen, while he does that twenty-five to life at Attica."

Stoney heard the commotion fade in the background, could tell that Tito had moved to a secluded area to be alone. After he heard a door slam shut, Tito asked passively, "How do I know this shit's for real? You could be just anybody calling to blackmail me with some shady info that ain't even correct. Us entertainers go through shit like this all the time."

"Here's what I'm going to do," Stoney said. "I'm going to send you a copy of the tape, which clearly identifies you making the purchase. This should take a few days. Then I'll call you again at the end of the week to tell you how we're going to handle this."

Tito complained heatedly, "You mother fucken no-good blackmailer! If I ever catch your ass, I'll stick my gun up you ass and unload the whole ..."

"Whoa! Whoa! Slow down," Stoney calmed. "All that shit gets us nowhere. It serves no purpose, as I know you don't want to join your buddy up at Attica. You're having too much fun out here, enjoying yourself with all those fly girls surrounding you in your videos. Be expecting a package at your doorstep in a day or so. Until then, hasta la vista, baby! Mr. Rap King!"

*　　　*　　　*　　　*

Revisiting another hustling episode, he inserted a few quarters into the pay-phone and made a long-distance call to New York City. The phone rang three times before a woman answered pleasantly, "Hello."

Laura Clark is a forty year old affluent ad executive who works for a television station in Manhattan. She's originally from a small town near Topeka, Kansas. She moved to the big apple with aspirations of becoming someone 'BIG' in the advertising industry. She's single, too busy for the institution of marriage and all of its fine intricacies. She graduated from Yale business school in 1982, then received a graduate degree from Boston University in 1984. Except for a couple of parking tickets, her life was spotless.

Three years prior, her organization had sent her to Boston, Massachusetts to attend a weekend convention and seminar at the John B. Hynes Civic Center on Boylston Street. Not to far from downtown Boston. One late Sunday evening, after having some drinks with a couple of sorority sisters, as she was driving back to her motel room at the Holiday Inn on Cambridge Street, she accidentally took a wrong turn down a quiet side street, which led her into one of Boston's poorer neighborhoods. Unfortunately, she had an accident, plowing her brand new BMW into a young woman; an English High School student on her way to purchase a bag of marijuana. Because Laura was intoxicated at the time, she fled the scene immediately for fear of criminal prosecution. She believed it would've destroyed her life.

Because the high school student was in a coma for two years, an in-depth homicide investigation wasn't launched until after she died, when he family finally agreed to pull the plug. After several days of tedious foot work, Spanky received a break in the case when he interviewed an ex-alcoholic/drug addict who had witnessed the accident. He remembered the license plate number because it was the same as the lottery number he's played for many years. He was reluctant to come forward at the time because he too was on his way to make a score for a few packets of heroin. The details of that horrific evening were a jumbled mess of a dark foreign sedan driving zigzag, screeching tires, a dull thump, and maybe an animal got hit.

Although Spanky got hold of this very important information, he reported to his superiors that the lead was incorrect. He did some quick research of how much Laura Clark was worth, then passed the information onto Stoney, and he ran his hustle.

Sometimes when Stoney established contact with his marks, he pretended to be overly compassionate. As if he genuinely liked the person. Oddly, this strange behavior added to his enjoyment. It created what he calls 'The Electric Shock Effect.' It raised the person blissfully to a heightened level of euphoria, before they were sent plummeting straight into the bowels of hell. The further the person was lifted, the harder they crashed.

He knew that there was much power in deciding a person's fate. A very addictive power. The higher up the ladder of authority, the more enrichment of feelings one got when exercising that authority. It's what makes some judges and magistrates feel dominant, as if they were above most people. Seemingly untouchable.

"Miss Clark," he stated. "Miss Laura Clark."

"Yes. May I ask who's calling?"

He showered her with much appreciation for the work she had done in the past, in the advertisement industry. "I'm a very good friend and fan of yours, Miss Clark. I'm calling to tell you that I think you're doing a fabulous job with your new soap commercial. I saw it for the first time last week, and I just love the way the time traveling soap bar dances across the screen, sliding from one era of time to the next. That's a pretty catchy slogan; 'The soap Julius Caesar one used.' I like the jingle too. That's absolutely wonderful. It takes a genius to come up with ad's like that. After I saw that ad, I realized that you were very gifted, and finally understood why they pay intellectual executives like yourself the top salaries."

As he piled on the compliments, flattering Laura to no end, she melted like a pat of butter in a searing skillet. That simpleminded slogan earned her a hearty fifty thousand dollar commission. He thought it was ridiculous, because he was sure he could've come up with a better idea than hers. Having her ego pumped the way he inflated it, she was exhilarated, on top of the world. She laid flat the back of her right wrist on her forehead and wooed charismatically, "Oh my! I don't know what to say, but that I really appreciate everything you've said. Um ... I didn't get your name."

"My name?"

"Yes." She wondered why he was reluctant to tell her. "Your name."

"My name is Sue Ellen McCockster."

She froze, thinking about the name, breaking it down, wanted to laugh. Hearing the silence, he explained, "I'm a little hesitant about telling people my name. When people hear it, they tend to not take me seriously. I think my old man was some kind of a prankster, giving me a girly name like that." He waited for a moment, then said, "Anyway, that's not important. What is is that you're doing an excellent job. I just thought I'd call to let you know that."

"Well, thank you. I think."

"You're very welcome. I also wanted to tell you that you did a wonderful job when you spoke at the seminar you attended more than two years ago."

Just as he mentioned that bit of information, a thick cloud of apprehension swallowed her whole, almost smothered her. He went on to say, "You know, when you spoke about the future of the advertisement business. I swear, I got so hyped about my career that I couldn't wait to go out and make a million dollars."

"You were there?"

"No. But a friend of mine was. She taped the seminar, then gave me a copy. I must've listened to it a million times."

"That's great. If I said something that was useful to you, then I'm glad you were able to benefit from my experiences."

He continued on a pleasant tone, as if everything were simply peachy, "Now, Miss Clark, for the real reason that I called." A few seconds after the drum roll commenced, he began, "You did attend that convention in Boston two years ago, didn't you?"

She thought the caller might've been one of the many people that she'd met there; a new connection, an interested client. Possibly an old friend from college. Then a different thought entered her mind, and she wondered if he was the over-bearing psychotic waiter who pestered her for nearly an hour to persuade her to go out with him. Oddly, having the accident with the high school student hadn't entered her mind, yet. Because she felt more paranoid than guilty about the whole episode, for two years straight, she drank herself into a manageable denial. She couldn't get out of her head the bits and pieces of the bloody scene; the young girls disfigured body soaring inelegantly through the air, as though she was a life-size rag doll hurled from a catapult. She wanted so much to believe that nothing about it would ever come back to haunt her. She tried adamantly to place the callers voice, then replied skeptically, "Of course. You already know that I did."

"Good. I hope it went great. I hope you enjoyed yourself."

"It was okay. Just another seminar and convention."

"That's not so," Stoney said, raising the hammer high to get the maximum striking affect. "That's not so at all. Ya see, I happen to know that after you left the convention late Sunday evening, you were kind of tipsy-tipsy." He released the hammer, braced himself, prepared for the collision. He thought it quite entertaining to see people go from cheerful to wretched on the same breath. It was like driving down the highway, then all of a sudden, an invisible brick wall springs up and does its damage. "When you had that little ... ah ... fender-bender, someone wrote down your license plate number."

Laura's worst fears wormed their way to the surface. Her guts cringed tight around her insides, and an indescribable warm wetness grew in her crotch area. Her eyes rolled downward and she discovered that she had wet herself.

She dropped the phone and ran hysterically around the apartment, amidst a storm of hysteria, crashing into objects, knocking other items over, screaming sadistically, "Noooooooooo! Noooooooooo! No! No! No! No! No!" For nearly ten minutes, the same thing, over and over again. Charging footsteps, loud crashing sounds, capped by horrific shouts of denial. Soon, some of the finer details of that horrible night returned, conveyed flashes of gruesome images filed with screams, a mangled body and blood gushing profusely from several sever injuries. Halfway through her irrepressible outburst, an idea came to her of what the telephone conversation might entail.

If she listened closely, in the background, she would've heard Stoney responding to what he heard. He was keeled over, lying splayed on the ground, clutching his sides, laughing up a storm, waiting for her to return to the phone. What in the hell is she doing? he wondered. I hope she doesn't hurt herself, because that can ruin my plans. This one's going to pay for that little cabin I've got my mind set on up in New Hampshire. Abruptly, his laughter trailed to nothing. He shouted into the receiver, "Miss Clark! Hello! Are you there? Come back to the phone? We need to finish this conversation."

She finally returned to the telephone, brought it to her ear slowly, and he could feel the terror in her stuttered breathing and incomprehensible babbling. He said calmly, "Miss Clark, you've got to calm down. Fleeing the scene of an accident, and you didn't even leave a calling card." He admonished her frivolously. "Shame on you, Miss Clark. Shame shame shame! Now, is that any way for a responsible and professional person to act?"

He could tell that she was too distraught to speak, maybe suffering a nervous breakdown. He could tell that she trembled with fear as she envisioned her life suddenly coming to a screeching stop. He could sense how dark and enclosed the immediate area around her had become, as if she was in solitary confinement, sucked into a big black hole.

Everything he imaged she was experiencing was true. That and a hell of a lot more, since only she knew in its entirety what was at stake. Not only did she envision her life and career coming to a devastating halt, she saw prison and some of its ugliness. She imagined the appalling viciousness of what life would be like for many years to come. The word 'jail' or anything that had to do with the subject of incarceration couldn't find its way past the tremendous lump swelling in her throat. However, she did manage to slur, "Wha-wha … do you … how … I don't … this … this is …" A mountain of horror sank deep, all the way to her toes, which remained curled tight with anxiety. Her thinking had become so jumbled that she couldn't turn the simplest thoughts into anything that made sense.

Understanding her present state of mind, Stoney said, "It's obvious that you're too distraught to go further with this conversation. So what I'll do is after you've calmed down, I'll call you back. Maybe later this evening sometime, and tell you what I want you to do. I'm sure it'll be quiet fair, considering what's at risk. Quite fair indeed."

Laura remained silent, still at a loss for words.

He continued on a cheerful note. "Anyway, you have a nice evening, Miss Clark. Miss … Laura Clark."

After he terminated the call, he snapped out of the trance and continued getting dressed for work.

CHAPTER 6

▼

Stoney had arrived at the Area C headquarters in Mattapan, Massachusetts at eight thirty to begin his shift. The fairly new station is located on the busy corner of Morton Street and Blue Hill Avenue, amidst a thickly settled minority neighborhood that has a higher than average level of crime.

Entering the station, as a few people walking by greeted him, he ignored them, as if they weren't even there. He didn't say a word. He appeared distant, in deep thought about something eerily inconceivable. Something that was trying to surface for the past hour while driving to work.

He went straight to the locker room located in the basement and began changing into his uniform. He opened his locker, stared at his uniform, and felt an abundance of unwanted attention flying toward his direction. He stepped into his pants, pulled them up slowly, glancing slyly at a few officers near, peeped them from the corners of his eyes. He grew outwardly paranoid, believing that other people besides Spanky and Sleeper knew about their secret operation; the Dixie Club. He studied a few of the officers nearby and believed wholeheartedly that they were wondering about what he's been into for the past ten years. Searching for some form of relief by sharing the blame, he wondered what kinds of hustles they were involved in. Surely, they had to have something going on on the side, as a mere paycheck could never appease anyone's lifestyle. He believed the more money a person made, the more they got use to spending. Charlie Vigota over there just got a promotion and a new speed boat, he thought. I wonder who he hustled to get it. McDaniel's in traffic has been dressing more fashionable lately. He might've stopped a tailor driving intoxicated, or with an expired license, then made a deal to get five new suit's, plus accessories, on the first of every month. Detective Peoples over there. I haven't heard him complaining about his mortgage payments lately. I wonder what he's into. I haven't heard Patricia Stone in narcotics complaining about the money she needs to finance her daughters kidney transplant. For something as serious as a lifesaving operation for her kid, I wouldn't blame her if she hustled the President out of his pension.

For no reason that anyone could see, he froze, thrown into a hypnotic trance. He descended slowly onto the wooden bench in front of his locker, then stared into it, at the badge on his shirt.

Suddenly, his subconscious grabbed him by the throat, choked him breathless and demanded that he give his complete attention. Rising shakily to his feet, a horrible feeling surged through his body, buried him deeper into a climbing iniquity separating his spirit from his soul. A ghostly feeling surrounded him, and he cowered and trembled with fear. His teeth shattered violently, and he felt like he had two-inch ice cycles hanging from his fingertips.

He made an attempt to shake the awful feeling by attempting to force himself back to his reality. A last effort ditch to save himself from being carried away to wherever *they* were trying to take him. He shook his head rapidly and looked around the room to absorb the environment. He tried to think of many everyday situations that made him feel normal. Sane.

He inhaled deeply, arduously, felt as though his lungs were about to explode. He gushed forward a heavy breath, exhaled exuberantly, and again, his body shook violently, like a dog ridding its coat of excess water. That was too close, he thought. Way too close.

From out of nowhere, a fellow officer who he had met at the police academy approached from behind, startled him. He plopped his dead weight onto the bench a foot away, sat hunched, his chin buried miserly into his chest. He had mentioned to someone earlier that he felt as though he had an eight hundred pound gorilla riding his shoulders, whacked his forehead viciously whenever he looked in the wrong direction. Pruning his lips sourly for the repulse stewing in his mouth, he wanted to spit the psychosomatic taste entailing his unpleasant circumstances onto the floor. He announced unenthusiastically, "The Stoneman."

"Capone. What's up?"

Nearly everyone in the department, and a few other precincts, knew of his regrettable situation, so he was often straightforward. Didn't want to relay that he was a coward hiding behind a cloak fabricated of self-pity and a steadfast denial. He used as few words as possible; the heroin quickened his pace with life. In a nutshell, his family, mainly his wife, noticed instantly the abrupt change in his social behavior. Their marriage grew estranged for his cold relations revealing only the basics; 'Hi, Goodbye, and I'm doing all right,' as with total strangers on the street. Empty talk that produced not the emotions that once delivered warm feelings of security, but robotic dialogue that delivered a chilled contempt for everything discouraging that's happened in his life since he introduced the needle to his veins. Because of the intimate personality that she had become accustomed to when they had began dating, she had come to believe that she was sleeping with a total stranger; someone that she didn't know from passing. A relationship akin to a prostitute and her John.

Having his status questioned, what barreled into mind was the incident that threw him over the top, sent his sanity zooming for cover, sent him to the Eric Lederman mental health center, where he was put on suicide watch for two months. One day, several months ago, he had arrived home from work and discovered his wife sitting in front of the fireplace, knitting needles and yarn resting on her lap, dead from a self-inflicted gunshot wound to the head. At her feet was a detailed suicide letter explaining how she felt about the monster that he had become. After enduring almost a year of his unsettling infidelities and problematic drug addiction, she could bear it no longer and decided to end it all. Before dialing 911, he stood frozen in absolute shock for nearly an hour, in a cocooned state of denial, staring at the gray brain matter splattered on the ceiling above her. Figured certain chunks to be reminisces of the marvelous life they started together some seven years prior; the first day he met her, their wedding, the birth of their only child. He then grabbed their wedding photo, fell to the floor and cried wretchedly for another hour. His therapists told him that his tears wouldn't compromise his strength, so he turned on the faucet whenever. Attempting to push the incident from his mind unsuccessfully, his eyes misted with remorse for the devastating occurrences crushing his life. Choking, he replied jadedly, "Tryinta do the right thing. Staying clean. It's not easy."

"No doubt." Stoney knew that he had created most of his own problems. Felt little compassion, but didn't show it. He could tell that he wanted someone to talk to. Needed someone to talk to, could feel the urgency squeezing his words. He felt the approaching testimony was inevitable. He asked anyway, "How long?"

He replied dismally, "Two months. Three weeks. Seven hours. Thirty-four minutes," he looked at his watch, "and ten seconds." Sounded like a countdown to his demise. His execution.

"Long as you keep on doing the right thing. I hear that heroin's a bitch." A curiosity entered his mind. "Hey, um," he lowered his head, not wanting to ask, "what's it like where they got you set up?"

"In the wash-ups unit, over there in the basement of headquarters?"

"I heard some things. Never had a chance to ask anyone there."

Capone looked to the floor with a cold solitude, his physique taut. "It's quiet over there, like a mortuary. Everyone walking around half dead, like zombies, hopeless, thinking about the mess we've made of ourselves. There's not much to do, mostly filing simple infractions, some light paper work to keep busy." As though he'd been stripped of all dignity, he grumbled, "They won't even let us answer the fricken phones, dammit! Got to keep the forces dirty little secrets on the down low. The company shrink encourages us to talk to each other while we're there, air our problems. Nobody does, cause nobody wants to listen to what anybody else has to say. It only adds someone else's misery to your own, as if we don't have enough to deal with. I'll be glad when I see the last of that fricken place. It's really starting to wear on me. I swear, it's like being in a cage, on exhibition."

"How long are you supposed to be there?"

"Not sure. Depends. They got a list of shrinks and higher-ups in internal affairs who we have to clear on first. Then maybe they'll let us see daylight."

"How's your family doing? How's your son taking all this?"

"They're with me on this. Supportive. I don't know why, as much shit as I've done against them. My son, sometimes I don't know what to say to him. I just pray to God that he forgives me. He means a lot to me, Stoney. I don't ever want to loose his respect. My girlfriend, I think she seeing someone else, getting ready to leave me. Not that I would blame her. But my sons respect, I wouldn't give that up for nothing in the world. My therapist says the hardest part of recovery" he corrected himself, "rehabilitation, is accepting responsibility." Stoney sat upright and exhaled exhaustively, felt like he'd been given a subliminal message. "Said I had to learn to live life all over again, like being reborn. Reclaiming and clinging onto the innocence, as if I ever was. I have to search for the old me, introduce myself, then get to know all about who I use to be." He complained, "That's damn near impossible. You know how stubborn we cops can be. He said I have to search for the passion to live life anew everyday, reasons to stay clean. Like when we were kids, a time of innocence. We didn't need nothing back then. Only playtime on a sunny Saturday morning, a playground, some friends, and a hand full of pipedreams. Life was so simple back then. Couldn't nobody tell us nothing, cause we had it all. Thought we'd live forever. Thought the happiness would last to the end of our days."

Stoney nodded indistinctly. Through his peripheral vision, he noticed Capone's eyes well with tears, noticed the dark arcs underneath from many sleepless nights. "I feel ya on that." He thought about Jake and Jessica, about what they were like before he stole their innocence—brought nightmares crashing into their world. He thought about his youth in deep contemplation, then added, "I remember. That was a beautiful time."

Capone spat wrathfully, "Then you grow up and meet someone called 'Life's a bitch,' and then you die."

"Then maybe we'll discover the correct reasons on how we should've been living."

Capone placed his hand on Stoneys right shoulder. "I don't want to find out then."

"Looks like you haven't been getting any shut eye."

"Yeah ... well." He faced Stoney. "I've been having a problem with that. Probably stress. Been having nightmares."

"You ... nightmares?"

Stoney felt a tremendous fright emanating from Capone's body when he began explaining, "Time to time, I wind up in this crazy situation that scares the hell out of me. I find myself assisting ... I don't know, a surgeon of some sort, in an operation. Instead of wearing a typical scrub suit and gown, he wears a bloodied butchers apron. He has two prosthetic limbs for arms, with hooks as sharp as surgical scalpels. When he operates, he only uses the hooks, and he sings these god-awful tricked-out nursery rhymes that drive me insane." Growing excited, his muscles tensed, his fists clenched tight, his breathing grew rapid. He wanted to explode with a burst of anger, but kept himself in check.

When Stoney recalled meeting a butcher several years prior, combined with his nightmares involving Jake, the details of Capone's nightmare hit him like a ton of bricks. He couldn't believe what he was hearing. It was all too familiar. It was as though his nightmare had taken on a life of its own; could breath, breed and lay fright to everyone connected to him in some way, shape or form. He asked disbelievingly, "You say he has two prosthetic arms?"

Capone eyed him penetratingly, nodded lethargically. "Yeah."

"And he wears a bloodied butchers apron?"

Breathed inaudibly, "Uh-huh."

"What's his name?"

"He says it's Dr. J. Like the seventies basketball star for the Philadelphia Seventy-Sixers."

"Jake!" Stoney alarmed. He punched his locker irately. "That fricken ..."

A few officers standing several feet away eyed them inquisitively.

"Who's Jake?" Capone asked. "You act like you know him."

"Probably just a coincidence. What else happened?"

"During the procedure, while he's cutting on … on the body, my job is to suck up the excess blood, so he can see what he's doing."

"Who's he cutting into?"

He stated weakly, evasively, "Just … just a body."

"Whose body?"

Capone hesitated a long moment, stammered frightfully, "M-M-Mine!"

"Let me get this straight. You're assisting in an operation …" he swallowed loud, "… on yourself?"

He nodded feebly. "And if I don't keep up with him, he scolds me excessively. Makes me fell like I'm an incompetent snot nosed kid fresh out of med school. If I make a mistake, he whacks me across the face with one of his hooks. Halfway through the procedure, my face is so battered and cut up that my eyes are nearly shut. Looks like someone fed my face through a meat grinder. And the miserable son-of-a …"

Going on and on, Stoney finally cut him off, "Whoa! Whoa! Take it easy." He paused, let Capone catch his breath, then asked, "You didn't just stand there and let him have his way. What'd you do?"

"Nothing!" he shouted. The officers standing in front of their locker eyed them again. This time, their eyes lingered. Taking in their probing stares, Capone stated timidly, "I couldn't do anything. I'm not under any form of anesthesia, strapped to a table, screaming in acute pain as he rips out my intestine, foot by foot. Watching the operation, I feel this indescribable pain inside my midsection, something gnawing into my spleen, tearing at my liver, ripping at my colon. I was so scared that I couldn't move a muscle, accept to piss my pants. He takes the organs he's ripping from my body and throws them into a trash bucket on the floor, next to his feet. And I look inside and see my heart, and it's still beating. All of a sudden, I look down and see that I'm a bloody mess, as though my midsection had been hacked to shreds with a meat cleaver. My organs hanging out of my body, I'm begging and pleading with him to stop, but he doesn't listen to a word I say. He totally ignores my pleas, as if they only make him more enthused about what he's doing … it encourages him. The images are so vivid that I can almost feel the pain he's inflicting, and I can smell the stench emanating from my rotting corpse on the table before me. When I try to look away, he forces me to watch the entire procedure. And for some reason, I feel helpless, inadequate. He humiliates me so much that I just want to run somewhere, crawl into a corner and die. Stoney, I don't know what significance he has in my life, but he scares me to death. Every time I go to sleep, there he is, a fucken eager beaver, waiting to do the operation all over again. When I awake, I'm so scared that I'm afraid to go back to sleep. He terrifies me so much that not once have I found the courage to look at his face. And he's only standing a foot away from me, just as close as I am to you." When he had finished delivering his sworn testimony, he remained silent, huffing and puffing arduously, sweat trickling the sides of his face, staring desperately into Stoneys eyes.

"That's ..." Stoney looked into his lap worriedly, his fingers entwined nervously, "... not good."

"Tell me about it. I don't know why it's happening, but I know it's for a reason. Nightmares like that only happen to send a message. A portentous omen. It's probably got something to do with the way I've been living, the things I've been doing." He looked away, stated remorsefully, "All that shit is finally coming back on my ass, and there's nothing that I can do to stop it." His body trembling, he rose shakily to his feet. He wiped his brow for the perspiration dribbling into his eyes, making him blink rapidly. Out of breath, he stated hurriedly, "I have to go. Later, Stoneman."

"Keep it real."

I'll keep it any way I can cling onto it, is what he wanted to say. Leaving, he threw over his shoulder, "No doubt."

Ten minutes later, he had just about finished getting dressed. He had put on everything but his clip-on tie. He held it to his neck, started to fasten it. He stopped, took a seat on the bench. Again, he fell into deep thought, knowing that something was attempting to take control over his mind, body and soul.

Reflecting conscientiously of his involvement with his illicit affairs—the ramifications for his participation in the Dixie Club had been consuming his sanity for the past couple of years—he began feeling disoriented, as if he didn't belong anywhere in particular. Wondering why his intellect was constantly challenged and haunted by his subconscious caused him to loose focus doing whatever.

Although the mansion and the Porsche Carrera GT were in title and registered to someone else, to cast suspicion, he couldn't stop himself from thinking that people were starting to see through the bullshit to take notice of his growth of wealth. For the most part, he couldn't stop himself from having sentiments for the faceless children who popped into his mind randomly to fire questions of liability. They bombarded him as though spat from an Uzi.

Staring into his locker, his boss noticed his strange behavior and approached wonderingly. Capt. John 'Shorty' Winslow is a fifty-five year old dedicated police officer, who's been on the police force for thirty-one years. He's five-foot-four inches tall and carries close to two hundred and twenty pounds on his portly frame. He wears a pair of black thick framed Buddy Holley type prescription glasses which magnify his eyes three fold. This often made people feel paranoid, because he tends to stand less than one foot away when conversing with then. Only a foot away, because he's usually chewing on a twelve inch long, fat cigar. One that he'll not dare light because he stopped smoking several years ago, after a few people mentioned that the habit would stunt his growth. However, at this age, rather than his height, his primary concern was his health. Until a person got use to his unconventional nature, as he stared through those binocular like spectacles, he made them feel as though he was examining every wee imperfection and minute blemish on their face. Actually, he studied their expressions. He realized that words said one thing, but the eyes and facial twitches; involuntary muscle spasms, seldom lie.

Besides his everyday dress blues, he wore a pair of black, size ten, wing-tipped Bostonians. To most people, they looked like clown shoes. The front toe sections bubbled up, tailor made that way to allow his corn infested toes to breathe. When it rains, or whenever his shoes absorb moisture, they produced a peculiar squeaking sound. The officers who knew him well could predict his mood by listening to this prophetic sound his shoes emitted. Most of the time, they were right on the money. Regardless of how Capt. Winslow said he was feeling, his shoes always told the complete story.

Since he's balding, to create the illusion at though he still has a head full of Elvis-like hair, he takes a few elongated strands of hair from the right side and tosses them constructively over to the left. Some days he bushed it so high that he resembles a television evangelist. Finally, not to mention, he's an eccentric man who reflects his insecurity by wearing a belt and suspenders.

Funny as it may seem, most people, somewhere down the line in their family tree, have either had, or has an uncle who resembles this man. This phenomenon. This Shorty. He's the illustrious man who shows up at family reunions or summer bar-b-ques, and lays splayed on the hammock with his hairy beer belly peeping gaudily from under his rib spattered t-shirt. He always has an ice cold beer clutched in hand, burps vociferously every few seconds, and tells corny jokes and funny stories to his nieces and nephews. Or anyone who'll listen. Sometimes he has them pull on his pinky finger for a gastrointestinal surprise.

Through all of his years of glory on the force, he's managed to survive the difficult times by sporting a very compassionate composure. He's a thoughtful leader who's always there for his officers; men and women alike, for when they have complex problems and need someone to talk to. Whether its professional or personal. He's a very important key factor in the station and plays a major role in keeping his men unified. Through daily maintenance; casual conversation, he keeps the threads of his outfit taut, because he's someone who knows how to listen.

He removed the cigar from his mouth, gripped it as though holding the small end of a pool stick, ready to fire away. With a croaky voice, a rasp that he's acquired over the years from berating his men on a daily basis, he said, "Hey, officer Brooks. What's with all the gloom? Ya look like someone shot ya dog or something. Ain'tcha gonna finish getting dressed? Where's ya tie?"

Stoney turned slowly to look at his boss, found his probing eyes, but said absolutely nothing.

Capt. Winslow eyed his overall appearance and quickly examined him for mental fatigue, exhaustion. A burn-out. He took considerable note of his spaced-out expression and realized immediately that something was more than wrong. This was definitely not the Stoney Brooks that he had come to know. He believed he was experiencing something other than just a bad day. He returned the cigar to his mouth, stated compassionately, "Stoney, why don't you come back to my office with me, so we can, ya know, maybe talk for a few minutes." He turned away, then walked to the doorway. Fifteen feet away, he noticed that Stoney hadn't budged. He stopped, turned halfway. "Officer Brooks, are you with me?"

Without saying a word, he rose slowly to his feet, then managed ineptly to throw one foot in front of the other. For some mysterious reason, taking steps, walking, felt strange. It's the first time in his life, since a toddler, that he's actually had to concentrate on doing it. When Capt. Winslow saw him conforming to his request, he continued to his office, leading the way.

On the way there, they passed Spanky and Sleeper. They were on their way to the locker room to get dressed, to begin their shift. As Stoney and Capt. Winslow walked by, Sleeper shouted, "Yo! Stoney baby. What's up?"

"How's it going, Stone?" Spanky asked, staring curiously. "We ... ah ... missed you last night. What happened to ya?"

Stoney continued stepping in a zombie like trance, not hearing a word his friends threw at him. Didn't even throw a glance of acknowledgement.

Spanky and Sleeper took considerable note of his dejected condition, the distant stare in his eyes. They glanced at each other momentarily, then back to Stoney, watching him trail their boss to his office. After experiencing rejection—the silent treatment—from someone who's supposed to be their close friend for many years, Spanky became suspicious. He had no doubt in his mind that something was terribly wrong. He turned to Sleeper and slapped his left shoulder lightly. "You see the way Stoney looked?"

"Yeah. Like he's on another planet or something."

"Let's go downstairs, to the locker room. We gotta talk. This shit don't look good at all."

They hustled to the basement, stepped to their lockers. They worked their combination locks for a moment, opened the doors. After they started getting undressed, Spanky blurted, "I don't like this shit!" He slammed his right hand into the palm of his left. "Damn! Something tells me that Stoney's gonna crack. He's gonna crack, and he's gonna take us down for the count. I can feel it."

"You really think he's gonna do something like that," Sleeper asked, "after all we've been through?" Shook his head. "We agreed to the code of silence, remember?"

Spanky's eyes hardened. He faced Sleeper, grabbed the lapels of his shirt in one bunch and fired, "Look, you fucken idiot! The hell with that code of silence bullshit. Didn't you see the look on his face? I've seen it several times in the past, and it ain't good." He released his shirt. "That's the look of someone who's getting ready to crack." "Wake the fuck up, you idiot! Do I have to tell you what that means for us if he does loose his marbles?"

Spanky looked to the left, but Sleeper could still see the anger etched on the side of his face, growing intense. He knew clearly of some of the dreadful penalties they'd face, had more than a good idea of the punishment they'd receive, if Stoney spilled his guts about the Dixie Club. And yet, he believed deep in his heart that their long time friend would never betray them. No matter what the circumstances. "I don't know, Spanky. I find it hard to accept that he would ever say anything against us. I mean, he may say something to implicate himself. But, about all of us, collectively, as a group of renegade cops, I say no way. Naaaw, Stoney's not that kind of guy. Think back on all those times he's covered for us. Think about the risks he's taken for us. Hadn't it been for him, your dumb ass would've been dishonorably discharged years ago."

Spanky leaned against his locker, and unexpectedly, an unforgettable incident entered his mind. One evening, as he and Stoney were leaving a sports bar in downtown Boston, they ran into and confronted a big-time drug dealer, one of Spankys marks. Two years before, Spanky had discovered crucial evidence implicating the man as a key figure in a fatal shoot-out amidst a drug-deal gone sour. While Stoney kept a vigilant lookout at the beginning of the alley, Spanky escorted the man into a dark alley, behind a hotel, and questioned him as to why he was late in making his weekly payments. The unarmed suspect refused to pay up, or even agree to it; he was fed up of being squeezed for his hard earned ill-gotten gains. Therefore, Spanky shot him once, then planted a small caliber semiautomatic handgun at his feet just before other officers arrived on the scene. Feeling he owed his career to Stoney, Spanky sighed, "Well, maybe you're right. But I still think we should keep a watchful eye on him. At least until we know for sure what's really going on. If he screws everything up, I don't want to be the last one to know about it. Like a Johnny come lately."

Sleeper looked into his eyes, tried to read what was on his mind. "You mean, we should put a tail on him, from time to time? Maybe tap his phone and all that sneaky backstabbing shit?"

"Until we know for sure. And I think you should keep in view what's at risk." He opened his locker, and an ugly picture entered his mind. He whispered, "You feel like giving up your freedom, going to jail? You feel like spending a few years locked in a six by five foot, sewer drenched shit hole of a cell, roomed with a psychotic asshole named Bolo who's gotten use to the idea that he likes men a whole lot better than women? You feel like letting another man move in on your wife? You feel like eating food that ain't good enough to feed to park animals? And what about your son, Junior? You want him to start calling someone else daddy? And what about your …"

Sleeper masked a sickening expression, absorbing the harsh realities of what Spanky hurled. Not being able to stomach anymore of the potential future atrocities, he became unnerved and gushed, "Okay okay! Enough already. I get the picture. Dammit, Spanky. Why do you have to rub in all that disgusting shit? Now I'll have nightmares for at least a week."

"Not me! I ain't going to jail for no fucken body, at no matter what the cost. No way in hell. By the way. I forgot to mention one thing. It'll be much worse for us in prison because we're cops."

For a few moments, they dwelled on the unsightly scenario in silence. They continued undressing in deep contemplation. Their minds worked overtime on the viciousness that Spanky had only moments before professed about their potentially explosive situation.

CHAPTER 7

▼

The door was shut tight to Capt. Winslow's office. Stoney sat in an aluminum folding chair placed directly in front of a huge oaken desk cluttered with mounds of paperwork; wanted posters and notepads, a computer, writing utensils, et cetera et cetera. His nervous hands clasped tight. His thumbs spun freely, playing a losers game of tag.

Capt. Winslow stared observantly from the perch of his high-back executive chair, his hands folded neatly on the desk. He studied him closely, without not saying a word. Every few seconds, he chewed on his cigar, then moved it from one side of his mouth to the other. Everyone who knew him understood that this meant that he was thinking about what he was going to ask. What he was going to say to initiate his plan of attack. After getting a feel of Stoneys physical disposition, he implied worriedly, "You got something on ya mind, kid?"

Staring into Capt. Winslows eyes intently, he didn't respond. He followed the shine on the lamp, on his desk, then fell into a deep trance. He then faded away to another place and time.

At his mansion, during a basketball halftime, while Spanky and Sleeper argued about who would win, Stoney placed a call on a disposable cell phone. As the phone rang, he told them, "Hey, you guys! Hold it down a minute." They stopped talking briefly, he continued, "Turn down the volume on the television for a sec. Dixie, I got a couple all set up." He pushed the speaker button on the phone so all could hear.

Spanky picked up the remote control, pushed the mute button. "This should be good, since the Nets aren't doing anything but getting me depressed. They look like a bunch of little old ladies at a mark-down at Macy's basement."

"All right!" Sleeper exclaimed, clapped his hands. "Now for some real excitement. On center stage, 'The Stoneman!' This tired ass game ain't doing nothing but putting me to sleep. We gotta come up with something better than this." He listened intently when Stoney rolled his lines, hoping to improve on his technique.

A man answered pleasantly, "Hello."

"Hello," Stoney said cheerfully. "May I speak to Helen Atwater?"

"Sure. May I ask who's calling?"

"Yes. My name's Father Donavan. I'm supposed to be replacing Father Mahoney at the rectory shortly, when he retires. He's given me a list of the members who have positions on the church board, so that I could call them, to learn of their functions."

Spanky whispered, "More like Father Bologna."

"I understand," the man said. "But, I didn't know Father Mahoney was retiring."

"One never knows what the next day will bring," Stoney said, "only the Lord. He lays all of our plans, and we live them. I just found out about it last Monday."

"I see. Well, my name's Kevin. I'm Helens husband."

"It's nice to meet you, Kevin. I've been hearing some exciting things about you, from Father Mahoney."

"Thank you, Father. It's nice to meet you too. I'll see if I can get Helen for you." He pulled the phone away from his mouth and called, "Helen, honey! Can you come to the phone for a minute?"

Stoney heard footsteps approach the phone, then heard Kevin fill his wife in on what they spoke about. She took the phone. "Father Donovan, how are you?"

"I'm fine, my dear," Stoney said. "I heard your husband fill you in on why I called. Also, I wanted to bring to your attention something that's very critical. Something that Father Mahoney has made me aware of."

"Yes Father. What is it?"

Stoney didn't hear Kevin footsteps, so he knew that he was still within earshot. "My dear, because you're on the board of directors, I have to bring to your attention an evil that Father Mahoney spoke of. An ugliness that's infiltrated our flock."

"This sounds serious," Helen said uncomfortably.

"It is," Stoney said sadly. "It's about a particular member in our congregation who's been involved in pornography. To be exact, underage-porn."

Helen expelled a breath of disgust. "Oh my God! Someone in our church is involved in underage-pornography. Father, that's disgusting!"

A thrash of heat swallowed Kevin completely. Panic slipped in and slapped him stupid. He blurted, "Wha-Wha-What did he say? Who-Who's he talking about?"

A sputter of laughter escaped Spankys lips, and Stoney held his index finger to his lips. "Ssshhh!"

Helen told her husband, "He's talking about someone in the congregation being involved in underage-pornography."

"Who?" Kevin blurted, staring at his wife, beads of sweat cropping his forehead.

"Father," Helen said, "who are you speaking about?"

"Father Mahoney said he'd let me know the next time I spoke with him. For the protection of the children, he's running background checks on everyone in the congregation. Especially those who work with the children. Then he'll confront the person directly."

"This is just awful," Helen said. She angered, "We have to get this sick person away from the children, and out of our parish. People like that are of the devil, and they should burn in hell. How did Father Mahoney find out about this terrible person?"

"He's a very resourceful man," Stoney said. "He has many friends in law enforcement. And I do share your sentiments about what should happen to them. They should burn in hell, or be castrated."

"Yes," Helen agreed, "or be castrated."

Not being able to contain himself any longer, Kevin grabbed the phone from his wife, then asked doubtfully, "You say this is somebody named Father Donovan?"

Helen told her husband, "Honey, you sound angry. Why are you speaking to Father Donovan in that tone?"

"It sounds fishy. Why would a priest call to talk about something like this?"

"Because it's disgusting," Stoney told Kevin. "And you're the person who I'm speaking about." He paused briefly to allow the information sink in. Marinate.

Kevin became so confused that he froze, mouth stuck agape. Many details of the lucrative underage-pornography business that he and two business partners began three years prior filled his mind. One of his partners was indicted a week ago, and the prosecutors are still searching for his accomplices. Stoney found out about Kevins involvement through one of their biggest customers. His wife asked, "Honey, are you all right? You look like you've seen a ghost."

With Kevins being unable to speak, at a total loss for words, Stoney went on to say, "I know all about the business, Kevin. I also know that you teach Sunday school at the parish I spoke of." He laughed, "And I'm sure that by now you know this isn't anybody named Father Donovan. As a matter of fact, I'm not a priest at all."

Kevin sputtered, "Who-Who-Who ..."

"Who am I?" Stoney asked casually. "I'm someone who doesn't want you to get into any more trouble than you're already in."

"What's he saying?" Helen asked.

She tried to take the phone away from her husband and he slapped the back of her hand violently and snapped, "Don't do that, dammit! Can't you see I'm trying to talk to the man?"

Incredibly surprised at his outburst of anger toward her, his wife leaned away from him, perplexed. "Why did you hit me like that? And why are you so angry?"

"Is your wife curious as to what we're saying?" Stoney asked Kevin. He laughed, "Maybe now's the best time to ask for some head."

Sleeper laughed, then whispered, "Stoney, you're crazy."

Kevin spat into the phone, "You miserable ..."

"Sweetheart," Helen said disturbingly, "how can you take that attitude with a priest?"

"Go ahead and tell her what we're talking about," Stoney told Kevin, laughing. "Of course, unless you want to keep this all under wraps, away from your community. I think you know what'll happen to your family if any of this information travels to that part of the globe."

Kevin remained quiet. Stoney continued, "It's time I stop messing around with you and tell you the real reason why I called, Mr. Atwater. It's all about the bucks, my friend. I know you got about a half million dollars stashed away in an off-shore account. I want half of it tomorrow. If not, I'll give your name to the authorities and they'll come knocking at your door by tomorrows end. Then I'll send the information to your job, and spread it throughout your community."

Kevin babbled, "What! You'll send it to ... you want a half ... but I don't have ..."

Taking in his distraught condition, his wife asked, "Sweetheart, what's wrong? And what are you two talking about?"

"I think that's quite fair," Stoney told Kevin. "Considering the repulse that you've helped spread throughout the internet. The World Wide Web. The world!"

*   *   *   *

After terminating the connection, he placed another call on the same cell phone.

A man answered, "Hello."

"Hi!" Stoney said. "May I speak to Coach Isaiah Henderson."

"This is he. May I ask who's calling?"

"My name is Peter Holt," Stoney said. "My son attends your school. He's not on the football team, but I simply called to tell you that I think you're doing an excellent job with training the players this year. The offense is strong, and the defense is tight," he emphasized, "right on the money. The starting lineup is fantastic. They're dynamite! Even the second stringers," he emphasized heavily, "the *replacements* are good. You're a great man, Isaiah. A strong leader. You're the kind of coach they need, if they plan to make it to the championship this year."

"Well, thank you." He felt much gratitude, but wondered why the caller stressed the phrase 'right on the money', and the word 'replacements.' "We're doing all that we can do. But it's ultimately up to the players to put forward their best. We merely encourage them to try."

"That's wonderful." Building the hype, showering him with praise, Stoney went on to say, "A man like you, you're the salt of the earth. I bet your players worship the ground you walk on. I use to play a little ball myself back them, but I never played in college. I remember when you played football many years ago, at Cal Tech. I read in the sports column that they nicknamed you 'The Snake', because of the way you slithered all over the field. I'll never forget that game you played against Florida, in seventy-two, when you ran a touchdown from a kickoff. The first play of the game. That was awesome! I still hear some people talking about it today, on some sports channels."

"That was a first for me. I was lucky back them."

Stoney drooled, "Aaawww! Don't be so modest. I'll never forget how it went in a million years." He said excitedly, "You were like Jim Brown, zigzagging all over the field. After you caught the ball, you took off like lightening. The opposition was hot on your trail, but you outran them all. The way you dodged them, moving in and out like that, it was totally amazing. You had crazy legs that day. You're feet had a mind of their own."

"Yeah, well." Isaiah proceeded gloomily, "But, it didn't last. Everything was going good until my junior year. I got clipped and my knee was never the same.

The scouts didn't want to consider me, and my career on the field came to a screeching halt. As far as the pros were concerned, I was through. Washed up."

"That's too bad," Stoney saddened. "And you had it all too. I remember when that happened. You took a bad one that day. But when you played, you were good. You were better than good. Heisman trophy candidate and all that good stuff."

Isaiah remembered his first college touchdown, revisited the excitement. He sighed gratifyingly. "Those were the times. I really enjoyed the game back then. That's why I enjoy coaching today. It makes me feel young, like I'm still on the field."

"Although, coaching can be very rewarding. Some positions are very lucrative; get yourself a nice big house, full-size luxury car, "he emphasized, "*fishing boat.* Once you get a good position, you've got to hold onto it with doing what you gotta do. Sometimes it can be hard out there, dog-eat-dog world. I mean, you bounced back from that college gambling scandal a few months ago, but everyone makes mistakes." He said shadily, "You know what I mean?"

"Oh shit," Sleeper whispered to Spanky. "Stoney's about to turn up the heat, bleed him midlevel style."

"I've had my ups and downs," Isaiah said, "and then some. You do your best, and no one can ask for anything more."

"In that first game that I mentioned," Stoney said, "when you reached the forty yard line, the crowd stood up and cheered, 'Isaiah! Isaiah! He's our man! If he can't do it! Nobody can!'"

Spanky whispered, "Hit'em low, Stoneman. "Pump the sucker dry." He waved invisible pom-poms and whispered, "Rah, Rah, Shish boom ba!"

Isaiah heard muffled laughing in the background, but thought nothing of it. He laughed weakly, "They were all on their feet after that touchdown, tearing the house down. Football wouldn't be football without the diehard fans."

Stoney told him, "You were the big hero that day. The big man on campus. The crowd cheered, "Gimme a 'T'! Gimme an 'O'! Gimme a 'B'! Gimme a 'Y'!

Isaiah hesitated for a moment, entirely confounded. He started to say, "What does …"

"After you got the touchdown, the cheerleaders on the side were going, 'Nit wack, paddy wack, give a dog a bone! You scored heroin to kill Toby Winfield, and now that man's gone!'"

He remained silent, waiting for Isaiah to get the gist of what he had just said. Waiting for the ugliness to sink in and zap him into disarray.

They heard an eerie silence on the other end of the line, Isaiah had stopped breathing. Horrified. Stuck on the gruesome images of what had happened only a month before, Toby's dead body floating face down in the Lassitude River.

Isaiah had found out through the grapevine in management that he was going to be replaced by Toby Winfield. A man whose record was unblemished on and off the field. To stop the impending replacement, he took Toby out for a few drinks on his fishing boat, and got him inebriated. After Toby fell asleep, Isaiah gave him an overdose of heroin, then threw him overboard. A drug dealer who Spanky was about to shake down volunteered this information to get him to back off. That's when Spanky put one and one together and figured out what had happened to Toby.

The three heard a weighty breath gush from Isaiah, a loud thud, and then nothing.

"You hear that?" Spanky laughed, "He's down for the count. I think you killed the son-of-a-bitch."

"That was smooth," Sleeper said. "Stoneman, you never cease to amaze me. You're stone cold to the bone. The Pope ain't got jack shit on you." He remembered two weeks before when he had spoken with a corrections officer who was caught on a surveillance camera purchasing a kilo of cocaine, to smuggle into a state prison. After he initiated the hustle; made contact with the mark, the corrections officer panicked. He quit his job immediately, then went to his secret stash and retrieved almost a half million dollars. Then he left the country. Now he's traveling abroad in the Philippines.

They heard rapid footsteps approach the phone, and a woman alarmed hysterically, "Isaiah! Oh my God! Honey, what happened? Did you remember to take your insulin today? Sweetheart, you just lay right there. I'll call an ambulance and we'll get you to a hospital."

Stoney terminated the call. "I'll call him back in a couple of weeks, after he gets out of the hospital. Fill him in on the details. The guy makes a pretty decent buck. He's only five years away from his retirement. I have a good feeling that he has a nice little nest egg tucked away somewhere. One that he's going to share with us."

"Sure ya right!" Spanky laughed. "That's *if* the poor bastard wakes up."

"I had a fainter last month sometime," Sleeper said. "And guess what? The guy's still in the hospital. Some CEO for a computer company in Waltham. I caught him with his pants down. Literally. A married man, nice little family in the suburbs. And there he was, in the back seat of his Mercedes, giving head to a transvestite."

"That's foul," Spanky said. "I wonder who was paying who."

"I have one more call to make," Stoney said. "How would you guys like to get in on this one? Have a little fun."

"What do you mean?"

Stoney went to the library, then returned a few minutes later, carrying six sheets of paper, and a pistol loaded with blanks. He handed Spanky the pistol and three sheets, explaining, "The gun's loaded with blanks. It's just a prop. I've been working on this script for two weeks, to use for my next hustle. It involves two people. It's about a whacked out home invasion gone crazy."

"Two people?" Sleeper asked. "How's that?"

"Well, first I'm going to call the mark, then let him overhear a deadly home invasion in progress. I'm going to play the role of the husband, a middle-aged man, married with two sons; age seven and nine. And Spanky, you'll play the role of the man who's committing the home invasion."

"What am I?" Sleeper asked. "Chop liver. I don't get a part?"

Stoney thought about it for a moment. "Along with us, you can be one of the screamers. But you'll have to scream with a high pitched voice, like a kid, or a woman. And every now and then adlib out of distress. Whine feverishly and throw a whimper into the air."

Sleepers flat response, "Oh really."

"When Spanky fires the gun, on cue, all of us will scream simultaneously, like someone had just been shot. We'll all move around the room, let him hear the shuffling feet of people cowering somewhere in a corner. After which, Sleeper, you'll continue to whine and cry at a whisper. Most importantly, we have to make it sound as real as possible." He told Spanky, "After I dial the number, I'll initiate the dialogue. Remember, you have to really get into the role. You have to feel it, if you want the mark to believe that's it's actually happening."

Spanky nodded, then chuckled. "Stoney, you're crazy. I never thought I'd admit this, but you're even crazier than me. I think I'm going to like this."

"Of course you will. It'll be fun. You'll see."

"What if someone else answers the phone?" Sleeper asked.

"He's single," Stoney replied, "and lives alone." He dialed the number on the cell phone, pushed the speaker button so all could hear, then waited for someone to answer. Moments later, the mark came to the phone and stated, "Hello."

Stoney read from a sheet of paper, alarmed hysterically, "Mr., you can't break into my house and threaten my family like this, waving that damn gun all over the place. Take what you want and get the hell out."

Spanky read from the script robotically. "Shut ... the ... fuck ... up!" He sounded like an amateur actor reading from his first script ever, pausing in between words, emotionless. Realizing he didn't sound realistic, he picked up the pace. "You know what I came for. And if I don't get it, then someone's going to get hurt. Now where's the ... the fucken money?"

Sleeper whined like a woman. "Oh my goodness! Oh my God!"

"What money," Stoney asked. "I don't keep any money in the house."

"Liar!" Spanky shouted. "I heard you keep at least a hundred grand, locked away in the basement somewhere. Probably in a safe. If you don't get it right this instant, then I'm going to blow your wife's brains out."

Sleeper screamed like a woman, "Nooooo! Please, don't do this."

"I told you, I don't have any money," Stoney claimed.

"Maybe this'll show you how serious I am." Spanky fired the pistol into the air, then flopped his dead weight onto the floor. All three screamed simultaneously.

Sleeper cried like child, "You killed my mommy!"

"My wife!" Stoney cried. "You've killed my wife. My precious wife! How could you?"

"Shut the hell up," Spanky angered. "If you don't give me the fucken money, then one of your kids is next."

"No!" Sleeper shouted, sounding like a child. "I don't want to die!"

"But I told you Mr.," Stoney pleaded, "I don't have any money in the house."

"Still wanna play games, do ya?" Spanky returned. "Maybe you'll take me serious if I do this." He fired the gun a second time, then flopped his dead weight onto the floor again.

All three screamed simultaneously. Stoney shouted hysterically, "My son! Mister, you killed my son. My child! What kind of a monster are you?

"The greedy kind," Spanky replied. "Now you got one kid left, then you're next. I'm going to ask you again. Where's the gotdamn money?"

Sleeper said, "Daddy, I don't want to die. Please don't let the bad man kill me."

"Mr.," Stoney begged, "Please, I told you ... I don't have any money in the house. Somebody lied to you. They misled you. There's no money here."

"Since you still want to head in that direction, play fucken games with me ..." He fired the gun a third time, then flopped to the floor again.

"Oh my God!" Stoney cried profoundly. "My whole family! You've just killed my whole family." He cried, "Whyyy? What have I ever done to deserve this?"

"You're a greedy man," Spanky replied bluntly. "Just as greedy as I am. This is the last time I'm going to ask, then I'm going to kill you. Now where's the gotdamn money?"

"Okay! Okay!" Stoney finally conceded. "I'll get it. It's in the wall safe, directly behind you. But I'm only going to give you half, since it's taken me so long to save it up."

"Okay," Spanky said. "Half is better than none, since I put all this work into killing you're whole family."

"I trust you're a man of your words," Stoney said. "So, before I open the safe, lets shake on it."

"So," Spanky stated, "you're not upset that I killed your whole family, are ya? I mean, I thought we could let bygones be bygones."

"Not too upset," Stoney replied. "I'll make up the difference on their life insurance policies. I'll be okay in the long run."

Stoney terminated the call, then told them, "Fred Baker is all about greed. He knows that it was all about the money. I got an inside tip that he had his wife killed in a staged robbery for a one million dollar insurance policy. I'll call him back after the basketball game to fill him in on what I've discovered, the irrefutable evidence. I'll negotiate, then comes the payoff."

"Stoney," Sleeper said, "You're stone cold to the bone! I really enjoyed that … the whole thing that we just did. You've taken hustling to a whole new level."

"Me too," Spanky laughed. "That was some serious shit, but I think I can top that. Gimme that fricken cell phone. The master's gonna show you boneheads how to take care of business." He placed a call, then waited briefly. When a man picked up, he began acting like a thirteen year old nerd with a sinus condition squeaking his voice, "Um, hellooo. Is this the Origami residence?"

Sleeper chuckled, then whispered, "Oh shit! Here we go."

"What in Gods name," Stoney uttered. He whispered to Sleeper, "He's lost his mind."

A man on the other end of the line replied, "Yes. It is."

Spanky asked, "Is Barbara Origami there?"

"Who's speaking?"

"The name's Horace Bagmire." Sounded as though Spanky had a speech impediment. "I'm with Quagmist and sons on the beach, luxury accessories. I'm one of the sons on the beach. May I please speak to Barbara?"

The man giggled at everything he heard thus far. The squeaky voice didn't help none. "Sure. Ah, hold on a sec." Laughing, he yelled into the background,

"Hey Barb! Pick up the other line. Some kid from Quagmire son-of-a-bitch accessories, or something."

A woman answered seconds later. "Barb here."

"Yes, Mrs. Oregano, I'm calling about the ..."

"That's ... Origami," she corrected Spanky. "Not oregano, sweetheart. I'm Japanese, not food seasoning. Get it right."

"Well, Mrs. Oregon, I ..."

"I said Origami. Are you an idiot or something? Would you like me to spell it out for you?"

"I'm terribly sorry, Mrs. Origami. I didn't mean to offend you. My dad ... I mean ... my boss's hand writing is very sloppy. You'll have to excuse me." Applying his preferred technique, he showered her with confusion. As if arguing with someone who wouldn't take no for an answer, he pulled the phone a few inches from his mouth and complained, "I told you, I went down to the kennel yesterday, but the guy wouldn't let me past the cotton-picking front door. He told me I had to put on pants, a gotdamn tee-shirt, and that I couldn't touch any of the fricken animals unless I first washed my hands and face."

Barbara became bemused. "Huh? What in the heck are you talking about?"

"I'm sorry, Mrs. Orangutan. I'm short staffed today. I got people coming in asking me all kinds of silly questions pertaining to ..."

"Look ..." she stewed briefly, slightly frustrated, "... you brainless twit! I told you my name is Mrs. Origami. Do you have a memory problem? Or are you just plain stupid?"

Spanky apologized again, "I'm sorry, Mrs. Organ. I suffer from a touch of A.D.D., from my moms side. Now my dad, that suckers got some kind of a weird antisocial disorder that got him locked up in a mental institution for seven years ..."

She cut him off, "Enough about your dysfunctional family tree. Now what's this all about?"

"It's about the party size Jacuzzi you ordered. I don't know if we can have it coated with fire engine red latex, as you specified."

"I didn't order any Jacuzzi coated with red latex from your company."

"You didn't?"

"No! Why on earth would I do something as crazy as that?"

"Well, it must be a typo. Anyway, about the other thing you ordered. The mechanical bull with the vibrating seat is not ready yet."

"A what?"

"You know, the double joy rider. It gives you twice the fun, as you ride."

"There's got to be some kind of a mix-up here. I've never ordered anything like that from anywhere."

"You didn't?" As if talking to someone else, he argued, "How dare you threaten me with an ass kicking. If I weren't behind this desk, and in this wheelchair, I'd rip your head off and shit down your throat. Now get the hell away from me, you inept moron. I'm talking to a customer." He sighed. "Now, Mrs. Oreo, about the double joy rider."

Figuring that he was too inane to get her name right, she bypassed the correction and fired, "I didn't order any such thing!"

"You didn't?"

"Hell no!"

"Then what about the slightly modified triple penetrator? We tailored it specifically to meet your needs. We made it three times as big, and put a turbo boost in for good measure."

Reeling in the disgust, Barbara had finally had enough. "Who in the hell did you say this was, from what company?"

"My name's Horace Bagmire, Mrs. Orgasm. Our company has a brochure that you can get on the internet ..."

Now highly upset for his continued mispronouncing her name, she fired, "I said, my last name is Origami!" She yelled, "Not oregano! Not Oregon! Not orangutan! Not organ! Not Oreo! Not Orgasm!" She calmed, "Are you a twisted dumb shmuck?"

Spanky dropped the act and used his normal voice when he stated, "No. But you are. I found out about the one million dollars you extorted from the insurance company you work at. Someone dimmed on you, gave me copies of the forged documents you used to have the checks drawn. It was easy for you to get away with it for so long because you oversee the loan approvals department." When Spanky heard a smothered gasping sound pouring through the line, he knew Barbara was going into shock. He knew he had her hook, line and sinker. Lock, stock and barrel. "I haven't told anyone because I have a feeling you wouldn't fair too well in prison, from you mingling with those high-society people you like to plant yourself around. Especially with your having gotten use to the lavish lifestyle you've set yourself up with. No, I want to put you in good hands, with Allstate. There's another way we can handle this, cutting out the nasty possibilities of your going to prison, trimming the fat. I think it'll be quite fair, considering what's at risk. Now here's what I want you to do. On Monday morning, I want you to bring two-hundred and fifty thousand dollars in a shoe box to the post office in Codman Square. Address it to John Taylor, post office box number ..."

Moments after Spanky had finished laying out the instructions, her husband approached from another room and asked, "Why are you wasting your time talking to that nut? I would've hung up a long time ago." Taking in her distraught condition, he asked, "Barbara, you look like you've seen a ghost. What'd the kid do, traumatize you with his stupidity?

"Shut up!" she threw at him. When he was close enough, she backhanded him across his face. "Leave me the hell alone."

He looked at her sideways, rubbed his cheek briskly. "The hell's matter with you? All I said was ..."

"I'll show you what's wrong with me." She dropped the phone and shouted, "I knew it was a bad idea to get involved with that stupid idea you conjured." Entirely enraged, she paint stroked him with her purse, cursed irately in Japanese. "Take the money, he says. No one will ever find out. They'll get lost in the paper trail. Jimmy, if I ever find out that you had something to do with this, just because I wouldn't give you the money to buy that Harley Davidson, I'll kill you!"

"What're you talking about? Have what arranged?"

The line went dead.

After their laughter ceased, Sleeper approached Spanky. "Not bad, for a beginner. Now, let the Obi-One Kenobi of hustling, the master Jedi, Yoda, show you nit wits how it's really done."

Spanky gave him the cell phone eloquently, as though giving a patron a menu at a five star restaurant. "Sir, the ball's in your park. In short, spit your shit." He sat on the couch. "Let's see what ya got, kid."

"This should be interesting," Stoney said. "I like it when he does that heightened emotional thing that he does oh so well."

Sleeper laughed, "You guys are funny. But you're going to get an even bigger kick out of this." He dialed a number. Waited for someone to answer.

Moments later, a young boy answered. "Yes." He couldn't have been any more that eight years old. "Who is it?"

"David Solomon," Sleeper told the kid. He rained praises immediately when he said, "Is your magnificent father, Paul Fisher, at home?"

The kid was slightly confused. "Um ... yeah."

"Could you please ask him if I could have a moment of his valuable time?"

The boy yelled, "Daddy! Mr. Solomon wants to talk to you."

Sleeper was very appreciative. "Oh thank you. Thank you so much. You're very kind."

Moments later, a man came to the phone. "Yes. Who did you say this was?"

"Oh my God, Mr. Fisher," Sleeper was nearly in tears, "I'm so glad that you could give me a moment of your precious time. I just called to thank you, and to tell you that I think you're an absolute angel."

"But, I don't understand. What's this all about?"

"This is the great and noble Paul Fisher, who works for the Boston Fire Department, isn't it?"

"Why, yes. But I ..."

"Aren't you the one who saved the lives of the thirty tenants at that recent early morning house fire, when you arrived just in time to warn everyone?"

Paul stated proudly. "Yeah. That would be me."

"Mr. Fisher, my wife and newborn were in that apartment building." To get the full effect, he dropped to his knees and cried pretentiously. "Had it not been for your heroism, a lot of people would've died, and my family wouldn't be with me today. As I'm speaking with you, I'm holding my four month old daughter in my arms. Mr. Fisher, she means everything to me. I'm able to be with her ... because of your unselfish heroism."

"Thank you. It was nothing, really. I'm sure anyone would've done the same thing."

"But it wasn't just anyone who did it," Mr. Fisher. It was you. I have you and only you to thank for this magnificent blessing. I find myself praising and thanking you all the time. My wife and I mention you in our prayers at night, and we tell everyone what a great man you are."

Sleeper had him feeling so elated and overwhelmed that he couldn't find words to respond. He floated on cloud nine. "Again, thank you. Thank you very much for your kind words. I'm so glad I could be of some service. But as you know, I'm a fireman. It's my job to perform as I have."

"And you performed well, Mr. Fisher. When the pressure was on, you pulled through with flying colors. Again, thank you, Mr. Fisher. Thank you very much. Thank you a million times."

"You're very welcome."

"And then they gave you a promotion to Captain, and a heroes dinner a month later. And they gave you all those wonderful gifts. Must've made you feel even more special."

"I really didn't want to accept the money, but I have kids also. I'm saving it for their college expenses. I'm sure they'll need the assistance, the way tuitions rise from year to year."

Sleeper felt that now was the time to nudge him to the roofs edge. "Well, as long as they don't have to *actually* count on it, they should be just fine."

"Push him off the pier," Stoney laughed. "He sounds like a non-swimmer."

Paul hesitated, slightly confused. "You wanna run that by me again?"

"I'm saying, you know how things happen," he emphasized, "*accidentally* and *coincidentally*. Sometimes a hundred grand can slip right through your fingers, within the blink of an eye."

"I don't understand."

"You will in a sec. Trust me on this. Have seat, Paul, and I'll fill you in."

"Bleed that son-of-a-bitch medieval style," Spanky whispered, laughing. "Hunker down and reel his ass in." He got to his feet and cheered, "The roof! The roof! The roof is on fire. We don't need no water, let the mickey fickey burn!"

"Now for the climax," Stoney snickered. He sung Nelly's hit, "It's getting hot in here. So take off all you clothes." He stated, "Take him to the bridge, Sleep."

"Within the last two years, that makes four fires that you've arrived at by coincidence. Just in the nick of time to save the occupants. Doesn't it, Paul?"

Paul grew somewhat uncomfortable, became angry. "What'n the hell are you saying?"

"I'm saying that those fires weren't accidents, Paul. I'm saying that I have evidence that you lit them, and then warned the occupants. All to make yourself look like some kind of a superhero." He taunted, "Didn't your mama ever tell you what would happen if you play with matches?"

Paul remained suspiciously quiet, having the guilt of his convictions thrown at his feet, on display for all to see and judge. Listening to an eerie silence ooze through the line, Sleeper went on to explain, "Yeah, buddy. I know *all* about it. I got the tape from the filling station you stopped at to fill the gas can. Nobody thought to look there, did they?"

Having the pieces come together in front of an invisible jury of his peers, Paul felt as though he'd been arrested, tried, and convicted, within the blink of an eye. He babbled incoherently, "What the ... but I didn't ... the fire was ..."

"Shut the hell up, Paul," Sleeper stated calmly, casually, sarcastically. "The next time you run into a burning building, one that you've lit, I think you should throw in the full effects. I think you should first run into a phone booth, slip into some fire retardant blue and gray tights, then throw on a red cape. In your case, the big 'S' on you chest will stand for 'Stupidman!'"

He babbled, "But I … I didn't … those people … the fire that they …"

"Shut the hell up, Paul," he ordered calmly. "Don't deny it, cause you're as guilty as sin. To alleviate you of the pressures of holding *my* money, here's what I want you to do. Of course, unless you want to deal with the tape finding it's way to the proper authorities."

He continued babbling, "But I didn't … I … I saved their lives, and I …"

"Shut the hell up, Paul. It's not me that you'll have to convince. But you will have to answer some very embarrassing questions at your disgraceful superior court indictment. The media will have a feeding frenzy during your trial. They'll probably give you a year in prison for each persons life that you endangered, then pretentiously saved. That's about fifty years hard time. And that, my friend, you won't be able to talk yourself out of. So what I'm gonna do, my little superhero, is help you out of the mess that you've made of yourself. Bottom line, you're going to send me the one hundred thousand dollars tomorrow, or go to jail for a very long time."

"But I … I didn't … I saved those people …"

"Shut up the hell up, Paul. P. O. box three-sixteen, under the name Joe Mama, in the post office next to the Prudential Center, on Boylston Street. Have the money there tomorrow, before the close of the business day, or *else.*"

Stoney and Spanky rose to their feet, gave a subtle applaud. "Not bad," Spanky said. You keep it up like that, and in about a hundred years you'll be almost as good as me."

*   *   *   *

Less than a half an hour later, in the parking lot, Stoney got into his car and started the engine. As he was about to put the car into gear, Spanky and Sleeper approached him. Spanky initiated the conversation by gesturing for him to roll down the window. He leaned over, placed his hands on the doorsill and asked politely, "How's it going …" he emphasized, "… old buddy?"

Sleeper smiled uncomfortably. "Stoneman. What's up?"

Seeing Stoney follow Capt. Winslow into his office with a spaced-out look bricked on his face had filled Spankys mind with many thoughts of treason. He couldn't help but to become even more suspicious when he noticed he wasn't wearing his badge or sidearm. He became paranoid. He had to know what went on in there—what crucial words were said between him and their boss.

Stoney sighed glumly. Appearing sedated, he replied, "Things could be better, I guess." His hands grasped the steering wheel firmly, as if driving speedily through an obstacle course. Every few seconds, he twisted the steering wheel, as if revving the throttle of a motorcycle.

Spanky threw a lighthearted question, but kept a serious expression when he assumed, "It's just my guess that you and the boss had a nice little wholesome chat."

"Yeah. Um ... we talked."

They expected him to say a lot more. When nothing else came out of his mouth, Spanky felt a little prying was in order. He changed his mind about being subtle, then asked point blank, "Look, Stoney. I'm not going to beat around the bush with this. Why don't you just tell me what's going on?"

In thinking of the conversation he just had with Capt. Winslow, his mind went blank. He looked at Spankys expensive watch, and the reflective shine on the crystal grabbed his attention. He followed the second hand for few seconds, and all of a sudden, there appeared an image of a child's face. He stared into the child's eyes, and again fell locked into a hypnotic state. He heard the child say, "Hey, Stoney baby. How do you like my jewels, and my Swiss movements? Pretty neat, huh? I'll tell ya what, my little buck-a-roo. You scrape together some of that money ya got stashed away inside of the fireplace, an you can get one just like it. What do ya say? How can ya pass up a deal like that? It's practically free." Moments later, the child demeaned him. "Even a miserable jackass like you couldn't pass up a deal like that."

Reacting to the child's trifling statement, Stoney replied irately, "No!" He shouted furiously, "Shut up! Shut the fuck up and get the hell away from me, you flat-faced son-of-a-bitch."

Extremely baffled at the unforeseen outburst, Spanky sprang upright. He crossed his arms and tilted his head to the right, curious like. The left corner of his mouth rose slightly to meet his closing left eye. He whispered, "What the hell ..."

Gazing in awe, Sleeper glanced curiously at Stoney, then at Spanky. To Stoney once again. Then back to Spanky. He didn't know what to make of the sudden unprovoked and heated eruption. Both didn't know what to think, or how to respond. For the moment, they found themselves to be like Stoney. Stuck in limbo.

Spanky believed that he was hiding something, since he was acting evasive. That he might've sold them out on a sweet deal, possibly for less prison time. Or maybe for no prison time at all; only a few months of probation. He grew angry at the various hideous scenarios. "Oh, I get it." He snickered sarcastically, "First we're buddies," the snickering died quickly, "and now you don't even want to talk." He turned to Sleeper. "See. I told you something was wrong. I think the woosp sold us out."

"I didn't say anything," Stoney said in his defense. "Not one word." He fired lastly, "I ain't no stoolie!"

One of the worst things that a police officer could call a fellow police officer is a stoolie. Or a snitch. Someone who sucked up to and kissed the asses of the few in internal affairs. The term, when labeled, beckoned a physical altercation. Or worse.

"Then where's your shield?" Spanky asked, throwing insinuations. "They took it after you gave them what they wanted to know, didn't they?"

From being bombarded with redundant questions that offended him and insulted the integrity of their long friendship, Stoney became enraged. Instead of returning the argument, he put the car in gear and drove off. Several feet away, he hollered out the window, "I didn't say anything!" Fifty feet away, he shouted, "I didn't!"

Spanky told Sleeper, "I think they had him under the lamp, then he cracked. He probably swung a deal to keep himself from going to prison. Something drastic has had to happen in order for the Captain to take his shield and piece. What do you think?"

"I don't know, Spanks. If he spilled his guts in there, implicating us in any illegal activities, then why hasn't anyone come out to arrest us. Or to tell us that the Captain wants to see us *yesterday?*" He glanced at Stoneys car as he drove away, then looked to the ground, feeling utterly dejected. "I don't know, Spanky. You know how loyal Stoney is to us. He would never do anything that would get us into trouble. Maybe he said something only about himself."

"Look at me, Sleeper. Lets be real about this shit." He tapped his badge three times with the tips of the fingers on his right hand. "This piece of metal don't mean shit to those people in internal affairs. We have our job priorities, and they have theirs. And the two are not the same. They're not going to believe that only one person could've handled all of those hustles, especially the way we have it arranged. It can only be managed with accomplices. Those nosy ass cop busters in I.A. are no fools."

"I feel you. I especially don't like that Johnson bitch. She initiated twenty financial investigations last month alone. Every time she talks to you, she gets in your face and examines you from the ground up. To see if you're wearing anything that looks as though it couldn't have been paid for with a cop's salary."

"I'd like to empty a clip into her myself. Those ass kissers know who relates to who, who's sleeping with who, and all our other semi-secretive personal bullshit. They know we three go way back to high school."

Sleeper thought about his words for a moment, weighed the pros and cons. "I can't argue that. But they can't staple us together in any illegal activities, unless one of us blabs."

"Sleeper, we've been doing good so far. Covering our tracks, keeping shit on the down low. But if Stoney cracks, what in the hell do you think he'll say?" He volunteered the answer. "If he's not in the right frame of mind, as it appears he's on his way there, any fucken thing may come shooting out of his mouth. Anything that may start an unpleasant investigation that'll lead to names, dates and payoffs. And chances are, after they investigate further, and I'm sure they will, they'll come down on us so hard it'll make our heads spin. Then we can kiss our freedom and everything we cherish goodbye."

Sleeper nodded solemnly. "I guess you're right about that. Anyway, what're we gonna do about all this?"

"First, we've got to find out what's going on; what Stoney told the Captain. If he's going to drag us down the gutter, then we'll do," he peered menacingly into Sleepers eyes, "what we gotta do."

"Meaning?"

"Sleeper, don't ask me what you already know."

Sleeper repeated more assertively, "Meaning?"

Spanky hesitated for a moment. "Meaning, we have to make the threat go away," "Make the threat, Stoney, go away." He paused, then asked, "And just how do we, make the threat, Stoney, go away?"

"If it's called for, we have to eradicate the son-of-a-bitch." Spanky jumped into his face and pushed him against a car they were standing next to. He ordered fiercely, "Man, you better getchor shit together, buddy boy! Don't start that babbling and cackling shit, like you're loosing your mind. Like our buddy. You know full well what I'm talking about."

Sleeper gawked awkwardly, knowing that asking anything would be a stupid question. Inane. Pointless. He wanted to say something rational. Because his tongue had swelled to the point where as he couldn't force a word past his tightened jaw and gnashing teeth, he fell unable to express words in any way, shape or form. He spurted, "Bu-Bu-Bu-Bu-Bu … huh?" His voice wavering, he whispered nervously, "You mean, you're gonna kill," he swallowed loudly, "Stoney?"

"Not me, you dumb fuck!" He proclaimed, "We, mother fucker! We! Both of us. We're in this shit together, straight to the end, till hell freezes over. I don't like this shit anymore than you do. But if I'm gonna have to kill that mother fucker with the loose lips to stop *us* from going down with a sinking ship, then someone's got to be there to watch my back. Since you're the likely candidate, that someone is *you!*"

Sleeper sidestepped to the right to get from out of the uncomfortable spot that he was in; in between Spanky and the car. He felt wholly overwhelmed with a frightful apprehension as he predicted Spankys next atrocious words of impending doom. His voice cracked with fear, he stuttered, "I-I-I don't know about this, Spanky. This is some heavy shit you're laying on me. This is our boy we're talking about. He's our friend. We've been through a lot of stuff together. He's been down with us from day one."

"I don't give a flying fuck how long he's been with us. He ..."

Sleeper stepped closer to him. "Doesn't he mean anything to you?" Spankys eyes rolled to the ground, sighed. Sleeper went on to say, "Think about what you're saying. Do you really expect me to swallow this shit, without giving any consideration to who we're talking about?"

Spanky bypassed the question altogether, then brought up what he thought was a more important subject. He asked, "Remember what I said about going to jail, that little scenario I drew up for you?"

"So."

"Are you ready for the long haul?"

Sleeper answered quickly, "No! Of course not. At least, I wasn't before. But now you're talking about doing something that's a lot worse than anything we've ever done in the past. Now you're talking about cold blooded murder. Even worse, you talking about cops killing another cop."

"Look, Sleep, I know its sounds bad, but did you ever hear the phrase, 'dead men tell no tales?'"

Sleeper had heard the phrase coined plenty of times before, a tired old cliché. But this time, it had a more direct meaning because of the personal application. After absorbing a good amount of the expression, he then had difficulties connecting it to their long time friend, bosom buddy, pal and forever chum, Stoney. However, in the back of his mind, another formidable word crept into the light of day. Accomplice! He replied weakly, "Ah, yeah."

Spanky glanced over Sleepers shoulder and saw Capt. Winslow approach, studied him intently. He couldn't tell what was on his mind by his infamous walk, because he couldn't hear his shoes make that foretelling sound they emitted, reflecting his true state of mind. Maybe Capt. Winslow turned the sound down to throw them off. It seemed to be working, because they had no idea where he was coming from.

As Capt. Winslow drew closer, their heartbeats raced to an explosive level. Caused them to pant and gasp with the expectation of the worst that was about to sledgehammer them into nothing but a faded memory. While Sleeper stood dormant, scared stiff, Spanky nonchalantly draped his hand on his gun. He loosed the leather safety strap slyly, then remained on full alert. Ready to do whatever he had to do, to stop from being arrested and sent to jail. Like Whitey Bulger, the notorious mob figure who took it on the lam during the early nineties to escape prosecution, he would've preferred to live life on the run. Hiding in disguise, camping in the cracks and crevices of some third world country that's not even on the map. He sighed anxiously. "Here comes the boss." He believed that if they were about to be arrested, he wouldn't have come alone. He whispered, "He's by himself. That's a good sign. We'll talk later."

Sleeper heard his footsteps just behind him, turned around and flashed a phony smile. Capt. Winslow asked, "What's up, guys?"

Spanky nodded. "Captain." His fingers itched to draw his gun and fire away.

"Hi Captain," Sleeper responded.

Capt. Winslow studied their faces for a moment, trying to read their expressions. He found nothing and asked, "Did either of you see officer Brooks out here, a minute ago?" His line of sight shot back and forth in between the two, as though watching a tennis match.

Since he didn't bring up the formidable subject of dishonor, disgrace and blackmail, they felt profoundly relieved, but tried not to show it. "Yeah," Spanky answered, then finally took his hand away from his gun. He wiped his brow. "He just took off. You just missed him."

"Dammit! I wanted to ask him something. But it's no big deal. I'll call him in a couple of days." He waited for a second. "Hey, since you guys are his buddies, I gotta ask you something."

Spanky glanced at Sleeper. "Sure, Captain. What is it?"

"Your buddy Stoney's not feeling like himself. Through the years, I've seen guys who were stressed out before. It appears as though your friend is way out there, in another dimension. When I talked to him in my office a few minutes ago, he started rambling off at about things that didn't make sense. That's when I realized he has some issues he needs to address. He looked kinda peaked. He became crazily enraged and attacked my desk lamp, so I sent him to see the company shrink to get a complete check-up. I also gave him a leave of absence." He looked to the clear blue sky, searching for a solution. He muttered unbelievably,

"Of all the things, he destroyed my lamp. He literally punched it out. I've had that thing for fifteen years and it's never caused any problems for me." He paused, shook his head unenthusiastically. He stepped closer to them and got back to the subject at hand. He looked into their eyes and asked suspiciously, "Guys, I know how messy it can get out there in the field. Did anything abnormal happen to him in the recent past? You know, like a break-up with his girlfriend, a death in the family, an unreported shooting. Anything unusual at all." He tried his damndest to make heads or tails out of their reaction to the question, but found nothing. He knew how stubborn his men were with their strict code of silence, but asked for the hell of it. Hoping something would give way. He understood that unless he could predict the future, you never knew what kind of a response he was going to get. Which could give him a hint of something to work with.

Spanky and Sleeper delivered looks of total perplexity, as many detailed recollections of the Dixie Club traipsed unreservedly through their minds. Spanky answered convincingly, "No, Captain. I can't say that I have."

"Same here, Captain," Sleeper said. "Nothing."

Capt. Winslow looked away for a moment, bewildered. "Well, I'll call the shrink in a little while to see if he's learned anything pertinent. Then I'll give Stoney a call in a few days. Maybe he'll be relaxed enough to get off what's on his chest. He was extremely tensed, like he had something on his mind that was giving him problems. Whatever it is, I hope it can be fixed." He paused. "Officer Sinclair, officer Knight, keep an eye on ya buddy for me. If anything turns up, fill me in as soon as you can." Returning to the station house, Spanky noticed that Capt. Winslow's head was lowered. It meant that he was thinking acutely of the conversation he had just finished. He could tell that he knew something was awry, but couldn't put his finger any where near it. Capt. Winslow looked upward and glanced off to nowhere in particular in an attempt to find something to focus on, to distract his confused thinking.

"Sure thing, Captain," Spanky said. "Will do, sir."

"You got it, Captain," Sleeper said,. "Goodbye sir."

Twenty-five feet away, Capt. Winslow turned halfway and yelled over his right shoulder. "You guys hurry up and finish getting dressed, and hit the streets. What do you think this is, a nursery?"

When he was out of earshot of their voices, Sleeper grew excited with relief. He asked Spanky, "You hear that? He doesn't know. That means we're in the clear. That means we don't have to do anything to Stoney."

"For the moment," Spanky corrected him. "You heard what he said. He's gonna talk to the shrink, then to Stoney in a few days. We can hope that he'll straighten out, then it'll be business as usual. Or we can gamble that he's gonna crack. And if he cracks, we'll be cracking too. Cracking boulders with sledgehammers in the federal penitentiary."

"I don't know about all this shit. Why don't we try to talk to Stoney, to see what's on his mind? Maybe it'll do him and us some good. Relieve all this stress. Maybe we can find out where he stands on all this craziness. I think we owe him at least that much."

Spanky thought about it profoundly, before he said, "All right. All right. We'll do that. But if things aren't looking our way, then we'll do what has to be done."

Without saying another word, the two returned to the station house to finish getting dressed, to begin their shift. As they walked, Sleeper glance at Spanky peripherally, wondering how in the hell did he get himself mixed up with this ruthless asshole. If the price were right, he knew he'd kill his own mother just to stop him from going to jail.

Meanwhile, what Spanky wondered about him was, here's another weak ass son-of-a-bitch I'm going to have to keep my eye on. Questioning me the way he did leaves his loyalty very doubtful. I hope I don't have to kill him too. Damn! Then I won't have anyone to watch baseball games with.

CHAPTER 8

▼

Shortly after Stoney had arrived home, his fiancé Katherine had stopped by at twelve noon to trip the light fantastic, with being the girlfriend and all. She had called down to the precinct at ten a.m. and spoke to Capt. Winslow, and he told her where she could locate him. She was out with one of her other beaus the evening before, a mere play thing. Her guilty feelings roused her, prompted her to drop in to see how her number one was doing. Maybe pamper him a little. Make him feel special, as though she couldn't wait to see him.

Stoney, the carefree and confirmed bachelor, treated her real good, like his mama taught him to. He pampered her constantly, and took her out on the town nearly every time they hooked up. He sometimes had his gourmet chef come in to prepare extravagant diners on special occasions, then showered her with gifts; maybe jewelry, or air tickets to a far away country for an exciting weekend get-away. He gave her all the freedom in the world for her to do anything she wanted, whenever she wanted. He also paid all of her credit cards bills and met most of her special attention needs. In all actuality, he's the only one of her boy-friends who actually cared about her. Although, he tried not to show it, under-standing the rules of engagement; making silent commitments. Somewhere along the way, he learned that some sentimental emotions came with a hefty price tag.

Using the spare set of keys he'd given her a week after they began dating, she gained entrance through the backdoor and searched for him. She ran into Carl-ton washing clothes in the laundry room, and he told her where she could locater him.

She made her way to the bedroom and found him sprawled across the king-sized bed, laid out in a pair of plaid boxer shorts, napping. The way he looked, lying there, one could tell that his last thoughts before he fell to sleep were 'God, please, I beg you. Come and take me away from this miserable place. I don't care if this is my last day on earth.'

She stood in the doorway briefly and studied his physical make-up. Quietly, she stepped from out of her shoes, then crept into the bedroom. Standing a few feet away, she gazed admiringly at his physique. She took considerable note of the tee-pee like structure his penis made out of his shorts and blushed lustfully as desires of eroticism filled her ravenous heart. Suddenly, an appetizing idea popped into her pretty little head and she giggled pleasurably.

Growing hornier by the second, she became overwhelmed with desires of eroticism. Her tongue floated seductively around the ridges of her lips; sampling her lipstick, wishing the flavor was of his flesh. She asked herself, why not take the opportunity to go for a joy ride? The pleasure trip vehicle is right in front of me. All I have to do is strap myself in, put it in drive, and I'm off.

Listening to him snore softly, she dropped her pocketbook on the floor, then shed her white leather jacket. She raised her mini-skirt higher, then and removed her nylon stockings. She seldom wore panties because they were too confining. Made her feel as though she was wearing a chastity belt

Staring feverishly at the zenith of his boxer shorts, a pair that she had brought for him on the Christmas last, she wondered if he was dreaming of her. She wanted to give him a twenty-one gun salute, place her hand over her heart and recite the pledge of allegiance. She wanted to run to the nearest roofs edge and shout, 'I'm as horny as hell, and I'm not going to take it any more.'

Suddenly, her urge to mount him increased, and she couldn't hold back any longer. Climbing onto the bed, it shook considerably. She knew that she wouldn't waken him because he was a heavy sleeper. One time, while he slept, she had entered the bedroom and changed her clothes while arguing with one of her girlfriends on her cell phone. During their on-line debate, he didn't loose a moment of sleep. His snoring went undisturbed. He didn't even hear the loud music she blasted on the stereo set in the next room.

She straddled him, as though mounting a stallion. He stirred, and it appeared as if he was going to awaken, but she proceeded anyway. She knew that even if he did, he wasn't going to do something crazy like make her get off. If anything, he would've helped her do just that, 'get off.'

Riding him wildly into ecstasy, he realized quickly the sensual feelings he experienced couldn't have been a dream. His eyes cracked open and he stared wonderingly at her. He cleared his throat, then asked casually, "Katherine, sweetheart. What're you doing?"

Questions didn't come any dumber than that.

She ignored his absurd question and continued riding hard like a rough rider, grinding her hips into him. She asked, "Baby, what'n the hell does it look like I'm doing?" She asserted, "I'm screwing you!" Now that he was awake, she felt it was okay to grunt louder and chant, "Yes! Yes! You mother ..."

He snickered at her exotic whim, then tried inconsequentially to thwart her actions. "But ... but ..."

"Shut the hell up!" she fired. "I know what I'm doing." She moaned, "You'll ruin the mood, Stoney. Just ..." grunt, "... don't move. I'm doing ..." grunt, "... just fine."

She trembled vibrantly, as if experiencing the withdrawal effects of a heroin addiction. Feeling she was near to her climax, he couldn't help but to join in the escapade. As she drew closer, he asked jokingly, "Sweetheart, are you cold or something?" She didn't reply. "You think maybe I should, you know, go back to sleep?"

Now that he was fully awake, all of his senses working properly, to the best of his knowledge, he couldn't stop his hips from swiveling, just a little. He threw his hands onto her hips, grasped hard and forced her weight down onto him.

"Baby," she moaned, riding feverishly, "you can do what ever the hell you want. Just don't ..." she grunted heavily, as if on her last breath, "... don't move."

Abruptly, she exploded and filled the room with her sizzling passion, shouted, "The handcuffs! Where are the fricken handcuffs?" She paused. "Dammit! Never mind. Screw the handcuffs. It's too late. It's too late!"

He looked at her sideways and smiled. Actually, he wanted to break out laughing, but held it in. For his pleasure and enjoyment, it was humorous to see her loose her mind when they had sex—the way she smudged her lipstick around the edges of her mouth with her hands, making it appear as though she had applied it during an earthquake. It was even funnier when she plowed her fingers through her hair and frizzed it, resulting with her resembling Phyllis Diller on a bad hair day.

However, when they made love, it was a whole new ballgame. They played by an entirely different set of rules. Their flamed sexual appetites sometimes lasted hours, which left them and the sheets soaking wet, some parts of the room in chaos; as in the aftermath of a tornado, and the surroundings areas filled with the unmistakable scent of amour. Essentially, they were more compassionate and seldom cursed. Often, a home-cooked meal is greatly appreciated, and well worth the time put in to prepare it. Other days, take-out will do just fine. Today, she just wanted to screw him silly.

After the effects of her third orgasm dwindled and faded to nothing, she inhaled deeply, then exhaled thoroughly, blew a heavy blast. Within seconds, her sanity found its way to the forefront. Returning to her usual self, she complained, "Dammit! I broke a nail. Do you know the trouble I have to go through to have these things put on?"

A trace of her last orgasm tackled her and she trembled briefly. A smile of satisfaction, accompanied with a moderate glow, flooded her face. "I love to get off in the morning. That was great!" She released a provocative sigh, a signal meaning, 'that's the end of that. I'm through.' After she got what she desired, she opened her eyes and looked down at him. Dog-tired and out of breath, she fell to the side and collapsed on the bed.

He mounted her immediately and proclaimed, "Now it's my turn."

She encouraged him, "Knock yaself out. I got mine, now come get yours."

"I intend on doing just that," he said. "No bout adout it."

He often quoted phrases that didn't make sense, only to him. Lately, because of the pestering appearances of the children, he's been saying them more often."

✳   ✳   ✳   ✳

After their short romp in the hay, they curled into each other's arms and fell asleep. Less than an hour later, Stoney awoke totally exhausted because his subconscious wouldn't allow him to sleep peacefully. While Katherine slept soundly, snoring like a champ, he paced the bedroom floor anxiously while looking over some mail he had received earlier that morning. He threw the letters on top of the bureau, then glanced into the mirror at his reflection, stared focally into his eyes.

Suddenly, he heard many indistinct whispers of children's voices which suddenly swelled in volume. Trying to make out what they were saying, a blurred image faded into view. Soon, the image sharpened, and it became apparent that he was looking at a little boy and girl returning his stare inquiringly.

The little boy, Jake, is nine years old. The girl, Jessica, is seven. They appeared related, having similar facial structures. Maybe brother and sister. The images quickly became crystal clear, and the children ceased talking. They stared at Stoney for a moment, absorbed as much of his aura as a lengthened gaze would allow.

After five seconds, Jessica broke the silence and told Jake, "Your teeth look like shit, all crooked and everything. They're so messed up that they don't know which way to grow. Mommy said that when you grow up, if you don't get'em fixed, you're gonna look just like a fricken buck tooth rabbit. Then we'll have to start calling you Bugs Bunny."

Jake nudged his sister. "Cut it out, Jessie ... you little bitch! So what if my teeth look like this. Daddy said he's gonna get'em fixed, as soon as he gets the money."

Stoney guessed that theses two children were members of one of the families that he had extorted money from. He was almost sure. There were so many people on his list that he couldn't keep track of who was who. He realized that in taking their money, he set off a domino effect that probably initiated many financial problems. Problems that had the family members at each other's throats.

Jessica danced mockingly around her brother, singing, "Bugs Bunny! Bugs Bunny! Bugs Bunny! Everyone's gonna call you Bugs Bunny!"

Jake eyed his sister viciously and grew upset. He shouted, "Stop it! Stop teasing me!" His little round face grew redder by the moment and he stomped his feet repeatedly. "You hear me. I said stop it!"

Since he knew how to get even with his sister, the thought of retaliation entered his mind briefly. The first few seconds of teasing often got the best of him. He composed himself to rethink his approach, and the desire to cause physically harm to her suddenly left. A better idea came to mind and he assured her, "My teeth ain't nothing compare to you." She stood still and listened carefully to his every word. "Daddy said that since we don't have any money, you can't go to the hospital to have your asthma looked at. "He grinned wickedly. "You don't have anymore of those inhalers, do you? And because you don't, you might get another attack and die and go to hell." He stuck out his tongue and gave her the raspberries. "My teeth may look funny, but at least I'll be alive."

After taking in the complete taunt, Jessica jumped up and down in dreaded fear of the worst thing that could happen to her. She cried frightfully, "Mommy! Daddy! Jake is making fun of my asthma again." She wiped the flowing streams of tears from her face and whined, "He said I'm gonna die and go to heeelll."

Suddenly, both froze in place, suspended in time, as if someone had pressed the freeze frame button on a DVD remote control. They turned simultaneously and looked at Stoney, and the expressions on their faces changed from them being upset with each other, to showing strong hostility toward him. Jake claimed, "It's not daddy's fault he can't help us right now. But we know whose fault it is." He looked at his sister, "Don't we, Jessie?" He nudged his horned rim glasses higher on his nose so he could see Stoney clearly. They were much wider than his head, and the left joint was patched with masking tape. Peabody and Sherman here.

Jessica pinched her left ear, then wiped her dribbling snot filed nose with the back of her right hand. She sniffled, then agreed, singing, "Uh-huuuh! We now whose fault it is."

Oh shit! Stoney thought. His anxiety shimmied higher.

Jessica pointed accusingly to him. The index finger of her right hand protruded menacingly from the mirror, and stopped to within a fraction of an inch from his face. Fixated, he stared frightfully at the tip of her finger. The tip swelled to the size of a basketball, and he felt something feather his nose. More than static electricity, a zap jolted his intellect and forced his brain to submit a current update of the direful circumstances at hand. Strangely, he felt more alert than he'd ever been before, thus making him more susceptible to respond to whatever unpleasant endeavors they had in mind.

As the children agitated his disturbed and screwed up sense of reality, he listened to the sound of his hammering heart fill his ears with a pounding that deafened him maddeningly. Staring acutely, his eyes bulged intensely, making him favor Capt. Winslow having a bad day. His sight shot back and forth in between the children, he sucked in each precious breath as if he was going to be robbed of the next. Because he believed that Jessica was going to touch him, maybe to inflict pain, or mental anguish, resulting in pain, he dared not take his eyes away from her. Now wasn't the time to challenge his waking conscious. Now wasn't the time to do a damn thing.

"You're right, Jessie," Jake agreed. He pointed a condemning finger to Stoney, his hand protruded from the mirror as well. Stoney thought that he was going to get poked in his right eye, and he flinched, reluctantly brought himself closer to their reality by accepting their existence. Jake proclaimed, "That man right there … he's to blame!" He explained, "Our daddy might've made some mistakes, but you're the one taking advantage of him. You blood sucking leech!"

Stoneys shoulders fell slump, his knees buckled with fear. He shook his head in denial and whined, "Nooooooo!" He played the blame game. "It wasn't just me. It was Spanky and Sleeper too. Why do you always bother me? Spanky's the one who started the whole thing."

Jessica replied, "Because you're the one with the fickle conscious. You're still in touch with your soul. We're trying to save you, because we believe there's still some hope for you." Her tiny voice peaked, "Can't you see that?" As if by rocket power or turbo-boost, her hand shot forward and poked Stoney in his left eye.

"Ouch!" he cried frustratingly. "Dammit!" He rubbed his eye briskly. "Why'd you poke me in my ..." He froze mid-sentence, his emotions ran amok because he couldn't believe what had just happened. He stopped rubbing his eye. "Wait a second." He stuttered, "H-H-How in the hell did you ..." At first, he thought that she had rammed him hard, and he felt enormous pain, as if he had in fact been poked hard. Then he thought that he had been poked lightly, and it felt as if a slight wind had grazed his face. As they tormented him to no end, he shook his fist threateningly at the two and blasted, "You little crumb snatchers! If I can get my hands on you, I'd rip you ..."

Jake broke in, "Aw com'on, Stoney! That didn't hurt. It's all in your mind. Besides, she's just a harmless little girl. She can't hurt you. But I can." His arm bolted forward and he punched him in his left eye with the ferocity of a cougar prancing on its prey. An Ali-Frasier flashback.

From feeling the full effect of the blow, as Jake said he would, his head snapped backwards. Whiplash! He stumbled to the side, drunkard like, shouting, "Shit! ... Shit! Shit! Shit!" He examined his left eye in the mirror and discovered that it had become puffed to a close. Feeling utterly dismayed, he brought his hand to his face, but feared to touch it. He was terribly confused.

To keep his sense of rational perplexed, Jessica cheered, "Good shot, Jake!" She clapped her hands and sang, "Hit'em again! Hit'em again! Hit'em again!"

Believing that he was about to be assaulted again, he became infuriated. Challenging the figment of his run-amok and fucked up imagination, he threatened, "Oh yeah! You wanna play tough, do ya?"

"Oh, shut up, Stoney," Jessica said. "You're a very bad man. What can you do to us, that you haven't done already? What's done is done."

The way she tossed her words innocently stabbed at his heart and stirred the many sympathetic feelings that he harbored for the way he actually felt about children. Truth being, he loved them. However, these two children from hell, because of the torment and anguish they brought upon him, he wanted them dead. Well, not breathing.

Searching frantically for total relief from their contemptuous mock, he ran to the side of his bed, reached under the mattress and pulled out a small caliber revolver. He ran to the foot of the bed, where he was before, then aimed it at the mirror. Appearing tremendously terrified, Jake and Jessica huddled together. They looked like a couple of children who had just received the terrible news that Santa Claus had been assassinated, and the North Pole was demolished in a catastrophic snowstorm. Jake wrapped his arms protectively around his little sister and both shouted, "Mommy! Daddy! A bad man is tryinta shoot us with a gun."

"Punch me in my eye, will ya?," he stated. "You don't know who you're fucking with. I'll fix your little red wagon … little punks talking that way to me. Disrespecting me, in my house?" He yelled, "Take this!" He squeezed the trigger repeatedly and fired three shot. **"POP!! POP!! POP!!"**

He asked sarcastically, "What's the matter? That's not enough? You want some more?" He fired the remaining three shots. **"POP!! POP!! POP!!"**

Katherine heard the deafening gunshots and snapped out of her sound sleep. She went directly into panic mode and screamed as loud as she could. She spanned the room anxiously and discovered Stoney standing in front of the mirror, pointing the empty smoking gun at what was left of the few shattered pieces of glass hanging loosely from the frame.

The hand holding the gun dropped and swung by his side. Breathing rapidly, like he had just finished fighting for the world heavy weight championship, he explained, "Don't worry. I got it all under control. I got the bastards." He pointed to his left eye. "Do you believe this? Look at what those little shits did to my face." He shouted angrily, "Look at my eye!"

Finding nothing wrong with his face, she tilted her head confusedly and asked, "Stoney, what'n the hell are you doing? What'n the hell are you talking about?" Her eyes spilled a tale of insanity in the making. "What in the hell's the matter with you? Have you lost your fricken mind or something?"

He pointed to the mirror and shouted, "Them! Those two assholes right there. They did it!" He mumbled complainingly, "Comin into my house … disrespecting me like that."

She looked queerly at the bullet ridden mirror through glazed eyes of fear, and saw nothing out of the norm, beside the fact that it was shattered into a zillion pieces. She spanned the entire room again, searching for something that she thought she might've missed.

Finding nothing, she tilted her head to the left, squinted her eyes curiously and her lips froze, asking 'What in the hell?' She pounded her fists into the mattress and pronounced, "Stoney, what—in—the—hell are you talking about? There's nobody here." She paused, then added, "There's nobody in this gotdamn room but you and me."

At that exact moment, Carlton barreled into bedroom totting a broom like a shotgun. He excited, "What's wrong? I heard the shooting. What happened? Is anyone hurt?" He glanced at the bullet-ridden mirror, then to the smoking gun in Stoneys hand, then to Katherine sitting in the bed, half naked. There was a delayed reaction pulling his sights from her exposed breasts. He cleared his throat and asked, "Are you two all right?"

Feeling his brief gawk, she pulled the bed sheets up to cover her breasts. Her facial features conveyed, 'how dare you?' She pointed to Stoney and yelled, "Ask him! He's the one doing all the fricken shooting, telling me they struck his face." She scooped a handful of hair dangling in her face and threw it behind her. "I think he's gone mad."

"What?" Stoney shouted. "You don't believe me? You think I've gone mad?"

Carlton brought the broom to rest at his side and shook his head disconsolately. He sighed. "Not again, sir." Now he had a good idea of what had happened. "Sir, why don't you go out for a while and get some fresh air. I'm sure it will do you some good."

Stoney looked at him as though he had two heads.

"That's it?" she pelted at Carlton. "Fresh air, and that's it?" Still quite excited. "He doesn't need fresh air." She draped the bed sheet around herself, then bounced hastily out of the bed. She continued on a note of sarcasm. "Naw, he doesn't need fresh air." She stated for sure, "He doesn't need fresh air at all." She shouted, "The man needs help, get it?" She spelled it aloud, "H … E … L … P! As for this little girl, who prefers to remain among the living, I'm getting the hell out of here before the next bullet accidentally finds its way into me." She grabbed her clothes and hoofed it to the bathroom, spewing along the way, "Stoney, I'm sorry baby, but it ain't safe around here no more. Shooting at the damn mirror like that." She shouted, "Sweetheart, you're dangerous!"

Knowing that she was right, he remained quiet, staring dolefully at the floor. On that note, Carlton glanced at him for a long hard moment, then left the room. Nearing the doorway, he threw over his shoulder, "I'll clean that up momentarily, sir."

Stoney looked up and stared heatedly at the mirror, beads of sweat pouring from the sides of his face. Feeling a sudden wave of fatigue, he stepped backwards until the back of his legs found the bed, then sat on the edge and stared at the revolver in his hand.

Minutes later, Katherine marched from out of the bathroom with intentions to head straight to the front door. The odor of burnt gun powder still fresh in the air, she eyed Stoney inconspicuously, watched him staring bemusedly at the empty handgun. The barrel still warm to the touch.

As she was about to walk through the doorway, she stopped in her tracks. She waited for at least ten long seconds, then sighed regrettably. Suddenly overwhelmed with sympathy, she felt that it wouldn't be right to leave him like that, in the wretched condition that she knew he was in. He appeared less than a morsel of a man, suffering from an insurmountable nightmare that haunted and debilitated him to a crippled state of mind. He searched desperately for an escape from a maze of madness. Soon, the claws of insanity would have its talons gripped around his soul, seeming never to release.

She wanted to help him in any way that she could, but second-guessed herself, feeling that she would've been of little or no help at all.

It was decided. She had to help. Even if all she could do was simply be there, to sit beside him and hold his hand, she decided she'd be there for him. At least, until the next time he went off his rocker and grabbed another loaded firearm, to shoot at objects that only he could see. She had her limits.

She approached him, and still, he hadn't removed his sight from the silent gun that only moments before fired its deadly intentions to kill. She sat beside him, said nothing, but placed her hand on his shoulder reassuringly. Finally, she advised him, "Stoney, sweetheart, maybe Carlton's right. I think it would do you some good if we went out to get some fresh air. Maybe grab something to eat from somewhere. I don't know. It might take your mind from whatever's bothering you."

With a heap of remorse riding his brow, he said nothing, but looked into her eyes appreciatively. Mouth agape, he tried with all his might to figure out what to say. Absolutely nothing came to mind.

She placed her hand against his lips gently to signal that an explanation wasn't necessary, for the moment. "Don't say anything, Stoney. Just take a shower and get dressed. Then we'll go out for a little while." He nodded drably in agreement, and she smiled halfheartedly. Rising to her feet, she went on to say, "I'm going downstairs to get something to drink." She pinched the bridge of her nose. "All this excitement leaves a body pretty thirsty." She kissed his forehead quickly. More like a peck. "Let me know when your ready to go, all right?"

She left the room.

Moments later, he rose shakily from the bed, peered at the shattered mirror suspiciously. When he didn't see Jake and Jessica staring back, he felt some relief. He walked around to the side of the bed, pulled open a drawer on the nightstand, then tossed the gun inside. He stared at it despairingly, then slammed the drawer shut.

He didn't take a shower because he had taken one earlier that morning, so he began to dress. As he did, he focused on what Jake and Jessica had mentioned only minutes ago, and knew that he was getting dressed by habit. Subconsciously, because he realized that his mind was surely not on what he was doing.

He entered the kitchen fifteen minutes later and found Katherine sitting on the edge of the table, drinking a glass of ginger ale. Pleased to see that he was in a better mood, she tossed lackadaisically, "Hi baby. I see you're ready to go."

He nodded unenthusiastically.

"Good," she said. She placed her glass on the table and rose to her feet. Her eyes lit up like diamonds when she announced, "We're going to the mall, to do some shopping. You haven't gone with me in ages." She took him by his right hand, then led him to the rear entrance, to the garage. "We're going to have a lot of fun. Trust me, you'll see."

When they arrived to the garage, she asked entreatingly, "Do you have any money on you?" She had plenty of money with her, but it was always a greater pleasure to spend his.

He nodded.

She smiled. "Good! Cause we're going to need plenty of it." It surprised him when she snatched the keys from his hand, then insisted, "I'll drive. Just in case."

For two good reasons. Jake and Jessica. This was one of the few times that he didn't argue about who would drive. Ever since she had a horrible rear-end collision two years ago, one which initiated a twenty-five car pill-up, he's always insisted on driving.

One Friday evening, amid after-work traffic on the expressway, as she zoomed along at over eighty miles per hour, she fell engrossed in a juicy conversation. Chatting her heart away about the latest around-town gossip involving one of her girlfriends, she took her mind off of her driving. Her one mistake initiated a chain reaction collision that some paramedics are still talking about around the water cooler.

$$*\qquad*\qquad*\qquad*$$

At that exact moment, while on his shift, Sleeper walked into a cafe and took a seat at the far end, out of earshot of the patrons. He placed a call on a disposable cell phone, then waited for someone to answer.

After the fifth ring, someone picked up and said, "Yes."

"Hey, Paula!" he excited. "I don't believe I finally found you! It's me, Theodore."

She didn't recognize the name, or the voice. "Excuse me. Who's this?"

"You know, Theodore. From high school. I don't believe this. How could you forget me so soon?"

She use to date someone named Ted during her last two years in high school. It was her first serious relationship. But she didn't know that they were now being called Theodore. Almost two decades had passed, so she gambled by assuming, "Ted? Ted Corey?"

To prepare for the hustle, after he found out where she lived, he went to the local high school library and found a dyad for the year that she had graduated. In it, he discovered a picture of her, with who the other kids called, 'the love of her life.' From studying the picture, and by reading a few comments the other students wrote about the couple, he assumed that it was her first serious relationship. He also assumed that Ted was the first person who she had made love to. If he was wrong in his assumptions and she disconnected out of disgust, then he would merely call again and get straight to the point of the actual business he had in mind.

He practiced this hustle to learn to use a new type of 'heightened emotional technique.' He wanted to develop his talents with improvising so that he could be as good as Stoney. If it worked out well, he'd use it for entertainment at halftime the next time the three got together to watch a football game. He kept his conversation general, like a fortuneteller, babbling things that nearly everyone did. "Yes. I was hoping you'd recognize my voice. How's it going?"

He felt some uncertainty in her voice. But she went along with it anyway because she was so excited to hear from him. "I'm doing great." She paused for a lengthy moment. "My God, Ted. I haven't heard from you in ages. How'd you get my number? And what made you decide to give me a call? This is, like," she expelled, "wow! Like out of the blue."

"I thought you'd get a kick out of it," he said. "I was going through some changes, some tough times, and needed some good memories to fall back on, to keep me going, That's when your name came to mind."

"That's so sweet, Ted," she drooled. "To be honest, I've thought about you several times in the past also. But I never expected to hear from you."

"Yeah, well," Sleeper threw in a small gamble, "you know how spontaneous I was."

"You had your moments," she agreed. "So, what's been going on in your life?"

"Well, I was just going through a terrible divorce and I ..."

She cut him off. "Oh Ted! I'm sorry to hear that. I didn't know that you and Cathy had broken up. I thought you two were going to be together forever. At least, that's the way it appeared at the wedding."

Whoever the hell Cathy was, he continued, "Yeah, well, it took a lot out of me. Since I was feeling kinda down about it, I just thought I'd call you, to try to lift my spirits. You're someone who I really enjoyed being with, in the past."

"I really appreciated being with you too."

"It feels good to hear you say that." As many wholesome and favorable memories flooded her mind and heart with strong feeling of elation, he anted the pot by telling her, "This may sound weird, but when I was with Cathy, every now and then a pleasant thought of you came to mind."

In confirming that they did have some kind of a physical relationship, she stated blissfully, "Oh really!" She was dying to know, so her natural curiosity prompted her to ask, "Why?" Waiting in rising anticipation for his response, the feeling of euphoria was on its final approach.

It was somewhat the response that Sleeper was hoping to hear. If she acted skeptical, only asking 'why' unemotionally, it would've meant that they didn't have much going on between them. Since he was on the right path, he felt that it was time to step up his approach. "Paula, did I ever tell you that you were the first girl I ever made love to?"

"Yes," she replied. "I already know that. You told me that a long time ago, remember?" She thought about it for a moment, before she asked, "What made you bring that up?"

"It's just that … it's something beautiful that we shared."

"I think I can understand where you're coming from. It was quite an experience."

"Was it as pleasurable for you, as it was for me?"

Floating on cloud nine, she sighed pleasurably, giggled, "Of course it was."

Since he had her at the roofs edge, he felt that now was the time to give her a cold-handed shove. "Was it as pleasurable as the time when you came to Boston six months ago, and got drunk and plowed into those two little kids riding their bikes across the Mass. Ave. bridge?"

For a lengthy period, he heard nothing but a ghostly silence pouring through the receiver. He tried to imagine the magnitude of the pandemonium that he knew was occurring on the other end of the line. After a long moment, she gasped several times in distress. As if after five long minutes she had finally remembered to breathe. She babbled, "Huh? … What? … But Ted, I thought that … Who … I … Who … Where did you … How?" Her mind went blank for a moment; she thought of nothing. Felt nothing. An out of body experience took her by storm. She was beside herself, standing next to the person who plowed recklessly into the children. She was in grave denial, had broken off all contact with that person years ago because she hated her. This unsympathetic killer of children. Not anyone she knew, or wanted to know.

Since she didn't deny it, he knew he had her by the throat. He squeezed mercilessly, filling her in on the rest, scolding her, "You dragged those poor kids through a living hell. One is confined to a gotdamn wheel chair, possibly for the rest of his life. The other has a fricken prosthetic leg. You put their families through hell, you ruined their lives." He spat forward, "You disgust me, you ignorant slut!"

As her world came crashing in on all sides, she became even more confused. Damn near traumatized. Her stomach cringed with repulse, and she wanted to scream as loud as she could. Instead, she continued babbling things that didn't make sense. "But I ... Who ... The kids ... What's the ..." She broke down and whined, "Oh my God! Shit! But I didn't ... I didn't ..."

"Don't try to deny it," he told her. He stated with conviction, "It was you all right. I got the information from a very reliable source. Simply put, someone saw the accident and wrote down your plate number. Lucky for you, I told them that the driver had already been caught. If they had reported you to someone else besides me, you would've gotten into some serious trouble. I also called a few insurance companies in the small town where you live, and discovered that you had some collision work done on your car the same week. Now isn't that a coincidence? At most body shops, the mechanics keep pictures of the damage done on file. They have portfolios, photo albums that show the before and after of the work they've done. But some people wouldn't call it a photo album, or a portfolio. They would call it evidence. Solid evidence that could get you into big trouble. Unmitigated evidence that can be used at your trial. Evidence that can be used to send your dumb ass to prison for a long time."

Feeling herself being swept away into a whirlwind of horror as images of ugly trials, repulsive newspaper clippings and prison life filled her mind, she finally managed to gush forward, "I think I'm going to be sick." She placed her hand over her mouth, and her guts muscles tensed several times. Abruptly, her mouth became overflowed with her breakfast and lunch. Her gut muscles tensed again, and she vomited her insides on the floor. Although she was completely empty, her guts muscled continued to spasm, delivering painful dry heaves.

Hearing the turmoil taking place over the line, Sleeper pulled the phone away from his ear briefly and laughed up a storm. After catching his breath, he told her, "I guess by now you know that this isn't Ted Corey."

She stammered, "Who? Who? Who?"

"You sound like an owl," he said. He mimicked an owl, "Hoot! Hoot! Hoot! Anyway, it's not important who this is. What I also discovered was that your father owns a car dealership. One that he's been operating for some time, ever since you were in elementary school. He should be doing pretty good by now."

She didn't respond. Telling her point blank, he continued, "This is all about the Benjamin's, baby. I want you to send me fifty thousand dollars in cash, and I can make this little nightmare go away. Tell your big papa you need some money to buy a house. I don't know, make up something. Or better yet, you might want to tell him the truth."

She still hadn't said anything. He went on to inform her, "I'll give you a post office box number, where you can send the money. I'm giving you one week to accomplish this. If you refuse, then I think you know what that means. If the money doesn't show up, I'll guess that you didn't get it because big papa doesn't believe a word of what I'm saying. If that's the case, when I call again, you'll give me his phone number, then I'll talk to him. Then I'll send him a copy of every-thing that I have, just to confirm that I'm not full of shit. He loves his little girl, and I'm sure he'll see things my way. Either he'll pay fifty thousand to some high priced lawyer, to bargain for your having to spend a few years in jail, with ten years of probation, or he'll pay me."

Since she still hadn't said anything, he filled her in on the details, giving her a good idea of what prison life would be like for a small town country girl like her-self. After terminating the call, he ordered lunch. He ate a hefty meal of steak and potatoes, with side orders of potato salad and collard greens. He drank a Pepsi, then returned to work.

*   *   *   *

Stoney and Katherine had just arrived at the Watertown Mall, then found a parking spot easily. Still not feeling like his usual self, he stepped unsteadily out of the car and stared oddly at his new surroundings. It appeared obvious to any-one observing that he had arrived to a place that he really didn't care to be. He rarely ventured the malls, believing it was only an impractical idea designed to accommodate shop-happy adults. Or for children to throw away their parents hard earned money by purchasing the latest video and arcade equipment, and for teenagers to congregate. It was the kind of place that his steadfast shop-a-holic Aunt Lucy in Gary, Indiana enjoyed immeasurably. She brought unnecessary items in bulk volume nearly every weekend because they were on sale, or were a bargain. The garage attached to her house is stocked to the gills and bursting at the seams, crammed full of new patio equipment, house wares and kitchen utilities, and clothes with the price tags still attached, designated for future Christmas and birthday gifts.

Although he liked expensive sports cars and nice houses, he kept his clothes wear simple. No name brands for this guy because he didn't believe in following fads. He believed in creating his own era, his own mystique. Mostly, and more importantly, if he was going to advertise for someone who he hadn't met, he wanted to get paid for it. Sadly, if it wasn't for her and Carlton, his mansion would be as dull as an empty box of raisinetts. No warm trimmings. An arctic bachelor pad, for a single polar bear.

He appeared immobilized, drifted in and out of himself. Katherine latched securely onto his left arm and led him through the malls entrance. It appeared as though she was assisting a blind or disabled person. He stared straight ahead, as if he wore a pair of horse blinders. As they walked, she glanced dreamingly at some of the glamorous shops, while he wondered drearily about everything he's been experiencing for the past few weeks. He realized that each time the children made their untimely appearances, he became more physically involved in their devious traps. He also realized that it took him a much longer time to recover; to regain his normal sense of being. Not wanting to admit, he knew he was loosing a hold of himself, loosing his mind, precious piece by precious piece. What's worse, he wasn't sure if there was anything he could do to stop it from occurring.

Fifteen minutes later, while shopping, she felt as though he was slowly returning to his old self when she noticed him staring favorably at a pair of dark gray Stacey Adams alligator shoes. He thought they'd go well with the new single-breasted, gray flannel Perry Ellis suit that she had purchased for him a month ago.

He broke his stare from the shoes, and opened his eyes wide, as if he had just awaken from a long slumber. Out of nowhere, he told her, "You don't have to drag me around like I'm a little kid. I can walk on my own."

"Oh," she said, surprised, "I see you're among the living." She released his arm. "For a minute there, I thought I'd lost you. Where'd you go?"

He felt he didn't need to explain himself. But he did search for an answer to pacify his needling conscious. He needed to know why these things were happening to him. Deciding to be considerate, he replied, "No where." Cleared his throat. "I guess I have some things going on in my head that I need to deal with. That's all." Truly the understatement of the year.

"Well, let's see if we can get them off your mind for now. Have some fun for a change. Just hang with me, and eventually, you'll enjoy yourself. And don't worry, babe." She nudged him playfully. "I'll try not to send you to the poor house."

A frail smile found its way to the corners of his lips. She could tell that it was as counterfeit as a three-dollar bill.

"All right," he said submissively. "I think I can hang with you for a little while at this ..." he glanced tiredly at few nearby shops, "... mall."

After nearly two hours of shopping, running from store to store, trying on this item and that, matching outfits to this accessory and that accessory, Stoney began to tire. Simply put, this wasn't his idea of having fun. Not at all. His idea of having fun was shooting a few rounds of pool, or sitting around the television in the company of his buddies; Spanky and Sleeper, watching sports, perhaps the super bowl, while drinking beer, eating chips and making a total mess of the place, while cursing sparingly and ranking on each others mothers. Real fun. Man stuff.

Katherine, on the other hand, was enjoying herself immensely. She couldn't remember when she had so much fun before in her life. She was ready to go for another two or three hours. No bathroom break, no eating, nada, zilch. He couldn't figure out this strange and mostly feminine phenomenon, and gave up trying to a long time ago.

At the checkout counter in one of the clothing stores, the cashier, a graying little old lady named Ester who worked there part time to supplement her meager social security income of three hundred and seventy five dollars a month, rang up their goods at the register. Her name was printed clearly in large bold letters on an identity plate pinned to the lapel of her white ruffled blouse. Gazing into her eyes, Stoney felt that she reminded him of Capt. Winslow. She wore a pair of thick framed prescription glasses which magnified her eyes three fold.

He pulled his wallet out of his back pocket and removed two-one hundred dollar bills to pay for the items. He handed them to Ester, looked into her eyes briefly, and discovered his reflection staring back at him. Unbeknownst to Katherine, he fell into another trance.

Waiting for the transaction to be completed, she turned away to admire a manikin fitted with a pair of fashionable Baby Phat jeans. She wondered if they'd look just as sexy on her. Apple bottom enhancement, no doubt. Why sweat it out at some smelly old gym to tone the gluteus, when you could easily buy a pair of pants designed to give you all the curves you want? It made her feel good to be able to turn heads, hear someone whistle like a wolf baying at the moon. A young man strolled by and ogled at the manikins round mound, and it suddenly became essential that she purchase a pair just like them.

She glanced at Stoney and sensed that something was wrong. She studied the fixation in his eyes and became worried. Growing exceedingly concerned, mainly because of the shooting that had occurred earlier, she asked, "Stoney, sweetheart, are you okay?"

Ignoring her, he remained staring at his reflection. All of a sudden, a clear image of Jake and Jessica appeared in Esters glasses—Jake in the left lens, Jessica in the right. He felt a thrash of heat rip through his body, as if he had stepped into the rays of a fifty thousand watt sunlamp hanging only a foot above his head. He breathed exhaustively, his heart beat tripled.

As the children played schoolyard games with each other, and sang slightly modified nursery rhymes, Stoney prayed to God that they wouldn't stop to notice to him. The last thing he wanted was another confrontation with the children from hell.

Abruptly, Jake informed him, "About that shooting," he shouted, "ya missed! Ya cockeyed son-of-a-bitch."

"Yeah!" Jessica threw in. She stuck out her tongue and wiggled it mischievously. "My mommy and daddy said you couldn't hit the broad side of a jackass, even if you were sitting on it. Ya filthy maggot!"

Watching the horrifying look on his face, Katherine noticed his jaw muscles tensed, and the veins on the sides of his temples and neck had swelled to twice their normal size. As beads of sweat puddled about his brow, like a volcano about to blow, he filled the area with his fury by yelling at Ester, "Oh yeah! You think I couldn't hit the broad side of a jackass? We'll see about that, you fucken rejects from a turd factory." His right hand snapped to his side by habit to where his service pistol was normally holstered. He was sure that just like earlier that morning, if he had access to one of his guns, he would've drew it and emptied the clip without hesitation.

Feeling his rage take her by storm, Ester stopped counting the change that she was about to give him and became frightened out of her wits—frozen stiff, paralyzed in utter shock. She sucked in a never-ending breath, clutched her heart, and leaned backwards to put distance in between herself and this madman. This raving lunatic. She dropped the money on the conveyor belt, then threw her trembling hands over her mouth in terror for the potential chaos that was about to explode. In the back of her mind, she heard a feeble voice echo, 'Oh Lord, somebody help me! I've fallen, and I can't get up!'

Stoney leaned over the conveyor belt and held a shaking fist to only inches away from Esters face. Staring fearfully at his idling knuckles, she discharged an earsplitting shrill that filled the store. **"NOOOOOOO!!!"**

Finally deciding to intervene, Katherine wrapper her arms around him and yelled into his ear, "Stoney! Wake up! You're doing it again. Stop it! Wake up!"

She broke his attention from Ester, and he shut his eyes tight for a moment. He snapped his head in every direction but loose, attempting to regain composure. A few seconds later, it finally came back to him where he was. He threw both hands onto his hips, lowered his head dejectedly, then exhaled deeply. He mumbled angrily, "No! No! No! No! No!"

The other shoppers in the store stared steadily on heightened alert. Not one person felt that it was safe to take their eyes away from the possibly escaped lunatic to return doing whatever.

Stoney glanced despondently to the ceiling, then spanned the store to take in his immediate surroundings, hoping desperately to keep surfaced his sinking sanity. He discovered that focusing on the everyday going ons of the people around him; life in general, created a distraction, and stole his attention from Jake and Jessica. He closed his eyes and lowered his head embarrassingly, as he appeared to all onlookers to be a figure of the battered warrior. He felt a surge of deep regret race throughout his body, and he trembled vibrantly in search of a release for his searing rage. He shifted his weight onto his left leg, then raised his shaking first high over his head. He allowed it to idle for a moment, then sent it crashing onto the conveyor belt. **"BANG!!"**

Hearing the crash, a few who felt his pit of anger stepped further away, believing that more violence was about to happen. A terrorist attack! Even worse, a shoppers rage over high prices.

All eyes glued to Stoney, Ester took a couple of steps backwards, spewing a nervous sputter, "S-S-Somebody! A-A-Anybody! G-G-Get him away from me. The man's lost his mind." She shouted, "Somebody call 9-9-1!"

She's probably right, he wondered of himself. I am loosing control, like a psychotic madman who should be locked away in a mental institution. An insane asylum. The house of asylum in Hawthorne, Mass. Damn! I can't even trust myself out in public anymore. This somber feeling has its arms wrapped around me tightly like a sopping cold grave. It's summoning me every chance it gets. It's pounding at my eardrums, beckoning me, pulling at my soul, or what's left of it. But I'm not done yet. The only thing that I can try to do to stop these hallucinations from occurring, is to try to stop myself from being drawn fixedly to anything that casts a reflection. I've got to stop listening to their voices. I can't give up. I won't give up. I refuse to give up.

Creeping up on them, a young burly man, an unarmed security guard approached from out of nowhere. Other shoppers near stared as though watching the great disco ball descend on New Years eve, in New York city's Times Square. After the ball, Stoney, hit the bottom, they believed that all hell would surely break loose.

The security guard had a black ugly night stick out, ready to drop a few lumps of sugar into Stoneys coffee. Everyone watching and waiting with anticipation figured the incident to be a 'COPs' reality show come to life. A tragic event! Excitement! The six o'clock news and you are there.

Another shopper switched on her video camera, then aimed it precisely at Stoney to catch his every hostile action. It was obvious that she was waiting for something thrilling to happen. Or better yet, something horrible. She was sure that selling the tape to Esters lawyers would net a small fortune. Or maybe she'd give it to Americas Funniest Videos. Or maybe a well known news correspondent would come to her home to interview her. She'd be on a first name basis with Oprah Winfrey. Fame and fortune, a chance to dance the light fantastic with Life!

If anything, she prayed to God that he would snap and pop that sweet little old lady right in the kisser. She wanted it to happen so badly that she could taste the blood pouring profusely from Esters age-wrinkled trembling lips.

Stoney, standing there, trying to look as normal as he possibly could made the amateur paparazzi feel as though she was wasting film. And mostly, her time. Although, she would've been more enthused if she knew he was a cop.

As Katherine embraced him securely, some shoppers standing nearby pointed condemningly as whispers of a maniac on the loose filled the store. The ridicule became too unbearable for him to handle. He felt that at any moment, two gigantic orderlies dressed in white t-shirts, slacks and sneakers were on their way with a straight jacket to restrain him.

When the security guard was close enough, he assessed the situation with as much as a glance would allow. He noticed how frightened Ester appeared, then asked concernedly, "Is everything all right over here?" He asked Ester, "You're not hurt, are you?"

Too frightened to respond, still trembling, she said nothing. She lifted her right arm, pointed a withered finger to Stoney, then babbled a mouth full of gobbledygook that didn't make sense to anyone. She ranted and raved to no end, like a terrified infant whose sleep was disturbed by a horrible nightmare.

The security guard eyed the couple, stepped to just behind them, then waited for them to offer an explanation. He asked authoritively, "Okay, you two. What's going on over here?" He passed an intimidating glance to Stoney, while rapping his nightstick repeatedly into the palm of his hand, warming up.

Katherine released him, but kept one hand on his shoulder consolingly. Attempting to downplay the situation, she told the security guard, "Sir, everything's all right. My boyfriend is just not feeling well. We ate at this sushi bar a short while ago, and he might've gotten a case of food poisoning, that's all." She added for good measure. "You know how risky it is with raw seafood."

Finally, Ester found a few words to throw into the mix. "I'll say he ain't feeling well. He was about to beat my brains in, is all he was gonna do. He needs help. He's dangerous, and people like him shouldn't be allowed to walk the streets."

The security guard examined him visually and observed his wretched condition, and realized that something was definitely wrong. Exactly what, he had no idea. With feeling that he wasn't an immediate threat, he decided to go along with Katherine and play the peacemaker. He pampered Ester with a little reassurance. "Don't worry, Ester. No one's going to hurt you. You'll be just fine."

"Humph!" Ester spouted. "A body ain't safe nowhere."

The security guard looked at Stoney again. "Well, it does appear as though something's wrong with him. I'm no doctor, but anyone can see that." He told Katherine, "Maam, your friend doesn't look too good. Can you please take him out of the store, immediately?"

"I'm taking him home right now," she said. "He'll feel much better after I help him flush out his stomach."

"See that you do that, maam. He's not safe walking around here in that condition. He's a liability. He could hurt someone," he slapped the nightstick into the palm of his hand, "or get hurt."

She guided him to the stores entrance. "Com'on, Stoney. Let's go home." As they walked, she thought about his violent outburst. She wondered if his deteriorating mental capacity had something to do with his illicit activities involving Spanky and Sleeper. She knew a few things about the Dixie Club, from catching a few details that had escaped his mouth one evening, amidst a drunken stupor. But she had no idea of the magnitude of the operation that's been going on for nearly ten years. She believed that they were involved in the mere shakedowns of drug dealers and other petty criminals. She couldn't have been more wrong.

She knew that he needed some form of psychotherapy, a few hours on the couch. But knew that he wouldn't accept it easily. Especially with knowing that in order to fix the problem, he'd have to divulge in detail what might've created them.

The idea to have him examined covertly by one of her psychologist friends entered her mind. Someone who she can invite by the house for a casual dinner to speak with him, and not let him know that he was being examined. Someone who wouldn't disclose to anyone their findings, because she was sure that one incriminating finding would lead to another. She didn't want to be responsible for him getting into any trouble.

As they were about to leave the store, Stoney turned slightly and told Ester, "I'm sorry, miss." His eyes grew misted. "I ... I didn't mean to ..." He choked. He wanted to say more, but his throat became clogged with the bitter fruit of remorse. A contemptible hatred grew inside of him to despise his free will for the illicit actions against those who he'd taken advantage of. Eerily, he wished he was a computer. Robo-Cop. A robot police officer programmed to uphold and apply the law ethically and evenly, straight across the board. He needed a computer program installed in his head to protect himself from his own folly. He also realized that this type of regretful thinking was always an afterthought, and not his reality. He thought about the repercussions after he screwed up. After he trashed his conscious, his soul. He tried the normal escape route by shifting the blame to Spanky, but it came back to him. Where it belonged. Where it lived.

Leaving the store, he kept his head bowed for the weighty embarrassment riding his shoulders. Didn't want anyone to see the torment he's suffering riddled across his face, the unfathomable misery choking his subconscious, the profound despair squeezing his heart pitilessly. If anyone glanced into his eyes, all of this and more would be easily seen.

CHAPTER 9

▼

It was a quiet drive from the Watertown Mall to his mansion in Dover. When they had arrived home, they went directly to the living room. He sat opposite the fireplace, on a lengthy couch fitted with the softest Italian leather he could find. She sat next to him, then finally broke the long silence. "I'll have Carlton bring the bags in later." She looked at him square in the face. "Stoney, I want you to promise me something."

He faced her. "Com'on Katherine." An uptight expression wrinkled his face. "You know how I feel about making promises."

She grabbed his shirt sleeve, said earnestly, "Stoney, promise me this." She grasped his chin gently. "Promise me you're going to get some rest."

He felt relieved that it was a simple request, and nodded slowly. She continued, "I think you need it badly. Maybe that's what we both need, a nice long vacation." She sat back in the couch and closed her eyes briefly, and an image of the Hawaiian Islands came into view. She pictured them relaxing on a beautifully architected hotel patio, amid a picturesque sunset, enjoying a moonlit Polynesian dinner and strawberry daiquiris. Hearing soft romantic music playing in the background, she sighed, "Yeah. Maui, that's where we need to be. On the beach, the beautiful sunsets, the natives, the luaus, the hula dancing ... I'm sure that's what we need."

"That sounds like a good idea," he agreed. "Sunshine, the clear blue water. Diamond Head. I think I'd like that very much."

"Remember the barefoot night walks we took on the beach, during our last visit?"

He closed his eyes and nodded pleasurably.

"Remember when we ran into that old man who told us the story about Mei Lei, the last girl his ancestors used as a sacrifice to satisfy their gods. Before they did away with the ancient rituals and customs?"

"I remember that."

She smiled. "Remember he told us the fable about Mahti Teilo. One of their last great warriors who fought in many battles, and killed over one thousand warriors?"

"That was pretty impressive. I still remember most of the details."

After getting the notion that he was feeling the moment, she smiled favorably. He was still with her, mind, body and soul. At least in body, and partially in soul. She felt relieved, but knew that he had to get some much-needed rest. She felt it imperative that he did.

She rose from the couch and straightened out her clothing, then stepped to just in front of him. "Sweetheart, we'll talk about this tomorrow, when I come back out to see how you're doing. If nothing comes up, and you know how things occasionally do with my having such a busy schedule, then we'll pack on Friday morning. Chances are, we'll be in Hawaii before Saturday evening, in time to enjoy a beautiful sunset dinner." She looked at her watch and grew excited, "My God! Where's the time gone? I almost forgot I have an appointment at the beauty salon." She ran her fingers through her hair. "I absolutely need this special treatment they have me scheduled for. In case you haven't noticed, it's getting pretty rough up here."

He remembered a few days before when he had tried to run his fingers through her hair, and they became entangled. He recalled it felt like trying to comb dreadlocks with a fine toothcomb. He decided not to comment on the matter to keep the peace. He thought about the fun they had the last time they visited Hawaii and responded, "All right, Katherine." His mind raced with the excitement of their probable upcoming getaway. "I understand." He reached out, took her right hand and squeezed gently. He looked into her eyes appreciatively. "Besides that little episode in the store, at the checkout line, I really enjoyed myself today." He stated questionably, "I'm pretty sure I did, somewhere along the way." He stated more convincingly, "I had fun." A fake smile made a weak attempt to surface. "Thanks for spending time with me today."

The sex, yes. The mall, no. Anyway, he thanked her for the effort at trying to get a few troublesome things off his mind. He wondered if they were really going to fly off to Hawaii for a few days of fun and sun, understanding how unpredictable her schedule was. He knew she sometimes made promises only to pacify the moment. The next time he'd see her would probably be in a week or so, their plans forgotten like so many times before. That's just the way their relationship was; her busy crashing parties every night of the week and shopping at the malls, and him busy pushing his hustles, keeping on his marks—conducting Dixie Club business. And hanging out with his cohorts, Spanky and Sleeper (A.K.A. Bonehead and T-Bonehead).

Nonetheless, she wasn't totally void of sentimental feelings for him. Feeling the way he squeezed her hand returned warm memories they once shared when they first began dating. She took it as a sign that he actually needed her to be there for him in his time of need, and he appreciated wholeheartedly the help she was trying to give him. She new those emotions were good for her, but felt that they came with the impending doom of commitment and restrictions on her freedom. Yet, still, she hoped that someday she'd receive them on a permanent basis, realizing that she wasn't going to be young forever. The thought frightened her because she had never been seriously close to any man before. Not even her father.

For now, at this particular time in her life, she didn't want to get use to his softer side, for fear that it might be ripped away on a moments notice. This has happened before. This has happened plenty of times before. In times of trouble, his serious side was seldom available to help her get through trying times. Simply for want, surrounding herself securely with a stable relationship was always at her fingertips. However, she didn't dare reach out and grab the golden ring, for fear that she might fall from the horse galloping promisingly around the carousel of her life. She knew that love cost no less than everything, and wasn't ready to leave her feelings open its sometimes harsh scrutiny, whichever way the wind blew. For this sole reason, she remains a 'no strings attached' kinda girl. Freestyle, it didn't cost a thing, but hell would catch up to her in the long run. Like a credit card, if the shit got too thick, then there was the safety net of bankruptcy. A roll of the dice on chapter seven come eleven. Baby needs new shoes, and I need a new life.

Paranoia was a considerable factor that crippled her in more ways than one. She believed it was only going to be a matter of time before she had the joy of being involved in his life snatched away from her. She somehow knew that it was inevitable, believing several dire circumstances were on the approach. She was forewarned, had ill-fated premonitions. Several times as she visited the malls to hang out with her girlfriends, she felt that she was being followed. Her paranoia grew so intense that one day as she jogged alongside the Charles River in Cambridge, she could've swore she was being followed by a police dog wearing a surveillance camera fitted on its collar. She figured it was trained to stay back at least fifty feet, to stop when she stopped, taught to turn away or face another direction whenever she looked at it.

There were also several instances of hearing unusually suspicious clicks on the other end of her telephone, and seeing dark shadows creeping stealthily around her apartment, and near her car. Once, when she had just finished shopping at Saks Fifth Avenue on Boylston Street, as she was about to cross Botolph Street, near the Copley Square Library, she had no doubt in her heart that she was being followed. She made a sharp right turn and hid in a doorway, then waited for the person to pass. After he made the same turn, then passed her, she came out of hiding and stood behind him. When the man thought that he had lost her, he stopped, spanned the immediate area, then found her standing just in back of him. His reaction was to be surprised because he had been caught with his hand in the cookie jar. To play it off, he asked her for the time. When she didn't respond, only stared distrustfully, he walked away immediately.

Wanting to believe that these unreasonable suspicions were only a figment of her imagination, she swept the thoughts from her mind with the bristles of denial. She leaned toward to him and pressed her lips against his. The kiss lasted only a moment, because the notion lingered that he wasn't back to his original self. The notion was verified when she felt his cadaver like cold lips press flatly against hers. He didn't blink once, as though he was in suspended animation. Apparently, something was on his mind, took a substantial precedent over everything that they had just discussed. Slow to release her hand, he looked as though he had and important question on his mind that he wanted desperately to ask. Before she knew anything, out flew, "Katherine, how do you feel about children?"

Caught of guard, her mouth snapped open in astonishment, her eyes full of surprise. No doubt, the question was a bombshell, and certainly the last thing that she had ever expected to hear come soaring from out of his mouth. She had no idea on how to respond. Didn't even know where to begin to search for an answer. From fearing its complicity, she didn't want to. She swallowed hard, replied sluggishly, "Well … I think they're … you know …" Her mind became filled distressingly with screaming babies in the middle of the night, shit clumped pissy diapers, exhaustive hours nursing and bathing the child, vomit on her wardrobes, a substantial loss of sleep, and an overhaul of her entire lifestyle, through the realization that another life would be placed before her own. Her face contorted vastly, went sour. She pulled away from him, turned around, then simply walked away. Before she left the room, she looked over her shoulder and glanced at him plainly, and it was her turn to flash a feeble smile that died quickly, even before she turned away. Then she left the room.

In referring to the unnerving inquiry, he figured that if he had a baby, he could show Jake and Jessica that he could love one of their own. That he could be unselfish, genuinely concerned about someone other than himself. Maybe they would have compassion for him, and leave him alone, go away and never return.

Several feet from the bedroom door, she paused, thinking about what he had asked. Over the many intricacies involved, what slowly surfaced was the idea that maybe that was his way of finding out how she truly felt about marriage, dealing with him entirely. Then, as with the other essential issues between them, the notion fizzled out to nothing.

Leaving, she couldn't help but to think of how distressed he was, and about what he was turning into. He had definitely come a long way from being the carefree man that she use to have a lot of fun with. He was definitely not the same person. Then there were instances when she felt as though she didn't know him at all. He appeared a total stranger.

When her footsteps were heard no more, he sat gaping at the busted floor model color television. Reflecting earnestly on his relationship with her, something that he seldom did, a few wonderful feelings came to heart, and he felt better than he did for the past few days. The same feeble smiled retuned and stayed a little while longer.

Minutes later, it left because a stark reality returned and crept up the cockles of his spine. Then all he could see were images of Jake and Jessica dancing merrily, singing modified nursery rhymes. Without a doubt, he figured them to be 'the children of the damned.'

To chase the unpleasant thought from his mind, he admired his prized winning gun collection encased behind smoke tinted glass. He rose from the couch and approached the wall-mounted casing. In the center is a fully restored impeccable 1964 Browning rifle. He had picked it up at an auction at Sotheby's three years prior.

He studied its fine craftsmanship and considered its deadly beauty. At the same time, he wondered of the numerous lives it possibly claimed during a special ops mission in Viet Nam. Beauty and the beast all wrapped up into one sweet little package. Truly an object to be respected.

Suddenly, his focus backed off a few inches to the glass, and he discovered a reflection of himself. He closed his eyes tight and remembered painfully how Jake and Jessica appeared indiscriminately on anything that cast a reflection. He wished wholly that he had seen the last of them, and he prayed to God that they'd never return. He thought that if it was his desire to never see them again, then he could take charge and block them out of his mind. He believed this, but not for long. A wavering thought.

Even before he opened his eyes, he heard the faded whispers of Jake and Jessica singing, their youthful voices rejoiced, "Santa Claus is coming ... to tooooown!" They stopped singing, and Jake went on to say, "But he's not coming to our house, because a pathetic rat-fink cop took all of our daddy's money."

Stoney shook his head maddeningly. "Nooooooo!" He whined, "Not again."

He opened his eyes and saw images of Jake and Jessica on the smoke tinted glass, and immediately his heartbeat tripled. Jessica asked, "Beating up on helpless little old ladies, are ya?" She brushed her index fingers against each other and admonished him frivolously. "Shame on you. That could've been my nana you was gonna hit. You boogieman!"

A rage never felt before surged through his heart. His eyes bulged to an ache, almost popped out of their sockets. His jaw tightened so stiff that one couldn't pry it loose, less it broke. He trembled violently, as though experiencing an epileptic fit. He heaved from the pit of his stomach a word that became stuck in his throat briefly. It filled his mouth like an explosive vomit, and he looked up and thrust forward with everything that he had. **"NOOOOOOOOOOO!!!"**

He ran frantically to the fireplace and grabbed the poker, and returned quickly to the gun collection with the sole intention of creating as much holly hell and destruction as possible. He raised the poker high above his head, then stopped for a moment to consider whether there would be any relief in his actions if he proceeded. Deciding there would be, he swung the poker so mightily that not only did he shatter the glass into a hundred pieces, but he knocked the entire casing from the wall. It went crashing to the floor, sending a loud boom resonating throughout the house.

Carlton heard the earth-shattering noise and stopped cleaning immediately. He ran to the living room to find out what had happened. He stopped at about ten feet from the entrance and observed Stoney holding the fire poker, breathing maddeningly, in the middle of another psychotic episode. He glanced to the floor and saw the demolished gun casing and the shattered glass sprinkled around it.

Taking everything into account, second thoughts to intervene entered his mind, and he figured he wouldn't volunteer an appearance. Plainly put, after what had happened earlier that morning, he didn't want to become a statistic. He figured that he was much safer right where he was, watching television in the comfort and safety of his room. Mostly, he didn't want to miss the final showcase on 'The price is Right.'

He turned around and went back to his room.

Stoney spanned the room quickly, searched desperately for someone to lay the blame. There was certainly no one there. He dropped his head, along with the passion to go on living, then mumbled, "Damn, this is crazy. I'm going insane. I'm going crazy. I'm going out of my fricken mind." He yelled to Jake and Jessica, "I've had enough of this shit!" He sprinted out of the living room, yelling along the way, "You're not coming back into my house." Amidst his shameless hysterics, he laughed wickedly, sinister like. "I know just how to stop you from coming back too."

CHAPTER 10

▼

Spanky and Sleeper had finished their shift at six o'clock, then drove out to Dover to check up on Stoney. Depending on the state of his mental health, their intentions would be honorable, or dishonorable. To Spanky, it really didn't matter which way it went. It only mattered imperatively that Stoney keep his mouth shut about the Dixie Club and all of its activities.

His mint condition 1969 Ford Mustang Grande Coupe is his golden trophy on wheels His boy toy, an extension of his ego. The car cruised heavenly on sixty and seventy series chrome plated wire spokes that are always fitted with fresh Goodyear racing slicks, and it has a beefed up racing suspension to allow maximum traction. The engine is slightly modified with a bored out 351 Cleveland Jet engine, and is crowned with a powerful air ram blower protruding through the hood. The primary power plant is tweaked with nitrous oxide; two huge tanks sat in the trunk. The total output at peak performance, over eight hundred horsepower. It has an immaculate black leather interior, and a ping and rust-free exterior, dressed with seven coats of lustrous midnight black paint.

It's the kind of monster that makes Corvette and Porsche owners cringe with fear and cower to the shoulder of the road until it rumbled by. It's the kind of sports car that enthusiasts and gear-heads love to flock around and admire through glossy eyes, while tossing a six-pack of cold ones. It's also the kind of vehicle that some men paid more attention to than their domestic relations. An unconditional mechanical love, charmed with a wrench. If only making adjustments in domestic relations were that simple.

Even if there's nothing wrong with the engine, drivetrain, steering or suspension system, mostly on weekend mornings, he spends hours underneath the hood, staring at the engine, touching parts, smelling areas, needlessly adjusting and readjusting everything. No wonder his friends thought he loved the car more than life itself. During the week, his hands remained soil free; totally clean. But when he got under the hood of his car, oil and dirt from the undercarriage covered his hands greatly, like a pair of black gloves. He considered the oil and transmission fluid to be 'love oil.' Sometimes he puts a few drop of the substance on the palms of his hands, and then rubs it in to feel the oils viscosity. It turned him on, proving that he was a bonafied gear head. No wonder he wasn't married.

Nevertheless, he hasn't abandoned the quest to find Mrs. Gear Head. He believed that somewhere out there, there's a woman who loves the early era muscle cars just as much as he does.

Some Saturday mornings, he drives down to the amateur race track in Franklin, Mass., where he and a group of gear heads get together and marvel at each others cars, some comparing them to their women. After so many beers, they sign insurance wavers, then open their engines full throttle, let their cars run wild on a quarter mile suicide track. They'd swear it was the most fun you can have with your pants on. Or off, making what they call a fast moon rising; flashing their glutes while the passenger held the wheel briefly.

If he could avoid having anyone else at the wheel of a car in which he was an occupant, he'd bitch, moan, gripe and insist to the high heavens that he do the driving. After being involved in a serious motor vehicle accident that occurred fifteen years before, when a friend of his was driving under the influence of alcohol—one which left him severely traumatized—he's learned never to trust another driver with his life. He wasn't critically hurt with any life threatening injuries. But for months to follow, he saw his life flash before his eyes repeatedly. Before he graduated from the police academy, his only request was that he do his own driving.

As he drove, Sleeper sat quietly next to him, grew nervous because of the diabolical ideas that he knew stewed in his head. In his wildest dreams, he never imagined that the three of them would come to a head over anything. It was like a bad dream come to life. The exhaustive thinking of their weary predicament and all of its grotesque complications plagued him incessantly. In trying to get some much-needed sleep for the past few days, he only tossed and turned and wrestled with his bed sheets. He wasn't granted the welcomed pleasure of an extended blink. Or, like Stoney, was it his subconscious he wrestled with? He couldn't tell. Most likely, he probably didn't want to know.

Staring out the window, watching the scenic suburbs rolling by, he thought about the long relationship that the three had constructed over the past fourteen years. Overshadowing his thoughts was an incident that had occurred when he was in his senior year of high school. One evening, as he walked home from varsity football practice, three-rivalry football players from a neighboring high school confronted him. They demanded that he surrender his money and jewelry, or suffer the wrath of a thorough ass whipping. Actually, they were jealous of his victorious football team that had broken their teams two month winning streak. Because he didn't give into their demands, they commenced to thrash him, hillbilly style, windmill fists ablaze.

Less than ten seconds into the massacre, Stoney and Spanky, who just happened to be passing by, after a lengthy deliberation, decided against their will—only because they didn't know Sleeper personally—to lend a helping hand.

Within seconds, the three attackers decided that it wasn't worth it to continue, and decided to high tail it out of there. Sleeper never knew that it was Stoneys idea to get involved, because Spanky only wanted to eat a Milky Way candy bar and watch.

From that day forward, the three began building a relationship that led them to be the best of friends. Although Sleeper is slightly taller in stature than Stoney, he always looked up to him with the utmost respect. At the back of his mind, he knew and believed that it was his idea to intervene. That's one of the reasons why he respected him so much.

As they were about to enter the town of Dover, Sleeper told Spanky worriedly, "I hope Stoney's doing okay."

Spankys flat response. "Yeah."

For years, Spanky had always gotten along better with Sleeper, than with Stoney. Sleeper was more of a follower, and would often follow him into his piles of shit. No matter how bad it smelled. No questions asked.

Stoney had more of an individualized conscious, which made him always second guess Spanky. And he didn't like to be undermined. Shortly after the three had graduated from high school, when he laid out the floor plans for a get-rich-quick business scheme for them, Stoney asked questions that he couldn't answer. At the back of his mind, he despised him because it made him feel inadequate. He was a Leo, and felt that he should be the leader of the three. Hearing a question, instead of the phrase 'yes Spanky', made him feel insecure. The more practical the question, the more insecure he felt. Because of his unyielding arrogance, his gilded pride, he wanted to make them feel that at any time, he could come up with the answers for whatever problems arose. Even if he didn't have the correct answer.

"Is that all you can say?" Sleeper asked.

"Well."

"Ain't this some shit."

"The fuck do ya want me to say?" He blew a heavy breath. "Look, Sleep, as I said before. This is business, nothing personal. We gotta take care of shit, before it takes care of us. It's just as simple as that, as long as you don't complicate matters by talking about friendships and loyalty. Unless ..." he peered suspiciously at Sleeper through slithered eyes, "... you plan on selling out also."

Sleeper became furious and fired, "Don't you throw that shit in my face and put me to sleep with your fucken bullshit!" He hesitated for almost five seconds, then asked, "This whole thing's beginning to get you paranoid, isn't it?" When Spanky didn't respond, he took his silence as an admission of guilt. "Yeah, that's it. Isn't it? All this shit has gotten you so paranoid, that you don't know who to trust anymore. All our years of friendship doesn't mean a damn thing, does it?"

"Me, paranoid? Perish the thought."

"Perish my ass! Who the hell do you think I'm talking to, the damn steering wheel?"

Spanky shrugged his shoulders. "Hey! I'm just trying to watch my back, that's all." Feeling that he was on the right path, he turned up the heat. "And you should be just as concerned, covering all the bases, since you do have a family to look out for. In times like this, it's good to go with your gut feelings. You see something wrong with that?"

"I suppose not. What's bothering me is that I never thought we'd have to watch our backs from each other; you, me and Stone."

"Well, this is one of the ugly realities of life. Sometimes it gets like that. And when it does, ya gotta deal with it." He took on a more serious note. "I guess I have to keep reminding you about what happens to cops who get caught up in the mix, don't I?" He glanced out the driver's side window for a moment. "You remember that cop ... um, what's his name?" He thought back, "Andy! Andrew Thompson! Yeah, that's his name."

Sleeper paused, searched through his mind. Then it all of a sudden hit him and he replied, "Yeah. I heard some things about him. All bad. Whatever happened to him?"

"If you go down to the corner of Mass. Avenue and Columbus, near where Stoney keeps that shitty little two-room studio apartment, you might run into him. Sometimes he stays at the Pine Street Inn, in the winter. It's a shelter for homeless people, bums and whatever."

"I know the place."

"In the summer, he lives in an alley, in the back of this greasy little Italian restaurant. He's an alcoholic now—couldn't stop soaking up the sauce even if he tried. He's been that way ever since they took his badge in disgrace and labeled him a worthless looser."

"How'd he screw up?"

"The way the story goes, during one of the biggest drug raids we've ever had—one in which we seized over eighty million dollars in cocaine and cash—he stashed over two million dollars worth of cocaine in a hiding spot on the premises. A week later, after the smoke cleared, he returned to claim it. Then he had the audacity to, of all the craziest things in the world, deal drugs covertly." He paused, shook his head deplorably. "At first, he was very careful and everything. He had a few tight connections with the right dealers on the streets, and he knew that as long as he kept everything on a professional level, that it was all going to be alright. The next thing you know, he blew up ... he was making dough hand over foot. But down the line somewhere, he made one itsy bitsy terrible mistake. Sometimes, that's all it takes."

After a lengthy hesitation, Sleeper grew restless and prodded. "Well, are you gonna tell me. Or do I have to use my nightstick?"

Spanky chuckled. "The asshole got sloppy and told his young play thing—a girl who was less than half his age—everything that was going on. He was married to, what I heard, was a descent woman, but he had a trophy girl on the side. He liked to impress her by playing the role of 'The Big Man!', and all that dumb shit. He gave her everything, sent her jet setting all over the globe. He was having so much fun that he had graduated to being a gangster, a thug in blue. A shot caller! A big daddy baller! He spoiled her rotten, and got her use to being spoiled rotten."

"So ..."

"When the money started running thin, because he was trying to take care of his family—setting up trust accounts for the kids, making sure that his wife was kept comfortable so she'd stay out of his hair—the girlfriend started getting a little paranoid, because he didn't help secure her future. She was once poor, and didn't want to return to the slum life; vowed never to return. Because of financial conflicts like this, they argued a lot. And that's when the shit hit the fan."

"What happened?"

"She thought he was going to break up with her, because she was becoming a pain in the ass. A nuisance. She knew that no matter what she did for him, his family came first. At least, financially."

"So ..."

"So one day, she threw her cards on the table and demanded a load of money to secure her future, and he refused. He told her that there wasn't enough left. She didn't take to kindly to that at all. To get something out of the deal, she decided to turn states evidence against him to collect a big reward that came with providing information leading to his involvement. Internal Affairs knew that it was an inside job, but they didn't have any evidence to corroborate a few theories. Meanwhile, Andrew only received a two-year sentence at a half-way house. And of course, a dishonorable discharge. Although the higher-ups promised to pay his girlfriend the fifty thousand dollars reward money, she never received a penny of it because she was in cahoots with him from day one. The crazy thing is that there was so much crazy shit going on during that period, that they simply tied her into some of it just that easy. To keep her quiet, they gave her a six month sentence for a jewelry store robbery that some say she's never even committed. Setting her up saved the state from having to pay off a reward to some lowlife back stabbing hussy who dimed on a cop."

"But the newspaper said that she ..."

"Fuck the newspapers!" Spanky blasted. "The bunch of nosy ass hound dogs." He stated threateningly, "They print what we tell them to print ... or else. Remember, since we're on the crime scene first, we control what the crime scene investigators get their hands on. Therefore, evidence is not evidence until we say that it is. If a fellow officer commits a crime, if it's been confined, we'll cover it up. It helps to keep our good name. Having a good name makes people trust us, and allows us to control the civilian population that much easier." He sighed. "Nowadays, Andrew does nothing but drink all day long, and sits out there on the sidewalk. Watching time go by, waiting to die.

"The state took all of the luxuries his family had, because they couldn't substantiate what was legitimate, and what wasn't. When he runs out of money, as he often does, he stumbles from out of that alley and whips out an old rusty ass badge on passerby's. He tells them that if they don't give him some spare change, he'll bust their asses and take them downtown."

Sleeper snickered, "You're kidding?"

"Do you see me laughing? Shit! The man looks deplorable, and smells like shit. Like a nasty ass bum who hasn't bathed in eons. No one takes him serious though. Even his own children have lost their respect for him. Most people he confronts merely laugh at him, throw him some loose change into a cup, then go on about their business. He takes the change and heads straight to the liquor store, so he can continue drinking. Perhaps so he can forget about everything that's happened with the entire ordeal." He sighed again. "Sleeper, the man is a disgusting sight, and smells like the sweat dripping from a baboons balls. I'll be damned if anything like that ever happens to me." He stated for sure, "I'd rather die."

I wonder how he knows what the sweat dripping from a baboons balls smells like, Sleeper thought. "Yeah. No doubt." He changed the subject altogether. "I still don't think Stoney will turn against us. He's just not that kind of a person. I know he ain't."

"Huh!" Spanky grunted doubtingly. "We'll soon see about that, won't we?"

CHAPTER 11

▼

They had arrived at Stoney mansion shortly before seven that evening. Not being strangers, they walked in unannounced through the rear entrance and ran into Carlton. He was cleaning up the shattered glass from a bottle of scotch that Stoney had just minutes before flung into the fireplace, because he saw Jake and Jessica dancing mischievously in the fire.

After Stoney returned home from the mall with Katherine, and after she had left, because of the formidable scene at the mall, and the hallucination with the gun trophy casing, he was feeling depressed and had downed a fifth of scotch. Then, to attempt to stop the children from reappearing, he went into every room in the house with a hammer and destroyed every mirror, and anything that could cast a reflection. All but the windows, since they were covered with either Venetian blinds or curtains. He grew desperate to save his dwindling sanity, and didn't want to take any chances.

At the onset of the demolition, Carlton decided to stay in his room, with the door locked securely, until the destruction was over. He wasn't frightened. He merely didn't want him to break his mirror. Or what's worse, his brand new flat screen color television.

"Carlton, my old friend. What's up?" Sleeper said.

Carlton faced him, smiled stiffly, but genuinely. "Mr. Knight. How are you, sir?"

Every time Spanky came by the house, he often toyed with Carlton by calling him different names. Using an airy English accent, he tossed nonchalantly, "Phipps, my good man. Have they gotten back together again?"

"I beg your pardon, sir."

"Answer the question," Spanky urged. "Have they gotten back together again?"

"Sir, who are you referring to?"

Spanky snickered. "Your ass checks." He laughed, "Get it? It's a joke." After the laughter died quickly, he came back with, "Are your teeth cold?"

"Officer Sinclair, I don't like where this is going."

"Com'on, Carlton! Just answer the question."

Carlton sighed resignedly, said tiredly, "No, Mr. Sinclair. My teeth are not cold."

Spank laughed. "Then why do you have that brown blanket covering them?"

"As usual," Carlton said jadedly, "you are in poor taste."

Spanky shrugged it off. "Anyway, Phipps, where's the master of the house?"

Holding a green trash bag in hand, he replied, "Mr. Sinclair, the name is Carlton. Carlton Rogers." He approached the trash compactor, explaining, "One gets respect by giving it. As for Master Brooks, he's in the living room." As they were leaving the kitchen, he warned them, "Mind the broken glass."

They wondered bewilderedly, broken glass!

Carlton despised him for his offensively idiotic jokes. He realized that he was only kidding, but just the same, he didn't like the guy. He considered him a wise ass. Considered him the kind of scoundrel that one should never get caught standing in front of, for an extended length of time. Meaning, he might put a knife in you back, or swing a heavy object over your head. The last time Spanky asked him for a glass of ice water, he went straight to the bathroom, dipped a glass into one of the toilet bowls, then threw a few ice cubes in for taste. As Spanky drank the water, he stood not too far away, smiling gratifyingly, laughing internally. In thinking of him, the phrase 'toilet bowl breath' often came to mind.

Leaving the kitchen, Spanky yelled to Carlton. "It's easier to take the respect! You know the country's policy. Look at what we're doing to the middle east. Or for that matter, the world." He muttered, "Damn softy."

On their way to the living room, he handed Sleeper a small devise and whispered, "First chance you get, put this into one of the phones. I'll be with you guys in a minute." He veered to the left. "I have to use the bathroom."

Sleeper arrived at the living room doorway and observed Stoney sitting slumped on the couch, staring out into nowhere. He was just about to break the seal on a fresh bottle of scotch, when Sleeper said concernedly, "Hey, Stoney, buddy. How're ya doing?"

Hearing Sleepers voice startled him, and he nearly jumped out of his skin. He turned halfway to view him entering the room, but didn't respond. Because

Sleeper didn't hear a word of welcome coming from someone that he's been close to for many years, he became troubled. "Stone, it's me. The Sleep man! What's going on?"

Still, he didn't respond. Only stared open-mouthed, as if he didn't know who this person was. He nodded indistinctly, his eyes filled with consternation.

When Sleeper was close enough, he noticed the distraught expression on his face. "Captain Winslow said you weren't feeling so good. What's wrong ..." he looked around the room, then back out into the hallway, "... and what's up with all the broken glass? Somebody break into your house or something?" He paused. "Katherine didn't do this, did she?"

He evaded the issue of the broken glass, but stuttered, "I-I-I don't know what's going on, Sleep. I guess I'm feeling a little stressed out. I probably have too much on my mind." He turned his body a few degrees toward him. Sounding anxious, he continued, "Sleep, I know I'm not crazy. But I keep seeing these ... these ..." He swallowed profoundly. He wanted to tell him everything, then he realized that if he did, he might've believed that he was going crazy. "Is Spanky here with you?"

"Yeah. He had to use the bathroom." He sat on the couch, next to him, about three feet away. "He'll be here in a sec." He glanced at the broken glass peppered about the floor in several spots. "I guess getting stressed happens to the best of us." It became imperative that he ask, "But, what're you gonna do about it? Are ya gonna get some help?" He placed his hand reassuringly on Stoneys shoulder.

He searched monotonously for what should have been an easy answer. It seemed a conundrum floating in his head. He looked to the ceiling, sighed wearily. "Sleep, I don't know. If I talk to someone, suppose I accidentally say something that might ..."

Spanky walked into the room, both turned to take note. Peering at Stoney, he darted viciously, biting his words. "Yeah! What're you gonna do about it," there wasn't a note of sympathy to be found in any of his words, "old buddy? And what the hell's up with all the broken glass around here?"

Stoney remembered the last words he hurled at them before he pulled out of the parking lot of the station house. He could only imagine what kind of confusion raced through their minds. He ignored the question about the broken glass. "I know what you're thinking, Spanky. But I have everything under control. I ... I just need some time to relax and ..."

He felt a splatter of spit shower him when Spanky got into his face and fired, "Are you sure you have everything under control? It didn't look like it back at the precinct. Actually, it looked like you were about to loose it altogether, like you were out of your mother fucken mind. And from the look of your house, I'd say you've already lost it. Look at this place. It's a fucken mess; broken glass everywhere." He stared into his eyes hard. "The fucks wrong with you, telling me all that crazy shit? Calling me a flat ..." he looked at Sleeper, "... what was that he called me?"

On the inside, Sleeper though it rather amusing. He wanted to laugh. Instead, he smiled indistinctly and replied, "I think he called you a flat faced, shiny son-of-a-bitch. Or was it a flat, skinny faced son-of-a-bitch? Or was it a prick faced, flat ass, wimpy son-of-a-bitch? Or was it a flat skimpy, lesbian faced son-of-a ..."

"Enough already," Spanky shot forward tiredly. "I think he knows what we're talking about." He faced Stoney. "Don't you, Stoneman? Or have you forgotten about our little Dixie Club arrangement? You know, the part about our never mentioning a word of our operation to anyone."

Stoney apologized solemnly, "Spanky, I'm sorry about what I said earlier. I had something on my mind. And you know I haven't forgotten about our arrangement. It's just that ..."

"You haven't forgotten, huh?" Spanky grabbed the front of his shirt, where his badge is normally pinned. "Then where's your badge and gun? I don't know about you, Sleep. To me, it looks like somebody might be trying to sell out on his buddies." He glanced to Sleeper. "What do you think? You think this whoosp is selling out on us?" He brought his face closer to Stoney, gritted fiercely, demanded to know, "What the fuck is going on with you? You cracking up, or what?"

Maintaining a tight grip on his shirt, Stoney didn't offer the slightest amount of resistance. He looked deep into Spankys eyes and saw the scales of their friendship sway beyond repair. He thought that even if he did tell him the truth about why he had snapped at him in the parking lot, that he probably wouldn't have believed him. He made an attempt anyway, feeling that he owed them that much.

He found the energy to free his self from Spankys vicious grip. He grabbed his thumb and bent it backwards; a martial arts slight of hand that ha had learned at the police academy. Spanky fell crumpled to the floor, yelling in pain. "Hey! That shit hurt." He rubbed his thumb knuckle. "Damn!"

Stoney warned him, "Spanky, if you don't stay out of my face, I'll kick your ass into the next millennium. The way things are going right now, I don't think I can take being pushed any further."

Somehow, Spanky harbored the notion that he could take him in fight, since he was a few inches taller, and was at least sixty pounds heavier. Periodically, someone like Stoney had to remind him that the theory of his overruling size was a crock of cold, hard shit. A pile of television hooey, a tall mans fantasy. A dream bubble that was often popped for a sample of razor-sharp reality. Throbbing pain.

While on the floor, on his ass, he slid back a few inches. Since he wasn't getting anywhere by using intimidation, he decided to take a different approach. "Well, look, Stone. How's this for your little intimidation effort? Ya putting me ta sleep. Ya gotta come up with some shit a hellova lot better than this. Ya been sitting there like a bump on a log, yapping all this crap about nothing, and I'm getting very bored. Let's hear it. The truth!" He stayed right where he was and folded his legs Indian style.

Listening to Spanky use his line, Sleeper sat up straight and gaped with twisted lips. You thief! How dare you steal what I so proudly possess.

Sleeper looked into Stoneys eyes and saw something that he'd never seen before, and it frightened him. He felt a chill deep in his bones, and trembled briefly. He looked into his lap, not sure of what he saw. But he was sure that he did see something terribly frightening.

"Sleep, look at me. This is your friend Stoney talking. I know you feel the same way as I do, about what we're doing. I can see it in your eyes, that you haven't been getting much sleep either."

Sleeper raised his head partially, peeked at him from the top of his eyes. Stoney pushed himself further into the couch, then released a heavy sigh. He straightened out his ruffled shirt. "Sleeper, when I was eight years old, one of the kids in my neighborhood was kidnapped. I remember the whole town was searching for him for days, but no one could find him. Then they found his body a week later, down near a place called the Glass Pond." He stated timidly, "I didn't see his body myself, but they said he was naked. What shocked everyone further was that his hands, feet and head were missing. For months, my parents warned me to stay away from strangers, because of the terror that they knew was out there, lurking to find another child. They were overprotective for almost a year, and they wouldn't let me go anywhere by myself. I had horrible nightmares that scared the hell out of me, and my little sister had to sleep with my parents for months. She kept waking up in the middle of the night, screaming her head off, yelling that the monster was coming to get her." He paused, before he proclaimed, "Sleeper, in this case, we are the monster!" He sighed horrifically. "My parents made us stay right in the backyard that summer, so they'd know where we were. That one hideous incident turned our town and my family upside-down for a long time. My mother came to me crying one day, and told me that people who could strike fear into the hearts of innocent children are cold-blooded and ruthless. She said that they'll never have any peace of mind, or any satisfaction in life, because their spirits are damned. Their souls are shredded, and they're condemned to suffer a dreadful existence. I don't know about you two, but I'm feeling it all, and it's haunting the hell out of me. It follows me everywhere, even in my dreams. And when I'm asleep, I think about some of the things that we've been doing, and I know it's not right. When I think about the pretentious child molester, who we put out there, I don't feel so hot. In fact, I feel like shit, because I know that we're the ones responsible for traumatizing innocent children. In my sleep, I see the frightened tear filled eyes of many faceless children who believe that there's someone out there, who's after them. Someone who's gonna take them away from their family, and do monstrous things to them. And I see them running away from this monstrous person, toward us, the ones who're supposed to be protecting them against lunatics like that. But since we put the threat out there, which is something real, it's in the hearts of the children. I feel like they're running straight into the arms of the threat. Which in this case, is us … the real sick perverted lunatics. I can deal with the Johns who've been arrested for solicitation of prostitution, the drug dealers, or even the killers, because we're teaching them a costly lesson. They're adults, and they deserved to be played. We're trailing from what they initiated. But the children, that's something different altogether. They're being victimized by us." Stoney stopped to catch his breath. "And when I'm awake, I see their eyes mirrored in the objects that I've brought, with the money that we've made from hustling the marks. They're not the eyes of the drug dealers, the killers, the johns, or any of the other adults. They're the eyes of the frightened children, and they won't leave me alone. The more I think about it, the more it collects into a big hideous something that taunts the hell out of me." He rose from the couch shakily, then walked unsteadily to the doorway leading into the room. He shouted, "Carlton, can you fix some coffee for us?" He turned around, propped himself against the doorjamb, then continued, "Ya kno, guys. We're cops." He approached Sleeper. "We may have the upper hand on the streets, and we may be able to get away with things that civilians only dream of doing. But we can't loose sight of something that keeps us on the same level as everyone else out there. That is the fact that we're just as human as anyone else. We wear badges and took an oath to serve and protect, but we're still subject to human emotions. We bleed, cry, hurt, and can be hurt. We have feelings just like everyone else, with minds that can only take but so much pressure."

He paused to catch his breath, then continued with, "When I awake, with no matter how comfortable I'm living, surrounded by all these luxuries, I feel like I've been sleeping in a filthy dumpster. Surrounded by all the disgust that I've allowed into my life. You guys know I'm not religious, but I'm getting a damn good idea of what hell is like. All I can say is it ain't a pretty picture."

Feeling an iota of shame, Spanky looked into the fireplace, knowing that he gave a truthful testimony. He sucked his teeth sarcastically, which prompted Stoney to lean toward him and declare solemnly, "For God sake, Spanky, my fucken cup is filled! Sometimes I can feel myself bursting at the seams. I-I-I gotta cool out for a little while. I need to get away from this madness. And that's exactly what it is, madness. Sheer madness. Only a person with no soul can go untouched. And Spanky, that ain't me. I simply can't do it."

Feeling his weighty insinuations, Spanky asked, "Hey, what do ya want from me?" He climbed to his feet, then stumbled around the room, clutching his heart, pretending to be in a painful distress. He cried facetiously, "Oh! Oh my heart. My fucken bleeding heart. It hurts so bad." He dropped the act, approached Stoney and drooled, "Boo ... fucken ... hoo!" He looked at Sleeper. "You believe the sack of shit he's handing us?" He eyed Stoney. "You think some childhood sob story about a psychotic pervert who thinks he's in diddler heaven is supposed to make me feel any different about the whole situation." He fanned Stoney off. "Man! Fuck that shit. But I'll tell you one thing, buddy boy. If our forefathers thought like that, you know, afraid to take the initiative to get paid from being a little assertive, or even aggressive, then we'd probably be slaves, living in huts, still using clubs, bows and arrows." He paused. "Man! I don't believe the soft shit he's pewking up on us. In this day in age, it's take, or be taken. That's the way it goes. That's the way it's always been. You can't play fair and expect to get on top. It wouldn't work. Because chances are, the guy on top is playing by a whole different set of rules. Possibly ones that he created for himself. If our government wasn't so manipulative, then just like Russia and a few other places, we'd probably be standing in a food line right about now, fighting for a piece of stale bread to take home to our starving families." He threw his hands to the air. "This is ridiculous! I give up. I don't want to listen to any more of this sad crap. I got things to do." He marched to the doorway, military style, as if still in training at the police academy. Just past the entrance to the living room, he turned and huffed, "Sleep, you coming?"

"Yeah. I'll be there in a second."

"Make it quick," he said, walking away. Voice fading, he griped, "Damn whoosp!" He mumbled to himself, "Ya start something like this, ya gotta stick by it. Ya can't let some figment of ya imagination start talking all that conscious crap. Ya gotta be strong, like me."

After he left, the room remained filled with his exasperating aura. It was as hot as a sauna.

"I understand what you're talking about," Sleeper told Stoney. "But, right now, it doesn't bother me as much anymore. Especially when I compare it to a lot of the things Spanky says. And he's right about it being a dog-eat-dog world out there. Ya gotta fight for the bone. Nobody's gonna give us the breaks we need to get on top. Sometimes ya gotta make ya own breaks."

"Yeah, well, maybe he's right … in some aspects. But do you ever stop to think that maybe you should be thinking about yourself, and your family, instead of listening to his glamorous lectures fueled by greed. One of the two you're going to have to live with for the rest of you life. Take your pick."

Sleeper looked deeply into his eyes, smiled weakly. "I see. I see." He said nothing else, because he knew it was difficult to argue with the final word. The truth. After a long silence. "Stoney, you take care of yourself. I know you won't let us down. And don't worry about Spanky. He's just popping off a little steam. You know how he gets from time to time."

Stoney placed his hand on his shoulder, sighed. "Yeah, I know. For now, go catch up to Spanks. Before he starts accusing you of conspiring against him."

Both forced weak smiles.

Sleeper rose from the couch, then walked to the room's entrance. Not looking back, he stated, "Take care, buddy!"

"Yeah. You too, Sleep."

Stoney delivered a word of caution. "Sleep! One more thing."

He stopped in his tracks. Didn't turn to face Stoney. "Yeah."

"Watch your back. I think you know what I mean."

He knew that he was referring to Spanky. He placed the note at the back of his mind, said nothing, continued leaving.

Seconds later, Carlton entered the living room. He carried a serving tray stacked with a few cups, saucers, a creamer, a sterling silver sugar bowl and coffee pot. "Sir, your guests are not returning?"

Stoney stared into the fireplace. "No, Carlton. My guests are not returning. At least, not any time soon. You can take the rest of the day off, if you'd like."

"Thank you, sir." He left the room and went to the kitchen, thinking along the way. Chucks! I wanted Spanky to sample some of my special blend. A combination of toilet bowl water, spit, topped with a dash of urine. He would've loved it, and probably begged for a second cup.

In the living room, Stoney wondered acutely about the conversation that he just had with Spanky and Sleeper, and became more depressed. He grabbed the bottle of scotch, raised it to his lips and took several hearty swallows.

In the back of the house, Sleeper had just gotten into the car. Spanky asked him, "It's about time. What were you two lovers in there doing? Crying over each others shoulders, swapping spit?"

Sleeper gazed awkwardly at him, stated earnestly, "Sure, Spanks. Whatever."

Not wanting to mix words, Spanky felt it imperative to get down to business. "Did you get a chance to put the bug in the phone?"

"I ... um ... I forgot." He lied. He wasn't about to turn dirty on his long-time friend.

"I had a feeling you would. That's why I did it on the way to the bathroom." He turned on the engine, put the car in gear and drove away, complaining, "If you want something done right, you have to do it yourself."

Not wanting to admit, he'd been having a reoccurring nightmare as well. He never said anything about it because he wasn't sure if it was a nightmare. Actually, he wasn't *aware* that it was a nightmare. Considered it *only* a weird dream. One that frightened him so much that he often woke up with a heightened exhilaration flooding his heart. It thrilled him so much at times that he preferred to return to sleep to continue the experience. He enjoyed the challenge, a race to the finish line

It always began the same way, him jumping into his '69' Stang, heading out in the wee hours for a fun cruise on a stretch of highway. He figured two a.m. a favorable time because the road was entirely deserted. He had it all to himself. Only tractor trailers rumbled by occasionally, on their way to and fro.

At the on ramp, as he was about to pass a hitchhiker—a middle aged Caucasian man dressed in fatigues, carrying a small duffle bag—he slowed the car to a stop. The man looked into the passenger side of the car, smiled exuberantly and asked, "Hidey hidey ho ho! Going my way?"

Spanky studied the man, contemplated the question. Figured him to be a war vet, seeing him fitted with two prosthetic arms. He assumed his arms might've been blown off by a grenade, a bouncing betty, or a land mine. Or maybe it was a mortar attack. Feeling a twinge of compassion, he replied, "Yeah. Sure. I could do that. Hop in, pal." He leaned over, pulled a lever and pushed the door ajar.

The man jumped inside, closed the door shut. "Thanks for stopping, son. This time of night, there's no telling how long I would've been waiting for a ride."

Spanky nodded, began to drive. "Just getting off work?"

"Yeah. Been a long day." He studied the interior of the car. "Nice ride ya got here." He inhaled deeply. "Smells brand new. Like you just got it from off the lot."

Spanky patted the dashboard. "This is a mint condition '69' Ford, Mustang. Slightly modified. I restored it myself. I modified it myself. You take care of your car, and it'll take care of you. By the way, I'm Robert."

"They call me Jake. I'm a butcher. I sell meats."

"Well, Jake the butcher, where are you on your way to?"

"No where in particular. I just needed a ride. That's all."

Spanky laughed. "Now, let me get this straight. You need a ride, but you're not going anywhere in particular?"

The stranger eyed Spanky. Told him plainly, "That's right."

Spanky chuckled. "All right. Whatever floats your boat, amigo."

"I don't sail boats, and I'm not your friend," the man stated gravely. "I sell meats. I make no qualms as to what I do for a living. I'm a butcher."

Feeling the intensity of his words, Spanky joshed, "All right already. Lighten up. I don't really care what you do."

"Or do you?"

Spanky stared at him for a moment, figured him a little touched. He did a little probing. "Anyway. I find it hard to believe that you're a butcher who's just gotten off from work. Most butcher shops close at five o'clock … p.m."

"Goes to show what you know." As if an actor in a banking commercial, he stated, "I'm not your typical butcher."

"How're you any different?"

"Spanky, trust me on this. I'm different."

Spanky paused, slightly confused. "Hey! How'd you know my nickname?"

"I know a lot about you, Spankster."

"What are you, clairvoyant or something?"

"Or something." Jake looked at the road ahead. "Hey! How fast does this thing go?"

Spanky floored the accelerator, put the peddle to the metal. The sudden increase in speed rammed them into their seats. "Let me show you what she can do."

"All right!" Jake cheered. "I'm down for a little joy ride." As Spanky brought the car close to one hundred miles per hour, Jake became thrilled. "Whoa! We're moving now." He reached into the duffle bag, yanked hard on something, and they heard a chicken scream. He withdrew a freshly plucked chicken leg, feathers still intact, blood dripping onto his lap. "This kind of excitement gets me hungry. You want a bite?"

"Hey!" he alarmed. "You're getting that shit all over the interior of my car. I just had the damned thing detailed yesterday." He eyed the chicken leg bizarrely, eyed Jake, then discovered that his facial features had changed considerably. He had grown several shades darker, his teeth grew menacingly larger. "How can you eat something like that? It's not even cooked."

"That's a matter of preference. Com'om! One bite, and you'll never stop … eating."

"Hell no! That's horrible."

"Shut up!" Jake returned sternly, started eating the chicken leg. "Don't look at me. Pay attention to the road. Go faster!"

Spanky eyed the speedometer, discovered them approaching one hundred and fifty miles per hour. "Hot damn! We're flying!"

"Go faster!" Jake muffled through the food packed in his mouth. He reached into the duffle bag, pulled out the rest of the chicken, began eating. Flapping its wings frantically, the dying chicken spat a few last bakaks, feathers floated liberally in the cars compartment.

Spanky turned his head slightly and became engrossed at what he witnessed. He discovered that Jake had changed into something hideous, an especially ugly demon. Not responding verbally to the transformation, since he was having so much fun watching the scenery whiz by, he stated only, "Aw man! That's really disgusting."

"Shut up, dickweed! Go faster!"

Spanky focused on the road, eyed the speedometer briefly. To his amazement, he discovered them approaching two hundred miles per hour. As if driving a formula racer, he spouted, "Wow! I don't believe this shit. We're almost airborne. I didn't even know this car could go that fast." Unexpectedly, and weirdly, a cow tail swiped his right side a few times. He heard lips smacking, teeth tearing into flesh and bone. Through his peripheral vision, he discovered Jake gnawing away at a side of beef. The cowhide still intact, blood and fat dressed the passenger side of the car. He exploded, "What'n the hell are you doing?"

"Shut up, ya dumb fuck!" Jake shouted. "Go faster!"

Spanky eyed the speedometer again and realized that they were moving at mach one; the speed of sound. Becoming extremely unnerved, he stomped the break peddle frantically with both feet, but the car only succeeded in going faster and faster. They were moving so fast that the passing scenery had become an indiscernible blur. Streetlamps whizzing by appeared as fifty yard long streaks of light, as if traveling at warp speed. Soon, he began to feel that something was grossly wrong, and the stimulation grew from what was exciting, to what was chilling. From what was chilling, to what was terrifying. He finally understood that what was happening was utterly impossible and began to feel misplaced. He felt as though they were going to crash and burn to cinders, and the terrifying feelings swelled twice fold. When he could take it no longer, he released a scream from the pit of his gut, swam amidst a turbulent storm and roused himself from the nightmare.

He sat up in bed, sweating profusely, out of breath, half cognizant, with Spike staring inquisitively, wondering what in the hell was going on. He wiped his brow, returned to sleep, mumbling, "Next time, I'll show that son-of-a-bitch that I can go twice as fast. I'll clean all that shit out my car tomorrow morning."

CHAPTER 12

▼

Halfway to Boston, both remained quiet. Not a word had been spoken since they had left Stoneys mansion. The loud silence made Spanky feel uncomfortable, and he became restless. Felt he needed to say something for a needling subconscious. Felt he had to justify the verbal abuse that he had administered to Stoney.

They arrived at a clearing stretching for miles on route 128, then he pulled to the shoulder of the road and turned off the ignition. He then said nothing, only stared straight ahead.

"What's wrong," Sleeper asked.

"Nothing. I just wanted to talk to you for a minute. That's all."

"About what?"

He threw in a lengthy hesitation before replying, "Let's get out of the car for a moment. Get some fresh air."

Sleeper spanned the area and saw nothing for miles. Only a scenic green landscape fading off into some blue mountains miles away, and a few motorists sped by regularly. "Spanky, we're out in the middle of nowhere. Why's it so important that you needed to talk at this particular spot?" The warning that Stoney had given him less than a half an hour ago came to mind and showered him with a ton of uneasiness.

"Because I wanted to show you something that's out here, and not in the city."

He got out of the car, then came around to the passenger side. He waved to Sleeper, still sitting in the car, unflinching, wondering apprehensively. "What're ya waiting for? Com'on."

Sleeper stared at him for a moment longer. Looked him up and down, trying to figure him out. He got out of the car and closed the door. Standing next to each other, they were startled when they heard some brushes stirring about fifty feet behind them. They quickly turned to notice a mother raccoon being trailed by three of her babies, probably on a forage expedition.

"Ya know, Sleep," he said, "it's like Stoney said. We're only human beings. Not that that means anything special. We're just another breed of animal. And sometimes, from taking into account some of the atrocious things that some humans do, I get the notion that some of us are no smarter than some animals. Ya gotta admit that we're not exactly the brightest of the food group. Animals kill when they're hungry, and rarely for sport. Man is just about the only breed that kills when his livelihood is threatened. We also do things like kill for future preference, perhaps to secure foreign oil fields. We do it with nuclear bombs, toxic chemicals, and all that other nasty shit, neglecting innocent bystanders; women, children and nature. I guess, what I'm trying to say is that, well, this is life, survival of the fittest and …"

Sleeper interrupted. "I don't need a history lesson to understand how I feel. How come you talked to Stoney like that, like he was some trash from the street? A typical criminal! That was some icy shit you laid on him back there. We've been hanging out for … for about fourteen years now. Doesn't that mean anything to you? Don't you care about the man at all?"

"Somewhat, I guess. Through my experience, all my fourteen years of friendship with anyone isn't going to put food on my table, keep me clothed, pay my bills, or secure my or my future children's future." He paused. "I was trying to give him some tough love. You know, that shit they throw at teenagers nowadays. I don't know about you, but I felt it did him some good. I smacked him in the face with the hard bricks of reality. Either I take a stab at it, or his future *inmates* will."

Sleeper didn't say anything, only stared reflectively at a few cars speeding by. A black Peterbilt eighteen wheeler cruised by, flooding the area briefly with the heavy rumble of it monstrous diesel engine. One of the huge tires snatched up a pebble with its knobby tread and flung it into the air. After it pinged into the left side of Spankys car, near the left quarter panel, he leered at the truck and cursed, "What the hell?" He ran to where he thought the pebble had made contact and inspected the area for a scratch." I should chase that son-of-a-bitch down and make him pay for that."

"Never mind him. Lets finish this up, so we can get out of here."

Spanky approached Sleeper, changed the subject altogether. "Hey, remember when we were in high school? Remember what I looked like? I had all the height in the world, but I was so skinny that everybody called me Goober. They use to laugh at me all the time, but not to my face. Sometimes when I walked down the hallway, I'd hear their whispered cackling, especially in the cafeteria. In gym class, when we wore those skimpy little shorts that revealed my legs, they use to call me beanpole. Or string bean. Luckily for me I filled out quickly the summer after graduation." He paused. "When they treated me like that, I understood that that's just the way some people are—they're just natural born haters. And because I wasn't that bright, I wasn't a rocket scientist, they voted me least likely to succeed at anything." He took a deep breath, then continued on a note of contentment. "If it wasn't for you, the Stoneman and a few others on the football team treating me normal, I would've developed a complex problem. And see, since I know that situations and people can change, I vowed to make everything in my life better, after we graduated. Remember that tenth year reunion we went to?"

"Yeah." He smiled. "That was pretty nice, seeing how everyone's life has changed. Finding out about what they've been up to."

"Yeah. Right. Wasn't that something? Remember how you, me and the Stoneman walked in there wearing one thousand dollar Italian cut suits? Man! They really stood up and took note then, didn't they? Remember that girl I use to be head over heels in love with, ah ..." he snapped his fingers a couple of times, "... Rebecca. Rebecca Dunne."

"I remember her," Sleeper replied. "She was kind of stuck up back then. Wore too much make-up for my liking. She was a cheerleader, and the best looking one too. Well, behind the girl who Stoney use to mess around with."

"She use to snub me all the time, hold her nose up at me damn near every time I tried to talk to her. As if she was better than me. That shit really ate me up back then. You know how tough on a person that teen peer pressure can be." He paused. "But at the reunion, when she saw how much I've changed, her eyes nearly popped out of their sockets. She came at me full force, and I let her. We had a few drinks, a few laughs, then I took her home and screwed her silly." He laughed, "Afterwards, while she was still naked, I dragged her out of my apartment, out into the hallway. I took a five dollar bill, crumpled it, then threw it on the floor. Then I told the heffa to go catch a cab." Both laughed. "And you remember those guys that jumped you? Remember when two of them showed up to hang around the reunion?"

A grand smile swallowed Sleepers face. "Oh yeah. I definitely remember those poor slobs. I especially like the part when we gave them a strip search right out there at that busy intersection. That was some serious payback."

"You damn straight it was. That was one of the best days of my life. I'll never forget it. That night, I felt like I had total control over the situation ... power. It felt great. Now that's what I'm talking about, Sleep. Power! Raw, naked power. There's nothing in the world greater than that. Let me ask you one thing, then we can get out of here."

"Sure. What's that?"

"You ever been up in an airplane?"

"Sure, and you already know that. I was in one last month, when I went to the Bahamas, remember?"

"I remember. And did you have a window seat?"

Sleeper nodded. "I like looking down on the clouds and everything. The cars and buildings look like toys. The people look like ants."

"Isn't it nice up there?"

"It's very quiet, serene. Sometimes I wish I could stay up there, just to get away from it all."

"Sleep, what do you think about when you're up there? What goes through your mind?"

"I just told you. It's nice and peaceful, probably like the place called heaven I hear some Christians talk about."

"That's it?"

"Well, yeah. There's nothing else up there."

"Well, let me tell you something else that's up there. Something that only people with prophetic vision can see." He pointed to the sky. "Up there is where it's all at. For some, being up there has inspired them to accomplish great feats. For others, it makes them understand why some people do what they have to do, to stay on top. Either you do what you have to do to make others conform to your wishes, or someone else will do what they want, to have you conform to theirs. Nothing personal, it's only business. Isn't that the way the system works? The necessity of conformity is one of the main reasons why we must maintain control over the mass media, and the general public, collectively. Life is a lengthy conditioning process. In this country, the powers that be have conditioned most people, through our history books and the media, to believe that it would be to their advantage to be culturally Caucasian. Hey, truth is truth. The history books are filled with situations that make us look good, even if we might've screwed up royally. To condition children, they even have cartoons on television that make people like Benedict Arnold look good. And I thought he was supposed to be some kind of a national traitor. Through our court system, and in our profession, we see everyday that minorities get more prison time when they commit crimes against Caucasians. This conditions them too have less regard for their own people; other minorities, knowing that they'll get a lesser penalty. The media generally downplays their race, makes them feel like they're not worth much. There's even a discrimination between light and dark skinned people. Now, how silly is that? Most people in America believe that the more fair your complexion, the more doors in America will be opened to you. Other truths of conditioning are the facts that many foreigners take on American names after they enter the country. They fade from their own culture. And they work hard to learn to speak English fluently, loose their native tongue. At least, the ones who want to be successful. I'm sure you know some people who've done this." He looked Sleeper up and down, sized him up. "And then again, you probably know plenty of them. Like Michael Jackson, many people go to plastic surgeons to have their faces altered; maybe streamline their nose. Meanwhile, they suppress some of the reasons why they had it done in the first place. Most will only say it's to enhance their beauty. But in all reality, what people are they simulating? Face it, Sleep. The worst thing that you can do is lie to yourself."

"But, some of our people wear dreadlocks. Some of our women go to plastic surgeons to have their lips injected with collagen. They want bigger asses; a sexy round mound."

"I can't explain their confusion. How do I feel about all of this? It doesn't bother me one bit. I don't have the time to think about it. In our chosen line of profession, I've meet *all* types. I've learned that there's good and bad in every pot. As far as people wanting to be of another ethnicity, race mixing and mingling, that's where all of these new fruits are coming from. I've heard some people explain that their mother was Indian, their father was Polish, their grandmother Chinese, their grandmother Indian. Their great-grandmother Black, and their great-grandfather Irish. The only thing I'm curious about is what they put on their job applications. I know blacks who prefer to be white, and whites who prefer to be black. Or Chinese who prefer to be Japanese, and vice versa. That's just the way life is. Either you accept it, or put one more thing on your list to find fault with. Life's already difficult in itself, without going around looking for problems. Pretty soon, there's going to be such a huge diversity of people in America, that no ones even going to care about things like racism and discrimination anymore. Of course, unless your stuck in the past, bound to repeat it—people not moving forward." Without hesitation, he turned from Sleeper and walked to the driver's side of the car, said along the way, "The next time you're up there, close your eyes and search your heart with your greatest desires. You'll be surprised at what you'll come up with." He pointed to the sky once again. "Sleep, it's all up there."

Feeling he made his point, he opened the car door and got in, while keeping an eye on Sleepers face. He searched for an expression that read, 'My God! It all makes perfectly good sense to me now. He's cleared up any problems I've ever had with trying to understand everything that's going on in life. Spanky is an absolute philosophical genius when it comes to proving theory. He knows everything! Einstein ain't got a damn thing on him. He can put L. Ron Hubbard of Dianetics to shame and out of business.

Meanwhile, what he actually thought was, the smart ass makes a descent point. From time to time he comes up with undisputable statements to back his shitty arguments. But that's okay. What comes around, goes around. One day, I'm going to shove his brought and paid for wisdom straight up his ass. As soon as I find something clever to say.

He opened the car door and got inside. He closed it, then glanced at Spanky, but didn't reflect despising his smug disposition. He stated, "I guess I can understand most of what you said, although you dodged my original question." Spanky didn't say anything, but his expression did read, 'Oh, you're still on that?' Sleeper asked, "How can you take fourteen years of an unblemished friendship, and step on it, as though it were a cockroach." He paused. "Out of everything you've said so far, you've only told me one thing I needed to know. If I started experiencing any difficulties, even if it's through no fault of my own, the first thing that I should be worried about ..." he looked him square in the face, "... is you."

Spankys eyes widened, totally surprised at what he heard. He felt profoundly insulted, but only stated, "Oh yeah?"

"Yeah. Furthermore, last week sometime when I ate at this Chinese restaurant, I read something written on a napkin that was given to me. It was something to the effect of 'He who fights solely to put himself high on a pedestal above all other men, can no longer see eye to eye with anyone. He's very brave, but unforgiving and paranoid. To maintain his position, he must sleep with one eye open.'" He paused when he finished reciting, then asked, "What do you have to say about that?"

Without hesitation, he replied, "I say, as long as you watch your back and cover your ass, you won't have to worry about any of that confusing 'Confucius say' bullshit."

Sleeper declared, "Mr. Robert, Spanky, high-an-mighty Sinclair, you have an answer for everything. Don't you?"

He smiled narcissistically. "Hey. What can I say? Some of us got it like that. Besides, if I didn't have an answer for whatever the problem, then it would be time to worry."

Most of the time he was convinced of his own superiority. Every morning before he leaves his apartment, he glances into the bathroom mirror and declares conceitedly, 'Kid, you've got the world by the kahoonas, and balls the size of Dallas, Texas. I'm proud of you, boy.'

Driving away, Sleeper had but one thought in mind. 'Smart ass!' He didn't have the correct words to debate with him, but he did have the common sense to know that there was something entirely wrong with his self-righteous logic; his conceited way of thinking. He was sure that if, per chance, he ever got hold a few intellectual words to debate with him, he'd grab each one by the gills and shove them straight up his ass.

CHAPTER 13

▼

Wednesday morning rimmed its daylight on Stoneys windowsill with a brisk chill. Or was it the shakes? There was always something about the morning that he found to be quite fascinating; the freshness of it. The way it happened, day after day. He believed it was a time for redemption, having another chance to accomplish today, what you didn't the yesterday. It didn't exactly make him feel like dancing around the house in his boxer shorts while singing delightfully, as if he was Luciano Pavarotti. It was merely something that he thought about, the first good feeling of the day. Probably because the troubles of living haven't begun yet. The brain hasn't loaded all the bullshit from the day before.

Another conundrum, who has the most important job in the world? Perhaps the insignificant and unknown city worker who paints the yellow traffic-lane stripes down the middle of the road. An irrelevant thought? Nevertheless, critically essential to all drivers and their passengers.

Since he didn't drown himself in alcohol the night before, the morning felt strangely unfamiliar. The air didn't scratch his dry throat and crack his tight skin, or seem substantially thick. The singing of the birds didn't torture his hearing until his lobes folded and stuffed themselves into the openings. The reinvigorating sunlight didn't horn its way through the Venetian blinds like a wooden stake through the heart of a vampire. His nerves didn't twitch from the alcohol leaving its calling card. And lastly, his vision was crystal clear.

This morning, the soft rays of sunlight creamed in like melted butter. Parkay, of course. He sat upright and realized that he didn't need to lean back or collapse against the headboard, because his sense of balance worked perfectly.

His eyes opened with ease, like well-oiled machinery. Unlike yesterday, he had to use his fingers to assist the left eye, because it was sealed shut for the sleep crust. The mucus was smeared on so thick over both eye lids, that it looked like a wad of that oozing green toxic stuff that some toy manufacturers have the audacity to sell to children as some sort of refined play dough.

While in his pre-teens, he was afraid to touch his eyes every time this phenomenon occurred. Fearing something infectious might spread to other areas of his body. He feared that if it got into his eyes, it would cause temporary blindness. Those old childhood myths; your inny or outty navel decided if you were going to heaven or hell, and you can't get pregnant the first time you have sex.

This morning was so beautiful that he thought he had died and gone to heaven. For once, he believed the place really did exist. That urge to lay back down and pull the covers over his head wasn't there. That dry mouth, leather tongue and fatigued body from the lack of insufficient sleep, wasn't there. Most of all, that intolerable wretched cluster headache, wasn't there. That earth shattering, kitty cat stomping across the floor, quarter stick of dynamite blasting, late in the evening kids upstairs bouncing around on the floor with no parents at home to supervise them, next door neighbors dog barking incessantly till the wee hours in the morning, continued with the early morning jack hammering migraine, wasn't there.

Because he's suffered these problems for nearly a half a year, this morning seemed foreign. He felt alienated, but not homesick. He had gotten use to getting up late for work, stumbling around in a belated stupor for the lingering effects of the alcohol, his eyes cracked open and out of focus. He dressed in the dark, with the shades drawn for fear of the dreaded sunlight. Sometimes he collapsed at least three or four times or banged a limb or his head into something on the way to the bathroom.

Before he left the house in the morning, sunglasses and a large brimmed hat were essential parts of his wardrobe. Even with showering himself with the strongest smelling cologne, when he arrived at work, just about everyone noticed the irrepressible residue of scotch or whiskey reeking through his pores.

Ironically, he believed that there was something wrong with being allowed to feel this good about himself, and he felt guilty. As though he was granted too much of what he's wrongfully taken, pleasure. He believed that there was a limit to how much a person could get away with, and his subconscious reminded him that he was well past that boundary.

He climbed out of bed and went to the bathroom. Normally he'd glance into the mirror over the sink, to find someone who he didn't recognize staring back through bloodshot eyes. He wondered depressingly at the circular cobweb design on his face—reflected from the cracked glass—then mumbled frustratingly, "Damn! The only mirror I didn't break was Carltons. I gotta go out and get an unbreakable one someday. Maybe a sheet of highly polished stainless steel."

After taking a piss, he washed his hands and returned to the bedroom. He went to the full length sliding windows parallel to and ten feet away from the right side of his bed, then slid the right side open. A gentle breeze from the north entered the room and masked his body. He inhaled deeply to capture a breath of morning air, and a feeling of rejuvenation swallowed him entirely. Feeling good, he yawned and stretched his arms upward, as far as he could.

He inhaled again and a hint of the ocean filled his nostrils, causing him to frequent a memory of some twenty years. He remembered the wonderful times when his father use to take him deep sea fishing on some Saturday mornings. He closed his eyes briefly, and an image of his father standing mightily at the helm of their twenty-foot motor boat settled comfortably in mind. His imagination pushed further and he heard the rumbling sound of the thirty horsepower Evenrude motor racing them to their preferred spot. He could almost feel the vibrations it sent throughout the boat. He could just barely smell a hint of the unleaded gas it burned, and feel the boat rise and fall against the waves, sending a fine mist spraying into his face. Fishing with his best friend, his father.

He wondered how he could spend his time today, and a few ideas entered his mind. Nothing too flamboyant. Some activity that can help him relax, alleviate some stress he knew he suffered. Something that he could do, that he hoped was far away from any kind of glass, mirrors or anything that could cast a reflection.

A comfortable smile creased his lips.

Cast. Casting. Fishing!

He decided he'd go deep-sea fishing. The excitement raced through his veins exuberantly, and he couldn't wait to begin reeling in the big ones.

CHAPTER 14

▼

Stoney had Carlton retrieve his fishing gear from the basement, a place that he hadn't ventured to in months. If he had retrieved the equipment himself, the search would've taken up the better part of the morning.

Within the hour he was on the road, traveling to Hyannis Port in Cape Cod, leaving his troubles behind. Temporarily. So he thought. So he hoped. So he prayed.

He dressed casual; blue jeans, a white tee shirt, black leather jacket, white high-top Nike basketball sneakers. Topping it off, for his eccentric quality, he wore a brown Rex Harrington hat. He drove his black 2002 customized Ford pickup truck, because he didn't want the smell of the fish to get into the interior of his freshly detailed Porsche.

An hour and a half later, he had arrived at the docks at Hyannis Port in Cape Cod. He became highly enthused when he saw hundreds of fishermen waiting to board their charter boats, and dozens of fishing ships docked at several piers. He found a parking spot easily, only a few hundred feet from the charter boat section. He grabbed his rod, tackle box, then waited near the docks to board a sixty-five foot charter boat that sailed for ten hour fishing trips. It has all of the latest high-tech gadgetry for finding fish, and nearly all of the home away from home conveniences, and a few luxuries. The rear of the boat was stenciled in big block letters 'THE VOYAGER.'

He didn't know anyone on the boat, but he made friends easily. Besides himself, there were forty two other fishermen going along on the trip. Excluding the Capt., there was his wife and two sons—who were the deck hands—six females and twenty-five males. Some of the passengers brought their children to continue traditions and pass legacies that their parents passed on to them.

Waiting to board the ship, he observed the other fishermen mingling among themselves, and glanced occasionally at the route the ship would take to leave port. Noticing the children standing next to their parents, he couldn't help but to frequent the warm memories that he had earlier that morning of fishing with his father. An obvious first timer, a six-year-old boy asked his father, "Hey dad. Am I gonna catch a whale today?"

The man looked at his son amusedly. "I hope note. I don't think we have enough room in the freezer for something as big as that."

"How bout a shark?"

"Son, out there, anything's possible. But today, I think we'll settle for something much smaller. That way we won't have any problems putting it in the car, and taking it home."

"Okay dad. I'll see what I can do."

The father rubbed his sons head and smiled. "That's my boy."

Suddenly, the Capt.'s voice boomed over the public address system on The Voyager, and filled the immediate area with a much anticipated announcement for all awaiting fishermen to hear. "All fishermen waiting to board The Voyager for charter can do so at the rear of the ship. After which, we'll be pulling out to sea immediately. Watch your step when boarding, and check to make sure that you have all of your equipment."

Boarded the ship, Stoney bumped into a seemingly twenty-five year old slender man that he mistook for someone he thought he knew. Possibly a perp that he had arrested not to long ago.

The man appeared the Don Juan player type, fit the bill of a full fledged ladies man. He was dressed like a city slicker/cowboy; a black Harley Davidson tee shirt, and skin tight blue jeans with a colorful rodeo trophy belt buckle filling his mid-section. He wore a black leather vest, a pair of rattlesnake skin boots, and was capped with a black Garth Brooks five gallon Stetson. His fifteen inch ponytail hung to the middle of his back, and he favored an aging actor named Sam Elliot. To complete the picture, his arms were inked from his wrists to elbows with black gothic tattoos. A skeletal grim reaper on the left, and on the right, Mickey Mouse posing as Merlin the Wizard, donning a cloak and cone hat. The combination clashed, probably his intent.

It was difficult for Stoney to make a positive identification because he wore dark aviator shades, and had a thick black moustache cloaking his entire mouth. He had a six o'clock shadow tanning the lower half of his face, and chewed on a toothpick—he whipped it around in his mouth vigorously, as though it were chewing gum. As he walked past, Stoney took considerable note of his stature, then glanced at his face. He attempted to place various sets of eyes on top of the dark shades, hoping that something would come to light.

It didn't work, so he dropped the thought of attempting to place him. Cop habits. Once he thought he recognized someone, he stayed on it until he was sure that he knew who the person was. Since there weren't too many places one could hide on a small ship, he figured that he could afford to put it off for now. Besides, Capt. Winslow took his shield and gun, making it difficult for him to arrest someone. What 's more important, he was out of his jurisdiction. He would've had to call to the local authorities and report it to them, drop the ball in their court. Since he wasn't sure of who the man was anyway, why go through all of that trouble for nothing?

After rolling the situation into a ball of jumbled complications, he put it out of his mind, fearing the complicity of the pursuit and capture, getting involved.

Feeling his stare from a few feet away, the man turned and peered oddly at Stoney. This prompted him to say, "I'm sorry. For a minute there, I thought you were someone I knew. A guy from another fishing trip."

A lie. However, it was a polite excuse. One that some people use to rectify mistakes of that caliber. Nowadays, in situations like this, especially in bars, the average conversation is chalked with lies. They have their disadvantages and advantages, if you were good at it. And just who wasn't? On occasion, even the pope has tossed a few whoppers into the air.

"That's all right, pardner" the man said, spewing a thick Texas drawl. He whispered under his breath, "Tum tassey." He threw on the last two words in a combination laidback blues-hip-hop fashion. He lowered his head a notch, peeped in between the brim of his hat and over his shades. "No problem." He whispered, "Bum rummy."

As Stoney figured, the man had a language all his own. Most of the time, when he completes a sentence, he gives it a personal touch by throwing a few homemade words onto the end. That je-ne-sa-phwah touch.

Absolutely no one, especially his psychologist, knows where this language was derived. And he's the only one that can understand it. It's exclusive, and makes him feel unique, important. Knowing that he invented something that can be used on a daily basis, only by him. Mostly, he didn't care if anyone understood him.

In considering his accidental brush with Stoney, the man speculated, I hope he's not a homo. One tried to pick me up last week in Maine, at my cousin's barbeque. The nerve of that jerk, whistling at my ass cheeks. So what. I like to wear tight jeans. I like clothes that fit. Or was it my ponytail that attracted him to me. Anyway, I wish they wouldn't do shit like that. That's very uncomfortable for a man like me. I ain't got nothing against them kinda people, parades and all. I just wish they'd leave me the hell alone. I wonder if this guy's looking at my butt cheeks right now.

Stoney found a spot to sit down and rest for the forty mile ride out to sea. He gazed out over the water and thought attentively of Katherine, about how his feelings were changing for her. Little did he know, he was growing comfortable having her around, enjoyed having a warm body lying next to him while he slept. Understandably, a natural concern for his mortality grew with age, as he often wondered if something terrible might happen to him while he slept. He knew his chances of survival would be greater if there were someone near, watching guardedly. Carlton was in the same house, but he was six rooms away, on a completely different floor. Seemingly in another country, galaxies away.

As the ships huge diesel engines grumbled and churned, they cruised slowly out of the marina. He looked to the blue skies and produced a mental image of her against a nimbostratus cloud. He then closed his eyes in deep contemplation. Never before had he taken the time to think seriously about her intellectualism. It wasn't relevant to his everyday activities. At least, he didn't feel that it was. Strangely, after a half hour, he felt as though he didn't know her at all, and many questions came to mind. What was her favorite color, her favorite food? What kind of music did she enjoy listening to? What relaxed her? Did she enjoy walks in the park during a starry night under a half or full moon, or only on clear nights?

The next thought highlighted itself, florescent as if, made him blush. Specifically, what turned her on? When they made love, had sex, screwed, he knew she wasn't faking her orgasms. He believed that her innermost feelings, which sometimes induced her to tears, didn't lie. So he thought. With remembering how genuine the tears appeared to be, he felt satisfied with himself, and that particular question disappeared.

Twenty minutes later, a few miles from the marina, he heard the engines power increase. The vessel picked up speed, increased knots, and he found the sea air to be three times as potent to what he had sampled earlier that morning.

As the ship bounced over the waters, slipped ardently over the waves, he gazed out over the horizon and his mind drifted away, back to when his father use to take him out to sea on their family boat. The memories he envisioned became twice as clear, more vivid. It all came back to him, especially the odorous smell of the burned gasoline mixing with the salt water. It wasn't appealing, but it helped complete the picture. A warm picture, like the one on the cover of Earnest Hemmingway's 'The Old Man and the Sea.'

Fifteen minutes into his daydream, he was disturbed when a heavy-handed person tapped his shoulder. He opened his eyes and discovered the Sam Elliot look alike standing over him, the man who he had bumped into when he had boarded the ship. Rocking with the sway of the ship, he held onto the banister with one hand, and with his free hand, an unlit cigarette. As if it were lit, by habit, he flicked invisible ashes over the side. He eyed Stoneys fishing equipment enviously and asked, "Hey pardner, yawl gotta match. Tulley tulley?"

Stoney searched the pockets in his jacket, advising, "Those things'll kill ya."

"I know," the man smirked. "That's probably why I smoke'em. Tokem moken." Seconds later, he laughed. "Just kidding. Frib abadoo."

"I don't think I do." He moved the all out search from his jacket to his pants. "Sorry." He wondered, what in the hell was that tokem mokem stuff all about? I never heard a language like that before. And what did he mean by it? I hope it wasn't an insult. Damn foreigners.

When his complete search turned up nothing, the man said disappointedly, "That's all right. I'll get one from someone else." He looked at some of the other passengers. "I know somebody on this tin bucket's got a match."

Stoney said nothing, but nodded vaguely. He thought the man was going to walk away, but he didn't. He tucked the cigarette into his right vest pocket, then extended his hand. "They call me Mike. Rump-ton-doody!"

Considering the last few words, Stoney eyed the toothpick hanging from his lips briefly, then accepted his hand. "I'm Stoney." Holding his hand briefly, from habit, he felt the texture. He searched for calluses, which told him that he might've been a hard worker, possibly in construction. Soft hands meant that he was an office worker, or did very little manual labor. He glanced at the inside of his arm, searching for needle tracks. To his fingers, searching for dark yellow Mary Jane stains on the tips of his index finger and thumb. People found the weirdest places to shoot up nowadays, like in between their toes and their armpits. But what if he uses an alligator clip for roaches? After finding nothing that mattered, he dropped the idea of giving him a further examination.

Mike chucked playfully. "The Stoneman, ta the bone."

"That's what a few of my friends call me. Stoneman."

Mike pointed both hands at him. "Hey. It fits you, pardner." With feeling that it was okay, he took a seat about two feet away from Stoney. He leaned over the bow and marveled at the water as it whooshed by. "So, Stoneman, what brings ya out here today? Nip boogie."

"Just getting a little fresh air, unwinding."

"Yeah. Fishing is good therapy. I've been doing it all my life. Ma father use to take me out here when I was nuttin but a squirt. Knee-high to a jack rabbit."

"Me too. That's probably why I'm doing it today. Brings back good memories."

"To the good old days," Mike toasted. "They only give out a few of em. My old man's gone now," he looked up and smiled admiringly, "to that great old fishing spot in the sky. Teebok."

"I'm sorry to hear that."

"That's all right. I didn't get a chance to know him that well. I was only eight when he died of cancer."

After a long silence, Mike caught a detailed glimpse of his fishing equipment and grew incredibly excited. On a lost breath, he asked, "What kinda equipment ya got there? Dang-o-shit!"

There was no misunderstanding the last word. Stoney picked up his rod and handed it to Mike, rolled nonchalantly, "Just basic equipment. A triple dyno-flex Shakespeare rod, and a fifty bearing signature edition McHenry reel."

Mike examined its fine craftsmanship and became even more excited, ran his fingers over the mechanical intricacies, cherishing every detail. "Basic stuff my ass! I only see gear like this in them 'Fishing and Stream' magazines. And in my dreams. This is some top-o-the-line gear ya got here. Ya must be rich. Climaxico!"

"No. Not hardly. I got it as a gift, last Christmas. I have wealthy friends, that's all." He remembered that he had told someone else that he had won the equipment in a raffle. He had told so many lies in the past few years that he couldn't remember who he told what to. The excuses seemed a blur of deceitful webs.

"Boy, I wish I had friends like that. If I did, I probably wouldn't have to bust my ass tryinta make a living," twisting his lips cagily, he finished, "doin what I gotta do." When commenting about his livelihood, he abstained from using his homegrown language. He left it alone, keeping it serious. Holding the rod and reel combination as if it were a precious newborn, he continued examining it, and then finally sighed in exhilaration. "Yeah boy! Ya got a winner right here. Ya stick this baby in the water, an the fish'll line up ta jump on the hook. Van-a-ding, pop doodly bash!"

As if it were a fragile piece of crystal, he handed it back to Stoney with both hands, cautious not to drop it. He declared, "That's real nice, whatchu got there." He nodded in anticipation. "One day, when my cash is right, I'm gonna get one just like it. You'll see."

Since the ice was broken. "What did you say you do for a living?"

Mike looked out over the water, then back at him with the most peculiar expression. He had a story-telling look in his eyes. Being a cop, Stoney had seen it plenty of times before. People fabricating alibis, telling the most unbelievable stories to elude capture. Or to stop the authorities from interfering with their unlawful ventures. As though police officers were judges, ready to pronounce sentence and send them to prison. That look was definitely there, in his eyes. There was no mistake about it.

Strangely, though, in this case, Stoney wanted to listen objectively. He realized that what this man was probably going to tell him, might be nothing compared to what he's been up to. The pot calling the kettle black. Besides, he had time to listen. Until the ship reached its first destination, he wasn't going to be doing anything else. Also, he figured that it might take his mind off of his personal problems.

Mike sat back on the bench, just as he did. He removed his cowboy hat and placed it in his lap. He brushed his hair with his free hand, then returned the hat to his head. Obviously a stall tactic, while he conjured an explanation. When he thought he had his story straight, he enlightened Stoney. It was his turn to sound unsure of himself. "I'm in computers."

Stoney considered the thought, and figured that he didn't look like a technician, or a geek. "You sell them, work on them? What?"

Mike contemplated the way he questioned him, sensed that there was something distrustful riding his tone. It brought to mind several episodes when he was pulled over, late at night, by state troopers for suspicion of driving intoxicated. To be questioned about where he had just come from, and his destination. Wanting not to believe his suspicions, he put it not to far behind him, realizing that some people were simply more assertive than others. He proceeded cautiously. "It varies," he finally answered. "All depends on what the buyer has in mind. I ..." Abruptly, he stopped talking and looked apprehensively into Stoneys eyes, only for a second. Sometimes that's all it took to read who you were talking to. He wondered, I could be setting myself up. I gotta watch that shit, telling total strangers my business. How do I know he ain't a cop.

Watching his words carefully, he continued, "It's kinda like, under the table stuff. You know, no taxes involved."

"Under the table?"

He thought for a second, smiled, then felt comfortable about saying, "More like, underground." He held his hands up, showing empty palms. "Gotta make a living, ya know. Got kids ta feed."

Stoney was very familiar with the feeling he experienced, talking to someone who figured him for a cop. In the middle of a sentence, the person stopped talking to organized their lies. To make sure their story would add up right. It had to sound credible to themselves, before they ran it by anyone else. Also, the eyes often flashed a look of caution. "How many kids do you have?"

A normal question. Mike felt relieved. "Three. Two girls; Sharon and Priscilla." He declared emphatically, "And a son, Benjamin." Anyone listening could tell that he cherished the ground his son walked on. "My boy!"

The way he said this made Stoney understand that he took more pride in his son, than in his two daughters. What if the girls turned out to be doctors or lawyers, and the son turned out to be a serial killer? Would he still feel the same way about them?

"Why didn't you bring your kids with you today?"

"The girls aren't into fishing. And my son, he's too young. Only two years old. He'd probably end up falling over the side or something. So I left them with my mom."

Stoney assumed he was married. A logical deduction. "Married?"

Mikes eyes frowned. "That old heffa, I ain't with her no more."

"Sorry to hear that," he said, for the sake of the children.

"Don't be. That bitch was getting on my nerves something powerful. We use to have so many arguments, I use to tell her everyday that one day she's gonna wake up, and I'm gonna be gone. But, what actually happened was that one day I woke up, and she was gone. She took the cat, but left me the kids and a stack of bills. Now, my credit ain't worth shit. She did leave one hundred and twenty five dollars that we had in a joint savings account. I guess she thought I'd need it, with having the kids and all." He sighed irritably. "That two timing whore fooled my ass good."

"You take care of three children, by yourself?"

"You damn straight." He made it a point when he stated, "Them's my kids."

"Must be murder. I don't mean to get into your business, but how do you do it? I hope I'm not insulting you by saying this, but you don't look like the well-to-do executive type."

"You got that right," he admitted. "That's why I said, I do what I gotta do, to make ends meet. Ya kno, Stone," Stoney could tell that he was loosening up, "just because a person does a few drastic things every now and then don't make them a bad person. Some people, including myself, will do anything to see that their kids are fed a good meal, before they get tucked into bed at night. I've been bone dry broke a few times, and it's not a pretty picture. Personally, I'll do just about anything to see that my kids have what they need. Not what they want, but what they need. There's a big difference, ya know."

"I think I understand where you're coming from."

"I weren't born with no silver spoon up my ass, and I've been scrounging ever since I left home at age thirteen." With malice burning in his heart, easily seen pruning his lips, he stated piteously, "It was ugly out there, on the streets. No matter what, you never get use to something like that. Unless you're mentally disturbed. After my Pa passed away, my Ma married this guy who was, and still is, a fricken bonafied dickhead. Although, she ain't with him any more, cause he died of cancer." He smiled bitterly. "It was the happiest day of my life. I prayed to God that he was in hell somewhere, with Satans hands wrapped around his throat.' He gritted fiercely. "I ain't never hated anyone more than I disliked that sadistic son-of-a-bitch."

Stoney felt the heat of his words, glimpsed him and saw the agony he's suffered scrawled across his face. "He use to beat my ass real good, like it was exercise and entertainment for some his rowdy ass friends. Then he wouldn't let me go to school for a few days, because he didn't want the teachers to see the black and blue marks all over my body. When I couldn't take any more of his shit, I left home and went to the streets. I couldn't go to school anymore because I was busy surviving." He paused, then stated disbelievingly, "My ma preferred to deal with that asshole, over me. Her own flesh and blood." He scratched his head. Disoriented. "I couldn't figure that for the world. But anyway, outta all that shit, I understood that I had to do one thing, and one thing only. That's take care of my kids. The way I was treated, I wouldn't want that shit to happen to them. If push comes to shove, I might end up giving custody to my mother, or put them in foster care." His last statement puzzled Stoney beyond comprehension. "I guess, as long as I don't get caught up, everything'll be all right."

Before he sold stolen computers, he ran a hustle boosting clothes. His clientele placed an order with him, and he fulfilled it. Around the end of August, just before his children returned to school, he visited a list of retail stores around the New England area to shop for their clothes. He visited only stores with hassle-free refund policies.

Step one: He strolled casually into the store with twenty dollars and bought a shirt and a pair of pants for his son, or a blouse and skirt for one of his daughters. Step two: He walked out of the store and left the items he paid for in his car. Step three: He returned to the store with the empty bag and receipts, and then put duplicate items into the bag. Step four: He went straight to the customer service desk and asked for a refund. Step five: He drove to several others stores and repeated the process until each of his children had at least seven outfits for the upcoming school year. The entire process was so uncomplicated that even a complete moron couldn't screw things up and get caught. At the end of the day, he still had the original twenty dollars. Enough to buy two packs of cigarettes and a six pack of beer.

One time, a security guard had witnessed him putting a couple of items into a bag and questioned him. He showed the security guard his receipts, proving that the items were paid for. He then explained that he had only come back into the store because he wanted to make sure that he bought the right sizes for his son. A likely excuse that induced sympathy, and his walking papers. He didn't loose a bead of sweat.

In thinking about the last statement he made, he felt that he had said enough. He realized how much of a chance he took by disclosing detrimental information, then decided to keep his conversation basic.

Seconds later, they heard a foghorn blow, signaling the ship had reached its first destination. The Capt., through data from his fish finding radar, had found a suitable spot for his passengers to drop their lines into the ocean, to try their luck.

The engines died quickly. After the ship slowed to a stop, they heard a muffled grumbling noise coming from somewhere near the front of the ship; the anchor dropping to keep the ship stationary.

The Capt.'s voice came over loud and clear on the P.A. system, he addressed his passengers, "This looks like a good spot, my friends. At this moment, we're tracking a large school on the radar, about two hundred feet down. In a moment, and I'll tell you when, you can bait your lines and drop them. While you're fishing, my crewmembers, who're also my sons, will be coming around periodically to check up on you. They'll deliver fresh bait, help get your lines untangled, and assist you in any way they can." There was a slight pause before he said, "Don't forget, your first catch goes into the pot for some of our delicious homemade chowder, which my wife will prepare. She'll also be working the concession stand inside the cabin, if you need any refreshments or snacks. We have soft drinks, candy, chips and bottled water. For your protection, we also have a minor medical kit, in case there are any mishaps. In case we need them, the life jackets are located under the benches that you're sitting on. Last, but not least, if you're interested in starting a pool for the biggest catch, come inside the cabin and enter. It'll only cost five dollars. We'll weigh what you have at the end of the trip. Yawl have a wonderful time. This is the Capt. of the Voyager, signing off."

The Capt.'s sons threw several buckets of bait into the water to draw the school of fish; get them going for anything in the area. "Now to do some serious fishing," Stoney clapped his hands and rubbed them enthusiastically. "I've been looking forward to this all morning." He picked up his rod, opened his tackle box, then searched for a ten ounce weight to tie onto his line.

"Me too. Blue ah blue," Mike added. He stood up, then stepped a few feet away to retrieve his gear. He returned a few seconds later. "Might as well fish right here, next to you. Being that I don't know nobody else. Sip cog."

"Sure. Why not? Hey, um ..." he felt that it was the appropriate time to inquire, "... do you mind if I ask you something?"

"Sure, pardner. Spit it. Zum book."

"I notice that every time you make a statement, you add a few words onto the end. What language is that? I've never heard it before."

"That only goes to show ya," he grinned, dodging the question. He felt he owed no explanation. It was too personal. "Ya ain't been everywhere. Kneeling bow." He whispered. "I got a couple of beers, if ya want one. Jam slop."

Stoney smiled. "Maybe in a little while. Right now, I want to get into this fishing stuff."

"Suit yourself." Mike took a seat on the bench, opened his tackle box, then searched for a suitable weight to tie onto his line. He wanted to ask Stoney what he did for a living. Since he had so many personal problems, he got some form of relief, as with a confession, when he tells someone about his. It's not important what the other person has to say. When he found a suitable ear, he transformed the average stranger into his personal psychologist. The only things missing were the notepad and couch.

At that moment, the Capt.'s voice boomed over the P.A. system again. "Everyone, bait your lines and drop'em!"

"It's about time!" Stoney excited. "He dropped his line into the water and told Mike, "Let's do it!"

"I'm with ya." Mike said. He threw his cowboy hat onto his head. "Soon as I find a good weight. Gum doop." He found one, then knotted it onto his line. After he baited the line, he dropped it into the water, then waited for the excitement to begin.

Stoney asked, "Care to make it interesting by placing a little side bet between the two of us, to see who catches the biggest fish?" His left eye brow jumped to his hair line. "Com'on, only five dollars. How about it?"

"Yeah. You're on, Stoneman. Moolah Moolah."

I understood that, Stoney thought.

Waiting for his line to tense, Mike looked admiringly at his rod and reel combo, and felt that the Stoneman had an advantage. Then he figured that at the bottom of the ocean, the fish see the same thing from line to line—bait on a hook. Growing impatient, he took a seat. He reached down and opened his six-pack cooler with his right hand, then retrieved a can of Budweiser beer. "You're sure you don't want a brewski, Stoneman?" He sat the can on the bench, closed the lid to the cooler, then lifted the pull-tab on the beer can.

"I think I'll wait a while."

"All right. It's here when you want it."

"Thanks. Mike, isn't it illegal to drink on a commercial ship that doesn't have a liquor license?"

"I don't think so. I believe it has something to do with us being this far out. Something about international waters, and all that political bullshit. I don't know. Zump de squad."

"I see."

Moments later, a spry looking teenager approached and asked, "You guys okay over here?" It was one of the Capt.'s sons, checking up on the passengers.

Mike presented his can of beer to toast, as if it were a special occasion. "You bet. Zumpty zumpty." He belched, loud.

Stoney replied, "Yes. Thank you."

"Good," the young man said. "I'll be back in a short while to check up on you. If you need help with anything, just holler. Either my brother or I won't be too far away."

The young man heard someone shout that their line was tangled, and walked away briskly.

"Of course you won't be too far away," Mike commented about what the teenager has just said. "How far away can you go on a small boat like this? Rapple tap."

Stoney chuckled at his wit. Funnyman type, he figured. He'll probably be a lot funnier after he gets a few of those beers into his system. Kinda reminds me of Spanky.

Only moments later, Mike felt a slight tug on his line. He grew excited and his adrenalin raced out of control. The tugging quickly grew into several hard pulls, his pole bending to an arch. He placed the can of beer on the bench next to him, then jumped out of his seat, proclaiming, "I think I got something here!" Spinning the handle on his reel rapidly with his right hand, he repeated, "Stoneman, I think I got something here." At that moment, whatever was on his line had pulled so hard, that it almost jerked the rod clean from his hands. Feeling the heavy pull, he figured that he had at the most a thirty pounder testing the line. "Yeah! I do believe I have something over here. Something big." He slurred, "Zippity dawg! Bop top zuey!"

The excitement gripped Stoney. He watched exhilaratingly as Mike tussled with his catch, awaiting eagerly for the same action on his line. He felt that he had an up front seat to a deep sea fishing show, on a sports network cable channel. 'How To Catch The Big Ones.' Incredibly anxious, his body twitched spasmodically. He cheered from the sideline, "That's it! Bring'em in. Not too fast now."

"Um reelin this sucker in!" he hollered, his right hand spinning the handle at five revolutions per second. He sang, "Sheeee's miiiiine! This baby's all miiii-inne." He laughed, "Come back Shane! Bippity bipitty dang."

As Stoney watched him tussling with his catch, riding on his hype, he became fascinated. He couldn't stop himself from shouting, "Bring'em in!"

It was nearly a three hundred feet drop, so he had a ways to go. It wasn't called deep sea fishing for nothing. Twenty seconds later, he stopped reeling and looked over the bow, at the ocean's surface, hoping to see what was on the end of his line. When he saw nothing, he grumbled, "Damn! This sho is some deep ass water."

Holding his rod firmly, Stoney looked at the water. On the end of Mike's line, a few feet under the surface, he saw a rainbow colored something swimming in circles.

As Mike was about to pull the fish from the water, the fish continued to fight fervently until its last breath, not realizing that it was only digging the hook deeper into itself.

Mike swung the fish over the bow and laid it on the deck, and the fish flopped wildly. Made several last ditch efforts to free itself, to return to the deep blue sea, home. Ogling at the size of his catch, he shouted, "Yes! Numero uno, and more to come. Dundee don dundee."

"Looks like a Pollock," Stoney guessed. "And a big one too. A twenty-five pounder, at least."

"She's a big one, all right. Looks just like my ex-wife. All mouth, same shape and everything. Even smells like her."

"That's funny."

"I don't think you can out-do this one," he bragged. "So ya might as well pay up now."

"I don't know," Stoney said, watching him unhook his catch. "But I'm gonna try."

"Good luck, pardner. Um gonna hold onto this one for the time being, and put my next catch into the pot, whichever is smaller. For that fish chowder the Captain's wife's makin."

Suddenly, Stoney felt his fishing rod pulsate. It stopped. It started again.

Could it be? He thought.

Ogling at the tip of his rod, he saw it bend. It straightened out. It bent again, and stayed bent, and his spirits climbed higher with the anticipation of the probable action to follow.

Eyeing him, Mike marveled at the way his Shakespeare rod flexed gracefully, like a ballerina in slow motion. He could swear he heard symphony music playing in the background. He stated, "I think it's your turn now, Stoneman. Get ready for some serious action. Wackadoodle wackadoodle!"

Stoney held tightly onto his fishing rod as it jerked non-stop. His adrenalin soared with the increased beat of his throbbing heart, and the palms of his sweaty hands made it difficult for him to maintain a solid grip. He persisted as though it were crucial that he hold on for dear life.

The noise coming from the other passengers drowned considerably, he heard nothing. Now feeling a much harder pull, because the fish had began to panic— its desperation to maintain its freedom grew tremendously—he released the safety, and began reeling in his catch.

As he spun the handle rapidly, before Mike baited his hook to resume fishing, he marveled in amazement at the beautiful sound emitting from the very expensive reel. The smooth mechanical clicking sound made him feel as if he was listening to the revving of a powerful Lamborghini engine. It was awesomely breathtaking, the way the fishing line threaded itself proportionately on the spool with ease, as if a built in electric motor did all the work.

Thirty seconds later, his catch was near to the surface. He stopped winding the handle for a moment and looked at the surface of the water. To his long awaited surprise, he saw something large swimming in circles, frenziedly in every direction but loose. The fish tried desperately to free itself from the impending doom of being filleted alive, then thrown into a boiling pot of fish chowder. He felt as though he was waiting for a pot of gold to be delivered from the murky depths of the ocean floor. No leprechaun, purple hearts, yellow moons or green clovers. His own little pot of gold. Mine mine mine. All mine!

Mike looked over the bow and directed him, "Pull'em up! Pull'em up! Humma zoom zoom."

Stoney pulled the fish out of the water, lifted it over the bow, then let it drop to the deck. He wiped his sweaty brow with his right forearm, watching the fish flop and danced like an enormous Mexican jumping bean. A slippery one with a big mouth, a tail and pointy fins. Nearly out of breath, he declared, "Wow! That was great. I can't wait to do it again."

"Same as mine. Pollock."

"About the same size too. Now, to unhook it." He sounded uncertain, unsure of himself. He cruised down memory lane to when his father had taken him fishing. He remembered one time when he had gotten pricked, no, more like stabbed, when he held a fish to remove the hook from its mouth. However, those were smaller fish; sunfish and porgies. This was different. This was a Pollock. It was at least five times the size of what he was use to. He imagined the pain would be five times greater. Feeling unnerved, he bent down and made several shabby attempts to remove the hook. All while keeping his eyes glued to the large fins.

Mike thought it amusing that every time the fish jumped, so did he. Don't tell me he's scared, he thought. I know a whole bunch of guys who are just like that. Macho men on the outside, crying little babies on the inside. Bummer! He offered a suggestion, explaining, "Step on the tail, hold the head down with one hand, then wiggle the hook out with your free hand. At least, that's the way I do it, so's I don't get stuck by one of them nasty looking fins."

"Ah … yeah." Mike could tell that he felt a little embarrassed. "I forgot. I haven't done it in such a long time." He did what he advised, and removed the hook with little difficulty. At that moment, the fish cried, "OUCH!" Like Cousin Joe from the Three Stooges, it sang, "Not so harrrrrrrrrd!"

He gaped disbelievingly. Filling his mind to the seams were all of the frightful feelings he's been experiencing since Jake and Jessica made their first debut. He stuttered "W-W-What?"

"I didn't say anything," Mike said.

"I wasn't talking to you. I was talking to …" He looked at the fish, then back to Mike, who stared at him with the most peculiar expression. Waiting for him to finish his sentence.

"Never mind. I thought I heard you say something. Forget it."

"Sure." Mike went back to tending his rod, but did keep a suspicious eye on him.

Stoney decided that give it to the Capt.'s wife, to throw into the pot of fish chowder that she was in the middle of preparing. The way that fish disrespected him, he was more than happy to get rid of it. Leaving, he told Mike, "I'll be back in a sec."

"That's a big one. Ain'tcha gonna keep it?"

"I'll keep the next one."

On the way to the cabin, he ran into one of the Capt.'s sons. "Mr., I saw the way you unhooked that fish. There's a much easier way to do it."

"Yeah?"

"Sure." He took the fish. "Ya just stick your hand inside the gills, like this. Hold it firmly, and you can take the hook out easily. There's nothing but soft tissue in there. Ya can hold it firmly, and ya can't get stuck. No matter how much it squirms."

He returned the fish to Stoney, and he held it by the gills. "Thanks a lot. I'll try that next time."

"You're welcome. Were you going to put that in the pot, for the fish chowder?"

"Yeah."

"I'll take care of that for you. Don't want you to miss out on the fun everyone's having."

"I appreciate that." Stoney said. He gave the young man the fish, then went back to where Mike stood and witnessed his line bending and bobbing wildly. "Looks like you're really cooking there."

"Yeah," he said, spinning the reel rapidly. "Now this is what I call having fun. Ya gonna try jigging anytime today?"

"Jigging? Sounds like some kind of a dance. What's that?"

Mike laughed, then pointed to another man in the process of tying a shiny, seven-inch long, kipper looking lure, onto his string. It had five triple hooks fastened to it. One at the head, another at the tail, and three in between. He explained, "It's what that guy right there's getting ready to do. Ya drop that jig into the middle of the school of fish, and let it hit the bottom of the ocean floor, where they're feeding. Then ya jerk it several times ... snap ya rod up, real quick like. Sometimes ya catch two or three in one drop. I use to do it all the time, but it's get to be tiring after a while. I like the old school way better. One at a time."

"That sounds interesting. I think I'll try some of that, a little later on."

Guessing that Stoney wouldn't have one, with not knowing anything about it, Mike asked, "You ... um ... you gotta jig?" His expression stated, 'I know, that you know, that I know, that you don't have a jig. I'm just asking to be a smart ass.'

Stoney fished around inside of his tackle box for a moment, since he didn't actually know what was inside of it. It was the first time he's ever used it. He thought he'd look just for the hell of it. People did things like this often for show, checking out things they already knew about. It's call 'playing out the moment.' Letting the flow of your natural idiosyncrasies unfold. He finally replied, "I don't think so." He pushed a few lures and hooks around, looked further.

Mike reached into his tackle box and retrieved a jig. "Here. Try this one. It'll do the job. I've used it plenty of times before. I call it the 'Mea West Jig.' Bomba dear."

"Mea West, huh?" He took the jig. "Thanks."

"Be careful," he cautioned. "I don't know how many times I done got stuck by that damn thing." He exaggerated, "Must've been a hundred times. It's got some serious hooks on it." He pointed into his tackle box. "That's why I carry some disinfectant, and a big box of bandages. It'd be an awful thing to go fishing, then have to go home with gangrene."

"I'll try to be careful." Stoney pulled a small folding knife from his pocket, then cut his line a few inches after the weight. It was an old Boy Scout model. He was never a member, but carrying it made him feel good about himself. It use to, anyway. He slid the jig onto his line, then knotted it securely in place. "That should do it."

Seconds later, he dropped the line into the water. He released the latch on the reel, and the jig dropped freely into the ocean. As the jig descended into the waters gloomy depths, the reel hummed an expensive charismatic melody. A pleasant tune that soothed Mikes senses with sweet dreams of having a rod and reel combination just like it someday. He glanced toward Stoney frequently and watched dreamily as the reels shiny casing sparkled its brand spanking newness. Like what Spankys car did to some people, it gave him goose pimples all over his body.

Finally, Stoney felt the jig hit the ocean floor, the reel stopped singing.

"Ya bottom out?" Mike asked.

"I think so."

Mike pointed to the other side of him, to another man. "Ya see what that guy over there's doin? Wapply dune."

Stoney turned to his left and witnessed a man snapping his rod repeatedly into the air. "Okay. I see."

"Then git to it. It's all in the wrist and elbows. When ya feel like ya got a gang of em tugging on ya line, reel em up. Bazoopa!"

Stoney snapped his rod into the air with the finesse of an amateur. Mike told him, "It takes a while ta get use to it, but you're doin okay. Just keep it up."

Moments later, after his fourth snap into the air, he felt the oddest sensation pulsating through his rod. It didn't pull up as easy. "All of a sudden, it feels heavy. This ain't right. I must've snagged onto something down there."

"Ain't nothing down there. You probably got a couple of big ones on the jig. Tutu zing."

"A couple!" he gasped. "Then how come the line's not pulling heavier than it did before?"

"If ya have a few on the jig, they might be pulling in opposite directions, going nowhere."

Since the theory did make sense, Stoneys face didn't have that confused look anymore. He grew excited at the thought of hitting the mother load, and began reeling in his catch. Struggling mightily, he stated, "Damn, its much heavier than before."

"Oh yeah! You definitely got a couple of them."

"A couple of em, huh? Yeah boy! This day is really turning into something amazing". Sparkles of delight gleamed in his eyes, and his heartbeat thumped with the thrill of an adolescent boy opening gifts on his twelfth birthday. A B-B gun from his father. A Lionel train set from his mother. A fifty-year-old series E collector's edition set of baseball cards from his grandfather. The stuff that youthful dreams are made of.

Almost two minutes later, he stopped reeling. He looked over the bow and saw his catch near to the surface. He saw a group of rainbow colored shadows swimming in a kaleidoscope fashion. Crossing over and under each other, flipping desperately like alligators amid the death roll.

The cluster of fish broke the surface, and he became amazed at the grouping of Pollock on the jig. He couldn't believe his eyes. There were three.

"Pull'em outta there," Mike said, then laughed. "It looks like ya got the Mr., the Mrs. and the mother-in-law. Hotch snick nicky."

Concentrating on the mother load, Stoney didn't hear his joke. He heaved the fish over the bow, with Mike assisting.

"Three!" Stoney exclaimed. "Wow!"

The Pollock flipped and flopped on the deck, blood poured profusely from their gashed wounds. He had snagged one through its belly, another through its tail—it was trying to get away—and the third through its right eye.

Prepared to use the method that the crewmember had suggested, he kneeled to unhook them. Looking into their human size eyes, his glance shot back and forth in between the three. He looked at the largest one, and it held his attention for a moment.

Suddenly, its jaws opened wide, gasping for a breath of much needed seawater, then closed shut. It opened wide again. But this time, it remained open. A frightful feeling searched its way through his heart, and he felt his throat swell around his tonsils. His eyelashes fluttered with fear, and he heard Jessica's little voice cry, "Look at what you did to my stomick. I'll never be able to eat again." Every muscle in Stoney's body tightened with fear, and Jessica went on to say, "An look at what you did to Jakes eye." Her baby voice cried a soft whimper, "Now he can't see no more. He's gonna look like a buck tooth, one eyed jack rabbit."

He sputtered disbelievingly, "No. No you don't. I thought it was only in glass, or in mirrors. I though you only showed yourself ..." he closed his eyes tight and groaned, tried desperately to erase what had just occurred. On bended knees, he beseeched, "Please, go away. I beg you. Please ... go away."

"You say something?" Mike asked.

Stoney said nothing, his awareness trapped deep in the abyss.

Watching him, Mike could've swore he was praying. He brushed it off and continued bringing in another catch, his third, all while keeping a leery eye on Stoney. Something wasn't right. Anyone could see that.

Stoney trembled in fear for the children from hell, peering at the Pollock with the hook lodged in its right eye. Before he knew anything, the Pollock grew a pair of gold trimmed horned rimmed glasses. Blood spilling profusely over its lips, Jake moaned excruciatingly, "Ooooohhhhhh! My eyeeeee! That bad man put a hook through my eyeeeee. It huuuurts. Somebody pleeeeease take it out."

Gritting his teeth, Stoneys nostrils and temper flared. He grumbled, "You gotdamn mother fucken miserable ..."

Hearing his choice of curse words as clear as day, Mike stared at him and became confused. "Hey, Stoneman. You okay?"

People in the immediate vicinity looked on warily, just as the onlookers in the Mall did the day before. Their suspicious eyes pointed condemningly, and some of the parents grabbed their children, brought them closer for protection. A little boy asked his father, "Daddy, is that man crazy?"

Feeling the child's weighty insinuation, Stoney rose to his feet and faced Mike. Breathing hard, his eyes reflected the strains of the destructive incidents from the past few weeks. He belched maliciously, "Those fucken bastards! They're here again."

Mike placed his rod down, propped it against the bow. Appearing incredibly baffled, he looked all around. "Who? What're you talkin about?"

Stoney pointed at the Pollock gasping for air, a limited amount of life left in them, sliding over and under each other, oiled orgy style, blood gushing from their wounds. "Them. Right there."

Mike looked oddly at the group of Pollock, then back to Stoney. "You, um, you feelin okay, Stoneman?" Crazy man, he figured. Just like the kid said. It's always the quiet conservative types, acting like he ain't been up to nothing. No wonder he didn't say much about himself.

His next thought was to rationalize. He glanced at everyone watching them. "Hey, Stoney. Relax, pardner." He held both hands up in front, his fingers pointing to the air. "Why don't we sit down, so we can talk about this?"

"Psssst! Hey, Stoneman," Jake said.

Stoney looked at the Pollock with the hook gashed in its eye, its other eye bulged grossly out at him. Jake continued, "We got something for ya, dear friend."

Jessica's giggled reverberated, causing Stoney to quiver. It sounded as though she was down the corridor, her voice echoed the walls, surrounding him with the effects of stereophonic sound.

Right before his eyes, the Pollock and the jig grew larger and larger, as if someone was blowing air into them, like blowfish. Growing to almost fifty times their original size, Stoney stepped backwards while shielding his face with his right arm, expecting something horrendous to happen.

Mike, as well as everyone else on board, pinned his eyes on his every bizarre movement. If the man were going to go berserk, he wasn't going to be the last person to find out about it. He whispered, "What in the hell?"

When it looked as though the Pollock couldn't get any larger, their skins stretched to their maximum displacement, they exploded in Stoney's face with an earsplitting boom that rocked the ship to a near capsize. A miniature fireball ensued and Stoney hit the deck. He curled in the fetal position and covered his head, shouting, "Aaaaaaarrrrggg!!"

Moments later, when it was completely quiet, he opened his eyes to view a human sized Pollock with horned rimmed glasses, Jake, standing a few feet away. Balancing on tail fins, his hands resting on his hips, he began dancing merrily like Rumple Stiltskin.

He stopped dancing and leered at Stoney. His now heavy voice echoed, "We fooled ya, didn't we? You're a born sucker. That didn't hurt you. But this will."

Before Stoney knew anything, Jakes right eye—the one with the large jig hanging from it—grew menacingly larger. It burst open and thrust forward a sopping stringy substance; akin to bloodied slimy veins and arteries. It surrounded Stoneys entire body and wrapped him in a tight cocoon.

Stoney swung wildly at him, attempting to stop the disgusting substance from smothering him in its death web. Taking handfuls, it oozed in between his fingers like warm spaghetti. He quickly reached into his pocket and pulled out his trusty rusty Boy Scout knife. He opened it quickly and began slicing through the air, attempting to rid himself of the slimy substance threatening his very existence. Fighting for his life, he shouted, "I'll kill you, Jake! I'll kill you … you and your fucken little snot nosed sister!"

For fear of being stabbed to death, everyone on the vessel moved further away, to the opposite side of the ship. Again, it almost capsized. Alarming screams of panic blaring from that side of the ship.

He attacked and stabbed the creature repeatedly, and it soon succumbed, fell to the deck. It's thunderous heartbeat had slowed to a snails pace. Then it had stopped beating altogether.

Moments later, Jake had disappeared. Stoney was totally exhausted from his skirmish with the creature from hell. He was dog-tired, but felt greatly relieved, as though his life had been spared.

He looked down and discovered himself covered entirely with the disgusting substance, and he dropped the knife and scrapped his clothes frantically with his hands; made futile attempts to grate the alien substance from his body. He gagged a few times, realizing that something was stuck in his throat. Jakes tennis ball sized eyeball had mysteriously found its way into his mouth, the nerve endings trailed his lips like boiled okra.

He ran to the bow, leaned over and spat into the ocean, attempting to rid his mouth of the disgusting taste flooding his palate. Just when he thought it couldn't get any worse, because he was inclined to believe it wasn't over—Jake and Jessica were just getting warmed up—a never-ending stream of bloodied saliva and phlegm exploded from his mouth and sprayed the waters below.

Mike gasped in amazement as he hung over the bow and puked his insides out; his breakfast, a coffee and donut. He gushed in awe, "Holy Mother! Must be LSD. It's gotta be LSD." He thought, I've seen this shit happen before when my cousin Ripley ran from that wild party we gave last summer, shouting and smacking his face, saying he had spiders crawling all over him. Then the damn fool doused himself with gasoline, then lit himself on fire. Probably thinking he was getting rid of the spiders. Or like my other cousin Darrel. One hit of that shit, and he was screwed up for life. When he gets ready for bed nowadays, he puts his pajamas in the bed, then crawls under the bed. Butt naked. Says he's been doing it that way ever since he could remember. Mike nodded for sure. Yeap. Now I know it's LSD. The Stoneman must be on a hellova trip. Screaming at no one, stabbing that knife at nobody, smacking himself like there're spiders and creepy things crawling all over him. Acting like there are bugs gutting up from his stomach, and pouring out through his mouth. It's gotta be LSD. It's the only thing that could make a person go through that kind of hell.

The Capt.'s sons approached Stoney cautiously. Darwin, the eldest, told his brother as they neared, "I wish dad can screen his passengers before they boarded. Remember a few months ago when that shady looking pervert went around the ship, grabbing all the women's butts?"

His younger brother Dwayne snickered. "Yeah, I remember. Lets see what's going on with this guy. He doesn't look to be sea sick, and it's too early to say that he might be drunk. Maybe he's on medication, and simply forgot to take it." He yelled over his shoulder at a few passengers huddled in a group. "It's okay. Nothing to worry about. We have the situation under control," he whispered to his brother, "I hope." As if they had done it plenty of times before, he said, "You stay on his right side, and I'll get on the left. And most importantly, watch out for that knife."

"Okay. Either it's what you've said, or we have an escapee from the loony bin. That place out in Bridgewater, Mass. The House of Asylum."

Stoney remained leaning over the bow, squeezing his midsection with both hands, ripping at his insides with dry heaves. The pain punched him like sledgehammer blow to the kidneys.

Standing a few feet from Stoney and Mike, at a safe distance, Darwin cleared his throat and asked, "What seems to be the problem here?" His voice took on a tone of authority. After all, it's their father's ship.

Mike responded, "It's my friend here." He wanted to say, I think he's freaking out, or having an LSD flashback. Instead, he told them, "I think he's sea sick."

Stoney faced the deckhands, still clutching at his stomach. He stood breathing feverishly, hunched, his skin tone faded to a sickly ashen. Streams of saliva flowed from his mouth, dripped from his chin, covered his shirt. His bloodshot eyes peaked their redness, the zigzag veins on his temples and neck inflated to twice their normal size.

He declared groggily, "I feel ... I feel ..."

"You look terrible, Mr.," Dwayne remarked, then threw his hands onto his hips. His head tilted to the left, curious like. "You wanna come inside of the cabin for a little while, to sit down? Take a load off. Sometimes this sea air, if you're not use to it, can cause ya to be real sick. Depending on what ya had to eat."

"My brother's right," Darwin added. His arms folded skeptically, his fingers twiddled the outside of his arm. "I've seen worse happen before." Although he lied, he felt it was a good thing to say, to put Stoney at ease. It didn't work. But it did make him feel good knowing that he made an attempt to comfort the stranger.

Stoney stumbled backwards and plopped onto the bench behind him. He leaned forward and brought his elbows to rest on his knees. He drowned his face into his hands, totally worn out from the relentless hallucinations plaguing him endlessly. Only one question came to mind. *For God sake, when will Jake and Jessica leave me the hell alone?*

He coughed a few times, cleared the last bit of vomit tickling his throat. He wiped his watery eyes with the back of his right hand. "Yeah. Maybe you're right. Maybe I should come inside for a little while, and have some coffee or something."

Mike asked skeptically, "Hey, Stoneman, are you gonna be all right?" He believed steadfastly that the incident was derived from a prior LSD trip. No matter what Stoneys excuse was going to be.

"Yeah," Stoney coughed. "I'm fine." *Insert lie here.* The scene was set for a doozie of a whopper. "I'm on some new medication that my doctor gave me last week. He said there would be some side-effects that varied from person to person." He paused. "I guess I just discovered one of the side effects."

Dwayne leaned toward his older brother, nudged him. His eyes relayed, *See, I told you it was something like that.*

After Stoney rose to his feet, Darwin stated, "For the safety of the passengers, I need you to hand over your knife, until we get back to the docks. Someone could've gotten seriously hurt a minute ago. For the sake of my dads insurance, we don't want to risk anything awful happening."

Stoneys tired bloodshot eyes shot back and forth in between the crewmembers. Normally, he would've offered a debate. But this time, he realized they were absolutely right. He picked up the knife, closed it, then handed it to Darwin. "I understand." He bent over to pick up his rod and tackle box, and realized that his clothes were spotless.

"Don't worry about that stuff," Mike said. "I'll keep my eyes on it for ya."

"All right," Stoney agreed. After walking past Darwin and Dwayne, he stopped, turned halfway. "Mike."

"Yeah."

"Can you finish breaking in that rod and reel for me? It's kinda rough around the edges."

Although what Stoney knew about Mike screamed 'THIEF!', he figured that since they were on a boat, he couldn't go too far. He seems like a descent person, he figured. Then again, who am I to judge?

He wasn't as possessive as he use to be, as when he first joined the Dixie Club. Now that he's come to light on the ramifications of his dishonest actions, the items he'd obtained with the money he made from hustling were of little significance, or none at all. Even the Porsche Carrera GT was tainted with rust spots and pings from a dented subconscious and battered soul.

Darwin and Dwayne followed him closely, in case there would be another violent outburst. Not that they could've done anything if he did snap and go on a rampage. They only wanted to comfort the passengers by making it appear as though they had everything under control. However, it did appear to a few bystanders that he was under cabin arrest. Both announced to the passengers, "Everything's all right! You can go back to fishing now." Dwayne threw in, "Yeah. He's okay. He just had some bad medicine, that's all."

Stoney heard the same little inquisitive boy ask his father, "Daddy, are they gonna put a straight jacket on him?"

The majority of the passenger's expressions spilled of their uneasiness for his presence. For nearly everyone on board, simply stating that everything was all right, wasn't enough. They wanted reassurances. Solid reassurances. They wanted him caged, locked up, as where all wild and sporadically violent animals should be.

Before he entered the cabin, he eyed the little kid and smirked, thinking solely of Jake. He did favor him, somewhat, with his inquisitive attitude. Entering the cabin, he found that the idea of having a cup of piping hot coffee seemed to get better as time cruised by. As The Voyager cruised the waters.

After Stoney was out of Mikes sight, the 'Star of David' twinkled in his eyes. Admiring the expensive fishing equipment, he became so elated that his beaming smile stretched completely around his head, displaying nicotine and coffee stained teeth. He dropped his rod immediately, the line still in the water. He rejoiced silently, "Yes! Yes! Topely dopely, boom boom dada."

He removed the three fish from the jig, then tossed them into a sack. He removed the jig, placed a weight and hook on the line, then baited it. He picked up the fisherman's dream rod and reel combo, then dropped the line into the water.

To complete the transformation, he cocked his hat to the side, cool hand Luke like. He stood with his feet spaced at least four feet apart, leaning backwards almost to a fall, toothpick clenched tight jutting from his flashy grin. Proud like, holding the rod firmly out in front and center. He was ecstatic, appeared to be a novice about to paint with a brush that Leonardo da Vince had once used. He snapped his head to the right, to the left, and glanced at the inexpensive equipment the other fishermen used. He smiled contentedly, with dignity. He mumbled, "Wait'll I tell the guys about dis. They'll never believe it." I knew I should've brought one of those disposable cameras with me this morning, he thought. Me, standing here, holding this rod like this would've made a hellova picture. He sighed, stated aloud, "Ah yes! I'm sitting on top of the world! Now dis here be what it's all about. Bipely bipely zoc, ring da mudda sucken fock."

Referring to Mike, the same inquisitive kid asked his father, "Daddy, is that man gonna attack the fish too?"

His father eyed Mike cautiously. "For God sake, son, let's hope not."

✳   ✳   ✳   ✳

Inside of the cabin, Stoney sat alone, drinking a cup of hot coffee. A few who witnessed his outburst walked by and gawked watchfully. He felt their negative vibes attack from all sides. He felt their probing minds poking questions, wanting to know what brought about his sudden extreme outburst; what triggered it. Was it drugs? Was he traumatized from something horrible that had happened to him in his up comings? Or was it something horrific that he was involved in that made him trip the light fantastic through a dark region in his mind, dance uncaringly through a place called Oz.

Some were genuinely concerned for his safety, an elderly man and his wife. Their sincere gestures made their presence when they delivered sympathetic stares of which he welcomed warmly. All others stay out.

The woman pulled from her husband, approached him warily. At first, he tried to stop her. She told him tenderly, "No, don't worry Herman. I'll be just fine."

She took a seat in the booth, opposite Stoney. For a long moment, she simply stared into his eyes, observed his wretched condition. She stated thoughtfully, "Hi there."

Stoney simply nodded an acknowledgement.

"Young man," she said compassionately, "ya got a lot on your mind, don'tcha?"

He didn't reply. Only lowered his head, contemplating, trying to figure where she was coming from. Where she was going with this.

"It's okay," she went on to say. "Ya don't have ta say anything. But I would like ya ta listen ta me for a moment, if it's alright with you." Since Stoney didn't respond, she felt it was okay to continue, "My son, God bless his soul, and yours, he had many problems in his life." She looked through the porthole, appeared comfortable, talked as if she had known him for years. "The way you were going at it out there, on the deck, ya kinda reminded me of him. Sometimes life can do terrible things to a person, get ya all worked up, make ya think the whole worlds against ya. I use ta tell him everyday not ta carry his own load. Tried ta get him to surrender his life ta Christ, lay his burdens down. But, he never listened. The load got so heavy that it crushed him under the weight of many wicked things, and now he's gone. He died only a year ago. Taken from this world because he made a few bad choices, went awry on the path of righteousness. I use ta tell him everyday that if ya wanna keep yaself out of harms way, ya gotta protect yaself with the shield and full body armor of Christ. The only way the devil can come into ya life, would be if ya invite him in. I know Satan like the back of my hand. He's tried to come into my life plenty of times. But I know one thing for sure. He doesn't stay where he's not wanted. I know this because my husband and I've been Christians all our lives. We've seen people get involved in and do the damndest things, only because they didn't believe in His name. They had no direction, they were lost. They went every whicha way." She told him point blank, "Son, I know you're lost, cause I can see it in ya eyes … on ya face. I can feel ya soul's seen better days. But that's alright, because I'm here to tell ya that Jesus loves ya, and He wants ya to be with Him someday, in His eternal kingdom," she looked at Herman and smiled blissfully, "where my husband and I will be someday." She rose from her seat. "Young man, you think hard about what I told ya, because it's never too late. The devil will lie to ya, and try ta make ya think that it is. But he's wrong. Always was, and always will be. He's the father of all lies." Leaving, she repeated, "You think about what I said. Ya hear me?"

She took her husband by the arm, and they left the cabin. Stoney looked through the porthole, watched a few ships floating near. The nearest, a white schooner, its sizable mask pinned itself against a low but steady wind. He tried focusing on anything that would take his mind far from 'The Voyager', and the incident that had occurred just a short while ago. However, his thoughts did linger on the old womans words of wisdom.

Feeling some comfort, he wished that he was somewhere else, around a new crowd of people, starting the day all over again. Around people who new nothing of his psychopathic behavior. People who didn't believe that he was crazy. People who didn't want to see him locked in a cage, like an uncontrollable wild beast.

He pushed the cup of coffee away, placed his folded arms on the table, then closed his eyes. He lowered his head, feeling completely dejectedly. He remained in that position until The Voyager returned to dock.

Twice, Darwin came by to check up on him, but didn't disturb him. He only wanted to make sure that he was still there, away from the other passengers. The other *sane* passengers.

As Stoney contemplated his unpleasant altercations with Jake and Jessica, he speculated if there was a sure way out of the madness that plagued him incessantly. He had broken off all contacts with the new marks who he had hustled just a few days before, but still felt the cold stabbings in and of his subconscious as Jake and Jessica turned the blade unmercifully and ripped him to shreds. He wondered how much more punishment they'd hurl at hi and his level of concern climbed yet higher.

At the back of his mind, he knew and believed that they couldn't hurt him physically. However, he couldn't help but to be moved by observing the terror in their eyes by witnessing the pain riddled expressions they masked. He wanted vehemently to pry open his head and scrape out the deeply embedded memories involving the misguided souls that he's taken advantage of. He was sure that there would be some sort of relief if he did. In all his days, he never thought that he could feel the kind of torment that he's experienced thus far.

The muscles in his face tensed, he groaned inaudibly, "God. Pleeeeassse.
—rip them out of my head—
—gotta get them out—
—I can feel them, their hands banging—
—clawing and scratching—
—clawing and scratching—
—their eyes, God, please, their eyes—"
The idea of committing a self-induced memory loss entered his mind; a bang on the head. But he had no idea of how hard he had to hit himself for the erasure to be successful.

He thought enthusiastically, I've seen it happen on television plenty of times before. But I don't know anything about the statistics; what my survival rate would be. And what if I accidentally damage myself critically to the point of having permanent brain damage? What if I end up in a coma, laying somewhere for years in a vegetated state? I'd have to rely on a total stranger to come by periodically to change my diapers. What if I accidentally kill myself? Then I'm sure to go to hell.

For a moment, the potential of the idea and some of its advantages soothed him. Then the nightmarish notion of him lying in bed in a vegetated state crashed through the door and screamed its hideous existence. He muttered, "There's gotta be another way. I know there has to be."

CHAPTER 15

▼

The charter boat cruised quietly into port at a little past five o'clock, then docked at its usual berth. The passengers packed their gear, prepared to go ashore and head home. Mike entered the cabin and caught Stoney steeling a few Z's. 'Stealing Z's, because it was what he had become, a thief. Stealing Z's, because he hadn't ask Jake and Jessica for permission. He hadn't asked them for forgiveness. Mike felt that what he needed was a few days of undisturbed rest, and didn't want to bother him. Listening to him snore his heart away in that little cubby hole, he tapped Stoneys left shoulder cautiously, prepared to jump back if he had to. In case Stoney would go on the warpath again, as if suffering from Viet Nam Syndrome.

'INCOMING!'

'FIRE IN THE HOLE!'

He sat upright and yawned thoroughly. He glanced at his surroundings, at his watch, and it quickly came back to him where he was. What came back next was the nightmarish incident that had occurred only hours before.

Mike placed his tackle box on the floor, next to his feet, then handed him the expensive rod and reel combo. He exhilarated, "Stoneman, that's a hellova rod and reel set ya got there, pardner. Shucks, man! I ain't had that much fun in years. Tweren't nothing but sheer ecstasy. The way that reel hums when the lines dropping, it's like it's made of eighteen carat gold. It's sweet music to my ears, like a symphony. And the way that rod feels in my hands, just as comfortable, it's like I'm holding a kings scepter, ready to rule the world." On the same note, he asked concernedly, "By the way. How're ya feeling, pardner? Them visions ain't come back, have they?"

A few people preparing to leave the ship looked at the two from a safe distance. Their eyes sang a gravediggers tune of 'Oh bury me on the lone prairie.'

Stoney yawned again and dragged his left hand over his face grudgingly, over the top of his head, then cupped the back of his neck. He stated insecurely, "Um, naw." He stated for sure, "No! But, I'm okay. I guess." He remembered his lie. "That damn medicine. You never know what you're putting in your system nowadays. Wait until I tell my doctor about this. He won't believe it."

Mike chucked it off, then looked into the cooler exploding with fish. "Stoneman, thanks to you, I've had a hellova day. I must've caught twenty-five fish. Shootma dip! Using that rod and reel combo of yours, I tell ya, it was nothing but sheer ecstasy. Bam! Deuce bam! Look here, pardner." He pulled a plastic bag out of his back pocket and opened it. "Seeing that I had a good day, ya can't go home empty handed. Why don'tcha take a few of the fish that I caught, to add with ones that ya did catch? Because ya let me use ya stuff, it's been an especially good day. One that I'm gonna remember for a long time, as long as I live. I would've caught the same amount of fish using my stuff, but I wouldn't have had as much fun doing it. Tum tum zang!"

"I couldn't do that. You really put a lot of work into it today. I think you deserve to keep what you …"

"Nonsense! Not another word." Along with his original four fish, he reached into the cooler and placed four more into the bag. He spun it closed, saying, "Here ya go, Stoneman. Zip doodly."

"Thanks Mike." He accepted the bag. "Thanks a lot. I really appreciate it."

"Sure thing. I'm gonna go home, clean and fry them up for the kids. Ain't nothing better in the world than fresh fried Pollock, doused in plenty of hot sauce. And a nice cold Budweiser beer. Man oh man, finger lick delicious zoletab!"

"That sounds good. I think I'm going to do the same." He paused. "Well," he stuck out his right hand, "Mike, it was nice meeting you."

He accepted his hand, and they shook as though they had been friends for years. "Yeah. Likewise." He whispered, "Hey, don't worry about that little episode, drum boogie. We all have bad days. You should've seen me the day I found out I was allergic to bee stings." He laughed, "Man! My faced puffed up like a blowfish, and I couldn't breathe for shit. I was all over the place, flapping my arms, like I was tryinta take flight. Like I was having an epileptic fit, swinging at everything. Who would've figured. Bee stings." He picked up his fishing gear, grabbed the cooler by one side—a set of wheels on the other—then strutted toward the cabins entrance. Ten feet away, he yelled over his shoulder, "Later, Stoneman. Stone ta the bone!"

Stoney placed his right index finger on his brow and snapped it away, as if to give a one-finger salute. "All right, Mike. Hey, you take care of those kids. Ya hear?"

Mike stopped walking, turned halfway and smiled, thinking, I hope he lays off that shit. That LSD will make ya have bad nightmares. My cousins were clear-cut cases. I know. I've seen it happen before.

Leaving, he sung one of his homemade songs. "Bop zidly cram da beep. To da ma ziggy ziggy, ram be dump. Castu pa heady lo ka zump, trump la dole lump tee rump ..."

Just after, the old woman who spoke to Stoney hours ago walked by with her husband. They stopped for a moment, the husband told him, "I hope you take into consideration what my wife talked to you about." He smiled at her, "She ain't never been wrong about the word of God. It's what kept me alive and out of trouble all these years. I know one thing. I couldn't have done it by myself." He paused, before he finished with, "You have a nice day. Ya here?"

His wife only smiled fraily.

Stoney nodded lackadaisically.

Holding the bag of fish, his last thought was to look inside. He rose to his feet, picked up his equipment and quickly got off the boat. When he arrived to the parking lot, a few passengers from the 'The Voyager' stared at him from afar, as though he had leprosy. He could only imagine what they were thinking. Their eyes felt like prodding fingers prancing on the sides of his head. He wanted more than anything to get the hell away from there as fast as he could, and knew it would be a long time before he returned.

Pulling out of the parking lot, the same young inquisitive boy pointed at his pickup truck and told his father, "There goes that crazy man!" Stoney saw his lips form words that were unmistakably clear.

Feeling their resentment, he grumbled, "What'n the hell does that kid know anyway? Kids like that, with their bellowing naive ignorance, have nothing but an underdeveloped sense of reality and reasoning. Wait'll he grows up and starts living life. Then he'll see what it's all about. The hell with him ... little now-it-all brat."

Suddenly, an image of Jake and Jessica came to mind. Certainly against his will. He closed his eyes tight, as if to squeeze the image from his mind. He was startled when he heard a car horn blow in distress. He opened his eyes and slammed on the breaks just in time, and the driver of a car that he had almost plowed into blasted, "You fucken asshole! Why don't you look where you're going?" He flipped Stoney the bird, then drove off.

He rubbed his eyes, then banged his right fist onto the dashboard. He looked at his aching hand, shook it a few times and spat, "Damn!"

Driving home, he became furious with everything that had happened that day, but kept only one question in mind. 'How in the hell am I going to get Jake and Jessica out of my life?'

∗　　　∗　　　∗　　　∗

At that exact moment, Spanky purchased a disposable cell phone for twenty-five bucks at a K-Mark, not to far from his apartment. He jumped into his car, but before switching on the ignition, he placed a call to someone living in a prominent Jewish section of Newton, Massachusetts.

The phone rang five times before a woman answered, "Hello."

"Hello," Spanky said. "May I speak to Maria Zangwill."

"This is she," she stated. Her thick Jewish accent pouring through the phone line. "May I ask who's calling?"

"My name's George. George Washington." Practicing one of his newly developed hustles that showered the mark with much confusion, he jumped right in, "I'm a gynecologist, calling in reference to your transgender son, Richard." He paused, allowing the astonishment of the disgust to sink in. He could tell that she was too shell shocked to speak. "You do have a son who goes to Newton North High School, don't you?"

"But, my son isn't gay. And why would a gynecologist be calling me?" She wondered about everything that he had said so far. Especially his name. "My son is okay, isn't he? Is he in some sort of trouble or something?"

"Well, he could be."

"What do you mean buy that? And what did you say your name was?"

"My name? It's Abraham Lincoln. I'm an enema specialist, calling about the probing anal activity going on behind your back."

Maria gasped in complete detest, "A what specialist? But, I thought you said your name was George Washington."

"George Washington, Abraham Lincoln, what's the difference? They're both dead ex-presidents, with their pictures on the money we spend. Get the idea?"

She hesitated for a hefty moment, then replied, "No. I don't." Her tone grew harsh. "If this is some kind of a sick twisted game you're playing, then I don't have the time for …" Since he did mention her son by name, the thought came to her that it may be one his friends, calling to play a cruel joke. Then she figured that the idea was unlikely, since this person sounded much older than any of her sons friends. At least the ones that she knew personally. She said firmly, "Young man, you'd better listen to me, and you'd better listen good. If you don't tell me what you want, then I'm going to hang up right this instant." Although, she should have done so a long time ago. As soon as she heard that his name was George Washington.

"I wouldn't do that if I were you," he warned her. "You do that, and you might destroy you and your son's life."

She spat at him, "Who ever this is, I've had just about enough of this nonsense. I'm going to give you just three seconds for you to tell me what this is all about, then I'm going to hang up and call the police." Although a blank name and address showed on the caller identification system on her telephone, she bluffed, "I have caller I.D., and I know just who you are, and where you're calling from."

Spanky knew that she was bluffing, knew that she was full of shit, so he gave her a new name. "Like I said before, my name's Benjamin Franklin. I'm calling about the hair I found floating in my bowl of tomato soup."

Having heard enough of this silliness, she fired, "That's it! I'm hanging up this very instant ..."

Fearing she would, he hurled quickly, "Mrs. Zangwill, your son's friend was busted when he tried to purchase a kilo of cocaine a few weeks ago, from an undercover police officer."

He didn't hear a click on the other end of the line, and knew he had grabbed her attention. Struck a nerve. She asked disturbingly, "What did you say?"

"Your son and his friend Joseph Greenbaum, who I'm sure you know because both attend the same high school, Newton North High, were busted in a sting operation in downtown Boston. Well, actually, only Joseph was arrested. Through some information from an eyewitness, they gave me your sons registration plate number, and I put one and one together. Since he was there, it means that he's just as guilty. It's called 'joint venture.' He's a co-defendant in a crime. When your son witnessed Joseph getting busted, he got scared and sped off, with no one in pursuit." He paused. "Mrs. Zangwill, now do you understand what this is all about?"

Taking it all in, she became confused. Her mind became fogged with troubling images of courts, prosecutors, negative media publicity and prison (for her son). His future ruined in disgrace. "But I don't ... I don't understand what this ..." a more important question hit her, "... suppose this whole fantasy story of yours is true. If you know that my son was present during this so-called drug bust bee sting operation thing, then why hasn't he been arrested?"

"If that happened, it would destroy both of your lives. I only called because I thought it would be to your best interests to see if we can reach an agreement on how to handle things. If I gave his name to the authorities, well, I think you know what'll happen from there. The Zangwill name will be stretched across the morning newspapers. There will be no future for him, and your family's name will be destroyed. Devastated. Life, as you know it, will come to a screeching halt. At least for your son. But you'll be ostracized and frowned upon by the affluent Jewish community, of which you live and play a significant role in, and ..." Instead of going down the list, he simply told her, "Mrs. Zangwill, I can guarantee you that it will get ugly."

"But ... But, I don't understand. What kind of an agreement are you talking about?"

"Mrs. Zangwill, for an intelligent person such as yourself, you haven't been listening to a word I've said. Remember I told you what my names were?"

"Well, at first you said it was George Washington. Then Abraham Lincoln. Then Benjamin Franklin. But that doesn't say much, except for that they're all ex-presidents."

"Mrs. Zangwill, I said *dead* ex-presidents, like on the money we spend. This all about the money."

She yelled, "Blackmail! You call my house with plans on blackmailing me with shady information that I don't even know to be correct."

Spanky sniggled briefly. As if it were as simple as that, he chucked into the air, "Well, yeah. But, I had a feeling you would say that. So here's what I'm going to do. When your son comes home from school, talk to him about what had happened two weeks ago, and he'll verify everything I've said. Then I'll give you a call tomorrow evening, sometime after dinner, and we can go from there. And if you know what's good for the both of you, Mrs. Zangwill, you'll tell him to never mention a word of this to anyone."

After terminating the call, he laughed, "George Washington, Abraham Lincoln and Benjamin Franklin." I have to get some new lines, he pondered. I'm staring to put myself to sleep with the stuff I use. I wish I could come up with some of the lines that Stoney uses. His stuff roles from his back like water. At least, it use to.

CHAPTER 16

▼

It was dark when Stoney had arrived home. Before he pulled into the driveway, he passed his neighbor, a young woman walking a five year-old Dachshund. The dog looked like an oversize kielbasa with four-two inch stumps for legs, and a three inch wagging nub. She waved hello, but since he wasn't paying attention, he had other things on his mind, he drove straight to the rear of his house.

He the kitchen and heard his servant in an adjacent room, cleaning up shattered glass from mirrors and other objects that he had broken just days before. To Carton, when it came to glass, clean wasn't clean enough. To the naked eye, those infinite crystalline granules were not there, but they'll find their way into bare feet or hands during the most inopportune time. Accidents do happen, and they happened to him often. Always remembering his past, he was well aware of the fact.

He placed his fishing equipment on the floor, next to the stainless steel stove. He then placed the bag of fish on the counter, next to a chopping block. Because of what he had experienced earlier that morning, he didn't dare look into the bag. That was the last thought on his mind.

Keeping his eyes on the bag of fish, from hearing Carlton mopping the floor, he approached the bathroom. He crept up on him, and startled him when he shouted, "Hey, Carlton! How're ya doing, buddy?" Carlton nearly jumper out of his skin, dropped the mop. "A tab touchy, aren't we?"

"I'm sorry, sir. I didn't hear you enter the house." He picked up the mop and continued cleaning. "Although I do smell fish, sir, it still leaves me to question. How was *chour* fishing expedition?"

He leaned against the doorjamb, and responded first to his slip of the tongue. "Carton, you're slipping." He paused. "The trip was all right. All that sea air and excitement, it was very invigorating." He sounded like he read from a script. Clearly, his expression didn't fit the words. He frowned, "I guess."

Carlton saw through it all. "Not a very good day, sir." He stared with a 'been there, done that' expression, his sky blue butlers apron tied snug around his waist. "Was it?"

Stoney knew that he couldn't mislead him. Not that he'll stop trying to. "I haven't been in a long time. It's going to take some time to get back into the swing of it, with all that jigging and snagging stuff going on." Updating his vernacular, fishing lingo, made him feel like a veteran fisherman. He needed practice, and plenty of it.

"Like riding a bike, sir?"

He brought to memory an episode of he and his father, fishing on their boat. He nodded pleasurably. "Yeah. Something like that."

After leaving the room, Carlton continued cleaning. He stopped when a thought came to mind. "Did you want to use the bathroom, sir?"

"I see you're busy in there. I'll use the one attached to the master bedroom. I want to get out of these smelly clothes and take a shower." At the foot of the stairs, he hollered, "I left some fish in the kitchen, on the counter. When you get a chance, can you fry up a piece for me?" As he was about to hit the third step, he yelled, "And make sure you cut the damn heads off!"

Carlton struck his head out of the bathroom and shouted, "Very well, sir."

He was relieved that Carlton didn't say anything about the broken glass that he was cleaning, because he wanted to push the chaotic incidents far from his mind. His theory, the less talked about, the less thought of. Out of sight, out of mind. He coined the phrase 'playing ignorant to the facts.' For some, that theory worked. Like standing in front of a two-way mirror, he wanted to look at people, without their being able to notice him. He wanted to study them, to be able to contemplate their next move, without them considering his existence. He wanted to believe that he was the last thought in anyone's mind. He wanted to go unnoticed. Especially when it came to the children from hell, Jake and Jessica.

*   *   *   *

While Stoney showered, he was disrupted when he heard a faint creaking sound, the bathroom door slowly opening. He stood still and listened intently. Although several spine-tingling thoughts flooded his mind, he wanted to believe that it was simply Carlton entering to retrieve his soiled clothes. To place them into the laundry bin.

Then a more treacherous thought came to mind. One that gave him cold shivers during a hot shower. JAKE! and JESSICA!

Abruptly, he froze in place, constrained by a dreadful thought of being subjected to another visit from the children of the damned. Even if he wanted to, he couldn't move a fraction of an inch. Over the sound of the spraying water, he listened to his heart throb stridently. Not being able to stop it from happening, the ugly horrors that accompanied the children's visits rushed into his heart and filled him with a shaky anxiety.

He heard someone say affectionately, "Hi, baby."

Feeling that he was out of danger, for the moment, his muscles thawed. Again, he felt as if he had been granted a reprieve; a stay of execution. He sighed exhaustively, then continued washing his body, acting as though nothing was wrong. Just to make sure, he checked by asking, "Katherine, is that you?"

Her voice approached the shower. "Yes, sweetheart. It's me."

"I thought I heard someone out there."

"Thought I'd come by to see how you were doing. Heard you went fishing today."

"How'd you know?"

"Carlton. Plus, I saw your fishing equipment downstairs in the kitchen, and I assumed."

Seeing her shadow move about behind the fogged glass partition, he could tell that she was up to something. Maybe shedding her jacket, because the bathroom was thick with steam, unbearably humid.

"I took off on a charter boat early this morning."

"Where'd you go?"

"Somewhere in Cape Cod. Hyannis Port."

"By yourself?"

"Yes, by myself. It was one of those 'on the spur of the moment' things. The morning called for it."

"How was it? Did you catch any fish?"

He hesitated for a long moment. "Um ..." he wasn't sure of how to respond. He had to think real hard. "... yeah. I caught a couple of them." Actually, he wasn't sure if he caught the fish, or if they caught him. It was all too confusing. He dropped the thought, went back to washing himself.

Seconds later, she slid the Plexiglas shower door open, and eyed him lustfully from head to toe. Standing in her birthday suit, she had an insatiable look sweltering in her eyes. Like what he had mentioned about an 'on the spur of the moment thing', she too had an 'on the spur of the moment' desire as well. However, her desire was a sexual itch that she yearned to have him scratch, to achieve a soothing gratification.

Had he been able to see her clearly through the steam, he would've seen how the tip of her tongue slid erotically across her upper teeth as she purred like a kitten. She drooled silkily, "I think it's time to get wet, handsome."

He couldn't tell what was about to happen. "Huh?"

"You need any help in there?" As if he couldn't bathe himself. He'd only been doing it for the past thirty-four years, that's all. Behind the ears and everywhere. Squeaky clean.

Her eyes remained focused on his body, certain areas more than others. She stepped inside and slid the door shut. In the shower, she knew the surprise she'd get if she turned her back on him, then dropped the soap, accidentally, on purpose.

Of course, there was that part of his life when he thought that sex was the only thing that mattered. When he got into his teens, getting his first piece was all he thought of, twenty-four seven. The day he lost his virginity, he wanted to work his peashooter until it fell off. He considered the burns on his kneecaps to be war medals, which he displayed proudly by wearing short pants most of the year. Even during the winter.

That crazed carefree period in his life lasted for more than fifteen years. With some guys, it never ends. That's why some ninety year-old men get heart attacks while pushing on a down stroke, for not knowing when to lighten up. They don't care if their penis is on its last leg, or needs the assistance of extra strength Viagra. What about that micro-sized mechanical gadget surgically implanted into the penis, with the manual pump surgically implanted into the scrotum sac? When the pump is pressed several times, it inflates the reinforced balloon planted inside of the penis. The man could sustain an erection that could last forever, even until after his demise. Or until his wife learns that he's been cheating on her with one of her closest friends, and she kicks him in the testicles, and deflates him.

Now that he's been updated to what's going on, he thought, I should've known she was going to get into the shower. She stops by, bangs my brains out, then leaves not too long after. Shouldn't these roles be reversed? I thought I was supposed to be the dog.

"Wash ya back yet?" she asked, looking for the soap. There was something about a mans back that left her utterly aroused. She couldn't explain why. It was just another one of those things, an idiosyncrasy. More like an oddity. Just like many women wonder what it's like to stand over a toilet bowl to pee, being able to grasp and supervise the steering of an extraordinary piece of equipment. Katherine became so curious one evening that she snuck up on him, as he was about to take a number one. She grabbed his penis from out of his hands and asked if she could direct the flow. To this day, he still couldn't believe that she had done that.

With him, it's the baby toe thingy complex. If an attractive woman has nice feet, no corns, perfect toes and arches, then she was all right. Good to get with. No taboo. If her baby toes did that curl under the ball of her feet, jelly jam crusty thingy, then it was an automatic turn off that made him nauseous. He made them promise to him, that under no circumstances whatsoever, either before, during or after the relationship, that she would ever remove her shoes in his presence. And if she did, then he'd shoot her. He hated toes with issues like these ever since he first saw the 'The Wizard of Oz.' Extraterrestrial toes like these made him think that the feet were about to shrivel or wither away, like the wicked witch of the west.

"No. Not yet," he replied waveringly. "I just stepped in a few minutes ago."

With a growing excitement dancing in her eyes, she removed the washcloth and soap from his hands, then rubbed them together. "I'll wash your back for you."

Although the water was steaming hot, the temperature just fifteen degrees hotter for him. Sometimes he wanted to tell her firmly, No! I can do it myself. Thank you very much. If he thought about it long enough, he would've definitely told her no, because he knew where she was going with the washcloth. Sometimes he didn't like it, but strangely, he never stopped her. When he thought about it long enough, an uncomfortable feeling surfaced, making him feel like he had just taken a long messy crap, and it was time to clean up shop. Something he'd been doing ever since his mom taught him. Simply put, her wiping his ass clean was something that didn't seem natural. Not at all. The idea of a woman cleaning a grown mans butt, especially when he was capable of doing it himself, just didn't sit right with him. However, and eerily, when she caught him at the right moment, the sky was the limit.

She worked at his back with a form of massaging, slash, cleansing technique. Her hands descended slowly and he felt an uncomfortable feeling approach. Suddenly, a red flashing light went off in his head. **'WARNING! WARNING!.'** Hearing sirens blare, he thought warily, not today. The idea to throw her a curve entered his mind, and he spun to face her. "Sweetheart," he said, embracing her.

"I wasn't finished," she said. "Turn back around."

Suddenly, something monumental and pleasurably astonishing caught her eye. Made her forget all about what she was doing only moments before. It was as if someone shook her mind like an Etch-a-Sketch toy, erased her thoughts. She stared glowingly at his fully erect penis, and a fresh idea entered her mind. "Oh my!" She gasped, "What's this?"

She knew perfectly well what it was. Sometimes a little dumb questioning added to the pleasure. Most blondes knew this little secret. That's why they have more fun.

He responded, as though teaching a child their ABCs. "You know what that is."

She soaped the cloth again, and implored lightheartedly with a schoolgirls voice, "Be gentle with me." She eyed his penis. "Did you wash it yet?"

He didn't reply. He knew that even if he didn't, that she'd wash it anyway. This, he didn't mind. In fact, he encouraged it. He stuck his midsection out, waiting for the delicate procedure to begin.

She wrapped the soapy cloth around his penis and grasped gently. Pulling the cloth toward her, she asked, "You'll let me know when it's clean, won't you?"

How could he possibly respond when the brain in her hand was now doing all of the thinking? During this, normal everyday words couldn't find their way to his lips. However, he figured that at this stage, he didn't need words.

The washcloth fell to the floor, so she used her hands, understanding that he liked that method much better. Suddenly, an idea to be barbaric entered his mind, and he felt the need to act prehistoric, like the Flintstones. He imagined Fred and Wilma slamming each other around like gorillas in the mist on that hard slab they called a bed.

He snatched her and delivered a deep, passionate kiss. Then pulled back and shoved her into the tiled shower wall. He lifted her up into his arms, and she wrapped her legs around his waist. Being soaped, he slid easily into her. Like an out of control animal, he grunted heavily, "Yaba-daba-doo!"

Holding onto him, she pressed her nails hard against his back, and three of her Jone' Clip-on-Nails popped off. Two on her right hand, and one on her left. Since she hadn't reached her climax yet, she hadn't noticed. Until then, it didn't matter. Enjoying her pleasure ride, she moaned, "Daddy! Ooohhh daddy!"

Several years back, when he first heard her say those words, he wondered if she was molested by her father. After asking her what it meant, she explained that it was just another one of her heated love calls; senseless rhetoric. Everybody did it. Those that didn't, probably want to.

What she never told him, believing that it didn't matter, was that she had the need to feel dominated, like to be roughed up a little. A little spanking never hurt anyone. If anything, it kept them in check.

His sense of humor found its way to his lips, and he returned the jest. "Ya want some candy, little girl? Will a nice fat peppermint stick do?" He gambled, never having responded to her 'daddy' call before. A smidgeon of curiosity found its way to his ears, and he waited anxiously for her response.

Gyrating her thighs, grinding them hips into his, she moaned and groaned, "Gimme candy! Gimme candy!" Her heated passion for him forced her to mutter, "All of it. Gimme all of it." Trying to get as much as she could from an out of balanced position, she swooned repeatedly, filled his ears with erotic whispers.

His rhythm was often one beat from hers. Sometimes she liked that. On a sloppy day, she liked it very much. Like having sex with several articles of clothing hanging from the body. Sloppy. Today was obviously a sloppy day. Anything went.

Feeling her legs tire, she dropped her feet to the floor, and they kissed passionately. She pulled away from him, and the lust in her eyes told him, 'You're not finished by a long shot.'

He welcomed the idea. But having a sexual encounter in a steam-filled shower often left him short winded. The thick air was difficult to breathe, challenged his endurance.

She turned her back to him, then grabbed onto the hot and cold shower knobs. She flashed her fanny and dared him to, "Saddle up, and lets go for a ride, my little buckaroo."

His hands embraced her hips gently, and his eyes ran to her heart shaped bottom. For some reason, an image of his elementary school teacher's chest cleavage entered his mind. The sexy young Miss Bottlestone, with her long red frazzled hair draping to her waistline. She use to wear tight fitting Marilyn Monroe cashmere sweaters that hugged her with the finesse of the puppy love that came from several of her young male students. The loose fitting short skirts she wore danced in the breeze at recess time, and peeped her magnificent legs in all their immaculate splendor. Her well-toned gymnast legs were as tall as the average student. She wondered why all of the little boys often circled her and insisted on playing 'here we go round the mulberry bush.' Bizarrely, she had the audacity to sit behind an opened end desk, with her legs crossed at the ankles, delivering a presentation, provide a view beginning with a journey that traveled up her well toned calves, over her perfectly cupped and sensuous kneecaps, fading off into a highly questionable dark 'V' shaped area of enchantment. Indeed, a rousing mystery to all the little tykes just discovering the world of being horny. Observation was always the beginning. Gawking, taking it all in, feeling with their eyes. Time to put away the Tonka Trucks.

When she was about to stand, thank God they didn't use swivel chairs back then. She had to take one leg and swing it out to the side, causing the highlight of the day. Some of the little boys leaned sideways, made desperate attempts to follow the infamous dark 'V' area, hoping for a slither of light to sooth their prying eyes. This desperate attempt to see more sometimes resulted in a few falling from their chairs. They prayed for just a smidgen of something more to dream on, a morsel to build a story to share at a Boy Scouts jamboree.

Peter Spencer, a little boy who made it a point to sit in the front row everyday, was considered very clumsy and accident prone at that time. He'd either drop his pencil, pen, notepad or book to just in front of his desk every ten minutes. Then he'd drop to the floor to retrieve it, lingering, suspended in time. All so he could get a better look at what was considered a phenomenon. He spent minutes on end, bobbing back and forth in his chair, gawking at her legs. They stole his attention from his studies, sometimes resulting in him falling into a deep hypnotic trance, and failing the class. He daydreamed daily, a goofy smile twisting his lips, his fingertips frolicking on his kneecaps. He showed strong dedication and ambition, all for a gamble that the next time she moved he was going to see more, hoping to get her right before she stood. When he arrived home from school most days, he went straight to his bedroom, locked the door and masturbated. Then he did his homework.

During the fall months, when she wore longer skirts, her calved were the topic of conversation in the little boy's room. Her muscular calves were pumped to the gills, perfectly toned. Their roundness must've been hand blown by the gods. Too bad for the little tykes all of this was no-boys land. Fortunately, some had questionable babysitters who couldn't wait to break a young lad into the world of fornication. Such a prestigious achievement, loosing their virginity at such a young age. Now that they're older, some would pay a fortune to spend the evening with a 'professional' babysitter. Someone from an escort service who dressed in costumes; maids outfits, nurses uniforms, tight fitting S & M outfits or whatever. Bondage. Fun stuff for some. Maybe for most.

Stoneys lower brain initiated his jockey like mentality, and he wanted to ride as if he was in the Kentucky Derby sweepstakes. His penis challenged him, asking, 'So, what's it gonna be, bro man? Ya don't need to breathe properly for me to have some fun. We've been this route plenty of times before. You just sit back and relax, and leave everything to me. I'll do all the work. I'll make ya feel real good, Stoneman. Good to the bone. I promise. Aren't you proud of me? Don't I always keep my promises? Always up and ready to go to work for you at a moments notice. Shiiiiit! I don't know how many times I busted my ass for you. This one time, how about you doing it for me? Do we have a deal? Whatdoya say, home boy? Brotha man! Home slice!'

With no doubts, he believed every word that his penis told him. Most men would've. And why not? His penis had never let him down before. It walked bravely into battle for him when he was a senior in high school. Minutes before a cheerleader who promised him a night he'd never forget, burned him. She carried at least a dozen Trojans in her knapsack. They were only for conversation sake, she seldom used them. Maybe one time. Nearly every high school has at least a handful of hussies who behaved in this fashion. Poor old Stoney had the drips for nearly a week before he finally built up the courage to tell someone about his searing problem. Actually, he didn't tell anyone. Spanky and Sleeper noticed him grinding his teeth in pain every time he went to the bathroom, while releasing his urine in short spurts. It was as if he was tapping out a message in Morse code. S-O-S! HELP! It—splash—hurts—splash—it—splash—burns.

Spanky and Sleeper talked him into getting the badly needed penicillin shots by ridiculing and chastising him. Back then, peer pressure was the only psychology they knew. They told him that they wouldn't come near him until he got the matter resolved. What really made him get help was when Spanky told him that he was going to announce over the school P.A. system the name of the burner, and of the twenty-five burnees.

Finally getting some enjoyment, some satisfaction out his life, Stoney gathered a cluster of her hair with his right hand, said inaudibly, Whoa girl! Back it up now!" He slapped her bottom. "Giddy-up there!

He didn't start slow, because he felt he was already past the foreplay of being gentle. Actually, there was no foreplay. That kind of consideration disappeared after the first time they had sex.

Because of the humidity, he proceeded sparingly, knowing his lungs were short on time. He knew he'd tire considerably quicker than normal, for the thick air factor. He rode Katherine wildly, like a bucking bronco, while trying to remember to keep his head low. Where the air was thinner, out of the stream of water. And so he wouldn't drown. Amazingly, his primary brain still had enough sense to realize this. As most intimate couples will admit, at this stage of intercourse, there was very little sense of reality.

Becoming lost in the heat of passion, she held onto the hot and cold knobs, and accidentally turned the cold water off. Quickly, they arrived to a period of utter confusion, a moment before their burning skin sent distress signals to their brains, 'THE WATER IS SCOLDING HOT! STOP WHAT YOU'RE DOING, AND GET THE HELL OUT OF DODGE!'

Both froze momentarily, wholly stunned. They yelled simultaneously as searing sensations blanketed many parts of their flesh.

After his midsection became enflamed, Stoney screamed, "Ouooo … shit!!"

"Aaarrrgggg!!" Katherine screamed painfully. "What the …"

He pulled from her, covered his groin with his left hand, pushed her to the side, then jumped out of the shower. The manly thing to do.

She jumped out afterwards, fell to the floor and banged her left knee. She sat leering at him, rubbing her lower back and kneecap, lips twisting into a sizable smirk of great disappointment. "Thanks a lot," she spat, "asswipe!"

"I'm sorry, Katherine," he apologized. "The water was burning the hell out of me."

She sprung to her feet and approached him, head snapping side to side with a plethora of attitude. "And I liked it, right?" She wound up and slapped him across the face as hard as she could, then threw at him, "You fricken idiot!"

He rubbed the left side of his face vigorously. "Dammit! The hell did you do that for? It wasn't my fault. You must've done something to one of the knobs by accident."

"No shit," she replied sarcastically. "You figure that out all by yourself, did you? Baby, your I.Q. is flying high today. My back and ass feel like they're on fire. Where's the shitten cold cream?"

Listening to her attitude, he had no doubt that the intercourse was over. For the time being. The mood was put on ice, like an arctic chill sliding in from the North Pole on the back of a frigid penguin. His Johnson had never shriveled so fast before in his entire life. A rapid sobering of both brains. He looked sadly at his limp penis, it delivered the bad news, 'Until next time, adios amigo.'

The last thing he needed was another unpleasant incident to spoil his already messed up day. He thought about what Mike had mentioned earlier about having a delicious meal of fried fish and beer, and it became something to look forward to. Something that he felt he could count on. Something that he hoped wouldn't let him down.

At that point, what barreled into his mind were the hallucinations that he's been experienced involving Jake and Jessica, and he prayed earnestly that it wouldn't happen again. He remembered telling Carlton to remove the heads from the Pollock, and hoped that he did just that. He walked to the bathroom door, opened it and hollered, "Carlton!"

From the bottom of the steps, he hollered back, "Yes sir!"

"Could you fix me a sandwich?"

"I though you wanted me to prepare the fish you've caught."

"I've changed my mind."

"Very well, sir. What would you like?"

"It doesn't matter." He returned to the bathroom and witnessed Katherine piling on globs of cold cream on her lower lumbar area. The scalding hot water had reddened her so severely, that it appeared as though only that part of her body had gotten tanned. Making eye contact with her, he found her expression to read, 'When all hell breaks loose, I can understand the every man for himself attitude. But you're a complete jackass! An asshole! Only a selfish piece of crap would do what you just did.

"Are you going to stay and have lunch with me?" He tried the puppy dog eyes routine. It never worked, unless he was on his deathbed.

"I don't know," she replied. "I have a couple of things I wanted to do with my girlfriends." It sounded like a poor excuse. After what had just happened, she didn't care how it sounded.

He asked distastefully "You hanging out with *them* again?" He grabbed a towel and dried himself, patted his groin area especially gently. "When's the next time you coming by?" He didn't want to sound overly concerned, but he was. It was difficult hiding feelings that he tried to keep from her. Didn't want her to know they were there.

"I don't know," She returned uncaringly. Felt that she had a right to respond this way, because of what he had just done to her. Even if she came back later on that evening, or the next day, she wouldn't have said so. She enjoyed the 'no schedule' routine. There were no promises to keep, allowing her to feel mysterious, as though she was an international spy; Mata Hari. "It all depends on how my schedule goes."

Schedule! he thought bizarrely. What fucken schedule? You don't have a fucken schedule. You never did have a fucken schedule, and never will a fucken schedule. You don't even know how to spell the fucken word. Until now, its never been in your vocabulary. After all this, he stated calmly, "Well, all right." He wanted to say a hell of a lot more, but figured who was he to complain. He threw in lastly, "Whatever."

A few minutes later, both had finished drying themselves. He grabbed a robe hanging on the back of the door, then slid into it. "You want something to eat before you go?"

She grabbed a large beach size towel hanging on a wooden rack nearby and wrapped it around her body, then glanced into his eyes and saw some of the disturbing events that have been haunting his soul. He had his ways of telling her that he wanted desperately for her to stay, and she knew about most of his carefully crafted sympathetic gestures. He didn't beg or plead or drop to his knees and pray to God to get things to go his way. It was all in the way he ended his sentences. The way the last word of his sentences rolled dolefully from his tongue with a whimpering effect was enough to indicate how he actually felt. She noticed that he always looked downward when he experienced these feelings. Looking down topped it off, as if he was too weak to hold his head up straight. Poor baby! He tried to play on the notion that there was still enough woman in her to make her feel for that mushy stuff. She couldn't help it, because she had no idea where those feelings came from. Otherwise, she would've done something to stop them from showing up. She only knew that they felt good, and understood that if pursued, those feeling might grow into something more pleasurable, lasting. However, she realized it was also a gamble. A risk she was thin to take.

"I guess I can stick around for a little while." Still present, a hint of antagonism riding her voice. "I'll have to call my girlfriends, to let them know that I won't be hanging out with them tonight. We were going to go to Boston, to check out this new club on Lansdowne Street. I think It's called Axis, or some shit like that."

She sounded as if her girlfriends, Pricilla and Dona, couldn't live without her. Stoney had to watch his back continually around these two beauties. Cinderella's sorority step sisters, Peat and Repeat. Been and Has been. Been there and Done that. Old bag and Deuschbag. The bell sisters, Ding and Dong. On one occasion or another, both have tried laboriously to take Stoney from Katherine. Failed attempts at seduction.

To this day, because he believed that some things should be left unsaid, she's never learned a word of their merciless back stabbings. He knew that if he had ever told her about what her girlfriends have tried to do, then he might've been accused as well. He had to have done something to initiate their efforts. He realized that it wouldn't have taken much to connect him to her exes. A few gigolos who came into her life only to use her for a temporary trampoline.

When she called and spoke with her girlfriends, they didn't sound too pleased at the news that she wouldn't be joining them for the evening. They even picked up a little attitude and took it personally when she mentioned that she was going to be spending the evening with her man. How dare that bitch! They handed her the 'he's no good for you anyway' routine. Amazing! All of this simply because they couldn't screw him and ruin their relationship. Making her situation like theirs. Making the three more compatible, as misery loves company.

Today they lost another round to hinder Katherines and Stoneys life. Feeling her tone over the phone line, they learned that they'd have to try harder in the near future. Or pay a professional to seduce him. Then they'd send her the pictures by email. And they call themselves best friends. With friends like these, who needs an enema?

Her girlfriend Donna invented the word jealousy. When Katherine invites her by Stoneys house, she did things that snakes would never do to their victims. Topping the list of a few things that she's done to try to separate the couple, especially while they were experiencing bitter times, she stole a few highly-prized CDs from his personal music collection. On another occasion, she walked around the house and broke insignificant items during parties and gatherings. She also blamed one of Stoneys male friends for urinating on the bed, something that a disturbed cat suffering from an anxiety disorder would do. She urinated into the mouthwash that's kept in the bathroom medicine cabinet, and poured a gram of cocaine into the sugar canister, along with some other strange chemical that she had got from her job at the waste recycling plant. During an intense argument between the lovers, she dropped a few cubes of sugar into the gas tank of his Porsche Carrera GT, hoping he'd blame Katherine.

Her other girlfriend Pricilla was more direct. She came by Stoneys mansion one day, unannounced, when Katherine wasn't there. She went directly to the master bedroom and removed all of her clothes. She laid across the bed and spread her legs as far as she could, then invited him to 'come get some.' Unfortunately for her it didn't work, because he didn't fall for it. At one of the parties he gave, through mingling and speaking with one of her ex-boyfriends, he discovered what her personality was like far ahead of time. To get her last boyfriend to break up with another one of her girlfriends, Pricilla seduced him into having oral sex. She then went to his girlfriends apartment—she only lived next door—and explained dramatically to her what he had forced her to do. Before she said a word, she spat the evidence on the floor, right at her feet. Once, while attending a cheerleader tryout in college, she was beat out by nine girls who hung in a clique. To get revenge, she screwed their boyfriends, nine jocks on the varsity football team. She'd swear to God on a stack of bibles that she came out ahead on that one.

CHAPTER 17

▼

Later that evening, Spanky was at his apartment, waiting for Sleeper to arrive. They were about to take care of some Dixie Club business in the downtown Boston area. Before he thought seriously about whatever he was going to get into, he normally threw down a few shots of Jim Bean Whiskey, with a Pepsi chaser. It helped loosen his nerves, increased the size of his ego; his balls. It pushed him closer to the edge. It tipped his balance with reality, made him feel like talking a boat load of shit. The only drawback, it sometimes made him ramble on in conversation about nothing in general—diddlysquat jack shit.

The last time the three headed out to ride a shakedown on a major drug dealer, Spanky and Sleeper stood in a vacant alley and psyched themselves by growling like wolves, slapping each other across the face. They didn't hold a damn thing back. Especially Spanky. It made them angry, go into a situation highly upset and ticked off. Ready to blow someone's head off at a moments notice.

After he took a shot and drank the chaser, he burped rowdily, blared his contentment. Spike looked at him sideways whenever this occurred. Like when Spanky passed gas, it wasn't the norm. Expected, but not the norm, if that can be figured. It came from out of nowhere. It didn't jive with the usual routine. It threw him off, puzzled the hell out of his little bulldog brain. Sometimes he spun in a quick circle, searching for a duck that he swore was nearby.

When Spanky looks into his big brown eyes, he finds peace and serenity. An undying friendship, because Spike is a suck-up. He's a dog. Most dogs grow to behave like this to anyone who, on a daily basis, feeds them, gives them a rubdown, scratches their necks and plays with them.

When he bathes him, the pooch enjoyed it immeasurably. He couldn't say so, but he loved it when Spanky washed his butt, freed the minute granules of hardened feces from his butt. When Spanky washed his lower back, he lifts his hind leg in anticipation, without having been instructed to do so. He looked forward to their Saturday evening bathing sessions, because there was little enjoyment elsewhere in his life. After all, animals get horny too. Most males, human or otherwise, love a good old-fashioned nut-rub.

When he was nine months old, Sleeper and Stoney use to come by mostly during the weekends to watch sports on cable television. Channel ESPN. To everyone's surprise, he'd come charging from out of nowhere, latch onto one of their legs for dear life, and hump his little rump until someone smacked him on his bulldog noggin with a rolled newspaper. He grew tired of Spankys leg and craved variety.

One time, while watching a football game, Spanky and Sleeper were drinking excessively, and had passed out on the couch. Naughty little Spike took advantage of, and molested Sleepers right leg. After he woke up, he noticed the stain on his pants leg, and merely thought that he had spilled special sauce on himself. He had wolfed down a Big Mac from a nearby McDonalds prior to the drinking. As he felt the stain for texture, Spike sat on his doggie bed with a relieved expression smeared across his flattened snout, craving a Newport cigarette.

Spanky asked him, "Hey buddy. Are we ready to go out and kick some ass tonight?"

Spike smiled. Sort of. He hadn't exactly mastered the English language yet, so he listened closely. He had nothing else better to do. He wasn't in the self-lapping mood this evening.

"When Sleeper gets here, old chum, we're gonna go out and have some fun. Ya wanna come? You can sit in the back seat and watch how the old man operates."

He understood questions. There was a certain tone to it that he'd come to recognize. A submissive ending to a sentence, the way Spanky stopped talking and stared expectantly. As if he was waiting for Spikes response. That's when he would sit up straight and deliver a look of encouragement, then bark. Usually twice.

"Woof! Woof! Woof! … Woof!" He was feeling talkative this evening. Sometimes he threw in a few extra barks for good measure. The forth didn't come like the first three. It was extended, like the way words tapered off at the end of a question. Spike asked him, 'Are you out of your fricken mind, you flaming moron? Shut up and get my grub, before I leave a little something something in the bathtub.'

Spanky rubbed his head. "That's my boy. I wish I can take you with us, but this is human stuff. Gotta make the bread. You understand, don't you?"

His tongue rested sticking out over his front teeth, in deep contemplation, trying to figure out what was going to happen next. He gave up and decided to sport the 'I have to go outside and take a crap' look. A deeply philosophical expression, accompanied with a slight whimper. He had hoped Spanky had learned to recognize it.

He didn't.

Seconds later, the doorbell rang.

"It's about time." He went to the door and pressed the talk button on the intercom system. "That you, Sleep?"

"Yeah."

Recognizing the voice, Spike barked at the intercom system. "Woof! Woof!" He tilted his head to the side, as if to ask, 'Master, why's Sleeper inside of that little box? Did he do something bad, and is on punishment?'

Spanky pressed the talk button. "I'll be right down in a minute."

CHAPTER 18

▼

Driving into Downtown Boston, Spanky filled the car, mostly Sleepers ears, with a bunch of gobbligook. Rambling off at the mouth about everything and anything, diddlysquat jack shit. Sleeper knew automatically what kind of a mood he was in, figured his behavior to be somewhat entertaining. He kept quiet and listened, wondered what kind of garbage was flying around inside of his head. "I wish I can get into the deep pockets of those pilfering bastards down at city hall. Man! They got it made in the shade, hustling heavy time, overtime, and any way you can look at it. They don't ever stop, with their fat ass bankbooks. Sleep, we're nothing compared to them. Out here busting our asses, dealing with the low-life scum of the earth. The boys in city hall are big timers, screwing every city contract and contractor they can lay their sticky little webbed fingers on. And the governor—oh that fucken governor—I'd like to take his ass, stuff him into a sling shot, then send his tight ass straight to the moon. And his buddy, the mayor—oh that gotdamn mayor—that bastard's got so many under the table things going on with helping his buddies get rich, they'll all retire billionaires. As for our senators, I can't even begin to tell you what those mother fucken freaks have been up to. And that ghostly looking city councilwoman with the mule ass, you know that bitch has three illegal immigrants working for her as servants. And that state-rep son-of-a-bitch, he ..."

Sleeper said flatly, "Spanky, my dear friend, don't you ever shut the fuck up? For someone who swore allegiance to uphold the integrity of the constitution, and protect its ruling members and citizens, you talk a lot of crazy shit against the system. You're pathetic, with your malevolent thinking. All the time, yap yap yap and blab blab blab, trash talking about things that don't even make sense. About people who've you've never even met. I mean, how old are you anyway?"

"Thirty-four. Why do you ask?"

"You can't be thirty-four. Nobody can get that full of shit in thirty-four years. It's impossible!"

Sounding like Al Pacino in the blockbuster movie 'Taxi', he asked, "You talking to me?"

"You don't see nobody else here, do you?"

"I see a scrawny little pamper wearing son-of-a-bitch sitting next to me. So you must be talking to yourself."

"No. I'm not talking to myself. I'm talking to you."

"Are you categorically and undeniably sure you're talking to me?"

Spilling a nonchalant attitude, Sleeper replied airily, "Most certainly."

"Well, my good man, since you've made yourself perfectly clear on the matter, I'd like to offer a suggestion for remedy."

"Pray tell, what would that be?"

"Why don't I simply pull over for a moment or two, then we can get out of the car? Then, with your permission, of course, I'd like to proceed in gracefully placing my steel toed shoe straight up your ass."

They broke out with laughter.

"You're a nut," Sleeper stated. "You're probably going to retire from some form of stress related mental illness."

"You're probably right."

While both laughed, for some ulterior reason, Sleeper laughed just a little bit longer, louder, as if to insinuate something. Because Spanky noticed, it lingered in the back of his mind, in an area marked 'caution!' It set off a warning. A red flag of warning. He believed it to be a distorted cryptic message. One that he's been giving more thought to translate, for his growing sense of paranoia. Perhaps it had something to do with the kind of risky business they were involved in. Or not.

They cruised down Boylston Street, heading in the direction of an area called the Combat zone. A locality infested with many filthy strip clubs and putrid bars frequented by many undesirables; prostitutes, their Johns, perverts and heavy drug activity. When they were exactly in front of a strip club called the Naked 'I', Sleeper noticed a familiar person standing just outside. He pointed in their direction and alarmed, "Slow down! There's Ricky Adams, standing next to those two women."

"He's not rolling anymore," Spanky informed him. "He's out of the business. Said he had a revelation, premonition, epiphany, or some bullshit like that. Said he found Christ during that hospital stay, when he had gotten shot three times over drug money. He almost bought the farm on that one. Now he's trying to clean up some of the criminal enterprises going on around here, preaching the word of God. Long as he doesn't interfere with my money, he ain't no threat to me. We have to find the Rasta man, Nate the skate. He's moving into the big time now. He must've made more than a hundred grand just last week alone, and I heard he's expecting something big. I heard he likes to hang out in the zone a lot. Tonight, our business is with him."

Dollar signs flashed in Sleepers eyes, he heard a cash register ring. 'Kaching! Kaching!' "A hundred grand!"

"That's right." As if it were a fact, he stated, "And half of it's mine. That's if he wants to stay out of jail. One of his cronies owed me a favor. Dropped his name, implicating him in that recent drug deal shooting over on Dudley Street. Two people shot, one fatality. I know that ignorant bastard's around here somewhere."

Turning left on Washington Street, Sleeper shouted, "There he is, coming from out of the alley, with that girl. Isn't that his new girlfriend? She looks familiar."

"That's ..." Spanky snapped his fingers twice, "... Marla, A.K.A., Sugar Babe. She use to work the streets in the Grove Hall section of Roxbury. Now she strips in a joint around the corner. I bet you she's forking over her money to that dumb ass."

Marla Johnson's a twenty two year old drifter who's been on the streets ever since she was eleven years old. She's originally from Billerica, Mass. When she was nine, her father sexually abused her, then her heroin-addicted mother threw her into the streets a year later. She thought her daughter was an evil child because she didn't tell her of the abuse. Instead of dealing with her husband, laying the blame where it belonged, she accused her daughter of having an affair with her biological father. Never mind the fact that he beat her senseless several times, then threatened her with a gun, promising that he'd kill her and her mother if she ever mentioned a word of the abuse to anyone.

She then stayed briefly in a housing project on the east side of Brockton with an aunt who was also a junkie. After the aunt was giving a life sentence for killing a teller in a botched bank robbery, she stayed at the apartment until the aunts boyfriend threw her into the streets. He tried to put her to work on hoes row, but she didn't like the idea of giving her hard earned money to someone who considered her to be less than a human being.

She's gotten use to living on the streets quickly. She somehow developed a sense of belonging, when she began associating with a group of people who had the same background as hers. People who've suffered the same kinds of abuse, and then thrown into the streets like yesterdays trash. Lost children of the night, searching for acceptance. She's been lost for many years, and lives with the unpromising expectancy that someday her mother will find her, and they'll rekindle the relationship they once shared. The fading quality times she holds dear to her heart.

Nathaniel Edwards, A.K.A. Nate the skate, is a thirty-two year old American born Jamaican. He's a very determined and strong willed individual who's been dealt an unfortunate hand of five skulls and crossbones at birth. He didn't just jump into the world of lawlessness, like most of his friends. His story goes all the way back to when he was born in prison. Twenty-five years ago, his mother was given a fifteen-year prison sentence at a womans correctional facility in Framingham, Massachusetts. She was found guilty of second-degree murder for killing his father for spousal abuse. Being dirt-poor, she had to use the assistance of a court appointed attorney who cared nothing about justice. She began serving her sentence two months before she gave birth to Nathaniel.

One day, because he could no longer take the mental and physical abuse delivered by some of the staff members in a state home for youths, he ran away, and they wrote him off. He's been on the streets ever since he was eight years old.

Because of the hard times he's experienced, he grew hostile inwardly, became extremely angry. He fed hatred into his ignorance, then allowed the countries preconceived beliefs of some African-American men to sink deep into his soul. He grew to believe that the only way he was going to get ahead in life was to steal, sell drugs, run con games, entertain or play professional sports. He swallowed the ideology completely, because he didn't get the proper guidance from anyone who cared enough to keep him marching in the right direction. He followed what he believed to be negative influential gestures coming from the few in control of dispersing the general news; television, the newspapers and so forth. He didn't realize that he was helping them to substantiate what they were misleading the public to believe, about the threat of black men to the general public. The menace to society.

Leaving the alley, Nate and Marla huddled closely together. Marla had just finished a set at a strip joint only ten minutes before. They chose to leave through the rear entrance to avoid some of her perverted fans and stalkers. Even a married city official waited to offer cash for a few extracurricular activities. A sinful evening of lace, pretty silk bows tied in bondage.

As they touched the sidewalk, Spanky nearly plowed into them with his car, grinding his wheels into the curb. He and Sleeper jumped out of the car quickly to confront them, and Spanky hollered, "Boston police! You two, hold it right there."

A few people standing near stopped to witness the confrontation. As Spanky approached Nate and Marla, he instructed Sleeper to, "You keep the people moving." His arms outstretched to stop Nate and Marla. "Hold up you two. We have to talk for a minute. Com'on back into the alley."

Sleeper waved his arms at a few persons walking by, shouted his authority, "Let's keep it moving! There's nothing to see here!" Pointing to three college students, he made it sound as though they were hindering police business. "You people, over there. Keep the sidewalk clear. Keep it moving!"

"Damn!" Nate grunted, shook his head in frustration. He whispered to Marla, "Don't tell them nothing, no matter what they threaten you with. They ain't got a damn thing on us, cept for what you give them."

Marla whispered, "What do they want?"

"What's happening, Nate," Spanky chucked airily. "How's it going, bro man?" A failed attempt at trying to relate.

After Sleeper got the people moving, cleared the area, he returned to where Spanky stood, pointing into the alley, telling Nate, "This'll only take a minute. Let's go."

Feeling that he didn't have a way out of the situation, Nate dropped his shoulders, along with a heavy sigh. "Shit!" He garbled angrily, "Mothers fuckers always fucken with me." He walked back into the alley with Marla tight by his side.

Spanky and Sleeper followed closely behind them, keeping a vigilant eye to make sure there were no witnesses. Before they arrived to a dark area where Spanky preferred them to go, Nate stopped short. He faced them and demanded angrily, "What'n the hell you taking us back here for? I ain't got no business with you."

Spanky grabbed Nate by the arm, then shoved him against a brick wall, on the side of the strip club. He gave him a quick pat down to make sure that he wasn't carrying a concealed weapon. He gave Sleeper an obvious look, urging him to do the same to Marla, but instead, he remarked, "I ain't touching this filthy thing. Besides, I didn't bring a pair of rubber gloves with me. You want me to bring problems home to my family?"

Marla frowned distastefully at Sleeper. Only grumbled, "Huh!"

"Listen up, Nate," Spanky stated, then got down to business. "Like the song says, Rasta man." He crossed his arms and assumed the likeness of a typical notorious rapper. "I hear you been sitting on the block," he clutched his crotch with his left hand, "holding your cock," he made like he carried a pistol in his right hand, "playing with a Glock, disobeying the law. You made a big messy score last week. A hundred G's of blood money. That's fifty thousand red bills for you, and fifty thousand for me." He flashed a pair of empty palms. "Hey, I'm a fair man. I'm only going to take half."

Nate's eyes bucked wide in shock, utterly stunned. Preparing to leave, he grabbed Marla by her arm and huffed, "Aw man! What kind of shit is this?" He told Marla, "Com'on babe. Let's get outta here."

Spanky grabbed him by the lapels on his jacket, and this time, pushed him violently into the brick wall in back of him. He placed his hand firmly on his chest, so he'd stay where he was. He asked calmly, "Where ya going, old buddy? I didn't say it was time to leave yet."

Marla released Nates arm, stared with a frightful expression. She clutched her purse firmly against her bosom and didn't say a word.

Nate attempted to free himself from Spankys grip, and he pushed him forcibly into the wall again, causing his head to smash into the bricks behind him. "Dammit!," he cursed. He rubbed the back of his head. "The hell's the matter with you? That shit hurt."

The thought to check Marlas purse entered Sleepers mind, knowing that people like Nate sometimes had their women hold their guns and drugs. He became leery of her nervous gestures and watched her with a cautious eye, as a blink from her was long in coming.

"Sleep," Spanky said, "Why don't you take this sad excuse for a woman for a joyride, and give it to her the way a real man should. She probably already did half the town tonight, and maybe a few women. One more won't make a difference. Meanwhile, I'll stay here and work on this sack of shit I got in my hands."

Marla looked at Sleeper, swallowed hard and whined, "Nooo!" The notion returned dire memories of an atrocious incident that had happened a few months before, shortly before she had promised herself that she'd leave prostitution for good. So she hoped. Quickly filling her heart was the horror she suffered when she was brutally raped by a Boston Police detective, and she dreaded the thought of anything like it ever happening again.

Sleeper pruned his lips sourly. "Com'on, Spanks. Ya putting me ta sleep with all this screw the trash business. I wouldn't screw her with my worst enemy's dick. In fact, I'd rather lay your dog. At least I know he's had his shots, and doesn't go around sniffing up other dogs asses for milk bones."

He smiled a peculiar sideways expression. "I'm sure Spike would appreciate that. I think."

Suddenly, Marla became frustrated at them, her twitching eyes shot back and forth between the two. She stuttered, "Y-Y-Yous two betta leaves us alone. We ain't botherin peoples."

Spanky caught her stare. "What the fuck are you looking at?" He addressed Nate. "You screwing this sad excuse for a woman, are ya Nate?" He laughed. "Ignorant bitch been whoring and hooking her way around the world, and still can't talk right. She's murdering the kings English. All that traveling, and the only thing that she's learned to do is say the word 'duh' in fifty different languages." He asked sarcastically, "How're ya doing it to her, Nate? Do ya take a shot of penicillin before, or after. Do ya have to use three or four rubbers? How about five?" He excited, "Oh! I get it. You just stick ya little whip in some melted latex, and you're all set for the night. Is that how you do it, Mr. Rasta man?"

Sleeper snickered. "That's disgusting."

Now highly frustrated, Nate tried again to free himself from his grip. "The only disgusting thing I see here is a couple of pilfering pimps for the system. The only thing you low-life maggots represent is 'cash over people.'

Absorbing the insult, Spanky wound up as tight as he could and punched him in the stomach. Nate fell to the ground on one knee, and vomited his dinner from two hours before on Spankys left shoe. As the corn like granules flowed from his mouth and splattered the ground, he gagged on the residue stuck in his throat.

Feeling as helpless as a baby, Marla trembled with fear, her whining climbed a pitch higher.

"Shut up, bitch!" Spanky ordered. "You want some of this too?" He snatched the purse from her hands. "Gimme that!" He used it to wipe the vomit from his shoe.

She leaned down to help Nate, placed her shaking hands on his shoulder. "It's okay, Nate. We's gonna get outta here. We's been in worst troubles before."

Laughing at her vocabulary, Spanky mumbled, "Ignorant bitch." He threw her purse at her feet, then leaned toward Nate and turned up the temperature. "Nate, as far as I'm concerned, you ain't been touched yet. Either of you starts talking cash, or I'm taken you downtown to book you for conspiracy of drug trafficking and accessory to murder." Nate looked at him fearfully, a very sensitive nerve had been struck. "One of your cronies who I interrogated in the recent shooting on Dudley Street dropped your name as his accomplice. Henceforth, you're a codefendant. You know, joint venture and all that togetherness shit. And to fan the flames on your already overcooked hide, I'm going to add to it that you tried to pull a gun on me to avoid arrest. At least, that's what it's going to read in the report I'll have to fill out. I know you have the money hidden somewhere, because people like you don't use bank accounts. You know the government will wipe out your account because you have no viable means of support. You can't explain where it came from. In short, you take us to the money, you give me half. If you're lucky, you can just hop on the next plane out of this country. To somewhere that doesn't have an extradition treaty with America. Personally, I think you should take the deal. If you don't, I'll take you in, and you'll be doing a lot of hard time up at Cedar junction. Walpole." He eyed Marla. "She'll go to jail too, Framingham for women. I'll string her along for the ride, add to the report that she tried to help you escape. Since you're a wanted and desperate criminal, they'll have no problem with believing every word of what I'll say happened."

"Nooo!" she whined. She picked up her purse with her thumb and index finger, stared at it revoltingly "I don't want to go back to jail. I didn't have nothing to do with ..."

Nate cut her off, "Shut up! You simple minded heffa."

Spanky said tiredly, "Will you shut the hell up? We're trying to do business here. I can't concentrate with you interrupting, sounding like a wounded animal. You're getting on my nerves with that shit. Cut it out." He told Nate, "What do you say, my Klu Klux Klan brother. Is it a deal, or is it off to the pokey."

"What?" he said. "I ain't no Klu Klux Klan man."

"Yes, you are," Spanky returned sarcastically. "You're just too ignorant to realize it. Malcolm X tried to tell you that you've been hoodwinked, bamboozled and led astray, but you didn't listen. Assholes like you never listen. That's why you're busy demolishing your own people, instead of helping to build them up. Busy fighting over the scraps that we scrape from our tables." He knelt down on one knee, got in Nates face, up close and personal. "Nate, let me ask you this. Do you personally know of any white men who dress up in white sheets, who've come to your neighborhood to kill black people and sell drugs?" He laughed. "You can't name one. Can you? But ask yourself honestly. How many black men do you know of personally, who've killed other black men, who are on the streets, as we speak, selling drugs and creating a shitload of havoc in their own communities? I bet you can name at least a few dozen easily. Can't you?" He paused again. "That means that people like you are doing more harm to your own people than the Klu Klux Klan, from your direct involvement. From what you've witnessed and know to be true. In fact, Nate, the Klan loves you, because you're volunteering your services without their even asking. And if you're helping them do their job, then you're what some in society call a Klu Klux Klan brother. You're doing their job, dumb ass! No matter how you look at it, no matter how you add it up, the bottom line is that you're a black man helping the Klan destroy his own people. The only difference between you, your friends, and the Klan, is that you don't wear the white uniform. Although, there are a few of your kind who like to wear pointed hoodies, just like the Klan. Same difference." Spanky stood upright, feeling wholly justified. "Nate, I don't have all day. What's it going to be? The money, or Walpole?" He pulled out a set of handcuffs and dangled them in front of him. "You've got just five seconds to make up your mind."

"Even for someone like you, Nate," Sleeper said. His sight ricocheted in between Spanky and Nate, "this should be a no brainer." He stared at the handcuffs. His adrenalin flowed swiftly.

After only two seconds, he agreed to settle. He answered submissively, "All right. All right." He coughed, then spat the last of the vomit tickling his throat, lingering in his mouth. "I'll do it."

"Good," Spanky nodded. "Now you're talking sense. Where's the cash?"

"It's at my place," he replied regrettably. "Not far from here."

"All right then. Let's go."

"When we get there, how do I know you won't take all of it?"

Spanky looked at Sleeper and smiled. "Well, since we're holding all of the cards, you're going to have to trust us on this."

"The hell should I trust you?"

"Simply put, because you've got no choice."

With that, Nate said no more, knowing that his back was up against a wall. Literally. Marla helped him to his feet, then all four walked to the alley entrance. Spanky and Sleeper walked directly behind them, almost touching their heels. In case they'd try to do something desperate.

"And remember," Spanky warned, "any tricks along the way, and I ain't gonna have no problems with making you two past history. As a matter of fact, put your hands behind you." He slapped on the cuffs. "We're going to keep these babies on, until we get to your place. Just in case."

Still clutching his midsection, Nate turned his back to him, mumbling obscenities under his breath. "Gotdamn fucken pilfering nasty ass …"

Spanky slapped him on the back of his head. **PAP!!** Nate stumbled a few feet forward, he told him, "I heard that. Watch you mouth, Klan brother."

Expecting the same treatment, Marla cringed with fear. Holding the vomit covered purse in her left hand, she covered the back of her head with her right hand.

Spanky pulled back a few feet, told Sleeper, "See. That's all ya gotta do. Ya let them know who's running things, what time it is, and boom! It's payday."

Sleeper shook his head and declared, "Man! You're one crazy son-of-a-bitch."

"Thanks." He assisted Nate and Marla into the back seat of his car, slammed the door shut, then told Sleeper, "I'm proud of that achievement."

"You know something, Spanks? I've never heard of that phrase you used on him back there. That Klu Klux Klan brother stuff. What's that about?"

He replied just low enough, so that Nate and Marla couldn't hear him. "It has something to do with a type of practice that an old slave owner named Willie Lynch once used during slavery, to school other slave owners on how to keep their slaves in line."

"Yeah?"

"Oh yeah. It's all about using proving techniques as a means to control a group of people, by psyching them into keeping busy with themselves. It breeds animosity among the ranks. You know, black on black crime. As long as they're caught up in the mix—preoccupied with the problems that we create for them—the system works its magic, and keeps things in line."

"Why don't people know about this stuff?"

"Some do. In his group, only successful African Americans know. That's how they get ahead, by knowing and applying this understanding to their lives. It's out there. It's just that it's not easy to get the word across in the inner-city. When you're caught up in the vicious cycle of oppression; battling poverty, you don't have the time to stop to listen to words of reason. To some caught up in the rat race, they don't have the time to pick up a book, because they believe words won't put food on the table, or help pay the bills. That's why there's a shitload of violence going on in some poor communities, fighting among their selves. Especially with these gangs running around out here, fighting over turf that doesn't even belong to them. They're fighting over crumbs, when the real deal is on a much wider scale. Something that they can't even see, cause it's too deep for them to fathom. When they get a speaker who tries to make them aware of what's happening, whether spiritual or otherwise, then the powers that be eradicates the threat. Or, like Dr. Cornell West of Harvard once said, they've been Santa Clausificationed—made to appear harmless, so no one will take their doctrine seriously. There's a lot of money to be made in keeping things the way that they are. You know, our way of life and all that good shit. You know how the old saying goes, 'with no bad guys, you need no good guys.'" He laughed. "We're supposed to be the good guys."

"That's some deep shit."

"Tell me about it. After we pick up the money, I'll give you a cut for helping me out. Then I'm going to make a short run out of state, to make a deposit at my secret hide-a-way stash."

"Does the Stoneman know about this stuff?"

"Yeah. He knows all about it. For a brother, he has a good working knowledge of the truth. That's why he's successful. He swallows it hard sometimes, but he knows how to accept. That's why I respect the man. He goes with what he sees, not with how he prefers it to be, like all that fantasy bullshit. He knows how society thinks. Remember what we talked about the other day, at the side of the road, about people and the things that they sometimes do to enhance their beauty?"

"Yeah."

"Well, to give myself an education, as I believe in getting firsthand knowledge, I went out with this very attractive sister. She has …"

Sleeper's squinted shadily. He laughed, "You tryinta get a little taste of honey? You tryinta put some flavor in your life? You got jungle fever?"

"Not exactly. The only color I see is green. When it comes down to it, that's all that matters to me. I call it the sum total. Anyway, about this woman, she's a very intelligent young lady. Sexy as all hell. I met her at a library in Copley Square. And you know something? I found out one thing. Never try to pull a fast one over on a positive sister who sports an afro. People who have an optimistic aura like hers are sure of their identities. This one in particular, she knows where she came from, knows all about her roots. That's why she wears that afro. We had a quiet dinner, and I appreciated dealing with her truth in realty. Rather than listening to someone caught up in the bullshit of living a fantasy. You know, all that Hollywood glamour shit. Sleeper, it was a hell of an experience. I think I'll call her at the end of the week, maybe plan something for the weekend."

"Will you be back before the shift ends?"

"Hopefully. All depends on the traffic. But then again, you know how I like to drive my '69' Stang." He proclaimed excitedly, "Like a bat out of hell!"

CHAPTER 19

▼

Thursday morning.

The dawns early light filled Stoneys morning with a glorious touch of daybreak, the rising sun brushed a soft pastel against his bedroom walls. The magnificent phenomenon entered his room as a symphony of music, awakening him graciously as it did the day before, and the pleasure succeeded in overwhelming him cordially.

Listening attentively, he heard the distant high-pitched melodious sounds of various birds chirping their morning verse. A delightful sound his ears welcomed wholeheartedly. And to think, Katherine was still by his side

Her flowing hair shading the side of her face, sound asleep, she laid undaunted by her unfettered dreams, but not shamefully so. Unmoving in a world all her own, she appeared ageless, as if a princess anticipating a kiss that would waken her from an eternal deep sleep.

Admiring his sleeping beauty, he felt that a completion of the fairy tale like encounter was in call. Eyeing her succulent breasts peeping themselves just above the edge of the white satin sheets, he took considerable note of her nipples, which stood full-bodied and ripe. He knew so much of the effects that a slight gust of wind would have on them, and entreated the soft winds circling the room to deliver a tender breeze. A gentle gust that would stroke her ever so delicately, to deliver one of natures delightful surprises. At first, a tingling sensation, resulting in a sudden swelling and hardening of the nipples. The two-inch diameter dark mounds encircling them, their flock of tiny sensuous pimples enhanced his desires furthermore, and he found them rather luscious. His lips quivered uncontrollably and his tongue swam in his mouth delightfully, as a newborn anticipating its next suckling.

A kiss. A stolen kiss is what he fancied. Her giving was simple and expected, a shared passion. Taking one whilst she slept, unbeknownst to her, stirred feelings of controversy, and **he** wondered how far he could go.

Lying beside him, she looked especially peaceful and free from the tangled web that she so tediously weaved during her waking days. Yes, a stolen kiss, perhaps.

He leaned toward **her** and inhaled a rousing fragrance, savored in her perfume of the evening before, entitled as so, 'The Evening Before.' He examined the fine details of her womanly facial structure, a rare moment of her being make-up free. From the morning light grazing her face splendidly, her naked beauty glowed vividly in all its natural form. From what society had conditioned her to believe, her naked beauty is what she shunned.

But alas, there remained moments of stolen glimpses. Moments that allowed the natural appearance of her exquisiteness to shine gracefully, whilst she slept. For him, now was the time to relish such a moment.

Leaning closer, he placed his elbow gently on her pillow, as not to disturb her. Her head turned slightly to face him, and it appeared as though she was going to open her eyes and greet the day. She was reluctant to do so, because it was not her time.

Before his lips touched hers, now only a fraction of an inch away, a trifling charge of static electricity connected the lovers and zapped them inconsequentially. She smacked her lips as though savoring a scrumptious delicacy from a foreign land, then opened her mouth wide and yawned exhaustively.

At that moment, at that very moment, he froze dead in his tracks, petrified, sporting an uncanny expression. His lips pruned awkwardly, he pulled back immediately, then questioned the eerie phenomenon crashing his storybook like encounter. Caused him to hold his breath, gag and choke.

He rolled to the opposite side of the bed, slid from it and rose to his feet. Heading toward the bathroom, he muttered, "Wow! I thought my morning breath stank. Girly over there done picked up some serious foul during the night. Must be all that raw seafood, beer and cigarettes she had last night. I keep telling her about those nasty cancer sticks, but she doesn't listen. She'll might consider quitting when she gets pulmonary emphysema, and they have to hook her up to one of those iron lung thingamajigs. I can see her now, coughing up wads of phlegm, carrying around one of those portably oxygen canisters in a knapsack, sucking in fresh air to keep herself alive. And chances are, she'll probably still be sucking on those things like they're going out of style. Just like my Uncle Buddy, can't tell her nothing.

Passing the bureau, he expected to see his reflection in the mirror that was once there. Abruptly, the dreadful details of the shooting came back to him, readily available to haunt him from top to bottom. Inside and out. There was no escape. The details of what had led to the temporary spurt of madness filled his mind, and he thought it strange that he didn't see Jake or Jessica while he slept. Shame on him. Will he ever learn? He had stolen a few more Z's.

He noticed Katherine's compact mirror sitting atop the bureau. She had placed it there the evening before. It was opened and facing him. He glanced into it briefly, became depressed and damned all mirrors for the ghastly hallucinations that he's experienced thus far. Until he'd seen the last of Jake and Jessica, he made it a sole priority to avoid anything that could cast a reflection. An impossible task that he believed he could achieve. He knew all to well he couldn't do it, unless he was dead. Damn the thought.

Breaking his sight from what was left of the shattered mirror to go to the bathroom, he mumbled, "I don't believe I went around the house and broke all of the gotdamn mirrors. I must be one sick mother …"

CHAPTER 20

▼

Within the hour, Katherine had gotten up, taken a shower, and most importantly, brushed her teeth and rinsed out her mouth. Stoney went to the kitchen to fix his breakfast, and discovered Carlton washing the dishes from the evening before. There was a dishwasher available, but he preferred to do it manually. There weren't many dishes anyway. He realized a dishwasher could never clean thoroughly, some areas on weird shaped accessories.

Hearing Stoneys footsteps approach, he greeted him cheerfully, "Good morning sir."

"Morning, Carlton." he stated insipidly. He stopped in front of the kitchen table, stared at the huge spread laid out before him. Bacon, sausage links, a few ham and cheese omelets, wheat toast, coffee and orange juice.

Carlton told him, "Through you fiancés instructions, I've taken the liberty of preparing breakfast for you." Donning his favorite sky blue apron, no ruffles. "I hope you will enjoy it."

Stoney inhaled the delicious aroma filling the kitchen, rubbed his hands together, appeared eager to begin eating. "It smells and looks great, Carlton. But, I don't want it."

"But sir. I don't understand"

"You're not getting paid to understand anything," he said earnestly, making clear the boss to employee status. "You're getting paid to take orders, with no questions, ifs, ands or buts attached. The breakfast looks great, but I want a bowl of cold cereal. I prefer to leave this most important meal of the day stuff to Katherine, and you."

"Cereal, sir." He waved his hand over the huge spread. With much repulse contorting his face, he stated, "This is more nutritional than a bowl of cold cereal. As I've said before, probably just yesterday, cold cereals are for children. For those who don't care about their health." Sounding like a commercial for Total Cereal, he continued, "This is a well-balanced meal. One that supplies all of the necessary nutri …"

Stoney grew a little irritated. "Carlton, I'm sure all of that's just dandy. But, we've been through this several times in the past. Now, I'm telling you, I want my snap crackle pop."

"But sir, I …"

"If you don't give me my snapple top pap, I'm gonna pull it out of your ass. Now where is it?"

Carlton knew that he was only joking. He knew he'd never attempt to do anything as viscous and remotely as what he had just threatened him with. He knew his outburst of hostility only meant that he was loosing his patience. He leaned back, eyes wide open. "Sir, did you or did you not hire me to take care of you?" This morning, he pushed the envelope.

His eyebrows rose in the center of his forehead, his eyes rolled submissively to the table. "Well, yeah."

"How can I, if you won't let me. My job is to see that you get off to a decent start. I can't do that unless you …"

He slammed the palm of his hand onto the table and dribbled, "Listen to me, Carlton. Katherine likes this stuff. When she comes down stairs, you and her can sit down and have a wonderful breakfast. As for me, I want my whipple snap pip."

"Very well, sir." He approached the cupboard and retrieved a bowl. He pulled open the silverware drawer and removed a spoon. He dropped the bowl onto the table, threw the spoon haphazardly into the bowl. His attitude heard clearly in his sloppiness.

He went to the pantry, opened it, and pulled out a large box of Rice Crispies. He placed it in front of the bowl. "There, sir," he said tiredly. "Your breakfast is ready."

"You got a problem, Carlton?"

"No, sir," he stated positively, then stated boldly, "but you do."

Stoney eyes widened, as if to say, 'How dare you, the hired help, talk back to me, your boss.' His arms crossed, resting his weight on one leg. "Since you're so well educated on such matters, Dr. Carlton, why don't you tell me what my problem is. Or have you changed your name to Dr. Phil?"

"Sir, I may not be the expert that you're speaking of," he explained sympathetically, "and I may not know the intricate details of what's going on in your life. But I do have enough common sense to know that something's wrong, and that you should take better care of yourself. Which in turn, may take care of a few *other* problems, that you seem to be experiencing?" He paused, before he stated suggestively, "If you get my drift, sir."

Stoney paused for a lengthy moment, allowing the truth to sink in. He lowered his head unenthusiastically. "Yeah. Well, I guess you might be right about that." He knew that there was no arguing with the truth. He understood that to do so, meant that he was in denial, and he disliked arrogant people. Never mind the fact he harbored some arrogance himself. As for the cereal, he loved his Rice Crispies. Growing up, he'd sit at the table with his family and fill his bowl to the brim, then eat until his hearts content. The average morning, he'd sit at the family table, feet swinging energetically underneath, stuffing his little round face, while marveling at the three cartoon characters on the front of the box.

Back then, he found them quite amazing. When he was five, he decided he wanted to be just like them, always happy and full of zest. The Peter Pan syndrome. Never Never Land. He loved to watch them fly around the screen in their commercial on television, defying the laws of gravity, dressed in their colorful skin-tight 'Wizard of Oz' outfits. Marveling as he did, he rarely blinked.

Shortly after his sixth birthday, the Kellogg's company had placed an advertisement on the back of the box, for children who wanted to send away for a doll-sized version of either of the three characters. Not being able to decide which one he wanted, it confused the hell out of him. It took him nearly three weeks to make up his mind.

After he finally did, he got his mother to help him mail in the ten dollars—he had to save his allowance all summer to accumulate—and ten box tops. For one solid month, during the end of a summer vacation, he sat on the front steps of their family home, and waited eagerly to greet the mailman daily in a heightened anticipation for the package to arrive.

Six weeks later, when the package finally did arrive, he was so excited that he snatched it from the mailman's hands, then sprinted to his bedroom and slammed the door shut. He jumped onto his bed, then tore the brown paper wrapping to shreds to get at the doll.

After opening the box, he removed the doll and stared at it for almost ten minutes, in total shock. It didn't look anything like either of the characters on the front of the cereal box. The flimsily constructed doll was made of a cheap rubber, and had a green face and painted on clothes. It had a pushed in nose—the guys down at the post office had used the box for a football during a lunch break.

It wasn't like anything he expected. He became very irate, and stomped on the doll until its arms and legs snapped from it. Then he launched the doll and flung it across the room, it landed in the dirty clothes hamper. After the carnage, for at least five hours, he sat at the foot of the bed, stewing, staring angrily at the doll. It reminded him of a creature from the movie 'Nightmare on Elm Street.' It looked like Freddy Crooger.

The doll couldn't do anything. It couldn't talk, dance, and it damn sure couldn't fly across the room. Or even sing the jingle. Little Stoney couldn't believe his eyes. The whole situation traumatized him incredibly.

Later that evening, when he had calmed down considerably, he collected the parts and threw them in the trash. Since that day, he's never sent away for anything advertised on the back of any cereal box. Just like he told the butcher he met near the Science Christian Monitor, 'unless I see it first.'

"Listen, Carlton," Stoney said apologetically. "I'm sorry for the attitude. The breakfast looks and smells wonderful, as I'm sure you put a lot into preparing it. For me, I'll pass, for today." He took a seat at the table, then asked, "Could you get the milk, please?"

"Certainly, sir." He brought the milk to the table, then returned to the sink, to finish washing the dishes.

Stoney prepared his cereal, began eating. He suddenly felt an urge to throw a little chatter into the air. "So, what's on your agenda for the day?"

"Well, sir, I had planned to get some shopping out of the way this morning. After I return, I'll give the place a once over. Unseen shattered glass has a way of finding its way into the feet, at the most inconvenient time. And you, sir, what are you going to do today?"

"Since I have the day off, I think I'll work on my manuscript this morning. The weatherman said to expect rain, so I think I'll stay in for a while. At least until the clouds clear."

"How's it coming along, sir?"

"Huh?"

"Your manuscript, sir. Are you making much progress?"

"Actually, I finished laying out the rough draft sometime last week. Now I have to type it into the computer, then edit it about a few dozen times. Maybe fifty. It'll probably take me a few months to do that, because it's over three hundred pages long. Plus, I really don't know how to write that well—I'm still learning. Then, as soon as I can find an honest literary agent, tread the traditional course, it's off to the presses. If not, then I'll have to go through a self-publishing house. One of those 'print on demand' houses. Provided I can find a decent one."

"That's sounds very exciting, sir. I wish you the best of luck. By the way, what are you writing about?"

"It's just a story about these three guys who've gotten themselves into, using your words, what you might call 'a pickle.'"

"Is this a real story, sir?"

He blurted quickly, "It's fiction!" He said calmly, "Purely fiction. Just a little something I made up and threw together."

Carlton wondered for a moment why his response sounded so strange. He thought about everything that's been happening for the past few weeks, then decided to put the thought out of his mind. "I see. Well, sir, as I've said before. I wish you the best of luck." He untied the apron strings, removed it, then hung it in the pantry. Before he left the kitchen, he asked skeptically, "Sir. Is there anything special you'd like me to purchase for you while I'm at the supermarket?"

Stoney entertained the notion briefly. "Nah!"

"Will you be okay, until I return?" he asked concernedly.

"Sure." He flashed a fake smile. "I'll be all right." He lifted a heaping spoonful of Rice Crispies to his mouth

Leaving, Carlton said, "Have a nice day, sir."

Through the Rice Crispies, he mumbled, "Uh-huh."

CHAPTER 21

▼

Forty-five minutes later, Stoney was in the library, sitting at the computer terminal. He scanned through his written manuscript, locating an area that he had been working on for the past two years. The three-month-old computer is the top of the line equipment in Dell hardware, complete with all the trimmings, stocked with all the latest software. Having a certificate in computer technology, he knew of the rapid rate of advancement in technology, and understood that computers were outdated the second they left the factory. He glanced to the stack of 'High Tech' magazines laying off to the side and considered updating his hardware. He then figured that since his was sufficient enough for the things that he needed to do, why go through all the hoopla with shopping for a new one. He pushed the on button, listened to the hum of the fan motor, waited for the windows program to begin.

Katherine entered the room. "Hey, baby. After I call my girlfriends, and then the bank to check out my cash flow, I'll be on my way out the door. Got some shopping to do, since I didn't pick up those cute jeans I had my eye on when we were at the mall."

He nodded. "When are you coming back?"

She kissed his forehead. "I'll give you a call. You know how my schedule is."

Here we go about that damn schedule thing again, he thought. What fricken schedule? He nodded doubtfully. "Yeah. Sure."

Soon after she left, he noticed the rain had began falling, hearing a cascade of droplets bounce and ping from the windowpanes in back of the computer. He looked to the windows, then back to the monitor, and thought it strange that the windows program hadn't begin; the introduction screen hadn't appeared. Waiting for the little yellow happy face to appear, which is normally what happened first, he felt a creepy sensation crawling all over his skin.

He looked out through the Venetian blinds and realized that the sky had grown exceedingly dark. He became startled when a sadistic thunder boomed and scared him shitless. A lightening bolt lit up the heavens, filled him with a wobbly anxiety. Listening to the rumbling afterwards, the creepy sensation increased and left him unnerved, all the way to his shivering bones. So unnerved that he felt it would be to his best interests to sit perfectly still, and not move a muscle. Just listen.

The rumbling faded to nothing, the only sound filling his ears was the fasted paced thumping of his heart. Somehow, he believed that soon he'd not be alone. Maybe Carlton would yell that he was on his way to the supermarket. Maybe Katherine would enter the room again, to tell him that she was finally on her way out through the front door. And that she might or might not see him later on that evening, depending on what her girlfriends, Priscilla and Dona, A.K.A. Piggy One and Piggy Two, had planned for them that evening. Maybe Spanky or Sleeper would come cascading into the room—unannounced, as they've done plenty of times in the past, no matter how many times he's told them to ring the doorbell before entering the house—laughing up a storm, bragging about the size of their genitals, or about how much money they collected from their latest successful hustle. Maybe a door-to-door salesperson would happen by, to try to sell him a set of Funk & Wagnells or Columbia encyclopedias. Or maybe the telephone was going to ring. He didn't know who or what, but he did have a bonafied feeling that he was expecting someone, or that something was about to happen. He believed they were coming. He knew they were coming.

Staring at the blank monitor, listening to its bleak silence, he heard a reverberating voice grow louder and louder, a down in the valley echo that whispered a word that scared him miserably. A cavernous resonance howled, "Ssstoooneeeeeeey!"

He trembled insecurely, as an abundance of fright made him aware that the emotions consternation and panic were in the same neighborhood, soon to make themselves prevalent. Gripping the edges of the desk with a vise like clamp, he dared not take his eyes from the monitor. He couldn't even if he tried.

The voiced howled again, "Ssstoooneeeeeeey!"

Again, "Ssstoooneeeeeeey!"

During a moment of silence, the monitor's dark picture tube hazed into an ashen shade of gray. A blurred image appeared in the center of the screen, and at first, it seemed like a face. Then it didn't. Then it did. A face much larger than the two-inch diameter yellow happy face that's supposed to appear when he first turned the computer on. The only difference is the face wasn't smiling. The computer was definitely not in a joyful mood.

Moments later, the face hazed into someone that he had recognized. It was Jake.

He became acutely stunned at his appearance, shoved with all his might, and jettisoned himself more than ten feet from the terminal, rolling backwards with his hands latched securely onto the arms of the swivel chair. He remembered Jakes last few visits, resulting in him being poked in the eye, and labeled a lunatic by nearly everyone on 'The Voyager,' and by all of the shoppers at the mall.

Jake stared penetratingly into his eyes, smiled and asked concernedly, "How're ya doin there, old buddy?"

Stoney felt as though he'd been commanded to stop breathing, and he did just that. He stopped breathing, stuck on a breath of relentless dismay.

Jakes face snapped into an image of his whole body, and he began doing a badly choreographed waltz, as though auditioning for Star Search. After the quick performance, he bowed gracefully, holding onto his glasses so that they wouldn't fall from his face. He stood upright and flared a gigantic bucktooth grin, then announced cheerfully, "And now, for my next trick. Presto!"

He disappeared. Poof!

After he vanished, he leaned toward the monitor, hoping that he had departed for all an eternity. He asked himself, "What'n the hell am I doing? Behaving like this, I'm only asking for it. I'm actually looking for him, when I'd prefer that he was the last thing on my mind. How dumb can I be?"

He shut his eyes tight, whispered repeatedly, "This isn't happening. This isn't happening. This isn't ..."

Before he finished the statement, he felt something on his lap. Someone, a small person, perhaps a child, was sitting on his lap. As curious as he was, he dared not open his eyes to find out who it was, or what it was. He was so scared that he didn't even want to steal a peek. He tried desperately to chase the occurrence from his mind, with no success.

Jake squirmed restlessly, wiggled his tush on his lap. Bouncing up and down as a hyperactive child, he said, "Aw com'on, Stoney. Of course this is happening. I came all the way over here to talk to you, and now that I'm here, you don't even want to look at me? Is that any way for a grown man to act? I came all this way to play the game with you, and you don't even want to cooperate. Aaawww chucks! If that don't beat all."

He started to respond, because he was curious as to what the game was all about. He thought that if he could beat Jake at the game, then hopefully, he'd never come back again. Maybe he'd leave him alone, in peace. He opened his mouth to speak, then pulled the breaks before any words reached his lips. I can't answer him, he thought. If I do, I'll only confirm to myself that he's here, sitting on my lap. No! I can't do that. I'll just stay like this, and ignore him. I can't give in and go along with this crazy shit.

Jake reached up and touched his right eyelid, and he felt a feathered touch graze him. At first, the touch felt warm, then cold. Then warm again. Then it felt as cold as ice. Jake bantered, "Peek-a-boo, Stoney. I see you."

Shaking his head grimly, he spat through grinding teeth, "No! No. No. No. No. No. There's no one there." He stated doubtfully, "There can't be."

"Guess what I can do, Stoney?"

He didn't respond.

"That's right. I can read your mind. And I'm reading it right now. You're thinking that I'm not here. But I got news for you, Stoney. I can prove that I'm here. All I have to do is ask you one question, and you'll be sold."

He tilted his head curiously, waiting.

"If I'm not here, then who are you listening to?"

Little did he know, that just by his inquiring into the matter, he had initiated himself into the game. Again, Stupid! He couldn't stop it even if he wanted to. He couldn't think about anything else. His subconscious spoke to him so loud and clear, that he had no choice but to respond. He could've believed that he was listening to himself, and he might've won the game, but he didn't consider the notion. He couldn't possibly erase the mental images of the children whose parents he'd taken advantage of. They popped into his head randomly, to ask many warranted questions. He believed they had assembled and picked a speaker to represent them. Jake! But, as everyone knows, that's crazy thinking.

While he deliberated the notion, Jake went on to say, "Now that you know I'm here, we can play the game." He grew excited, "Ooooooohhh! I've wanted to play the game with you for some time now, now that you're fully involved. You'll be such a fine challenge."

Searching desperately for a way out of the madness plaguing him, he came up with a solution. A chance, a gamble that he was more than willing to take. He thought of his parents, about how they had nurtured and raised him with tender loving care. About everything they've meant to him, their unconditional love and continued support.

Moments later, amazingly, Jake was gone.

Still on the issues, he thought about the cherished relationships that some parents have with their children. Suddenly, an image of a woman holding a baby entered his mind. He thought of the hardships that she'd face in taking care of the child. Not being able to stop himself, he added to it the many problems that he created when he extorted their money. He thought of the big things, like their futures, draining their college savings accounts, leading them to continue a legacy of uneducated lower class laborers. He thought of the small things like typical holidays, about how empty their Christmases and birthdays would be, with not being able to afford presents—about how sad and empty their lives would be.

Unexpectedly, his mind became filled with a multitude of impoverished women, holding hungry children layered in tattered clothes. Feeling as though he had something to do with their misery, he became severely depressed. He eyed a young boy standing next to and holding his mothers hand, and realized that the boy looked dreadfully familiar. Looking closer, he discovered him to be Jake. Bingo! He had knocked himself back into the game.

Now that Jake was in his mind, he realized that he couldn't be on his lap. He took the chance to open his eyes, ever so slowly, and discovered that the room had grown dark. Absent from any form of light. The only light flashing occasionally, the lightening still going on outside.

He glanced through the window and caught glimpses of jagged luminous streaks, fragments of lightening dancing from cloud to cloud. They zapped and fizzled into nowhere in particular, searching for lightening rods, telephone poles, trees and golfers.

The storm neared its peak, and the sound of the thunder clapped louder and more frequent. Strangely, even though the windows in the room were closed, he felt a draft graze his face. It puzzled him, and he wanted to know where this breeze had come from.

From out of nowhere, he released a loud burp, and his stomach gurgled loudly, as though suffering from a sever case of gastritis. He looked to his midsection and saw his shirt rippling as the waves of many turbulent waters. There was definitely something moving around on the inside of his stomach. He was nine months pregnant with an energetic child expected at any moment. The baby was on its way, and there was absolutely nothing he could do to stop it.

He cringed at the thought of giving birth the usually way, an impossibility, so the idea of having a C-section entered his mind. He could dash to the kitchen, get a knife, cut himself open, and be rid of the damn thing. Whatever the hell it was.

It puzzled him as to why the idea came later that if he attempted to do anything like that, chances are, he'd die. A more reasonable solution came to mind, and he figured that the only available opening that he could use for the impending birth was his mouth. His ass was definitely too small. He believed t that that would've pained something awful.

Slithering, inch by inch, jerking his body to and fro, Jake made his way out of his stomach, scratching and clawing at anything he could grab onto, moved through his esophagus at a crawl rate of speed. Listening to the sound of his ribcage cracking, Stoneys chest expanded wide, like blowfish. He felt an enormous pressure on his backbone, caused him to sit up as straight as a studious student.

His chest area had swelled to the size of a three-foot diameter beach ball, and his breathing became laborious, as though he suffered from an acute asthma attack. He tried to force Jake out by expelling the air in his lungs, and it appeared to be working. As Jake ramrod his way through his trachea, his eyes bulged intensely. He gagged repeatedly, as though he was being strangled to within an inch of his life. He felt a pair of clawed hands scrapping the insides of his cheeks, ripping the sides of his face to strips of bacon, like a piece of paper fed through a shredder. As pieces of his flesh dangled from his jaws, he felt his warm blood dribbling onto his neck, chest and back.

As Jakes head filled his mouth, his cheeks expanded to the size of two bowling balls clad with bloodied racing stripes, strips of mangled skin. For some reason, the idea to reach inside of his mouth and pull him out never entered his mind. It was because he was afraid to touch him.

Jake grabbed onto his jaw and pulled downward with all his might, and Stoneys mouth stretched to more than a foot in length. As he made calamitous efforts to extrude, Stoney looked over the top of his lip, and could just barely see a crop of short blonde curly hair, haloed with a strip shiny metal—the upper ridge of Jakes gold trimmed horned rimmed glasses.

When the head was completely out—Stoney rimmed his neck with his lips—Jake turned around to face him, then asked comically, "Tight fit, wasn't it?"

Within the blink of an eye, he had disappeared, leaving no trace that he was ever there. Stoney smacked his lips repulsively, still tasting a head full of greasy hair.

Suddenly, a clap of thunder boomed and resonated throughout the house, shaking it on its foundation. A flash of light filled the sky like burning magnesium, blinding him for an instant. It lit up the room for a fleeting moment, and to his shocking surprise, through the corners of his eyes, he caught a hair glimpse of a tall dark figure standing only a few feet away. He didn't get a good look at the person, because it had happened so quickly. He prayed to delay another strike of lightening, which would've given him the opportunity to affirm what he saw. Confirmation was the last thing he wanted.

When the lightening had struck again, he saw that there was nothing there, and he breathed easy. Trying to bring any form of rationality and stability back to his life, a zillion and one formidable thoughts ran through his head.

In this moment of reprieve, amidst an absolute dark silence, believing the worst was over, another burst of lightening thundered from the heavens and crashed through the two windows behind the monitor. Broken glass and debris whooshed violently into the room. The computer equipment; speakers, keyboard, printer, flatbed scanner, mouse, and the High Tech magazines were swept from the desk and sent flying into the air, swirled around the room amid a vicious cyclone. Like a twister that would uplift the house, taking him zooming to a place called Oz.

He felt the aggressive winds strike his body and toss him to and fro. When he believed that what was going on was physically impossible, the winds simmered to nothing but a gentle breeze, and he felt only a slight gust of wind graze his body. Although the winds had slowed, the computer equipment still hovered and circled him, as if the winds still carried them. He couldn't figure it out, it made no sense at all. Never mind the idea that his giving oral birth to a nine-year-old kid was preposterous to begin with.

Trying to comprehend the madness haunting him, he had no idea that he was only placing himself deeper into the game. Then it grew even darker, and he could no longer see glimpses of the objects whizzing around him. Before he knew anything, either the room had grown in size, or he had shrunk. It was a toss up. The wall behind the computer terminal had backed away until it had vanished. It was still there, but far away, seemingly unattainable. He looked up and realized that the same thing had happened to the ceiling. It was gone. There was nothing over his head but a pitch-black heaven, with a few black clouds brewing angrily.

For some weird reason, he felt as though he was an amoeba. A one celled protozoan swimming relentlessly on a glass plate, underneath a microscope lens. He believed that there was a gigantic someone up there, watching him, examining him, waiting to dissect him. Then toss him in a jar filled with formaldehyde.

He looked up and saw the dark clouds bubbling in place, then realized that the lightening had simmered to but a fading flicker. The sound of the thunder was no more, and it was as quiet as a mortuary.

Curious to his new surroundings, he rose wearily from his chair. He turned in a complete circle and found nothing. Even the chair he was just sitting in had vanished into thin air. Now, it was so dark that he couldn't even see the nose on his face.

Amidst an ominous silence, he heard a dwindled clomping at a distance. Shortly, he could tell that it was the sound of people walking, nearing him. When they were about thirty feet away, he stared at the vague images moving through the darkness, and could tell that they were small in stature. They were definitely children.

When they were close enough, he strained to pierce the darkness, and could just barely see the many shadows standing directly in front of him. But what he couldn't make out were their exact identities. He couldn't even tell what color they were, or their genders. Since he couldn't see them, he listened to them whispering among themselves, like little busybody's. "He heard a little girls soft voice say just barely, "He's the one. He did it to my father a few months ago." She complained to a Raggedy Ann doll clutched firmly in her arms, "See, Miss Huckabee—named after Rudy Huckstable of The Cosby Show—I told you we'd get him for what he did to our family."

Another little girl clutching a Twinkie accused him blatantly, "He's the one! He did it to my father a few months ago, and sent our family to the poor house. We couldn't even have Christmas this year."

A young boy holding a kite fired, "He did it to my family too. Before my mom went to jail, he took all the money we had saved up."

"My parents gave him the money they were saving for my college education," a young girl said. "Now I'll have to work at McDonalds for the rest of my life."

Another little boy threw in, "We had to move into a poor peoples house, in the projects. And they made us get rid of Benji, our dog. I don't like the school in that neighborhood. They're always fighting all the time, and we never have fun anymore."

"We had to move into a poor people's house too," another child testified, "and I don't like the schools in that neighborhood. They're always and shooting guns every day."

Feeling the weighty accusations of their possibly truthful testimonies, Stoney grew paranoid. He believed that their claims were justified. Among the broken sentences he absorbed, he heard the children walking, then realized that they were forming a huge circle around him. A human chain. After they had completed the circle, they held hands and continued whispering. "Same with us," a little girl said. "I can't even go to sleep at night, because I hear people arguing all the time. Trying to kill each other for drugs and everything."

Staring at the dark shadows, he noticed the children had began swaying rhythmically from side to side. Their insignificant dark shadows—that's what they were to him, little insignificant nothings. Little nobodies who meant nothing—they remained faceless and in the shadows. As they had always been to him, unseen. Out of sight, out of mind.

While the children swayed and carried on in conversation, Stoney fought arduously to bring himself back to where he knew he should be. Where he knew he belonged. He thought that if he could break their play by concentrating on anything with a connection to the real world, then maybe the children would go away. At the back of his mind, he also realized that the children were going to thwart his attempt to leave their presence. He would have to try with everything he had.

He tried to focus on something totally irrelevant to the issues at hand, and he felt himself leaving their presence, fading away. Then, they brought him deeper into the game by doing something that he could relate to. Something childlike. Something that he use to do when he was their age. Something that his mind would not refuse. That's when they began singing, "If you're happy and you know it, clap your hands. If you're happy and you know it, clap your hands. If you're happy and you know it, and you really want to show it, if you're happy and you know it clap your hands …"

In between the phrases, the children clapped their hands and stomped their feet respectively to the song. Singing their ghostly melodies, their voices grew louder and louder with each verse. He attempted to cover his ears, to block the earth shattering sound, but discovered that he only muffle it somewhat. He thought it odd that he could hear the roaring sound that they made, but not feel the heavy vibration that should've been thrust around his body. When he could no longer tolerate what was happening, he looked up and screamed from the pit of his gut, **"NOOOOOOOOOOOO!!"**

His voice echoed into the dark heavens, and a mind numbing thunder boomed from the skies above. A lightening bolt exploded overhead, split the clouds and lit up everything for miles around, then crashed to the ground at a distant not too far away. The singing had stopped, and once again, it was as silent as a hushed breeze.

Just then, he heard a deep voice whispering in an area just behind the children. It was definitely a man. A huge figure of a man. Peering keenly in hopes to make out who the person was, he had no success. The tall stranger told the little ones, "Children, you can go now. I believe we have his attention."

Immediately, Stoney heard the clomping of little feet. At first amassing, then walking away, until their footsteps faded off into nothing. For what seemed like forever, the man hadn't spoken a word, and he wondered if he was still there. Another mistake on his behalf. Wondering about the stranger, therefore giving belief to his existence. He gave it placement in his mind. Certification. Again, certification, like confirmation, was the last thing that he needed.

"I'm still here," the stranger said, using a laid-back tone. "Don't worry, Stoney. I ain't gonna leave you, boo. You've been calling me for the past few years. Now that I'm here, I'm all yours." He snickered, "Ma man Stoney. Stoneman! Stone to da bone. How're ya doing," he emphasized, "old friend?

Shaking nervously, he stuttered, "Wh-Wh-Who are you?"

"The question is not 'who am I.' The question should be 'who are you?'"

His mind labored drearily on the question. He thought that if he could get the stranger talking, then maybe he could figure his weakness. And then, maybe the way back home. A place that he so badly desired to be.

At the same time, he realized that the more questions that he placed around strangers existence, the deeper he dragged himself into the game. He had to be careful. Ever so cautious.

All of a sudden, he heard the pounding of weighty footsteps approach. Now, exactly in front of him, at less than three feet away, he saw the silhouette of a man who was the same height as he, with the same build. He leaned forward and focused intently, peering keenly through the blackness of the night. He stared at the strangers face, trying to make out the details, attempting to place him. He saw nothing but a sinister cloud floating above his shoulders.

He leaned even closer, and the haze thinned somewhat, and he was almost able to see the strangers face. Before he could be sure of anything, the stranger stepped backwards, fading into the darkness, and his facial features became hazed. The stranger stated, "You've seen enough. Now it's time to get down to business."

"B-B-Business. Wh-Wh-What business?" He asserted, "I have no business with you."

The stranger leaned toward him, got to within an inch of his face. He filled the area with an explosion when he shouted, **"You know perfectly well what business I'm talking about, boy! Don't you fuck with me, Stoney. Don't you ever fuck with me!"** He asked calmly, "Who do you think I am? Perhaps, one of the suckers that you think you can hustle out of their life savings."

As if a frightened infant, he pleaded submissively, "But, I honestly don't know what you're talking about. I really don't know."

"In that case," the stranger calmed, "let me remind you." He stepped further backwards, released a contemptuous laugh. One that brought goose pimples that were afraid to rise.

From out of nowhere, he saw a phosphorous glow illuminating in an area surrounding the stranger's right shoulder, and he assumed that something was about to happen. Within the blink of an eye, he heard a whooshing sound, and saw something flying toward him at full speed, as though jet propelled from a rocket launcher. The stranger's right hand made solid contact with the left side of his face like a battering ram. "**BLAM!**"

Upon feeling the brutal blow, he flew several feet into the air, did several cartwheels along the way. At first, he thought that he had been punched hard, and the pain he suffered was tremendous. He focused on what might happen to him when he landed, and didn't feel the injury that he thought was inflicted to his face.

Before descending, wherever the ground was, he turned to a random direction that he believed was down. He suddenly became lost and confused for the total blackness. Weirdly, his sense of balance, his equilibrium, existed no more. Therefore, there he remained floating, suspended. Lost in space.

With believing that people were supposed to see stars when they were punched that hard, he focused on one spot at a great distance, and saw the twinkling of a shiny object. He turned from it and glanced all over, still searching for the ground. Or anything that might help shed light to his present situation.

Being unsuccessful, he turned back to observe the shiny object, and discovered it racing toward him faster than a locomotive. When the object was close enough, he realized that what he thought was one shiny object, were actually two objects, side by side. They were connected, as the barrels of a double-barreled shotgun.

When it was just in front of him, he got a terrifying idea of what the objects were. Now, he could clearly see that they were Jakes gold trimmed horned rimmed glasses. "I know you. You're Jake!"

Now that Jake was only a few feet away, he took in the detailing of his face, which was now ten times its normal size. What struck him as being strange was that his facial features had changed drastically. He lost all of his boyish charms, and had aged considerably. He was all grown up. His jaw line was structured like Stoneys, but he had a cleft chin. The overall structure was like his, but the ears were much larger. However, the hair wasn't black like his at all. The new-fangled Jake had a head full of golden curly locks, just like the original little Jake. The dark red skin covering his face was glazed, like the finish on a vase. But the gold trimmed horned rimmed glasses and angry eyes, the cold piercing eyes, they were unmistakably the original little Jakes. The eyes remained to give Stoney the full effect, as no one was angrier than Jake.

The altered Jake smiled broadly, flashing a gigantic buckteeth grin. Stoney noticed that his teeth were crooked, chipped, tartar ridden and rotten. Looked like he hadn't brushed and flossed in years. Didn't know what a dentists office looked like. Looking even closer, he studied his hairline for a moment, and something bizarre caught his attention. On the corners of the front of his head, near his temples, through his golden curly locks, he spotted a pair of ivory colored horns. Jake smirked. "Not quite!"

He moved several feet backwards, then pointed in a random direction. "What's the matter, Stoneman? Having a problem finding your way back down?"

Now that he was made aware of the downward direction, he plummeted like a rock released from a slingshot. A meteorite! He fell at such a high rate of speed, the wind whistled past his ears, stretched and contorted his face to a great extent. He was moving so fast, it felt as though he was whizzing through a wind tunnel, at over three hundred miles per hour.

What he thought was strange, was that he didn't feel the friction on the rest of his body. Only his face. He glanced to the direction that he fell, and discovered something in the distant. When he gave the object considerable thought, although he continued plummeting, for an instant, he didn't feel the wind against his face anymore It seemed that he had stopped falling. He thought about the wind again, then suddenly felt it in spurts.

Now that he was much closer to what he thought was the ground, possibly dirt, pavement or concrete, he saw something resembling a huge square. A grid of some sort, almost one hundred square yards in size. One hundred feet away, he could tell that there were numerous objects riddling the pattern. Objects that swayed back and forth like three-foot tall blades in a sea of blue grass.

Now, much closer, it became terrifyingly clear what he was about to crash into—a dense field of a few thousand animated, razor sharp, double edged swords, spaced a few inches apart. Their lethal tips yearned to pierce his flesh, cried for his blood, and screamed for his death.

Realizing the approach of what he considered to be an extremely gruesome death, he tensed all of the muscles in his body, attempting to thwart the impending doom. He closed his eyes for a moment, and his heart thumped as if he was about to have a major heart attack. He thrust his hands forward, as if to assist in stopping himself from falling. Amazingly, it worked.

He felt that the fall was only a figment of his imagination, as if he hadn't experienced it at all. As if he had just awaken from a terrible nightmare. Just in time, before he bottomed out and died. So it was entailed in the myth.

Hovering a few feet above the swords, he stared at their deadly tips, feared them in every respect. They whispered his name softly, over and over again, beckoned him to come closer. He felt the wind gushing past his body, and his clothes fluttered as if he was still freefalling. Oddly, he didn't hear the whistling sound that's supposed to fill his ears.

He then heard the giggling sound of a group of children, who annoyed him persistently with their pestering squeaky chatter. Some called out his name, others taunted and jeered him. He didn't reply, his mind focused solely on the tips of the life threatening swords. Their intimidation reined supreme and terrified him so much, that it chased all forms of rational thinking from his mind. The threat of the swords served their purpose well.

Suddenly, his whole life flashed before him, realizing that he was on the verge of death. An essential idea entered his mind, and he thought about his family, about what his life has meant to him. About what he was leaving, and where he was going. What outweighed these thoughts was his understanding that whether a person went to heaven or hell, depended solely on the condition of the heart before the passing. Had heard it somewhere … in passing. He wondered if he was forgiven for his transgressions. What staggered his mind afterwards was the notion that he had never asked to be forgiven. He was too busy to give it any consideration. He was caught up.

In between the swords, at the darkness near the base, he caught glimpses of the children's eyes leer accusingly. They saw him for his true value, his net worth. They saw his wicked deeds as clear as day. He felt the fire from their heated stares—dark circles traced their eyes from many sleepless nights—and he began experiencing an intense burning sensation at the back of his skull. Some with no eyes, only hollow dark sockets, death staring him square in the face, nameless children, their identities or anything personal about them remained mysterious. They attended all of the gatherings, but were without spirit.

Most of them did not understand finances, but knew that he was responsible for placing many hardships in their families lives. They didn't know much about good and evil, but did believe that he was a very bad man. The type of stranger that their parents had warned them over and over again never to speak to, or go near. If you see someone like this, run like hell in the opposite direction. As you're running, scream for help as loud as you can, to let unsuspecting adults in the immediate area know that an evil bastard, a terrible monster, the boogeyman, is trying to get you.

Ironically, he thought it odd that he had experienced something like this many years before, when he was a teenager. Walking from high school, he sometimes stopped by the 'Five and Dime'—a cute little Indian mom and pop corner store—and brought a little bag full of penny candy to hand out to his neighbors children. After turning onto his street, when the children spotted him—there were at least fifteen—they stopped doing whatever and ran to him, screaming frenziedly, as if charging an ice-cream truck on the hottest day of the summer, eager to buy their favorite brand of Hood product. Or as though he was Santa, making a mid-year special delivery. They surrounded him and bounced up and down like little human springs, chanting, 'Me first, Stoney! Can I have a piece, Stoney! Can I pick out which piece I want?' Cindy Lee, an especially cute little Asian girl stood out from the crowd. With an orange popsicle ring circling her lips like the ring of Saturn, she spilled a thick Chinese accent, breaking his name expressively, 'Stow-Knee! Please, Stow-Knee!"

Smiling at their little happy faces, he found much gratification when handing out the candy, always saving a few pieces for his siblings. Yes in deedy, give to the needy. The outstretched entreating hands is what he remembered. Tiny beseeching fingers imploring the pleasant sweet tasting nectar of sugar cane.

However, this time the children weren't smiling, or thinking pleasurable thoughts of receiving candy, presents or ice-cold refreshments. This time, they frowned irately as they begged incessantly for his blood, cried relentlessly for his demise. Their graven desires poured profusely from their hearts, easily seen on their faces, in their angry eyes. They tried their damndest to pull him into the swords. They wanted his hide. As what he wished of Jake and Jessica, they wanted him 'not breathing.' They wanted him dead.

He knew the children's hands waving frantically was an elaborate attempt to keep his attention fixated. Slowly, the hands rose higher, to just a few inches past the swords. They yelled, "Grab him!"

Another shouted, "Pull him down! Bring him closer!"

As their little hands grazed and snipped at his clothes, he fought relentlessly, slapped their hands frantically. He yelled, "Get the hell away from me! Don't touch me, dammit! Leave me alone!"

The children persisted mercilessly, determined to pull him downward into the swords, to kill him. Fighting vigorously, thrashing wildly, an important thought entered his mind once again. The myth of what would happen to a person if they died in their sleep. They may not have died the way it happened in the dream, but the end results did mean death. Literally, physical death. He was frightfully sure.

Fighting the children unremittingly, he watched their arms and hands collide with the blades, and became confused at what he observed. What puzzled him thoroughly, was that he didn't see any blood whatsoever gush from the opened wounds that he was sure were inflicted upon them. This discrepancy clashed with his sense of reality, made him understand that what was happening couldn't have been real. If this occurrence wasn't real, then none of it was real. Either it was entirely a reality, or it was entirely a nightmare. A dream. One in which he knew he could somehow return from.

Not watching where he swung his hands, he accidentally grazed his right hand against a sword. He felt the blade slice into his skin, and gash the knuckles of his right hand. He felt the stinging sensation, as the ripped muscles and tendons wriggled about on the inside of his hand, stretching the gash painfully wider.

Immediately after, his hand grew numb, cold. He became horror-struck, and his level of fear climbed yet higher. There was no doubt in his mind that he had indeed suffered an injury.

From out of nowhere, Jake appeared hovering a few feet above his body, just behind him. "What you need is a shove. And I'm just the person who can give it to you." He lowered himself slowly, feet first, onto his back. Stoney looked at his hand, and stared at the open wound, feeling lightheaded. He closed his eyes to shake the feeling, but it wouldn't subside.

Watching the blood from his wound trickle down onto the swords and coat the children's hands like red paint, as they continued to make desperate attempts to pull him down, he began to feel more dazed. He felt a whirling sensation and spun in place, faster and faster, until the swords and the children's hands became a total blur. It was if he was tied to a knife throwing target, like the one some entertainers use in the circus. In an attempt to ward off the symptoms of a seemingly heavy inebriation, he shut his eyes tight, and shook his head repeatedly.

At that moment, he heard his deep voice shower from above, "**Get back here, Stoney! I'm not through with you yet. You can run, but you can't hide. Come back here, Stoney! Come back!**"

Spinning wildly, his rage fading, "**Come baaack! Come** baaack! Come baaack!"

Stoney looked behind him, and witnessed his enlarged hand reaching out to grab him. The hand grew a hundred times in size, to almost twice that of his entire body. Suddenly, the hand lunged toward him, fingers outstretched as a huge dragnet. As he was just about to snare him, the entire scenery hazed into an indistinct whirling cloud. Once again, he had stumbled into the depths of the formidable abyss. Once again, he could see nothing. It was pitch black everywhere.

Seconds later, he began to come around, returning to his body. Back to the reality that he knew did exist, the world he desired unremittingly to play an active part in.

He opened his eyes wide, and to his amazement, he became overwhelmed with an intense feeling of incongruous repugnance. He discovered that in all that time, he was in his mansion, in the library, sitting in the swivel chair, with his back to the computer terminal.

Spanning the room, he discovered that everything was in its usual place. Everything was the same, but the throbbing in his right hand continued. It was still cold and numb, and pained greatly. He lifted his right hand up to view, then became totally astounded. It looked like it had been fed through a meat grinder. Streams of blood dribbled steadily from several gashes along the knuckles, covered his entire lap, and puddled about his feet.

Staring in disbelief at the wounds, he blurted, "Oh my God!" He held his hand pressured tightly against his right inner thigh. He jumped out of the chair and ran toward the master bedrooms bathroom, leaving a trail of blood on the carpet. Before leaving the library, he looked back at the computer terminal, and discovered that the monitors screen had been shattered into a hundred pieces. The jagged edges of glass were tainted with his blood, he suddenly realized what he was swinging at in the nightmare. At that moment, he also realized how the game was being played.

He entered the bathroom, went to the sink and turned on the cold water. He placed his hand under the stream to rinse out any fragments of broken glass, in case there were some there. He opened the door to the medicine cabinet, and spotted a bottle of alcohol on the top shelf. He pulled it down, opened it, then set in on the edge of the sink.

As the water cleansed the wound, he looked straight ahead at the shattered glass covering the cabinet door, but wondered if he'd see Jake in water. A deplorable thought.

Watching the water funneling in a clockwise direction, as it entered the drain, it held his attention briefly. Attending high school, in a physics class, he discovered that in places below the equator; in South America or Australia, the water entered the drain funneling in the counterclockwise direction. Bizarrely, the fact totally amazed and stymied the hell out of him.

He grabbed the bottle of alcohol, removed the cap and drenched his hand. Gritting his teeth in pain, he released several intense grunts as the burning sensation traveled throughout his hand, and shot up his arm. It made him feel like he was holding onto the business end of a searing hot iron.

When the worst was over, he discovered the bleeding had slowed considerably. He spanned the room in search for a towel to wrap around his hand. He looked next to the bathtub, twenty feet away, and found a few towels of various sizes on a wooden rack.

Approaching the rack, a peculiar feeling set in and touched him all the way to his frightened bones, delivering a dispirited chill. Growing in his heart was a perceivable notion that something eerily horrible was about to happen.

He attempted to chase the fear away, with no success. He pulled a towel free from the rack and wrapped it around his right hand. The second time around, to keep it from falling loose, he tucked the remaining tail under the wrap on the inside of his hand.

Now that his thoughts weren't entirely on his hand, he thought about the altered Jake, about how much he had changed. Mostly, he wondered why he had changed. He considered what he could try to do, to stop himself from being swept into the maddening turmoil, when and if Jake and Jessica returned. A thought entered his mind about what brought him back the last time. He wondered if it would work again.

Abruptly, the notion that something was about to happen grew inside of him like a quickly rising fever. A creepy sensation crowded the room and flooded his heart. It overwhelmed him so quickly, that he didn't have enough time to think of a way to stop it from occurring.

Suddenly, the bathroom lights dwindled to an evening dusk. Behind him, he heard a loud dribbling sound. Not turning to see where it was coming from, he heard what sounded like a wire brush being pulled through a small pipe; a hollow scratching sound. He had no doubt that someone or something was coming through the drainpipe.

Dreading the thought of Jakes formidable return, he exploded with rage and punched a gapping hole through the wall. He faced the sink and witnessed an enormous propulsion of high-pressured steam spouting from the drain, mushrooming to the ceiling.

Seconds later, he observed the altered Jake standing antagonistically over the sink, his arms folded intolerantly. Leering at Stoney, he frowned a wicked grin from ear to ear, nodded slowly. He was confident, smug, as if he was damn sure that he was going to get what he came to claim. He released a deep cavernous laugh so thunderous, that it propelled him into the wall behind him. **"HA HA HA HA HAAAAAAAA!"**

Holding his wrapped hand over his thumping heart, his adrenalin soared out of control. Staring horrifically at Jake, he shook his head gloomily, in absolute denial. He whispered, "There's no one there. There's absolutely no one there. There's no one …"

Jake extended his right arm, it stretched like a rubber band, and he grabbed a handful of Stoneys hair. He pulled him closer, shouting, **"Round two, bitch!"**

Stoney grabbed onto the flimsy towel rack, and held on for dear life. Imagine that. As if a flimsy piece of wood was reliable enough to save anyone's life from a gruesome creature. A hideous nightmare.

Nevertheless, he tried frantically to hold his ground, fighting tooth and nail all the way. Too bad he believed it was impossible for him to prevail, holding onto a pathetic piece of wood. As the will of the people who he's taken advantage of unite to build one strong force, Jakes provocation was much too persuasive for Stoney to resist. Understanding the towel racks weak construction, he knew that it would only have been a matter of moments before it collapsed and gave way. Before he knew anything, it buckled and snapped like a meager twig. The actual reason it collapsed so easily, was because he had no faith in it. Otherwise, it would've remained anchored, like a cement pylon. As Jake dragged him clawing, scratching and kicking, he attempted to grab onto several other items that he passed along the way. Sliding past the wicker constructed hamper, he attempted to wrap his arms around it, but it was much too bulky. Not weighing much, only a few pounds, he merely dragged it along easily, as though he wasn't holding onto anything at all.

A few feet from the sink, he stared at Jake inexplicably, and witnessed him entering the drainpipe, going down. He didn't know how it was happening, only that what he was doing was outright impossible.

He sought to give it one last attempt to save himself from only God knows what kind of hell Jake was attempting to inflict upon him. That's when the life-saving toilet bowl came into view. It's cold ceramic weighty presence offered an abundance of security, because of its renowned stability. That wouldn't move, he believed. It's attached to the floor, anchored in place. They're clamped down so tight that nothing can move it. Not even an earthquake.

Clawing at the tiled floor like a vicious German Shepard, digging a hole under a fence to get at the loud-mouthed poodle in the next yard over, Jake pulled strenuously to haul him to the sinks edge. Passing the toilet bowl, Stoney reached out and wrapped his arms around the base, and hugged it as though it was a dear long lost friend.

Eyeing Jake through the corners of his eyes, Stoney looked up and saw his stretched arm hanging over the sinks edge, pulling him mightily with everything he had. A cropping salty perspiration puddled about his head, trickled into his eyes, and he blinked repeatedly to clear them. An abundance sweat did the same to his hands, and greased his grip.

Fighting relentlessly to maintain his grip, many hopeless thoughts raced through Stoneys head, weakened his dwindling will to persist. The bastard's trying to take my life! he figured. There's no way in hell I can fit into where he's pulling me. It's impossible! He declared assertively through gritted teeth, "I've got to hold on, just a little longer. Can't let go."

Suddenly, he grew tired, his grip weakened, and a heavy sentiment of profound grief swelled within him. He felt sorry for himself, for the grim circumstances of knowing that he couldn't possibly hold on much longer. But if he did let go, then what?

Along with his arms and hands, his aspirations to fight Jakes will grew weary. Since he believed he was in the middle of a relentless nightmare, a place where doing the impractical was possibly achievable, his thoughts turned to survival by adapting. What if I simply go along with what he's trying to make me do, he wondered. If I don't have the power to control what's happening, then maybe I can simply go with the flow, and do some manipulating of my own. I could improvise.

With the idea in mind, along with a weak prayer tucked in his fearful heart, he released his grip from the base of the toilet bowl. Jake yanked him to the edge of the sink, sent him whooshing through the air. Stoney screamed in mid flight, "WHOOOOOOA!"

He finally saw what was occurring inside of the sink, and his eyes bucked open in absolute disbelief, as wide as his gaping mouth. To his shocking surprise, Jake was trying to pull him into the drainpipe.

Envisioning the horrendous occurrence delivered second thoughts about what he was going to attempt, challenged his imagination, so he held tightly onto the edge while Jake pulled relentlessly. Fighting insistently, the idea of adapting to the circumstances surrounding him entered his mind once again. He somehow knew that the only way he was going to accomplish such a feat, would be if he cleared his mind of all doubts challenging him. Unfortunately, this meant keeping his mind clear of all physical properties of the real world. Ironically, he had to place more of Jakes world, into his.

He closed his eyes tight, and concentrated not on the incredulous view that he witnessed—Jake, a demon from hell, struggling to pull him mercilessly into a two inch drain pipe—but solely on what he wanted to achieve, negating its impossibility. He mumbled, "If I go down the drain pipe at my normal size, I'll die. I don't know how, but I know I will. I've got to block out the viciousness of being brutally forced down the drain. This is a nightmare. A dream. I have to believe that I can do anything, even change my body's shape. Mostly, I have to believe that there will be absolutely no pain whatsoever.

Suddenly, several unusual feelings crept inside of him, took over his mind, hazed his thoughts. He felt animated, able to experience many supernatural abilities. He felt like his soul had been separated from his body, changing him into a spirit that had the unearthly characteristics of a ghost. He felt fictitious, like a cartoon character. Something that can defy the laws of nature and be molded, stretched and contort into whatever shape he desired. Defy the laws of nature, like the Rice Crispies action figure he mailed away for when he was a kid.

The notion soothed him, and he discovered a smidgeon of relief over the horizon, and scurried to its salvation. Weirdly, now he felt more comfortable about going down the drain. He released his grip from the edge of the sink, and Jake dragged him to the drain opening. As he was about to enter the two-inch diameter pipe, he felt an uncanny tingling sensation whisk over his body, and his head stretched out like rubber and thinned to within an inch in diameter. He had established the transformation, but it frightened him drastically. All because a few lucid thoughts concerning reality entered his head, and challenged his awareness. This is fucken ridiculous! he thought. It's illogical. I can't do this shit. Nobody can do this shit. It can't be done.

Managing to hold onto what he's accomplished thus far, his body elongated and he entered the drain pipe, sliding easily into the opening. He held his breath for fear of drowning, and kept his eyes closed as tight as he could. Soon after, he discovered himself submerged in cold water.

After being violently pulled into the drain, he felt his body taking several twists and turns, swooshing through a dark tubular maze of several tightly constructed plumbing elbows, straight-aways, 'T' sections.

He arrived to what he believed was the septic tank. Floating around him were a few everyday items normally flushed down the toilet bowl. He visualized these items, because he never knew where things went, when they were flushed down the John. He also noticed that Jake had released the grip on his head, and once again, had vanished.

Searching frantically through the polluted waste filled water; raw sewerage, he soon discovered what some of the items floating around him were. Just in front of him hovered a few dead rats; some were still alive, dogpaddling their way to wherever. Many clusters of knotted hair twined with string, maybe dental floss. A few discarded feminine napkins, and an abundance of shit. A copious amount of brown, yellow, black and green excrement belonging to Katherine, Carlton, Spanky, Sleeper and him. Or maybe the mailman or an appliance technician happened by for a quick one.

Growing alarmed at this disgusting discovery, he became nauseous and flapped his arms hysterically to push the repulsive items away from him. Attempting to take a step backwards, his fears climbed higher when he realized that his feet were stuck in place. He looked down, and discovered them planted ankle deep in a mound of gummy sludge.

Suspended in a plague-ridden, disease infested raw sewerage, he flapped his arms exasperatingly, made drastic attempts to swim upwards. Again, he couldn't budge, something stopped him from ascending. He pulled strenuously to lift his right foot, but his shoe rose to only a few inches from the ground, and then he felt the tension of something elastic pull him back down. He discovered the soles of his shoes were laced with a gooey cement, holding him in place.

Making another attempt, he exerted a great deal of energy, flapped harder and lifted himself gradually. A few feet above the ground, he looked down and saw the gummy substance on the bottom of his shoes string itself thin, like a stretched rubber band.

After being pulled back to the bottom a second time, it finally hit him that the only way he was going to escape this madness, was if he slipped out of his shoes. He bent down quickly, stuck his hands into the thick sludge, and untied them. After he was free of his shoes, he flapped his arms liberally and floated upwards, on his way to the surface. Moving in this direction offered some relief. Very little. An unnoticeable amount, because he was still there. Wherever there was.

Fifteen feet from the bottom, a terrible feeling spurred him. The notion to look down crossed his mind, and he did. Searching through the dead mice and rats, discarded feminine napkins, hairballs and a copious amount of shit, he saw something zooming toward him through the murky depths, approaching like a rapid torpedo.

He became nervous and spanned the immediate area, searching for a glimmer of hope to attain some form of relief from the nightmarish hell sucking him into an underworld deep inside of himself. A place where darkness and deceit toiled hand in hand.

When the object was only a few yards away, it was almost clear to him what it was. He saw a diagram of five, not quite round objects, almost equally spaced apart in an imperfect circle. Now much closer, he realized that they were the tips of the fingers on Jakes right hand. Five gigantic outstretched fingers, forming a net to snare him, mind, body and soul. The gargantuan hand spanned three times the length of his body. Jakes deep voice rumbled through the shadowy depths, **"Stoney! Get back here. I'm not done with you yet. You'll not cheat me. I'm gonna abuse you like a twelfth generation step child. I'm gonna rip you to shreds like a malicious back alley abortion. I'm gonna cleave off your testicles, then shove them in place of your eyes, so that you can see with what you so much pride."**

Completely disoriented, Stoney looked upward, to where he thought the surface should be. He continued his ascent, remembering how the surface layer was suppose to grow nearer with each stroke he took. However, this time, no matter how fast he swam, it didn't. So he wandered aimlessly, swimming in random circles, rather than heading in a fixed direction. Weirdly, the surface layer changed its position sporadically. He didn't even feel the surface pulling at him anymore, as it normally should for the oxygen in his lungs.

Suddenly, he became more confused when he realized that there was no oxygen in his lungs. Only muddied water, combined with a few everyday natural ingredients. Disgusting and repulsive ingredients that made his breathing difficult, made him choke. Made him gag. Made him cough. His breathing became laborious.

At that moment, Jakes gigantic hand clutched his left leg with a grip so tight, that Stoney felt like he had stepped onto a brutal bear trap. It felt as though a Tiger shark had wrapped its jaws around his shin, calve and knee area, tried desperately to dismember him. To eat him. To kill him.

As he kicked at the enormous hand with his right foot, Jake laughed wickedly, **"AAAHHH HA HA HA HA HAAAAAAA!"** He roared, **"Gotcha!"**

Stoney flapped his arms anxiously to break away from Jakes grip, shouting, "Getchor gotdamn hands off me, you evil bastard!"

"NO!" Jake shouted. **"I've been waiting for you for a long time. You owe me your soul, and now you must pay."**

"Let me go!" Stoney hollered back. "Stay away from me."

"Who gives a fuck what you want, boy. Your ass is sold," Jake declared, **"to meeeee!"**

He glanced to where Jake held his leg, and saw a twinkling of glitter, a sparkle reflecting from his gold trimmed horned rim spectacles. Jake grabbed hiss other leg, but the thought of tiring never entered his mind. He persisted, flapping his arms frantically.

At that moment, an explosion of light flared in front of him. A fire burst of intense colors haloed the immediate area surrounding him, stunned him to disarray. After Jake released his legs, he coughed and gagged, felt lightheaded. Although he had indeed been released, he still felt the severe pains of Jakes nails digging pitilessly into his legs. He also felt a pounding in his head, as if he suffered from a sever migraine headache. As if someone were on the inside of his head, jack hammering to break out.

The display of colors grew blindingly brighter and brighter. Jake yelled, **"Come back here, you insignificant sniveling bastard! I thirst for your soul. I shall not cease, lest it be mine."**

He swam toward the light in front of him, believing it offered some salvation. He heard the phrase coined several times, 'Always move toward the light!' Kicking fervently, he flapped his arms hysterically. Feeling his body glide through the infested waters, as he put more distance in between him and Jake, he heard his fading voice cry, **"Come baaaack! Come** baaaack! Come baaaack! Come baaaa …"

Moments later, he felt a hand on his shoulder, rousing him. Someone delivered a cold slap to his face. "Wake up, Master Brooks!" Carlton yelled in distress. He coughed a few times. "You have to get out of here. You'll die if you stay in this place."

He shook his head a few times, cracked his eyes slowly. He closed them and fell unconscious. Amidst a garage completely filled with carbon monoxide emitting from the exhaust of his Porsche, Carlton worked zealously to revive him.

He leaned inside of the car, turned the key, and the engine died. His stinging eyes squeezed out a trail of tears, and he began to feel woozy for the poisonous fumes taking their toll on him.

He struggled to pull Stoney out of the car, then both tripped over some shopping bags that he had placed on the garage floor. He climbed to his feet quickly, grabbed his shoulders and roused him again, ordering, "Getchor ass up, Stoney! We have to get the hell out of here."

The thick poisonous fumes filled Carltons lungs and near incapacitated him, as if he was being chocked by a sadistic chemical killer. He ran to where the garage door switch was located, pressed a button, and the door rose slowly. When it was about four foot high, he stepped outside, coughing persistently. He took in a deep breath of fresh air, and quickly felt rejuvenated.

The rain had stopped falling, but it was still a bit cloudy. The afternoon sun, its radiance could be seen over the horizon, hadn't as yet made its way through some hovering clouds. As gloominess had its way of hanging around to rub things in.

After taking in a third breath, he ran back to where Stoney was, and grabbed him by his arms, struggled to pull him out through the garage door entrance. After both were well outside, Carlton laid him on the wet grass. He knelt beside him and checked for vital signs. After discovering that he had stopped breathing, he panicked, became scared shitless, damn near lost his mind.

He sat him upright, grasped his chin and shook his head a couple of times. He ordered hysterically, "Wake up, Stoney!" Near crying, he begged, "Please, don't do this to me. You've got to wake up."

To Carltons increasing frustration, there was no response. From the skies above, a mountain of ugly circumstances fell on him like a ton of bricks. This is terrible, he thought. A dead cop, here, with me. They'll be questions for eons, until the day I croak. They'll come down on me as if I had something to do with it. I know how his people at the station do things. I know how they think. I've heard him, Spanky and Sleeper say how they like to put people in little smoke filled rooms, and coerce them into admitting things that they didn't do. Giving them the 'bad cop, good cop' routine. And what if they ask me about the Dixie Club? What if they try to imply that I had some involvement? I may not know much about it, but they'll assume I knew about everything that was going on. They'll think his death had something to do with it. They'll make me an accessory. If I try to run, they'll put a dragnet out on me. They'll put me on an intercontinental most wanted list, and hunt me down, as if I was Whitey Bulger. I won't even be able to go back to my own country, without the fear of an extradition haunting me every moment of my existence.

He figured he should try harder to bring him back to life. It became imperative that he give it everything he had. That's when the idea of using C.P.R. entered his mind.

Scared out of his wits, and unsure about how to proceed, he laid Stoney flat, then checked again for a pulse. He placed the tips of his fingers on an area on the side of hiss neck, held it there for ten seconds. To his greatly desired relief, he felt a weak pulse beat every two seconds.

He pinched his nose shut, and blew a breath of air into his lungs, gave him mouth to mouth. He straddled hiss lifeless body, placed his hands, one laid flat on top of the other, to just over his heart, and delivered several lifesaving thumps. He repeated the process over and over again.

After the fifth time, he waited for a reaction. To his growing dissatisfaction, there was none. As the likely ramifications of Stoneys possible death clouded his mind, knocked him beyond comprehension, he was prompted to continue using C.P.R.

Moments into his second attempt to bring him back to the land on the living, he received a long sought after reprieve. A slight cough spurted from Stoneys lips, which moments later turned into him fighting desperately to suck in huge scoops of air, as if suffering a major asthma attack. One in which he almost didn't survive, hadn't it been for Carlton. These signs of life prompted him to glance toward the sky and whisper appreciatively, "Thank God he's alive, Father almighty! Thank God." He urged him, "Yeah, that's it! Take in more air. Keep breathing. You're going to be okay now."

Abruptly, Stoney snapped his eyes open as wide as he could, waved his arms feverishly, as though fending off an attack by someone attempting to snatch his life. He shouted, "No! Dammit, Jake. Stay the hell away from me!"

Carlton grabbed his arms, attempted to calm him. "Whoa, Master Brooks. It's just me, Carlton. Your servant."

Hearing Carltons voice, he felt greatly relieved. Gasping for air, he sputtered, "Wha-Wha-What happened?" It felt as if someone had stapled his lungs shut with fish hooks. Almost like the time when he learned how to swim in 1979, when he was nine years old. His parents had sent him to a salvation army camp for the summer, and he had a know-it-all, smart ass camp counselor who believed that the best way to learn to swim, was by first-hand experience. He simply threw little Stoney into the deep end of the pool, then told him to swim or sink.

The first time in, after swallowing a few cups of water, he almost drowned. The camp counselor had to jump in to retrieve him, then administer C.P.R. The second time he was thrown in, he struggled to get to the edge of the pool doing the panic stroke, with only a few ounces of water splashing around in his sinuses. On the third trip, he had the doggie paddle licked.

"Sir," Carlton replied. Feeling they were out of danger, he spoke more calmly, "you were in the garage, in your car, and the motor was running. You could've died. I should take you to a doctor, to have you examined thoroughly."

"No!" he spat hastily. He coughed a wad of saliva onto the left side of Carltons face, then wheezed, "No doctors, and definitely no hospitals. I hate those fricken places. If they can't find anything wrong with you, then they'll give you a few problems. They'll keep me until my insurance runs out." He paused, then stated, "Damn, my legs hurt."

"But, your lungs, sir. There may have been considerable damage. You could have respiratory problems for the rest of your life." Noticing the blood spotted towel wrapped around his right hand provoked him to ask worriedly, "What happened to your hand?"

Stoney glance at his right hand, delivered an uncanny expression. His mouth cracked open, but no excuse came forward. He's talking about the rest of my life, he thought. But I'm worried about the next few hours. If I go to one of those hospitals, they'll be glass windows and mirrors all over the fucken place. I'll see Jake or Jessica, then go into another blackout. If I do something crazy in a public hospital, they'll never let me leave. They'll strap me in a straight jacket, throw me in a padded room, then keep me heavily medicated. Besides, I don't want anybody thinking that I'm crazy. I know I ain't crazy.

He coughed the words, "No! No damn doctors or hospitals. I'll be okay. And you'd better not tell anybody about this. Especially Katherine. If you do, you're through here. And I think you know what that means."

His threats didn't mean that much. But if he ever make good on them, it meant that Carlton would be left in a very precarious predicament. One that only they knew of.

Carlton thought of his termination in more ways than one. He frowned and sighed heavily, then replied despondently, "Yes sir. Not a word to anyone. Especially Katherine."

"Good," Stoney coughed and wheezed. "Now help me get up from this wet grass, and into the house." Feeling several sharp pains in his legs, he grunted, "Damn, my legs are killing me."

"Yes sir." Carlton assisted him to his feet.

Taking a few wobbly steps, Stoney groaned painfully. Carlton asked, "What's wrong?"

"It's my legs," he wheezed. "All over the front area."

Both looked to the front of his pants legs, and discovered small blotches of blood stains riddling his knee, shin and ankle area. "Oh my God!" Carlton gasped. "Sir, this is just too much." He asked disbelievingly, "What happened to your legs?"

He flashed a baffled expression, and stuttered, "I-I-I don't know. I guess I must've …" He lifted his left pants leg carefully, up to the shin area, and both stared appallingly at the bruises and gashes dressing the front his knees and shin area.

"You honestly have no idea of how this happened?" Carlton asked in astonishment.

Staring off into nowhere, an abundance of horror filling his eyes, He repeated, "I-I-I don't know."

Inside the car, as he swam in the nightmare and kicked at Jakes hand, he acquired the bruises when his legs banged repeatedly into the underside of the dashboard, into the steering wheel column, and into the break and accelerator peddles.

"Are you absolutely sure?"

His voice cracking, he replied, "I can't explain it. I simply don't know what happened." He dropped his pants legs, and as they slid over the wounds, he groaned in agony, his face contorted insufferably.

"Lets get you inside, cleaned up and into bed," Carlton suggested.

With Carlton assisting, he hobbled slowly toward the rear entrance of the house. "I'll get in the bed and lie down for a little while, but I ain't going to sleep." He asserted adamantly, "Hell no! No fucken way! You can bitch, moan and gripe to the high heavens all you want, but I ain't going to sleep. Not for an instant."

CHAPTER 22

▼

After they got inside of the kitchen, Stoney flopped into the first chair that he managed to stumble to. Carlton returned to the garage to retrieve the groceries that he had left beside the Porsche.

Waiting for his return, he lifted his pants carefully, and again examined the damage done to his legs. Studying the many nicks, cuts and gashes, some of which were down to the shin bones, streams of blood trickled his legs and absorbed into his socks. Staring awkwardly, he realized that the terrifying night-mares were occurring more frequently. Each time he went under, he stayed capti-vated longer than the time before. What's worse, the hallucinations were more vivid each time around. More real.

An ugly feeling surfaced and sent shivers rocketing through his body, and he smelled an unfamiliar grotesque chemical odor fill the kitchen. He became wholly unsettled, felt nauseas, wanted to vomit his insides until his stomach lay at his feet. Recollections of the terrifying anxiety he suffered through the recent nightmare returned, and he felt the room's temperature drop fifty degrees. Rigor mortis had set in, and he couldn't move a muscle.

He turned from examining his wounds, looked to the center of the table and there they were. Lenses facing him, sitting there in all their hideous glory. Exactly in the middle of the table were Jakes gold trimmed horned rimmed glasses. The frames flashed sparkles, as if they were brand spanking new. Still present, the strand of tape holding one corner together.

Staring at them, he fell shocked and dropped the pants cuffs. As they slid over the gashes, he grunted excruciatingly. He felt like he was descending in the first steep drop on a roller coaster ride, without a seatbelt. Included were the gravity defying effects of hovering above his seat, and his organs being compressed into his chest area. He couldn't believe what he saw, because he thought he had returned from the nightmare. He gasped dismayingly, "Wha-Wha-Wha ..."

A chair on the opposite side of the table slid four feet from the table, Poltergeist like. The original little Jake appeared from out of nowhere, sitting in it. He stared at Stoney with a pretentiously concerned look, then reached for his glasses, exciting, "Heavens to mergatroid! My glasses. For a minute there, I thought I'd lost them. If I did that, my daddy would've whooped my hinny real good. Glasses are expensive nowadays." He put them on, looked at Stoney and smiled. "Ya kno something, Stoney, old buddy? You don't look so good." He asked facetiously, "What's wrong?"

Staring back, he said absolutely nothing. He looked to the blood soaked towel wrapped around his hand, then to the ceiling, a look of regret fixed on his face. He asked sorrowfully, "Why me? Why is this happening only to me? Spanky and Sleeper were doing it too. Why do you only come to see me?"

Jake sat back in his chair, sighed. "Stoney Stoney Stoney. Always with the questions." He paused briefly, then went on to explain, "Spanky's nothing but an empty shell of a man, walking around dead. He died in his heart a long time ago. He already has a seat reserved in hell. No matter how much he tries to straighten out his act from this day forward," he laughed, "he's still going straight to hell. No detours. It's already written in the books. The damage he's caused is irreversible. He sold his soul a long time ago. He just doesn't know it yet. Through a compromise with the big man upstairs, we've decided to let him stick around for a little while. And why not? Soon, for him, it'll be just like hell anyway. Ya see, my man Stoney ... The Stoneman ... Stone to the bone, when you signed onto the Dixie Club, you pledged your soul to me. Whether you go to heaven or hell all depends on what kind of life you're living. Sadly, most people are living a sort of ... hell. A lot of you people have the conception," he clenched he right fist and pointed his thumb to the floor, "that hell is down there." He yelled, "Wrong! Hell is in your mind, it's in your soul." He pounded his chest lightly, explaining, "It's in your heart. It's what you've conditioned yourself to believe about your existence. What's even funnier about you people," he pointed the same thumb to the ceiling, "is that most of you believe that the Lord Jesus is up there somewhere. But if you were on the other side of the world, Stoney, which direction would you be pointing in, and looking at? Better yet, if you were in outer space, which direction would you consider to be up?"

As Jake spoke, his voice grew menacingly deeper. Frightfully familiar. He continued, "When Spankys finished here, he'll come to see me. And that's when the fun will really begin. He'll be a student of which I'll hardly have to teach. In hell, they'll crown him king of the atheists. As for your friend Sleeper, he's like a sheep. Constantly being led to the slaughter by Spanky. He's devoted to him." He paused, thinking of his status. "And yet, believe it or not, he's a toss-up." Jake smiled proudly and proclaimed, "As for *my* children, I have an abundance of work for them. Since they want to do my work, I will gladly accommodate their desires, and their schedules will be filled. Since they want top bestow grief, I will teach them merciless pain. Since they want to embrace what is unholy, I will teach them how to live a satanic damnation. The ongoing battle for souls has been fought since day one. It's a billion year old war, and I'm winning." He stated acutely, "That's a fact! Just look at your diminished earth and its pitiful people. The Father has granted you ample opportunity to earn your way into His eternal kingdom. A place even I desire to be. And yet, your selfish greed has drained you of nearly every drop of hope that He has granted you. All for petty material possessions that fade as the sands of time." Jake laughed. "And I thought I was disgusting." He exhaled deeply, filled the kitchen with his odious breath. "There is more to life than simply what is superficial. Because of your undying vanity, your excessive pride, you have over sighted this seemingly trifle, but considerable fact." He looked to the heavens and proclaimed victoriously, "Against my Father, I am winning!" He protested, "How dare He denounce me, His son! I am a part of His plan for His children to have free will. Without me, there cannot exist the other. There would be nothing for which to compare with good."

On that note, Jakes physical structure changed dramatically. From the little blonde haired innocent kid who bow guarded into Stoney waking days, into the full figured demon that's been trying desperately to drag him into the bowels of hell. He wore a tattered police uniform, the sleeveless shirt torn to shreds, looked as though he'd been flogged with a cat-o-nine tails. His police hat cocked to the side, cabby style, and his rusted Boston police officers badge seemed a millions years old. He was completely out of breath, as though he had just seconds before returned from an exhaustive clash with a devout enemy, appeared a wearied soldier fresh from battle. A smug disposition iced his smirk, twisted his lips inexplicably.

He pulled a pack of Newport cigarettes from his shirt pocket, stuck one in his mouth, inhaled deeply, and it lit itself. He blew a puff into the air casually, and it resemble a nebulous skull and cross bones briefly, then quickly dissipated to nothing.

Stoney stared at the graven image floating over the table, looked over Jakes dilapidated uniform, figured it to be as battered as his soul. Just over his pocket, he noticed the medal of valor that he had received a few years prior. During a shootout with a bank robber who had taken hostages, he had run in between a hail of gunfire to heroically save a child playing unaware of his deadly environment.. He felt good about himself that day. But the feelings died quickly, washed away by a fervent conflict of interest; his involvement in the Dixie Club.

Suddenly, Jakes glasses grew shaded as a complete solar eclipse. Black, like ebony eyes. He sat back in the chair smug like, totally composed. He crossed his legs, then placed one hand on top of the other, and brought them to rest on his left knee. His fingers parlayed a dead mans drum roll frivolously on his kneecaps. His glazed muscular face sported a manikin likeness. A solemn stare. Cold, clammy and collective.

Jakes lengthy yellowish-brown rustic nails snatched his attention; the tips jagged from scrapping the bottom out of the pit of life in an effort to fill his lot. With the left leg strapped over the right, his foot tapped out a sacrilegious ceremonial war dance in the air. The bottom of his bare feet thick with the insensitive calluses for treading through many battles, the ongoing encounters between the forces of good and evil.

As Stoney peered deeply, a contemptuous fire blazed aglow in his eyes. A reflection of how he felt about Jake. About himself.

"But you, Stoney, in all fairness, I must say. You, like Sleeper, are a borderline case. You're an interesting challenge—one that I find very intriguing. One that I placed upon myself to deal with. As with some of my greatest victories in the past, you're a fine selection of the choicest meats from everything that is superior … grade 'A' prime. I can't wait to throw you into the boiling pot of *my* redemption. You'll make succulent jambalaya." He licked his chops and rubbed his belly. "Yummy yummy, good for my tummy!" He closed his eyes tight, and feelings of extreme elation took him by storm and he moaned profoundly. Pleasurably. He slid his tongue across the ridge of his upper lip. "I can almost taste your soul as we speak." He opened his eyes and sighed. "I have work hands, but they're my students." He chuckled, "my slaves. I couldn't trust them with someone as special as you. You'll have to be filleted just right, so I can get the most bang for my buck." He leaned over the table and whispered, "It would bring me nothing but sheer pleasure to win your soul. And win it, I shall."

Stoney looked into his lap despondently, shook his clenched fists into the air. He looked to the ceiling and screamed, **"NOOOOOOO!!"**

Hearing the scream, Carlton rushed into the kitchen, carrying the bags of groceries he had retrieved from the garage. He placed them on the floor, just past the threshold. "What's wrong, sir?"

He looked at Carlton with a field of horror sizzling on his face, then pointed a trembling finger to the chair on the other side of the table. Carlton glanced puzzlingly to the chair, then back to Stoney. "Is there something that's supposed to be there, sir?"

Stoney looked at the chair, and became appalled, because Jake was still sitting there, smiling wickedly from ear to ear. He informed Stoney, "No one can see me, but through your eyes, Stoney. As I am in you."

Jake rose from the chair, then walked backwards. "I will see you soon, Stoney. I will not cease, lest I possess your soul." He turned and simply walked through the kitchen wall. Disappeared. "My man Stoney," he voice faded. "The Stoneman! Stone cold to the bone."

A shower of fear rained over his body as he shivered at the thought of Jakes ill desires. He found a dejected expression muddled across Carltons face and said, "Help me get upstairs. Afterwards, I want you to call my pharmacist, and have him deliver me the strongest prescription sleeping pills that he has. And I need something for the pain in my hand and legs."

"At once, sir." He helped him to his feet. "Would you like me to prepare lunch for you?"

He studied the thought for a moment. "Um ...," he coughed, patted himself on the chest, "Yeah. I'll have a ham and cheese on wheat, with a ..." he cleared his throat, "... a little mayo. And throw in two of those kosher dill slices on the side."

"And to drink, sir?"

He coughed, then wheezed, "Ginger ale."

"Splendid sir. I'll bring that up to you, as soon as I can. After I call the pharmacist."

CHAPTER 23

▼

He had finished eating the tasty lunch that Carlton had prepared for him when the doorbell rang. Lying on his bed, clad in a pair of plaid boxer shorts, he stared at the ceiling and contemplated his grisly fate.

He spent nearly two hours locked in this position. Hadn't moved an inch, except for the beating of his heart, the flowing of his blood, and an occasional blink. He was struck in a form of paralysis, defenseless against a power that he believed could never exist. No matter how vivid the nightmares appeared, he wanted to believe the sightings were only in his mind, a figment of his condemned and run amuck imagination.

Never had a nightmare in his past come anywhere close to what he'd been experiencing for the past few days. Unfortunately, never once did an inclination of bitter regret enter his heart. He felt somewhat sorry for the children living the repercussions of his actions, but not enough to drop to his knees and beg for the Lords forgiveness, plead his case before a court of angels, appeal for mercy. His many convictions were buried deeply within, remained etched in his soul, never to see the light of empathy.

Practicing a great deal of caution, Carlton entered his bedroom quietly. He observed him briefly, wondering what kind of horrible demons had taken over his spirit, battered his soul. He cleared his throat. "Sir. Are you awake?"

There was no reply.

He spoke louder. "Sir!"

"Huh?" Stoney garbled. "Yeah. I'm awake."

"You have a visitor waiting for you, downstairs in the reception area."

"Who …?"

Carlton pronounced, "A Mr. Greg Norton, your pharmacist. He has an important matter that he wishes to discuss with you."

The eccentric perverted weirdo, he thought. Let me go downstairs and see what this sideshow freak wants.

He swung his legs over the side of the bed, then heaved while standing to his feet, "Tell him I'll be down in a few minutes." He coughed, patted his chest area, traces of the carbon monoxide lingered to remind him of the nightmare he had just returned from. "Where's my robe?" The thought escaped him for a minute. He remembered he saw it last in the bathroom, hanging behind the door. Just where Carlton always hung it after he completed the laundry.

Walking to the bathroom, the pain in his legs lashed at his nervous system with each hobbling step he took. He felt like a dilapidated cripple, pitied himself. After slipping into his robe, he walked to the beginning of the staircase, where he stood paused, leaning over the banister. Using the handrail for assistance, he stepped down cautiously, placed all of his body weight onto his right leg. An excruciating pain shot up the length of his shin, exploded internally, but he only released a slight groan. Tried his damndest to minimize the suffering, kept it in check.

He descended unsteadily with his left foot, bracing for the same amount of pain. At least, this time he expected it. Repeating the process, the notion hit him that this was definitely going to be the longest time it's ever taken for him to walk downstairs. Usually a simple task. Never even a thought.

After five long excruciating minutes, and twenty-five damn steps later—he cursed each one—he had arrived to the first floor landing. He glanced loathingly to the top of the stairs and dreaded the thought of an unbearable return trip. He leaned against a three legged antique table, a place where there use to sit a priceless Ming vase, then called aloud, "Mr. Norton!"

Just around the corner, Greg Norton stood in the waiting room; a small den located off the side of the living room. When he heard Stoney calling, he approached the voice. When he saw him, he flashed a pretentious smile. He had a fresh haircut, freshly manicured nails. He wore a freshly pressed suit, wore freshly polished shoes. Refreshing! He extended his right hand, and his freshly polished teeth gleamed when he stated freshly, "Hello, officer Brooks?"

Stoney extended his right hand, and Greg stared inquisitively at the blood soaked towel wrapped around it. He explained, "I'd shake your hand, but as you can see, I've had a little accident a short while ago."

Greg dropped his hand by his side, twisted his lips curiously. "So I see." He asked concernedly, "Are you going to be all right?"

He nodded unenthusiastically.

"That's a lot of blood there," he stated, staring worriedly at the towel on his hand. "Shouldn't you go to a hospital or something? Infection could set in."

He glanced at his hand. "No. It's nothing. Really."

"Suit yourself, officer Brooks. Just trying to give you a little good advise."

"I appreciate your concern. But, it's okay. I'll be just fine."

"You know, I haven't seen you since the party you had a few months ago." He smiled indistinctly "I believe you were a bit inebriated when I showed up." He paused for an uncomfortable moment, then asked, "So, how's everything going?" He knew it was a stupid question.

Stoney shifted his weight uneasily from one aching leg to the other, tried to conceal the stabbing pains filling the lower half of his body. Since he was plastered to the gills at the party, he didn't remember seeing him at all. It took him a good long minute for the incident to become familiar. He replied gloomily, "I've seen better days."

Carlton entered from the kitchen and inquired, "Would your guest fancy a refreshment, sir?"

Stoney asked Greg, "I'm sorry. Where are my manners? Would you like something to drink?"

He waved his hands dismissively, replied casually, "No, thank you. I can't stay long. I have pressing business to tend to in Boston."

"A glass of ginger ale for me, Carlton. That's all."

After Carlton returned to the kitchen, Greg went on to say, "Carlton contacted me and explained that you needed something to help you get some rest. And something for pain. Told me that things were a little rough around the edges."

"Yes. Something like that. Give me the strongest stuff you've got. I've got to get some serious rest. Seems like I have a touch of insomnia. Whatever, it's driving me up the wall. I'm so out of it from lack of sleep, that I wasn't paying attention to something that I was doing earlier—you know, working around the house." He elevated his right hand. "That's how this happened." Giving no explanation wouldn't have felt right.

"I understand," Greg smiled. "No problem. I have it right here." He reached into his pocket and retrieved two plastic vials. One slightly larger than the other, both capped with child restraint caps. He uncapped both, then removed one pill from each. He handed Stoney the pills to his left hand. "I'm sure you'll want to take these as soon as possible." He placed the vials on the mantel over the fireplace. "I'll leave these over here, since I have to be leaving now. I'm running late."

Hands clasped behind his back, he stood modest. Seemingly humble. "Well, that should be it."

There was definitely something suspicious in his tone that made Stoney think hard. Made him feel a little uncomfortable. He glanced at the containers, and became curious when he noticed that there were no labels on them. Feeling it didn't matter, he decided not to ask questions. After all, this was an under the table kind of thing. He placed his life in his hands with no hesitation or doubts as to his sincerity. Probably because he was preoccupied, looking forward to the much needed rest that he'd soon receive. Greg explained, "I made these special, just for you. The larger vial contains tranquilizers. They'll relax you, and help you get to sleep. The smaller one contains a combination oxicodine and muscle relaxer, for the pain."

"Thank you very much, Mr. Norton. I really appreciate it. I didn't mean for you to have to go out of your way, to get these to me."

"Nonsense. No bother at all. It was along the way." By habit, he inserted a commercial plug. "We, my employees and I, pride ourselves on our customer satisfaction policy."

"That's good." He forced a weak smile. "So, how much do I owe you?"

"I'll bill you later. You'll probably want to get some rest now."

"Thanks again. I won't keep you any longer from your business in Boston."

Greg turned away and approached the front door. He threw over his shoulders, "You shouldn't have any problems with the pills. They'll get the job done, I guarantee."

The same uncomfortable feelings surfaced again. Since Stoney couldn't substantiate its significance, he dropped the notion.

After Greg left, Carlton returned with a glass of ginger ale, and Stoney took the pills and washed them down. Returning to the master bedroom, he had twice as much of a hard time climbing the stairs. It took him almost eight minutes to reach the second floor landing. He sat on the first step, paused to catch his breath. He was totally exhausted, like he had just finished climbing Mt. Washington. Sweat ran abundantly from his face, and his robe was soaked with perspiration. The pain in his legs was so intense, that on the last few steps, he was on all fours, crawling like a baby, moving at a snails pace. He appeared a lone foreign legion soldier, dying of thirst in a torturous desert. He called out, "Carlton!" Waiting for a response, he massaged his aching kneecaps gently.

He came to the bottom of the staircase and glanced upwards. His expression was one of great concern, relayed that he was greatly worried about Stoneys overall health. He tossed upstairs, "Sir!"

"Could you bring me another glass of ginger ale?"

"I shall be there in a moment, sir."

"On the mantel, over the fireplace, you'll find two vials. Could you bring them also?"

"Certainly sir."

He crawled into the bedroom, then hoisted himself onto the bed. Carlton entered the bedroom less than a minute later. "Sir. Your prescriptions, and your ginger ale." He placed everything on the nightstand, eyed Stoney mournfully. "Will that be all, sir?"

"Yes. Thank you." As Carlton was about to walk through the doorway, he added, "One more thing."

He faced him. "Yes."

"Go to the library, and you'll see a brown leather encased book, with no title on it, sitting next to the computer. Could you bring it to me?"

"Certainly sir." He returned less than thirty seconds later. Entering the bedroom, he held the book up to show. "Is this what you were referring to, sir?"

"Yes. That's the one." He took the book from him, placed it on the nightstand. "I think I'll do some editing, before I take a nap."

"I trust those sleeping pills will do the job, sir."

"They'd better," he said, opening the larger of the containers. "I think I'll take two more, a triple dose of the sleeping pills, just to make sure."

Carlton delivered a cautious stare. "A triple dose! Are you sure that's wise, sir?"

"They're just tranquilizers," he underplayed. "How dangerous can they be? If I took a handful, then I'd have a serious problem."

"I suppose your right. If anything, you'll probably get enough rest to last a lifetime."

"That's my point. You know what they say about sleep deprivation. You start seeing things that aren't there. That's probably what's wrong with me."

"Respectfully sir, I couldn't agree more." He smiled fraily. "Will there be anything else, Master Brooks?" He felt relieved that he was finally going to get the essential rest he needed. Soon, he figured there would be an end to the madness of glass and mirror smashing, of shooting at objects that only he could see. And of shouting belligerently at everyone who he happened upon.

"Aaahhh, nah. I'm all set. And if I don't wake up tomorrow morning, then fine. Let me sleep through the day."

"Certainly sir."

"Another thing, Carlton."

"Sir."

"I ... um ... I want to apologize for the way I've been treating you recently. We've been together for a long time now, and if anything, my respect for you should've grown. I should know better than that."

"That's all right, sir. A little rain must fall into everyone's life."

He managed to find another frail smile. "Goodnight Carlton."

"Goodnight sir. Pleasant dreams." Before he left the bedroom, he peered at him through the corners of his eyes. He smiled insecurely, then left the bedroom.

Stoney opened the drawer to his nightstand, then pulled out a set of hand-cuffs. The set that Katherine was looking for when they were having sex. His intentions were to handcuff himself to the bedpost right before he fell to sleep, so he wouldn't be able to follow through on whatever deadly plans Jake and Jessica had in mind. He figured that they would try to get him to commit suicide, by sticking his head into a gas filled oven, or by sleepwalking into oncoming traffic, or by diving face first from the roof of the mansion. Figured an once of prevention was less bloody than a pound or cure.

CHAPTER 24

▼

It didn't take him long to fall asleep. He was out so fast that he didn't have the opportunity to glance through his manuscript. Ten minutes into his siesta, he began experiencing the most unusual sensations, entered an extraordinarily vivid dream stage.

Into the phase, abruptly, he felt a ton of weight on his chest, as if he had been flattened by a steamroller. His heart thumped a monumental beat—it surmounted like the high point of a symphony; the apex—and he thought he was suffering a massive cardiac arrest. A dense cacophony of silence ensued, and he felt his body descend slowly at a sharp angle. During the descent, his arms extended perpendicular to his body, as far as he could stretch. He felt the piercing of cold steel ream the palms of his hands and crossed ankles, nailing him, then all of his body weight fell on his shoulder sockets and upper spinal column. All of this, and he didn't feel the excruciating pain that he was sure he was supposed to suffer.

The only pain he experienced was a mere soreness in his throat. A pain stemming from the intense emotions of severe grief, cruel sorrow and deep regret. All of which made it very difficult for him to swallow.

On the journey downward, passing through a dark ghastly expanse, he stopped briefly at a formidable area filled with the timeless shadows of his jaded past. Paused on the cross, staring out into the darkness, he somehow knew that his judgment was about to be rendered. The records of his life would be opened for all to see, his story would be told in its entirety.

At that moment, a huge golden book appeared in the distance, emitted sparkles of bright lights, made a slow approach. Now only a few feet away, the binder facing him, he wondered what significance it had, if any at all. It rotated slowly and opened to the middle, showing blank yellow pages. A picture hazed into view on the left-hand page, flashed an indiscriminate episode in his life, a still picture of his uncomplicated birth at Mass General Hospital. A joyous occasion.

The page flipped to age three: His first day of preschool he cried for nearly two hours, because it was the first time that he had been separated from his parents. His first heartbreak. He accepted the fact that *all* good things must come to an end.

Age five: He observed himself sitting on the foot of his bed, stewing irately, extremely heated after opening the package he'd received from the Kellogg's Corporation, only to discover great dissatisfaction. The mutant disfigured Rice Crispies doll. A rude awakening, he learned to accept discouragement and disappointment, then move on.

Age six: He watched himself riding a small bicycle unsteadily and insecurely, on the day his father removed the training wheels. He learned that it was in him to be secure within himself against great odds.

Age seven: Sitting at the head of the table at his birthday party, he flung handfuls of ice-cream and cake at his playmates. He learned to give and take. Tit for tat.

Age nine: He watched himself struggling desperately to swim to the edge of the pool. Taught him to stare death in the face, then overcome it. Courage under fire.

Age ten: He observed himself sitting in a pew, crying incessantly from the death of his grandmother. A realization of mortality, everyone must die someday.

Age fifteen: He revisited the magnificent disaster of the first time he had sex. A premature ejaculation. A right of passage, a pubescent learning experience for most young men. He accepted it as practice, then adjusted fittingly, with more practice.

Age sixteen: Walking across the stage to receive his high school diploma, the entire student body chanted dynamically, 'Stoneman! Stoneman! Stoneman! He smiled internally, but showed no emotions. He learned that it was up to him and only him to boost his own ego, so that no one could lead him astray under false pretenses, with self-serving compliments.

Age twenty: He discovered that his tech school certificate had about as much bang as a firecracker floating in a bowl of chicken noodle soup. He learned all about the dollar, and acquired the need for much more. A time of reckoning.

Age twenty four: The day he graduated from the police academy initiated the challenge between his integrity, his honor, and the phrase 'Cash Over People.'

Age twenty five: The day he hustled his first mark, he put his soul up for sale to the highest bidder. He learned that nearly everyone can be brought for a price.

After his eulogy, the book slammed shut, rotated ninety degrees, then flashed the front cover. The title in a biblical age calligraphy read, 'The Book Of Life.'

Moments later, the pages that he had just viewed ripped themselves from the binder. Each caught fire in mid-flight and disintegrated to ashes, like the remains of his life. These memories he knew no more.

He continued descending.

Again, he stopped briefly at a spacious place with crystal clear blue skies overhead. The air was so crisp and clean that it appeared as though the earth had been made anew. It was unspoiled, the environment in pristine condition. In this picturesque setting, in a wide open field of green, he found himself standing amidst a vast gathering, a multitude of people of a wide diversity; black, white, brown, yellow; young and old alike, dressed in white flowing gowns. Looking at their joyful faces, he attempted to place who they were, but nothing appeased his recollections. Although some were people who he once new, he denied knowing them because they weren't into the ways of what he had come to know. They were unfamiliar to him in spirit.

He noticed that all were looking to just in back of him, and turned around and became thunderstruck for the astonishing sight of what he witnessed. His eyes lit up like watchtower beacons and the breath gushed from his body; he was beyond fascination, frozen in complete awe. Before him, its enormous foundation planted at more than a few hundred yards away, he saw the likes of a grand castle built to a tremendous height, spanning to the firmaments above, designed like none ever seen before, unimaginable to the human mind. Its great walls and towers stretching toward the heavens were constructed of gold and ivory, the moat surrounding it created of thick bubbling clouds. Taking in its full height, he looked upward, became disoriented and almost fell backwards.

He saw two Greek symbols etched in the two colossal wooden doors at the base of the castle; alpha on the left, and omega on the right. As he wondered of their meaning, they opened slowly, and a bearded man appeared standing just past the entrance, carrying a huge book that was as old as time itself. He opened it to its beginning, looked into it briefly, then smiled delightfully at the masses standing before him. He closed the book, nodded blissfully, and the people began moving forward.

Entering the castle, treading the paved road of gold laid before them, no one had uttered a word, but some nodded ecstatically to the old man in passing. Not one word had been said by anyone, but their pleasant smiles spoke immensely of their steadfast anticipation of the wonderful lives that they would soon began to live. Their eyes filled compassionately to overflowing with the hopes of finally receiving the gifts that had been promised for their unwavering belief in His name.

When Stoney tried to make an effort to approach the castles as well, he discovered that his feet wouldn't budge. For they were stuck in place by his ignorance to approach this beatitude when the opportunity was readily available. "My feet," he stated uncomfortably, a lump swelling in his throat. "What's wrong with my feet." He asked the people walking by, "Please, can someone help me?" He reached out to no one in particular. "I want to go inside too, but my feet are stuck to ..."

A few looked at him sorrowfully, as if they wanted to help, but realized that it was beyond them to do so. An elderly woman walking by grazed her hand softly against his shoulder. Humming an old spiritual hymn, she stopped briefly and mumbled inaudibly, "No one can help another get through these gates. The responsibility is solely your own."

Trying desperately to place her features, he felt that she reminded him of someone who he use to know. Perhaps his grandmother, for the hymn was one that she sang occasionally as she did chores around the house.

A young mother of some thirty years walked by, holding her children's hands. The eight year old girl on the left eyed him briefly, smiled frailly. The boy on the right, a few years older, with golden curly hair, smiling a huge bucktooth grin, his face capped with gold trimmed horned rim glasses, looked at Stoney, then nudged his glasses higher so they wouldn't fall off.

The three were in a fatal car accident not long ago, for the mother being unfamiliar with the rules of the road. Usually, her husband did most of the driving. He was taken from their lives abruptly when he was incarcerated for taking a life unjustly, and it left her stressed and severely depressed. She had problems concentrating on everything. Sometimes unusual circumstances initiate unusual circumstances.

At that moment, a commanding voice bellowed from somewhere inside of the castle, "Thou shall have no other gods before me."

"Thou shalt not make unto thee any graven image, or any likeness of any thing that is in heaven above, or that is the earth beneath, or that is in the water under the earth: thou shalt not bow down thyself to them, nor serve them: for I the Lord thy God am a jealous God, visiting the iniquity of the fathers upon the children unto the third and forth generation of them that hate me; and shewing mercy unto thousands of them that love me, and keep my commandments."

"Thou shalt not take the image of the Lord thy God in vain; fore the Lord will not hold him guiltless that taketh his name in vain."

The proverbial words of the bible touched him profoundly, but he wondered why the ten commandments were being recited with such vigor. Listening to the words, he heard a growing rage emanate from somewhere far away. Feeling the ground tremble beneath his feet, he turned slightly, and in the distance, saw a huge horse-like creature trudging furiously in place, stomping his giant hoofs into the ground with a graven bitterness, pointing accusatory fingers at several persons walking past him. Cursing to the high heavens, a shower of saliva burst from his mouth when he complained heatedly, "… and this one right here, with the sick twisted things he's done in the past—You know he's unworthy of entering. I have more of a right to be inside than he."

As he hurled many groundless accusations, the people merely walked around him, paid little or no attention at all. They feared him not, for they knew in their hearts that they were beyond his touch. Knew that they were saved, protected by the full body armor of Christ. A group of thirty persons walked by him as a procession, marching up the aisle as they once did in their local Baptist church, singing a hymn from the depths of their souls, praising the Lord their savior. Their voices roared, 'We come this far by faith.'

Lucifer pointed elsewhere. "And this woman over here, you saw how she denied her own child. You saw the neglect and abuse she inflicted. We discussed what her punishment should be, remember?"

He pointed to a young boy keeping in step with the procession. "This kid was past the age of reckoning; he was old enough to know better. He knew right from wrong. Having autism is no excuse."

The young boy stopped walking, smiled naively and asked, "O death, where is thy sting? O grave, where is thy victory?"

Others individuals strolling by peeped Lucifer from the corners of their eyes, remembered the persistent battles they've had with him from day one, their times of unrelenting strife. To conciliate themselves, they remembered the many times they've dropped to their knees and begged for His forgiveness, cried endless pools of shameful tears, pleading for His mercy to deliver absolution. Because of the shallowness of Lucifers deprived vision, he saw only what was superficial, negating to fathom the atonement in their hearts.

Stoney looked down and focused on his feet again, tried to figure the significance of everything happening. He closed his eyes briefly, and while departing from this place, he heard the fading ominous voice orate, "Thou shalt not kill."

"Thou shalt not commit adultery."

"Thou shalt not steal."

He opened his eyes and discovered himself to be as he was before—nailed to the cross, descending through the blackness filling his heart. He then arrived to a vast desolate region where he heard a dull humming sound cruising in a small patch of fog. It's the kind of sound that stereo speakers made before the damned thing blew, went kaplat! Nothing. It surrounded and pressurized his body briefly, then coasted off to another area not to far away. He became highly puzzled, because it was the first time that he was able to see what a sound looked like. He also realized that he was free of the cross, it had dissipated to nothing. Gone.

Overhead, gloomy skies crowded with swirling black clouds emitted soft sparks of lightening, simulating the Aurora Borealis. What was frightfully strange was that during this particular dream, so he believed it was a dream, his senses were fully active. He felt the environment around him, as an unfamiliar chemical stench filled his nostrils and lungs with a thick gaseous mixture. Delivering a contemptible impression, he smelled a fine blend of sulfur and lime. The place was void of any temperature, tweren't none. It was neither hot, nor cold.

Standing, he felt the dirt ground beneath his bare feet, granules crumbed in between his toes, a jelly jam crust. He searched the immediate area for a sign to help him find out where he was, but could see nothing for miles and a distance hazing off into some cloud peaked hills. A deserted wasteland, forever in the distant. There was absolutely no greenery to be found anywhere, no life in the ground. Only death filled the atmosphere with a grim persona of impending doom.

He spanned the area and discovered a few misshapen objects laying scattered about, camouflaged in the terrain. He thought it bizarre that a few rocks, broken tree limbs and other inexplicable objects resembled withered human remains. Even the tumbleweeds rolling by appeared as bulky growths of knotty dreadlocks. In passing, the bush whispered inaudibly, "A rolling SSStone gathers no mosssss. My man SSStoney. The SSStoneman! SSStone cold to the bone."

A pasty white tongue slithered through a pair of ashen lips imaged on a rock, made futile attempts to moisten itself. The crusted lips cracked ajar and out came, "What do ya say, the drinks are on you tonight, Stoneman?"

At that moment, the altered Jake approached him from the side, just out of his view. He found it favorable to catch someone through their blind spot, take them by surprise. This time, when he addressed Stoney, he was self-assured. He exhibited a strong confidence, demonstrated his authority as he informed him of what was coming to pass.

Upon hearing his footsteps, Stoney turned quickly to the right, and his eyes reflected the fright curdling in his heart. His voice danced waveringly on a shaky breath, "I-I-I thought that if I slept hard, that you wouldn't ..."

Jake chuckled, then jested amusingly, "Aaahhh! Trying to fool the Master. Sorry, Stoney." Shook his head disapprovingly. "No dice. I'm the one who invented the tricks of deceit. Or have you forgotten that little detail?" He paused, sighed deeply, then walked a few feet to just past Stoney. He turned halfway, said earnestly, "Let me explain some things to you, my forever child. Come, walk with me."

Feeling he should comply, he caught up to him, but stayed at what he thought was a safe distance. He stepped cautiously, as if treading on eggshells, didn't want to step on his toes. Feeling that he was in too deep, up to his ears in hock, he thought that if he listened to Jake attentively, that maybe he could discover a way out of the madness haunting him. A possible escape. A fruitless chance that he had to take. Fruitless, because Jake knew ahead of time exactly what his thoughts were. He was even aware of his future thoughts. And strangely, he had just realized that he didn't feel the excruciating pain in his legs and hand any longer. It was as if he never suffered the injuries at all. Even the nick inflicted while shaving the day before had disappeared.

The same tumbleweed rolled by again, and through glazed eyes of fear, Stoney hushed frightfully, "That bush looks awfully familiar, like someone I know." He stepped closer, hovered, peered down intently.

Tears dribbling down its cheek, the tumbleweed slurred as a cobra, a whispered hissing trailed his words, "SSStoooneeey! My man SSStoooneeey. The SSStoneman! SSStone cold to da bone, ya dig me booooo? I knowsss ya knowsss where I'm coming from. We usseta hang tight. Ya feel me, bro? Tighter than tight, when we wasss up there having a good ole tiiiiiime, shaking our assesss on the dance floor. Finger popping and all that good shit. Ya rememba, SSStoney? Couldn't nobody touch ussssss. We had it aaalll, baby. Just like I said in the beginning—power, pressssstige and privilege. We wasss on top of the world, ma. We had everything. We told everybody to kissss our mutha fucken assesss. Didn't we, SSStoney?"

Staring into its eyes, Stoney discovered an inkling of identification. He blurted disbelievingly, "S-S-Spanky! I-I-Is that you?"

"Hidey hidey ho ho, SSStoneeey. Ya right on the money with that one, old buddy. Only difference isss, I done lost ma limbs, but I gained a few more eyesss. Know I can sssee them mutha fuckasss sssneakin up on me. It's just what I've alwaysss wanted. Can't beat that with a basssseball bat. Now can ya, SSSSSSS-toneeey?"

"But ... how? I mean ... why?"

"SSStill wit the dumb assssssss questionsss. I can tell ya ain't leart a damn thing while we wasss up there," Spanky laughed, "jusss like me. It's just like the butcher sssaid. One bite, and you'll never ssstop ... eating."

"Never mind that beautiful sack of shit," the altered Jake said. "He arrived shortly after you did." He eyed Spanky. "He's gonna do all right here. He likes my meats just fine. Loves the way I season them; without an ounce of regret, not a drop of shame, not a speck of conscious, nor a dash of awareness. No side dishes. I love him because he tells the truth, straight up, shaming me. You might've heard of the phase, 'Tell the truth, shame the devil.'" He laughed. "He'll do anything I say. Just like ya buddy Sleeper, with no questions asked. Never any questions asked. I love Sinclair because he loves me and everything I stand for. He did me proud when he was up there. He showed my Father who's in charge—who has a greater flock." He stated boastfully, "They love my influence ... my meats. Not His. Proving that His other is a mere fallacy, and not I. Nobody believes that garbage he's putting out." He proclaimed conceitedly, "They all want me, the real deal Holyfield!"

He strolled casually, his hands clasped modestly behind his back. Holding his head high, he explained arrogantly, "My son, in life, there extends to everyone a perpetual gamble, of which everyone has been given the freewill to, or not to, speculate on." To remind Stoney, he repeated, "He, our Father, grants all of his children the freewill to place good or evil on their minds. Where it will eventually proliferate into their hearts, then consequently take over their souls."

As they walked, Stoney didn't notice that the scenery had changed gradually from what was grim, into what was undoubtedly unearthly. The lightening above their heads escalated into an exhibit of perilous whirlwinds and treacherous thunderstorms. As if they had left a calm world, and entered a disastrous environment reeking its havoc of an apocalypse. A place suffering the destruction of a thermonuclear war. Being cautious of his every step, he attempted to avoided puddles of bubbling lava, and stubbed his feet into and tripped over huge stones.

He looked up and glanced at his surroundings, and noticed many eerie transformations occurring. The features of a few mysterious objects changed from what was unsightly, to what was repulsive, to what was irrefutably hideous. He also noticed that the pitch in Jakes voice had become much deeper, and his height increased with each few steps they took. With the increase in height, came an increase in weight. Each ponderous step he trudged thundered to the ground, sending shock waves straight through his backbone, settling at the base of his skull.

Expressing amusement, Jake asked sarcastically, "What is it with you humans anyway? Our Father has explained very clearly, using simple words, in nearly every tongue known to man, what you have to do to get it into His eternal kingdom of heaven. A wonderful place that even I desire to be. The place that I have been cast out of eons ago, for a little misunderstanding." He sighed. "Tell me, Stoney, because I fail to understand what's going on here. On earth, is my practice desired *that* much? I often find delivering my persuasion much too easy, even boring at times. A long time ago, as the serpent in the garden of Eden, all I had to do was work a slight influence on the first Eve. As for you, Stoney, how did you come about?"

Stoney began experiencing a gradual deletion of his recollections, and the everyday knowledge of what he had acquired became obscure. His thought process failed him miserably. He felt naïve, like an innocent child. In hell, this process wiped out all pleasant memories, leaving him to fill his heart abundantly with what is unholy. In heaven, it wiped the slate clean of the pain he's endured through his strife through life, leaving him to know only the glory of the Lord Jesus Christ.

Not looking at Jake, he lowered his head to focus on where he tread. What came to him slowly, dragged its feet for his big fat denial, was the understanding that this place didn't exist anywhere on Gods earth. What scared him more than anything was that he was finally coming around to accepting that his fate was sealed forever. The arrival of this revelation left him severely petrified. With some repentance in his voice, finally, he replied solemnly, "They … they make it hard for you up there … there's so much pressure. Life shouldn't have to be so difficult, just to exist." As if it would justify his irresponsible actions, he sounded like a troublesome misfit when he stated, "Everybody else was doing it too."

Jake peered deep into his eyes, said gravely, "I understand, my child. You had what you needed; the basic necessities, but you wanted a hellova lot more. You could've survived just fine on what you were making when you graduated from that shitty second rate tech school, but you had to have more, for your gluttony. As gluttony is a sin. You lie to the Father, and He'll forgive you, for His abundance of mercy and compassion for His children. You lie to me, and like I said before, I'll cleave off your testicles, them shove them in place of you eyes, so that you can see with what you so much pride. The truth, Stoney. Remember, I know when you're lying. You are of me. Therefore, I am of you. What you meant to say was that my temptation was much too strong for you to resist. I had more of an influence over you than our Father who is in heaven. Isn't that what you meant to say, Stoney?"

Not wanting to admit the truth, he didn't respond. He was preoccupied jumping over the small lakes of bubbling lava, leaping over large rocks and climbing over gigantic boulders.

Jake smiled, flashing yellowish razor sharp teeth. "All for the almighty dollar. Yes, my child. I know all about the dollar. My Father didn't invent money." He asserted, "I did! I did it because I knew that most of you people would grow to cherish it, then subsequently me. I know what it's like on earth, with some of your kind praising scratch tickets, all packed wall to wall at casinos, practically kneeling in front of slot machines, praying for the million dollar jackpot," to sum it all up, he threw in, "worshiping me. Before me, in the Garden of Eden, everything was as free as the air you've once breathed. As free as the choices you've once made. Hence the phrase 'Free will.'" He paused, then explained, "Stoney, my forever child, *your* death brings absolute truth. It is time you understood that truth. Man is only man … nothing more, nothing less. The higher one puts himself above other men, the further from His grace he will fall. Man is not judged by his actions, so it's been deemed on earth. Another misconception, with your fables of 'a man is this, and a man is that', supported by vanity." He shouted "Bullshit! He's judged by his overall worth, by only one who is capable of making that judgment. Certainly man is not capable of passing judgment on any man, all being bred of sin. Only the Father is in position for that. On earth, a mans life is but an iota of the entire civilization, when you take the time to graciously consider the overall picture, to keep the life granted to you in its proper perspective. One must always stand back to look at the overall picture, to find the truth in his own self worth. The truly honorable and meek understand this truth, that they must remain humble and modest, neglecting what is arrogance and egotism. That is why *they* shall inherit the earth and all its goodness. Not you. They are the sweetness of truth, who birth an eternal salvation. You are the epitome of a lie, who will die an endless death."

He stopped walking and faced Stoney, discovered him fatigued to a near collapse. He fell to his knees, leaned against a boulder to rest for a moment. Feeling a strain in his neck, he glanced upward and witnessed Jake transforming into a massive centaur strutting sternly in place. Half man, half beast. His strapping arms grew to several feet in diameter, his burly muscular chest expanded robustly. His upper body strength developed from digging in the chapters of time to fill his lot, to show his Father that he was just as good as Jesus. When his transformation was near complete, a pair of ivory horns bolted from the front corners of his head and flared to the span of fifty feet. Resembling a pair of gigantic tartar ridden elephant tusks.

Stoney found that his legs resembled a mammoth Clydesdale. His pylon like hoofs weighed tons easily. His long thick tail swayed heavily in slow motion, launched dirt-filled whirlwinds, swept huge boulders several feet out of place. Now in his complete transformation, Lucifer stood monumental at more that two hundred feet tall. He threw his hands onto his hips and glared down at Stoney. His eyes blazed fires of eternal damnation, his nostrils blasted snorts like Nasa's Discovery rocket engines prepared to launch.

He cradled himself securely for the flying debris and hellfire. He felt the ground shake beneath him when Lucifer stomped his mighty hoofs and pranced in place. He released a sinister laugh that shook everything for miles around, his servants trembled drearily with fear. Now, understanding that his fate was forever lost in the doom of this forsaken creatures world, he wept ruefully, "For God sake, why me?" He wondered why some individuals while amidst a world of serious troubles asked that very same question. He understood that there were several parables in the Bible that were not understood by man. Mysteries. He knew that he wasn't among the living any longer, so that particular mystery was disclosed to him. A thought came to mind for clarification, and he found his answer when he switched the words around. 'Why me? I have forsaken God.'

"My forever child, the more you traveled my road, the closer you came to me." His breath showered Stoney as if amidst an angry hailstorm. Holding his arms outstretched, he announced proudly, "And now, for what you so desired ... you are here!" He glanced to the heavens and shouted, **"Welcome to my kingdom! Bow to me, my child! My forever servant!"** He strutted a pompous swagger, spanned his terrain. **"Wake up, my children! It's time to pay homage, to meeeeeeeeeeee!"**

Stoney witnessed some of the stones and branches gradually transform into deformed figures of man. Some took the shapes of snakes and slithered on their bellies. Others disfigured into an extreme loathe of indescribable repulsive creatures, rocking back and forth in place, lodged in their complete transformation. Their bent, broken and twisted limbs nudged them across the ground at a snails pace, leaving trails of flesh and blood stained with their vile iniquities.

He felt an overpowering compulsion to splay outstretched on the ground. His arms and legs cracked painfully at the joints, bent into impossible positions. His skin grew thin and stretched frailly over his bones. His head twisted completely to the left until his neck snapped, and his jaw twisted to the right until it popped from the hinges. His backbone snapped in three places, then his head fell backwards. His nose, now a snout, found its way into his ass. The toes on his feet rounded off to stubs. The space in between his fingers grew meshed as a web, for swimming the tides through his oceans of regret. His ears fell off and he swallowed his tongue. All of this surely happened, but his sight remained to bear witness to the miserable suffering in Lucifer's eternal kingdom.

Stirring amidst his profound disgust, streams of saliva drooled from the corners of his mouth, he slurred, "SSSSSSommmebody ... eeeeelp mmmeeeeeee!"

At that moment, several large muscular Gladiators appeared from out of nowhere, and dispersed themselves among Lucifers flock; his forever servants through to the end of time. A Gladiator told Stoney, "It's too late for that, you lame fuck! You had a chance to straighten everything out," he laughed, "when you were up there having a *grand* old time. Swinging your ass and partying every night, as if everyday were your last day on earth."

A few ran in between some of the scattered figures lying on the ground and kicked them about, shouting obscenities. "Get the fuck over here, you repulsive shits! There's plenty of work to do."

A few Gladiators carrying whips cracked them into the air. Some merely pointed at the disfigured piles of repulse and laughed. Others carrying shepherd's staffs jabbed the figures violently, as if herding cattle to the slaughterhouse. As this happened, cries of grief, despair and sorrow filled the air and covered the skies for a distance over the mountains.

A Gladiator knelt down to one of the deformed figures weeping persistently, and listened to him beg repentantly, "I'm sorry! I didn't mean to do it. I'm sorry! For God sake, please, have mercy on my soul."

The Gladiator responded sarcastically, "Aaawww, what's the matter, widdle baby? Not feeling well, are we? Well, let me see if I can fix that for you. As for your soul, you have none. Ya blew it, kid." He reached down and plucked out his eyes. "You won't be needing these babies anymore. Me and the guys are going to play a little game of pool later on. These'll come in handy. Thanks."

The captain of the guard—a Gladiator wearing a weighty brass breastplate—approached Stoney, then stood over him with a great deal of intolerance perverting his mind. He grumbled, "I get to break in all first timers." He raised his shepherd's staff high over his head, then came down with such brutal force, that it traveled straight through Stoneys back and entered the ground. Stoney cracked the atmosphere when he cried excruciatingly, **"Aaaauuuuuuurrrggggg!!"**

A small rock beside Stoney commented facetiously, "Ooohhh! I know that must've hurt like the dickens." It laughed. "But don't worry. The pain will go away in a minute. Luckily for me, I'm just a rock. I only get kicked around when they play soccer. But I get these suicidal migraines every now and then. The kind that make me pray for someone to swing a sledgehammer at me, and be done with it."

Lucifer looked at Stoney and smiled gratifyingly. The Gladiator yanked the shaft out of his body, and the wound healed within seconds. Then he pierced him over and over again, until the end of time. Then Stoney would surely die. Dissipate as a vapor in the wind. Fade to nothing.

Absorbing an unfathomable satisfaction, Lucifer turned from his flock and galloped to the top of the highest mountain nearby. There, he stood proud, and peered proudly over his domain.

To God, a billion years is but the blink of an eye. Therefore, merciless tyrants like Hitler, Caesar, and their sorts have arrived just moments before Stoney. Lucifer knew that now was the time for him to be crowned fittingly for his accomplishments. He brought his clenched fist high above his head, pointed to the sky and commanded his followers to, **"Summon the Master!"**

At the four outermost corners of his world, on four pillars built of stone, four scantly clad men stood poised, each holding a rusted brass longhorn. They raised the horns to their lips, then blew simultaneously a sound heard like none before. The reverberation of the horns in sync produced a pitch so high that it shattered boulders, and sent shock waves through the depth of several oceans. A sonic boom thrashed from the heavens and stimulated the black pot bellied clouds just above Lucifer's head, stirring them energetically.

Just then, all heard the galloping of clomping hoofs approaching from the south. Soaring through the sky overhead, they saw an unknown messenger approaching on a gray chariot pulled by ten white Arabian Stallions. When the chariot was just over Lucifer's head, the messenger reached into a cask and pulled out a sizzling bolt of lightening. He hurled it into the black pot bellied clouds, and they exploded upon impact like a nuclear explosion, dispersing the black clouds into a blue heaven above. After the rumbling subsided, the messenger yelled to his stallions, "HOOOOOO!" The stallions pranced in place for a moment, then galloped on their way to a region in the north. When they were no longer visible, for a few moments, it was quiet.

When Stoney thought that the silence would last an eternity, the thunder of thunders, the demanding voice of God filled the heavens. It was felt as deep as the magnitude of many earthquakes throughout time. He declared, **"I AM!"**

Lucifer pronounced, "Father, I have tallied Your precious earth and its images made in Your likeness. I have won their souls for their committed belief in me. Do I not deserve to be the sole ruler of Your kingdom?"

"Lucifer, thou have won the empty souls of those who did not believe in Thy name. Mine who truly believe for their devoted hearts are Thy real treasure. Nevertheless, thou hast forgotten that judgment is not passed upon man until their final call. At mans demise, no matter how putrid his soul, who does his heart call upon?"

Lucifer stomped his hoofs heatedly, stewed as an idling volcano about to blow. He lowered his head in anguish and whispered a grunt of despair through gritted teeth, "Nooooooo! You deceived me. I won fairly. You can't do that. I won!"

"Since this time, the earth is anew. Since this time, I have left the vision of your image open, so Thy real treasure could know thou kingdom of hell." God paused to allow an ageless defeat to brew in Lucifers heart, then surmised, "At last, thou have made Thy example to ensure Thy name on the new earth. My child, you have served me well."

Now extremely irate because he realized that he had been used as a thing, a mere object to be manipulated, he shouted, "You tricked me! I am better than Your other beloved Son, and have a much greater following. It was Your image who crucified Him."

"I have always been in Thy Sons heart, the Prince of light. There, I will remain, and never in yours. I am content. As I promised, I crown three fittingly, the prince of darkness. Thou has his kingdom ... in hell!"

Gods voice faded, and the black stewing clouds gathered once more above Lucifers head, as they'll remain. Standing on the mountain of stone, poised high on his pedestal, he raved and ranted his case fiercely. Only to be heard by his kingdom, his forever servants through to the end of time.

CHAPTER 25

▼

Early Friday morning.

Capt. Winslow, while in his office at the station house, telephoned Stoney's primary care physician, Dr. Ivan Wolfgang Kaplan, to get the results of his three hour long, arduous, physical examination. He was at his office, a private practice in Brookline, Mass. He's a sixty-year-old German-Jew, born in Munich, near the Bavarian Alps. He grew up in Bern, Switzerland and studied at a distinguished University in Vienna, Austria. His family had fled from Germany in the early forties to escape the religious prosecution of Jews. He came to America shortly after completing an internship in 1965, and has been the Brooks family doctor ever since Stoney was five years old.

When Stoney came to see him the day before, in the company of Katherine, after giving him a thorough physical exam, he found no signs of a physical disorder, although he recommended that he seek immediate diagnostic psychiatric procedures. He's six-foot-three inches tall, rawboned, walks with a slight limp, and carries a giddy disposition. He speaks several languages fluently, but flaunts his thick Austrian accent proudly. His shoulder length gray hair is frizzed like a clown's hairpiece, making him favor Albert Einstein. He gets excited naturally when talking, his voice sporadically jumps higher in tone from word to word, spilling the heavy Austrian accent that he's managed to hold onto for many years. "Yeaz, Captain Vinslow. Ztoney came by for un examination un de Monday last."

"Vell, I mean, well," the doctors accent was very catchy, "how'd he make out?"

"Vrom vhat I can vecall," he explained considerately, "Ztoney haz always been a nize boy. Alvays vit de yez maams, und de no zirs. He'z neva had diz kind of trouble before in his life. At least, not dat I can vecall. During de examination, ven I vaz tesding de veflexis un de knockers o de kneecaps, his vight leg vlung up like kapow, und he kicked me un de groinin."

Capt. Winslow pulled the phone from his ear and muffled, "Ouch!" He returned the phone to his ear. "That must've hurt."

"You damn skippy it did. Dis high tone of de voice um zpeaking vit iz not my normal tone. Und ven I was checkin de eyes und de pupils, he looked into my eyes, den called me zomebody named Jake," he shouted, "… **und VHAMMO!** He hauled off und punched me in da la bonza. My blackened eye is ztill qvite zvollen und puffy. Und I don't even know diz Jake person—I have no affiliations vit him vatzoeva. Howeva, I do believe dat Ztoney muzn't like him at all." He stuttered, "I-I-I've neva seen anyding like diz before, and I know zat abnormality of da noggin doez not vun in hiz vamily." He said plainly, "I dink Ztoney needs to zee a head doctor on a vegular basis, until ve get zome control on de matter."

"A head doctor? You mean a psychiatrist, or something like that?"

"Yeaz!" he excited. "Zomeding like dat von dere. Dat's vhat he needs alvight. Um glad you zaid it, cause I have problemz vit bik vords like zat von dere. You zee, he may have a temporary mental dizorder, vhich probably involves emotional dizturbances zat are vendering him incapable of adjuzting realistically to hiz zur-rounding environments."

Capt. Winslow sat with a confused expression iced over his brow; his eyes squinting confusedly. He was hoping and prayed that the good doctor wasn't going to throw in a pop quiz at the end of their conversation. "Vhat, I mean, what would you suggest that I do? I don't know of anyone in the business. At least, anyone really good."

"I have a vriend at zee Harvard School of Medizine. I'm going to call him vight now, und tell him to be expecting a call vrom you. You should call him about a half hour vfrom now."

"Great! What's the number?"

"Hold on a moment, Captain. I got it vight here zomevere."

While Capt. Winslow waited patiently, in the background, he heard what sounded like a shuffling of papers being whooshed around in a hefty pile. That's exactly what it was. Dr. Kaplan's secretary's been sick for a few days, and he's been too busy to hire a temp. His cluttered desk was blanketed with a huge mound of paperwork, of which he had to clear to find his roller deck. He flipped through a few cards, then continued his conversation with Capt. Winslow. "Here vee go. You got a pen?"

"Yeap. Shoot."

"Zee number is area code 781, 522, 7610, extension 428. After you call, you vill ask to zpeak to Dr. Ipshaw. After you make zee appointment, you make sure you take Ztoney to zee him as zoon as you can." He scratched his head. "I neva thought zat little Ztoney vould grow up ta be a qvacky qvacky. He vas alvays zuch a good little boy. Alvays vit de yez maams, und de no zirs."

"Don't worry Doc. We'll take care of him on this end. Thank you for your time."

"You're velcome. Toodle-loo, Captain Vinslow."

"Toodle-loo, back at ya," he said, before terminating the call.

*   *   *   *

Twenty minutes later, Capt. Winslow was on the phone with Dr. Ralph Ipshaw, a psychology teacher at the Harvard University school psychiatry. He dreaded the thought of conversing with another egghead, because he knew that most of the psychiatric jargon he was going to hear was going to fly right over his head. Nevertheless, he managed to hold onto what was necessary for him to grasp the gist of what they were trying to relay. He informed Dr. Ipshaw of Stoneys symptoms, and was listening to what he had to say.

"Well, if you've described his exact symptoms, it sounds like officer Brooks may be suffering from a condition that we in the profession term psychosomatic. His symptoms include a disturbance of reality appreciation (hallucinations and delusion), severe deviation of moods (depression and mania), lack of, or inappropriateness of apparent emotional response, and severe distortion of judgment."

Capt. Winslow took all of this information in, then agreed, "That sounds like him all right. Is there anything that can be done about it?"

"We can certainly try. You see, in most psychosomatic conditions, there is usually some interaction between psychological factors and a psychological predisposition to the illness. For example, ulcers are sometimes caused by a combination of external stresses, anxiety, and, or by having a susceptibility to ulcers. The treatment of psychosomatic ailments ordinarily involves a medical regimen, as well as some form of psychotherapy for the patient. It also involves an interpersonal relationship between the therapist, the patient, and sometimes a deeply concerned third party, such as yourself. In turn, the patient will find relief of the symptoms in order to initiate therapy. However, this does require some commitment on the part of the patient."

"Oh, don't you worry about that part right there," Capt. Winslow assured. "He'll commit. I'll see to that. Even if I have to drag him in screaming, kicking and biting."

"Excellent! In addition to a psychoanalysis—this requires some understanding of the psychoanalytic theory—there will be other forms of stress therapy, which should help him to examine his own ideas about himself and life in general. If there's no progress through conversation and readjustments of his lifestyle, I'll start him on a regiment of psyche drugs, order an EEG, cranial x-rays or whatever's necessary."

"That sounds great doc. Will you be his therapist?"

"Heavens no," he laughed. "I only teach nowadays. However, I will put the matter into the hands of one of my most dearest and trusted friends. Someone who I use to study with. Then I will do an inclusive follow up. During the therapy, I'll look in on him from time to time, and give you a progress report as we go along. How's that?"

"That sounds vonderful."

"Sounds like you've been talking to Dr. Kaplan."

"I have. He's a nice guy."

"He's been a good friend of mine for many years. Every now and then I accidentally throw in a 'V' instead of a 'W', and a 'Z' instead of an 'S.' But for now, Captain, I have some very urgent business to attend to. Bring officer Brooks down here as soon as you can."

"I'll do that, doc. Thanks a lot."

"You're very velcome. I mean, you're welcome. Goodbye."

"Goodbye."

CHAPTER 26

▼

An hour later, after ingesting a pastrami submarine loaded with onions, Capt. Winslow telephoned Stoney to see how he was doing. When someone answered the phone, he heard an unfamiliar voice say, "Hello."

The voice didn't sound anything like Stoneys or Carltons, and he heard a suspicious bustling going on in the background. He grew suspicious. "Ah, yeah. Is officer Brooks there?" He listened intently.

"Who may I ask is calling?"

"This is his boss, Captain Winslow, of the Boston Police."

The listener paused for lengthy moment, then sighed mournfully. "Captain Winslow. This is Captain Bogart of the Dover police department. And, well, all I can say is that there's been a terrible accident out here, at officer Brooks' residence."

Premature thoughts of mayhem dazed Capt. Winslow. His heart raced out of control, his anxiety climbed. He paused to let it sink in, then excited, "Is it officer Brooks?"

He hesitated, then replied solemnly, "Yes. I'm afraid so."

Capt. Winslow pulled the phone from his ear, then slammed his fist furiously on the desk. He shouted irately, "Damn!" He returned the phone to his ear. "How bad is he?"

"Captain Winslow, I'm sure you're familiar with standard procedure. I know you're very concerned, but this is a public telephone we're speaking on."

Shooting through Capt. Winslows mind was the conversation he had with Stoney earlier in the week, in his office. Believing that if it was so bad that he couldn't mention it over the phone, then obviously, it was something gravely serious. He spat forward, "I'm on my way out there right now."

"All right. I'll be waiting. When you get here, just come through the tape. I'll tell my men to be expecting you."

Capt. Winslow dropped the phone, sprang from his desk, then rushed to the dispatchers station. He flung open the door and ordered, "Wendy! Get officers Sinclair and Knight on the horn. Tell them to meet me at Stoneys place in Dover. And tell them it's urgent."

"Yes sir," Wendy replied. "It's already done."

He left the dispatchers station and rushed down the hallway, bumping into and nearly knocking everyone out of his way. After he got to his cruiser in the parking lot, he jumped inside and switched on the ignition. Seconds later, he sped from the parking lot, almost hitting several civilians on the sidewalk. Lights flaring, siren blaring, tires screeching and smoking. Anyone observing would think that he was on his way to a shoot out in progress, in which one of his family members were critically wounded, or being held hostage.

At that moment also, Sleeper called Spanky on his cell phone. He sounded frantic when he asked, "Sinclair! Did you get the call?"

"Yeah. I'm on my way out there right now."

"I'll see you there."

CHAPTER 27

▼

At approximately ten thirty a.m., the three had arrived at Stoneys mansion in Dover, Mass. They noticed the late model black coroners wagon parked haphazardly in front and shot directly into panic mode. Capt. Winslow approached Spanky and Sleeper anxiously, eager to learn information relevant to anything. The uneasiness was clearly heard in his voice when her asked, "Officers, I don't know what's going on, but this doesn't look good. Before we go in there, so that I won't end up looking like a fool for not being informed of my own officers folly, I want to ask you something." He cautioned, "And you better think real hard before you answer." He paused, staring into their eyes. "Was officer Brooks involved in any illegal activities? Anything at all? I don't care how long ago … does anything come to mind?" His sight shot back and forth in between the two. Waiting for a response, he studied their expressions, every wee blemish on their faces. He waited for an eye to twitch spasmodically, for either to clear their throat uncomfortably, for a brow to jump from being caught off guard, or for a mouth to form the first letter of a word of culpability. He listened for their breathing to waver hesitantly, watched their hands for nervous fidgeting, and studied their posture, waiting for an uncomfortable shift in weight from one leg to the other.

Visions of hustling episodes swarmed through Spankys mind, scenes of Stoney rolling his spellbinding lines. He thought about the money he accumulated hand over foot, the off shore bank accounts, and the Swiss account he opened the year before. Mostly, he thought of the five thousand dollars that he had bulging in his front left pocket. He stuck his hand inside, felt the wad, then swallowed awkwardly.

Anytime Sleeper was confronted with anything that made him feel uncomfortable, his thoughts ran to his son, Junior. He thought of the ramifications of his unlawful actions, and how they'd effect his own future, if he did get caught. He thought of his wife next, then his thoughts went blank.

Deciding to answer first, Spanky stated confidently, "I don't think so, Captain. I know Stoney pretty well. If he was involved in anything illegal, I'd know."

Sleeper looked at Spanky, waiting for him to conjure up a lie for him. Spanky returned an expression reflecting 'You're on you own with this one, buddy.' He shrugged his shoulders, stated simply, "No, Captain."

Capt. Winslow considered their responses, and saw an inclination of something he didn't trust, but decided to put it away for now. He eyed them skeptically. "Lets go in and find out what's going on."

They flashed police credentials to a Dover police officer standing guard at the front entrance, then slipped under the yellow tape marked 'POLICE CRIME SCENE. DO NOT CROSS'. Just past the threshold, in the receiving room, they observed a heavy commotion bustling about on the inside of the mansion. A slew of Dover police personnel scuttled about; some vacuuming every possible clue that they could sniff out, a few fingerprinting experts dusted and lifted every fingerprint that they could possibly find, and a couple of DNA experts swabbed every crack and crevice in the entire house. Standing in the middle of the room, they saw a man who appeared to be the head honcho. They assumed this because of the weighty commands he shouted. Indeed, it was Capt. Bogart, talking sharp to a few of his people.

Capt. Winslow remembered what he looked like from attending a League of Police Capt.'s convention a few years ago. Their meeting was brief. Few words were spoken. However, Capt. Winslow never forgot a face. Everyone had something under their belt that they were good at. His was remembering faces. He remembered that Colombo (Peter Faulk) persona that he had mastered, and the Ben Franklin style bifocals hanging on the tip of his nose, which looked like they were about to fall off. Mostly, he remembered the ageless beat-up Stetson Hat he sported, which he wore slightly cocked to the side.

Since their outfit was located in the deep burbs, they were allowed to dress casual. More relaxed, than if they were located in a big city like Boston. Capt. Winslow could tell that it took many years for Capt. Bogart to become the master of his own character. The ongoing strive for human individuality, things that people do to bide their time. Eccentrics.

The three rushed to where he stood, bumping into and nearly knocking people out of the way. Capt. Winslow blew the cigar from out of his mouth and cuffed it in mid-flight. He addressed Capt. Bogart, "Captain Bogart, I presume?"

Capt. Bogart turned from talking to a detective. "Yes. And you must be Captain Winslow."

They looked the other up and down briefly; scanned each others identity, as there was a lot to be absorbed in a glance. Especially to investigating eyes. They shook hands quickly. Not like a merry 'Hi! How ya doing?' hand shake. But like a cold business gone wrong 'Let's get this very disturbing matter out of the way' hand shake. There were many types. Each had a discernable distinction.

Normally, Capt. Winslow could tell simply by looking at a persons face what the situation was. In the case of bad news, there was normally a hill of distress riding the brow, or maybe a sour feeling pruning the lips. Much more was said in the persons stance. Slump shoulders meant 'get ready to receive disappointment, because someone's paid their due to the devil.' However, Capt. Bogarts expression threw him off completely. Most likely, because he's been in the same profession for just as many years, with witnessing all the disgust that he's seen, as far as murder investigations went. He's learned to hold his composure, as well as keep a dispassionate facial expression. In short, he was numb to it all. Or just plain use to it. Dealing with decapitated and mangled bodies occasionally had become a way of life. It had gotten so that both could observe an autopsy while eating their lunch. Be it Spaghetti or lasagna.

"Yes," Capt. Winslow replied. "And these are two close friends of officer Brooks. Since they know him better than anyone, I brought them because I thought they could possibly shed some light on what could've possibly happened. By your tone, I assumed it wasn't good news." He nodded to the right. "This is officer Knight," to the left, "and officer Sinclair." Because he didn't see Stoney anywhere, he got straight to the point. "Where's officer Brooks?"

With feelings of deep discouragement hidden behind his eyes, Capt. Bogart gestured to the staircase, stated grimly, "He's upstairs." His dismal response unraveled a gruesome tale in the making.

Capt. Winslow shoved his cigar into his mouth, turned around and marched toward the staircase. Spanky and Sleeper right on his heels. As he was about to climb the first step, Capt. Bogart told them, "Before you go upstairs, I think there's something important you should know."

All three stopped in their tracks. The ratings of the grim tale increased by two X's. Capt. Winslow feared the sound of his voice. He turned around and approached him. His magnified eyes blinked rapidly. His cigar froze in place. "What's that?"

Capt. Bogart lowered his head briefly, almost evasively. He couldn't possibly have held back his emotions for what he was getting ready to say. After a long moment, he looked up, then declared calmly, "He's dead. The coroner's just informed us that he's been dead for almost twenty-four hours." His eyes couldn't find an expression to accompany what he had just said. Not that he was looking for one. He realized that applying any emotions on the job only complicated matters.

Seconds after the words left his lips, a heavy silence crowded the room. Everyone from the Dover police department stopped doing whatever it was they were doing to observe their expressions. Their responses.

Capt. Winslow couldn't believe what he had just heard. A heavy breath gushed from his body, and he stumbled backwards a few feet, as if the word 'DEAD' was thrown at him with the force of its severe meaning. Hearing the news of Stoneys death pounded at his chest with the sledgehammer of the Mighty Thor. A wave of heat rushed threw his body and drained him of nearly every ounce of energy. His shoulders dropped gloomily, his cigar fell to the floor. He wobbled briefly, rocked back and forth on his wing tipped Bostonians. Appeared as though he was about to faint. He felt completely incapacitated.

Spanky stood gawking in total disbelief. Wide eyed and on a still breath, the word 'DEAD' echoed throughout his head. Instead of it fading, it grew louder and louder until it deafened him. He cringed shakily, as though a marine drill instructor blasted his eardrums with drill commands. His fists were clenched so tight that his fingernails almost broke the skin in the palms of his hands. A strenuous expression etched the contour of his face, and he remained perfectly still, eyes shut tight. It looked as though he tried to force the grotesque word 'DEAD' and all of its grisly meanings from out of his head. It couldn't be done no matter how hard he tried. It was too concrete to erase, or accept as something not precise. The meaning of the word was unambiguous.

Sleeper felt like someone had thrown a bucket of cold water into his face, waking him from a deep comfortable slumber, into a waking nightmare. Like Spanky and Capt. Winslow, a heavy breath gushed from his body when he received the news of his friends death. Pulling air in pained his chest. He became weak in the knees and his vertebrae felt as though it were made of rubber. Holding his balance was extremely difficult. From utter disbelief, he shook his head in grave denial. No!

Capt. Winslow approached Capt. Bogart. He picked up his cigar along the way, almost crushing it. Capt. Bogart informed them, "Someone named Carlton found him early this morning, and he called us immediately."

Because it didn't sink in, Capt. Winslow asked disbelievingly, "Officer Brooks ..." he swallowed contritely, "... is dead?"

Sleeper shouted under his breath, "Nooooooo!" He cried strenuously. "It's gotta be a mistake! Stoney ain't dead! He can't be dead! He can't be ..." He ran to the foot of the staircase, shouting, "Stoooneeeeeeeey!"

Everyone in the room felt his outburst of grief, watched him sprint hastily toward the staircase. Following his lead, Spanky ran close behind.

"Captain Winslow," Capt. Bogart said.

He whispered inaudibly, "Yeah."

"About your men. I know you're familiar with departmental procedure."

"Yeah. I know the routine."

"Good. Can you remind your men?"

"Sure. Yeah." He hustled to the bottom of the staircase, saw that Spanky and Sleeper had just made it to the top landing. He shouted, "Hey, you two!" When they faced him, he instructed, "You can look, but you can't touch anything. You hear me? It's not our jurisdiction. They're responsible for the body, and all of the evidence at the scene. I'll be up in a minute."

Spanky and Sleeper nodded simultaneously. "We understand," Spanky said.

Capt. Winslow asked Capt. Bogart, "Any ideas about how it happened?"

"We're not sure yet. I think you should know that at the time of his death, he was handcuffed to the bedpost, and highly intoxicated. My forensic expert thinks he might've been poisoned."

Capt. Winslows eyes bucked in disbelief. "Poisoned? Handcuffed to the bed?"

"Yes. But he's not sure what kind of poison was ingested. Only an autopsy can give us that information. In addition, we're not sure if it was murder, or self-inflicted." He showed Capt. Winslow two pill containers inside of a plastic evidence bag. "We found these vials on the nightstand, next to his bed. Strangely, the labels are blank. There's no information about who filled the prescriptions or anything. However, we did get some information from Carlton that someone had dropped them off yesterday morning. One is a tranquilizer. The other, a painkiller. Supposedly. At the moment, we're not even sure about what he used to put himself to sleep with. From finding an empty two-liter bottle of scotch lying on the floor, next to the bed, I'm sure the booze was enough to knock him out. Who knows? Could be it was alcohol poisoning. Alternatively, there's no sign of a forced entry onto the premises, or of a perpetrator having been present.

We're questioning Carlton in the next room. I don't think he had anything to do with his death. We're just digging up all possible leads. You wouldn't happen to know if officer Brooks had any sworn enemies. Domestically or otherwise."

Capt. Winslow lowered his head, wondering about the question. "Not that I now of. I'll have to look into that. If I find anything, I'll definitely let you know."

Capt. Bogart stepped closer, whispered, "Was … ah … officer Brooks under any kind of departmental investigation? You know, internal affairs, or anything like that."

Capt. Winslow leaned back almost to fall, as though he was pushed. He looked at him like he was talking crazy. He assured him that without a doubt, "No!" He paused, wondering of Stoneys bizarre behavior with his desk lamp, then said indecisively, "Not that I know of. What makes you ask something like that?"

"We found a bug planted in the telephone, in the kitchen." He opened his right hand.

"A bug!" He gawked at the miniature electronic device. "Are you sure?"

He nodded gravely. "It's a bug, all right."

Capt. Winslow looked to the floor, highly confused. He walked away, mumbled inaudibly, "A bug!" He turned around and approached Capt. Bogart. "This is all so … so strange. I don't understand, and I don't know of anyone who disliked him *that* much." He sighed. "Captain Bogart, thanks for everything that you and your department are doing. I'm sure the investigation is in capable hands. I think I'll go upstairs to take a look at the body."

"I'll come with you. I have to talk to a few of the detectives up there. And possibly your men, since they were his closest friends."

Less than a minute later, both were in Stoneys bedroom, viewing his rigid body—the crime scene. After taking in enough, from staring at his manikin like face for almost five long minutes, Sleeper had collapsed and sat at the foot of the bed, slump, his head hung low. Dejected. He appeared very distraught and distant. He babbled incoherently, "This ain't happening." He turned around and viewed Stoney's body and repeated, "This just ain't happening." His eyes grew misty, a stream of tears dribbled his cheeks. Out of the blue, many images of what Stoney had meant to him flashed through his mind, filling his heart with a painful remorse. He reviewed some of the fun times they shared in high school, their graduation party, and the learning experiences that they shared at the police academy, throughout their lives on the force.

Spankys thinking went blank altogether. He stood beside the nightstand and stared down at Stoneys expressionless face. In thinking that he wanted him dead earlier in the week, he felt a shadow of guilt blanket him completely. Now that Stoney was actually dead, he realized that he didn't mean what he told Sleeper about killing him, to stop them from going to jail. He thought about everything that Stoney had meant to him in the past also. However, his thoughts lingered on the Dixie Club.

Capt. Winslow took one brief look and fell stuck on a still breath. The air in the room suddenly grew utterly thick. He went to the window and opened it wide. He stuck his head outside and inhaled deeply, took in as much fresh air as he possibly could. Being a leader of men, he often kept his emotions hidden. But on the inside, the pain burned him like a ravaging cancer. The shock of seeing one of his men dead interfered with his normally rational way of thinking. He didn't know where to begin to look for answers. He was completely baffled. Stymied beyond repair.

Like the time when his parents were killed in an automotive accident fifteen years prior, involving a hit and run drunk driver. Upon hearing the very disturbing news, he left the station and rushed to the hospitals emergency unit. Once there, he learned that they were pronounced D.O.A., 'dead on arrival.' His reaction was to sit on the outside of the emergency unit for nearly three hours, unflinching, in shock and in denial. While his wife drove him home, it was a long quiet drive. After they arrived home, he went into the garage, locked the door and closed the windows, and then cried like a newborn for over an hour.

His wife is the only person who's witnessed the misery and suffering he's endured for many years after. For years to follow, drunk drivers were his worst enemies, next to cold-blooded murderers and pedophile's. He threw the book at, and came down hard on anyone who smelled of a hint of alcohol.

At that moment, Detective John Sloan, Capt. Bogarts second in command, approached the nightstand, and picked up a brown leather shrouded book. The manuscript that Stoney was working on. He opened it, scanned it briefly, told Capt. Bogart, "Sir! This might be of some help. I think it's a diary of some sort. Maybe he rights down his thoughts or something." He read the title on the first page. "The Dixie Club!" He rubbed his chin wonderingly.

When Spanky heard the phrase 'The Dixie Club', a cold flash ripped through his body as he shuddered at the diary's condemning contents. He leered at the diary contemptuously, wishing that he had ex-ray vision. If he was Superman, he could examine its contents with his x-ray vision, then burn it to a crisp with his super heat vision. I don't believe this shit! he thought. That bastard had the audacity to keep a shitten ass diary of every gotdamn thing we did. What kind of a fricken moron would do something like that? Names, places and dates … shit! He betrayed us! We swore we wouldn't log anything.

Every nerve in his body tormented his muscles to snatch the diary from the detectives hands and run like hell. But he couldn't do it. He wanted to kill everyone in the house to keep the matter hushed. But he couldn't do it. He became so visually unnerved that he had to sit down, next to Sleeper.

When Sleeper heard the phase 'The Dixie Club', he damn near jumped out of his skin. The phrase pounded at the sides of his head, sending him into a tizzy. He felt the room grow in size, he wanted to shrink until he disappeared. He glanced at Spanky with a big question mark on his face, trembling, hoping that everyone watching would relate his condition to being upset from learning of the death of their good friend. He also wanted reach out and grab the damn book and run like hell. But he resisted the notion to do so.

"Let me see that," Capt. Bogart said. Detective Sloan handed him the book. "A diary, huh? I'll take it home and run through it. Who knows? It might be able to tell us something." He opened it and flipped through a few pages; scanned it briefly. He mumbled, "This is pretty interesting." He told Spanky and Sleeper, "I'm really sorry about your friend, and I know this is a bad time for questions. But do either of you have any information that could help us find out what might've happened here?"

Spanky eyed the book in his hand, shook his head despondently. He cleared his throat, said drearily, "Um … no, Captain." Meanwhile, a Dixie Club episode of him hustling a bank executive pinned for extortion wandered aimlessly inside of his head.

Sleeper remained perfectly still, said only, "No."

Capt. Bogart told Capt. Winslow. "I can understand them being distraught, especially if they were close friends. I'll call you later if others questions arise. After they get over the shock, their grieving."

"Thank you for your understanding," Capt. Winslow said. He addressed his men. "Officers Knight and Sinclair, there's nothing we can do here for officer Brooks right now. He's in their hands." Spanky and Sleeper rose to their feet, and Capt. Winslow approached Capt. Bogart. "I know the procedure. But since I know his parents personally, is all right if I break the news to his family? They're very nice people, and I'll probably be spending a lot of time with them, preparing for the funeral and everything."

He closed the diary. "Sure, Captain. I understand." He extended his hand, and they shook. "No problem. And please, give them my condolences."

"I will. And thanks for everything."

Capt. Bogart nodded, then addressed Sleeper and Spanky. "Sorry about your friend, officers. I'm sure he was an outstanding officer."

Both shook his hand before leaving the room. As Spankys hand neared the book—Capt. Bogart held it cradled sacredly, as if it were the keys to heaven or hell—his right arm twitched spasmodically. Again, he felt the notion swell in him to grab the damn book, kill everyone to keep the matter hushed, then run like hell. But again, he suppressed the compelling notion to do so. He considered the book a verdict about to be read by a jury of his peers. Acquittal, or life behind bars. Freedom, or the formidable hell of living in the belly of the beast. The handshake he gave was firm, a little aggressive. Sleepers handshake was nervous, his palms laced with a chilled perspiration. When his hand neared the book, his heart beat doubled and he trembled with fright. He wanted to snatch it from his hands also, then simply disappear. He figured the book to be an accumulation of everything in his life that he's worked for. Then his thoughts ran back to the sacredness of his family. How much his wife and child meant to him.

"Let's go," Capt. Winslow told his men. He slipped the cigar into his mouth, then approached the staircase. Spanky and Sleeper followed close behind. He didn't say so, but he did catch their awkward expressions when Detective Sloan had mentioned the phrase 'The Dixie Club.' He saw the way Spanky stopped breathing, briefly. And the way Sleeper shut his eyes tight in some form of mental anguish, then opened them wide, as if a doctor had just delivered the grave news that he was dying of cancer, and had only six months to live.

On the way to their cars, he stated, "I wonder what's in that diary." He stopped walking and faced Spanky. "When the detective read the title, you looked as though you'd seen a ghost. You know anything about it?" He held his hand up to stop the response, said seriously, "Sinclair, I want a straight answer. I know you can fudge your way through anything. I've read some of your filled reports in the past, and then compared them to the crime scenes. Simply put, more than a few don't add up."

Spanky felt the pressure of his magnified eyes staring him down. He was on the spot. Staring at Capt. Winslow, Sleeper became paranoid. His ears grew twice their size, like satellite dishes. He became tense. He knew that Spanky always pocketed quick believable excuses. Lies. He prayed silently in hopes that he was going to conjure up something real good, then execute it without flaw. Everything was riding on it.

Spankys mind went to work quickly. It only took him an instant to fabricate the entire story. Sleeper often joked with him about being the 'Picasso of liars.'

When Spanky was ready to roll his tall tale, he looked into Capt. Winslows magnified eyes and smiled hazily.

Watching his comfortable expression, Sleeper felt at ease. He knew that the master was about to paint stroke a masterpiece of which Monet would've been proud.

When he began talking, the only things missing were a group of eager children, a black night under a full moon, a campfire, and the phrase 'Once upon a time.' He explained convincingly, "Captain, writing was one of officer Brooks pastimes. It was a hobby of his. He mentioned to us, officer Knight and I, that he was one day going to publish a fiction novel. Although, we never took him seriously. We thought it was only talk. You know how people are always talking about doing things like that."

After he finished explaining, Sleeper waited anxiously for the Capt.'s response. He wanted to add to the story, to make it sound more viable. But it was complete in its entirety. Besides, he didn't want to destroy a magnificent creation.

Their ears twanged, waiting on baited sound. They were eager for quick relief, as time seemed to linger on a welcomed positive gesture. Seeing the Capt. shift his weight from one foot to the other, they nearly exploded with anxiety. Like they were at the end of a great 'who done it mystery', about to find out who the murderer was. The drum rolled silently.

Capt. Winslow lowered his head for a moment, then looked at Spanky blankly. He removed the cigar from his mouth. "You know. I kinda thought it was something like that. He seemed like the writer type. He had a candid imagination, which is essential for writing. He was always comparing things or situations. You can tell by the way he talked, using clichés that writers use. Only writers do things like that."

Greatly relieved, Sleeper sighed thoroughly. It was as if someone had just informed him that his cancer was in remission.

"He was definitely the type," Spanky said. "He sometimes carried a note pad, all the time writing down notes to add to his stories. He took many of the situations that transpired in his everyday life, and exaggerated on them. To make them seem more interesting. When we hung out together sometimes, he'd run these crazy situations by us, to get our opinions about books that he was planning to write."

"Yeah. He did that all the time," Sleeper added. "He had some really good ideas. Although, some were a little too strange for my taste."

"That sounds like a pretty smart idea," Capt. Winslow said. He looked down profoundly. "To bad he can't see it through. Who knows? He might've made a hellova writer." He looked to the sky and whispered, "God, I don't know what the master plan is, but You always take the good ones first." He asked Spanky, "About the handcuffs, any ideas about those?"

"Well, Captain," Spanky said, "as weird as this may sound, he mentioned to me that Katherine like to use them when they were, you know," he stated uneasily, "having sex."

Sleeper was surprised at Spankys answer, thinking, I knew she was a freak.

"I don't doubt it," Capt. Winslow said. "But, a little novelty never hurt anybody. I'll call Captain Bogart when I get to Boston, and give him this information. You never know where it might lead to."

Sleeper eyes smiled at Spanky nonchalantly, congratulating him for a job well done. Capt. Winslow suggested, "I think we better get back to town. I want to start our own investigation, pronto." Heading to his cruiser, he pinched the bridge of his nose frustratingly, then huffed, "Dammit! I can feel the headaches already, and see the many sleepless nights ahead of me. For the next few months, the governor, the mayor, the commissioner, and the news hounds are gonna be riding my back for answers." He faced them. "Since you're his best friends, you're gonna hear some of it too."

He got into his cruiser and slammed the door shut. He stared straight ahead, searching desperately for answers. Obviously angry about the suspicious death of one of his favorite officers. Wondering of the days events, he sighed grievingly, shook his head in total disappointment. He turned on the ignition, and began an arduous drive back to Boston.

As Spanky and Sleeper stood watching his every move, when his cruiser was out of sight, Sleeper rejoiced, "Man, that was a hell of a story you gave the Captain. I almost believed it myself. Writing a novel. I would've never thought of something like that."

"Well, part of what I told the Captain is true. A few years ago, Stoney told me that he was a moonlight writer. I just threw the book into the mix."

"I believed it," he said convincingly. "And the Captain swallowed it entirely."

"I don't know. He might've swallowed it, but lets just hope that it stays down. I just hope he relays the same story to Captain Bogart."

"I get it. We plant the seed, then let it grow from there. Lets also hope that they don't do a thorough investigation of the diary."

Suddenly, Spanky felt like he'd been pounded in the face with a cinderblock. He blurted, "Not do a thorough investigation? Let's be real about this shit, Sleep. Of course they're gonna do a thorough investigation. For Christ sake! A fricken cop was killed. Nobody's gonna shake that shit off lightly." He spat, "Nobody! If the answer of who did it was up a gnats ass, they'll dissect it to find it. Especially if the Feds get involved. Those fingernail scrapping asswipes will search everywhere." He lowered his head and spat to the ground in thorough detest. "Damn! That fool actually kept a diary of the shit that we were doing. When we started the Dixie Club, we agreed not to document a damn thing, remember? If Stoney were alive, I'd kill him myself. Of all the stupid, idiotic things to do."

"I don't believe it either. But, lets stop to think about this for a second, since we knew him better than anyone. Suppose he *was* writing a fictitious novel. Suppose he changed the names, dates and everything. Suppose the book is harmless."

Spanky paced in front of him. "He used the actual name of our group, Sleep. What does that tell about its contents?" He sighed. "I don't believe this shit. As libelous as that book probably is, he should've kept it locked in an underground vault. At least a hundred miles down, in hell!"

Sleeper fell slump against the driver side of a Dover Police cruiser, appeared very depressed. He saddened, "I don't believe Stoneys dead." He looked at Spanky and asked irately, "Who in the hell would do something like that? I hope they find the bastard before I do." He raised his clenched fists and shook them violently into the air. "I could strangle that fucker by the throat until his neck snaps. I could ..." He looked to the sky, a tear fell from his left eye. He felt drained and fell slump once again. "Spanky, none of this shit means anything anymore. I mean, we've been racking up pretty good, but now that this has happened ... now that Stoney gone, it feels like it was all for nothing. I feel like I just want to ..."

Spanky grabbed his arm. "Oh no you don't, you little slobbering shit! You better not start talking like that. You're starting to sound like Stoney. You cut that shit out right now, and suck it up. You hear me? I don't want to hear anymore of this negative bullshit. I feel for Stoney too. But with all this melancholy malarkey you're spitting, it feels like you're trying ta put the lid on the coffin and bury me."

"Yeah. Right," Sleeper said facetiously. "You're actually feeling down about Stoney, are you? I find that hard to believe. Just a little while ago, you were dogging him like a sixty year old douche bag." He spewed furiously, "You don't care about nobody but yourself. You selfish son-of-a-bitch! I been around you long enough to know how you think. You'd sell-out your own mother, if it could save your ass from going to prison." He peered into Spanky's eyes and asked skeptically, "What happened the other day when we stopped by here? After you planted the bug in the telephone, did you stop by the kitchen and drop some arsenic off somewhere?"

Spanky pushed himself away from Sleeper. "What the fuck is this? I don't need this shit from you. You think I killed Stoney?" He rushed Sleeper and rammed him violently into the cruiser and shouted, "You're crazy! I don't want to hear anymore of this dumb shit. How do I know you didn't drop a little plop-plop fiz-fiz into his glass, when I went to the bathroom? You were alone with him before I came into the living room, remember? You had the same kind of opportunity as I had. He trusted your dumb ass too."

Sleeper grabbed him by his shirt collar and got into his face. "You bastard! He was my best friend. I'd never think about …"

Spanky interrupted, stated calmly, "Sleeper. Look at the window, on the second floor. They're watching us."

Still holding his shirt, Sleeper glanced to the house, saw Capt. Bogart and Detective Sloan studying them intently. Their expressions highly questionable.

"We can't let them see us going at it like this," Spanky whispered. "They'll get suspicious." Sleeper released his shirt, Spanky went on to say, "Let's just get in our cruisers, and leave. We'll talk more about this when we get back to town. Let's hope that they took this little skirmish as two distraught friends of the deceased looking for answers.

"All right," Sleeper agreed, still quite angry. "I'll see you when we get back to town. This conversation ain't over yet."

Walking to his car, Spanky leered at him through the corners of his eyes. Both jumped into their cars and drove away.

In Stoneys house, Capt. Bogart and his men had their hands full. Scrapping up every bit of evidence they could possibly find, they put the coffee pot on, ordered Chinese take out, and made plans to campout over night. Through the initial stages of the investigation, many things puzzled Capt. Bogart. One was the enormous size of one of Stoneys bank accounts, which he had reassigned to his dead uncles trust account. Another, the accumulation of receipts that Stoney had saved from making costly purchases. They were stored in a filling cabinet in the basement of the mansion. They were sure that finding the answers to these mysteries would be like cracking the case of the century. They knew that most cases weren't as tricky as what some television shows made them appear to be. Most of the time, all of the clues to catch the perps, or perpetrators, were right out in the open, waiting to be pieced together by a trained eye.

Capt. Bogart dropped a few Alka-Seltzers into a glass of water, removed his glasses, then drank the entire contents. When he finished, Detective Sloan asked, "What do you think about that little incident out there in front? Looks kinda suspicious, I'd say. You think we should do a follow up on those two?

Capt. Bogart removed his hat, then rubbed the top of his balding head. He sighed resignedly, replied, "I don't know. Maybe they're simply distraught over the death of their friend. But, it did look suspicious. For the time being, let's finish sifting through what's in front of us. If we can't find what we're looking for here, then we'll branch out to wherever it leads us. But, I gotta tell ya, and I pray to God that this isn't one of those cases. The last thing I want on my hands is an inside situation, with cops killing cops. It doesn't get any messier than that. Because of the way things look so far, I'm gonna make it a priority to get to the bottom of this, even if it kills me. The one thing that I despise the most is when cops go bad." He sighed. "Go back in there and see what else you can get from Carlton. If you have to, sweat him a little. He may not have killed officer Brooks, but I know he's holding out on information that could lead us to who might've. Find out if he has a girlfriend, then get in touch with her. Bring her in for questioning. Then question his family members. And find out who paid for this house, and all of the furnishings. I know Brooks couldn't afford anything like this on a cops salary." He laughed dryly. "Look at the little house I have."

CHAPTER 28

▼

After Spanky and Sleeper returned to Boston, they were excused from returning to work for their bereavement. After changing into their civilian clothes, they drove to Rhode Island to visit Spankys Uncle Boomer. He's a sixty-five year old ex-vet and retired-cop. His real name's Henry Doyle. He's six foot-two inches tall and weighs close to three hundred and fifty-five pounds, obviously overweight for a man his age. Spankys family members and Old Boomers primary care physician have tried with much difficulty to get him to diet for many years. The venture was unsuccessful because he loves gourmet foods, and dines mostly at Italian Restaurants. His favorite dishes are Spaghetti, linguini, and lasagna.

One time, after a failed diet attempt, Old Boomer went on an eating binge for three entire days. When his family had finally located him in East Boston, he was sitting at the back of an Italian restaurant called Little Italy, drinking wine, stuffing his fat face with lasagna, spaghetti and sesame seed bread sticks. When they tried to get him to leave the restaurant, he became utterly enraged. He threw bread sticks at everyone, shouting belligerently, 'No! No! You can't do this to me. It's not right. I'll die if I don't get something to eat. This is America, land of the free. I'm allowed to eat as much as I want.'

He made a spectacle of himself that day, with showing everyone how bad he needed intervention. What he actually needed was a weight-watching Guru on his tail twenty-four seven. If they hadn't stopped him, he would've eaten until he imploded.

When Boomer was on the police force, he received warnings from his superiors nearly every week to loose weight. At least fifty pounds. He was given the nickname 'Boomer' from his fellow officers, because they called on him often when they needed a door battered down. They coined the action 'Lowering the Boom.' A few times, while he and his partner were in the midst of a scuffle with a suspect, he sat on the person. He used his weight to mobilize the culprit, while his partner slapped on the cuffs. Unfortunately, one time, he rendered a one hundred and twenty pound purse-snatcher unconscious, accidentally knocked the wind out of him—bent him out of shape a bit. He couldn't return to his feet because he suffered a collapsed left lung and had some kidney damage. When they realized how bad he was injured, they had to use CPR, call and then wait for an ambulance to arrive to administer aid. The poor little scrawny guy didn't have a snowballs chance in hell of surviving. His legs were never the same after that takedown. Now, both knees bend toward the right slightly. Since the perp didn't have health insurance, the problem wasn't fixed correctly. The hospital for the poor and underprivileged merely slid a knee-wrap on each leg, and gave him a few aspirins. They handed him a walking stick, then sent him on his way, telling him, 'Good luck!.'

On a positive note, the purse-snatcher has since then retired from the profession, after that spiritually enlightening run-in with Boomer. Since he can no longer run fast, he's turned his life around completely. Now he's working part-time at a Shiners hospital, helping crippled children cope with their traumatic experiences.

Sometimes when Spanky had doubts about himself, or questions about his profession, and needed answers, he drove to Providence, Rhode Island on weekends, to spend a few hours conversing with his uncle about the good old days. The times when cops didn't have to draw their weapons to approach a vehicle stopped for a minor traffic infraction. The days when law officials didn't have to flood the media with top-cop shows, to try to get the public to understand that their jobs were crucial. And that they should be respected, regardless of what went on after the cameras were off.

Fully aware of their unstable situation, Spanky and Sleeper remained hyped. Knowing that at any given moment they might be called in for questioning about the reality-like implications of Stoneys so-called fictitious manuscript. That seemingly quiet leather bound book that entailed loud accusations of many illicit activities, that have been going on for the past ten years. Perhaps, it was all written in that manuscript—the actual names of the marks, the felonious crimes they committed, the outrageous and disgusting psyches used to initiate the hustles. The payoffs that were extorted—the Dixie Club hustle. No matter how Stoney wrote it down, it all spelled one ugly word that would be on the lips of every federal prosecutor around the country. Indictment! Capped with a lengthy prison sentence.

Five minutes before they had arrived at Boomers house, Spanky explained to Sleeper a few of his uncles eccentricities, so that he'd know what to expect. Unless one was aware of the mans nature, one might think that they were being offended. "My uncle was one of those sensitive cops. People use to tell him all the time that there was no room for guys like him in the department. He's one of those nice guys, the type that's always giving people a second chance. Especially kids."

At this stage, Sleeper developed an 'I don't give a shit anymore' attitude, and it was starting to show. He was thinking about his wife and son, and welcomed nothing but solid solutions to their chaotic state of affairs. He felt that any other conversation wasn't worth the effort or his time, as his time was the one thing that he was running short on. He replied snidely, "That's not what I heard about your uncle. I heard that he was so shell-shocked from the Viet Nam war, that every time someone in the office popped a paper bag, he'd drop to the floor and yell **'INCOMING!'** They said that one time he even woke up in the middle of the night, sleep walking, and had grabbed his gun and shot up the neighborhood. Looking for somebody named Charlie."

Spanky eyed him crossly, twisted his lips, sucked his teeth. "Why you wanna dog my uncle like that? He's been through a lot of shit in his time. He's a deco-rated war veteran. A hero. He's got the Medal of Honor."

"Suuure! A big war hero. Right! That's not what I heard from Sergeant Murkowski. He and your uncle were in the same platoon back then. He told me that when that mortar round came in from the next village over, your uncle was in the latrine at the time. As he sat there doing his *doody* for his country, a piece of shrapnel came flying through the canvas and gave him the spanking of his life." He chuckled. "That's why he was awarded the Medal of Honor. And that's how he got that limp."

"So, you think that's funny?" Spanky said earnestly, peered slyly at Sleeper. "My uncle goes over there to put his life on the line for us, so we could live the American dream, and you sit there and laugh at him. You know what? You dis-gust me! And that Murkowski ain't nothing but a brown-nosing jackass. The hell does he know? The man's a proven nutcase. That's why he's in the wash-ups department right now. In the basement at headquarters, with all the other cops who have anger management and addiction issues."

Dealing with the truth wasn't one of Spanky strong points. Because of his tre-mendous amount of pride, if he caught a case of the drips, he'd wait until his penis fell off before he got medical treatment. Coaxing Stoney into getting medical attention was one thing. Getting him to deal with his realities was an entirely different ballgame. No matter how close the truth was, it remained out of reach. He preferred to bend the truth to meet his standards. Life was more comfortable that way. He inherited this deceptive behavior from his father. His mother considered his father to be one of the biggest liars to ever hit the east coast. Being a man of the world, and of more that a dozen state prisons, Spankys father is still doing time at Cedar Junction, Walpole State prison, for a fouled bank job, resulting in murder. In his heyday, he's done time for embezzlement, robbery, wire and welfare fraud, art theft, grand larceny, and for non-support of his only child. Spanky.

The man couldn't help himself. He liked money. He simply didn't like to work honestly for it. Many people share this same desire. He use to tell Spanky things like 'if you don't take what you want, then you'll never have it.' And other things like 'If you're gonna tell a lie, then keep a serious face. And tell it so that it sounds like something that even you'd believe.' It was a miracle that Spanky didn't end up on the wrong side of the law when he was a juvenile. Unbelievably, knowing how terrible his father lived is what kept him straight. Apparently, it scared the hell out of him.

Before his mother and father were divorced, when Spanky was fourteen, his father use to tell his mother regularly that he was going to hand her the world on a silver platter. What he actually gave her was a world of migraine headaches, a mountain of aggravation, a slew of hard ways to go and a few brutal ass whippings, all on a shredded paper plate. The man lied so much that he started believing his own lies. The only person that he never lied to was Spanky. He didn't mind his wife hating him for letting her down all the time. But lie to his son, never. This is the only reason why Spanky held his respect for him. He doesn't talk about him much, but he does respect him.

Last weekend he went to check up on the old man, see how his pop was doing in the big house. Wanted to know if he had lost his mind completely. He wasn't exactly in the best of health; he had a rare form of degenerate arthritis scaling his spine, and was put on a exasperating regiment of various pain relievers that whacked him pitilessly with several very annoying side effects. When Spanky observed his posture as he slowly approached to where he was seated, he thought he reminded him of his grandfather, the way he struggled with much difficulty to heave one foot in front of the other. When the same debilitating arthritis crept in and swallowed his life, he had died less than ten years later. Probably willed himself to die, since there wasn't much pleasure elsewhere in his life.

During the short visit, it was just like it had always had been in the Sinclair household. Few words were spoken, but he felt that the quality time spent in each others company was worth something. He didn't know what, and didn't want to figure it out because he had grew comfortable with the way things were.

What makes him draw the ugly scenarios of incarceration to Sleeper was what he had heard in the visitors lounge; absorbed broken pieces of dialogue coming the other inmates and their family members, girlfriends, wives, whoever. During a moment of torrential silence between him and his father, he listened to a couple seated to his left. A young black man in his early twenties serving a fifteen year to life sentence for a second degree murder conviction told his girlfriend sympathetically, 'You know I gotta do this bid, baby girl. It's just me and you, riding it out. I hope you're gonna be there for me?'

'You know I am, baby,' she pampered. 'I'll be sending you money for your canteen, pictures of me with nothing on and everything. All the shit we been through ... you know I ain't gonna leave you like that.'

He thought about the hard times that she faces every day; her mounting bills and her children's every day necessities—she complained of these often as they talked over the phone every other day. She was dependant solely on him, and would face devastating odds of survival if she remained on her own, stayed single. He felt that she would succumb to the pressures of an inflating society if presented the right opportunity to move forward. His imagination ran too fast and he couldn't handle the complicated details, so he dropped the thought and took off with another. Remembering the many evenings of lovemaking that they shared, he imagined her lying naked in a bed before him. Reminiscing the taste of her delicious brown skin in his mouth, he wasn't able to contain himself and stirred uncomfortably in his seat. Torturing himself further, he knew that it would be eons before he would be able to see her as he imagined, and the harsh reality crashed into his dream bubble and screamed its insufferable existence. She was a needy woman, in more ways than one—had strong sexual desires. From out of nowhere, he grew exceedingly angry for the tsunami obliterating his emotions and flipped the script. He angered, 'Yeah. You'll tell me anything, now that my ass is in here. You probably couldn't wait for me to get caught up. Girl, if I ever find out that you had something to do with me getting sent up, I'll ...' He bit his lower lip and slammed his fist onto the armrest. A corrections officer heard the noise and looked in their direction guardedly, and the inmate lowered his voice. 'You probably giving it up to somebody already. That new neighbor down the hall, ain'tcha? The one that got the new Maxima.'

'Oh stop it, Dee. I ain't doing no such thing.' She asked, 'Why you wanna say some stupid shit like that? You paranoid or something?'

Shook his head gravely, stared her down. 'Naw. I know how it be out there, on the streets. Brother gets locked up, his girl comes up and feed him all kinda dumb shit … be lying out they ass. And I'm supposed ta swallow that shit, like I'm an all-day sucker. Maybe you working for the feds now, tryinta get information outta me about some other shit, for a reward. Tryinta get into that witness protection shit that moves you to a nice sunny spot down south, and pays for everything.'

'I don't believe this shit, Dee. I bust my ass to come all the way up here to see you, borrow money for a bus ticket, and you treat me like this. Is that what this place has done to you? If I gotta hear this shit, then I might as well not come up at all.'

When she sprang to her feet, he flipped the script again. He grabbed her arm gently and begged with nil shame. "Aw com'on, baby. Please don't go. Com'on back. I was only kidding. This place be fucking with a brothers mind. I hear all kinda shit everyday about what somebody else's woman is doing out there, and it makes me think these crazy thoughts. You know how much I love you baby.'

'Don't worry, boo.' She descended slowly to her seat, said convincingly, 'I'm not gonna leave you.' He looked blissfully into his lap for a moment, delighted that she had decided to stay. At that exact moment, she glanced lasciviously across the room at a well groomed young man who had come to visit with another inmate. She smiled nonchalantly, thinking that maybe she could hook up with him on the way out. She didn't see him on the bus on the way up, therefore she believed that he must have drove a car. And if he has a car, then he has a job. Maybe he could help her with her bills, and show her children how a real man is supposed to be with taking care of his responsibilities. She figured that when he was about to leave, she'd leave also, and bump into him on the way out—an accidental meeting. She told her boyfriend, 'You know I'm better than that. I ain't never let you down before. I ain't thinking about nobody but you, my baby's daddy.'

To Spankys right, he overheard a young Hispanic man talking with an older woman. Perhaps his mother. He was serving a life sentence for killing his girlfriend amid a domestic dispute. Hunched over to conceal his wretched condition, while a stream of tears trickled his cheeks, he plead with the woman, 'Mrs. Menendez, I swear, if I could give her back to you, I'd do that in a heartbeat. You've got to believe me.'

She eyed her daughters name tattooed on the back of his left hand, stared at it sadly. She placed her hand consolably on top of it, squeezed gently. "I know, Juan.' Tears filling her eyes also. 'I believe you.' She pulled out a napkin and dabbed under her eyes, sniffled. 'I know in your heart you didn't mean to take her from us. I tried to hate you for it, but it only made me feel bad. I've even asked God to forgive you, to show you mercy, so you won't have to suffer much.'

His head fell on her shoulders, he began to cry, "Mrs. Menendez, I'm ...' he choked, '... I'm so sorry. I think about your daughter, Manita, all the time. She was so beautiful. She was my heart. Every time I close my eyes at night, she's all I see in my dreams. Every night, before I lay down, I fall to my knees and pray, and curse myself for the fight we had that night. I wish I could take it all back; the horrible words I told her ... everything.' He looked away for a moment, faced her and continued in Spanish.

Not understanding them, Spanky focused his attention to two men seated five feet in front of him. One of the men had brought a four year old boy to see his biological father, a man sentenced to a life sentence for killing a store clerk in a robbery four years prior. When the inmate saw his son for the first time, he couldn't contain himself, broke down and cried miserably. He held his arms outstretched to receive his son, who he thought would come running into his arms. But the child ran to the other man and cried, 'No, daddy! I wanna stay with you.'

For some reason, this incident touched Spanky the most.

"I didn't say it was funny," Sleeper stated. "I only said that your uncle caught a piece of shrapnel, using his ass as a catcher's mitt." He looked surprised when he stated, "What? Isn't that how it happened?"

Spanky turned away, studied the traffic. After a lengthy silenced oozed by, he tossed casually, "You make sure you have that sense of humor when you get to the prison. You can tell jokes and keep'em laughing all day long. It'll keep their minds off that pretty mouth of yours. But it won't stop them from wanting to do strange things to you in the middle of the night. Now stick that in your pipe and choke on it."

Sleepers smirk faded to nothing. He hated it when Spanky reminded him of the fear pacing cowardly in the back of his mind. A haunting dilemma of a probable impending reality, only when Spanky reminded him. At the back of his mind, he created many comfortable and positive scenarios of what he'd like to see happen, to smother Spankys unenthusiastic and depressing outlook. He imagined that Spanky talked a tough game, but if sent to prison, he'd drop his soap in the shower, on purpose, then bend over in anticipation of the warm welcome he'd receive. Spanky rattled on, saying, "I brought us down here because I though that maybe my uncle can help us with our situation. He knows this guy who's full of solutions. He works in the state house, in the neighborhood planning department."

He and your uncle are probably full of shit, Sleeper figured. Something tells me that if he keeps throwing me these curves, I'll probably start thinking just like him. However, since I'm in it this far, I'll listen for a little while longer. He told him, "I know a few of those guys who work up there too. I saw a couple of them on the news last night, laying out plans to do some construction in the South End of Boston. On Tremont street, closer to downtown.

"No," Spanky corrected. "Not those guys. I'm talking about the people from the *real* neighborhood-planning department. There exists two separate and totally different departments."

"What in the hell are you talking about? What do they need two separate departments for?"

"The first department is above the table, so that the public can see them at work. They plan typical things that the public is allowed know about, for show, and make progress speeches and all that other kind of bullcrap. The second department that I spoke of is on the hush hush tip. They do the actual planning. These people have a very complicated job to handle. They're responsible for creating situations in neighborhoods that control the population flow, for financial reasons. They have a hidden agenda."

Sleepers head twisted like a curious puppy dog. "Control the population flow! How in the hell can anybody do that?"

"You wouldn't believe some of the things that they do. These people are incredible. They run scenarios and plan situations years ahead of time. It's almost like what they do at the stock market, preparing a prospectus. For example, lets that say for financial reasons, you want to relocate a group of poor minority people to a deserted place somewhere on the outskirts of the city. How would you go about accomplishing that?"

"I don't know. But I want you to humor me. How would you do something like that?"

"First of all, you have to remember that the country's in a bit of a recession at the moment. Probably a planned recession. A few decades ago, when the price of gas was bearable, and when most affluent middle class yuppies had money, and were just starting out, they moved to the suburbs and brought nice big cars and houses. They left the inner-city areas to minorities and poor people. There's also less crime in the burbs. However, now they're suffering financially because of inflation. Most people aren't doing so good nowadays. It's more economical to live in or near the city of Boston. Where most of the good jobs, hospitals, and major businesses are located.

"That department that I spoke of, through running scenarios years ago, knew that this was going to happen. What they're doing now is forcing the minorities out, by making it very costly and unbearable to live in the inner-city. The people on welfare and those who have section eights certificates are the easiest to handle. Since they have no resources, no voice, they're simply shipped out to problematic towns; places like Lynn, Chelsea, Framingham and Springfield. Ya know, out of the way somewhere."

"How does this so-called secret department make things costly and unbearable for inner-city people?"

"Well, adding to the present situation of crime, you know how the politicians handle things for a number of poor inner-city communities. They just throw them a bone once in a while to show them that they're not forgotten constituents, and they're okay. There are normal bills that you have to maintain, rent, utilities and so forth. In addition, there are expenses that are created by that second department that I spoke of, that do nothing but fame the flames of an already overburdened financial structure. I'm sure you understand that living in a high crime area raises your auto and home insurance. A smaller example is how the streets are maintained. In poor neighborhoods, when maintenance and upkeep of the streets conditions are disregarded by the politicians, it becomes costly to maintain your vehicle. A chopped up street with plenty of potholes can do treacherous things to a cars suspension—it loosens and tears up everything; breaks it all to hell. One of the ways that you can increase the rate of deterioration of a street is to use a cheaper quality of asphalt that breaks up in months. Another thing that makes your insurance go up is having accidents. The misplacement of things like yield or stop signs at dangerous intersections is also a part of neighborhood planning. Another thing you may have noticed is that at most stoplights in the inner-cities, the yellow light lasts only three seconds, before the red appears. In the burbs, you get five to six seconds. That may seem insignificant to you or me, but it was planned that way so that inner-city drivers are ticketed frequently for moving violations, which increases their auto-insurance. These are just a few of the many things that are going on as we speak. Since people are busy trying to make ends meet, they don't have the time to stop and try to figure out what's going on. Every time you see digging and construction going on in the city of Boston, it doesn't necessarily mean that they're repairing something. Sometimes it means that they're using up excess funds, so they can get the same amount allocated for the following year. That's just the way the budget works." He smiled haughtily at Sleeper, then finished, "Yeap! It's called neighborhood planning, and keeping the books balanced."

"And I thought we were hustlers. We ain't got jack on the city."

"You better believe it, buddy-boy. When Francis Bellamy wrote 'The Pledge of Allegiance' in 1892, because of the state of social affairs in America, he knew it wouldn't apply to everyone. Just like the constitution. With liberty and justice for all, my ass!"

Sleeper didn't say anything, only listened to his pointless rhetoric. "You ever notice that on the nickel, the dime and the quarter, the presidents face the left. But on the penny, Abraham Lincoln faces the right."

"Ya know, out of all my years of handling money, I've never noticed that."

"Yeah? Well, think about it for a second. They've turned their backs to him for a reason." He turned left on Pemberton Street. Driving down a tree lined street, he spotted his uncles house at maybe fifty yards away. "He lives right there. I'll just pull up in the driveway, then we can get out. Be careful of the front porch. It's ... ah ... kinda booby trapped."

Boomer lives in a small four-room house that's falling to pieces. The trim work is in dire need of a coat of paint, and the siding is missing in several places. Most of the gutters leak, or are non-operational, and at least a few hundred shingles need replacing on the roof. The huge oak trees surrounding the place over-shadowed the house and front lawns, and the grass couldn't possibly grow for the lack of sunlight.

As Sleeper looked at what could've easily have been a junk dealers house, images of firefights and dismembered bodies flashed through his mind. "What! You mean to tell me that he believes he's still fighting a war? Is your uncle suffering from Alzheimer's, or from some kind of postwar traumatic syndrome?"

"Will you shut it?" Spanky angered. "Don't be stupid. I'm only talking about the steps leading to the front porch. They're kinda shaky. He hasn't had the time to repair them."

Sleeper sighed with relief. "Oh! I thought it was something ..."

"I know what you thought it was. And my uncle's not crazy either."

"Looking at this place, I can't tell. Anyway, we'll soon see about that, won't we?"

Spanky delivered a tired expression, obviously fed up. "Honestly, Sleep. I don't know about you sometimes." He parked the car just in front of the house, killed the ignition.

Sleeper got out of the car and stared at Boomers house, figuring how long before its collapse. "It's kinda small, ain't it?" He observed the vast compilation of garbage and junk decorating the grounds, surrounding the house. Bizarrely, he saw a corroded Craftsman riding lawnmower parked next to a dilapidated one car garage riddled with more than fifty bullet holes. Believed it to be the garage where they staged the St. Valentine Days massacre. The doors wide open, they saw an antique car that was so rusted that they couldn't tell the make or model. Just the evening before, a transient passing the house stopped by and caught sight of a toilet bowl sitting in the middle of the front lawn. Without hesitation, he pulled out a newspaper, then took a midnight dump. The terrible odor filling the immediate area was because he didn't flush, let alone wipe himself. There are several bald tires scattered about, and half a canoe rested sticking from out of the ground, looked as if it fell from the sky like a meteorite. And there's a Stop and Shop shopping cart filled with a few dozen empty cans and beer bottles parked next to the front steps. The neighbors complain about the house on a regular basis because it brings down the property value of the entire neighborhood. "What's all this shit all over the place. It looks like Sanford and Son lives here. Where's the grass?"

"He lives alone. What do you expect? And stop picking on everything you see. The man's practically handicapped. He can't do maintenance and all that other stuff."

In the middle of the lawn, next to the toilet, Sleeper spotted a fifteen-inch high cement figure of a little boy sitting on a stump. Strangely, its head was missing. "Looks like somebody lost their head."

"Lawn mower accident. Uncle Boomer said he almost got his foot severed that day. That's why he gave up on gardening."

"Sure Spanks," he stated doubtfully. "Anything you say."

Twenty seconds later, after maneuvering through the many piles of junk and dog shit spread evenly over the front lawn—Sleeper tripped over several items along the way—they managed to make their way successfully up the rotting wooden stairs, then onto the fail-safe porch. Both looked through the smudged windows to determine if there was anyone home. They couldn't tell. Spanky pressed the doorbell a few times. He waited a few seconds, then pressed it again.

"I don't think anyone's home," Sleeper said. "The placed looks abandoned." He mumbled, "Even condemned."

"Enough with the wise cracks." Spanky leaned on the doorbell a third time. "He should be home. He never goes anywhere, except to a few restaurants not to far away."

Seconds later, a hoarse voice trumpeted from behind the door. "Stop ringing the gotdamn doorbell!" He sounded just like the doorman to Emerald City, on the Wizard of Oz. "An old man can only walk so fast. I'm coming. Shit!"

Sleeper flashed a befuddled expression.

"Oh! I forgot to mention something. He's a hell of a character also."

He cocked his head to the left, peeped through curiously squinted eyes. "Is there anything else you wanna tell me before I step into this ..." he looked the place over, "... house? Anything that I really need to know, about *anything* that could be detrimental to my health. Huh, Spanks, anything at all?"

Moments later, the door creaked opened, and a mountain of P-funk whooshed through the doorway and almost debilitated both. Standing in the doorway was Spankys Uncle Boomer, a man cloaked in all his glorified bliss. He was shirtless, barefoot, and his half unzipped filthy pants hung desperately from the cliff of his cellulite ridden buttocks. His beer belly hung low, and his unshaven face rained of the nubs and a plethora of razor burns. His short uncombed hair was in complete disarray. Clutching a cold can of Budweiser beer, he burped, looked at Sleeper, then to Spanky and grew excited. "Hey boy! Ya don't normally come around here until the weekends. What's up? I was just speaking to ya mama the other day. An ya daddy, I ain't going up ta that Satans hell ta see him. They got more infestation up there than I got in the back yard." He burped, and a gust of residue from the beer, it could have been phlegm, flew out of his mouth and landed on Spankys shirt. "Sorry about that, son." He held the beer can up to view, looked at the label. "If it don't come out down there somewhere, then it'll come flying out ya mouth, nose or ears." He showed no shame to the game. His eyes rolled to Sleeper, staring buck eyed and in complete awe. "Who's ya friend, standing there gawking like that? Oh, I'm sorry. I forgot my manners. You two wanna come in?" He turned from them and waddled into the house. When he didn't hear them enter behind him, he shouted, "Don't just stand there! Com'on in! Shit. I ain't got all day, and I ain't getting no younger. And don't forget to close the damn door. All these gotdamn flies in here bout to drive me up the shitten wall."

Spanky nudged Sleeper with his elbow, snapped his head. "You heard the man. Let's go."

Following Boomer, they couldn't help but to observe the crack of his ass; a blubbering mound of hairy flesh peeking out at them. His pants hung so low in the back, that it looked like the chest crevice of an extremely obese woman. The nipple impression on the left cheek is the disfigurement from when he caught the shrapnel.

Walking through a short span of hallway, the loose floorboards creaked disharmoniously. An odious smell of stale everything crept up their noses and flooded their senses sickeningly with an air of grotesque repulse. Spanky's offered to help his uncle clean the place many times in the past. But just like him—it must run in the family—Boomer has too much pride to accept.

Now that Sleeper couldn't hold his breath any longer, he expelled a heavy breath, inhaled deeply, and felt a dizzy spell take him by storm. He gagged inconspicuously, held onto a wall to steady himself, then wiped his misted eyes. He couldn't help his mouth from contorting insufferably.

Spanky noticed his odd behavior. "You okay?" He smelled it too, without a doubt. Since Boomer was family, he had to play it off.

"I'm fine," Sleeper wheezed. He cleared his throat. "I'll be okay, soon as I get use to this Godforsaken …" Spanky reached in back and shoved him lightly.

They turned left and entered a small den. A crowded room dressed with a twenty-year old worn-out recliner that's patched moderately with duck tape, an end table with a shaded lamp centered in the middle, a nineteen inch color television, a fifteen year old loveseat, a couch with a wooden coffee table placed in front of it, a non-working fireplace, and a trophy case stuffed to the gills with war medals and knickknacks from several places that he's traveled to in the past. He spent most of his time in this room, watching satellite television, eating snacks, drinking beer and reminiscing through his compilation of service memorabilia.

Above the fireplace, resting on the mantel, is an antique Japanese sword. In the middle of the swords blade is a dime-sized notch. To people who inquire, to make the notch appear interesting, he placed an exciting story around it, explaining that that's how he received the Medal of Honor. He tells everyone that he took the sword from a Vietnamese soldier, after wrestling with, and then killing him with his bare hands. Tells them that the notch was placed when he used his rifle to stop himself from being decapitated.

Of course, that's not what really happened. But it's a lot more exciting than the truth. Having an encouraging excuse for how he obtained the Medal of Honor mended his injured pride, from catching that piece of shrapnel with his ass. The truth was that after his discharge from the service, he brought the sword from a secondhand pawnshop in downtown Boston. After his wife told him that she wanted a divorce, he was so broken up that he used the sword to decapitate the little cement statue sitting in the front yard. Inside of the statue is a piece of steel rebar, used to reinforce the concrete.

In the den, Boomer plopped into the easy chair, and every small object not anchored in place either rattled or shook. He reached downward and pulled a lever attached to the side of the chair, and his feet elevated to a foot above the carpeted floor. He reached to the end table and grabbed a can of beer, then said plainly, "I heard about your friend, officer Brooks. Stoney Brooks. Why don't you boys have a seat and let's talk about it?"

"Bad news travel quick," Spanky said, just before he sat on the love seat. He dropped his left hand to in between the cushions and pulled out a handful of pretzels. He placed them on the coffee table. "How'd you find out about it?"

Sleeper sat on the couch opposite the loveseat. "It hasn't even been on the television yet."

Boomer sipped his beer. When he felt the time was right, he released a deafening burp, and didn't excuse himself. He pulled himself forward in the chair until his feet hit the floor. Reaching for the pretzels, he released a heavy grunt. He scooped them up and examined them briefly, looking for lint. Not that it would've mattered. He shoved them all into his mouth. Through the food, he muffled, "I got friends on the force, Spanky. You know that. Damn! Asking me a dumb ass question like that. What's the matter witchu boy?" He looked to Sleeper. "Who the hell's this?"

He reached to the end table and retrieved a fly swatter, then quickly nabbed one sitting on the arm of the chair. He proclaimed excitedly, "Gotcha! Ya little freeloading bastard. Ya won't be leaching offa me no more."

"This is Bruno Knight," Spanky said. "We call him Sleeper. We go way back. He's on the force also. We're tight." He stated these facts as if informing Boomer, 'These are his qualifications. He's one of us. You can confide in him.'

"Nice to meet you, sir," Sleeper told Boomer. He swatted at a fly buzzing around his head, annoying him. "I've heard a lot about you."

"All fucken lies, I tell ya!," Boomer shouted. "Believe half of whatcha see, and none of whatchu hear, and you'll be all right, son." He nodded. "Nice ta meet chu, boy. Any boy who's a friend of my nephew, is a friend on mine. By the way, the names Henry. Henry Doyle. But my friends call me Boomer. You can call me Boomer. And another thing. Neva call a man sir, unless ya respect him. An ya don't know me from a bucket-o-beans. Let that be a lesson to ya, boy." He turned his attention to Spanky. "I know this ain't a pleasure visit. That ain't until the weekend. This is business, and I can feel something's on ya mind, boy. And I bet it's got something ta do with ya dead friend. Go-ahead! Tell me I'm right, boy. Whatchu come here for?" He sipped his beer. "You boys want something ta drink? I got some beer and soda in the fridge. If ya want a snack, I'm sure there are some more pretzels in between them cushions yawl sitting on. Them's good snaking. I ate the rest of them during the super bowl, earlier this year."

Sleeper flicked a sour expression. "I'm okay. Thanks anyway."

"No thanks, Uncle Boomer," Spanky said. He swatted at a fly giving him the buzz treatment. "I just ate a short while ago. But, we're here because something's come up, and I need your advice." He swatted again.

Boomer sipped his beer, looked into his lap frustratingly, then said, "Getting in over your head with the Dixie Club, no doubt."

Sleeper fell shocked. "In didn't know he knew about that."

"Where do you think I got the idea from? I told you it wasn't an original idea."

"Boys!" Boomer interrupted. "Your squawking serves about as much use as tits on a Tasmanian Devil. Now let's get down ta business. Whatchor problem?"

"The officer that the Dover Police found dead this morning was a close friend of ours. He's the other one in the Dixie Club. You're not going to believe this, but he actually had the fricken pigheaded audacity to keep a diary about everything that we've …"

*   *   *   *

Two cans of beer, thirty burps from Boomer, and fifteen minutes later, Spanky had finished explaining about their potentially explosive dilemma. Boomer stared at the two with a serious expression, remembering the jams he use to get into. More so, he remembered how he got out of them. Every few seconds, he looked thoughtfully into his lap, contemplating their ugly situation. When he looked up several times, they thought that he was going to say something, but he didn't. False starts.

He reached over the side of the chair and pushed the lever, and his feet hit the floor. He scooted his overweight bottom to the edge of the easy chair, then struggled, climbing to his feet. Without a word, in total silence, he paced in front of them. Only the floorboards creaked, a few odds and ends about the room rattled liberally.

Minutes later, he stopped in his tracks, looked to the ceiling and scratched his chin. It sounded like someone was using sandpaper. Or were out in the backyard, cutting down a tree. He looked at Spanky and Sleeper, then finally broke the discomforting silence. "Ya kno, it seems ta me that that little ole book's hanging over your heads like the sword of Dangle-leas. Or however that damn Canadian saying goes. I don't know what'n the hell ya came ta me for, because you're wasting precious time. I'm sure ya already got the answer ya been looking for. Ya probably just wanted to hear that it's the right thing ta do." He mumbled inaudibly, "Damn! As old as this boy is, he can't even make up his own mind." He said, "Spanky, boy, I done told ya this a thousand times before. I'm sure ya might've even heard it from ya daddy too. If ya gotta get reinforcement of ya thoughts, then you're in doubt of yourself. It means your heart's not in it. Otherwise, there would've been no questions. No doubts. Only actions. And ya know what they say about he who hesitates." He returned to the easy chair, released a heavy grunt, sitting. He ordered, "When ya find that shitten ass book, at no matter what the cost, destroy it, and anyone who can connect ya to it. No matter who the hell it is."

As Spanky and Sleeper absorbed his formidable reply, Boomer sipped his beer until the cans bottom faced the ceiling, slurped the suds. He pulled it down, crushed it. "Well, what'n the hell yawl waiting for? Move it! Get outta my sight." He gave them a grave piece of advice. "Yawl got urgent things ta do, because everything you've worked for is at stake. Your careers, freedom, and everything ya cherish is on the line, up for grabs." He stated earnestly, "If you know what's good for ya, ya better consider it a matter of life or death."

Without hesitation, they rose quickly to their feet and left the room. Before they reached the front door, Boomer hollered, "Yawl let me know when ya get a hold of that diary. But don't tell me what ya had ta do to get it. I don't wanna know." He thought about some of the disturbing incidents from his shaky past, then muttered, "I already got enough shit creeping up on me from back in the day."

"Thanks Boomer!" Spanky yelled. "Later!"

Scratching his prickly five o'clock shadow, Boomer yelled back, "An make sure ya close the gotdamn door! All these gotdamn freeloading flies in here bout ta drive me up the shitten wall."

After leaving the house, and making sure the door was shut tight, Spanky and Sleeper hustled to the car. Sleeper peered at Spanky slyly and noticed a formidable aura growing from within. It wasn't like the one he had when he said he was going to kill Stoney, but a much colder look. He wore an arctic frown etched deeply on his face, his fists were clenched tight, and he marched like a soldier on his way to battle, neglecting the well-being of his undying soul.

A scary picture, Sleeper thought. I can only imagine what's going through his mind. Up to now, all I had to do was imagine the worst, and I could figure what he was going to do. This time, it feels like I'm standing next to something dark and sinister. Something absolutely evil. Something that's blocking my vision from determining what I should do for my sake. For my sons sake.

CHAPTER 29

▼

Spanky drove mostly depending on how he felt. On their return trip to Boston, on the highway, he passed cars like he was in a middle of a high-speed pursuit. Sleeper was forewarned before he pulled a haphazard maneuver. His right hand snapped a fraction of a second before he jerked the wheel left or right, showing how he drove his Harley Davidson. He gripped the steering wheel so tight that the skin on his knuckles remained taut. The way he clipped a few curbs on his turns, Sleeper knew that he was out for some serious business. He was so preoccupied that he hadn't turned on the cars headlights, and wasn't using turn signals. The ride scared Sleeper so much that he had aged two years, and his hands never left the dashboard for fear of a head on collision.

All was quiet until they reached Boston, but it was fifteen minutes before they had arrived at Sleepers apartment in Roslindale. Although they weren't looking at each other, they felt each others presence asking many critical questions. Feeling an enormous amount of pressure growing between them prodded Spanky to ask, "You know what we gotta do, don't you?" The answer embossed in his lethal gaze.

Sleepers response was hesitant, already knowing what the answer might be. Actually, he wasn't sure of how to answer a question thrown with such conviction and final jeopardy. Therefore, he took the wise approach. He answered a question with a question. His eyebrows lifted surprisingly, and his mouth formed the first letter of the word seconds before he replied calmly, "What?"

Staring intensely, Spanky looked him dead in his eyes and shot forward, "We're gonna get that gotdamn mother fucken book!" While images of damning illicit hustling episodes flooded his mind, he bit the bottom of his lip so hard that he nearly drew blood.

Sleeper expected him to say more a hell of a lot more, so he remained quiet, as times of imminent chaos raced through his mind. He wondered how was a lengthy description of what he thought he was going to say, explained so easily. With just a few simple words. Since he appeared stuck in limbo, Spanky went on to say, "From here on, everything, and I mean *everything*, depends on how successful we are in getting our hands on it. You get what I'm saying?"

After a long moment, Sleeper sighed dolefully. "Spanky, we don't even know where it is." Unsteady nerves in his throat riddled his voice with signs of ambiguity. "I mean, I heard what your uncle said back there. But tell me, what're you thinking?"

"I'm thinking that at no matter what the cost, we have to get that gotdamn book." He paused, then continued, sounded more assertive. "That's it! That's what we're gonna do. You look as if I was supposed to say something else. Maybe some fairytale shit coated with sugar. That damn book could disgrace us, and send is to prison for a hellova long time. Since I'm a gambling man, I'm gonna gamble on the notion that Captain Bogart is a meticulous bastard. You saw how curious he looked when he and Detective Sloan were discussing the possible connections it might have involving Stoneys death. You saw that probing expression he had when he flipped through a few pages. When we were in Stoneys bedroom, when you were sitting at the foot of the bed, all incapacitated and shit, I heard him say that he was going to take it home with him tonight. Chances are, he's gonna go through it with a fine toothcomb. If what I think is in that book, or what ever the hell it is, then I'll bet he's going to do some bedtime reading, to get all of the fine details of our operation."

Sleeper swallowed uncomfortably. "That means we have to …"

Spanky finished for him, "… go by his house in a little while, and take it."

Gruesome images of mayhem from a full out assault on the sanctity of a brother police officers home flooded Sleepers mind, and he fell dazed. The ghastly repercussions filled his head and knocked him silly, then his thoughts went blank. He couldn't handle it, his hard drive crashed. The potential ramifications played with his head, kicked his conscious around, as if it were a soccer ball. "Even if it's there, how are we going to get our hands on it? We can't just walk up to his front door, ring the doorbell, then kindly ask him for it. He's not going for that."

Spanky tossed a somber chuckle, before stating, "You simple ass son-of-a ..." He reached over and opened the glove compartment, stuck his right hand in and retrieved a .45 semi-automatic handgun.

"You keep a .45 in your ..." A frightful look consumed his heart, easily seen in his bulging eyes. He stuttered, "Wha-Wha-What are you gonna do with that?"

Spanky placed the gun in his lap, then reached under his seat and pulled out a brown paper bag. He handed it to him. "Take this."

"The hell's this?"

"Open it," Spanky ordered.

Sleeper reached inside and felt something metallic. Approximately eight inches long, tubular in shape, and very cold. Having a good idea of what it was, his hands trembled.

"Take it out and attach it to the gun. I had that silencer made special a few years ago. Although, you can get them through the mail order, from several foreign countries. Especially Russia. The KBG ain't nothing nice over there."

Sleeper pulled the silencer out of the bag, then stared at it for a lengthy period. It was one-third the weight of the gun, but it felt ten times heavier. It felt ruthless, like what the whole situation was becoming. It moved him further from the light of his dwindling conscious. His voice trembled when he asked, "Y-Y-You're gonna kill Captain Bogart?"

"That name dropping mother fucken book!" he blasted. "At no matter what the cost, we gotta get it, destroy it, then destroy anyone who can connect us to it. And it's not me, buddy boy. It's we! Ya heard me? We!"

"B-B-But Spanky, that's murder! Cold blooded murder."

"No shit, Sherlock. You figure that out all by yourself?"

Sleeper threw the gun and silencer onto his lap. His voice strained, "In the ten years I've been on the force, I've never had to kill anyone on duty. I've never even shot at anyone before. Spanky, this shit ain't right! This can't happen. This can't possibly hap ..."

"Gotdamn your ass! I guess I have to remind you of what's at stake. Again!"

"I already know. You've told me over and over again, and I'm getting sick and tired of hearing it."

"I'm not gonna tell you anything this time, old buddy. This time, I'm gonna show you."

Sleepers eyes widened. "Show me! How are you going to show me?"

There was no reply. On route to his apartment, Spanky took a detour, prompting him to ask, "Where're you going? I don't live in this direction."

"Sit tight. I'm taking you to meet someone. Like the old saying goes, 'One picture is worth a thousand words.'"

Whoever it is, I know they can't possibly be all that bad, he thought. I already met his Uncle Boomer.

CHAPTER 30

▼

Minutes later, they were driving down Massachusetts Avenue. Spanky turned right at an intersection leading onto Columbus Avenue, then quickly found a parking spot. After getting out of the car, Sleeper walked around to the driver side and asked him blankly, "Now what?"

Stone faced, Spanky walked away. "Follow me." He was through with using verbal scare tactics. He hoped this little see-and-say seminar would make Sleeper understand the dreadful predicament they were in. A predicament that Spanky hoped would force Sleeper to call his bluff.

Seconds later, they were standing at the beginning of a very narrow, dimly lit sixty-yard long back alley that's located in the rear of a near century old, three-story Brownstone apartment building. Stuffed trashcans and green garbage bags lined the two-foot wide sidewalks on both sides. Close to the end of the alley, about fifty feet away, they saw a huge dumpster located a few feet from the rear door of an Italian restaurant. The dumpster was filled to overflowing with garbage from the tenants living in the brownstone apartment building, empty food crates from the restaurant, rats and other disgusting disease carrying creepy crawlers.

There's a large cardboard box located several feet behind the dumpster. It was directly under an alley lamppost, next to the rear entrance of the Italian Restaurant. There were large black letters printed on the side of the box. **'WHIRL-POOL'**

Walking the length of the alley, Sleeper kept his hand over his nose and mouth, and gagged repeatedly for the tremendous stench misting his eyes.

Watching Sleeper reel in the nauseating environment, Spanky said, "This place is cleaner than some prisons. It even smells better."

Almost to the middle of the alley, Spanky called out, "Yo! Andrew!"

No one replied, but a stirring noise coming from inside of the dumpster did cease. He tried again. "Andrew! I need to talk to you for a minute."

That's the name of the disgraced cop who he told me about, Sleeper wondered. The one who'd gotten busted, then kicked from the police department dishonorably for stealing and distributing confiscated narcotics.

Moments later, when a garbage can lid fell from a trashcan, Spanky snapped his sights to that direction. Sleeper became unsettled and placed his hand on his gun. A Mange ridden alley cat scrounging for something to eat sprang from out of a trashcan and dashed by their feet, exiting the alley. Sleeper sighed in relief, then proclaimed, "There's nobody here. Let's get out of this stinking hell hole."

At that moment, they heard a rummaging emanating from inside of the large cardboard box. They glanced at each other curiously, then back to the box, stared intensely. They heard someone cough, then clear their voice, coughed up a loogie. A cutout like door on the front of the box cracked ajar, and a homeless man stuck his head out and spat on the ground. Before he looked up, his alcohol strained voice fired, "Who da fuck?"

A frail figure of a man crawled out of the box on his hands and knees. Partially inebriated, he stumbled toward them. Badly dressed in grubby rags that haven't seen laundry detergent in years, he opened his eyes wide to focus, then leaned toward the strangers. He reached into one of his tattered pockets and pulled out a timeworn brown wallet. He opened it and flashed a rusted Boston Police officers badge, spewing, "Okay, ya mutha fuckas." He shouted, "freeze!" He slurred, "If ya don't gimme some gotdamn spare change, um gonna bust ya asses for trespassing, an take ya downtown an let the boys work ya ova."

Spanky and Sleeper remained staring at the repulse before them. However, Spanky expected to see nothing less than what had just happened, going by the rumors of what he had heard. Meanwhile, Sleeper, still covering his nose and mouth, couldn't believe his eyes. He was totally bewildered. Beside himself.

The homeless man stumbled closer, holding an empty hand extended. "Well! Com'on wit it, Beevis and Butthead. I ain't got all day, ya kno. I gots important things ta do. I gotta stake-out ta go to. Me and the crew are gonna bust some big-time mobsters in the North End."

"We're police officers," Spanky informed the homeless man, then flashed his badge. "We heard a disturbance, and came to investigate." An obvious lie.

Sleeper looked at him, leaned toward him and mumbled, "What'n the hell …"

Spanky returned a stale expression. 'Shut up!'

"Dat's bullshit. No cop in the right mind would come down an alley like this to check out a disturbance, less he first got his gotdamn piece out. Either you're very brave, or very stupid. Or your just plain fulla shit. I'm prone to believe all three of the above. What'n the hell do ya want?"

A thought came to Spanky. "If you're ex-officer Andrew Thompson, my uncle Boomer said you'd be here. I saw him a little while ago, and he asked us if we could check up on you, the next time we were in the neighborhood. And, well …"

Sleeper knew it was a lie, but hoped it would work. This was no art den, but the painting commenced.

The homeless man looked downward, paused for a long moment, thinking back. Something was coming back to him. Perhaps fragments, bits and pieces of fading recollections of his jumbled past. He looked into Spankys eyes with an expression filled with warm memories, and said considerately, "Ya say you're Old Boomers nephew, huh?"

"Yes, I am. I'm officer Robert Sinclair, and this is officer Bruno Knight."

"Why didn't ya say so in the first place? Instead of talking all that crap about hearing a disturbance. The nerve of you, comin down here and scaring the shit out of an old man." On the same breath, he stated, "By the way, the names Andrew. Most people call me Andy." He rambled on, "Anyway, how's Old Boomer doing? I ain't seen him, going on for now, bout ten years. Has he gone on a diet yet? Did his wife ever come back ta him? It really hit him hard when she gave him that divorce." He looked down, shook his head despondently. "Talk about a broke man." On the same note, he laughed, "Did ya uncle ever tell ya about the time we busted a coupla ten year old kids for stealing fruit from a food market in Dorchester?"

Spanky thought back. "I don't think so."

"After we caught them, we threw them in the back of the cruiser, and told them that we was gonna take them down to the station and use a rubber hose on them. We drove around the block a few times and talked shit to them for a half hour. I'll neva forget it. Scared the shit outta them. One of them cried the whole time, kept asking for his mama. The other pissed his pants. It was the damndest thing. I wanted to send them down to juvi, lock them up for a coupla hours. Let them sweat it out. Old Boomer just wanted to teach them a lesson, scare them a little. He was like that with kids. Bless his soul." He paused, then asked again, "Anyway, how's my old friend doing?"

"He's managing," Spanky said, while thinking, Compared to you. "Boomer's still Boomer. He still lives in that same little house down in Providence, Rhode Island. He hasn't changed much. About you, how've you been?"

Andrew turned and stared at the large box that he had just minutes before crawled out of. "Well, as you can see, I went condo. It's got central air, heating and everything in between. I put it right in front of this warm air vent, leading out of the restaurant. That way, I'm all set for the winter. It'll be waterproof as soon as I line the outside with some plastic wrap. As far as eating is concerned, I do all right. I dine on Italian cuisine almost every night." He looked at the huge trash bin. "As long as I can get to it before the rodents do. Besides that, everything's just peachy." He pulled a dinner roll from his pocket. It looked as though it was made soggy from the tears he wept nightly from self-pity. He offered them, "You guys want something ta eat? I got a lot more of these back inside. The restaurant throws them out by the bundles. I just scoops them up, an takes them inside. They're good for midnight snacks, while I'm reading a book by candle light."

Sleeper looked at him as though he was insane. "No thanks." He swallowed with a repulsive taste simmering in his mouth. "I'm not hungry, at the moment."

Just then, a mangy mongrel stuck its head out from inside of the huge cardboard box. It looked like a cross between a German Shepard, a Collie, a Poodle, a Beagle, a Siamese cat and a rabid squirrel. In fact, it looked more like a capybara; the largest know ancestor to a rat. There were homeless dogs, and then there were homeless dogs. This was truly the homeliest flea-bitten, mange infested, biscuit eaten homeless dog that ever scuttled the face of the earth. Nevertheless, it belonged to Andrew because no one else would claim it. Even dogcatchers won't attempt to snare it, for fear that they might catch some awful infectious disease that hasn't even been given a name. Once, a pitbull simply ignored it, believing that it was already dead.

The dog waddled out of the box and ventured close to the strangers. That's when Spanky placed his hand on his gun. Not because the dog was huge or appeared vicious, but only because it was extremely unsightly. Actually, he wasn't even sure if it was a dog at all, but some kind of a prehistoric rainforest animal that's managed to evade the border patrol authorities when it slipped through the cracks, probably because they thought it was a statue of a gargoyle, or was dead.

When the dog was close enough, it lifted its nose and sniffed the air, trying to figure out if the strangers were friends or foe. "He probably smells my dog on me," Spanky guessed. "I have a Bulldog. His name's Spike."

Andrew leaned down and rubbed the pooch's head, flashed a mustard stained smile. "This here's my little dog. We go way back, been through some trying times together. I call him Dickhead! He's all I got, on account of my family don't know me no more. Although, he only comes around mostly when I got something to eat. But, he's still my friend. He's the only one that comes around not expecting to get something."

"Is that so?"

"Hell yeah! Ya probably heard about that bust that happened ta me a few years back Ain't no secret. Anyway, a few people involved in taken me down come round here sometimes looking for some of the money that got lost in the shuffle. They think I have it stashed somewhere in an offshore account, waiting for the heat ta blow over, so's I can run off ta claim it. So much shit was going on back then that this person over here dipped their hands into the pot, and that person ova there dipped their hands into the pot. It was chaos! They come round threatening ta do a whole lot of shit ta me. Maybe send me ta jail, ta do some time." He huffed, "Humph! I know what time it is. It's half past the monkey's ass, and a quarter to his nuts." He laughed hysterically, then danced the jig briefly. "But I fooled them. I ain't got nothing worth threatening for. As long as I stay like this, they can't touch me." He grumbled, "Buncha gotdamn do-gooders. There was nothing wrong with what I did. My only mistake was getting caught." He thought about the woman who helped the authorities set him up for his tremendous fall from the ranks of one of Bostons finest, and suddenly, his mood changed drastically. He became hostile and quarrelsome. "That no-good back-stabbing two-bit whore … I still owe her a hell of an ass whoopin." He swung his clenched right fist into the air, as if punching an invisible adversary, then complained further, "An them gotdamn public defense lawyers," he swung again, "and them lying ass district attorneys." He swung twice. "They wouldn't know the truth if it crept up and bit'em on the ass."

Growing more aggressive, Andrew swung madly at his invisible opponents, only in his mind. Spanky and Sleeper stared watchfully, took several steps backwards. The dog became so frightened for the sudden outburst, most likely because it had experienced it many times before, it scuttled into his rent controlled condo for cover. Andrew continued raving and ranting like a lunatic on a rampage, swinging like a champ. "An them nasty ass close-minded judges, an them stinking ass divorce courts, an them fricken media people, twisting the facts and distorting all the evidence ta sell a good story, blasting what they don't know ..." filling the alley with his uncontrollable rage, he shouted, "Lies! Lies! All lies!" Highly excited, he screamed, "I hate'em all! I wish they were dead. They ain't no good. As far as I'm concerned, they're all on the take, and they can kiss my stinking ass. If I had a gun, I'd blow all their fucken heads off." His temper flaring, he jumped up and down in a maddened frenzy.

Watching him loose his mind, creating a whirlwind of pandemonium, Spanky and Sleeper took a few more steps backwards. Andrew blasted, "Who in the hell do they think they are? I did one fucken think wrong, and everybody blames me for a whole lot of other shit." He wrestled in place, choking an invisible adversary, spewing, "I'll kill the bastards! I'll squeeze the life out of them. I'll choke them! I'll kill them all!"

With a burst of speed, he ran toward the wall-to-wall newspaper lined condo, his home, and jumped into the air and kicked a large gapping hole into its side. The box caught his leg, and he fell to the ground. He rose quickly to his feet, and kicked another hole into the same side. This time, he accidentally kicked the dog. It came barreling through the cardboard flap door, with its tail tucked securely between its legs, throwing several high-pitched yelps into the air. "Yyaaarrrk! Yyaaarrrk! Yyaaarrrk!"

On the way out, the dog kicked a Kentucky fried chicken bucket over, and it rolled out to just past the doorway. Andrew picked the bucket up, then flung it high into the air. Its contents flew out and spattered over the immediate area, half of it landed on him. Obviously, this was his toilet. Clad entirely in feces and urine, he shouted hysterically, "Fuck'em all! Every single one of them!"

Spanky and Sleeper continued stepping backwards, listening to Andrews rage. To what they witnessed, no explanations came to mind. They were thoroughly flabbergasted. Sleeper more than Spanky, because Spanky was forewarned. However, neither could pry their eyes from what they observed. Andrew, a man constantly haunted by his past mistakes. A man whose sanity was challenged daily by the slightest hint of everything that had occurred when he was busted for his greed. A slight miscalculation. A tiny error in judgment. Now living a life sentence, struggling in the epitome of his nightmares.

Standing at the beginning of the alley, they stood watching Andrew jumping up and down zealously, listened to his fading voice rave furiously. In between leaps, he swung into the air at his invisible adversaries. The adversaries in his mind. His needling subconscious. He sees all of the people who he complained about as clear as day. They were around him all the time. Gathered to infiltrate his every waking moment. To remind him of what he had done.

Spanky stole a moment to observe Sleeper through his peripheral vision, and found a look of putrid disgust stained on his face. He remarked, "That's what happens when you don't take care of your possible liabilities. The loose ends." He faced him. "You seen enough?"

Sleeper didn't reply. For a long moment, he pictured himself at the backend of the alley, acting like a rampaging maniac. Dressed like a bum in tattered clothes, pulling the hair out of his head, shouting obscenities as though they were going out of style. He wondered if all of the terrible things that Andrew had mentioned would happen to him. He wondered if his family would disown him the same way. Especially his son. Factoring in the idea of a lengthy prison sentence, something that Andrew didn't receive, he imagined that it would be more horrifying for him. Considering everything thus far, he finally turned away robotically, then returned to the car. When he heard Spanky's footsteps just in back of him, he asked solemnly, "If I ever get like that, could you do me a favor, please?"

"Sure. What's that?"

"Take out your gun, then shoot me in the back of the head. Blow my gotdamn ever lovin brains out! I'm sure I'll appreciate it."

"Sure thing. With much pleasure."

I'm sure it would be a pleasure, Sleeper thought. He brought to mind what Spanky had mentioned earlier about loose ends. For a moment, that's what he considered himself. A possible liability, because of his wavering uncertainty. He knew that Spanky wasn't sure that he could count on him.

*   *   *   *

After arriving at Sleepers apartment, Spanky told him, "I'll be back here to pick you up at eleven o'clock *sharp*. Be ready, and wear all dark clothing."

Sleeper got out of the car. Before he closed the door, he nodded. "I'll be ready." His look was decisive, feeling as though he wanted to pull the trigger himself. If he had to.

After Spanky drove off, he went into the apartment building to break the news of Stoneys death to his wife. In the hallway, before he entered the apartment, he stood at the door and an image of what Andrew had become; a maddened fool, a raving lunatic, flooded his mind and overwhelmed him. He felt dizzy for a moment, braced himself against the doorjamb, trying to collect himself. He couldn't believe that his best friend was dead.

*   *   *   *

Minutes later, when he felt that he was ready, he entered the apartment and called out to his wife, "Elizabeth! Honey, I'm home."

In thinking about how much his wife and child meant to him, to secure his life with them, he believed that he could manipulate his feelings like a light switch. *That* was the type of callous person that he had to be, in order to do the job that they might have to do, when he and Spanky got to Dover. He had to be someone so unscrupulous that he could turn from being a loving warmhearted family man, to a merciless cold-blooded killer at the drop of a hat. A sterling soldier of misfortune.

He gave little concern to the notion that visualizing the bowels of hell from belligerent thinking was one thing. Going there by committing a damnable act of cold-blooded murder was something else altogether. He's yet to discover the difference. He'll feel the difference. Therefore, he'll live the difference.

A soft voice called from a room at the back of the apartment. "Hi sweetheart! We're in the nursery."

Contemplating the days events, Sleeper removed his jacket, then hung it on the wooden coat rack standing a few feet from the front entrance. Right next to the fifty-gallon fish tank. He approached the nursery. When he arrived to the doorway, he looked in and discovered Elizabeth sitting in a bentwood rocking chair, cradling their son in her arms, humming a soothing lullaby.

"Hi baby. Hard day at the office?" She was always happy to hear her husband coming through the front door. Because he was a police officer, at the back of her mind, she sometimes has disturbing visions of receiving an alarming telephone call from his boss, spilling of gunplay and hospital emergency rooms.

Most days, when Sleeper arrived home, he'd normally have a brisk air about himself, signaling that it was business as usual. Just another day. There was a usual vivacious kick in his step that told her that everything was okay. His movements throughout the apartment were quick and lively. He was full of energy, pep, raring to go back out on a special detail on a moments notice.

However, today, because Stoney was dead, his mood was stifled severely. Because the quality of his life was in jeopardy, it sank him deeper into a impenetrable shell of despair. He was somewhat confused about the matter altogether, because he couldn't understand why feeling remorse for his dead friend, was difficult to surface over the idea that he could shortly be hauled off the streets in handcuffs, and thrown in jail. Disgraced! Shamed! Dishonored! Repulsive words found somewhere in the neighborhood of scandal, indictment, prison, divorce, etcetera etcetera. In short, Andrew!

Leaning dolefully against the nursery doorjamb, his head lowered glumly, she knew immediately that something was awry. In preparation for what he was about to tell her, he managed to slip on a smidgen of remorse. He sighed exhaustively, then announced flatly, "Elizabeth, Stoneys dead."

The rocking chair came to an abrupt stop. She looked at him with a frozen expression, not believing what she had just heard. Given the distressing news, she stopped breathing for a moment. She cupped her mouth with her right hand in total shock and muffled through her fingers, "Oh … my … God!" She stuttered, "B-B-Bruno … what do you mean Stoneys dead?" She waited for a response, then rambled hysterically, "How can he be dead? I mean, when did this happen? How? I didn't see anything on the news this afternoon about anyone in Massachusetts getting shot. Especially a cop!" She looked at her baby profoundly, a deep concern dribbling her face. "There must be some kind of a mistake. Stoney … he can't be dead."

"He's dead," Sleeper said assuredly. He approached his wife, knelt on the floor beside the rocking chair. "It's true, and he didn't get shot. Actually, they're not sure of how he died. Spanky and I just came from Stoneys uncles place out in Dover a short while ago." He explained dolefully, "I … I saw him lying there, in the bed, not moving. He looked as though the life had been sucked right out of him." He stated again, "He's dead. I can't believe it. He's actually dead!"

She persisted, asking the same useless questions. "But, how? What I mean is, what happened?"

"They don't know yet. Although, they think he might've been poisoned." As if she had the answer, he asked, "Who in the hell would do something like that?"

"I don't know, Bruno. But I still find it hard to believe that he's dead. I mean, I wish they could tell you something … anything about what happened."

"All I know is that Carlton found him in bed this morning, unresponsive. Dead. Gone. Just like that."

"This is unbelievable!" she declared, still quite shaken. "He was one of your closest friends. And now …"

He sighed. "Yeah. I know."

Because she knew her husband intimately, she felt that his emotions didn't coincide with what he had just told her. She felt that he should've reflected a lot more remorse for the death of someone who he considered to be one of his closest friends. There was definitely something he held back on. "His family … his poor parents, I can just imagine the hell they must be going through right about now.

I'll call them tomorrow sometime and give them our condolences. After they get through the initial shock." She asked sympathetically, "Bruno, sweetheart, are you all right?"

His head rolled upward mournfully, he found her eyes. "I'm okay, I guess."

"No. I mean, is everything all right … situation wise?" She thought for a moment that Stoneys death might have implications leading to illicit activities connected to him.

He realized that she knew him better than anyone else, and the line of questioning made him paranoid. "Of course everything's all right." He lied with a straight face, then quickly changed the subject. "How's Junior? Did you feed him yet?"

She felt it was an evasive response, but replied anyway. "Yes, I did. Shortly before you arrived." After a long hesitation, "I have to use the bathroom." Holding the baby in her lap with her left arm, she ran her right hand over his head consolably. She kissed his forehead, then asked compassionately, "Baby, are you hungry?"

She rose carefully from the rocking chair, and was about to put the baby into the crib when he informed her, "I don't have much of an appetite, at the moment. There's been so much going on today, with hearing the news of Stoney death." He stood to his feet. "For the life of me, I just can't figure it out."

"Try not to worry about it too much," she said, placing her son in the crib. "He's in Gods hands now." She remained still for a moment, pondered Stoneys demise. "My God! There's going to be so much going on for the next few days, with his funeral in all. It'll be chaos." She looked at her son and smiled frailly.

"Let me hold Junior, while you go to the bathroom."

She placed the child into the crib, staring at him as if he had two heads. "Bruno, are you crazy or something?" She pointed at his hands. "I didn't hear you wash your hands when you came into the house. What're you trying to do, give our son problems he doesn't need?"

He eyed his grime-ridden hands. "Oh, yeah. I forgot."

Walking out of the room, she threw over her shoulders, "And you'd better not touch him until you wash your hands *and* face." She threw in for good measure. "And brush your teeth too. Babies his age don't know how to talk yet, so he can't complain about the onion loaded sandwich you might've had for lunch."

He found a little humor and stated facetiously, "A little dirt never hurt anyone."

"It's not the dirt that I'm worried about. It's what might be in it that concerns me."

He said affectionately, "Okay baby. You're right. As usual."

"Of course I am!" she hollered from inside the bathroom. "I'm always right!"

Before he left the room to wash his hands, he leaned over, looked into the crib and admired his son. Staring wonderingly into his innocent eyes, he felt as though he was trying to communicate with him. His eyes, together with his little hands gestured several possible expressions. It actually had more to do with his subconscious, than the idea of what he wanted to believe he was saying. Observing his sons innocence had a way of reflecting self-criticism. Like staring into a mirror.

Wondering about his son, with considering Stoneys inexplicable death, and his involvement in the Dixie Club, he quickly fell into a trance. At that moment, and only for a moment, he lost his sense of coherence and thought he heard his son say, "Hi daddy. I love you, daddy. Do you love me?"

"You know I love you," he replied. "You're my son."

"That's good. And that means that you'd do anything to make sure that you'll always be around to protect me. Right, daddy?"

Dreamy eyed, he smiled, then replied, "Of course I ..." He shook his head, peered keenly at his son. "What'd you say?"

At that moment, Elizabeth entered the room. "Sweetheart, who're you talking to?"

"No one, honey. I was just talking to myself."

She picked up a soiled diaper resting on a change table, a few feet from the crib. Started to carry it out of the room, but stopped in the doorway. "Be careful, Bruno. That's the first sign of loosing it." She appeared extremely worried, crossed her arms, said suspiciously, "I find what happened to Stoney ... all so strange. I still can't believe he's dead."

"Me neither."

"You think he could've been involved in something crazy? You see him hanging around with any strange people lately?"

Deliberated briefly. "Not that I can recall."

She looked down fearfully, wondered if the perpetrator who committed this damnable act would come for him next. "Well, I hope they find out who did it. Stoneys family won't have any peace until the killer's caught."

He nodded, whispered, "Yeah."

"Why don't you go wash up."

When she left the nursery, he followed her into the hallway. "Oh, I forgot to tell you something, honey. I have to go on a special stakeout detail tonight, with Robert Sinclair."

Upon hearing Spankys name, she stopped dead in her tracks and he collided with her. She turned around and fired, "They expect you to work tonight? Even with after what's happened to Stoney?"

"It's a big case they've been working on for months now," he tried to explain. "And no ones more familiar with it. Through our confidential informant, we're expecting something to go down soon. Maybe tonight."

She shook her head disbelievingly. "How do they expect you to concentrate?"

He shrugged his shoulders.

"I simply don't believe this. First your friend gets himself killed, and now they got you paired with that idiot gigolo again." She sighed deplorably. "This doesn't look good at all." She didn't like Spanky mostly because he wasn't married. She considered him to be irresponsible, unstable, unreliable, a total slob, and mostly, unworthy of wearing his badge.

"It's not going to be too difficult to handle, light work. Mostly waiting in a cruiser, observing a few suspects, waiting for the deal to go down."

Once, when Spanky had invited them over for dinner, she went into nearly every room and finger tested many areas for dust collection. Just as she had figured, the place was filthy; a haven for germs. Her philosophy, how clean the home is, is a direct reflection of the person who lives there. She asked coldly, "How's he taking it? Knowing him, he might've had something to do with it."

He said nothing, but made an effort to peel away into the bathroom. She latched onto his shirtsleeve. "Sweetheart, you know how I've always felt about that nutcase. He's nothing but a dishonorable discharge waiting to happen."

He looked into her eyes. "That's not a nice thing to say about my friend."

"Remember what I told you about that a long time ago. You pick your friends. Don't let them pick you."

"You don't hear me talking like that about any of your friends."

"Sweetheart, that's because none of my friends are lowlifes."

"Elizabeth!" He ordered gently, "That's enough, please. I've already been through enough for one day."

"Don't tell me that that's enough," she argued. "That's not enough."

Normally, she wouldn't fly off the handle for no apparent reason. But ever since she discovered that secret bankbook that he kept tucked under a few items at the back of the closet, in their bedroom—one that listed staggering figures—things just haven't been right between them. His excuse was that it didn't belong to him, and that it was a coincidence that he and his friend, Brad Klaus, have the same initials. Never mind the fact that in the five years he's had it in his possession, she's never met the man. Sleeper was never good at lying. He always left that job to Spanky, since he had the golden tongue. Spanky was an expert at it. Hence the phrase, 'A natural born liar.'

He knew that if he pushed the issues, the argument would lead back to the secret bankbook, so he put the whole thing on ice. He turned from her, entered the bathroom, acted like he was preoccupied cleaning himself. She stuck her head in the bathroom and persisted, "You're a good man, Bruno. Robert isn't doing anything but dragging you down. Believe me, I know the type. If he gets into trouble, he'll string you right along with him."

Tired of hearing what could be the truth, he tried to ward her off by closing the bathroom door. "Do you mind, sweetheart? Can I have some privacy?"

"Privacy my foot," she pelted at the door. "You just don't want to hear it. I've seen everything you have before—saw you take a number one, two and three—so what's the problem?"

Not responding, he looked frustratingly at his reflection in the mirror. Damn that woman, he thought. Why don't she leave it alone? She has no idea what's going on. I have to keep my mind straight to do what's planned for tonight. If I don't get it right, then …"

Another image of Andrew flashed before him, and he assumed a devilish expression capped with an ugly frown. His jaw tightened severely, a malicious taste foamed in his mouth, he spat into the sink. "Shit!"

She called to him from the kitchen, broke his concentration. "Bruno! Come to the kitchen when you finish. You have to put something inside of yourself, to keep you going."

Not hearing a response, she tried again, approaching the bathroom. "Bruno!" She opened the door and stuck her head inside.

Hearing the door squeak startled him, scared the hell out of him. He turned around and fired, "What'n the hell's the matter with you, sneaking up on me like that?" She stood frozen, mouth agape, he spewed crossly, "Don't you know how to knock on the fricken door?"

Peering deeply into his eyes, for a moment, she felt as if she didn't know him at all. He appeared distant, far away, in another world, in another place and time. She had never before experienced such open and enraged hostility coming from him. She remained motionless, completely baffled. Highly perplexed, she chucked it off toward his feeling remorse for his dead friend. She said peaceably, "Come and try to eat something before you leave. It'll make you feel better. Or if you want, I can make some coffee for you."

He realized that she was only trying to help. He lowered his tone and calmed, "Listen, sweetheart, sorry about snapping like that. It's just that … I've got so much going on in my head right now."

"It's okay Bruno. I understand. But you really should try to put something in your stomach."

"I told you before, I'm not hungry." He inhaled the enticing aroma entering the bathroom, then changed his mind. "Well, maybe I might nibble on something."

"Good," she said, smiled weakly. "I'll have it ready for you in a minute."

She returned to the kitchen, and he continued washing, glanced occasionally into the mirror. In thinking of how he had snapped at her, he realized that he had many doubts about his identity. Knew that he was slowly loosing a grip on himself, his identity seeped slowly down the drain.

He entered the kitchen, pulled up a chair and sat down opposite her, in front of a plate of steaming hot food. Without saying a word, he studied the plate for a moment, while she eyed him suspiciously. She crossed her arms frustratingly, then broke the silence when she said, "Sweetheart, I know I've asked you this before. But I'm going to ask you again. Are you all right?"

He replied unsurely, "Sure. I'm fine." There was a drab tone lingering in his voice. "Why do you ask?"

Shook her head pessimistically. "You've never spoken to me like that before, in all the days we've been married." She rose from her chair, walked around the table, then sat in the chair next to him. He knew she wasn't going to let up on him that easy. Remaining composed, she persisted. "Bruno, I'm going to ask you again … one more time. Is there something going on that I should know about?"

Forking, toying with the pork chop on his plate, he replied calmly, "No. There's nothing going on. I'm just freaked out about Stoneys death." He sighed. "That's all."

He discovered during their first month of marriage, that keeping his answers short and simple kept him out of the doghouse. It worked out fine for him, but she often got on his case for not going into depth with expressing his feelings. She tries constantly to get him to be in touch with his feminine side, and he disliked it immensely, claiming that he didn't have one. He's a closet homophobic. He thought that being too soft, forthcoming or friendly, especially in his profession, might let the bad guy see his weaknesses. Which would allow him to be caught off guard. Instead, he remained undaunted, so the results of whatever would be less self-inflicting.

She persisted, watching his every movement, examining his emotions. "No matter what you say, I still think there's something going on. Something I believe I have a right to know about, since you *are* my husband." She leaned toward him, got in his face, examined every discrepancy that she came across. "Just the way you're acting, Bruno ... it's not you. I like to think I know you intimately. I've seen you mourn the loss of a loved one before, and this isn't it. This isn't how *you* express grief."

He placed a piece of pork chop into his mouth, then muffled, "What do you mean it's not me. I'm still Bruno."

"Dammit Bruno!" Her head dropped exasperatingly, her jaw tightened. "Don't play games with me. You know that's not what I mean. Don't get sarcastic, and most of all, don't patronize me. It's your personality I'm talking about. You're ... You've changed in some way or another. I can see it. Mostly, I can feel it."

He placed the fork on the table, next to his plate, faced her. "Look, honey, you're getting yourself all worked up for nothing." Said earnestly, "Everything's all right." Told her sincerely, "I promise."

She sat back in her chair, thought, I don't care what he says. Something's wrong, and I'm sure it has something to do with that damned bankbook I discovered at the back of the closet. Since I can't put my finger on it, then I can't go anywhere with it. He'll just keep leading me in a circle, just like he's doing. I'll just have to wait and see.

He picked up the fork and continued eating, pretending to enjoy his meal. When he thought about the food, it tasted delicious. In between those times, his mind drifted, took his palate along for the ride.

Feeling as though she was barking up a tree, because it might have something to do with 'the blue wall of silence', she finally threw in the towel, stated submissively, "Okay. It's okay if you don't want to talk about it. But for my and our sons' sake, I'm going to keep my eye on you."

He smiled halfheartedly, and she went on to say, "You did the same thing last night, while you were sleeping."

He dropped the fork next to the plate, looked into her eyes bleakly. In just an instant, many ghastly visions of a reoccurring nightmare traipsed inconveniently through his mind, chased out the warmth he normally felt while enjoying a home cooked meal prepared by his wife. Seeing the name Jake flash intermittently before him, his jaw grew rigid and he shivered furiously. He looked into his lap, sighed, said plainly, "I'm not hungry anymore. Got too much on my mind right now." He rose to his feet, left the kitchen. "I think I'll go watch television for a little while."

The year before, on the Forth of July, at a cookout that headquarters had given for the police officers and their families, Capt. Winslow had mentioned to her to be aware of the symptoms of an occupational stress that some police officers may experience during their time on the firce. Since he's been tossing and turning and wrestling with his sheets for the past few days—sometimes he screamed the name Jake at the top of his lungs—she's been giving it more consideration to give him a call. She threw at him, "I'm keeping my eye on you, Bruno. What time is Robert coming by?"

He threw back into the kitchen, "Bout eleven o'clock."

She excited, "Why so late?"

"We can't help it, honey. That's when the bad guys come out to play."

"Well, you just make sure you wear your bullet proof vest."

Walking to the living room, he mumbled, "Yeah. No doubt."

CHAPTER 31

▼

Eleven o'clock came quickly, and Sleeper was as ready as he thought he'd be. He was psyched to the gills. Pumped! In just that short amount of time, he's managed to condition himself to believe that what he was getting ready to do—kill unjustifiably—was unquestionably right, and politically correct. He had that, 'All the other kids are doing it' attitude.

Spanky pulled up to his apartment building and honked the horn a few times. Sleeper kissed his wife and child goodbye, then left. She ran to the window facing the street, peeked out and saw Spanky waiting in a dark red Dodge Charger, a car that she had never seen before. She thought nothing of it, understanding that they sometimes used rental vehicles for surveillance duty.

Watching her husband climb inside, she couldn't help but to believe that there was something strange about his goodnight kiss that warned her of imminent danger. A rickety anxiety building in her heart, she felt it was inevitable.

After he closed the car door, Spanky asked immediately, "You ready to do this?" He had hoped he wasn't in there getting butterflies or the willies from experiencing warm moments with his wife and child. When he didn't want to hang out late with the guys sometimes, the first thing that came out of his mouth was something about his family. Never mind the excuse being legitimate. To the guys, any excuse was a disappointment. They didn't want to hear anything about the genuine responsibilities that he had promised to uphold. They didn't want to hear, what was to them, bullshit. They wanted Sleeper to be just like them, carefree and single, with no one to needle them about anything. They wanted him to be without conscious, immature and irresponsible. Actually, they were envious— green-eyed with jealousy—because he had a family. He had someone waiting for him when he came home from a hard days work. People who respected and loved him unconditionally. People who he could reveal his deepest thoughts and desires to, and know that they'll keep them confidential. Without having to worry that it'll be on the six o'clock news, or be a topic in some internet chat room.

Straight faced, Sleeper replied assuredly," Let's do it." He looked over the Dodges interior, inhaled the freshly detailed interior. "Where'd you get this piece of junk from?"

"I stole it." Spanky smiled indistinctly, feeling good that his level of confidence had climbed a notch from the last time he had spoken with him. Peeling away from the curb, he stated, "Lets get this over with."

*   *   *   *

It took them no time at all to reach the small suburban town of Dover, Massachusetts. This time, instead of Spanky driving like a maniac, he took his time for good reason, as to not draw attention from any of the small town deputies that occasionally parked stealthily behind billboards advertising 'buckle up for safety' slogans. He cruised as though he had all of his faculties, and Sleeper appreciated every moment of the ride. Not once did he have to latch onto the dashboard for dear life. Not once did his thoughts run to his life insurance policy.

Pulling into a quiet residential area, a beautiful country setting surrounded them. Not a soul was visible, but a few lights were on in each house. Sleeper asked, "How'd you find out where Bogart lives?"

"I plugged his name into an online computer, at a coffee house on Boylston Street. That way there's no trail as to who inquired. No problem at all."

Spanky pulled quietly to a stop at the corner of a reasonably lit cul-de-sac. He looked around for a moment, caught sight of their intended destination, then announced, "That's his house." He pointed. "Right over there. The white one, with the light next to the front door."

Capt. Bogart and his wife of forty years loved the serenity and tranquility of their peaceful home, now that their two children have moved out on their own. Their daughter, the eldest, was married only ten months ago, and lives with her husband just a few towns over. She returns frequently to give her mother a hand around the house, because of her degenerating arthritis. The son is a senior at Boston College, studying electrical engineering.

The house is medium in size, and there's plenty of open land around the estate to keep the neighbors at a respectable distance. There were eight rooms in the house; three bedrooms, two whole baths, a living room, a library and a den.

There was a sensor light beside the front doorway, set to switch on automatically at sunset. It was fitted with a sixty-watt bulb emitting a soft incandescent glow of security, like the Oaks Bluff Watchtower at Nantucket Bay, in Cape Cod. It's the kind of light that the family members sat under at dusk, after suppertime, during the warm months to enjoy their after diner coffee. It's the kind of light that a young girl had her first kiss under, after her first boyfriend took her home from her first date; perhaps her junior prom. It's also the kind of light that allowed Capt. Bogart and his wife to spy on them, to make sure that they didn't get too carried away.

Spanky turned off the ignition and sighed thoroughly. He reached inside of his jacket and pulled out the gun fitted with the silencer. He looked it over, made sure it was ready for action. He ejected the clip, checked to see that it was fully loaded, then reinserted it into the butt of the gun. He pulled back the slide to make sure that a round was chambered. When he was sure that all of the 'T's' were crossed and the 'I's' dotted, he slid it into his jacket.

He reached into the backseat, grabbed a bag, brought it forward and gave it to Sleeper. "Luckily I knew your shoe size. Put these new sneakers on. I got them two sizes too big on purpose. They'll be looking for someone taller than you." He explained, saying only, "Footprints."

It took Sleeper less than a minute to switch shoes. Before they got out of the car, Spanky told him, "Most importantly, don't touch anything on the outside of the house, and especially on the inside. Fingerprints!"

"Got it."

Without hesitation, both exited the car and approached Capt. Bogarts house. At the back of his mind, Spanky was still surprised that Sleeper was eager to get the whole thing over with. He tried to image what encouraged him, gave him reassurance. So much promise.

Nearing the house, under his breath, Spanky cursed the lamp glowing next to the front doorway. He lowered his head a few degrees to shade the upper area about his face, understanding that darkness was preferred mostly for one doing a diabolical deed in the middle of the night. It was Satan's false security blanket. A tainted blanket with many doubtful rips and suspicious holes torn all through it. It made one feel comfortably inconspicuous. Less guilty about the transgressions that they were about to commit.

Now standing at the door, they stared at each other in absolute silence for a lengthy period. Both gazed at the door, a threshold that would lead them to the darkest regions of their souls.

For a fleeting moment, Sleeper wasn't sure of whom he stood next to. However, he believed that whatever differences in behavior separated them, the next few minutes would place them in the same category of species, join them at the hip, bond them for life. He considered the darkness haunting Spankys shredded soul. Then his thoughts ran back to himself, and he searched desperately for something to balance his lopsided conscious. Searching drastically, he turned over every bit of fault he's ever had with himself in the past, to find a touch of sympathy to cast a shadow of doubt on the venture that they were about to embark upon. He was sure it would be a trip to an unexplored region in the back of his mind. To an area with a small room that has a big sign on a door marked 'HELL!' He had no doubt whatsoever.

They sighed simultaneously.

Spanky knocked on the door.

Less than a minute later, they heard footsteps nearing them from the inside the house. At that moment, Spanky placed his hand on the small caliber back-up pistol tucked in his right jacket pocket.

Whoever it was that came to the door, settled behind it for a moment. Maybe to tie the sash in their robe, or maybe to put their glasses on. Then someone moved the curtain away from the narrow stained glass trimming accentuating the doorway, and glanced out onto the doorstep.

It was Capt. Bogart.

He eyed them curiously for a moment, then both arms swung to the left to unlock and crack the door ajar. He stuck his head outside and announced, "Officers Sinclair and Knight. This is a rather strange visit, wouldn't you say?" He looked at his watch, insinuating the evenings late hour. He tilted his head upwards, peeped at them through the bottom of his bifocals.

This is a good sign, Spanky thought. He didn't look suspiciously at us. That means he's not onto us yet. He was most likely at Stoney's house all day, and just got in a short while ago. That means he hasn't read the book yet. This is gonna be a piece of cake. I just hope that that gotdamn book is in there somewhere.

Sleeper didn't respond. He figured he'd let Spanky do all of the talking, since he had the gift of gab. Spanky started, "Sir, I know it's late, and I know this may seem odd, but officer Knight and I stumbled across some very important information, that we thought may be crucial to your investigation into officer Brooks death. We were wondering if we can come inside, to talk to you about it for a few minutes." He said respectfully, "If you don't mind, sir." Spankys mannerism reigned supreme. It's how he got most people to trust him, just before he placed the knife into their back. You scratch my back, I'll claw yours.

When he spun his yarn, Sleeper always waited anxiously to see if the person who he was talking to would reject the story, or accept it entirely. It was like sticking his hand into a grab bag. Like potluck.

Solving a case was always the foremost thing on Capt. Bogarts mind. After learning of the attention-grabbing news, the late hour seemed irrelevant. It was like waving a side of beef in front of a starving tiger.

Last spring, Capt. Bogart had gotten so preoccupied in a double homicide investigation involving two children murdered by their parents, that he had completely forgotten about his marriage anniversary. His wife forgave him, but he knew that she'd keep the incident tucked away in the back of her mind, ready to be used as leverage during a dispute. Or in case she wanted something like a vacation, or a new diamond ring.

Capt. Bogart lowered his head, gazed at his visitors over the top of his glasses. His sight traveled curiously from Spanky to Sleeper. He tightened the sash wrapping his robe, then stepped to the side, and opened the door wide. "Gentlemen, I'm glad you're here. I need to talk to you about your friend, officer Brooks." He urged them to, "Please, come inside."

He welcomed them warmly, because he believed it was safe to do so. What could possibly go wrong? He thought. This is official business, and these were two veteran police officers. Men in the same profession as I.

Upon entering the house, Sleeper released a faint sigh of satisfaction, as if they had already accomplished what they had come for. Capt. Bogart closed the door behind them, then led his guests into the living room. He pointed to couch. "Have a seat, right over there. I'll be back in a minute or two. I just left the crime scene at officer Brook's house a half hour ago, and I haven't had dinner yet. I had Chinese take out earlier, but you know how fast that goes. I get these miserable cramps when I'm hungry. Can't think straight or anything. I was in the middle of fixing a sandwich. Would either of you like something to drink, or eat?"

"No thank you, sir," Spanky replied. He sat in a chair opposite the couch that Sleeper had just sat on.

"No sir," Sleeper said.

Capt. Bogart held out his hands, showing empty palms. "Anything at all?"

They replied simultaneously, "No, sir."

"Okay." Capt. Bogart pointed the index finger of his right hand to the ceiling. "I'll be right back." He left the room.

Just as he did, Spanky spanned the immediate area, searching drastically. He was sure the diary was somewhere near. So close that it gave him goose pimples in just thinking about it.

Observing his actions, Sleeper whispered, "What're you doing?"

He whispered angrily, "Don't ask me a dumb ass question like that! What'n the hell did we come out here for, you fricken moron? I'm looking for that damn book. I swear, if you start pulling a Stoney number on me," he flashed a shaking tight fist, idling knuckles, "I'll break every gotdamn bone in your body. Starting with your head."

Sleeper got the message. "Sorry. I forgot."

"Stop apologizing, and start looking. We don't have all night. We've wasted enough time already. We've should've been in and out of here by now."

He did forget. His mind became overfilled with so much uneasiness about what they might have to do, that his thought process took it on the lam. He was so nervous that he had difficulty remembering his own name. While both looked thoroughly for the diary, he became more nervous. Clusters of sweat puddled about his brow as he listened to the pounding of his fearful heart fill his ears with a deafening pandemonium. He looked in between the cushions on the couch that he was sitting on and saw the binder of Stoneys book. He froze in place, his heart ceased to lob another beat. He felt every nerve ending in his body tingled with static electricity. He became greatly confused with anxiety, thinking, If I tell Spanky that I found the book, then we'd have to kill Captain Bogart. If I say nothing, and Captain Bogart reads it, then our lives will be over. Andrew! Damn, he's got it real bad. I don't want to end up like that. Hell no! I ain't going out like that. The hell with that shit! My wife will get a new husband. My son will never get to know me. He'll start calling somebody else daddy. My self-respect, gone. I'll be marked for life. Andrew!

Suddenly, a tiny voice bellowed persuasively from the inside. 'Take the book, you bumbling idiot! Show it to Spanky, quick!

He reached down and pulled it out, then stared at it, as if it were the keys to heaven or hell. He didn't know.

Spanky noticed him holding the book, ran to him and snatched it from his hands. "Gimme that, you fucken moron! What'n the hell do you think this is, a staring contest?" He tucked the book securely in the back of his pants waist. "Sitting there posing for animal crackers, like we have all the fricken time in the world." He reached inside of his jacket, pulled out the gun fitted with the silencer.

Sleeper saw the gun and stuttered frightfully, "S-S-Spanky, we got the damn book, and he hasn't read it yet. "His eyes implored, "C-C-Couldn't we just leave?" He felt like he was pleading the case of the century. Bigger than the Lindberg kidnapping. Bigger than Watergate. Bigger than O.J.

Spanky leaned toward him, peered angrily into his eyes. "Captain Bogarts no fool. Once he realizes it's gone, and he knew that we were the only ones who were here, he'll come to us with very embarrassing questions about Stoney death. Questions that can lead to a fucken indictment."

"An indictment for hustling only. We can bounce back from that."

"Just like Andrew did?"

"No. But we don't even know what happened to Stoney. There's no way that anyone can tie us to anything that he might've gotten himself involved in."

"We can't take any chances on that. Once they start snooping up our asses, if they find anything suspicious, it'll be just like what Andrew said. After they get the ball rolling, they'll tie us in on a whole bunch of other shit that has nothing to do with anything." He released the safety switch on the gun idling behind his back, then waited for Capt. Bogart to reenter the room.

Each passing second felt like an hour. The loud ticking sound emitting from Sleepers watch had slowed to a deafening click … CLICK! … **CLICK!!** Sitting on the edge of the couch, he gaped steadily at the gun, his adrenalin raced out of control. Somehow, the silencer appeared more frightening than the gun. It made the gun look mysteriously devious, more dangerous than others not fitted with silencers. Not only did it mute the sound of the gunshot, but it silenced the death as well.

Hearing Capt. Bogart approach the living room, Sleeper held his breath. Frozen like a statue. Any moment now …

Hearing the footsteps also, Spanky raised the gun and aimed it toward the doorway. He stood firm, as though it was business as usual, only target practice. It always puzzled Sleeper as to how Spanky could do such a thing, without feeling the slightest remorse. Like the time when he shot an unarmed suspect in the knee, merely because he didn't want to pay up. Since he allowed these events to unfold before him, he was beginning to understand.

Feeling totally immobilized, a thought of redemption crossed his mind. He felt as though he wanted to jump out of his chair and make an attempt to stop what was about to happen. Nevertheless, he didn't move a muscle. Could it work, he wondered. I'll grab the gun from him, and wrestle it away, to show Capt. Bogart that I was trying to save his life. I'll be labeled a hero. For the extenuating circumstances surrounding the entire ordeal, instead of kicking me off the force, they'll give me an early retirement. But, what if I fail? Spanky will feel that I turned against him, and he'll try to kill me too. No. No. I'll just sit right here and …

At that exact moment, Capt. Bogart entered the room, stood in the doorway and figured immediately that something was wrong. Holding a glass of milk in his left hand, a plate with a sandwich on it in the other, his mind went blank with absolute shock. He stared at the silencer on the gun that Spanky held aimed at him, then searched for words to express his dreadful surprise.

Before any solid ideas of what he should do came to his mind, at least one that he'd act on, Spanky pulled the trigger several times, and they heard what sounded like a vipers' hiss. "PHSST. PHSST. PHSST."

With every shot fired, Sleeper jerked in his seat, as if the bullets had ripped through his chest. The first shot sealed Capt. Bogarts fate, killed him. The second shot confirmed it. The third shot was for extra measure. Spanky would've pulled the trigger a forth time, but he ran out of reasons to keep firing.

The bullets tore through Capt. Bogarts body, and he jerked backwards dynamically. Looked like someone pounded him with a battering ram. His bifocals flew from his face, and he dropped the items he carried. Chances are, he was dead even before he hit the floor. His eyes never opened again to span the room in search of answers as to why it happened.

Moments after his collapse, the blood gushed from his open wounds, puddled around his body. As it filled his lungs, a moment of life returned briefly and he gurgled a few incomprehensible words, nothing which made sense. "Arahg—zzzpt."

He coughed twice, hurling spats of blood into the air. A flow of blood poured from the corner of his mouth, streamed toward his left ear, absorbed into his hair.

Spanky couldn't make heads or tails out of what he was saying. He didn't want to. He didn't care. It was irrelevant to the mission.

Sleeper realized what Capt. Bogart asked over and over again. **Why?**

Finally, Spanky lowered the still smoking weapon slowly. Although it took less than one second to kill Capt. Bogart, they waited for the gravity of the moment to subside. It was slow in coming, dragged its feet. Everything moved in slow motion.

Seconds later, they were startled when they heard footsteps quickly descending a flight of stairs. They gawked curiously at each other in total silence, then heard a roughly sixty year-old woman ask, "Dear, are you all right?" Nearing the living room, she asked, "It sounded like you fell? Did you drop something?"

She arrived to the living room and saw her husband lying splayed on the floor, halfway in the doorway. Instantly, she became greatly alarmed, and her heart skipped a monumental beat. Since she didn't hear gunshots, she assumed that he might've had a heart attack. When she noticed the blood pooling around his body, her eyes pained with an intense heat. A weighty breath gushed from her body, seeming never to return.

She glanced to the strangers frighteningly, and wondered why they weren't doing anything to assist her husband. It was a few moments more before she realized that they were certainly not there to help. Staring as coldly as they were, she realized that they were responsible for her husband being as he was. On the floor. Dying. Maybe already dead.

She noticed the silencer fitted gun in Spankys hand, and every inch of her quivered wildly with fear. She inhaled deeply, prepared to release a thunderous scream. One that they were sure would wake up the entire community, and maybe a few neighboring towns. Before she could let the first syllable fly, Spanky raised the gun and fired. "PHSST. PHSST. PHSST."

Again, as if he had felt the blows himself, Sleeper twitched in his seat three times. Now, he felt completely numb. Especially his tongue. He felt dizzy, and the room spun out of control, as though he was amidst a perilous tornado. He could've sworn that he was going through an out of body experience, because he damn sure didn't want to be where he was—in Capt. Bogarts house, committing cold blooded murder.

He threw himself into a substantial denial, and imagined that he was safely at home with his wife and child. In the midst of doing something completely innocent. Like sitting in front of the television with her, while holding his sleeping son in his lap.

At who they guessed was Capt. Bogart's wife, the woman dropped to the floor and fell slump over Capt. Bogart's body. Because of her failing health, she died quicker. Her blood puddled about her body, coated her husband, mixed with his. It filled her lungs and stomach quickly, and she expelled a weird bubbling sound. Spanky thought it strange that it sounded like a child blowing air into a glass of milk through a straw.

Releasing every muscle in her body, they noticed a wet spot growing in between her legs. All self-control dissipated. All signs of life, vanished. Long gone since written in the books that will be opened at the end of time, on judgment day

Starling them again, they heard a young lady ask worryingly while swiftly descending the stairs, "Mom! Dad! Is everything okay down here?" The Bogarts oldest child, their daughter, came into the room, looked at the two strangers, then saw her parents lying dead on the floor. Wobbling unsteadily on shaky knees, she cried hysterically, "M-M-Mom! D-D-Dad!" She looked at Spanky and Sleeper and cried hysterically, "What in the hell did you do to my pare ..."

Without hesitation, Spanky raised the gun and fired. "PHSST! PHSST! PHSST!"

The woman fell to the floor, a few feet from her parents, never took another breath. They were startled when they heard a newborn crying upstairs. They glanced at each other, Sleeper looked to the staircase landing. He remained fixated, thought it strange that the child sounded exactly like his son.

An endless amount of silence thrashed between them, drowned out the crying infant, filled the living room with a high-pitched shrill. Gawking at the dead bodies, since Spanky had never killed cold bloodedly before, he searched for an expression suitable for the moment. He decided to comfort himself by appearing featureless. It was the simplest emotion to grab a hold of. It was the cheap way out. Inexpensive; it didn't cost much. At least, not for the time being. Again, like using a credit card to buy something you couldn't afford. Enjoy now, pay later. After the interests incurred. Paying out more than what you're taking in.

Sleeper sat on the edge of the couch with anxiety hanging from the tip of his tongue. His eyes bucked open wide, his jaw hung low, his chin nearly resting on his chest. He'd seen death before, but never had it been so cold, free of any emotions. Never unflinching. Never so ruthless. Never so resolute.

Spanky closed his eyes tight, then opened them wide, attempted to erase a hideous vision swarming with his wickedness. It didn't work. How could he have thought it would have? He stuck the gun inside his jacket, and upon seeing Sleeper temporarily locked into a deep trance, he leaned toward him and shoved his shoulder repeatedly. "Wake up! We got what we came for. We're in the clear. No witnesses, no nothing. It's smooth sailing from here on." He ordered, "Com'on. Lets get out of here."

He sprinted to the front door. Half way there, he noticed that he didn't hear Sleepers footsteps trailing him. He turned around and witnessed him still sitting on the edge of the couch, staring at the dead bodies, looked just like a zombie. Perchance, what held his attention were the souls leaving the dearly departed. He could see them as plain as day. Looked like he was trying to offer an explanation as to why they did, what they had just done. The only thought that appeased him, was that he didn't pulled the trigger. The notion swelled quickly as a comfortable denial.

Spanky ran to him, wound up and slapped him hard across the face. **"WHAP!"** It knocked him off the couch, down onto the floor. He fired, "The hell are you doing, waiting for the Dover Police to get here? Get the hell up, and let's get the hell out of here. Before someone else comes downstairs."

Sleeper rubbed the right side of his face briskly. Overly nerved, his motor skills wavering, he finally stood upright. His movements were unsteady. Shaky. He tried to take a step and tripped over his two left feet, then fell to the floor. He fumbled over his words as well, "Yeah ... um ... all ... all right. All right."

He shook the moment off quickly, then climbed to his feet. Shaking off a moment of torrential chaos, he staggered once, twice, then stood firm, still unsure of any direction. Following closely behind Spanky, he couldn't rip his sight from the dead bodies. Hustling clumsily to the door, he bumped into several pieces of furniture along the way. The walking soon became manageable. Ripping his sight from the bodies was difficult to achieve. He felt them pulling at him. Summoning him. Holding him responsible. Making him accountable.

They passed a doorway leading to another room off to the side. It was the family room at one time, when the children stayed at home. Sleeper looked inside briefly and caught glimpse of a baby grand piano positioned in the middle of the floor. On it was neatly fashioned a collection of assorted family portraits, a dozen smaller framed photos placed around one huge family photo of Capt. Bogart, his wife, their two children, and their only grandson. The smaller photos were of their children's high school graduations. One of their daughters college graduation. One of Capt. Bogarts graduation from the police academy. One from when he received his college degree in criminal justice. Another of him on a platform, receiving a commendation for outstanding police performance, shaking hands with the commissioner. One of his wife's recent graduation from a community college. She had placed caring for her children before considering a career. The rest, several still photos of their only grandchild.

Staring absorbedly at the photos, he was beginning to understand the magnitude of the irreparable damage that had just been inflicted. Two generations of Bogarts had just been wiped out, within the blink of an eye. He knew an abundance of devastation would plant itself deep and be felt by many people near to the Bogarts. He was sure that their misery would be insurmountable. Their surviving family members would never get over it.

Had Spanky seen these photos, he would've thought, 'Hey! Rather you than me. Sorry about the blood stains we left on your living room floor, but I ain't going to jail for nobody.'

At the front door, he told Sleeper, "You better get your shit together, you hear me? When we walk out of here, we can't let anybody see us acting suspicious."

"I'm cool," he said timidly. Even he didn't believe what he had just said. He tried his damndest to control himself physically and emotionally. He straightened out his clothes and stuttered, "D-D-Don't worry about me." He sung weakly, "I-I-I-I-I can handle it." He looked like an elementary school boy, after having been caught looking up a girls dress.

"Yeah, right," Spanky said doubtfully. "I saw the way you were in there handling things."

"But I …"

"Don't tell me who you are. I already know. You're a combination Danzel Washington, Clint Eastwood and John Wayne, all rolled into one. Or better yet, Superman. Nerves of steel, and all that other bunch of fake bullshit." He paused, then stated, "I'm telling you for the last time. Get your shit together, and straighten up." He cleared his throat, then opened the door slowly. He whispered, "Act normal. Walk calmly to the car. Whatever you do, try not to call attention to yourself." He stuck his head outside and looked up and down the street, searching for anyone; late night strollers, dogs walkers or insomniacs. He saw no one. When he felt that the coast was clear, they left.

As they walked, Sleeper felt an overwhelming urge to turn back repeatedly and glance at the house. He heard voices whispering his name. Voices that grew louder the further he separated himself from the house. Because he wasn't looking where he stepped, he tripped over his feet and fell to the ground. In attempting to handle the turmoil they were amidst, his brain had difficulty sending walking impulses to legs.

Watching him lay splayed on the ground, Spanky whispered angrily, "Get the hell off the ground, you moron." After Sleeper climbed to his feet, he said calmly, "Look, everything's going smooth. A few minutes, and we'll be on our way. Away from this place, back in Boston. It's just like monopoly. We past 'GO', then collect two hundred dollars." He opened the car door and slipped inside. He picked up the screwdriver he had used to start the car, inserted it into the ignition, turned it, and the engine sprung to life.

As Sleeper entered from the passenger side, Spanky removed the book from his pants waist, then tossed it onto the gearshift console. Before he put the transmition into gear, Sleeper, from out of nowhere, slammed his right fist violently into the dashboard. "Dammit!"

"Hey!" Spanky alarmed. "The fucks the matter with you?" He clutched his chest, felt his pounding heartbeat. "You scared the shit out of me." He sighed. "Look … just stay cool, and everything will be all right." He then drove away.

Sleeper couldn't help but to think, *three people dead, and this asshole's telling me that everything's going to be all right. Dammit! I'll be glad when this fricken night's over.*

For the moment, he actually believed that his feelings about what had happened would be different in the morning. As if a good night's sleep would take care of everything. Set things straight, make everything all right. Don't worry. Don't fret none. Go home to your wife and child, get some shuteye. It's all in a good nights work. Capt. Bogart, his wife, and their daughter will be just fine in the morning. You only brutally gunned them down. Murdered them in cold blood, that's all. A few aspirins, a couple of bandages and they'll be okay in the morning. Anyone can get over this.

He realized that this was only wishful thinking, and had slowly came around to acknowledge their vicious actions. The repercussion always came later. Now, in thinking back, he realized that if he had it to do over again, he would've definitely sprang from the couch, then done something to stop Spanky. Now that the ramifications were climbing to fruition, he felt that he would definitely have done something to stop the carnage. *If* he had it to do all over again. If! As in should've, could've, would've.

Leaving the street, he turned around and looked through the rear window. He couldn't help but to believe that someone was watching their every move. That little peaceful area didn't seem so tranquil anymore. It plagued of freshly spilled blood and murder, and haunted of ghosts from just sent bodies.

His head fell back against the headrest, he shut his eyes tight. Minutes later, they were on the expressway, returning to Boston. Along the way, they tossed the new sneakers out onto the highway.

While Spanky drove, he reached to the console and picked up Stoneys book. He opened it somewhere toward the middle, thumbed through a few pages. Because he had to concentrate on driving, he could only glance sporadically at the pages, absorb bits and pieces of several paragraphs. He became highly disappointed by what he read, then slammed the book shut. He tossed it onto Sleepers lap. "Yeap! That's us, all right. That fool wrote down exactly what we did, damn near word for word." He cursed the book. "Manuscript my ass!" He cursed Stoney. "That son-of-a-bitch must've been crazy to write that shit down about hearing children's voices, a bunch of little crumb snatching boogas. That crazy bastard!" He cursed himself. "How in the hell did I ever get mixed up in this mess anyway? Fuck!"

Sleeper didn't hear a word he had said, because his mind had drifted. Staring out the window, he whispered plainly, "You killed all three of them. Just like that."

"Let's get something straight," Spanky corrected. "To express the term politically correct, the proper phrase is 'we!' Not me, mother fucker. *We* killed them!

You were there also, you chicken shit son-of-a-bitch!" He paused before he said, "If they come to get me, they'll take *us*. Isn't that what the book's all about?"

Searching for words to dispute, Sleeper decided not to respond, but focused solely on the book resting in his lap. He wanted to touch it. But for some reason, he couldn't bring himself to do so. He knew that they should have it, but didn't want to know that it was in their possession. Catch 22. An enigma. A real life conundrum. Riddle me this.

Suddenly, conflicting thoughts entered his mind and bombarded him from all sides. Feeling as if he was coming under attack, he took the easy way out. He emptied his mind and thought about nothing.

CHAPTER 32

▼

Exiting from the Mass. Pike, upon entering Boston, Sleeper frequented one of his hustling episodes. Unaware of what he was doing, he brought his hands to rest on the book. Feeling the texture of the leather, he felt that it was as soft as a newborn, but deadly. He shut his eyes briefly, traveled back to the week before, and discovered himself a few blocks from where Spanky lives. He stood huddled at a telephone booth, conducting Dixie Club business. He called one of his marks to initiate a hustle. It was three o'clock in the afternoon. He was on a lunch break.

After a man answered the phone, he cleared his throat, said groggily, "Hello." He sniffled twice. "Bobby here. Who's calling?" He gave another long sniffle. Not like a cold and flue sniffle. More like a cocaine addicts, runny nose sniffle. It sounded like he ingested cocaine on an hourly basis. For sure, Sleeper knew what he was into. No doubt. He noticed the wavering speech immediately, the long drawn extension of words. The man sounded like a stressed out paranoid alcoholic. The monkey often escaped its cage.

"Bobby? Bobby Slatter?"

"Yeah. Who's this?" He sniffled again, scratched the inside of his left arm. An area riddled grossly with heroin tracks. A few scabs loosed themselves and fluttered to the floor like black snowflakes.

"I'm new in town, from the west coast. San Francisco area, to be precise. I got your number from a friend. He says you're pretty good at what you do." Sleeper snickered "Said you have a hellova set of lungs on you."

Bobby sniffled, said smugly, "Well, you know. My reputation does precede me."

"I heard that you were so good, that I had to call to check you out. Are you available to come by sometime? You know, so we can get busy."

"Is the money right?"

"How's three hundred, for a half an hour?"

Bobby thought about it for a moment. "I think I can manage that." He sniffled. "By the way, who am I speaking to?"

"Who I am isn't important," Sleeper said, then decided to turn the tables. Because of the way the conversation was going, he felt disgusted with himself. Experiencing these ugly feelings, with not being able to lay them aside and play the hustle to get the maximum excitement, he realized that that was why Stoney was so good. Stoney would've kept going until he had the Bobby salivating like a dog in heat. "What's important is that I know where you were last Thursday night, at about ..." he paused for a long second to let the moment linger, prepared to unleash what was already on the tip of his tongue, "... ten thirty."

"Yeah, so." It hadn't come to him what the caller referred to.

Sleeper repeated the statement. This time, he emphasized, "At exactly *ten thirty*, Bobby."

Sleeper heard a crash. Bobby dropped the phone to the floor. Obviously, he was too shocked to bend down and retrieve it. Sleeper shouted into the phone, and Bobby heard the caller ask, "Hey! Are you still there?"

Hands trembling, he finally picked up the phone, brought it to his ear. After having some very disturbing details of what had happened the week before return to him, he stuttered, "S-S-So!" Throwing a tough guy image, he called Sleepers bluff. "Who the fuck is this? And what the hell do you want?"

"Well," he chuckled, "I just happen to have a piece of evidence that places you at a particular homicide scene. If I hand it to the authorities, I can guarantee that you'll be doing a natural. No parole, ever." He threw in lastly, "No more chirping birds for you, Mr. Fancy Pants. Mr. Liberace. Mr. Richard Simmons."

Bobby thought about the misplaced health insurance card that admits him into the local methadone clinic, but continued suspiciously. "Oh yeah. What kind of evidence?"

"It's a purple health center card, with your name and address on it. It also has traces of cocaine on it. I guess you and that deceased loans officer had a good old time. Didn't you?"

He didn't respond, but Sleeper could hear his nervous breathing.

"What happened?" Sleeper asked facetiously. "My guess is that when you two started to mix it up a little, he reached down in between your legs and discovered that little package. He found out that you weren't a woman," he laughed, "didn't he?" From doing some research, Sleeper discovered that the recent homicide scene had the exact same M.O. as an unsolved murder from a few months before. The dead man wore the same unusual colored lipstick, from kissing someone. Same as the loans officer. He had cocaine in his system, his penis was exposed and mutilated, and he was strangled to death. The authorities believed it was unlikely that a woman had committed the crime, because the perp must have been stronger than the victim. They believed that it was possibly a transvestite. Or a drag queen. "He found out that you were a homo, and didn't want anything to do with you? It's happened before, hasn't it? That makes two bodies, doesn't it?"

"Screw you!" Bobby blasted. "I don't know who this is, but you can kiss my ass. And screw those bastards too. They had it coming to them, the sleazy dumb fucks. I treated them good. Real fine, like a lady should. Then they up and told me to get lost, only because I didn't have the right equipment. They should've known better than to reject me like that. You don't get nobody half-way there, then tell them to get lost ..." Abruptly, Bobby stopped talking, after realizing he might've said too much, incriminated himself.

"Is that why you killed them?"

Bobby tried to recant. "I never said I did anything."

"Look, Bobby, for Christ sake. Ya gotta come up with something better than that. Ya putting me ta sleep with all this denial bullshit. I've got you flat busted. Luckily for you, I'm the only one who knows that it was you, because of the identification card you left behind. You didn't get nabbed for the first homicide, because your fingerprints aren't in the system. And yet, you left them all over both crime scenes. If I match the ones on the I.D. card that I stumbled across, to the ones at both crime scenes, then notify the authorities, you'll be going to prison for the rest of your life."

From hearing so much talk of fingerprints, homicides, and being sent to prison for the rest of his life, Bobby guessed, "You must be a cop."

"Could be. But what we should discuss is how we're going to patch things up."

"Huh? Patch things up? What are you talking about?"

"You robbed the loans officer of fifty thousand dollars, after you killed him. He was supposed to make a deposit earlier that day, but didn't. He had the bank deposit slips in his pockets, and the money never turned up anywhere. I believe you have it, or what's left of it. If you haven't already ingested it, or shot it in your veins." Bobby remained quiet. Sleeper continued, "But I'm not going to bust your chops about that. I only want half of what you've got, and you can keep the rest."

"Is that it? You want me to give you twenty-five thousand dollars, and you'll leave me alone? I'll never have to worry about this again."

"Of course not," Sleeper chuckled. "I also found out that you like to work the streets every now and then."

"So."

"So, from now on, you'll be working for me."

He became irate and yelled, "A pimp! I don't need no blood-sucking pimp. You no good piece of shit. You mother fu ..."

Sleeper cut him off, calming, "Tut tut now. Such language. All this cursing you're doing, I have virgin ears, ya kno. I'm a sensitive guy. I'll break down and cry on ya in a second."

On the other end of the line, he heard Bobby grinding his teeth down to the gums. He explained, "Every Friday, I want you to drop off a payment at the post office, down on Huntington Avenue. I'll expect the first one to be large, considering it'll contain the twenty-five grand that we spoke of. After that, you'd better work your little tush off to keep it coming, to keep yourself out of jail. I got a family to feed. The baby needs new shoes. The wife needs a day at the spa, and I need a vacation, and a new play station." He snickered, "You think you can manage that?"

"Suppose I don't want to go along with your little game. What's to stop me from getting out of town?"

"Listen, Bobby, you're a drug addict. You won't do too good on the road, hiding out in every small dirt town you accidentally happen upon, giving head on the run for discounts, because you won't have the time to haggle. This way, you can keep on being a perverted drug addict, without having to worry about when you're going to get nabbed to be sent to the big house. A life on the run is no good, and you know this. Dealing with drugs the way you do, it'll only be a matter of time before you'll hear the music," he sang, "Bad boy, Bad boy, whatchu gonna do? Whatchu gonna do when they come for you?"

He heard a submissive sign on the other end of the line, then instructed Bobby, "I'll give you the post office box number, and you'd better use it. If not, well, don't say that no ones never given you the opportunity to remain a free and perverted fool. I hope you have a pen, because the address and post office box number is ..."

*   *   *   *

Spanky pulled up to Sleepers apartment building, then put the car in park. When he noticed him daydreaming, he reached over and shoved him lightly. "Hey! Wake up, Sleep. We're at your apartment."

He looked around to see where he was, then said unenthusiastically, "Oh, yeah." He noticed his hands resting on top of the book.

Spanky ordered sternly, "When you get inside, you look at your wife and kid, then decide how much your freedom and reputation means to you. And think about Andrew. Then you destroy that piece of trash book in your lap, and be done with it. Take it out to the back porch, put it on the Hibachi, and burn it. Send it straight to hell! I don't ever want to see it again. You hear me?"

"Yeah. Yeah." He placed the book inside of his jacket, then got out of the car. He tossed inside, "I got it. As soon as I go inside, destroy it." With nothing more to say, he slammed the car door shut.

From inside of the car, Spanky shouted, "You asshole! What're you trying to do? Break the gotdamn door." He slammed the cars transmission into gear, then sped off into the night, grumbling, "Shit! This ain't my '69' mint Stang, but it is road worthy. Dual pipes, total racing package and all that good shit." He patted the dashboard gently, told the car, "Don't worry, baby. Papa's gonna take you home and buff you out a little. Maybe give you a drink of S.T.P.... some of that good shit." He paused, then finished with, "Then I'm gonna send your scrap ass to the bottom of the harbor."

*   *   *   *

When Sleeper entered the apartment, he noticed that all of the lights were off. All but a luminous glow emanating from the bathroom nightlight. By habit, he found his way through a short span of hallway, then to the couch in living room. He took a seat on the end of the couch, then switched on the lamp centering the end table. He pulled out the book, opened it, and began reading.

Ten minutes into the reading, he paused, amid a profound revelation. Something wasn't right. An awkward feeling crept under his skin, worked its way throughout his entire body, and his breathing grew rapid. Tense. Growing faint, he felt out of sync, as if traveling through a time tunnel. His next stop, the twilight zone.

Hands trembling, he flipped through more pages, accidentally ripped a couple. He searched zealously for something that he believed was missing. Something very crucial. He gushed frightfully, "Nooooooo! He didn't." He looked to the ceiling and cried, "Stoooneeeeeey, you bastard!" He released an unbridled fury that filled the apartment. "Nooooooo!!" He said, "Nothing—he, we did it for nothing." He lowered his head and cried ruefully. "Oh my God!"

Feeling his faculties slip away, his hands went numb. He dropped the book on the floor, then kicked it several feet away.

Hearing his rage, Elizabeth sprang from the bed and dashed to the living room. She stood in the doorway and stared at her husband for a long moment, took considerable note of his distraught condition. On a slow approach, she noticed the tears streaming down his cheeks. Believing that he was finally grieving the death of his long time friend, she asked distressingly, "Bruno, sweetheart. What's wrong?"

He didn't respond, only stared perplexedly out into nowhere.

Listening to his hyperventilated breathing, she thought that he was having an anxiety attack. She examined him closely, then realized that she had guessed wrong. She sat down next to him, cupped the back of his neck with her right hand. Feeling him tremble, her concern climbing, she asked, "Baby, you've got to tell me what's wrong?"

He didn't reply.

Several terrifying thoughts entered her mind. Is this because of Stoney? Did something happen on the stakeout? Was there a shooting? Did somebody get hurt?

She glanced to the floor, spotted the book, then wondered if his condition had anything to do with it. A sinister thought entered her mind, leaving a distasteful impression. Spanky!

She placed her left hand over his forehead and excited, "Bruno, you're burning up! You're running a temperature." She wiped the sweat from his brow. Approaching hysteria, she cried, "Bruno, you're starting to scare me. You've got to talk to me. Tell me what happened."

Thoughts of suicide filled his mind and incapacitated him extensively. Swelling inside of him was the strong desire to go somewhere, crawl in a corner, and die. He wanted to disappear. His face reflected strains of intense grief, and he had difficulty sucking in air past his pouting lips. His tear-filled eyes squinted an oriental expression. His fists were clenched so tight, that they nearly pierced the palms of his hands. He released his bubbling anger and slammed his fist onto the end table, breaking two of its legs, sending it crashing to the floor. He stomped his feet hard, sending shock waves throughout the floor, making the glass in the china cabinet shudder, as though the entire building experienced a minor tremor.

Elizabeth became terribly frightened for the violent outburst and scooted a few inches away. Her conscious yelled, 'CAUTION!' She leaned over, slid from the couch and fell to her knees, all while keeping her eyes on her husband. She picked up Stoneys book, thought nothing of it. She closed it, then placed it on the couch, less than a foot from her husband. The thought to look inside never entered her mind. A mere book could never cause that much turmoil, she believed.

For a few moments, she sat on the floor in front of him, attempting to rationalize with what was happening. Like barking up a tree stump, nothing made sense. Pointless. She implored, begging him to, "Talk to me, baby! Please, tell me what happened."

Still, no response.

She rose to her feet and paced nervously in front of him, chewing on the fingernails of her left hand. She stopped briefly, stared skeptically at him, wondering if his condition was created from some awful deed that he had initiated. She tightened the sash to her robe, folded her arms, and many controversial thoughts filled her mind. At the forefront was the secret bankbook that she had discovered while doing some spring-cleaning several years ago. It was hidden in the back of the closet, tucked in a shoebox. Quickly, her thinking went haywire. Blood money! Extortion! Hush money! Payoffs! The mob!!

She lowered her head in serious contemplation of many troubling scenarios, and paced again. This time, her pacing was more like a stiff marching. A though of what she should do made an attempt to squeeze its way into her head. Through the clusters of her sweltering frustration, nothing came to light.

＊   ＊   ＊   ＊

At Spankys apartment, he stepped out of his car, wondering precariously about Sleeper. Out of the blue, a frightful thought popped into his head and scared the hell out of him. Delivered the shakes. "Wait a minute," he said to himself. "What in the hell am I doing?" I gave the book to Sleeper, he thought, and told him to destroy it. I must be getting as crazy as Stoney. I must be out of my ever-loving cotton-picking mother fucken mind. Damnit! This insanity shit must be spreading among the troops. I gotta watch myself, because I damn sure can't rely on him to do get things done. He's a bungling fool. An idiot! The way he acted out there in Dover, I should've known better. I gotta go back to his place and make sure that that damn diary is past history.

With the thought of the entire situation blowing up in his face, he shuddered grimily. He jumped into his '69' Stang, slammed the door shut. He turned on the ignition and rammed the shift stick into first gear. Driving like a madman, he returned to Sleepers apartment. Tires screeching, peeling rubber, almost side swapping several cars along the way. His determination, fueled by his paranoia, drove him to complete the sequence. His determination, fueled by his paranoia, drove him damn near insane. His determination, fueled by his paranoia, would not let him rest easy, until all loose ends were tied. *All* loose ends. Just like his Uncle Boomer had warned him.

*   *   *   *

He arrived at Sleepers apartment less than twenty minutes later. He jumped out of the car and ran into the apartment building with only one thought in his mind. Getting his hands on, and then destroying the diary. He leaned on the buzzer incessantly, then waited impatiently for a response. With sensing the urgency of the visitor, Elizabeth came to the door swiftly. She pressed the talk button on the intercom system. "Yes?"

"It's me, officer Sinclair. I need to talk to Sleeper. Can you let me in?"

Maybe he can help Bruno, she thought. Maybe he can tell me what happened while they were out on that so-called stakeout.

She pressed the buzzer, it opened the main door to the apartment building. Seconds later, Spanky was at the front door to the apartment. Not seeing it open, he knocked several times.

On the other side of the door, she looked into the peephole and stared at his antagonistic expression, then became afraid to open the door. She asked warily, "What do you want, Robert?"

He wondered why she was hesitant to open the door. He noticed the apprehension in her voice. "Mrs. Knight, I have to see Bruno. Is he here?" The more time that fell in between his not having his hands on the book, the more his anxiety mushroomed.

She looked to the floor concernedly, then to the ceiling, stalling, thinking of an original idea. She told him, "I'll open the door in a minute, Robert. I ... I have to get my robe. I'll be right back in a minute."

She already had it on, but needed time to decide whether or not she should let him into their home. Or should she call someone of a higher authority—maybe his boss. His showing up unexpectedly was very suspicious. She didn't know what to do. The question standing out in her mind mainly was, why was her husband so distraught? She had to know what happened.

Where's Sleeper, he wondered. Why didn't he come to the door? He just went into the apartment a half hour ago. Unless he's on the back porch, burning that damn book. Then again, I wonder.

Ten seconds later, he grew more impatient, then knocked on the door again. This time, much harder. He heard the bolt retract into the lock. She opened the door and fired, "Get your ass in here!"

He stood in the doorway for a moment, surprised, and a little confused. He wasn't sure of what to make of her heated attitude. Now what? he thought. I'm getting this shit from all sides tonight.

He stepped precariously into the apartment, looked everywhere. "Where's Sleeper?"

She grabbed him by his jacket sleeve and yanked him through the threshold, into the apartment. She dragged him forcibly through the dimly lit short span of hallway, to where Sleeper was sitting, in the living room. Not focusing on his surroundings, he accidentally knocked over the wooden coat rack. The head of the coat rack crashed into the fifty-gallon fish tank, and shattered the glass on one side. Moments later, goldfish and other tropical fish were flopping around the immediate area like an assortment of large Mexican jumping beans.

"Look at what you made me do," he told her.

She ignored the accident with the fish tank entirely, having more pressing matters in mind. They arrived to the living room, and both stood in front of Sleeper, observed his almost comatose state. He was a hog's breath away from sliding into shock. He was somewhere off the coast of Algiers, floating in limbo, without a life preserver. Elizabeth shouted irately, "Look at him, Robert! He's been acting like this ever since he came home. He won't say anything. He just sits there." She faced Spanky, pointed her finger in his face. "I know that you know what happened, because you were with him. Tell me what happened. And dammit, Robert Sinclair, don't you lie to me."

He stared confusedly at Sleeper, his head twisted slightly to the right. He whispered, "What the fu …" He noticed Stoneys book, and his eyes darted a cold disdain for it. He glanced to Elizabeth, then back to Sleeper. Again, his eyes came to rest on the book. Again, if he had heat vision, like Superman, the book would've exploded into a ball of fire moments ago.

He looked at Sleeper once again. "Is he … Is he gonna be okay?"

She threw back at him, "That's a hellova stupid question, Robert." She shouted in his face, "Look at him! Just look at him! He's just sitting there, like a bump on a log. What kind of a stakeout did you two go on, that would leave him in this condition? Or was it a stakeout at all?"

"I don't understand," he said convincingly. "I just dropped him off here a short while ago. He was fine then."

"Something's had to have happened since then" she said. "I've been trying to figure it out. So far, nothing. Now tell me, Robert, without all the extra crap that you usually attach to simple explanations." She spat at him, "what in the hell happened out there?"

He ignored the question and faced Sleeper. Peering into his eyes, he joshed lightheartedly, "Hey, Sleep, old buddy." He got down on one knee, then snapped his fingers in front of his face. "Hey, Sleep. You in there?"

Sleepers eyes rolled slowly to meet his. He wept neurotically, explaining, "Stoney ... he didn't tell. He didn't tell." He laughed hysterically, "Don't you see, Spanky. He didn't let us down. Stoney's really is our friend. And those poor innocent people out in Dover, oh my God, Spanky, it was for nothing. It was all for nothing."

"What in the hell are you babbling about?" he asked. Feeling that Sleeper was having a fit of delusion, like what Stoney had experienced, he grabbed his shoulders and shook vehemently. "Wake up, Sleep! You gotta start making some sense out of what you're saying."

His eyes rolled to the book. He placed his hand on it, thinking, I thought I told him to burn this trash. Dammit! I knew I shouldn't have trusted him to get rid of it. What in the hell is he trying to pull?

Seeing his hand on the book, Elizabeth spouted, "That book! It's got something to do with that book, doesn't it?"

At that moment, they heard the baby crying in the nursery. Spanky picked up the book, and she snatched it from his hands. "Let me see that thing." She cracked it open, flipped through a few pages. "I bet its all in here."

Spanky sprang to his feet and snatched the book from her hands, then pushed her several feet away. "This is none of your business!" he fired. "Why don't you go take care of that yapping kid?"

She took several insecure steps backwards, asking, "What's in that book, Robert? Payoffs? Names, dates and places?"

"Nothing," He returned. "It's just a stupid book."

The baby's crying grew louder. She left the room and dashed to the nursery. She returned less than fifteen seconds later, carrying her son. Patting him on his back, she charged Spanky, "You bunch of no-good crooks! I had a feeling that something like this was going on. All the times that Bruno ran out in the middle of the night, I just knew it! That secret bank book I found in the back of the closet, it's all a part of the same shit." Cradling her son, she said, "Just a book, huh! I know there's a hellova lot more to it than that."

Having the book safely in his possession, Spanky felt relieved. With nothing more to say, he marched to the front door. Stepping over the broken glass and fish, he told them, "I ain't got no time for this bullshit." He looked over his right shoulder, peered at Sleeper. "I'll be back to check up on you tomorrow ..." he said snidely, "... old buddy!"

She watched him leave, and over the sound of her crying child, she threw at his back, "Don't ever come back to this house again! You hear me, Robert Sinclair? Don't ever come back here again." She ran behind him, carefully stepped over the fish and broken glass, then slammed the door shut. She ran to the telephone.

She sat in a recliner, pressed the speed dial, called Capt. Winslow. In most emergencies, or when something was wrong with Sleeper, he was the first person that she got in contact with. He made her feel like she was talking to her father. It was a deep comfort.

The phone rang four times before someone picked up and cleared their throat. A voice said groggily, "Captain Winslow here. And at this hour, it better be good."

Being highly excited, she spoke rapidly. "Captain Winslow, this is Elizabeth Knight. Officer Bruno's Knights' wife. Something's terribly wrong with Bruno, and I don't know what to do. He came into the house just a short while ago, from some kind of a stakeout that he went on. Now he's acting like he's been traumatized from going through hell knows what. Right now, he's just sitting on the ..."

He interrupted, "Whoa! Whoa! Slow down, Elizabeth. You're going so fast that I can't take it all in. I guess my ears are still asleep. Once again, start from the beginning. This time, run it a little slower. I almost missed everything you said. First, I have an important question. Are you and the baby okay? I hear him crying in the background."

"Yes, we're okay."

"Good. Now tell me about Bruno. What's his condition like?"

She glanced at her husband, became panic-stricken and cried, "I don't know. He's just sitting there. He won't talk to ..." she whined, "... meeeeee."

"Is he sick or something?"

She sniffled. "I don't think he's sick. He's acting like a zombie. I think something happened. Something horrible. I don't know what, and he won't tell me. He won't say anything."

He hesitated for a moment, thinking. "Is there anyone else there, with you, at your home?"

"No. Just me, Junior and Bruno. Although, Robert Sinclair was here just a few minutes ago. But then he left."

He sounded surprised. "You say officer Sinclair was there?"

"Uh-huh."

"What did he want?"

"He wanted to talk to Bruno."

"That's it? He just wanted to talk to him?"

"Yes. Since Bruno didn't say anything, he took a book that was here, then left."

He listened to the fear in her trembling voice, then warned her to, "I want you to listen very carefully to what I have to say. Don't leave the house. And most importantly, don't open the door for anyone. Especially for officer Sinclair, if he should return. I'm on my way. I should be there in about twenty minutes, or less."

Feeling a little better, her crying faded. "Okay."

"And make sure the front door is locked."

She sniffled. "All right."

"Ill see you shortly".

*   *   *   *

Capt. Winslow's wife was lying next to him, took in bits and pieces of the conversation that he just had. She rolled over, yawned, and asked sleepily, "Another emergency?"

"I think so." He yawned., opened his eyes wide. "One right after the other."

"You think it has something to do with officer Brook's murder?"

He slipped into his pants, neglecting to remove his pajamas. He pulled the zipper up. "Could be. But sweetheart, you know I'm not supposed to talk to you about cases like this. Everything's confidential until ..."

She cut him off, "Confidential smontidential." Yawned again. "It's all alien to me. Just give me a call when you can. And if there's more than one hooligan, make sure you call for backup. All right, honey?"

"Sure, sweetheart. I'll do that if the occasion arises. And I'll give you a call when I get a chance. Now, go back to sleep. You know how you are when you don't get at least a solid eight hours of rest."

"You make sure you put on that heavy vest thing that stops the bullets."

"Sure, sweetheart. I'll bring it along."

He disliked wearing his bulletproof vest. Especially during the summer months. It weighed over fifteen pounds, and made him feel as though he wore a short mink coat, in the middle of the Sahara Desert.

Less than five minutes later, he was completely dressed, and on his way out the front door.

*   *   *   *

Twenty minutes later, he had arrived at the Knights' residence. Elizabeth was in the nursery, placing her son into his crib. When she heard the shrill of a siren, she dashed to the front door and opened it. Seconds later, Capt. Winslow rushed into the apartment, and spotted the dead fish lying scattered around the immediate area. "What hap ..." Remembering what she had told him over the phone about Spankys deteriorating physical condition, he changed the subject abruptly and asked, "Where's officer Knight?"

She led him through the short span of hallway, then pointed to the couch in the living room and whined, "There he is!"

He asked concernedly, "Is the baby okay?"

She nodded wearily. "I put him in his crib. He went back to sleep a few minutes ago. He woke up when the coat rack accidentally fell over, and crashed into the fish tank. It must've frightened him."

"As long as he's okay," he said. He approached Sleeper worriedly, looked into his eyes, and discovered an evil that he was sure would develop into a horrid tale of illicit repugnance. He searched immediately for answers on his face, even before he asked questions.

Sleeper sat trembling, staring out into nowhere with a dazed and distant expression. Sweat poured liberally from his forehead, covered his face copiously, and he mumbled what sounded like a rare Cantonese dialect.

Capt. Winslow came even closer. Only a few feet away, he leaned over, to only inches from his face. "Officer Knight?"

There was no response.

"Officer Knight. You want to tell me what happened?"

Sleeper looked into his eyes and babbled, "Stoney! He ... He didn't tell. Don't you see, Captain? He's my friend. I ... I knew he wouldn't let us down. I just knew it. And those people ... oh my God, those poor people. They didn't have to die."

Capt. Winslow stared at him for a moment longer, trying to figure out what he meant. Thinking about Stoney, he though his condition seemed familiar. He told her, "He's acting like officer Brooks did." He looked to the ceiling and clenched his fists, highly frustrated. "If it's the last thing I do, I'll get to the bottom of this."

She sat on the couch, a foot from her husband. Staring at him, she asked Capt. Winslow, "Is my husband going to be all right?"

He stood upright. "I don't know, Elizabeth. I honestly can't answer that. He seems to be in some kind of shock." He sighed exhaustively. "Dammit! Where's the telephone?"

She reached to the other side of her, and found the cordless phone lying on the couch. She handed it to him.

"I have to call an ambulance," he said. "There's no telling what might happen to him, if we don't get him some help immediately."

He punched a few numbers. "This is Captain Winslow of the Boston Police. This is a code four-eighty-two." Which meant, after taking the person in for observation, hold him until further instructions by the authorities. "I need a bus at 126 Birch street. Pronto!" He paused. "Officer Bruno Knight." He paused again. "Third floor, apartment number three." After terminating the call, he gave the phone to Elizabeth, telling her, "They should be here in about ten minutes." Taking everything into account thus far, he paused in contemplation. "On the phone, you mentioned something about a book that officer Sinclair took with him, when he left. What'd it look like?"

"It was brown, leather encased. It didn't have any writing on the cover."

He held up his hands to simulate the overall size, from corner to corner. "Was it about this big?"

"Yes. I think so."

"And about an inch thick?"

She nodded. "Uh-huh."

Stoneys manuscript, he thought. There's got to be a connection between that, Sleeper, Spanky, and what's going on. But, I thought Capt. Bogart had possession of it. If it's the same book, I wonder how Sinclair and Knight got their hands on it.

Many questions came to mind concerning Capt. Bogart. Just to be sure, he asked again, "Are you sure that that's what the book looked like?"

Again, she nodded. "Yes. And when I tried to look into it, Spanky wouldn't let me. He got aggressive, acting like it was something sacred. I bet all of this has something to do with that damn book. Including Stoneys death."

"You could be right."

"Aren't you going to put out a dragnet on Robert Sinclair?"

"A what? Oh, you mean an 'all points bulletin.'"

"Yeah."

He pondered the though. "No. I don't want to do that. We don't even know if he did anything wrong yet. Besides, if I did that, it might scare him into doing something drastic. I want to catch him by surprise. If he knows I'm onto him, he might try to destroy the book. It may contain evidence about what's been going on. Something tells me that the crucial answers we're looking for, are in that book." He sighed again. "I'm going out to Dover, Mass. Most importantly, if officer Sinclair calls to inquire about Sleepers condition, tell him that you called an ambulance, and they came and took him away. Another thing, don't tell him that I came by. You got that?"

She nodded. "All right."

He rose to his feet and approached the door. Half way there, he instructed her to, "Keep this door locked." He stressed, "And don't let anyone in here, except for the E.M.T.'s."

Seconds later, he was gone. She peeked through a set of Venetian blinds facing the street, watched him peel away into the night. Speeding recklessly, he drove like a maniac on a rampage. The blinding lights on top of his cruiser flashed intermittently, his ear-piercing siren whined aloud, alerting drivers to get the hell out of his way.

As he drove, more questions cluttered his mind. Soon, a ball of confusion filled his head, surmounted with a great uncertainty of the next few hours. He searched for answers to illicit going-ons buried deep within the department's code of ethics, the blue wall of silence. Answers that may be found by digging and prying into forbidden areas; personal and sacred space. Answers that might be tossed aside, to be later explained as a possible figment of someone's eerie imagination. Then maybe, even the truth will be cast off as a hoax. As some hoaxes are man made.

*   *   *   *

Almost an hour later, at one o'clock in the morning, he had arrived at Capt. Bogarts home. Upon seeing a few lights on the inside, at this late hour, he assumed that someone was out of bed, up and about. He glanced in through the front windows briefly, but saw no one. He went to the front door, rang the doorbell a few times, then waited impatiently for a response.

After a few moments, he grew more impatient. He knocked on the door, and accidentally pushed it ajar, it was unlocked. He pushed it open a little wider, then stuck his head inside and looked around. Someone has to be here, he figured. The door was unlocked, the lights are on. Unless …

He yelled, "Hello! Captain Bogart! Mrs. Bogart! Anyone here?"

He waited a few seconds.

There was no response.

Suddenly, a dangerous sensation tingled throughout his body, sent up a red flag. He pushed the door open and crept inside. Moving stealthily, an eerie silence filled his ears, throttled his heart. He pulled out his gun, and removed the safety. He pulled back the slide and chambered a round. He gave another attempt at making the occupants aware of his presence by yelling, "Hello! Is there anyone here?"

Not hearing a response of any kind, he proceeded to give search. With his gun held up in front, ready to shoot, prepared to take life, he tiptoed through the house. After entering the living room, he looked to the floor, and fell shocked at the sight of three dead bodies laying in a pool of blood. Two people, a man and woman, one slumped over the other. A third body, a young woman, a few feet away.

He succumbed to a feeling of helplessness, and began to weaken. Frozen on a breath of fear, he felt like someone had jabbed his eyes with a pair of knitting needles. Trying to catch his breath, he felt like his lungs were attempting to force themselves through his mouth. He realized quickly that the male was Capt. Bogart. Assuming, the woman slumped over him must be his wife. The young woman, having similar facial features, he was sure that she was their daughter.

He snapped his head a few times to revive himself of the horrendous sight, trying to stay alert for what he might run into. Maybe the perp, or perps, who committed this vile and unthinkable act, were still in the house.

Keeping this in mind, he checked the bodies for vital signs. To no avail, all three were dead. Rigor mortis had began to set in. Taking note of the powder burns, he figured that the shooter had to be no more than a few feet away. The assault was up close and personal. Capt. Bogart was caught with his guard down. He must have known his attacker.

Damnit! Capt. Winslow thought. Three dead bodies! I have to check to see if there's anyone else in here. Other family members, or the preps.

Listening to the sound of his heart beat fill his ears, a distraction, he remained quiet and searched the house thoroughly. As he walked, he cursed his squeaking shoes. Every thirty seconds, he pulled off his fogged spectacles, then wiped them clean. Although the house was very quiet, the presence of the dead bodies blasted **'PROCEED WITH CAUTION!'**

While on the second floor, he crept into one of the bedrooms at the end of the hall, and noticed a crib in the far right hand corner. He approached quietly, looked inside, and to his dreadful surprise, discovered an infant sleeping soundly. He cringed miserably. The child couldn't have been more than a few months old.

He observed it for a moment, to make sure that it was alright, unharmed. Feeling satisfied that it wasn't harmed, he continued his search throughout the house.

Less than fifteen minutes later, after completing a thorough search of the entire house, including the basement and garage, he made his way back to the living room. Standing over the dead bodies, he spanned the immediate area, in case there was some detail, or piece of evidence that he might've missed. He found the cordless telephone and dialed 911.

Seconds later, an operator answered robotically, "911 emergency. This call is being recorded. What is the nature of your …"

He cut her off and huffed, "This is Captain Winslow of the Boston police department. I'm at Captain Bogart's house, in Dover, and there's been a multiple shooting. Getchor people over here," he shouted, "now!"

"Is the person still alive??"

"No." He stated sadly, "I'm pretty sure they're dead."

After terminating the call, he sat on the couch, and removed his bifocals. He wiped the sweat from his brow with the back of his right forearm, imagining the magnitude of the chaos that would soon arrive at the front door. Staring at the dead bodies, the pieces of the puzzle slowly connected themselves. At that moment also, three names planted themselves firmly in his mind like a pulsating migraine. Officers Robert Sinclair, Bruno Knight and Stoney Brooks. Spanky, Sleeper and Stoney. He also wondered about the significance of Stoneys manuscript, and the role that it might have played in initiating the Armageddon in Dover.

*   *   *   *

Less than a few minutes later, Capt. Winslow was startled when he heard screaming sirens approach the house. He rose to his feet and hustled to the front door. Even before he got there, Capt. Bogarts second in command, Detective Sloan, the officer who found the diary, came barreling into the house. He started to ask Capt. Winslow, "Where's Captain Bo ..." Abruptly, he caught sight of the three dead bodies, and rushed to them. Too devastated to speak, as the room became congested with many detectives, police officers, E.M.T.'s and firefighters, he stood over the bodies, unmoving. A gorge of horror could easily be seen on his face, squeezing his heart devastatingly.

After the living room became crowded to its capacity, Detective Sloan managed to say unbelievably, "Captain Bogart, his wife, and their daughter ... dead!"

"I don't believe this shit!" another detective angered.

A police officer angered, "Somebody killed the boss, his wife, *and* Debra?"

"Naw, this shit ain't happening," someone said in straight denial. "No fucken way!"

Several others made similar statements.

A mass of anger swallowed Detective Sloan completely, and he became tensed, enraged with extreme anxiety. He turned slowly to face Capt. Winslow, and approached him. Discharging sputtering breaths through his tightened jaw, he spat wrathfully, "What psychotic sick son-of-a-bitch did this?" His eyes fired a vicious contemptuousness that Capt. Winslow felt all the way down to his frigid bones. Detective Sloan wanted to reach out, grab him, and beat the answers out of him. He felt he would've been wholly satisfied in doing just that.

Abruptly, the room fell silent to the detectives question. Capt. Winslow felt the room shrink around him, accusatory stares fired from all sides. He looked to the floor, then sighed severely. He removed his bifocals, steamed them with a short breath, then pulled out a handkerchief and wiped them clean, all while returning their stares. He inhaled deeply, then announced regrettably, "Gentlemen, I'm just as confused as you are. However, what I do know, is that we have a long evening ahead of us. In this case, if we pool our resources, I think we can find all of the answers that we'll be looking for. And you might want to get someone from children's services over here. There's an infant upstairs, sleeping, in a crib in one of the bedrooms. The child was unharmed, thank God." He told Detective Sloan, "I think we should go into another room to talk, you and I. There, I'll give you my hypothesis as to why I think these three homicides are connected to the demise of one of my officers. Officer Brooks." With no further words, Detective Sloan led Capt. Winslow into another room off to the side, where they talked for at least fifteen minutes.

*   *   *   *

After Capt. Winslow gave Detective Sloan his theory in its entirety, he pushed further into his chair. An alarming thought came to mind, leaving him to feel an abundance of uneasiness. Realizing how far Spanky had already went, gave him a good idea of how far he might go. It gave him a clear indication of what his next move might be. He mumbled, "Dammit! I must be out of my mind. What in the hell am I still doing here?"

He pulled out his cell phone, then dialed Sleepers telephone number. Detective Sloan waited patiently, in hopes to gather more information by what he might overhear. He stared at Capt. Winslow skeptically, wondering if he might've deliberately withheld crucial pieces of evidence, because the officers in question were under his command.

With each unanswered ring, Capt. Winslow's frustration grew more intense. After the phone rang eight times, he became distressed. Unsuccessful in attempting to contact Elizabeth left him thinking, She probably didn't pick up because she might've thought that it was Spanky.

With a heavy grunt, he sprang from the chair and dashed to the doorway, telling Detective Sloan hurriedly, "I have to leave! I know how important capturing the perpetrators means to you, so I'll give you a call as soon as I can."

Before he could pass through the doorway leading into the living room, Detective Sloan caught up to him, then latched securely onto his right arm, seeming never to release. He explained resolutely, "Where do you think you're going? You're not supposed to leave, until we say so. You've forgotten that you're in our jurisdiction, to be subjected to our procedures."

Everyone stopped talking briefly, stared at the two standing in the doorway. All cheered internally, the solemn challenge became intense.

Capt. Winslow spanned the entire room, and noticed an undue response of malicious stares. He felt the unfriendly environment pressure him to throw his hands into the air and concede. Moreover, he absorbed bits and pieces of hostile innuendos that called for his detainment, or possible arrest. Why? Because they were angry, and because someone had to pay. He was the likely candidate, because he's the only outsider. He felt like he was in a foreign country. A place where the people lived devotedly to become martyrs, by setting off dirty bombs in the middle of a bustling times square traffic. Or by flying airplanes into American skyscrapers.

He eyed the hand on his coat sleeve, then replied calmly, "If I don't leave right this instant, then this blood bath could get larger. Innocent bystanders may get hurt. Do you want to be responsible for that?"

Detective Sloan's hand dropped and swung by his side. He peered deeply into Capt. Winslow's magnified eyes, and everyone watching stood idling, waiting on a slight gesture to back their fellow officer. All waited for the conclusion to unfold.

Capt. Winslow stepped closer to him and got personal. He explained confidently, "Young man, I'm almost twice your age. And from your actions, I think my wisdom is twice that of yours. If you ever disrespect me, and grab me like that again, I'll break every bone in your hand." He paused before he asked, "You got that?" The fierce stare he delivered was enough to make his point. He seldom cursed, or lost his cool. He understood that if a man knew the words that he was trying to relay, he didn't have to resort to degrading and deplorable diction that advertised low self-esteem, and poor intellect.

He hustled through the doorway, on the way to his cruiser. Detective Sloan trailed him through the front door, shouted into the street, "Winslow! I want to hear from you within the next hour. If not, I'm coming to Boston to find you."

Before he got into his cruiser, he replied, "You want me to stay, shoot me." He jumped into his cruiser and sped off. Like Spanky, he was on a life and death mission. He was in a race to beat the clock against his opponent, Spanky, who was now, what he considered to be, a recruited member in Satans den of unholy disciples. He considered Spanky to be a man caught up in the web that he so tediously weaved. He believed that he was a man on the edge, and that he'd do anything to prove to himself that it wasn't too late for him to save himself. No matter how many people he had to kill to do so. He would try to prove to himself that he could fix the entire ordeal with a little medieval bloodletting. He believed that he was a man whose time was winding down, like a watch with invisible hands. Only he could see the relevance of his bloodthirsty appetite.

CHAPTER 33

▼

At Spankys apartment, he paced the floor nervously and contemplated his bloody trail. His faithful companion Spike was right on his heels, every step of the way. He had a peculiar expression that could've been taken for one of several possible gestures. He could've been trying to say, 'Hi Master. How did your day at the job go?' Or maybe it was, 'you're late with my grub again.' And then again, it could've been, 'since you didn't show up on time, I couldn't hold my number two. I'm sorry about that little something something I left over there in the corner. Also, I humbly apologize for tinkling in front of the refrigerator. Furthermore, since I'm unloading my burdens, I'm sorry about your new Stacey Adam shoes I chewed to pieces. There's just something about that fine Italian leather that tastes so good. Why do I do these things? you might ask. Simple. Because I'm a dog with an anxiety disorder.'

Every few seconds, when he strode by the diary—he had placed it on top of the television—he leered at it with much revulsion, despised it condemning content. He wanted to erase its history from existence. As he labored in the trenches of Satans domain, marching at a dreadfully disturbed pace, sweat poured profusely from his brow, his shirt became soaked with perspiration. His nerves tangled and bunched like the rubber bands inside of a golf ball. His knees twitched spasmodically, like he was a black panther, about to prance on its main course. His guts tensed erratically with the cramps of his ill fate, he wanted to vomit his insides.

Tracing his deadly path for nearly an hour, he ran into a snare. He realized that the only way he was going to succeed at keeping the whole ordeal under wraps, would be to eradicate everyone who could connect him to the manuscript.

The names Bruno and Elizabeth Knight entered his mind, and he whispered devilishly, "Sleepers cracking up. In the distraught condition he's in, anything can slip from his lips. He's probably over there right now, spilling his guts, telling his wife about everything we did. Especially with killing the Bogarts." A psychotic look fell into his eyes, his soul drifted further from the dwindling light of what little empathy he had. He rambled on, "I gotta think about this shit. I gotta pour myself a stiff drink, and think about this mother fucken shit real hard."

Ten minutes later, he reached a solid conclusion. "I can't let this shit happen. No! No way in hell. I'm not going to leave my fate in the hands of a babbling idiot. He can take himself down for the count, but he ain't dragging me along with him." He shouted, "Hell no! No way! I can't let this happen. And his wife, that stuck-up bitch don't like me no how. In court, they'll gang up on me like white on rice, like stink on shit. They'll say that I was responsible for initiating everything. They'll say that I was the leader of the Dixie Club. They'll turn states evidence, and put everything on me. And the prosecutor will shove every single one of those indictments straight up my ass, sideways. Hell no! I can't let that happen. If they throw me in jail, I'll never see the light of day for as long as I live. I'll have to live my life as a disgraced recluse, locked up in solitaire confinement for twenty four hours a day, in protective custody." A more formidable thought came to mind, and he pictured himself sitting next to Andrew. They were at the far end of the alley, inside of his 'WHIRLPOOL' rent controlled condo, nibbling on day old biscuits, arguing over a bottle of cheap wine.

He looked at Spike and spewed deliriously, "What do you think I should do? I know you have some good ideas floating around inside of that head of yours. You never say anything, but I know you can talk. Don't deny me that."

He paused, waiting for Spikes response. He was sure that Spike was going to open his mouth, and speak. He waited for his blubbery bulldog lips to form the first word of a sentence.

Because Spike was thrilled that his master was giving him some much-needed attention, he gave Spanky a hearty look of encouragement. He seemed to say, "Yeah! Do it, master! Atta-boy! Kill those worthless bastards! Send all those conspiring sons-za-bitches straight to hell in a doggie basket You can't go to jail, the dog pound. If you do, then who's going to take me for walks, feed and bathe me?" He whined cheerfully, his tail stub wagged briskly.

Spanky forced a sick twisted smile, then sneered psychotically. He told Spike, "I knew I could count on you, old buddy. You're always with me." He reached down and rubbed his head. "After tonight, it's just you and me, babe. The hell with those fools. They don't have what it takes to hang with us. I wish they were like you. Then I wouldn't have to worry about them talking, and writing all that shit that got this whole mess started in the first place. They're not like us at all. You ... you're perfect, because you know how to keep your mouth shut. And mostly, you don't keep a diary of everything you do."

He nodded assuredly, resolute on what he needed to do. He was determined to clean the slate of all witnesses; potential or otherwise. Until he accomplished his mission, he felt that he wouldn't have a moments rest. Until then, his feelings of extreme anxiety would not subside.

He grabbed the car keys and ran out of the apartment, like a man who had very little time to save himself from the epitome of existing an eternity in the bowels of hell. Maximum security prison, an institutionalized hellhole. Maddened deliriously into an ambiguous state of paranoia, he persisted on an arduous quest to see that all witnesses against him, potential or otherwise, were taken out.

CHAPTER 34

▼

Twenty minutes later, Spanky had arrived at the Knights residence. He reached into the glove compartment, and retrieved the gun that he had used to kill the Bogarts. He reached into his jacket, pulled out the silencer, then attached it onto the barrel. With no hesitation, he got out of the car and approached the front door of the Knights apartment building. He tried to clear his mind of anything that would make him hesitate to pull the trigger; their fourteen-year friendship, an unarmed and helpless woman, and the well being and safety of their only child.

Instead, he focused on Elizabeth's never liking him. He recalled the sneering expressions she gave him, when he and Stoney came by occasionally to take Sleeper out for a few beers. He felt her despised leers of disapproval, prodding at the back of his head. He felt her badgering stares nudge him to the front door, mentally bopping him up beside his head, urging him to get lost. With her sarcastic responses to any question he asked, she told him in so many ways to stay away from her husband, and their home. If she knew how to use hypnosis, she would have persuaded him to leave the country the moment she met him.

He always thought of her as the goody-goody two shoes type. She's the type of woman who was overly concerned about who her husband hung out with. She's the type of woman who stood by her man, regardless of what everyone else thought. She's the type of woman that he secretly admired. She's the type of woman that he wanted to be with, and knew that she'd be the best thing for him. She's the type of woman that he'd been searching for, for many years. But he could never find a woman like her, because of his loud obnoxious personality. He loved and loathed her all at once.

As for Junior, the Knights newborn, he considered him to be collateral damage; a casualty of war, and not just an innocent bystander. The thought of making him parentless never entered his mind, because he was cruising in overdrive. Now, his warped idea of mercy was to kill Bruno and Elizabeth, then raise Junior as his own.

The gears in his head churned exclusively on self-preservation, and the ignorance of greed. For what he so mind-numbingly searched for, the need to be a self-proclaimed god rendering judgment, was somewhere in the neighborhood to be relished. He focused solely on his continued freedom, and to be able to command and have authority over the general public. And his reputation as a police officer, to be respected and admired by many people.

Under the cover of the blackness of the night, standing in front of the Knights apartment building, he pulled the gun from his jacket, and checked it to make sure that it was ready for action. He approached the intercom system and pressed a few buttons, in hopes that one of the other tenants would simply open the door. It worked.

He entered the apartment building, then hustled upstairs to the Knights apartment. He stood in front of the door, just for a moment, hyping himself up. When he was ready, he gripped, then turned the doorknob slowly.

To his surprise, it was open.

He crept the dimly lit apartment, and discovered that all of the lights were off. All but the soft nightlight emanating from the bathroom. They must have gone to bed, he assumed.

Tiptoeing through the apartment, the only sound he heard was the slight creaking of floorboards. When he reached their bedroom door, he stood poised, lurking in the darkness of his arctic abomination. Because he was slipping, loosing his sanity, he was tormented by conflicting thoughts. The human element of compassion battled with his egotistical and cannibalistic wants.

Urging himself into continuing, feeling it was all for the better, he drew a blank. Now, he had only two things on his mind. The only things that he could see and feel; the door in front of him, and the gun in his hand. A few other images floated indistinguishably in the back of his mind, then forced their way to the forefront. The words disgrace—dishonor—incarceration—protective custody—Andrew!

Seeing the door cracked ajar, he reached out and pushed it open. The squeaking door hinges tried their damndest to rouse the occupants, but failed miserably.

He crept into the bedroom.

It was extremely dark.

He strained to pierce the darkness, and observed the wooly mass of a lumpy comforter. He didn't know if Sleeper slept on the right side, or on the left. At this stage, it really didn't matter. It only mattered that he kill whoever was there.

Reeling in the hype, his adrenalin pushed him to the point of no return. He raised the gun, aimed at the clump of life lying dormant, and fired fourteen times, until the gun was empty. "PHSST! PHSST! PHSST! PHSST!...."

He was trained to count his shots fired, so that he'd know how many bullets he had left in the clip. A crucial detail used for survival. The fourteen shots he had just fired, each one killed a year of their friendship. Now, Sleeper was a complete stranger. Now, it was as if he never knew the man, or his family. He considered him, his wife and child, to be total strangers. Simply nobodies.

Amidst a room filled to the brim with gun smoke, the comforter innards floated liberally like huge snowflakes. He glanced to the right, and fell alarmingly distressed when he discovered someone returning his stare. It startled the hell out of him, and he jumped backwards, nearly out of his skin, and the person jumped backwards at the same time. Then he realized that he was looking into a mirror sitting atop of the bureau. The incident scared him shitless. Almost gave him a heart attack.

The reflection captured his attention for a moment, and he looked deeper. He realized that what looked like him, was actually what he had metamorphically changed into—a devilish monster with a battered soul. The huge horns dressing the sides of his head scrapped the ceiling, their massive weight caused his head to bow in deep regret.

Looking down, peering through the gun smoke, he saw the caverns of a thriving hell welcoming him warmly. Fire, smoke and brimstone, the combination he inhaled delighted him at first. Years ago, when he started the Dixie Club, it made him feel indestructible. Capable of serving the dark master, without feeling he owed repentance. He wanted to purchase the butchers meats, on credit. Now, he realized that the tab must be paid in full. The bright lights of greed blinded him, and always forced that day into an endless amount of tomorrows. A time which is actually today, because tomorrow never came. The period remains in the future, never to arrive.

Listening to the sound of death, a high pierced shrill filled his ears, deafened him to a maddening incapacitation. He dropped the gun and covered his ears, in a futile attempt to block out the mind-crippling sound. His throat tightened, and he found it difficult to breathe. His heart pounded a beat so heavy, that every nerve ending in his body throbbed intensely. Riding a very unstable moment, he remained perfectly still, unmoving. Even the blood racing through his heart earlier refused to flow.

Suddenly, he heard a low persistent whining coming from another room across the hallway. The baby, he thought.

He left the room, paused in the hallway, listened attentively.

The whining continued.

Moving toward the nursery slowly, he noticed the pitch of the whining had changed slightly. It sounded more like that of an older child, or perhaps a woman.

His curiosity flared, ran rampant, like a raging bull in a rodeo. At the threshold of the nursery, he discovered the door was closed. He raised a trembling hand, twisted the doorknob, then pushed the door open wide. The light was off, it was so dark that he couldn't see a thing, only the fuzzy shadows of pieces of furniture. Venturing forth, straining to see through the darkness surrounding him, he was finally able to make out what several items in the room were. Spanning the room, he saw the front side of the crib, the bassinet, the change table, and the Bentwood rocking chair. Last of all, he noticed an object sitting on the floor, in the middle of the room. Unsure of what it was, he took a couple of steps backwards. He reached to the light switch, then flicked it on.

After his eyes adjusted to the sudden light, he recognized what it was, and the utter shock jolted him into the next millennium. He felt like someone had reached into his chest and squeezed his heart pitilessly. The pain he suffered weakened him, forced him to his knees, forced him to surrender.

He saw Elizabeth, sitting on the floor, with her baby clutched in her left arm, while holding her husbands service revolver in her right hand. A Smith and Wesson revolver. Stocked, cocked and ready for action.

His mouth fell open in full gawk. Staring disbelievingly, he babbled incomprehensively, "Ah … I … ah … I-I-I thought … you … S-S-Sleeper … I thought …" he pointed to the bedroom across the hallway, "… you … um … Sleeper … I thought …"

"You worthless bastard!" she blasted, biting her words. The baby woke up and began crying. "I know what you thought. Bruno told me never to trust your miserable ass, and he was right. He told me that you'd come back to kill us, and you did. You worthless piece of trash."

His hands rose slowly to surrender. He implored, "No, Elizabeth. You got it all wrong. I wasn't going to kill you. I … I just wanted to …"

"Lies!" she shouted. "All lies! You filthy bastard. But that's okay, Robert Sinclair. Because where I'm going to send you, you'll fit in just fine."

Entirely at her mercy, he collapsed onto the floor, fainted. His face buried into his hands, sniveling with profound shame, he begged desperately for her to spare his life. "Elizabeth! Please … please don't kill me." Looking into her eyes, his hands clasped to pray. "I'm begging you. Please don't do it."

Holding the gun on him, the notion to see him dead filled her heart with a bitter satisfaction, chased out all rational emotions. As her grip grew tighter around the trigger, from just outside of the nursery, they heard someone say, "You can take the gun off him now, Elizabeth. It's okay now."

It was Capt. Winslow. His gun aimed directly to the back of Spankys head.

She found it very difficult to pull the gun away from him. Grunting like a maddened bull with the sole intentions of killing in her heart, she held it targeted point blank to in between his eyes.

Capt. Winslow said again, "Lower the gun, Elizabeth." He asked sympatheti-cally, "Please! You don't need this kind of grief riding you for the rest of your life. You have a baby to take care of. You let me deal with him. All right?"

The muscles in her right hand and shoulder began to cramp, but her elbow remained locked. Feeling lost in time, seconds felt like hours. In thinking about what Capt. Winslow said about grief riding her for the rest of her life, she came to a reasonable conclusion, and understood that the right thing to do would be to comply. Nonetheless, she also believed that even if she did kill him, no one would blame, persecute or prosecute her.

She understood that taking a life needlessly, would most likely brand many resentful feelings deep into her heart. Bitter feelings that she'd reflect toward her son in the near or distant future. As he grew older, those feelings would magnify, and their relationship would become stressed and estranged, separated because of an alien anger that would not subside. She understood that some police officers and members of the military had to endure several weeks, months, or even years of grief counseling, after taking a persons life. She also understood that some peo-ple never got over it.

Her arm grew tired, and descended slowly. When the tip of the gun barrel touched the floor, she dropped it. She clutched her son even tighter, and wept. Though, she did keep one eye on Spanky.

Capt. Winslow walked to in between Spanky and Elizabeth, then kicked the gun further away. He looked into Spanky eyes, then shook his head deplorably. He stepped to just behind him and stated, "Sinclair, you know the procedure." Spanky disliked it when the Capt. used a commanding tone of voice. It meant that the person who he was speaking to was hopeless. Through! "Put your hands in back of you. You're being placed under arrest for the murders of Captain Bogart, his wife, and their daughter. And for a slew of other things that I've yet to sort out." He pulled out the handcuffs, and put them on Spanky. "Now where's Stoneys manuscript?"

With no hesitation, he replied sorrowfully, "It's at my apartment, Captain." His feeble voice spilled of remorse. He wept erratically, "I … I left it on top of the television, in the living room."

Capt. Winslow grabbed him by his right arm, then pulled him to his feet. He turned him around to look at his face, and asked, "Why?" His expression begged for a reply. One that he could hopefully understand. Then he thought it good that he not understand any excuse that Spanky handed him. "What made you do something so hideous?" He sighed heavily. "What I mean to say is …" he threw his hands into the air, "… I just don't understand it." He allowed his anger to build for a lengthy moment, then exploded. "What in the hell happened?" He turned to Elizabeth, said calmly, "Excuse me. I was beside myself for a moment."

Now that Spanky was living the first few repercussions of his criminal actions, he remained quiet, staring confusedly. He finally managed to get a few words past the swelling in his throat. "I-I-I don't know, Captain." He lowered his head in shame. "But, I guess it doesn't matter anymore."

Capt. Winslow locked the handcuffs with a notch on the tail end of the key, then corrected him. "Oh, it does matter, ex-officer Sinclair. It matters to Captain Bogart's children and grandchildren. It matters to all of the members of the Dover police department, and to everyone in Dover who knew the Bogart's to be exceptionally descent people." He told Elizabeth, "I'm taking this sad excuse for an officer down to the station to be booked on murder, attempted murder, extortion, blackmail, several violations of departmental policy, and hell knows what else he's been involved in. You should be all right now."

Elizabeth's crying simmered to a whisper. Focusing on her child, she forced a frail smile, a flow of tears trickled her cheeks. Feeling safer, she rocked her son gently, whispered softly, "Everything's okay now. Mama's here."

Capt. Winslow picked up Spankys gun, and slid it into his waits band. He frisked him, and found a small caliber back-up pistol in his right jacket pocket. Escorting him to the door, he told Elizabeth, "Come lock the door." Opening the front door, he said, "You, ex-officer Robert Sinclair, have the right to remain silent. If you waive that right, anything you say may be used against you in a court of law …"

Although he knew the Miranda—a warning which he had recited to criminal suspects thousands of times in the past—he was awe struck knowing that it was being recited to him. It was as if Capt. Winslow spoke in a foreign tongue, cursing him.

After Capt. Winslow heard her lock the front door, he proceeded to the cruiser. Halfway there, they were approached by four strangers. One of the men stared heatedly at Spanky, then asked Capt. Winslow, "Is this the sick son-of-a-bitch who killed Captain Bogart and his family?" It was Detective John Sloan of the Dover police department. He bobbed from side to side like a caged panther. He was so anxious that he couldn't keep still. His right hand twitched repeatedly, dying to pull his gun, then empty the clip into Spankys heart.

Another detective made it apparent that he was tremendously distressed when he grumbled, "I vote we lynch the crazy fuck! String his ass up."

"I say we use our night sticks," another detective spat forward. "Let him suffer a little, before we send him to hell."

Through the climbing tension, Capt. Winslow realized that they were all detectives from the Dover police department. Before things got out of control, he hurried Spanky into the back seat of the cruiser. He slammed the door shut, told them calmly, "He might have some involvement. We won't know for sure, until we paste together a few odds and ends. What are you guys doing here, in Boston?"

No one replied.

Detective Sloan and his men stepped even closer, approached the car and looked inside. The desire to kill easily seen blazing in their eyes, firing from their angry hearts. Detective Sloan pulled out his gun quickly, and slammed the butt against the rear window. After the glass shattered into a million pieces, he aimed his gun at Spankys head. He removed the safety, then pulled the hammer back. His clear-cut convictions remained firm.

Without hesitation, Capt. Winslow stepped boldly in front of the gun. He placed his hand on his own, knowing that he wouldn't have had a snowballs chance in hell of surviving, if they start shooting. It was four against one. Yet, he stood resolute. Brave heart struggling for a lost cause. Now, Detective Sloan's gun was aimed directly at his midsection.

The remaining three Dover Police Detectives pulled out their weapons as well, and Capt. Winslow was sure that it was going to be Viet Nam all over again. A hailstorm of shots fired, the screams from agonizing pain filling the immediate area, the stench of death in the air as blood gushed profusely from several wounds. He felt that a seemingly never-ending amount of grief and misery would surely ensue, and be felt by everyone nearest and dearest to all involved.

Capt. Winslow drew his gun from his holster—for some reason, it felt like it weighed ten times its normal weight—the three detectives took aim on him. The tension climbed a thousand times higher, as racing hearts beat a cacophony of earsplitting silence. Soon, the apex would occur. Eventually, the drama would subside. He told them, "I understand your anger, but this isn't the way to handle things. Think about it for a second. You do this, and you'll be just as bad off as him. It's not worth it."

He lifted his gun slowly, uneasily—all noticed the shaking gun for his trembling hands—beads of sweat dressed his brow and misted his spectacles. He took aim at Detective Sloan, held his ground.

A weighty moment struggled by, then he broke the silence, when he stated assuredly, "Officers, I think you should lower, and then holster your guns." He ordered with authority, "Now!"

Detective Sloan fired, "Hell no, dammit! You're not in any position to tell us what to do. Besides, the bastard's got it coming to him."

Capt. Winslow lowered his gun, then holstered it. "Officers, for your sake, and for my own as well, I would suggest that you take a look around you."

The Dover Police Detectives spanned the immediate area, and observed the setup surrounding them. After realizing the new turn of events, they lowered their weapons. Circled around them, hiding stealthily in various spots at not more than fifty yards away, were a few proficient individuals dressed in black fatigues. Some crouched behind cars, a few hid partially around corners, and a couple of sharp shooters were positioned on a roofs edge. They were all members of the Boston police departments S.W.A.T (special weapons and tactics) team. Now, the greater persuasions were the infer-red laser beams aimed directly at their bodies. On route to Sleepers apartment, Capt. Winslow had radioed for backup, on a gut hunch that things were going to get a bit sticky. A smart move, for his sake.

He informed them, "Ya see, gentlemen, now you're in *my* jurisdiction."

The Dover Police Detectives faced him, and without hesitation, quickly holstered their weapons. Detective Sloan promised, "This isn't over, Captain."

"For your sake, you better hope it is." With nothing more need be said, the Dover Police Detectives marched quickly to their vehicle. They jumped inside, then sped off. In the car, Detective Sloan told his men, "If it's the last thing I do, I'll get that son-of-a-bitch. I want his ass dead!"

A detective in the back seat suggested, "Why don't you call Benny, the residential sniper. After Winslow takes the prisoner to the station house, eventually, they're going to take him to their headquarters in downtown Boston. For him to be fingerprinted and processed. Then they'll take him to Superior Courthouse, where he'll be indicted. You know how Benny is. He's got the patience of a rock. That's why he's got a one hundred percent kill rate. Besides, he'll be happy to do it. He and Captain Bogart go way back. They grew up together."

"I might just do that."

*   *   *   *

Back at the scene, in front of Sleepers apartment, the S.W.A.T. team members had come out of hiding, and had gathered around Capt. Winslow's cruiser, asking a horde of questions. In pertaining to the Dover Police Detective's antagonistic behavior, he merely replied, "It was just a little misunderstanding. I can understand their anger. I'd expect the same behavior from some of you if I … well, we'll let it go, for now."

A few Boston police officers gazing inside of Capt. Winslows cruiser examined Robert Sinclair, whispered tales of extortion and blood money. A few chastised him with leering eyes, feeling the shame of it all. Some merely stared at him from the corners of their eyes, feeling mortified that he had slandered their heritage, integrity, and badge of honor.

Feeling their heated stares, Spanky dropped his head forward remorsefully, then closed his eyes tight in an attempt to erase the events from the past ten years. It didn't work. The thought to return their curious stares never once entered his mind.

A sergeant accompanied by a new recruit approached the cruiser, and instructed his protégé to, "Go ahead. Take a good look at him. I want you to remember his face."

The rookie stepped to the cruiser, and looked inside with a deep resentment pruning his lips. He nodded earnestly. "What do you think they'll do to him?"

The sergeant released a heavy sigh. "The question should be, what hasn't he already done to himself?" He told a few other recruits standing near, "I want you guys to remember this. Seeing situations like this …" he pointed to Spanky, "… is the best way to learn about what *not* to do."

Capt. Winslow spoke to the leader of the S.W.A.T team. "I have what I believe to be the gun that may have been used to kill Captain Bogart and his family. But we won't know for sure until ballistics confirms it. You can get a statement from officer Knight's wife," he emphasized, "*if* she's up to it. She's been through a lot already. Don't pressure her." Although he believes that she ignored subtle hints about certain illicit events; i.e. Spankys secret bank book that she discovered one day while cleaning the apartment, he felt comfortable in telling them, "Officer Knight kept her in the dark about everything." He glanced into the back seat of the cruiser. "As for me, I'm taking the prisoner back to the station house, to see if I can get anything out of him. There are still a lot of loose ends to this case."

The word prisoner stabbed deep into Spankys heart, like a searing hot branding iron, sizzling with the intense heat of its sinister ways. A sweltering fire that won't extinguish itself for years to come. Maybe never. Sitting slouched in the back seat of the cruiser, a place that he use to hurl suspects into, as his ex-colleagues gawked at him mercilessly, he thought of the handcuffs, and realized that that was how things were going to be for the rest of his life—restricted. Imprisoned! Caged, like an out of control wild animal.

Weeping woefully, a stream of burning tears trickled his cheeks, etching his face with scars of his jaded past. A huge lump of self-pity fell lodged in his throat, caused him to gag, and he choked for the lack of a breath of fresh air. A smidgeon of leniency, his vision of having any form of satisfaction in life, gone.

Inappropriately, one of his hustling episodes entered his mind. Stoney, Sleeper and Spanky each had unique styles of hustling. Spanky sometimes used a style that caused much confusion, before he got down to brass taxes. While walking a beat at a construction site in Mattapan Square, he took a fifteen minute coffee break. So that the construction crew couldn't overhear him, he stood about fifty feet away from them, then placed a call on a cell phone. A man answered, "James Pakowski here. What can I do for you?"

"Mr. Pakowski," Spanky saddened. "I know I shouldn't discuss this with you over the phone, considering the significance of the call, but it's an emergency. I had to call."

James felt the sincerity in Spankys voice, and asked worriedly, "What seems to be the problem?"

"It's your wife, Ashley," he wept pretentiously. "She's had a terrible accident, on the way home from the grocery store."

"My wife!" he excited, panic stricken. "What happened to her?"

"She was nearly killed when a huge prick ran a red-light and plowed into her. It was awful, I tell ya. It nearly split her in two. Mr. Pakowski, there was yogurt, apples, oranges and tits all over the highway. It was a total disaster!"

He became perplexed. "You say a what ran into her?"

Spanky cried, "A Dodge pick-up rammed her right up the ass, from in back. It was just terrible. There was blood and feces everywhere. Before she passed out, as I was holding her hand, she told me to tell her husband that she loves him very much. And that she's sorry that she cheated on you with the busboy at the House of Pancakes."

"Huh? I mean, is she still alive? Where did this happen? What hospital did they take her to?"

"I'm not sure. But when the train ran over you sons car, there was nearly nothing left of it. His body was destroyed beyond recognition. There were pieces of the wreckage scattered for miles on both sides of the tracks. If it wasn't for the license plate, they wouldn't have been able to tell who was driving."

"Wait a minute," he said. He hesitated, entirely puzzled. "I'm a little confused. Did my wife have an accident, or was it my son?"

"Mr. Pakowski, they need you to come down to the morgue to identify the body, before the cremation. They want to know if your son was wearing a red mini skirt when he left the house this morning. Or did the mailman come by for quickie with your wife?"

A heightened confusion hit James by storm. He became irate and fired, "What in the hell is this? First you say that my wife had an accident. Then you say my son had an accident. Now you're talking about some shit that doesn't even make sense. What in the hell is going on?"

Now that Spanky had him by the scruff of the neck, he felt it was time to yank with everything he had. He got to the real reason why he called, stated calmly, "Mr. Pakowski, you're the assistant vice president at the Bank of America in Hyde Park. I've discovered evidence that says you've been embezzling money hand over foot, for the past three years. I'm not going to tell you who turned on you, because it doesn't matter to me. What does matter to me, is that we keep everything on the hush hush side of things. I'm sure you know what'll happen to you and your family if any of this gets out."

James wet himself, choked and babbled incoherently, "But I ... who said ... the bank ... what did ... I didn't ... when did ... they didn't ..." He finished off with, "Oh my God!"

"Now to rectify the matter," Spanky said. "Here's what I want you to do ..."

*   *   *   *

On the way to the station house, Capt. Winslow had many morals that he wanted to preach to Spanky. Instead, he remained absolutely quiet, allowing a somber silence to fill the cruiser and slap him beyond comprehension. He realized that sometimes talk only made matters worse. He understood the seriousness of Spankys crimes, and yet, he was still a man of mercy. Hence the phrase 'a leader of men.' Captain.

CHAPTER 35

▼

Less than an hour later, after Capt. Winslow had dropped Spanky off at the area 'B' station house—he put him into protective custody for his own protection—he went to Spankys apartment to retrieve the diary.

He entered the apartment—in Spankys haste, he had forgot to lock the front door—flicked on the lights, and was greeted by Spike. He scuttled to the front door eagerly, with his bowl clutched firmly in his slobbering chops. He was very happy to see Capt. Winslow. Actually, he was happy to see anyone, considering he hadn't eaten all day. In all the commotion, Spanky had forgotten to call home earlier to ask a neighbor to go into his place to fix his diner. Even though he sported a 'who in the hell are you?' look, he welcomed Capt. Bogart with open arms.

Just an hour before, he had scurried around the apartment in haste and emptied the trash buckets, in hopes to find a morsel to nibble on. A tiny insignificant nothing to fill his empty belly, to sooth his savage ways. A crust of food to restrain him from traveling back to his Neanderthal ways laying dormant at the back of his skull. He had a Jones for the Bonze. Had it been a few days later, he would've bit first, then felt guilty about it on the morning after. Although, this time he most likely would've gotten a bullet in his English pushed in snout for his troubles.

Ignoring the filthy apartment, he reached down and patted him, looked at a word stenciled on his collar. "It says here your name's Spike. You're a cute little fella. Ya kinda remind me of myself."

He went to the kitchen and found a can of Alpo dog food sitting stacked in the cupboards above the sink area. He opened it, scooped its contents into Spikes dog bowl, then watched him grub out until his hearts content. "You stay here and eat ya pedigree heart out, little fella. As for me, I'm going into the living room to do some reading." He mumbled, "Maybe I can find out what all this mess is about, since your master wouldn't tell me anything that made sense."

Spike shoved his nose deep into his bowl and ate as though he'd never see food again. He pushed the bowl from one side of the kitchen to the other, finally trapped it into a corner, then worked at it until every bit of the dog food was gone. Including the smell.

Capt. Winslow went to the refrigerator, opened it wide and an awful reek gushed forward and knocked him back a few feet. After viewing the contents—he became disgusted when he saw mold growing on almost everything—he decided quickly not to take any chances on the food, and reached for a can of Pepsi. "I don't think Sinclair will miss this," he told Spike. He closed the door quickly, then wiped the top against his jacket. He popped the lid and took a sip. Exhaled exhilaratingly, "Aaahhh, that's good."

He took another sip, then released a loud burp that filled the kitchen. He looked at Spike. "Excuse me, little fella." He rubbed his throat, thinking, That gas always comes back on me. No wonder I stopped drinking the stuff years ago. Stings the back of my throat; makes me feel like I've swallowed an ice cube. Gets my heart pumping something fierce also. Must be all that caffeine.

Spike stopped licking the inside of the bowl briefly, stared fixedly at Capt. Winslow. His expression read, 'So what! Spanky does that all the time. And much louder too.'

He left the kitchen, headed for the living room. Passing the bathroom, in the brief scan that he took, he saw a ring around the tub, the toilet bowl and the sink. A three ring circus, it smelled of lions and tigers and bears, oh my! Lions and tigers and bears, oh my!

Altogether, the apartment looked like a fraternity stayed there and partied hard every night, like in the movie 'Animal House,' which stared John Belushi.

Returning his focus to what was more important, he searched for the manuscript. After he found it perched on top of the television, his heart raced with much anticipation of the knowledge he'd soon acquire. For some strange reason, perhaps because of the trouble that it caused, he believed that he had struck gold. A radioactive gold.

After a lengthy moment of staring at it in a heightened suspense, he picked it up, went to the couch and sat down. He placed the can of Pepsi on the end table, then placed the manuscript in his lap, or what little bit of it there was. He grazed his hand slowly over the exterior, felt the texture, expected to learn something from it even before he opened it. He wondered how something that could appear so harmless, be as deadly as the bubonic plague—had people dropping like flies for their direct connection.

After a long minute, he opened it and began to read. Studying the first page, the title, he mumbled, "The Dixie Club! Finally, something to read with substance. Now maybe I can get down to the bottom of what's been going on."

CHAPTER 36

▼

Less than four hours later, as the sun was coming up, Capt. Winslow had finished reading the entire diary. He slammed the book shut, then sat staring at Spike with a puzzled expression. Spike returned the same inquisitive stare.

I wonder what in the hell all of the hoopla was about, Capt. Winslow thought. I've never heard of these three lawyers before. And there isn't anything in here that's worth following up on. Unless there's something that I might've missed. Something that I overlooked. Something in between the lines that I was supposed to pick up on. Maybe the whole thing's written in code. Or maybe Sinclair replaced incriminating information, evidence, with something innocent. With intentions on allowing the book to be discovered by the authorities, to mislead, or add confusion.

He grew excited, spouted, "He's had to! With all the trouble that he went through to get it, he's had to."

He opened the diary again and flipped through several pages, scanned it quickly, searching for writing that's been edited or altered in any way. Coming to a quick conclusion, he mumbled, "It doesn't look like anything's been changed. Not the names, places or dates. Not even any of the information given about any of the hustling situations—it all looks original."

He looked at the page numbers to see if any were missing. Again, another disappointment. He sat quietly with the same confused look on his face. It was as if he was blindfolded, attempting to figure out the solution to a brail version of Rubics Cube.

As the fog lifted slowly for the light of day, he was hit with another idea. Thinking back on a very violent episode in the diary, a part described in such fine detail, he felt that it could've been taken from an actual real-life situation. He said, "No way! Considering that officer Brooks was an amateur, that part is just too good to be fiction. The threats that that pharmacy guy made to the main character, because he was being blackmailed, it sounds too real. The hallucinations that one of the main character experienced for taking advantage of all of those people, that's enough to play with anyone's conscious. No! I say either officer Brooks was a hell of a writer—a natural—or these things really did happen."

He paused for a long moment in heavy contemplation, considered the personalities of the three main characters, the facts of the case collectively. Searching drastically for motives and answers, his reasoning for what had happened thus far rose to the surface, became clear for the light ahead. Now closer, his thoughts became more definite. Eureka!

He declared, "That's it! The main character is officer Brooks!" Feeling assured that he was headed in the right direction, he nodded with confidence. "And the other two lawyers are officers Knight and Sinclair. These characters, their personalities, its them all right. It's got to be them. The stress, frustration and sinister doings that they've gotten involved in led them to harbor feelings of insecurity and mistrust among themselves. Which in turn created a mountain of paranoia. Deadly paranoia!"

Among a few understandings that were finally coming to light, it explained why Stoney had experienced a violent outburst, suffered a hallucination, during the last conversation that he had had with him in his office. It looked as though he was shouldering a heavy burden that distressed him rigorously. A burden that was destroying him from the inside like a merciless terminal cancer. One that blinded him sight and soul, until both were rendered useless. That spaced-out transparent look he had in his eyes—the main character was definitely him. He might've changed the names and occupations, and exaggerated on the hustling situations, but the emotions remained the same. In writing the story, if he had changed the emotions in any way shape or form, the story wouldn't have made sense. As much as he wanted to throw suspicion, he couldn't deny the authenticity of it. The emotions were real. They were very clear and precise. Anyone who can explain emotions as deeply as these has had to experience them. He was living them. And they were living inside of him, inside of his soul.

"Damn! Now the only problem I have is trying to figure out what parts are real, and what's been fabricated." He thought, figuring this out is going to be like trying to hit a piñata with a five foot stick, from ten feet away.

He picked up the telephone and dialed the Dover police department. The phone rang twice before the switchboard operator answered. Capt. Winslow didn't give the person a chance to say anything before he hurled, "This is Captain Winslow of the Boston police department. Connect me to your homicide unit, at once."

With no delay, his connection went through.

"Captain Winslow, this is Sergeant Simms. I'm acting in place of Captain Bogart. What seems to be the prob ..."

"I think I know what happened to officer Brooks."

"Yeah?"

"Yeah. This is just a hunch, but did you find a bottle of prescription pills anywhere, at the scene?"

"Yes. There were two bottles there. But neither had labels on them. Our lab confirms that one prescription was for pain, and the other for sleep. They checked out okay. We've even dusted them for fingerprints. Only officer Brooks were on them."

Talking to himself, Capt. Winslow said inaudibly, "This doesn't add up. I still think it was the pharmacist who ..."

Sergeant Simms cut in, "I never said anything about a pharmacist. How'd you know about him? All of our reports are supposed to be kept confidential until the case is closed. I just thought I'd extend some information as a matter of courtesy, in hopes to get some back. Carlton, officer Brooks uncle, told us that he had stopped by the day before yesterday. He said that he forgot to mention it because the visit was brief. Said that when the pharmacist came into the house, he gave officer Brooks the prescriptions and instructions about the required dosage, and that was that, cut and dry. He informed us that officer Brooks was taking tranquilizers because he was having a difficult time getting some shuteye. Said he was taking the pain medication because he had a couple of in-home accidents. The initial autopsy shows that he had a gashed right hand along the knuckles, and suffered multiple bruises along the lower frontal area of both legs. We don't why or how it happened, but we know that he hurt his hand when he put his fist through his computers monitor, as though he was angry with it. I have cheap one at home that crashes every now and then, makes me mad enough to take a sledgehammer to it, so I can understand how that happened. But Carlton didn't explain how he hurt his legs."

"What kind of poison was used?"

"The M.E. confirmed that it was arsenic."

The pharmacist probably pulled a switch-er-roo on Stoney, Capt. Winslow guessed. He most likely molded the poison to the same shape and color as the other tranquilizers. Chances are, when he was there, he took a time released, arsenic lased capsule from his pocket and gave it to officer Brooks, then urged him to take one right there and then. He wanted to kill Stoney, but didn't want him to die instantly.

He also guessed that there would be a serial number on the underside of the caps, which may give them something to explore. "Do you have the bottles with you?"

"They're down stairs in the lab."

"Could you get them, please? It's very urgent."

Sergeant Simms pulled the phone from his ear for a moment, thought, I shouldn't be giving him all this information. This is our case, and we should have all the opportunity to get the first crack at solving it. What does he think this is? A free-for-all.

He returned the phone to his ear. "I don't think I can do that, Captain Winslow. Some information in this case is confidential, until our investigators go through them with a fine tooth comb. We're not aloud to ..."

Capt. Winslow interrupted, snapping, "I don't care about what's aloud in your department ... this is very important. Officer Brooks was one of my men. I'm sure you can understand how important it is for me to find his killer."

"I know he was one of your men, but Captain Bogart was *my* boss. This case is more personal for us, because compared to your big city, this is a small town. Things are more personal here. Besides, me giving you all of this information over the line is sloppy business. Especially if it's uncorroborated."

Priorities, Capt. Winslow wondered. Sometimes pride is more important than the crime that's been committed. If the public ever found out about the many cases that were bungled because of someone's pride or haughty attitude, we would've been forced out of business a long time ago.

He understood the rules and regulations well, but also knew that when you applied the human factor element to them, they fluctuated sporadically. If the boss had to sleep on the couch the evening before because he and the misses were not getting along, then on the very next day, everyone at work might get the big end of the shaft. Subsequently, when the underlings applied their angry attitudes to their routine work, the outcome could be detrimental to their subordinates, straight on down to the customer.

"Okay. Okay. I see your point. Well, thanks for your time. I know you're very busy, so I won't hold you up any longer."

"You're welcome, Captain. So long." He hung up the phone quickly, before Capt. Winslow could ask for anything else.

"Dammit!" He cursed. "I hate it when they throw that 'by the book' bullcrap."

Without hesitation, he sprang from the couch and darted toward the door, with the manuscript in tow. He believed that the only person who could give him the crucial information he needed was Carlton. Stoneys uncle. Or whatever his relationship was to him. His gut feelings made him suspicious of their relationship many years before. Every time he called Stoneys house, he noticed that there was something unusual about the way he answered the phone that shouted 'ABNORMAL!' Because he knew an authentic English accent when he heard one, he felt that Carlton's accent sounded like it was borrowed from an old Sherlock Holmes movie. It sounded manufactured. Brought and paid for.

Also, there was another thing that bothered him even more. At the beginning of the manuscript, Stoney had wrote that his character never let any of the people he hustled see him. They never knew his identity, which leaves a question. How did the pharmacist discover who was hustling him?

Somewhere, there was a missing link.

Before he walked through the door, he hollered, "Com'on Spike! You gotta get outside to get some fresh air, and stretch your little limbs," he mumbled, "and all that grass and fire hydrant stuff. I hope you can make it a quickie, because you're going with me. Got some important things to take care of."

Less than ten minutes later, he was on the highway once again. Being a very resourceful man, he relied on his exceptionally praised detective skills to lead the way. In thinking about the manuscript, he remembered reading something about a man who was a servant to the main character. A once poor, but modest man who came from a foreign country. He's the type of person who has a lot of patience, possibly because he didn't want to call attention to himself. In an average street altercation, he'd play it down at all costs. Even if the other guy was a total asshole.

An example being the way Spanky belittled him almost every time he came by to see Stoney. Carlton believed that defending himself by telling him where he could stick his dry humor would make him challenge his credentials. Or his status as an American citizen. Capt. Winslow had to check him out. He radioed to the dispatchers station and got in touch with Wendy, who told him, "Captain, your wife's been trying to get in contact with you. She's been calling every half hour. You know how worried she gets when you take off in the middle of the night in an emergency. Isn't your cell phone turned on?"

"Yeah. But I leave it in the car from time to time. If it went off while I was try-ing to sneak up on someone, it would give away my location. Ruin the element of surprise. Besides that, as you can tell, I'm pulling an all-nighter." He sighed, "Wendy, this one is so close, that I can taste it like it's on the tip of my cigar."

She snickered. "What can I do for you, sir?"

"I want you to pull some information from the computer for me."

"No problem, sir. What's the name?"

"Carlton Rogers. It could be an alias, but check it out anyway."

"Will do, sir. It should only take a few minutes. I'll dig it up, then run a copy of what I find through the computer in your cruiser."

"Thanks Wendy. I don't know what I'd without you."

"Knowing you, sir. You'd manage."

"Oh. And if my wife calls again, tell her I'll call her as soon as I get a chance."

"Will do, Captain."

CHAPTER 37

▼

At approximately five a.m., Capt. Winslow had arrived at what he thought was Stoneys uncles house, going by the rumors. The paper boy hadn't as yet cruised his route, and the trash collector had just been by only minutes ago, to pick up the one garbage bag that Carlton had placed on the curb at dusk the day before. It was still quite dark outside, and about half of the residents in the area were up and about, readying themselves for their endeavors. Before long, the sun would rise on the quiet little town of Dover, Massachusetts, breathe life into the day. Soon, what will be, will be.

Before he pressed the doorbell, he stood in front of the mansion for a moment, marveling at the almost three acres of beautiful estate grounds. Absorbing the surrounding scenery, something that Stoney had enjoyed for only a fraction of any given day, he took great pleasure in all that it had to offer. He also took note of the five foot tall, perfectly manicured rose bushes planted on each side of the stairs, wanted to reach out and take a few home to his wife.

Having his fill, he rang the doorbell.

Less than thirty seconds later, Carlton had opened the door. He was a little surprised, but very frustrated, because he had answered a cavalcade of thorny questions just hours before—he was drilled until he broke down, collapsed, cried dramatically on the mercy of the kitchen table. It was more like an intense interrogation, excluding the smoked filled room with the only lamp positioned a few feet above his head, a halo of light circling three feet around the chair he was seated in. He wiped his eyes, yawned, then stated unenthusiastically, "Captain Winslow, I presume." Even at this early hour, in his robe and slippers, still dignified.

"Yes," he replied. "Sorry to disturb you at this early hour, but I ..."

"It's no problem, sir. The last of the Dover police department just left a short while ago." For a split second, it seemed as though he wanted to vent his frustrations, curse out loud, call them every four letter word in the book. "I didn't have the chance to go to sleep anyway."

"Good. Then may I come inside? Ya see, some particular questions have been brought to my attention, and I'd like to discuss them with you. It shouldn't take too long, only a few minutes." He stood patiently, his hands clasped behind his back, rocking back and forth in his Bostonian Wingtips. He appeared a seven year old child who had a secret that he couldn't wait to unload on anyone who'd listen.

Carlton stated whiningly, "No disrespect, Captain, but I've already given a complete statement to the Dover police department." Lowering his head, he added, "They've told me not to discuss the case with anyone who doesn't represent their department."

His speech was impeccably sharp. He had made his point. No. He wanted to believe that he had made his point. Like most civilians, it made him feel good to be able to tell a person of authority that they couldn't speak with them. It was like saying 'Here's a dose of your own medicine.'

But what he would've preferred to say was, 'I'm busy. Go away. Beat it! **Get lost!! Scram!!!**'

Capt. Winslow smiled comfortably. It was more like a smirk. One that told him, 'Guess what, amigo? The jig is up.' He asked, "Is that so ..." he emphasized, stretched the name extensively, "... *Mr. Perezzz?*"

Suddenly, Carlton had the strangest feeling that he was about to have his unconstitutional rights crammed straight up his ass. No grease on the splintered stainless steel shaft, a running head start from fifty yards away, kicked into high gear by a jet propelled one thousand horsepower, nitrous oxide engine. With turbo! Somewhere in the background he heard the phrases **'IMIGRATION!'** and **'DEPORTATION!'**

At that moment, he remembered several years before when he was pulled over by a Dover police officer. While running a few errands; frequenting the laundry mat to pick up a few of Stoney shirts, and some light grocery shopping, he was stopped because he had ran a red light. Because he couldn't produce the proper identification, he was arrested on suspicion, brought to the police station in cuffs, then questioned about his citizenship status. Later that evening, Stoney was called to the Dover police station. As a courtesy for a fellow officer, Carlton was released into his custody, under the terms that he'd register immediately. Simply put, he never did. Hearing his true surname, he grew uneasy and began to perspire. He had no idea about what was going to happen next. Was the Capt. going for his gun? His handcuffs? A rubber hose? Was there a charter van full of illegal aliens parked just outside, hidden around the corner? His stuttering reply was, "Y-Y-Yes sir."

Capt. Winslow pulled a fresh cigar from out of his shirt pocket. He positioned it into his mouth—it looked like he was about to suck the flavor from out of a hotdog. Or about to fire a blow dart to its intended target. He shifted it to the left, then clamped down hard. "Well, in that case," his teeth didn't separate when he said this, "I didn't come here to discuss the case concerning officer Brooks." He hesitated before he finished with, "I came here to discuss your illegal residency in this here fine country of ours."

Carlton's eyes widened to their maximum displacement. He felt like a bully had just stepped on his shoes, punched him in the left eye, then demanded that he apologize for not existing in another place and time. Feeling every nerve ending in his body tingle, he clutched the lapels on his robe, threw several gasps into the air. With a South American accent, he asked, "Would you like to come inside, sir?"

His English accent faded to nothing. Fizzled out to zilch. Vanished.

Noticing his abrupt change in lingo, Capt. Winslow smiled dimly. "I do believe I will."

Leading Capt. Winslow to the living room, he walked solemnly, head hung low, dragged his feet, like a condemned man on his way to the gallows. What he had hid for many years was about to be revealed. Soon, he would be naked to the elements. In rare form. Exposed to the bone.

After they arrived to the living room, Carlton gestured toward the couch. "Would you like to have a seat, sir?"

Before Capt. Winslow sat down, he eyed him suspiciously. "Now we're getting somewhere."

Both took a seat, opposite each other. When Capt. Winslow questioned someone, he wanted to be close enough to observe their facial expressions and body language. Especially if it was someone who he felt had something to hide. "Now, tell me ... Mr. Perez." Eyes piercing Ramon, he hesitated before he asked, "What in the hell's been going on around here?"

As he showered him with his truthful identity, Ramon turned from him, stared into the fireplace, appeared far away, somewhere where he preferred to be. Using an obvious delay tactic, he asked, "Would you like something to drink, sir?" Still donning an extremely polite demeanor. It grew to be second in nature.

In thinking about how Stoney had been poisoned, he replied positively, "No thanks! Not from this house." Cleared his throat. "Now, stop stalling and tell me about everything. I want to know all of the details, and don't hold anything back. I've already got some of the details, so don't lie to me. You'll only dig a bigger hole for yourself." His cigar slid from the left side of his mouth to the right. His magnified eyes zoomed in on Ramon, as though examining an ameba through a microscope.

Ramon spoke softly. "That is my real name, Ramon Perez." Sounded like he was announcing a matador entering the arena when he proclaimed proudly, "Ramon Jesus Guadalupe Perez!" He paused to gather his thoughts, then continued flatly, "I came to this country some ten years ago, from South America, to make a life for my family and I. I had entered with my wife and three year old child. We snuck across the border, hiding in back of an old delivery van." A formidable incident came to mind, his eyes misted, and he bowed his head forlornly. His voice full of anguish, his eyes shut tight to erase a disturbing image before him, he went on to say, "Less than two miles after entering California, we had the most terrible accident." Capt. Winslow heard a gulp when he swallowed hard. "It was horrible. I think the brakes failed, or something like that. I was knocked unconscious, and thrown clear of the van, into some tall grass. When I woke up the next day, I saw that the only injuries I suffered were a fractured elbow, a twisted ankle, and a few scrapes on my head." Choking on his words, he continued, "I also discovered that my wife and daughter ... they ... they had died instantly." Through a moment of unfathomable grief, as though it were somehow his fault, he expelled a heavy breath, "Since there was nothing that I could do for them, I let them stay where they were. After another day of rest, I struggled to get to the nearest town, which was almost ten miles away. I went to a terminal and boarded a charter bus, and it took me to South Station, in Boston, Massachusetts. I was supposed to meet some relatives there, but they never showed up. Since I didn't have their address, I stayed in that area until my money ran out. I didn't have much, only fifty dollars. Since I didn't have the proper papers to get any kind of a start, I was homeless for a while. I didn't know anything about the system, how it operated, so I did nothing. I didn't ask questions because I thought I would've gotten caught, then sent back to South America. I lived in a cardboard box, behind the bus terminal." From out of nowhere, he declared ardently, "That's where I met officer Brooks. He was walking by one day, and saw me sleeping on the ground. He stopped to talk to me, and we shared a cup of coffee. Ever since then I've been working for him as his valet. His man Friday, waiting on him hand and foot."

Capt. Winslow glanced around the living room, took note of the luxurious furnishings. "This beautiful house and its contents were paid for by ..."

Ramon finished, "... with the money that officer Brooks made from hustling criminals. I know that this is of no consolation, but he was very good at it. He was so good that officers Sinclair and Knight envied him greatly for his natural ability to improvise." He thought of his last statement, then decided to be more forward and blurted, "They were jealous! I could see on their faces, and in their eyes. Officer Sinclair, more than officer Knight. When they hung out here, sometimes to watch sports on television, they'd take a short break to hustle a new criminal. They'd turn off all the lights, except for the one pointed at the person doing the hustling. The next thing you know, it was like they were on stage, playing a role in a movie. When officer Brooks spoke to these people on his cell phone, I saw a whole different side of him. He sounded like somebody I've never seen before; a total stranger. He was very warm and appreciative one moment, showing the person with many warm praises. And on the very same breath, he turned into someone that was very cold and unforgiving ... damning the person extensively. And I could tell that he meant every word he spoke. I can't see how, but they enjoyed this behavior enormously. At the end of the performance, they'd stand up and applaud, bring down the roof." He paused. "I knew that these things were going on when they had first started, some ten years ago. But, I kept my mouth shut. As long as I did, I knew I'd have a decent job. Officer Brooks paid me good wages." Before volunteering this next piece of information, he hesitated, then went on to say, "Captain, over the years, officer Brooks has had many visits from other police officers from your same department. As they spoke, most of the time, I would never be too far away. In case they needed refreshments, or appetizers. From listening to them, I gathered that most of them wanted to be on top of the world. It was never enough for them to merely exist. They acted as though they were not going to be satisfied until they had everything, all the luxuries in life. Captain, how is it that so many people wish to be put on pedestals, like kings without a country to rule? I use to believe that this was because of conditioning from television and Hollywood. You know, all of that glamour stuff. But then I realized that someone has to govern even the politicians, the celebrities, and professional athletes. Anyone with fame, fortune, or a lot of money.

"You must understand, Captain, your country has a head; the government. But the body will only be as pure as the minds thoughts. I've heard many strange things during my stay here. I was, how you Americans say, like 'a fly on the wall.' The officers who stopped by to see Mr. Brooks never paid any attention to me.

Chances are, it was because I never interfered with what was going on. I never said much. I stayed in my place." He peered at Capt. Winslow shadily when he said, "Captain, there were many many *strange* things going on. Many crazy things. I've learned of one officer who was also a hit man. He was paid fifty thousand dollars to make a witness disappear. Another officer manufactured evidence, just for the sake of a few dollars, and a promotion. He said that because it was an election year, he had to help make the commissioner look good to his constituents. Plus, you know, one hand washes the other, as far as favors are concerned. He also planted evidence at crime scenes, just to get people convicted. Another officer, um, I forget his name," he believed that it would be in his best interest to say he forgot his name. He knew their names well, "he use to arrive at accident scenes, and have a bidding war with the people involved to see who would get his report to be in their favor. At some places where people left their cars abandoned, if the car was worth anything, he'd radio his friend with a pick-up truck to come and get it. Before anyone else found out about it. Then that friend towed the car to a chop shop, and they made money from selling the parts." He stopped talking for a moment, sat back in his chair. He asked, "Captain, why is it so important to obtain great wealth at the risk of loosing your self-respect? And these are supposed to be men of honor and integrity. From experiencing this, I was beginning to understand why so many in your country disrespect your system of leadership. I know that corruption goes on in the country where I come from, but your system is a wonderful one. It's the abuse of an individual's inalienable rights that I find very … very …" He looked into his lap. "… Captain, I'll tell you one thing that my grandfather use to always tell me when I was young. He would always ask me 'how do you find clear solutions, in a bucket of dirty problems?'"

"I don't know. How do you?"

"You don't. You simply empty the bucket, clean out the residue, then fill it again. It's just that easy. Most of the time, the only thing that makes it difficult is the sticky arrogance of some who know that they should be replaced. In this country, Captain, you've got a whole lot of cleaning to do. And if you don't get it done, then the bucket is going to rot, and then leak. Then you're going to have a much worse problem on your hands."

Capt. Winslow nodded dismissively. His ears were filled to the brim with Ramón's self-righteous rhetoric. He disputed, "Look, buddy, I don't want to get into a pissing contest about ethics and who has the best country. Sometimes we all have problems with doing the right thing. If you country was any better, you'd still be there, wouldn't you? In referring to the accident involving your wife and child, at no matter what the situation, I would've never left them, until I knew that they were laid to rest properly. For that matter, I would've never chanced their lives in a beat-up death van." Ramon lowered his head regrettably. "But anyway, let's get down to business. "Tell me everything you know about the manuscript, officers Brooks, Sinclair and Knight."

"Yes, the manuscript. It was supposed to be a work of fiction. One that officer Brooks said that he was never going to publish. He couldn't, because he knew it meant his neck. He only joked about doing so. Said he might change it all around, restructure it, then get it published under a friends name, just to see how it would do in the mainstream media. Mostly, he wrote it for practice. It was hobby of his. The title, 'The Dixie Club', is the name of the actual group that the three had formed. As far as the situations entailed inside of it are concerned, involving the type of hustling that they were into, everything is true. It all happened. Officer Brooks only changed the names, places and dates, so that he wouldn't directly involve himself, officers Knight and Sinclair."

Capt. Winslow mumbled, "Before Sinclair and Knight killed Bogarts family, they assumed that Brooks kept an authentic diary of what they were into." Thinking back, when he was at the house earlier, with the Dover police department, he finally understood why officers Sinclair and Knight had flashed bizarre expressions when Detective Sloan discovered the book, then read the title. He said, "This confirms that they would've done anything to get their hands on it. Include murder Capt. Bogart and his family, in cold blood."

Ramon's eyes nearly popped out of their sockets. He lost all coordination involving his breathing and speech. He stuttered appallingly, "Th-Th-They murdered somebody?" Growing hysterical, he rambled, "I don't doubt it about officer Sinclair. He's the ring leader. He talked the others into doing it. If you ask me, the man es moy loco. He's merciless! He'd sell out his own mother, if it would save him from going to jail. I heard him say so."

"Forget about what I just said." He paused, thinking. "Um, yeah. Uh-huh. It's all coming together now. A solid motive. Now, for the fifty million dollar question. What's the name of the pharmacist who came by to see officer Brooks?"

Ramon looked upward, scratched his head. "His name's Norton. Greg Norton. He's a very strange man, that Norton character. One second he runs hot, and the next, he's as cold as an ice cube."

"When he was here, did you notice anything unusual about him? Something that he might've done."

Ramon lowered his head, thinking. "No. Not really. As they talked, I stepped out of the room momentarily, to get a glass of ginger ale for officer Brooks. When

I returned, Mr. Norton was gone. But the man does have nice manners, in a weird kind of way."

"What do you mean by that?"

"He may fit right in with everyone out here, but I think he's a phony. He pretends to be someone that he's not. If you observe him long enough, you can see right through him. He's plastic."

Capt. Winslow took out a small notepad and began scribbling. "Greg Norton, huh?"

"Yeah. Greg Norton."

"You notice anything else strange about his character?"

"Yeah."

"What's that?"

"He's a married man. But I heard from officer Brooks that he's a womanizer, all the time chasing the senoritas."

Capt. Winslow wrote all of this down. "Okay. This should do it, for now." He stuck the note pad into his shirt pocket, then rose from the couch. He walked to the doorway, but before he left, he turned around as said, "You know, all of this makes you an accessory after the fact. And a material witness. You knew about all of these crimes committed, but never said a word to anyone. When if you had acted, you could've worked out a deal with the state, and maybe have gotten your citizenship."

Ramon clasped his hands, humbled himself. "I thought of that, sir. But, who would've believed me even if I did tell? They would've had a hit man erase me from existence. Besides, I'm merely a peasant from a poor country. An immigrant. A foreigner. It would've been my word against such law men. As I've said before. Officer Brooks treated me good. He treated me with respect. It's not easy to bite the hand that feeds you."

Capt. Winslow swallowed the realities of his last statement, then asked, "When the detectives from the Dover police department questioned you, what did you tell them?"

"Since they didn't find out about my true identity, I told them exactly what officer Brooks told me to say, if the occasion should arise. That I was only his uncle, who came from England to get a fresh start, because I was on the skids. At first, I though that they already knew who I was. Eight years ago, when I was on an errand to pick up some dry cleaning and buy groceries, I was stopped by a Dover police officer for a minor traffic infraction. Luckily for me, he retired three years ago, and took my secret with him."

"Did you give them the name of the pharmacist?"

"No."

"Why not?"

"I told them that I didn't know."

"Why did you do that?"

"Because they would've wanted me to stick around for a follow-up on this and that, involving me deeper into everything that's happened. Stoney told me that if anyone were to question me about anything, to say as little as possible, and never volunteer information. He said that that's how some people got themselves into trouble."

Capt. Winslow nodded. "I see. Well, do you know what can happen to you, if and when they find out the truth about what you've just told me?"

Ramon didn't reply. He waited anxiously, knowing that Capt. Winslow would inform him regardless.

"You could go to jail for a hellova long time. I'm not going arrest you because you're not in my jurisdiction. But mostly, because it'd only be a waste of my time. As far as I'm concerned, the only thing you're guilty of is your ignorance." He turned and walked through the front door.

After he left, Ramon hustled to the window facing the street, watched Capt. Winslow hurry to his cruiser. He radioed Wendy to request Greg Norton's home address. After it flashed on the computer screen, he turned on the engine and sped away.

After he was out of view, Ramon ran to his room to pack his belongings. His newfound plans were to put as much distance as possible, in between him and the mansion, the fastest way that he could. He wanted to be history, long gone before the Dover police department woke up to what Capt. Winslow had just learned.

CHAPTER 38

▼

At six thirty a.m., Capt. Winslow had arrived at Greg Norton's residence. He lived only a few miles from Stoney, on the west side. In a conservative part of town that's family orientated. Before he stepped out of the cruiser, he threw his cigar onto the dashboard, then closed his eyes tight. He yawned exhaustively, and his body reminded him that he hadn't gotten that much sleep the evening before.

He took out his note pad to make sure that he was at the correct address, then observed the fine-looking mansion, speculated on everything that he had learned thus far.

The beautifully crafted and meticulous seven year old mansion was custom built to Greg Norton's exact specifications. In thinking of the diary, he remembered reading a few paragraphs that explained in fine detail what it had looked like.

He remembered reading that it was layered in a French White vinyl siding, and was finely trimmed with many personalized and precious possessions characterized by the well-to-do. It relayed to all who marveled at the house that that particular family put their all into every little thing that they did. From the many assorted and cleverly arranged eye-catching plants dressing the entire landscape, to the French white doghouse positioned to the right of the four car garage.

The colors differed somewhat, from what was written in the diary—Stoney never knew the difference between light beige and French white—but the description of the layout was the same. Even the mailbox was a miniature version of the house itself. Even it had a four car garage, and a doghouse sitting off to the side.

The same chapter gave a thorough and detailed description of each of the family members personalities; their individual traits. He figured that either Stoney knew them well, or admired them from afar. Chances are, it was the later of the two, knowing what kind of clandestine business he was involved in.

He remembered reading about how close-knit they were in all aspects of their family life. About how Greg was a longtime member of a prestigious country club and Capt. of the community's bowling team. He was also a crewmember of the yachting club and scoutmaster of the local chapter of Boy Scouts. He remembered reading about how his wife was on several community boards, and was heavily involved in the PTA. She chaperones nearly every event that their children's elementary and junior high school held, and has won ten blue ribbons for five years straight, for her award winning apple preserves.

He remembered that the following chapters described how a man could achieve such a desirable foundation in life, had a wonderful family who worshiped the ground he walked on, but allowed himself to sink deep into the epitome of some of the states most notorious undesirables. He was ivy league educated—graduated from the Harvard school of pharmacology in nineteen eighty-four—and his roots led to a prominent family from Connecticut. All this, but he enjoyed tripping the light fantastic on the dark side. Probably to break the monotony, he had developed a split personality.

Capt. Winslow stepped out of his cruiser, slammed the door shut. He proceeded to tread the thirty yard long cobblestone path leading to the eight foot tall beautifully crafted mahogany double doors. Along the way, he glanced at the landscape and became astonished for the perfectly cut grass. Each strand stood exactly the same height. Each the same width. Each the same shade green. The bushes sitting off to the sides of the steps leading to the front door, two on each side, never had he seen shrubbery so perfectly shaped in all his born days. It was as if they were computer trimmed with a laser to a fraction of an inch.

He climbed the four steps leading to the front door, looked upward, paused to admire the roman design implemented into the doorways arch. Lowering his line of sight, he observed the full-length colorfully stained glass dressing the sides of the door, and the brass night lamps complimenting them. They looked like they were taken from a historic castle in jolly old England centuries ago. This was definitely the place that he had read about. There was no mistake about it.

He unfastened the strap on his holster, just in case. He lifted the large brass knocking ring centering the left door, studied it for a moment. There were two; one on each door. When he dropped it, he heard the dull thumping of metal against wood. He waited patiently.

Less than fifteen seconds later, an occupant of the house appeared behind the left stained glass and stared inquisitively at him. Observing the colorful patchwork design on their face, he heard a mans muffled voice say, "Yes. Is there something I can do for you?" A dog began barking, the man ordered, "Go away, Caesar!"

"I'm Captain Winslow of the Boston police department. I was wondering if I could speak with Greg Norton for a moment."

"Excuse me," the man said, "but can you please show some identification?"

He pulled out his wallet, opened it and flashed his badge. He heard a bolt retract, and the left door opened slowly. When it was opened halfway, the aroma of fresh potpourri seeped outside and filled his senses pleasurably. It caused him to frequent the heartwarming memories of his dearly departed mother. She kept a full basket of what smelled like the same on the living room coffee table, in the front hallway, the bathroom, and in a few of the bedrooms.

Capt. Winslow was amazed at how such a seemingly heavy door with large gothic like rustic hinges could operate so quietly, with the slightest effort. A phenomenon, as if there were zero force of gravity.

The morning chill whipped through the front door, embraced the man and he shiver briefly. He opened his eyes wide, assisting them in making their morning adjustment to the abrupt change in light. He stood humbly, dignified, in his Polo designer silk robe and cozy fur slippers. He stretched, covered his mouth and yawned. "Good morning, sir." As with Carlton, his mannerism reigned supreme. Such niceness. Such politeness. Such courtesy. Such ... "What can I do for you on this brisk morning?" He extended his hand, keeping in mind that this officer was out of his jurisdiction. He figured that he would limit his responses. He knew that too many words opened the doors to rooms he wanted to stay out of.

Capt. Winslow returned his wallet to his pocket, reached out and shook his hand. As they shook, he thought that his skin was as soft as a baby behind. No calluses, manicured nails and the whole nine yards. I could never trust a guy with hands like these, he thought. He's probably never done a hard days work in his life. He probably doesn't even know how to put the gas into his own car. If he's responsible for officer Brooks' death, I'd rather break his hand than shake it. But until I know for sure, I'll play his little game of Fantasy Island. I wonder if Tatu is in there somewhere, strutting around with tea and crumpets on a silver platter held high over his head.

Remembering what he had read about Greg's personality, he felt as though he knew the man well. He quickly grew familiar with the way he stood poetically, leaning off to one side. The way he tilted his head, as if to wonder continuously why things were, the way that they were. He noticed the way the left corner of his lip rose slightly, it remained in snubbing position. Like Elvis Presley. He noticed the way his bottom lip frowned, as if someone had just christened his two thousand dollars Italian shoes by stepping on them. His demeanor made him feel guilty. As if he had done something wrong, even before he committed the act. He proceeded cautiously, as if not to step on his toes. As if not to insult by insinuating that he might've done something even remotely wrong. This is America, and undeniably the rich do get preferential treatment.

"Sorry to disturb you at this early hour. Are you Greg Norton?"

The man stated shrewdly, "I am. How may I be of some service?"

Capt. Winslow tried to slip one by him. "May I come inside for a moment? I'd like to ask you a few questions."

Unlike most American citizens, Greg understood that he didn't have to permit the officer to enter into his domain, unless he had a search warrant, or probable cause. Realizing that neither existed, he replied, "I'm sorry, Captain. I have a wife and daughter who are not dressed properly as yet. We're just now getting up for the day. I'm sure you can understand that." He looked to the street and saw the marked police cruiser parked at the curb. He looked up and down the street to his neighbors houses, to see if any were outside, watching the unusual early morning events—an out of town police officer at the front door of the Norton's Estate. He was sure that the incident would raise many eyebrows. Give birth to many unfounded rumors. There would be talk.

Capt. Winslow threw his hands onto his hips, sighed. "Ah, yeah. Sure. I understand. No problem. Then I'll ask you the questions right here, if that's okay with you?"

Greg thought about it for a moment, spewed threw pruned lips. "I guess I could spare a few moments."

Capt. Winslow dived right in and got straight to the point. "Do you know a police officer named Stoney Brooks?"

He looked up for a moment, searching through his memory. "Stoney … Brooks?"

"Yes. He *was* one of my men."

"The name does ring a bell." He repeated, "Stoney Brooks. Stoney Brooks." He exclaimed, "Ah, yes! Now that I recall, I delivered some prescription medication to him a few days ago, when I was on my way to another appointment. It slipped my mind briefly, because I had made three deliveries that day. He was at his Uncles house." He looked down for a moment. "Excuse me, Captain. Did I hear you speak of him as in the past tense?"

"Yes. That's what I said … *was*." He looked away despondently. "He … um … he passed away." The eyes being the mirror to the soul, he looked deep into Greg's eyes when he stated, "He was poisoned."

Greg's hands covered his mouth in shock. He expelled, "Oh my Goodness! I saw some terrible news on the television last night. About something that had happened to a police officer. I wasn't paying close attention." He drooled sympathetically, "Captain, you have my utmost condolences."

Not for an instant did Capt. Winslow look away from his eyes. No matter how deep he had to dig, no matter what he had to uncover, he was determined to find the truth. Unexpectedly, he saw an inclination of what could've been perceived as genuine sincerity in his outpouring of emotions, actual grief. Although, skeptically, he wondered if it was for Stoney, or for himself. He became confused and didn't know what to think. He suddenly wondered if he had any involvement in Stoneys death whatsoever. Maybe he was an excellent actor.

He believed that he had enough intuition to be able to tell if Greg was lying. As in the past, with other suspects, there were several signs that he had come to recognize right off the bat. Sometimes the person would get nervous or fumble over their words and movements. Make inconsistent statements. Or they would stutter, or avoid eye contact. Regardless, he couldn't arrest the person until he found solid evidence that they had committed the crime in question.

As for Greg Norton, the man was cool. Too cool. Ice! Hot ice! He didn't twitch, fumble or sweat, and kept solid eye contact. He stayed in total control of himself. He remained self-assured, as if he was the President of the United States, stating at a press conference before his joint chiefs of staff and the American news media, 'I was misled into believing that weapons of mass destruction really did exist. Even my Taro palm reader told they existed. As God is my witness, I don't think she'd lie to me, just because she has stock in Halliburton industries.'

"What happened when you were at his uncles house?" He peered deeply into his eyes, placed his hand on his gun. His fingertips grazed the hard leather, an elaborate attempt to incite a nervous response. Stunts like this worked sometimes. Today, it didn't.

Greg's self-assurance remained intact. His integrity, unbendable. His responses very sharp and accurate. "It was a brief encounter," he explained. "After I entered the house, Carlton brought me in to see officer Brooks. We talked for a few moments about the strength of the prescriptions, and I explained to him about the dosage. When Carlton left the room to get some refreshments, since I was in a rush, I left before he had returned." His head tilted slightly from the left to the right from sentence to sentence. His statements were precise, as if he had been rehearsing them for twenty-four hours a day, beginning a week before Stoneys demise.

Reading in between the lines, Capt. Winslow felt that what he would have preferred to say was, 'You have all of the information you requested, now be gone from my doorsteps you vagabond. Hurry, before any of my neighbors notice your eerie presence. I have much better things to do, than to stand here and converse with the likes of someone in your menial line of work.'

Capt. Winslow felt a negative vibe, chucked it to the understanding that most people simply don't like talking to police officers. Especially when one arrived at your doorstep so early in the morning. It made them feel as though they were instantly placed under suspicion. Life was difficult in itself without someone from '*the system*' adding more complications. "That's it? That's all that happened?"

Greg nodded. "That's it, Captain." Holding a faint smile, not an eye twitched spasmodically. Not one hair jumped out of place. Capt. Winslow figured his nerves were bronzed eons ago. He leaned closer. "You didn't have *any* words with him at all?"

Greg delivered a harmless expression. "Goodness no." He chuckled, "Why on earth would I?"

Capt. Winslow felt as though he was playing tag in the dark. Therefore, he switched games and pitched horseshoes. He asked point blank, "Wasn't he blackmailing you?"

Greg's eyes popped open wide and he laughed uncomfortably. "Officer Brooks, blackmailing me?" Clearing his throat, his sight shot cautiously over his left shoulder, back into the house. He stepped out onto the landing, then closed the door shut. Out of the side of his mouth, he whispered, "Captain, can we step further from the house to finish this conversation? You know, um, near the curb. Near your car." His head remained tilted, but his snobby expression dwindled slowly. His new expression read, 'Oh! I see! So you caught me trying to plug the dike with my ... well, you know.' He appeared the inexperienced farm boy who tried to milk a bull.

Capt. Winslow nodded, "Now we're getting someplace." Because of the drastic change of his demeanor, he finally understood Ramón's statement when he informed him that he was a phony. Now he was looking at a whole new side of the man. A Dr. Jeckle, Mr. Hyde.

Feeling vastly paranoid, Greg opened the door partially and glanced into the house once again, to make sure that no one had heard what Capt. Winslow had just mentioned.

"Sure. We can do that." I'll go along with his little game, he thought. At least until I find out for sure about what actually happened.

Greg closed the front door, then both tread the cobblestone path, leading to the curb. Along the way, he glanced back at the house several times to see if any family members were peeking through any of the windows, observing their every move. They reached the sidewalk, stood a few feet from the cruiser. He said, "So he's the one who sent me the letters, with the pictures."

"What letters. What pictures?"

"A few years ago, my wife and I were on the threshold of a divorce, because of my fleeting infidelity. This may sound far fetched, but I had cheated on her. One Friday evening, I was in Boston on business, to attend a very important meeting. After we closed a big deal, a few of my colleagues and I celebrated by going out on the town. I had become entirely inebriated, and I knew I couldn't drive home in that condition. So I sat in my car and drank a few cups of coffee, waiting to sober up. As I did, I was approached by a prostitute who propositioned me." He hesitated before he said regrettably," Maybe if I wasn't drinking, I would've turned her down. But that's not what happened. I accepted, and we had sex, in the back seat of my car. As she was getting out of the car, we were arrested by the Boston police. We were taken to the police station, where I was booked for having unsolicited sex with a prostitute. She was booked for prostitution, and robbery. During the tryst, she had stolen my wallet." He took a deep breath, then, "I called my lawyer, and he came to bail me out. When the court day arrived, I was sentenced to probation for three months. And I had to pay a one thousand dollar fine. But mostly, it was all hush hush. You know, on the down low. My lawyer handled the situation, so that I didn't even have to show up at court for my sentencing. Since it occurred in Boston, none of it got back out here, to my family and community." Shadowed by a cloud of remorse, he lowered his head shamefully. He expelled a heavy sigh before he went on to say, "Less than a month after my arrest, I received a letter and some pictures. The letter explained that I was going to be blackmailed, and told me how much I had to pay on a monthly basis. The pictures were of me and the prostitute having sex. I also received a copy of the police report and court documents. If word ever got back here about any of this, my family life would've been ruined." He paused again. "Although I walked right into it, I felt like I was set up. I never knew who was doing it to me, until now."

Capt. Winslow recalled reading that out of the sixty-seven people that Stoney had hustled, he knew only three of them through typical business relations.

Those were the ones that he had sent letters to, because he didn't want to chance them recognizing his voice over the phone.

"Please, help me understand this. You mean to tell me that you never knew who was blackmailing you ..." his eyes opened wide, "... until now?" His arms crossed, tremendously perplexed.

"That's correct. And man was I paying through the nose. It was like having a black cloud following me around, everywhere I went. I mean, granted, I made a mistake. I paid my debt to society, as required by law. It was supposed to be a done deal. A dead issue, in the past. I shouldn't have had to keep paying for it like that. I was sentenced to pay the state, and I did." His temper flared and got the best of him when he stated furiously, "Not some renegade cop! What he did nearly destroyed my family. I had fabricated these ridiculous excuses to explain to my wife where the money was going. I told her that I gave to many charities on a weekly basis, and she passed around talk that I was into the business of philanthropy. The next thing you know, everybody was asking for money. It was getting so bad that I was running out of reasonable excuses ... and money. Once, I told her that I was taking lessons on how to be a better lover." He smiled insecurely. "This, she welcomed wholeheartedly. Another time, I told her that I was taking flying lessons. And I don't even like getting into airplanes."

Capt. Winslow refastened the Velcro strap securing his gun in place, and Greg felt relieved that he did. Appearing curious, he repeated, "Flying lesson?"

Greg nodded distastefully. "Yeah. Flying lessons."

"But, if your wife is an understanding woman, and I hope that she is, wouldn't she have forgiven you, if you had simply told her the truth?"

"Captain, take a look around you. It's not just my wife whose forgiveness I would've been asking for. There are also my kids, and all of the respectful organizations that we're associated with. In this wealthy community, when people discover skeletons in your closet, whether they're only accusations or rumors, the scandal begins immediately. They'll oust you with no reconsiderations whatsoever." He spanned the area, admiring the breathtaking scenery. "My family and I, we've built so much here. We've come so far. We have solid roots in this community." He swallowed hard, then stated adamantly, "I just couldn't let them down like that. I'm the head of my family. They look to me with great respect, and I want them to continue to do so. Keeping their respect means everything to me. I'm sure you can understand that, with your being a man of honor."

"I guess so. But, let's go back to when you were in the house. Try to focus now. Is there anything that you might've forgotten to tell me? Something that might've slipped your mind."

Greg looked slightly to the left, his eyebrows sank curiously in the middle of his forehead, just over the bridge of his nose. "No, Captain. It was a simple, you know 'stop by and drop off' situation." Seconds later, he added, "But, you know something, Captain? That Carlton fellow and officer Brooks had the strangest relationship. There's just something not right about it."

Capt. Winslow figured his last statement to be a deterrent to shift suspicion. Remembering that Capt. Bogart had mentioned that there was a listening device found planted in Stoneys telephone, he asked, "Mr. Norton, do you know anything about electronics?"

"No. I'm a pharmacist. Not an electrical technician."

Capt. Winslow sighed. "Well, I guess that's everything. I'm sure you can understand why I had to ask all of these probing questions. It's just procedure."

You miserable wretched asshole, Greg thought. The nerve of you to come out of your jurisdiction, to question me improperly in front of my own home ... I hate your guts! You disgust me. Suppose someone were watching. Suppose they saw you. How am I going to explain that? Consider yourself fortunate that I gave your pilfering roly-poly ass the time of day. I know the acronym C.O.P. stands for 'Cash Over People.' I saw it written in a book somewhere. Everybody knows about it. Greg smiled pretentiously. "I understand, Captain. Just procedure." Signaling that the interrogation was over, he took a step backwards, then stuck his hands comfortably into the pockets of his robe. "Well, Captain ..." he extended his right hand, "... I wish we could've conversed under more pleasant circumstances."

Capt. Winslow had noticed that within the blink of an eye, his demeanor had reverted back to his usual self. His head tilted slightly to the left, the left corner of his lip rose like Elvis Presley's, his lower lip arched into a frown.

Through his transformation, he thought, that damn diary, manuscript or whatever the hell it is ain't nothing but pure hell. Just when you think it leads you somewhere solid, it throws you a curve, and you're right back to square one. I guess this takes me to the one person who I haven't talked to yet. Stoneys girlfriend. Her number is bound to be in that little black telephone book I saw resting on the coffee table, in the living room. Or in the memory of one of his cordless phones, of which I can only hope that the Dover police department didn't take. "Okay, Mr. Norton." He shook his hand. "Sorry I had to bother you with all of this stuff, so early in the morning." He said this to get him to lower his guard. To hang lose. "You won't be hearing from me again. Thank you for your time."

"You're welcome, Captain." Greg flashed a pearly white smile. "Have a nice day." Before he returned to his house, he glanced precariously up and down the street at his neighbor's houses to see if anyone was watching. After finding no one, he sighed with relief. He made his way up the cobblestone path, and stopped when he got to the first step. He picked up the newspaper that was thrown haphazardly on the dew ridden grass an hour earlier, then went inside. He looked through the stained glass accentuating the doorframe, and observed Capt. Winslow's cruiser pulling away. He whispered, "Thank God! No more payments. The bloodthirsty greedy bastard got just what he deserved."

His wife approached from behind, startled him. "Did you say something, dear?"

Greg turned to her. "Oh!" He embraced her, said affectionately, "My dearest Pamela. I didn't know that you were up yet, my pet." His kissed her gently on her forehead.

She smiled. "Who was that, honey?"

"It was just one of the guys from the bowling team. He's going away on a business trip, and came by to inform me that he won't be able to make the upcoming tournament. That's all."

"Oh. That's a shame. Anyway, sweetheart, what would you like for breakfast on this magnificent morning?"

$*$ $*$ $*$ $*$

Driving to Stoneys' house, he wondered about the conversation that he had with Greg Norton. He's a little rough around the edges, but a softy, he thought. He doesn't seem like the type who would kill a cop who was blackmailing him. The type that is, I can normally smell them from a hundred miles away. Damn that Book! It's like looking at a 3-D picture puzzle, through a kaleidoscope.

CHAPTER 39

▼

Capt. Winslow had arrived at Stoneys mansion at seven-fifteen a.m.. Before he got out of the cruiser, he observed the estate momentarily while considering the conundrum of Greg Norton's identity—wondered what kind of a man was inside of the man.

Besides the notion that he reminds me of a few two faced politicians I know, he thought, there's something about him that I just can't put my finger on. He's just like Ramon said. All chatty and professional one second. Then after you pull a few skeletons out of his closet, he gets all hush hush and paranoid, spewing dumb excuses like 'I have a more pressing engagement to attend. You'll have to ask my lawyer about that. I'm not at liberty to say so.' Then he slips the crowd a professional liar, a veteran politician.

He grabbed the cigar from the dashboard and threw it in his mouth. He chewed on it a few seconds. His face went sour, thinking, I have to start chewing on a different brand. A day or so with these cheap ones, and the taste goes all to hell. They start falling apart in your mouth. Maybe I'll try a Cuban brand when I get a chance. I've been hearing some good things about those babies. Sgt. Thompson picked up a box when he went to Mexico last week. I'll see if I can get one from him when I return to Boston.

He stepped out of the cruiser, walked across the lawn, and slipped under the tape marked 'POLICE CRIME SCENE. DO NOT CROSS.' Being overweight, he sometimes emitted a hefty grunt when he bent over. His lap bunched to his chest area, compressed his lungs, caused him to practically suffocate. His wife has been trying for years to get him to loose a couple of pounds, but it's been an unsuccessful voyage. He likes to watch television most evenings, and those dagnabit food commercials are murder. The only exercise he gets nowadays is from running back and forth to the refrigerator for snacks, during commercials. At nearly every important business meeting that he attends, food is always the center of attraction. There was no way around it. As for trying to regulate his amount of caloric intake, his wife, relatives, and concerned friends figured they would've had more success in trying to take a juicy pork chop from a starving Pit-bull that hasn't eaten in days.

He opened the front door, but before he entered, he stood in the doorway and wondered if anyone was there. Listened to a creepy silence filling the empty mansion, he believed the coast was clear, then entered the house. Never mind the fact that he was breaking the law by entering a restricted crime scene. Being out of his jurisdiction, he was like the average civilian, subjected to their rules, their laws.

After his last visit, he figured Ramon to be long gone. He couldn't have been more right. However, along with his personal belongings, he took Stoneys silverware, his jewelry, a combination VCR/DVD player, some of Stoneys finer clothing, a pair of gold plated candleholders, the entire stereo system; including Stoneys personal music collection, an undetermined amount of cash, and a few other miscellaneous items. He also took the fishing tackle. He couldn't take the computer system because it had been confiscated by the Dover police department.

Listening to the loud silence haunting the mansion, he walked apprehensively to the living room. The weighty clomping of his Bostonian Wingtips echoed the halls and left him feeling somewhat uncomfortable. Walking through the mansion, he figured Stoney was a lonely man, not seeing many family portraits anywhere.

He looked on top of the glass coffee table and discovered that the little black book was still there. It belonged to Stoney, but was stenciled with the name 'Carlton Rogers.' That's probably why the Dover police department didn't take it. Capt. Winslow figured Stoney did this to throw suspicion.

He picked it up, scanned through it quickly and became disappointed to the fact that there were not many telephone numbers listed in it, less than a dozen. He would learn later that Stoney kept all of his important telephone numbers in his computer. Telephone numbers of the marks who he had blackmailed. The long list was filed under 'D.C. #s.'

He took a seat on the couch, then plopped his feet onto the coffee table, nearly shattered the glass. He crossed his feet at the ankles, sighed heavily, shook his head discontentedly. He whispered to the book, "Tell me something. Anything, please." Damn that Stoney, he thought. Since his life was all screwed up, I wonder what his girlfriend was like. Something tells me that she's going to take me on the ride of my life down 'Crap street', left onto 'Bullshit avenue, straight on through to 'I don't give a damn highway.' I remember running into her at the retirement party we had for Abe Johnson three years ago. She was stumbling all over the place in a drunken stupor, and going back and forth to the bathroom as though her bladder is the size of a golf ball. The girl ain't nothing but pure hell walking around on two feet. And those manners, oh my God! She'd fit right in with some institutionalized convicts. I wonder what Stoney found so attractive about her in the first place. But then again, I suppose if I was the kind of guy who thought with the brain in between my legs, I'd like her too. The jeans she wore that day were so tight, that they appeared to be spray painted on. I'm sure she wore crotchless panties, if any at all. What's funny was that nearly all of the wives badmouthed her as if she was nothing but a two bit slut, rubbing elbows with the elite for an evening of jaw jacking and slamming down a few boilermakers. Their husbands backed every word they said, even though some had playthings who looked just like her, on the side. She's nothing but a gussied up home wrecking vamp who does nothing but party and shop at the malls.

He cracked the small book open, then fingered through a few pages. Since he never knew her last name, it took him a few minutes to locate her first name. If it wasn't for his cousin having the same first name, he would've forgotten it.

He picked up the phone resting on the coffee table, dialed her number.

The phone rang six times before someone answered. An out-of-breath woman said exhaustively, "Hello!"

"Katherine?"

"Yeah," she grumbled, "Who the hell is this?"

Even at this early hour, she was her usual self. No wonder Stoney never introduced her to me, he thought. He was saving himself some embarrassment. People who wake up with this kind of attitude should go back to sleep, then never wake up again. That's all I need is for some sassy mouthed heffa to fill my ears with a bunch of hogwash. Thank God my little girl didn't grow up with a mouth like hers. I would've disowned her a long time ago. It's amazing the attitudes that some people can develop. Of course, unless she was born with hers.

"This is Captain Winslow of the Boston police department. I'm Stoneys boss. That is, his ex-boss. I called you because I wanted to talk to you about something very important."

She started right in and complained, "Look, Captain, I just got in from partying, and I'd kinda like to get some rest." She had the nerve to ask, "Do you mind? Besides, I already gave a statement to the Dover police department. They gave me explicit instructions not to discuss the case with anyone who doesn't represent their office. So, you're only wasting your time. Besides, I have some very important things that I have to ..."

Essentially, what she wanted to say was, 'go stick your head in a bucket of shit, then inhale.'

Meanwhile, what she actually thought was, what in the hell ever possessed me to get with that asshole in the first place? Because one of them got into some crazy shit, and got himself killed, someone's been calling me every half an hour, asking me about things that I don't even know about. This is starting to get on my nerves. So the man was hustling, big deal! He's not the only one on the force doing it. He's just the only one who got caught, so far. Wait until the good Capt. finds out about Spanky, Sleeper and the Dixie Club. For that matter, wait until he finds out a few others in his department. That should keep their internal affairs department busy for about a good twenty years.

Katherine's belief is that everyone on the planet earth is damned from day one. If you've ever told an innocent little white lie, then that's the same as telling a big bold face lie. To her, God and His eternal salvation is a yes or no situation. There is no such thing as being just a little bit pregnant. Either you are, or you aren't. St. Peter is not going to stand at the pearly gates with a measuring rod, and say, 'I think we'll let this seemingly harmless one slip by. He won't cause *too* many problems up here.'

She believes that in heaven there are no faults. Allowing one person in who has ever told any kind of a lie, would be like having a repeat of Adam and Eve in the Garden of Eden. Capt. Winslow cut her off, explaining, "I understand that. But Stoney was one of *my* men. He was one of my best men. As for what he was into, I'm just now finding out about his other side. I know he had a lot of problems, but he also saved a lot of lives, and helped a hellova lot of people. He only took advantage of those who were bad in the first place. I don't condone his illicit actions one bit, but we all have problems. Besides, I feel I owe it to him to find out who his killer is. I know what the rules are, but this one is special."

She thought about what he had said. In the background, he heard someone yawn. It was definitely a man. She pulled the phone from her ear and covered the mouthpiece with her hand. He heard her muffled voice say, "I thought I told you to keep quiet before I answered the phone? I'm talking to Stoneys boss. He's a cop."

"Aw shut up!" the man told her. "You stupid chicken head. He ain't nobody to me. After I get dressed, I'm getting the hell up outta here. You just make sure that you pay me the money you owe me for all that shit you snorted last night." He angered, "I need it tonight!"

She chucked him off, "Yeah yeah yeah. Just get the hell out of here!" She removed her hand from the phone, sighed wretchedly, then asked Capt. Winslow, "What do you want to know?"

Ignoring what he had heard in the background, he asked, "Do you know Greg Norton? He's Stoneys pharmacist."

"Yeah! I know that two-faced son-of-a-bitch," she huffed. "I introduced him to Stoney at a party one time"

Feeling her attitude, he said, "I don't understand." He did understand, but he wanted to probe, so that she'd throw the full affect of her own understanding of him. "I just talked to him a short while ago, and he seemed like a pretty decent guy. I understand that he made some bad choices a while ago, but you sound like there's more to it than that."

"There is! You don't know his other side. He's a sneaky bastard with a split personality. While he's in Dover, he's kind, respectable, and acts like he really cares for his family and close friends. But when he goes to the big cities, like Boston or New York, he becomes one of the lowest back stabbing homo-sapiens who've ever crawled on the face of the earth. He's a drug dealer and he …"

"What did you say?"

"I said he's a drug dealer and he …"

"Why do you say he sells drugs?"

"Well, he's been selling Oxicontin to one of my girlfriends for the past two years. And she told me that he has a list of people who he serves to."

"I see. What else can you tell me about him?"

"He's a sex pervert. All the time trying to …"

"Why do you think he's a sex pervert?"

"I don't think he's a sex pervert." She yelled, "I know he is! Every time I see him, he's always trying to come on to me. He's married, but he says he doesn't get any at home. He said his wife is so frigid it ain't funny. They have two kids, and that tells you how many times they've had sex. Least that's what he told me. He even grabbed my ass a couple of times, then tried to make it seem like it was an accident. Believe me, it was no accident. I know his type. And I know when someone is trying to cop a feel on my ass."

"Wow! That doesn't seem like the man I met a little while ago."

Katherine laughed. "It seems like he sold you on that nice guy shit too, huh? He sells everybody on that pitch. It makes him seem less suspecting, so that he can go on being the asshole that he really is. I should've kicked him in his nuts the last time he grabbed my ass."

"There's something else I have to ask you. Stoney kept a brown leather encased book of some sort. And I ..."

"I know. He was preparing a manuscript for a fiction suspense novel. He said that he was going to get it published someday, by putting it in a cousin's name. He thought it would create a lot of controversy if he did it himself, because of its nature. I don't know. He use to go on and on about that stuff, as if he was going to make it big in the publishing industry someday. I guess he wanted to be a big shot, and all that high-life shit. He wanted to be a writer. An author."

"Did you, per chance, ever get a chance to read it, or look into it?"

"No." She lied. "I don't have the time to read much." Like Carlton, she knew that Stoney was writing a manuscript based on the actual situations that have occurred in the Dixie Club. But she also realized that if she had admitted to what she knew about it, it would've incriminated her. Spanky and her would've been great together. She's the Mrs. Picasso of liars.

"Who else knew about the manuscript?"

"A few people, I think." She scratched her head. "Let me think for a second here." She paused. "First, there's Carlton. I'm sure he knew about it, because he lives there. And I think Spanky and Sleeper knew that he was working on a couple of manuscripts, but probably didn't know of their content." She excited, "Oh yeah! And then there's Greg Norton, and I think one of my girlfriends might've ..."

Capt. Winslow gushed forward, "Whoa! Hold it a second. Back up a little. Did you say that Greg Norton knew about the manuscript?" All kinds of alarms went off in his head.

"Sure he did. I saw him reading it one day."

"Katherine, are you absolutely sure about this?"

"Hell yeah! Why would I make this up?"

"But ... when? How did he get a chance to?"

"When Stoney gave a party a few months ago, he had passed out on the couch from drinking too much. Greg assisted him to his room, and put him to bed. While in the room, he probably found it on the nightstand, or laying around somewhere. I came into the room and saw him reading it. I can tell that he was really getting into it, like it was all about him or something. After he noticed that I was standing in the doorway, he almost jumped out of his skin, then dropped it next to Stoney. He left immediately, but I could tell that he was very upset about something. He was highly agitated. And on the way out, as he went past me, he tried to grab my ass again. He ain't nothing but a dog in heat! If it wasn't for Stoney, I would've shoved my foot up his ass a long time ago. The next day, I told Stoney about it, and he told me not to worry about it. Said he'd take care of it later. Like he had something else in mind for him."

So Greg did know about the manuscript, he wondered. This means that he did know who was blackmailing him. I had a feeling the case was heading in this direction. I should've known.

In remembering the conversation that he had with Greg a short while ago, he mumbled, "That lying son-of-a-... he did know about the book."

"That's what I just said. Aren't you listening to a word I've said? Damn! I feel like I'm talking to myself."

"Oh, yeah. I'm sorry. I was just thinking about something else." He sighed. "Katherine, you've been a great help. I won't mention to anyone that I've had this talk with you. You have a nice day."

"But Captain ..."

He hung up the phone, then ran to the cruiser. He jumped inside and told Spike, "Hold on, little fella. This is going to be one hellova ride." He turned the ignition on, put the pedal to the metal, returned to the Norton's home.

CHAPTER 40

▼

Capt. Winslow arrived at the Norton's residence, parked the cruiser haphazardly in the driveway, in front of the four-car garage. It sent a clear message to anyone looking on, meaning, 'I have no respect for these people anymore, because they did something illegal.' Not that he had much respect for Greg Norton in the first place.

He got out of his car and tread boldly across the grass. After he stepped to the front door, he marveled at the spectacular arch bridging the doorway, only for an instant.

He unfastened the strap to his holster, then knocked on the door. This time, the knock was more assertive. Unlike before, he had more confidence about his position. He was ready to kick some ass.

He whispered a quick prayer under his breath, seeking the Lords forgiveness ahead of time, in case he had to use his gun. He wasn't much of a religious man, but it did offer some comfort.

Waiting for a response, he thought, I would've never known. Man by day, beast by night. He lied convincingly, without batting an eye. And I thought I've seen it all. He must've been running lies like the one he ran on me for a long time. He had me fooled completely. But that's all right. It all comes out in the end anyway.

A woman opened the door slowly, stuck her head outside. She took note of the police cruiser parked untidily in their driveway, then tossed politely, "Good morning officer." She was spying on her husband earlier because she knew of his ways intimately. She was aware of his sinful practices, no matter how much he promised he had changed. "Weren't you here earlier? You were talking to my husband."

"Yes. I was."

She opened the door wider, clutched the lapels on her robe. "Is there something I can do for you?"

"Yes, there is. Are you Mrs. Norton?"

"Why, yes." Her eyes widened. "Are you looking for me?"

He crossed his arms, looked down intolerably. Rocking back and forth in his shoes, his patience wore thin. "No maam. I'm looking for your husband. Is he home?"

"Is he in some sort of trouble?"

"I'm not at liberty to say so. Is he home?" His eyes played no games.

"But what …"

"Maam!" he asserted, "is your husband home?"

A few neighbors were leaving their houses, on their way to work. They stopped, stared, wondered inquiringly. A patrol car in the Norton's driveway this early in the morning simply wasn't an everyday event. It wasn't the norm. It thundered, 'UNUSUAL! SOMETHING IS WRONG IN THE GARDEN OF EDEN! **TROUBLE!!**

Returning his stare, she called frightfully, "Greg, honey! There's someone here to see you." There was clearly a tone of danger curdling her voice.

Waiting for her husband to arrive, she made several futile efforts to read the calamitous message in Capt. Winslow's eyes. She felt perilous whirlwinds radiate around his body like an intense heat source, and took a few steps backwards so that she wouldn't get burned. To her, situations like this were almost unheard of, only scattered bits and pieces of 'Top Cop' television shows. Things that happened to other people. Unlawful, corrupt and evil people—no one she knew. Fearing the unbearable content, she could stand it no longer and finally looked away, wondering what kind of havoc would soon be released into the sanctity of their happy home.

Seconds later, from hearing someone's footsteps approach, Capt. Winslow placed his hand on his gun. Even before he pulled it out, he switched the safety off.

After Greg had arrived to the front door, he stood beside his wife. Ironically, they posed identical to the pewter framed wedding photograph placed over the fireplace mantel. The picture was taken on June 20, 1989, amid a picturesque scenery in front of placid lake. However, this time, they were not surrounded by the brides maid, the best man, and a host of maid of honors and ushers. And this time also, she wasn't wearing a turquoise wedding gown, and he wasn't wearing a matching tuxedo, top hat and tails. She was fashioned wearing a pink plush robe from Tiffany's, and he was clad in a gray flannel Brooks Brothers suit, carrying a brown leather Gucci attaché. And this time, for sure, they weren't blaring monumental smiles, or thinking delightful thoughts of living happily ever after.

She was caught in a catch twenty-two situation, wondering what was happening to her perfect world. And he, psychotically, believed that he was on his way to work. As if it were simply going to be another day at the office. He wanted wholeheartedly to believe that. Something everydayish, the norm.

Greg looked into Capt. Winslow's eyes, and broke sweat immediately. He knew exactly what he had returned for. Eerily, the doorway shrank around him, and they heard him swallow loudly. Feeling that the worst was about to happen, he realized that his time had come. In the back of his mind, he felt it would've only been a matter of time before someone had put the pieces together, figure that he had killed Stoney Brooks. In a nutshell, his anger got the best of him, and he gambled on the notion that maybe he could've gotten away with murder.

Playing the moment through, he proceeded as though nothing was wrong. He tugged at his collar to release the steam his nervousness produced around his body, then cleared his throat. "Captain, I … um … I …" At a loss for words, he turned to his wife. His denial dwindled. "Sweetheart, I … I have to go with this man."

Confusion took Pamela by storm, her heart raced out of control, her emotions grew disorderly. She looked at Capt. Winslow confusedly, then back to her husband even more confusedly. A lump of everything unpleasant crowded her throat, and she found it extremely difficult to breath, choked by everything occurring. Now very tensed, she quivered frightfully, her voice trembled with trepidation. "W-W-Why? What's wrong?"

Greg looked behind Capt. Winslow, across the street, and saw his neighbors looking on with inquiring appetites that beckoned their senses to look, listen, determine prematurely what was going on, then call a friend and have something interesting to talk about. He told his wife, "It's a …" he expelled a heavy breath, "… it's a very long story, sweetheart."

While keeping his eyes on Greg, Capt. Winslow removed the handcuffs from the clip attached to his belt. With an abundance of horror dancing on her face and in her heart, she asked, "But, I don't understand. What did you …?"

Capt. Winslow didn't dare take his eyes from him for an instant. Like several times in the past, he realized that the suspect might suddenly become hysterical and violent, from realizing that he was about to be incarcerated for possibly the rest of his life. He recalled one time that an innocent looking eighty-five year old drug dealing grandmother, had transformed into a bat-wielding banshee within the blink of an eye. She was *only* trying to supplement her social security income. At the moment of her arrest she became desperate and was willing to do anything, so that she would not have had to spend her twilight years in prison. This lively grandmother had her sights set on Palm Springs, Bingo, and the Chippendale dancers.

While Greg glanced at a few of his neighbors, a million and one despicable thoughts filled his head and gushed through his mind. His wife stepped closer, latched onto his arm, seeming never to release. Her eyes misting, she whined, "Greg, is this something new? Honey, I knew about what happened in Boston, when you were arrested for sleeping with that vile woman. Now what are they accusing you of doing? What's this all about? When are you coming home?" A fit of delusion launched her next words, "Greg ... but I ... the children ... what are they ..."

Staring deeply into her eyes, he didn't reply. He handed her the attaché, then kissed her gently on her right cheek. He grasped her hand, then squeezed reassuringly. "I'll call you the minute I can, to let you know what's going on."

Capt. Winslow neared him with the handcuffs, ordered firmly, "Mr. Norton, put your hands behind your back. I'm arresting you for the murder of Stoney Brooks."

Feeling the cold steel of the handcuffs touch his wrists, he knew that once they were on, it meant that he'd never be allowed to do whatever he wished, from that moment on. In all likelihood, for the rest of his life.

His wife heard the outrageous charge and froze solid, her heart refused to lob another beat. Bizarrely, she felt as if someone had pulled the ground from underneath her, falling into a deep chasm. She gaped in total disbelief, stammered frightfully, Mur-Mur-Mur.." she finally blurted, "Murder!" She told her husband, "Sweetheart, you didn't murder anybody." She told Capt. Winslow, "This has got to be a terrible mistake. My husband hasn't killed anyone." She told her husband, "Honey, I know you didn't do anything like what he's talking about. You don't have a violent bone in your body. I know you mess up every now and then ... but murder?"

Staring confusedly into her husband eyes, she saw something that she'd never seen before. Returning her stare, he had a look of definite guilt in his eyes. One that told her that he did know something about the change that Capt. Winslow had mentioned.

Capt. Winslow handcuffed his left wrist, and Greg became panic-stricken. He faced him and implored, "Captain! Please! Look around you. This is a peaceful, dignified and undisturbed neighborhood. If you put these handcuffs on me, while we're standing here, the neighbors and the entire community will label my wife and children. Everyone in the church, their schools, and in the whole town will ridicule them." Looked as though he was reciting jurisprudence when he proclaimed, "In this country, a man is innocent until proven guilty by a court of law. Putting these things on me now will sentence my family the second we leave." He was sure his philosophy would win the Capt. Over.

He took a chance, glanced up and down the street, saw several of the Norton's neighbors observing their every move, staring in complete awe. Greg continued, "Can't you spare my family the grief of my actions, until we get inside of the cruiser?"

"Sorry, Mr. Norton. You should've thought about that before you decided to kill officer Brooks. And like you said. Those were your actions, not mine. I'm simply doing my job."

Feeling the cold steel constrain his wrists, a gloomy feeling emerged from deeply within. Out of the blue, he felt like taking a last ditch effort to escape. But he decided not to. He wouldn't have been able to get to his gun. It was locked in the drawer of his desk, in his study. Three rooms away.

After Capt. Winslow had cuffed both hands, he read him his rights. Feeling the cold braces deprive him of his liberty, all thoughts of what his life had entailed filled his mind. In thinking about the family's house, many warm thoughts embraced him briefly. He thought of the many birthday parties, Thanksgiving and Christmas day celebrations. He remembered one Christmas, when after they put up their tree, the dog chased the cat underneath it, resulting in its collapse. It caused some damage, destroying a few presents surrounding it. He remembered how they laughed, thought nothing of it, understanding how privileged they were. It was like a scene taken from the movie 'The Grinch who stole Christmas.' He then remembered the honor of being accepted into such a graceful community that prided itself on nothing but sheer perfection. In that household, up until now, nothing but uninterrupted happy times filled their hearts.

Now, his thoughts were chilled and clammy, like the handcuffs, causing a vast emptiness to fill his soul. An emptiness as bleak as a cavernous void filled his head rampantly. No freedoms to come, go, and do as he pleased. No family or close friends to communicate with. No privacy. No fine living. No fine Italian suits; only a set of standard issue denims and sneakers. No nutritious meals. No manicures, nor pedicures. No friendly community activities to fill his days in ways as it had been in the past. No random casual, or pleasant conversations. No more morning deliveries of the Wall Street Journal to accompany his breakfast. No more chirping birds to enhance his mornings. No more sampling of the spice of life; variety. And most importantly, no more fluff dried cotton underwear.

Seeing her husband in chains, Pamela began to cry. She felt weak, drained. Her knees became unstable. She felt wobbly, as though she was about to faint. She propped herself against the door jamb for support, with her hands laid flush against her cheeks, a chasm of horror filling her soul. Believing that her world had come to a collapse, she became disoriented. She couldn't hold herself upright any longer and slid down the door jamb, weeping hysterically. As her husband was led to the police cruiser, she cried aloud, "Greg! Come back! You can't ... You can't just leave. The children, Greg. What about our babies? You can't just leave them. You ... You can't ..." Her faced buried in her hands, she continued weeping. "This ... This isn't supposed to happen to people like us. It's a nightmare! It's not supposed to happen."

At that moment, their two children emerged from the kitchen, dressed in pajamas and robes. They were having breakfast. Seeing their mother on the floor in tears, they ran to her, and Jake asked worryingly, "Mama, what happened? Where's daddy?"

The children looked outside and saw their father in the most peculiar situation, and knew it wasn't good. Seeing his hands constrained, they knew that he was being taken against his will. Jessica asked her mother, "Where's that man taking daddy?" She shouted at Capt. Winslow, "Where are you taking my daddy?"

Somehow, they knew in their naive hearts that their father would not return. From what they had experienced in the past, because of the unduly pressure that Stoney had created in their lives, they realized that this would be much worse.

Capt. Winslow disliked this part of the job. It made him feel like he was shredding the fabric of the most sacred of relationships. A family. Nowadays and very often, it had to be done. He'd never gotten use to it, though, trying to make himself believe that it was certainly for the better. No matter what the adults may have done, the children never deserve what they get.

Approaching the cruiser, Greg turned halfway and glimpsed his children standing in the doorway, over their mother, his wife. Absorbing their misery, he persisted in pleading, "Look, Captain, I'm sure that you're a reasonable man of *fair* intelligence. A man with a good head on his shoulders. How much does the state pay you anyway? About fifty or sixty grand a year. What do you say we make some kind of a deal? Look back at my house." He smirked. "My family's loaded.

I can get enough money so that you can retire in another country, if you wish. It's easy. All you have to do is tell everyone that I left town before you arrived, or that I escaped. After I pay you off, about a million, that'll give me enough time to leave the country. I've passports from over thirty countries I've traveled to. All for a duffle bag full of money. What do ya say, huh? You think we can make a deal?" He joshed nervously, "For Christ sake, com'on! Get ya self a new car, a new house … a new personality, and you'll be good ta go."

Capt. Winslow noticed that as the more he talked, the more he sounded like the sleazy person who Katherine had told him about. When they got to the cruiser, he finally replied, "Shut up, Mr. Norton. You're only making matters worse, trying to bribe me." He opened the back door to the cruiser. "Get in. Watch your head."

When he slammed the door shut, Greg nearly jumped out of his skin. Hearing the loud noise, he imagined it to be the closing of a cell door, locking him in permanently.

After Capt. Winslow climbed into the car, he hurled promises of wealth as fast as he could fabricate them, offering everything conceivable. He persisted, "Com'on Captain! The state doesn't pay you enough to do things like this." He paused briefly, then continued with a different plan of attack. "Captain, I know how you guys in blue think. I know how you do business. I read somewhere that C.O.P stands for 'Cash Over People', and you're just like the rest of them." Because Capt. Winslow didn't respond, he angered, "You won't be able to make this stick, you filthy son-of-a-bitch! I have very important people on my side, and in my pockets. Very influential people. I know judges who owe me favors. You'll see."

Capt. Winslow started the engine, pulled away from the house. From Greg Norton's empire. His noble kingdom. His pretentiously humble domain.

Seated in the doorway, as her children made feeble attempts to console her, Pamela watched dismayingly through a heavy rainfall of tears. As the cruiser departed, grew smaller on the horizon, dwindled to nothing, so did her future hopes of ever having any kind of a decent life in that little part of town. In that corner of the world. A life she cherished so deeply, never to return.

As a few of the neighbors watched the cruiser go by, some pointed fingers at Greg Norton, whispered unfounded rumors of a major scandal. The gossip filled the air, the smear campaign had begun, the libelous insinuations were being delivered. The Norton's were branded for all an eternity.

Greg continued. "You think you're better than me, don't you? Look at the life I live, verses yours. I wouldn't trade a few of mine for a million of yours. You're nothing but a street pimp for the system, and the system is a lie. It's a lie, and you're helping it live that big fat stinking lie, as if they really care about you. When you retire, they'll give you a rusty ass piece of costume jewelry, then send your roly-poly ass out to pasture. Then you'll sit around the house for the rest of your short fat life, waiting to die, struggling with diabetes, severe arthritis and high blood pressure. Forgotten! Is that anyway to live?"

Checking to make sure that his seatbelt was secure, Capt. Winslow kept his composure. He looked into the rearview mirror, then replied calmly, "Mr. Norton. How does it feel to have your few years of fine living come to an abrupt end? It was quick, wasn't it? You're only in your mid thirties, and you're going to loose all respect from everyone who's ever known you. Even people who don't even know you will probably give your family members a hard way to go. In the next few years, maybe just after the trial, your wife will leave you. Your kids will grow up not knowing who you are. They probably won't want to. You won't be there to see them graduate high school, college, or anything. You'll miss their proms, first dates, and all of that good stuff that makes life worth living. The things in life that really matter. But you're so far gone that you probably don't even know what I'm trying to say. Among what I've just told you, another man will be taking your place. Your wife will remarry, and your kids will call somebody else *daddy*. He'll be someone who your children will learn to respect a great deal more than you. You won't even be a thought in their minds, only a vague recollection of someone who they use to know." He laughed, "Of course, unless you expect that your wife will be faithful, and wait for your release someday. This is highly unlikely." He sighed. "You won't even be a person anymore—just a number. A misplaced, forgotten, eight-digit number with very little significance. From here on, for you, time is no longer of the essence. You won't even have the need to wear that fancy watch anymore. Your whole life will be governed by bells and buzzers that'll tell you when to eat, sleep, piss and shit. You'll rot away in a urine drenched poop-hole, a disgusting place that you'll learn to call 'home sweet home.' And at night, you won't have your wife or kids to kiss goodnight. Just some horny muscle bound psycho named Blade who will tuck you in, *after* he gets into the bed with you." He warned, "And don't you go ahead and do something stupid, like try to put up a fight. That'll only get him more excited. He'll snap your neck so fast that you won't even have the time to wet yourself. Hell! If your dog ever sees you again, he'll most likely piss on your shoes, if he doesn't first bite you on your ass."

Greg sat quietly, stewing, leering at the back of his head in deep consternation. Capt. Winslow went on to say, "What bothers me is that you don't even know your own wife. You have no conscious of her being. She said that she knew about that situation that had happened in Boston. It sounded like she already forgave you, without your even having to ask." Greg's only response, a heavy sigh. "Doesn't it bother you that you took a mans life?"

He still had some respect for Stoney, so he referred to him as a man. However, he wasn't going to disgrace himself by calling him a fellow officer. It didn't feel right.

Greg looked out the window, watched his town go by. Tried to capture as much as he could, feeling that he may never see it again. He angered, "Hey! I do what I have to do for my family. The bastard was milking me. He had no right to do that. He had it coming to him. If I didn't kill him, then somebody else would've."

"And now it's your turn."

Suddenly, Greg's temper flared and he shouted, "Look, you fat bug-eyed, pork rhine chewing son-of-a-bitch, why don't you shut up? Just … just shut the fuck up."

"Now, ya see that, Spike?" Capt. Winslow laughed. "That's the irate Greg Norton I've been hearing about. Babbling in all his brilliance."

The remainder of the ride to the Dover police department was quiet. After giving Greg a good understanding of what his new life was going to be like, Capt. Winslow switched on the radio to an oldies station that he often listens to. He stated, "Oldies but goodies. My favorite music." He sang merrily, "Let the midnight special, shine its light on me. Let the midnight special, shine its ever lovin light on meeeeeeee."

He reached inside of the glove compartment, pulled out a fresh cigar, stuck it into his mouth. He switched it from side to side, getting the taste and feel of it. He mumbled inaudibly, "Damn these things stink. They taste good, but they stink."

CHAPTER 41

▼

After Capt. Winslow had dropped Greg off at the Dover police station, he went to the observation ward at Boston City Hospital to check up on Sleeper. Upon his arrival, he went to the rear of the building and saw one of his men, Sgt. Bradley, escorting Sleeper to a bulletproof cruiser. Two men dressed in full riot gear stood near the rear of the car, listening on their radios to other officers positioned guardedly not to far away. They were on their way to police headquarters, where Sleeper was going to be booked, then subsequently indicted. A typical process. There would be no favoritism.

Observing Sleeper, he saw a man self-degraded by the actions of his unprincipled will. His badge and gun removed. His pride demolished. His honor obliterated. His head hung low, his shoulders slump. Dragging his feet discouragingly, it appeared as though his ankles were cuffed in leg irons. Now a forever slave of the state.

Approaching them, he removed the cigar from his mouth and requested, "Sergeant. I want to speak to the prisoner for a moment, please. In private, if you don't mind."

When Sleeper heard the word 'prisoner', he felt like he had been stabbed pitilessly, and grunted despairingly. The word echoed in his head, got louder and louder, he cringed shakily.

"Sure, Captain," Sgt. Bradley said. "It's ashamed about what happened to Robert Sinclair."

Capt. Winslow froze. During the ride from Dover, he had turned off the police radio to listen to his favorite oldies station. "Wh-Wh-What're you talking about?" His eyes bucked opened in astonishment. "Something happened to him?

How could something happen to him? I just dropped his off a short while ago. He was in protective custody. The security around him was so tight that a gnat couldn't have gotten in."

"But, I thought you knew."

Capt. Winslow shook his head gravely. Sgt. Bradley continued, "He got sniped as they were taking him to headquarters. Someone blew his brains out. They said it came from out of nowhere. It took his handlers by total surprise."

"Sinclair's ..." he said in amazement, swallowed, "... dead!" He looked to the sky, his eyes shut tight in anguish.

"Yeah. That's why I got orders to put a bullet proof vest on Knight, and take him straight to headquarters, pronto."

There was absolutely no response from Sleeper, verbal or physical. He kept his head bowed. It was almost as if he had expected to hear the bad news. Wishing that he was anywhere but there, for an instant, he traveled back to a few weeks before. He was sitting in the rear of a Legal Seafood's restaurant, with a Boston Red Sox's baseball cap pulled low over his face. Disguised in a pair of dark shades, and a fake moustache. He held a menu in front of his face to conceal his whereabouts. He also wore a hearing aid size cellular Bluetooth inserted in his right ear.

Before he entered the restaurant, he overheard two men talking just on the outside. A sixty year old man ripped the corner from a fifty dollar bill, and gave the hefty portion of the bill to the thirty year old man, probably his apprentice. He told him to go into the restaurant and buy a cup of coffee. He also told him to wait outside for a half hour.

The old man then entered the restaurant and ordered lunch. After he had finished eating, he summoned the waiter. He told him that he'd like his change for the fifty dollar bill that he had given him a short while ago.

The waiter swore that he had never given him a fifty dollar bill, and they began to argue. Then waiters supervisor came to intervene. The old man told the supervisor that he had given the waiter a fifty dollar bill to pay for the meal. And that the waiter must have forgotten that he had received it. The old man also told the supervisor that the fifty dollar bill that he gave the waiter had one corner ripped from it, then showed him the piece that had fallen off.

The supervisor checked the cash register, found the fifty dollar bill with the ripped corner, then gave the old man his change.

Small time petty hustlers, Sleeper thought. The old man's probably trying to scrape together a few bucks for his retirement. Filling out all that paperwork just for a slap on the wrist misdemeanor would be a waste of my time. Handling cases like that only put me to sleep.

He pulled out a cell phone. But before he dialed a number, he paused, thought back, recalled an incident of a young man who'd been pushing a cigarette scam for almost five years. The way it went, he purchased a carton of cigarettes, opened each pack carefully, as not to tear the seal on the outer wrapper. He filled the boxes with balsa wood, then sealed the packages as they were before. Then he'd walk into a connivance store, or any place that sold cigarettes, with four of the false packs. He then purchased four packs of the same brand, took a brief walk around the store, out of view of the clerk. While doing so, he switched the real packs, with the false ones. Then he returned to the desk, and told the clerk that he had purchased the wrong brand. Leaving the store with four packs of real cigarettes, he profited almost twenty-five dollars in less than three minutes. After traveling to twenty stores, in about four hours time, he supplied cigarettes to everyone in his neighborhood at discount prices. He kept a checklist of over one thousand stores tallied, and over a years time, had made enough to finance his college tuition. He's now as assistant district attorney for superior court in downtown Boston.

At another table about twenty feet away, a few professional looking individuals clad in business suits were having a retirement party for one of their own. A man stood from his chair, tapped the side of his glass with a butter knife, then announced, "People, I'd like to say a few words for the man of the hour, Thomas Healy. A man whose thirty years of service to the firm has assisted us, his colleagues, to climb through the ranks of the fortune five-hundred, to number two hundred and twenty-three. We owe him a great deal of appreciation for his undying dedication," he looked at Thomas Healy, "and Thomas, we thank you from the bottom of our hearts. We couldn't have done it without you. You're a great man."

A few people sitting around the table gave applaud and cheered. After the clapping faded, the man asked Thomas, "Would you like to say a few words?"

The people around the table cheered, "Speech! Speech! Speech! Speech!"

Thomas removed the napkin from his lap and rose to his feet. "Thank you, Mr. Billings, for your kind words. I really appreciate it." He told the others, "Guys, it's been a pleasure working with all of you. I couldn't have gotten what I wanted out of life, had I've not been with such a fine company, with fine people. I remember when I first came to the firm, some thirty years ago. I had an office the size of the janitor's closet. But when I ..."

At that moment, Sleeper brought the cell phone up to his mouth and pronounced, "Thomas Healy". Within an instant, the voice activated cell phone dialed Thomas Healy's cell phone number.

The phone rang a few times. A man answered, "Healy here."

"Thomas Healy," Sleeper said excitedly. He peeped over the menu, observed Thomas speaking into his cell phone. "How're you, sir?"

Thomas didn't recognize the voice. But due to the hype that he was amidst, he replied cheerfully, "I'm doing excellent. Who am I speaking with?"

This was one of the times when Sleeper was short on time, so he got right to the juice of things. "That's not important right now. But what is, is that I called to tell you that you've won a five hundred thousand dollars grand prize, in a sweepstakes drawing. How do you feel about that, sir?"

Thomas remained silent for a moment. He proceeded cynically, "You're kidding? This is a joke, right? A sick joke. Oh, I get it. There's a catch. You just want to sell me a set of encyclopedias. Am I correct?"

"No sir," he said earnestly. "I'm not trying to sell you anything. No encyclopedias, no purchase of anything necessary, and mostly, it's no joke. You've been selected at random by our computers, and you're the big winner. Last summer, when you were on Martha's Vineyard, you unknowingly entered a tri-state sweepstakes contest, when you signed your name for the check at the sushi bar you dined at. And, well, you're the big winner."

Another moment of silence, then Thomas blurted in shock, "I-I-I don't believe it! I simply don't believe it." He held his hand over the cell phone, and Sleeper heard him tell his co-workers, "Hey guys! Someone on the phone just told me that I won a half a million dollar grand prize, in a sweepstakes contest. Is that amazing or what?"

His colleagues released a small ruckus, someone cheered aloud, "Hey! That's great, Thomas!"

Another person said, "Way to go! It couldn't have come at a better time."

The two people sitting to the left and right of Thomas rose to their feet. One shook his hand, the other patted him on the back, congratulating him on his sudden windfall. Having Thomas already at the front door to paradise, Sleeper decided to lower the boom. He told Thomas, "Oh, I'm sorry, Mr. Healy. I made a terrible mistake. What I meant to say was that you're going to pay me a half million bucks, just that so you won't rot in jail for the rest of your life ... for murdering an escort." He laughed, "How's that for a retirement?"

"What'd you say?" Thomas asked disbelievingly.

"You're going to pay me a half million bucks, just so that you won't rot in jail for the rest of your life. You're friends think that you're some kind of a big shot lawyer. But I know the real deal. Don't I, Mr. Healy? The truth of the matter is, you're a killer."

"B-B-But I ..." He became paralyzed with fear.

"Com'on with all that B-B-But I, jazz. Ya putting me to sleep. Ya gotta come up with something better than that. Since you're probably at some unimportant dinner function at the moment, I'll get right down to brass taxes. Last summer, you strangled a woman to death on Marathas Vineyard. She was employed by one of the island escort services, and had a date with someone who used a fake name. You did that so that your company wouldn't find out about it. The authorities found her naked body washed ashore on one of the beaches, and they're sure that she was killed by someone that she knew. That would be you. You can't deny it, because I have the only piece of evidence that ties you to the murder. The autopsy revealed that the victim ingested sushi the night she was murdered. I found a container from the only sushi bar on the island, with what chances are, your fingerprints, on it, near the crime scene. It was hidden in some shrubbery. What led me to this conclusion was that after I found out about what type of sushi the woman consumed, I went to the restaurant and discovered that you had ordered the same type listed on the menu. You paid for it with your Diners Credit Card. As far as the payments for the half million are concerned, I'll call you in an hour and fill you in. Unless you want to retire to prison, you'll pay me."

Thomas Healy clutched his heart, groaned aloud, then fainted right where he stood. His colleagues gathered around him to give assistance. Someone stated, "I think he's having a heart attack."

Sleeper rose from his chair, then walked right past them, on his way out of the restaurant.

*   *   *   *

Sgt. Bradley nodded earnestly. "I'm sorry, Captain. But I thought you knew. Otherwise, I wouldn't have blurted it out like that. It's all over the radios and the televisions. Now that the mainstream media's gotten a hold of it, their going at it like crazy. I heard talk that they think it's tied into the triple homicide out in Dover; Captain Bogart and his family." He released the grip on Sleepers arm, then walked to about fifteen feet away. "I'll be over here."

What he meant to say was, 'I'll be watching.' In a society where sometimes you were not sure about who to trust, because of the monkey business that Stoney, Spanky and Sleeper were involved in, you took all of the necessary precautions to protect yourself. Sgt. Bradley trusted his boss, Capt. Winslow, but he understood the theory of the changing tides. Besides, the responsibility of transporting the prisoner was given to him. His neck was on the line, and he wasn't about to ruin his career for even his boss. As much as he admired and respected him.

"I don't believe this shit," Capt. Winslow complained. "First Brooks, Captain Bogart and his family, and now Sinclair." He grabbed Sleeper by the scruff of the neck, jerked him fiercely, then exploded, "For crying out loud, Knight! Do you see the mess you guys have gotten started? All of this hell is going on just because a couple of gluttonous bastards..." he stopped short, totally stymied, "... Dammit, Knight! You're despicable! You know that? That's all we need is an open war from cops killings each other, and the Feds on our backs, monitoring every gotdamn thing we do. The entire department will be walking on eggshells for years to come. The good guys that I have working for me, they don't need internal affairs or the feds probing into every aspect of their personal lives. Just because a couple of ignorant fools got greedy. What you, Brooks and Sinclair have started will make our jobs a thousand times more difficult." He stuck the cigar into his mouth, stared intently at Sleeper. Through a moment of torrential silence, his facial expression blasted, 'Why? How could you? So young, and so stupid.' He ordered, "Hold your head up straight when I'm talking to you."

Sleepers head rose partially. He couldn't manage to look his former boss directly in the eyes. Instead, he focused on the cigar. Capt. Winslow composed himself. "You use to be able to look me in the eyes when we talked. What happened?"

He sighed resignedly. "Captain, I ... um ... I don't know." He searched for words to explain his actions. He found none. "I ... I guess things got out of hand."

Capt. Winslow's eyes widened. He asked sarcastically, "You think, maybe just a teeny weenie bit?" Tired of the corruption that's plagued the department thus far, he threw his hands into the air, and started to walk away. He stopped in his tracks, turned halfway. "Sleeper, I know that money is the root of all evil. But this time, please, tell me something different." He begged, "Please! I'm getting tired of hearing the same old thing." He sang, "It's getting monotonooouuuus!"

Never looking into his former bosses eyes, he dropped his head to as it was before. His chin rested on his chest. He started to say something, then changed his mind. Thought it better to keep his mouth shut.

"Sergeant," Capt. Winslow called out, "take this ... this person to the station." He was so disappointed with Sleepers actions that he couldn't find a proper word to describe what he had become.

Sgt. Bradley approached them, then grabbed Sleepers arm. "I'll see you at the station, sir."

"Yeah yeah yeah," he spat with a bad taste stewing on his palate. "Will ya take this ... this ... take him outta my sight? I can't even stand to look at him anymore."

Returning to his cruiser, he shook his head deplorably. He looked to the sky and asked, "Lord, will they ever learn?"

After Sgt. Bradley put Sleeper in the back seat of his cruiser, his cell phone rang. He spoke with the caller for a few seconds, then yelled, "Hey boss!"

Capt. Winslow turned around, approached Sgt. Bradley. His gut feelings told him that there was more bad news on the way. "Yeah. What's up?"

"You're not going to believe this," he said sadly. "It's about Knights family; his wife and child."

Capt. Winslow looked at Sleeper. In the back seat of the cruiser, he couldn't hear a word that they were saying. "What about them? I just left them a few hours ago. They're okay, aren't they?"

Sgt. Bradley sighed, lowered his head sullenly. "Captain ... they're dead."

Capt. Winslow hesitated for a long moment, not believing what he had just heard. He stated disbelievingly, "E-E-Elizabeth ... *and* their son?"

"Yeah. She was killed execution style. Hands tied behind the back, shot once in the back of the head. And you're not going to believe this, but his son was decapitated. The ... the nursery looks like a blood bath. They say it was a professional hit. The killer sent a message. Carved the initial 'B' on her chest, in three places."

Capt. Winslow shut his eyes tight in anguish, pinched the bridge of his nose. He felt he was going to be sick, placed his hand over his mouth. "Oh my God! I don't believe this shit's happening. It's like a nightmare come to life." He slapped his holster. "Something told me I should've put protection around them." He cursed himself, "Dammit!" He gritted heatedly, "I just knew I should've."

Sgt. Bradley looked back at the cruiser, at Sleeper. "You ... you think I should tell him?"

"No! No! Absolutely not. He almost went into shock last night, after discovering that he and Sinclair had made a terrible mistake. You give him any kind of news like that, and either it'll kill him, or he'll commit suicide. When you get to headquarters, tell everyone not to mention to him a word of what happened to his family. Do you understand?"

Sgt. Bradley nodded forbiddingly. He waited a long moment before asking, "Captain, you think it's going to get any worse than this?"

"For God sake, let's hope not."

CHAPTER 42

▼

Twelve o'clock that afternoon, Capt. Winslow had returned to Spankys apartment with Spike. As soon as he opened the front door, Spike scuttled around his legs and dashed straight to his dog bowl. He looked inside with the great expectancy of it being filled to the brim with his favorite brand of dog food—Beef flavored Alpo.

He followed him into the kitchen. Stood next to him with his hands resting on his stout hips. "Something tells me that you're hungry."

Spike threw a few barks into the air, obviously agreeing with him. He didn't know many human words. But the words hungry, food, and bathroom, he had down packed. He picked up his dog bowl, then dropped it on his Bostonian wingtips.

"All right already, little fella." He bent down and patted him. "You ready for breakfast?"

Spike sat up straight, delivered a look of encouragement.

"I guess that means yes." He picked up the dog bowl, carried it to the cupboard, then placed it on the counter underneath. He opened it, saying, "Let's see what we got in here for ya."

He found another can of beef flavored Alpo, opened it, then scooped the contents into the bowl. He placed it on the floor, then stood over Spike, watched the food disappear. "After you finish, you're coming home with me. For now, enjoy yaself."

He nodded a few times, smiled. "Yeah, you're definitely coming home with me. And you can stay too. Of course, unless my wife disagrees. Then it's off to the dog pound."

Abruptly, Spike stopped eating and dropped to the floor. He covered his ears with his paws and whined feverishly.

"Okay! Okay! I'll talk to her. But she's going to make me pay dearly for this."

On his way to the living room, he exclaimed, "Gracious! What a sensitive little fella." Throwing over his shoulders, he added, "Hurry up, Spike. After I drop you off at the house, I have to make another run to take care of some important business. Tie up some loose ends."

That reminds me, he thought. Some of the guys from the lab will be down here in a little while to check things out. From knowing what I know now, there's no telling what they'll find in this place.

He glanced over to the right, into the kitchen. "Damn! That Spanky is one sloppy mother ..."

He went to the living room and sat on the couch. He picked up the manuscript and stared sullenly at it. He opened it, and noticed that the title page was stuck to another page. After separating them, centered in the middle of the page, he discovered the words, 'Optional title, C.O.P. (Cash Over People).' He stated earnestly, "Not all the time."

From out of nowhere, a young boy said, "Hey! Uncle Shorty."

Believing that he was hallucinating, he shook his head a few times to chase off the moment. Chucked it off to his being tremendously exhausted. "I must be hearing things. I could've sworn I ..."

This time, a little girl said cheerfully, "Hi, Uncle Shorty."

Totally confounded, he spanned the room. He stared at the answering machine, and thought that maybe ..."

"Over here," the voices said simultaneously. "In the television set."

He snapped his sights to the television, and at first, he saw a regular dark gray picture tube. Moments later, two blurred images faded into view. Quickly, the images sharpened. "What in the world ..."

He saw two children standing beside each other, holding hands, staring at him, smiling with great relief. As though they could finally return to thinking childlike thoughts. As though they didn't have a care in the world. As though everything was going to be okay, from that moment on.

Fumbling nervously, he sat back in his seat. He removed his glasses and wiped them against his jacket. He put them back on and stared intently, eyes bucked wide.

"Thank you, Uncle Shorty," Jake said, smiling a bucktooth grin. "Maybe now I can get my teeth fixed."

Jessica's eyes gleamed. "Yes, in deed! Thank you, Uncle Shorty. Now maybe I'll live forever." She clutched her favorite Barbie doll, one that she'd forgotten about temporarily, because there was much fighting and arguing going on in between her parents, for Stoneys greed.

Abruptly, the images faded to nothing. The picture tube was a dark gray once again. Ogling at the television set, he mumbled, "If that don't beat all."

He brushed the occurrence off to a possible malfunction of the television set. This, because he didn't want to believe that he was seeing and hearing things; experiencing hallucinations. In his book, if he believed that it occurred, it would've been a sign telling him that he was loosing his mind. Maybe it was time to put in for an early retirement. Nonetheless, it warmed his heart, and he smiled. He called out, "Hey Spike! Are you about ready to go?"

Spike came barreling in from the kitchen, with the dog bowl clutched firmly in his chops, his stubby tail wagging briskly. He dropped the bowl at Capt. Winslow's feet, looked at him encouragingly, then barked, "WOOF! WOOF!"

"Don't worry. I wasn't going to forget your bowl. We'd better get to know each other real quick. Something tells me that after I take you home to meet the misses, we'll both be sleeping in the doghouse tonight."

978-0-595-44729-9
0-595-44729-5

Printed in the United Kingdom
by Lightning Source UK Ltd.
125586UK00001B/122/A